PLAY DIRTY

SANDRA BROWN

PLAY DIRTY

POCKET BOOKS
New York London Toronto Sydney

Pocket Books
A Division of Simon & Schuster, Inc.
1230 Avenue of the Americas
New York, NY 10020

This Pocket Books trade paperback edition June 2009

POCKET and colophon are registered trademarks of Simon & Schuster, Inc.

For information about special discounts for bulk purchases, please contact Simon & Schuster Special Sales at 1-866-506-1949 or business@simonandschuster.com.

The Simon & Schuster Speakers Bureau can bring authors to your live event. For more information or to book an event contact the Simon & Schuster Speakers Bureau at 1-866-248-3049 or visit our website at www.simonspeakers.com.

Designed by Jaime Putorti

Manufactured in the United States of America

10 9 8 7 6 5 4 3 2 1

Library of Congress Cataloging-in-Publication Data is available for the hardcover edition.

ISBN 978-1-4391-6633-8
ISBN 978-1-4165-4541-5 (ebook)

PLAY DIRTY

CHAPTER

1

"THAT IT?"

"That's it." Griff Burkett tossed a small duffel bag onto the backseat of the car, then got into the front passenger seat. "I didn't bring much with me. I'm sure as hell not taking souvenirs." He wanted no memorabilia from his stint in BIG—official code name for the Federal Correctional Institute in Big Spring, Texas.

He made himself comfortable on the plush leather, adjusted the air-conditioning vent to blow straight at him, then, realizing they weren't moving, looked over at the driver.

"Seat belt."

"Oh. Right." Griff stretched the belt across his chest and latched it. Tongue in cheek, he said, "Wouldn't want to break the law."

As lawyers went, Wyatt Turner was okay. But if he possessed a sense of humor, he kept it under lock and key. He didn't crack a smile at Griff's wry remark.

"Come on, Turner, lighten up," Griff said. "This is a special day."

"Unfortunately, we're not the only ones commemorating it."

Turner drew Griff's attention to an ugly, olive green car parked in a handicapped space. Illegally it seemed, since there was no tag hanging from the rearview mirror. Griff didn't recognize the make or model of the car because it was younger than five years old. Nothing distinguished the no-frills sedan except the man sitting behind the wheel.

Griff cursed under his breath. "What's *he* doing here?"

"It's been all over the news that you were being released today, but I don't think he brought champagne."

"So why'd he come all this way to see little ol' me?"

"I assume he wants to pick up where the two of you left off."

"Fat chance."

The object of their conversation, Stanley Rodarte, had parked where he couldn't be missed. He had wanted Griff to see him. And Griff would have recognized him anywhere, because Stanley Rodarte was one ugly son of a bitch. His face looked like it had been hacked out of oak with a chain saw, by a carver too impatient to smooth out the rough edges. Cheekbones as sharp as knife blades cast shadows across his ruddy, pockmarked skin. His hair was the color and texture of dirty straw. Behind the lenses of his opaque sunglasses, his eyes—yellowish, as Griff recalled—were no doubt trained on Griff with an enmity that even five years hadn't blunted.

Griff shrugged with more indifference than he felt. "It's his time he's wasting."

Sounding like the voice of doom, Turner said, "Obviously he doesn't think so."

As they pulled closer to the other car, Griff flashed Rodarte a big grin, then raised his middle finger at him.

"Jesus, Griff." Turner accelerated toward the prison gate. "What's the matter with you?"

"He doesn't scare me."

"Well, he should. If you had a lick of sense, he would scare you shitless. Apparently he hasn't forgotten about Bandy. Steer clear of him. I mean it. Are you listening? Do not cross him."

"Am I gonna get billed for that unsolicited advice?"

"No, that advice is on the house. It's for my protection as well as yours."

Despite the blasting air conditioner, Griff lowered his window as Turner drove through the gates of the federal prison camp that had been his home for the past five years. The area in which he'd been incarcerated was classified minimum security, but it was still prison.

"No offense to the folks in Big Spring, but I don't care to ever enter the city limits again," he remarked as they left the West Texas town and headed east on Interstate 20.

The air was hot, dry, and gritty, perfumed by diesel and gasoline exhaust from the well-traveled highway, but it was free air, the first Griff had tasted in one thousand, eight hundred, and twenty-five days. He gulped it.

"Feel good to be out?" his lawyer asked.

"You have no idea."

After a moment, Turner said, "I meant what I said about Rodarte."

The sand-bearing wind scoured Griff's face and flattened his hair against his head. "Relax, Turner," he said, speaking above the noise of a foul-smelling cattle truck roaring past. "I won't wave red flags at Rodarte. Or at anybody else. That's in my past. Ancient history. I took my punishment and paid my debt to society. You're looking at a rehabilitated, reformed man."

"Glad to hear it," the lawyer said, heavy on the skepticism.

Griff had been watching Rodarte in the car's side-view mirror. He'd followed them out of Big Spring and now was matching their speed, keeping at least three vehicles between them. If Wyatt Turner realized that Rodarte was on their tail, he didn't mention it. Griff started to say something about it, then figured there were things his lawyer didn't need to know. Things that would only worry him.

Three hundred miles later, Griff stood in the center of the apartment's living area, which was a laughable misnomer. A person might exist here, but you couldn't call it living. The room was so dim it bordered on gloomy, but the poor lighting actually worked in its favor. A crack as wide as his index finger ran up one wall from floor to ceiling like a jagged lightning bolt. The carpet was gummy. The air conditioner wheezed, and the air it pumped was damp and smelled like day-old carryout Chinese.

"It's not much," Turner said.

"No shit."

"But there's no lease. The rent's paid month to month. Consider this only a stopover until you can find something better."

"At least Big Spring was clean."

"You want to go back?"

Maybe Turner had a sense of humor after all.

Griff tossed his duffel bag onto the sofa. Not only did it look uncomfortable but the upholstery was stained with God-knew-what. He remembered fondly the high-rise condo he used to live in, in the ritzy Turtle Creek area of Dallas. Suffused with natural light during the day, a spectacular view of the skyline at night. Outfitted with countless amenities. Half of the gadgets and gewgaws he hadn't even known what they were for or how to work them. But the important thing was that he'd had them.

"When you sold my place, weren't you able to keep any of my stuff?"

"Clothes. Personal items. Pictures. Like that. It's all in a storage unit. But the rest . . ." Turner shook his head and nervously jiggled his keys as though anxious to get back in his car, although the drive had taken them nearly five hours with only one stop. "I liquidated everything in the Toy Box first."

That had been Griff's pet name for the extra garage he'd leased in which to store his grown-up toys—snow skis, scuba equipment, an Indian motorcycle, a bass fishing boat that had been in the water exactly once. Stuff he had bought mostly because he could.

"The Escalade and Porsche went next. I held off selling the Lexus until I had no choice. Then I began emptying the apartment. I had to sell it all, Griff. To pay off your fine. Consulting fees."

"*Your* fee."

Turner stopped his bit with the keys. Under other circumstances, the combative stance he took would have been humorous. Griff was more than half a foot taller, and he hadn't slacked on workouts during his incarceration. If anything, he was harder now than when he went in.

Wyatt Turner had the pallor of a man who worked indoors twelve hours a day. A workout for him amounted to eighteen holes of golf, riding in a cart, followed by two cocktails in the clubhouse. In his mid-forties, he had already developed a soft paunch in front and sagging ass in back.

"Yes, Griff, my fee," he said defensively. "I get paid to do my job. Just like you do."

Griff looked at him for a moment, then said softly, "Did. Just like I *did*."

Turner backed down and, looking slightly embarrassed by his momentary testiness, turned away and laid another set of keys on the stick-furniture coffee table. "Our extra car. It's parked outside. Can't miss it. Faded red, two-door Honda. Not worth anything as a trade-in, so when Susan got her Range Rover, we kept it for emergencies. It runs okay. I had the oil changed and the tires checked. Use it for as long as you need it."

"Will the daily rental fee be added to my bill?"

Again, Turner took umbrage. "Why are you being such a prick about everything? I'm trying to help."

"I needed your help five years ago to keep me out of fucking prison."

"I did everything I could for you," Turner fired back. "They had you. You do the crime, you do the time."

"Gee, I need to write that down." Griff patted his pockets as though looking for a pen.

"I'm outta here."

Turner moved toward the door, but Griff headed him off. "Okay, okay, you're a prince among lawyers and I'm an unappreciative prick. What else?" He allowed Turner a few moments to fume in righteous indignation, then repeated in a more conciliatory tone, "What else have you done for me?"

"I put some of your clothes in the closet in the bedroom." He gestured toward an open doorway across the room. "Jeans and polos haven't gone out of style. I picked up some sheets and towels at Target. You got toiletries?"

"In my duffel."

"Bottled water, milk, eggs are in the fridge. Bread's in there, too. I thought there might be roaches in the pantry."

"Safe guess."

"Look, Griff, I know it's no palace, but—"

"*Palace?*" he repeated, laughing. "I don't think anyone would mistake this dump for a palace." Then, to keep from appearing ungrateful, he added, "But as you said, it's only a stopgap. Do I have a phone?"

"In the bedroom. I put down the deposit for you. It's in my name. We can have it disconnected when you get your own."

"Thanks. What's the number?"

Turner told him. "Don't you need to write it down?"

"I used to carry a couple hundred plays inside my head. I can remember ten digits."

"Hmm. Right. Don't forget to check in with your probation officer. He'll need to know how to contact you."

"First item on my list. Call Jerry Arnold." Griff drew a check mark in the air.

Turner handed him a bank envelope. "Here's some walking-around money until you can get a credit card. And your driver's license is in there, too. Address is wrong, of course, but it doesn't expire until your next birthday, and by then you'll have a new place."

"Thanks." Griff tossed the bank envelope onto the table beside the keys to the borrowed car. Taking handouts from his lawyer was almost as humiliating as the first day of prison, when he'd been told the rules as well as the punishments for breaking them.

"Well, then, I guess you're good to go." The lawyer clapped him on the shoulder, which seemed an unnatural and awkward gesture for him. He turned away quickly, but at the door he paused and looked back. "Griff . . . uh . . . folks are still pissed at you. To a lot of people, you committed a cardinal sin. If someone gives you flak, don't let it bother you too much. Turn the other cheek, okay?"

Griff remained silent. He wouldn't make a promise he couldn't keep.

Turner hesitated, looking worried. "Getting out . . . It's a tough transition."

"Beats staying in."

"Those classes they have for inmates about to be released . . ."

"The Release Preparation Program."

"Right. Were the sessions helpful?"

"Oh, yeah. I learned how to fill out a job application. Was urged not to scratch my ass or pick my nose during an interview."

Looking chagrined, Turner asked, "Do you have any idea what you're going to do?"

"Get a job."

"For sure. What I mean is, do you have any prospects lined up?"

"Do you know an NFL team looking for a starting quarterback?" Turner's face went so flaccid, Griff laughed. "That was a joke."

The estate was enclosed by an ivy-covered, twelve-foot-high brick wall.

"Holy shit." Griff pulled the red Honda up to the call box at the gate. He'd known by the address that this was an affluent part of Dallas, but he hadn't expected it to be *this* affluent.

Instructions on how to contact the house were printed on the box. He punched in a sequence of numbers on the keypad, which he supposed rang a telephone inside. In a moment, a voice came through the speaker.

"Yes?"

"Griff Burkett to see Mr. Speakman."

Nothing else was said. But the iron picket gate opened and he drove through. The brick lane was bordered by cultivated beds of low shrubbery and flowers. Beyond them the tree-shaded lawn looked like a carpet of green velvet.

The mansion itself was as impressive as the landscaping. Older than Griff by several decades, it was constructed of gray stone. Some of its walls were ivy covered like the estate wall. He followed the curving driveway and parked directly in front of the entrance, then got out of the borrowed Honda and approached the front door. It was flanked by urns containing evergreen trees. Idly Griff wondered how in hell they got a tree to grow in the shape of a corkscrew.

No cobwebs clinging to the eaves. Nary a stray leaf anywhere. Not a smear on any of the windows. The house, the grounds, the whole place was freaking perfect.

When he'd told Wyatt Turner he didn't have any prospects, he'd lied. Not that job offers were pouring in. Right now, Griff Burkett was arguably the most detested man in Dallas, if not the entire Lone Star State. No, that was still limiting: He was despised in the whole football-loving country. People sneered his name, or spat after saying it as though to ward off an evil spirit. Nobody in their right mind would want him on their payroll.

But he did have this one prospect, however slim.

A few days before his release, he had received an invitation to be in this spot, on this date, at this time. The stiff card had been engraved: Foster Speakman. The name was vaguely familiar, although Griff couldn't remember why it would be.

As he depressed the doorbell, he couldn't imagine what a guy who lived in a place like this could possibly want with him. He had assumed the appointment portended a job offer. Now, seeing this spread, he thought maybe not. Maybe this Speakman had been a diehard Cowboys fan who only wanted his own pound of Griff Burkett's flesh.

The door was opened almost immediately. He was greeted by a waft of refrigerated air, the faint scent of oranges, and a guy who looked like he should be wearing a breechcloth and carrying a spear.

Griff had expected a maid or butler—someone in a white apron, with a soft speaking voice and polite but aloof mannerisms. This guy didn't come close. He was dressed in a tight black T-shirt and black slacks. He had the wide, flat features of Mayan royalty. His skin was smooth and beardless. Straight hair black as ink.

"Uh, Mr. Speakman?"

He shook his head and smiled. Rather, he revealed his teeth. You couldn't really call it a smile because no other feature of his face changed, even moderately. He stood aside and motioned Griff in.

A vaulted ceiling loomed three stories above. Oriental rugs formed islands of subtle color on the marble floor. Griff's image was caught in the enormous mirror that hung above the long console table. The curving staircase was an architectural marvel, especially considering when the house had been built. The space was vast, and as hushed as a cathedral.

The speechless man motioned with his head for Griff to follow.

Again it occurred to Griff that Foster Speakman might be lying in wait. Did he keep thumbscrews and whips in the dungeon?

When they reached a set of double doors, the butler—for lack of a better word—pushed both open, then stood aside. Griff stepped into the room, obviously a library, the walls on three sides consisting of floor-to-ceiling bookcases. The fourth wall was almost entirely windows, affording a view of the sweeping lawn and flower gardens.

"I wondered."

Griff turned at the unexpected voice and got his second surprise. The man smiling up at him was in a wheelchair.

"Wondered what?"

"How physically imposing you would be in person." He sized Griff up. "You're as tall as I expected, but not as . . . bulky. Of course, I've only seen you from the distance of a stadium box, and on TV."

"TV adds ten pounds."

The man laughed. "To say nothing of shoulder pads." He extended his right hand. "Foster Speakman. Thank you for coming." They shook hands. Not surprisingly, his hand was smaller than Griff's by far, but his palm was dry and his handshake firm. He pushed a button on his fancy wheelchair and backed away. "Come in and have a seat."

He motioned Griff toward a grouping of comfortably arranged pieces with appropriate tables and lamps. Griff chose one of the chairs. As he sank into it, he experienced a pang of homesickness for the furnishings of similar quality he used to own. Now he had to keep his bread in a fridge with an irritating hum.

Taking another glance around the room and the acreage beyond the windows, he questioned again just what the hell he was doing *here,* in an ivy-covered mansion, with a crippled man.

Foster Speakman probably had five years on him, which put him around forty. He was nice looking. Hard to tell how tall he would be standing, but Griff guessed just shy of six feet. He was wearing preppy clothes—navy blue golf shirt and khaki slacks, brown leather belt, matching loafers, tan socks.

The legs of his trousers looked like deflated balloons, not much flesh to fill them out.

"Something to drink?" Speakman asked pleasantly.

Caught staring and speculating, Griff shifted his attention back to his host's face. "A Coke?"

Speakman looked over at the man who'd answered the door. "Manuelo, two Cokes, *por favor*."

Manuelo was as square and solid as a sack of cement but moved soundlessly. Speakman noticed Griff watching the servant as he went to the bar and began pouring their drinks. "He's from El Salvador."

"Huh."

"He literally walked to the United States."

"Huh."

"He tends to me."

Griff could think of nothing to say to that, although he wanted to ask if Manuelo, despite his smile, kept a collection of shrunken heads under his bed.

"Did you drive from Big Spring today?" Speakman asked.

"My lawyer picked me up this morning."

"Long drive."

"I didn't mind it."

Speakman grinned. "I guess not. After being cooped up for so long." He waited until Griff had taken his drink from the small tray Manuelo extended to him, then took his own cut-crystal glass and raised it. "To your release."

"I'll drink to that."

Manuelo left through the double doors, pulling them closed behind him. Griff took another sip of Coke, becoming uncomfortable under Speakman's blatantly curious stare.

What was this? Invite a con for drinks week?

The whole scene was beginning to make him uneasy. Deciding to cut to the chase, he set his drink on the end table at his elbow. "Did you ask me here to get an up close and personal look at a has-been football player? Or a convicted felon?"

Speakman seemed unfazed by his rudeness. "I thought you might be in the market for a job."

Not wanting to look desperate or needy, Griff gave a noncommittal shrug.

"Any offers yet?" Speakman asked.

"None that have interested me."

"The Cowboys aren't—"

"No. Nor is any other team. I've been banned from the league. I doubt I could buy a ticket to an NFL game."

Speakman nodded as though he had already determined that was the way things were with Griff Burkett. "If you can't do something related to football, what did you plan to do?"

"I planned to serve my sentence and get out."

"Nothing beyond that?"

Griff sat back, again shrugged as though he didn't give a shit, reached for his Coke, and took another sip. "I've toyed with some ideas but haven't settled on anything yet."

"I own an airline. SunSouth."

Griff kept his features schooled, trying not to show that he was either surprised or impressed, when actually he was both. "I fly it. Or rather, I used to fly SunSouth often."

Speakman flashed an unself-conscious smile. "So do a lot of people, I'm pleased to say."

Griff looked around the beautiful room, his gaze stopping on some of its treasures, then came back to Speakman. "I bet you are."

Despite his drollness, Speakman's smile remained in place. "I invited you here to offer you a job."

Griff's heart did a little jig of gladness. A man like Foster Speakman could do him a lot of good. Now he remembered why the name had sounded familiar. Speakman was an influential force in Dallas, owning and operating one of the region's most successful enterprises. An endorsement from him, even a minor nod of pardon, would go a long way toward winning back some of the favor Griff had lost five years ago.

But he tamped down his bubbling optimism. For all he knew, the guy wanted him to strain the shit out of the sewage tanks on his airplanes. "I'm listening."

"The job I'm offering would give you immediate financial relief. I understand that your assets were liquidated to pay the fine the court imposed on you."

Hedging the truth, Griff said, "Most of them, yeah."

"Those proceeds were also used to cover substantial debts. Is that correct?"

"Look, Speakman, since you seem to know anyway, stop fishing. I lost everything and then some. Is that what you wanted to hear? I don't have a pot to piss in."

"Then I suppose a hundred thousand would come in handy."

Taken aback by the amount, Griff felt his irritation turn to suspicion. He'd learned the hard way to be wary of anything that seemed too easily come by. If it seemed too good to be true, it probably was. "A hundred thousand a year?"

"No, Mr. Burkett," Speakman said, smiling, enjoying himself. "A hundred thousand to seal our deal. Using a term you're familiar with, it would be like a signing bonus."

Griff stared at him for a count of ten. "A hundred grand. U.S. dollars."

"Legal tender. It's yours if you say yes to what I propose."

Griff carefully removed his ankle from his opposite knee and set both feet on the floor, buying time while his mind spun around the amount of money and how badly he needed it. "Are you thinking about using me to advertise your airline? Billboards, commercials, ads? That kind of thing? I wouldn't cotton to posing naked, but it could be negotiated."

Speakman smiled and shook his head. "I realize that endorsements were a significant part of your income when you were the starting quarterback of the Dallas Cowboys. That Number Ten jersey sold a lot of whatever it was advertising. But now I'm afraid an endorsement from you would repel customers, not attract them."

Even knowing that was true, Griff was pissed off to hear it. "Then what did you have in mind? Who do I have to kill?"

Speakman actually laughed out loud. "It's nothing that drastic."

"I don't know anything about airplanes."

"This isn't airline related."

"You need a new yardman?"

"No."

"Then I'm fresh out of guesses. What do I do to earn my hundred thousand dollars?"

"Make my wife pregnant."

CHAPTER

2

E XCUSE ME?"

"You heard correctly, Mr. Burkett. Another Coke?"

Griff continued to stare at his host until his question sank in. At least the crazy bastard was a courteous host. "No thanks."

Speakman rolled his chair over to the end table and picked up Griff's empty glass, carried it along with his to the wet bar, and placed both in a rack beneath the sink. He used a bar towel to wipe the granite countertop, although from where Griff sat, he could see that it was highly polished, not a single drop of liquid or streak of moisture on its glassy surface. Speakman folded the towel, lining up the hem evenly, and threaded it through a ring attached to the counter.

He rolled back to the table at Griff's elbow and replaced the coaster he'd used in its brass holder, gave it three taps, then put his chair in reverse and resumed his original place a few feet from where Griff sat.

Griff, watching these maneuvers, thought, *Courteous and* neat.

"Let me know if you change your mind about another drink," Speakman said.

Griff stood up, rounded his chair, looked back at Speakman to see if his lunacy could be detected at this distance, then walked over to the windows and looked outside. He needed to ground himself, make sure he hadn't fallen into a rabbit hole or something.

He felt as he had those first few weeks at Big Spring, when he would wake up disoriented and it would take several seconds for him to remember where he was and why. This was like that. He felt detached. He needed to get his bearings.

Beyond the windows, not a Mad Hatter in sight. Everything was still there and looking perfectly normal—the emerald grass, stone pathways winding through the flower beds, trees with sprawling branches shading it all. A pond in the distance. Blue sky. Overhead a jet was making its final approach into Dallas.

"One of ours."

Griff hadn't heard the approach of Speakman's chair and was startled to find him so close. Prison would do that to you, too. Make you jumpy. Linemen topping three hundred pounds used to charge at him bent on inflicting injury and pain, teeth bared behind their face guards, eyes slitted with malice. He'd been prepared for them and was conditioned to take their abuse.

But even in the minimum-security area of the prison, where the inmates were white-collar criminals, you stayed nervous twenty-four/seven. You kept your guard up and other people at arm's length.

Of course, he'd been that way before prison.

Speakman was watching the jet. "From Nashville. Due to touch down at seven oh seven." He glanced at his wristwatch. "Right on time."

Griff studied him for several seconds, then said, "The hell of it is, you seem perfectly sane."

"You doubt my sanity?"

"And then some."

"Why?"

"Well, for starters, I'm not wearing a sign that says sperm bank."

Speakman smiled. "Not the kind of job you thought I'd be offering, huh?"

"Not by a long shot." Griff glanced at his own wristwatch. "Look, I've got plans tonight. A get-together with some friends." There was no get-together. No friends, either. But it sounded plausible. "I need to get going to make it on time."

Speakman seemed to see through the lie. "Before declining my offer," he said, "at least hear me out."

He extended his hand as though to touch Griff's arm. Griff's flinch was involuntary, no way to prevent Speakman from noticing it. He looked up at Griff with puzzlement but pulled his hand back before making actual contact. "Sorry," Griff muttered.

"It's the wheelchair," Speakman said blandly. "It puts some people off. Like a disease or a bad-luck charm."

"It's not that. Not at all. It's, uh . . . Look, I think we're finished here. I gotta go."

"Please don't leave yet, Griff. Do you mind if I call you Griff? I think this is a good point at which to shift to first names, don't you?"

Speakman's eyes reflected the bright light from the windows. They were clear, intelligent eyes. Not a trace of madness or the kind of wild glee that signaled insanity. Griff wondered if Mrs. Speakman was aware of it. Hell, he wondered if there *was* a Mrs. Speakman. The millionaire might have been completely delusional as well as compulsively tidy.

When Griff failed to reply to the question about his name, Speakman's smile relaxed into an expression of disappointment. "At least stay long enough for me to finish making my pitch. I would hate for all my rehearsing to be for naught." He gave a quick smile. "Please."

Fighting a strong urge to get the hell out of there, but also feeling guilty for the physical rebuff he'd given the man, Griff returned to his chair and sat down. As he settled against the cushions, he noticed that the back of his shirt was damp with nervous perspiration. As soon as he could gracefully make an exit, he would *adiós*.

Speakman reopened the dialogue by saying, "I can't father a child. By any method." He paused as though to emphasize that. "If I had sperm," he added quietly, "you and I wouldn't be having this conversation."

Griff would just as soon not be having it. It wasn't easy to look a man in the eye while he was talking to you about losing his manhood. "Okay. So you need a donor."

"You mentioned a sperm bank."

Griff nodded curtly.

"Laura—that's my wife. She and I didn't want to go that route."

"Why not? For the most part, they're reputable, aren't they? Reliable? They do testing on the donors. All that."

Griff knew little about sperm banks and wasn't really interested in how they operated. He was thinking more about what had happened to Speakman to put him in that chair. Had he always been paraplegic, or was it a recent thing? Had he contracted a debilitating and degenerative disease? Been thrown by a horse? What?

"When the male partner is incapable of fathering children, as I am," Speakman said, "couples do use donor sperm. Most of the time, successfully."

Well, apparently he wasn't embarrassed by or self-conscious about his condition, and Griff had to give him credit for that. If he was in a situation like Speakman's, needing somebody like Manuelo to "tend" to him, he doubted he could be as accepting of it as Speakman appeared to be. He knew he wouldn't be able to talk about it so freely, especially with another man. Maybe Speakman was simply resigned.

He was saying, "Laura and I desperately want a child, Griff."

"Uh-huh," Griff said, not knowing what else to say.

"And we want our child to have physical characteristics similar to mine."

"Okay."

Speakman shook his head as though Griff still wasn't quite getting it. And he realized he wasn't when Speakman said, "We want everyone to believe that the child was fathered by me."

"Right," Griff said, but there was a hint of a question mark at the end of the word.

"This is extremely important to us. Vital. Mandatory, in fact." Speakman raised his index finger like a politician about to make the most important statement of his campaign. "No one must doubt that I'm the child's father."

Griff shrugged indifferently. "I'm not going to tell anybody."

Speakman relaxed, smiling. "Excellent. We're paying for your discretion as well as your . . . assistance."

Griff laughed lightly and raised both hands, palms out. "Wait a minute. When I said I wouldn't tell anybody, I meant I wouldn't tell anybody about this conversation. In fact, I'm not really interested in hearing any more. Let's consider this . . . uh . . . interview over, okay? You keep your hundred grand, and I'll keep my sperm, and this meeting will be our little secret."

He was almost out of his chair when Speakman said, "Half a million. Half a million dollars when Laura conceives."

Arrested in motion, Griff found it easier to sit back down than to stand up. He landed rather hard and sat staring at Speakman, aghast. "You're shittin' me."

"I assure you I'm not."

"Half a million?"

"You have blue eyes, light hair. Like mine. It's hard to tell now, but I'm taller than the average five feet eleven. We have similar genetic makeups, you and I. Similar enough anyway for a child you sire to be passed off as mine."

Griff's mind was spinning so fast it was hard to hang on to a thought. He was thinking dollar signs, Speakman was talking genes. "Those sperm banks have books." He pantomimed leafing through pages. "You go through them and find what you want for your kid. You pick out eye color, hair color, height. All that."

"I never buy anything sight unseen, Griff. I don't shop from catalogs. Certainly not for my child and heir. And there's still the risk of disclosure."

"Those records are kept confidential," Griff argued.

"Supposedly."

Griff thought of the gate with the disembodied voice, the high wall surrounding the property. Apparently privacy was a real issue with this guy. Like neatness. The psychologist at Big Spring would have had a field day over the obsessive way Speakman had removed the drinking glasses from view, folded the towel, and replaced the coaster.

Intrigued in spite of himself, Griff studied the millionaire for a long moment, then said, "So how would it work? I'd go to a doctor's office and jerk off into a jar and—"

"No office. If Laura was inseminated in a doctor's office, there would be talk."

"Who would talk?"

"The people who staff the office. Other patients who might see her there. People love to talk. Especially about celebrities."

"I'm a fallen star."

Laughing softly, Speakman said, "I was referring to Laura and me. But your involvement would certainly add another element to a delicious piece of gossip. It would be too tempting even for people bound by professional privilege."

"Okay, so I don't go to the doctor's office with you. You could take my semen in and claim it as yours. Who's to know?"

"You don't understand, Griff. That still leaves room for speculation. My condition is obvious. A specimen I claimed as mine could have come from the pool boy. A skycap. Anybody." He shook his head. "We're emphatic about this. No nurses, no chatty receptionists, no office open to the public. At all."

"So where? Here?" Griff envisioned taking a dirty magazine and a Dixie cup into one of the mansion's bathrooms, the mute manservant standing outside the door, waiting for him to finish and deliver the specimen.

No way, José. Or rather, *No way, Manuelo.*

But for half a million bucks?

Everyone had their price. He'd proved he did. Five years had decreased it considerably, but if Speakman was willing to pay him five hundred grand for doing what he'd been doing for free for the past five years, he wasn't going to let modesty stand in the way.

He'd walk away with six hundred thousand, counting the "signing bonus." The Speakmans would get the kid they desperately wanted. It was win-win, and it wasn't even against the law.

"I assume you'd have the doctor check me out first," he said. "For all you know, I could've taken up with a lover in prison and have HIV."

"I seriously doubt that," Speakman said drily, "but, yes, I would require you to undergo a thorough physical examination and bring me back a clean bill of health, signed by a physician. You could say it was for medical insurance."

It still seemed too easy. Griff wondered what he was overlooking. Where was the catch? "What if she doesn't get pregnant? Do I have to return the first hundred grand?"

Speakman hesitated. Griff tilted his head as though to communicate that this could be a deal breaker. Speakman said, "No. That would be yours to keep."

"Because if she doesn't conceive, it might not be my fault. Your wife may not be fertile."

"Who negotiated your contract with the Cowboys?"

"What? My former agent. Why?"

"A piece of advice, Griff. During a business negotiation, once you've won a point, drop it. Don't mention it again. I've already conceded that you could keep the initial hundred thousand."

"Okay." They hadn't covered that in the release preparation sessions.

Griff weighed his options, and they boiled down to this: he didn't have any options, other than saying no and walking away from mega cash. To turn this down, he'd have to be crazy. Crazy as Speakman and his old lady.

He raised one shoulder in a negligent shrug. "Then if that's all that's required, we have a deal. One point, though. I want to do my thing in the privacy of my own bathroom. The doctor will have to come to my place to pick up the stuff. I think you can freeze it, so I could give him several samples at one whack." He laughed at the inadvertent double entendre. "So to speak."

Speakman laughed, too, but was serious as sin when he said, "There won't be a doctor, Griff."

Just when he thought he had this figured out, Speakman hit him with something like a linebacker coming around on his blind side and knocking him on his ass. "What do you mean, no doctor? Who's gonna . . ." He made gentle thrusting motions with his hand. "Put it where it needs to go."

"You are," Speakman said quietly. "I'm sorry for not making this clear from the beginning. I insist on my child being conceived naturally. The way God intended."

Griff stared at him for several seconds, then he began to laugh. Either somebody had set him up for a whopper of a practical joke or Speakman was out of his frigging mind.

Nobody in Griff's life cared enough to play an elaborate joke on him. No one in his present life would go to the trouble. No one from his past would give him the time of day, much less invest the time it would take to set up this bizarre scenario and talk Speakman into going along.

No, he was betting that Speakman went beyond being an eccentric millionaire and neat freak and was, in fact, certifiable.

In any case, this was all one huge waste of time, and he'd lost patience with it. Flippantly, he said, "My job would be to fuck your wife?"

Speakman winced. "I don't care much for the vernacular, especially in—"

"Cut the bullshit, okay? You're hiring me to play stud. That's basically it, right?"

Speakman hesitated, then said, "Basically? Yes."

"And for half a mil, I guess you get to watch."

"That's insulting, Griff. To me. Certainly to Laura."

"Yeah, well . . ." He didn't apologize. Kinky sex was the least offensive factor of this whole interview. "About her, does she know your plan?"

"Of course."

"Uh-huh. What does she think about it?"

Speakman rolled his chair toward an end table where a cordless phone stood in its charger. "You can ask her yourself."

CHAPTER

3

UPSTAIRS, IN HER HOME OFFICE, LAURA SPEAKMAN CHECKED the clock on her desk. Only half an hour had elapsed since Griff Burkett's arrival. *Punctual* arrival. Being on time would definitely have won him marks with Foster. But of the other impressions he was making, were they good or bad?

For thirty minutes she'd been reading a new flight attendants' contract proposed by their union. She retained none of it. Giving up the pretense of working, she left her desk and began pacing the width of the office. It was a bright and airy room. There were drapes on the windows, carpet on the floor, crown molding at the ceiling. It was designated an office only by the desk and the computer setup concealed in an eight-foot-tall French antique armoire.

What was being said downstairs in the library? Not knowing was driving her mad, but Foster had insisted on meeting with Burkett alone.

"Let me test the waters," he'd said. "Once I get a sense of him, I'll ask you to join us."

"And if your sense of him isn't good, if you don't think he's suitable, then what?"

"Then I'll send him on his way, and you will have been spared an awkward and unproductive interview."

His plan made sense, she supposed. But it wasn't in her nature to

delegate decision making. Certainly not on something this important. Not even to her husband.

Of course, if she and Foster weren't in complete accord about
Griff Burkett's suitability, he would be rejected. Nevertheless, she
hated to miss seeing his initial reaction to their proposal and gauging
that reaction for herself. How he reacted would tell a lot about him.

She looked across at the closed door and, for a moment, considered going downstairs and presenting herself. But that would violate
Foster's careful planning. He wouldn't welcome the interruption to
his schedule.

The pacing was only making her more agitated. She returned to
her desk chair, reclined in it, closed her eyes, and utilized relaxation
techniques she had taught herself while still a university student. After going days without a break from her studies, when her head was
so packed full of information it couldn't tolerate any more, she would
force herself to lie down, close her eyes, do her deep breathing exer-
cises, and rest, if not sleep. Practicing the technique helped. If nothing else, it slowed her down, made her admit to the limitations of
mind and body.

Difficult as it was for her to accept, right now there was nothing
she could do but wait.

As her agitation gradually abated, her thoughts drifted back to
the events and circumstances that had brought her to this point in
her life, to this day and hour, to hiring a total stranger to make a
baby with her.

It had begun with the color of the uniforms . . .

Headlines on the business pages had blared the news when Foster
Speakman, last in line of the prominent Dallas family who'd been
made wealthy by oil and gas, bought the distressed SunSouth Airlines.

For years the mismanaged airline had been teetering on the brink
of total collapse. It had suffered a lengthy pilots' strike, followed by
a blistering media exposé on its slipshod maintenance practices; then
a disastrous crash took fifty-seven lives. Declaring bankruptcy had
been the airline's final hope of recovery, but unfortunately that last
gasp hadn't saved it.

Everyone thought the Speakman heir was insane when he spent a huge chunk of his fortune to buy the airline. For days the story dominated local business news: COSTLY HOBBY FOR MILLIONAIRE? SUNSOUTH'S SALVATION, SPEAKMAN'S RUIN? The acquisition was even mentioned with mild derision on national broadcasts. It was implied that yet another rich Texan had gone and done something crazy.

Foster Speakman further surprised everyone by immediately grounding the airplanes, laying off thousands of employees with a promise to rehire them once he'd had time to conduct a thorough analysis of the airline's situation. He closed the doors to all media, telling frustrated reporters that they would be notified when he had something newsworthy to tell them.

In the ensuing months, Foster sequestered himself with financial and operational experts and advisers. Upper-echelon executives of the old regime were given the option to retire early with fair retirement packages. Those who didn't opt to do so were fired outright.

The firings weren't vindictive, only sound business acumen. Foster had a vision, but he also realized that, in order to bring it about, he would need people around him with knowledge equal to or greater than his. With his enthusiasm, charisma, and seemingly bottomless bank account, he lured the best in the industry away from cushy positions with other airlines.

Almost three months after taking over, Foster called all the new department heads together for the first of many roundtable discussions. Laura was there, representing the flight attendants. It was at that meeting she saw the man in charge for the first time.

She knew what he looked like from all the media coverage he had received, but photographs and television images had failed to capture his crackling vitality. Energy radiated from him like an electric aura.

He was lean, handsome, confident, personable. He strode into the conference room dressed in a perfectly tailored pin-striped suit, soft gray shirt, conservative tie. But soon after the meeting was called to order, he removed his double-breasted jacket, draped it over the back of his chair, loosened his tie, and literally rolled up his sleeves. By doing so, he indicated that he intended to do what needed to be done, that he didn't consider himself above applying elbow grease, and that he expected the same work ethic from everyone in that room.

The date had been set for the airline to resume operation. It was circled in red on the large calendar placed on an easel where all could see. "Target date," Foster announced happily. "Following our review of the budget, each of you will get a chance to tell me why I'm out of my mind and that there's no way in hell we'll make that deadline."

Everyone chuckled as expected. The meeting commenced.

The new CFO—hired because he was a notorious penny-pincher who had won his reputation by saving an American auto manufacturer from going under—was asked to talk them through the proposed budget item by item.

In his monotonous drone, he went on uninterrupted for a full ten minutes, then said, "Flight attendant program, the allotment remains the same. Next is food and beverage. Now here—"

"Excuse me."

The CFO raised his head and, looking over his reading glasses, surveyed the table to find the voice that had interrupted him. Laura raised her hand to identify herself. "Before moving on, this figure begs discussion."

He lowered one bushy eyebrow into a near scowl. "What isn't clear?"

"It's perfectly clear," she replied. "What needs discussion is how sorely underbudgeted this department is."

"Everyone at this table thinks his department is underbudgeted." He squinted at her, referred to the agenda for the meeting, and then squinted at her again. "Who are you, anyway?"

Before she had a chance to answer, Foster Speakman spoke from the head of the table. "Ladies and gentlemen, for those of you who haven't met her, this is Ms. Laura Taylor."

Her lips parted wordlessly. It came as a shock to her that Foster Speakman knew she existed.

The CFO removed his reading glasses and, after giving Laura a glance of consternation, asked Foster, "Where's Hazel Cooper?"

He said, "Ms. Taylor, will you do the honors?"

She rose to the challenge, saying evenly, "Ms. Cooper tendered her resignation day before yesterday."

"She did, that's right," came a voice on the other side of the table. The man was director of Human Resources. "I sent a blanket e-mail. Didn't y'all get it?" His gaze swept around the table, but there was a unanimous shaking of heads. "Oh, well, Hazel took early retirement. Said as long as there was a major shake-up, she might just as well make the move now, 'cause she planned on retiring next year anyway. I asked Ms. Taylor to sit in for her until another director for the department can be hired."

The CFO coughed behind his hand. "All well and good then. Once a new director is in place, I'll take up the budget for that department with him."

"Or her," Foster said.

The CFO turned red-faced. "Of course, I was speaking generically."

"As long as we're here, let's discuss the budget for this department," Foster said.

The CFO gave Laura another irritated look. "No offense to Ms. Taylor, but is she qualified to conduct that discussion?"

Foster riffled through a stack of file folders he had carried in with him. He found the one he wanted, stacked the others precisely, leaving no edge overlapping another, then opened the one he had withdrawn.

"Laura Eleanor Taylor . . . hmm, I'll skip down to . . . Here we go. Graduated with honors from Stephen F. Austin State University. Two years later she earned an MBA from Southern Methodist's business school. Again with honors.

"Applied and was accepted into the flight attendant program for SunSouth Airlines in 2002. Advancement, advancement, and another advancement," he said, consulting her employee record in the file.

"Promoted to do training and performance evaluation in 2005. Was a thorn in the side of the previous management and has made a nuisance of herself with Ms. Cooper by writing memo after memo, copies of which I have," he said, holding up a handful of sheets, "criticizing standards and practices now in place and suggesting ways in which the department could be vastly improved." He read directly from one memo. " '*But*'—which is underlined—'not without insight, intelligence, and plain common sense on the part of the new owner.' Who happens to be . . ." He paused for what seemed to Laura an eternity. "Me."

He replaced all the sheets in the file folder, then set it on the top of the stack. Only after lining them up to ruler-edge exactness did he stand. "Will you accompany me outside, Ms. Taylor? Bring your things."

She sat stunned, cheeks flaming, feeling every eye in the room, except Foster Speakman's, on her. He was already at the door of the conference room, going through it, expecting her to follow.

With as much dignity as possible, she retrieved her handbag and briefcase, then stood up. "Ladies, gentlemen," she said. Some, embarrassed for her, averted their eyes. Others gave her nods of sympathy. The CFO, with whom this had started, opened his mouth as though to apologize, then thought better of it and gave a regretful shake of his head.

She stepped through the door and pulled it closed behind her, then squared her shoulders and turned toward Foster Speakman, who was standing in the empty corridor. "You're not nearly as ferocious looking as your memos led me to expect, Ms. Taylor."

Her cheeks still burned with humiliation, but she maintained her composure. "I didn't realize my interdepartmental memos were being forwarded to you."

"In view of her impending retirement, I suppose Ms. Cooper felt the issues you raised were no longer her problem but mine."

"I suppose."

"Would knowing I was reading the memos have changed your opinions?"

"Not at all. But perhaps I would have softened the tone and language in which I expressed them."

He folded his arms across his chest and studied her for several moments. "Satisfy my curiosity. Why, with an MBA from SMU's highly regarded business school, did you become a flight attendant? It's an honorable profession, but you were overqualified."

"Four times I applied to SunSouth for an entry-level management position and was passed over each time."

"Were you told why?"

"No, but the positions went to men."

"Gender discrimination?"

"I'm making no accusations, only telling you what happened."

"So you settled for a flight attendant's position."

"I accepted it, but I didn't settle for it. I thought that once I got my foot in the door—"

"You would distinguish yourself and work your way up to the level for which you had applied in the first place."

"More or less."

He smiled. "Having studied your file, I thought as much. For all I know, you have your sights set on my job, Ms. Taylor. In a way, I hope you do, because I admire ambition. But today I'm offering you Ms. Cooper's position as director of the flight attendant program. Add to that the title of vice-president in charge of . . . et cetera."

For the third time since she'd laid eyes on him, he had stunned her. First, just by knowing who she was. Second, by calling her out of the meeting for what she thought would be immediate dismissal. Now this. "Just like that?"

He laughed. "I never do anything 'just like that.' No, this offer comes after careful analysis of your employment record. I also ran credit and criminal background checks, as I did with every person in that room. You passed, but you have an outstanding parking ticket that hasn't been paid."

"I mailed the check yesterday. Grudgingly. There was no sign posted, but it would have cost more to contest the ticket than simply to pay it."

"A practical decision, Ms. Taylor. I believe your drive, ambition, and talent have been wasted by managers who lacked 'insight, intelligence, and plain common sense,'" he said, his smile widening as he quoted from her memo. "I assume you accept this position?"

Still shaky, but with relief instead of the humiliation of being summarily terminated, she said yes.

With no more ceremony than that, he said, "Good. Now, shall

we return to the others?" He reached for the door, then paused. "A word of warning: You'll have a fight on your hands over that budget. Are you up to it?"

"Absolutely."

Murmured conversations ceased when they reentered. Foster startled the others by introducing her by her new title, but most seemed more pleased than not. "Mr. George," Foster said, addressing the human resources director, "following this meeting, I, you, and Ms. Taylor can go over the contract I prepared in advance and with the hope that she would accept my offer. I think you'll both find it satisfactory." He slapped the table lightly. "Now, Ms. Taylor, it's your first official duty to tell us why the budget allotment for your department is inadequate."

Out of the frying pan. Laura took a deep breath, knowing this was an acid test and hoping she didn't blow it. "While we've been grounded, we've lost a lot of flight attendants. Some have gone to other airlines. Others have left the industry altogether. Now I'm faced with hiring replacements. I can't entice the best applicants if I can't offer them starting salaries and benefits equal to those offered by our competitors. I'd like to offer them better, but I'd settle for equal. Second, the uniforms are ugly and drab."

"I thought attendants paid for their own uniforms."

"They do," Laura said. "But there's no budget for a new design. Which brings me to another point."

"The 'look of the airline'?" All heads turned toward the head of the table. Foster tapped the top file folder on the stack. "To quote from your latest memo, Ms. Taylor. Will you please elaborate?"

Things were moving along too quickly. She hadn't counted on being elevated to an executive this suddenly. Nor had she planned on being placed immediately in the hot seat. But she had been dwelling on this topic for weeks. In her idle time, she had thought long about what she would do if she were running the show. Now the new owner of the airline had invited her to elaborate on the bullet points of her many memos. She was ready.

"Days ago, Hazel, Ms. Cooper, gave me a copy of the proposed budget so I could familiarize myself with it in advance of this meeting. You're spending a lot of money to make drastic changes in the infrastructure and in total reorganization of the airline's operation," she said, addressing Foster directly. "You're making it brand spanking new. But you've stopped short at conveying its newness to consumers."

"Changing the color of the flight attendant uniforms is easy," someone remarked. "Ticket and gate agents, too."

Laura acknowledged the comment with a nod. "Their appearance is important because they deal one-on-one with our customers. So the impression they make is vital. But we're aiming for an about-face in public opinion of SunSouth Airlines. With that as our goal, I don't think changing the color of the uniforms is sufficient." Her gaze moved around the table, ending on Foster. "But as the most recently appointed department director, I don't want to overstep my bounds."

"No, please," he said, indicating she should continue.

Holding his gaze, she said, "When we relaunch SunSouth, if we look the same, consumers will figure we *are* the same."

Another of the directors said, "It's been suggested that we change the name of the airline."

"That suggestion was voted down by the new board of directors," someone else contributed.

Laura said, "I agree we should keep our name. It's a good name. An excellent name."

"But?" Foster said.

"But it suggests light. Sunny days. Bright skies and open landscapes. Our planes are the color of storm clouds, and so are the uniforms." She paused, knowing the proposal she was about to make was destined to raise a chorus of protests. "Even if it means making cuts in other areas, including the flight attendant program, I propose we budget to retain a first-rate design company to revamp the entire look of the airline."

"Hear, hear!" This from the well-liked head of advertising and marketing, a genial young man named Joe McDonald. He always wore an outlandish bow tie and suspenders. Everyone at SunSouth knew him because he made it a point to know everyone. He was an equal-opportunity teaser, from executives to the janitors who came in after hours to clean the offices. "Thank you, Laura, for putting your butt on the line, thereby saving me from having to place mine there."

Everyone laughed. The discussion continued but in a more light-hearted mode.

Laura's proposal, seconded by Joe McDonald, was ultimately acted upon, although not without many lengthy meetings and hours of debate. Cost was the major factor. Designers of the caliber she proposed didn't come cheap. Then, revamping a fleet of airplanes inside and out was exorbitantly expensive. Every coat of paint on an airplane added weight, which required an increase in the fuel needed to fly the aircraft, and therefore an increase in operational costs that was passed on to passengers in the form of ticket prices, which Foster Speakman had gone on record saying were going to be the lowest in the industry.

With that in mind, the design company suggested stripping the planes of paint and applying the newly designed logo to the silver metal. Eventually the shade of red used in the logo became the signature color of the new flight attendant uniforms. They were tailored and professional looking but conveyed a vivacity and friendliness that the media picked up on and extolled. The pilots' uniforms went from navy blue to khaki with red neckties.

The first flight of the renovated airline departed at six twenty-five the morning of March tenth—its scheduled relaunch date. That evening, Foster Speakman and his wife, Elaine, hosted a lavish party in their home. Everyone who was anyone in Dallas had been extended an invitation to the black-tie event.

Laura's escort for the evening was a friend with whom she played mixed-partners tennis. Their friendship was uncomplicated and un-romantic. He was divorced, owned his own accounting firm, was at ease with strangers and consequently someone she didn't have to cater to, worry about, or look after.

Indeed, shortly after they arrived at the mansion he excused himself to go look at the billiard room. Once featured in an issue of *Architectural Digest,* it was reputed to be a guys' fantasy room. "Take your time," she told him. "I'll be busy mingling."

Mrs. Speakman, Elaine, was a gorgeous woman, impeccably turned out in an understated designer gown and breathtaking jewelry. But hers was a frail beauty, fragile, like that of a character F. Scott Fitzgerald might have conjured. Like her husband, she was blond and blue eyed, but hers was a watercolor version. Standing arm in arm with him, she paled in comparison, literally.

"It's so nice to finally meet you," she said to Laura warmly when Foster introduced them. "I serve on the board of SunSouth—one of the few to survive the shake-up when the new owner assumed control." She gave her husband a nudge in the ribs.

Leaning in, Foster lowered his voice to a whisper. "I understand he can be a real bastard."

"Don't believe it," Elaine said to Laura.

"I don't. My experience has been that he's tough and knows what he wants, but he's a pleasure to work with."

"And a sweetheart at home," his wife said. The two smiled at each other, then Elaine turned back to Laura. "We on the board have heard about your excellent ideas and innovations. On behalf of the board members, the investors, and myself, thank you for your valuable contributions."

"Thank you, but you give me far too much credit, Mrs. Speakman."

"Elaine."

Laura acknowledged that with a slight nod. "Foster has made it known that the new SunSouth is a team effort. Every employee has a voice in the company."

"But some voices offer substantially more than others," Elaine said, smiling.

"Thank you again. However, I still maintain that our success will be attributed to your husband's motivational and management skills."

"Am I blushing?" he asked.

Elaine regarded him adoringly, then to Laura she said, "The gentleman I saw you arrive with, is that your—"

"Good friend," Laura said, cutting her off and hoping to avoid having to explain her single status. Although thousands of women in their thirties remained unmarried, it seemed an explanation was still required.

The truth of it was that no one, not even the occasional lover—

and there hadn't been many—had been as important to Laura as the pursuit of her career. But somehow that simple explanation fell short of satisfying people's curiosity. "He's dazzled by your billiard room. I may have to drag him out."

They chitchatted for a while longer, but Laura was aware of others who wanted time with the couple. She shook hands with both and moved away.

Later, as they were leaving, she let her friend deal with the parking valet while she looked for an opportunity to thank her hosts. She spotted them across the room, their heads together, talking privately. Foster leaned down and said something that caused Elaine to laugh. He pressed a kiss on her smooth temple. Laura was struck again by what an attractive and obviously enamored couple they were.

"He's devoted to her."

Laura turned to find a co-worker standing beside her. She, too, had been observing the Speakmans.

"And she to him," Laura said.

"She's lovely."

"Inside as well as out. A real lady."

"Yes," the woman sighed. "That's what makes it so tragic."

Laura turned toward her. "Tragic?"

The co-worker, realizing her mistake, touched Laura's arm. "I'm sorry. I thought you knew. Elaine Speakman is ill. In fact, she's dying."

The sudden laughter coming from downstairs was muted by distance but loud enough to rouse Laura from her reverie. She didn't recognize it as Foster's familiar laugh, so it had to have come from Griff Burkett. What could Foster possibly have said to bring on a laugh?

A few moments later, the telephone on her desk rang. *Finally,* she thought. She picked up the phone before the second ring. "Foster?"

"Can you join us, darling?"

Her heart bumped. His summons meant that, at least so far, it was a go. "I'll be right down."

CHAPTER
4

WHILE WAITING ON SPEAKMAN'S WIFE TO JOIN THEM, GRIFF had been studying the globe. Suspended within a polished brass stand, it was as large as a beach ball and made of semiprecious gems. It was quite a trinket. He speculated you could buy a damn good car for what it cost.

Funny how having money, or not, changed your perspective. Recalling the rarely used, superfluous items in his Toy Box, he couldn't think too badly of Speakman for having a fancy globe he could well afford.

Griff turned toward the library doors when he heard them open. He expected to get his first look at Mrs. Speakman, but instead the stolid Manuelo came in.

He went straight to Speakman and extended a small silver tray. On it were a prescription bottle of tablets and a glass of water. Speakman took a pill, washing it down with three sips of water. They had a brief conversation in Spanish, then Speakman said to Griff, "While Manuelo is here, can he get you anything?"

Griff shook his head.

Speakman looked up at the Central American and dismissed him with a soft *"Nada más. Gracias."*

Manuelo and Mrs. Speakman met in the open doorway. He stepped aside so she could come into the room, then he left, pulling the double doors closed behind him. But Griff was no longer interested in Manuelo. He was focused on Mrs. Speakman. Laura, her name was.

She didn't give off crazy vibes. In fact, she seemed perfectly composed and in control of her faculties. She didn't look toward Griff, although he created a sizable silhouette even in a large room like this one. Instead, she crossed to where her husband sat in his wheelchair. She placed her hand on his shoulder, leaned down, and kissed his cheek.

When they pulled apart, Speakman said, "Laura, this is Griff Burkett."

Since she had ignored him up till now, he was surprised when she walked toward him, right hand extended. "Mr. Burkett. How do you do?" He met her halfway, and they shook hands. Like her husband's, her handshake was dry and firm. A businesswoman's handshake.

Griff limited his greeting to a simple "Hi."

She dropped his hand but maintained eye contact. "Thank you for coming. Didn't you get released just this morning?"

"We've been over that," Speakman said, humor in his voice.

"Oh, sorry. I would ask you about the long drive, but I rather imagine that topic has been exhausted, too."

"It has," Griff said.

"Small talk sounds even smaller in this particular situation, doesn't it?"

He wasn't going to touch that with a ten-foot pole.

She said, "I'm sure you were offered something to drink."

"I was. I'm fine."

"If you change your mind, let me know."

They might have been missing critical marbles, but their manners remained intact.

"Please sit down, Mr. Burkett." She took the chair nearest her husband's wheelchair.

Griff hadn't had time to speculate on what Foster Speakman's missus would be like, but if he had to define his initial reaction, it would be surprise. There was nothing in her handshake or straightforward gaze that could be interpreted as nervous, flirtatious, or coy. Nor did she seem embarrassed by the topic they now had in common. He could have been there to talk about cleaning their carpets.

She didn't act submissive or browbeaten, either, like this was something her husband had cooked up for his own gratification and she had agreed to go along with it under duress.

Hell, he didn't know what he had expected, but whatever it was, Laura Speakman wasn't it.

She was wearing a pair of black slacks and a white shirt, sleeveless, with pleats—he thought that was what they were called—stitched in rows down the front. Like a tuxedo shirt. Low-heeled black shoes. A serviceable wristwatch, a plain wedding band. Some of the players on the football team had worn diamonds in their ears much bigger and flashier than the ones in hers.

Her hair was dark and cut short. Sort of . . . swirly. He figured it would curl if it were worn longer. She was on the tallish side of average, slender, and, judging by her bare biceps, fit. Tennis maybe. A couple of times a week, she probably did yoga or Pilates, one of those women's workouts for toning and flexibility.

He tried to keep from staring, tried to avoid looking at the features of her face too closely, although his overall impression was that if he had spotted her in a crowd, he probably would have done a double take. She wasn't a babe, not like the kind of silicone-fortified Dallas dolly who used to hang out in the nightclubs frequented by him and his teammates, single or not. But Laura Speakman wasn't homely. Not by any stretch.

And another thing, she looked healthy enough to have a baby. Young enough, too, if she didn't waste time. Mid-thirties, maybe. Around his age.

He felt awkward, standing there in the center of the room, the two of them looking at him as though waiting for him to entertain them.

"Mr. Burkett? Griff?" Speakman nodded toward the chair facing them.

He'd told himself that the first chance he got, he was going to say "Thanks, but no thanks" and bolt. But he felt compelled to stay. Hell if he knew why.

Well, there was the six hundred grand. The figure had a nice ring to it that was pretty damn compelling.

He walked over to the chair and sat down. Looking directly at Laura Speakman, he said, "Your husband told me you're all for this. Is that true?"

"Yes."

No hesitation. Not even a blink. "Okay. But, excuse me for saying, it's . . ."

"Unorthodox?"

"I was going to say it's freaking nuts. A guy asking another guy, *paying* another guy, to sleep with his wife."

"Not sleep with, Mr. Burkett. Not in the context that implies. Impregnate. As for the freakiness of it, it's not unprecedented. In fact, it's scriptural. Genesis. Remember?"

In the household where Griff had grown up, there'd been no Bible. When he went to school and learned the Pledge of Allegiance, he was shocked to hear that it had the cussword *God* in it. He soon realized that *God* wasn't always used in combination with *damn*.

In any case, it came as shocking news to him that anything like this was in the Bible.

"We want a baby very badly, Mr. Burkett," she said.

"There are other ways to get pregnant."

"There are, yes. Our reasons for doing it this way are personal and shouldn't concern you."

"They do."

"They shouldn't," she repeated.

"We, uh, do our thing, I go home and sleep with a clear conscience. Is that it?"

"That's what it amounts to, yes."

He looked at her, wondering how she could speak so calmly about the two of them getting it on, when her husband was sitting right there holding her hand. Griff looked from her to Speakman, and the man seemed to read his mind.

"Before you joined us, Laura, Griff suggested that . . . well, that I would be observing the two of you while you perform."

She'd been looking at her husband as he explained. Several seconds passed before she turned her gaze back to Griff, and he took exception to her affronted frown. "Hey, don't look at me like *I'm* the pervert here."

"You think this is perverted?"

"What do you call it?"

"Would you think it was perverted if we were asking you to donate a kidney? Or give blood?"

He laughed. "There's a big difference. To donate a kidney you don't have to . . . touch," he said, quickly substituting the word he'd been about to say. "You never even have to meet."

"Unfortunately, the reproductive physiology is such that *touching* is necessary."

The hell it was. He didn't have to plant the seed personally to yield the crop. But he'd already argued that point with her husband. Speakman was determined for her to conceive naturally. She didn't seem to have an ethical or moral problem with it, so why was he making an issue of it? Mentally shrugging, he reached a decision: They wanted him to fuck her, he could fuck her. It wasn't like she had three eyes or something.

He addressed Speakman. "A handshake and I get a hundred grand?"

Speakman rolled his chair over to a desk and opened the lap drawer. He took a manila envelope from it, and when he came back and extended it, Griff was reminded of having to accept a cash loan from his lawyer like a kid getting an allowance. The sooner he was no longer obligated to anyone, the better.

He took the envelope.

Speakman said, "Inside is a key to a safe-deposit box and a signature card. You sign it. I'll see that the card gets returned to the bank tomorrow, where it will remain on file. While I'm there, I'll deposit your cash in the box. You can pick it up, um, say anytime after two o'clock tomorrow afternoon. Laura and I have a meeting in the morning with representatives of the flight attendants' union to discuss their new contract."

Hiring a stud was just another entry on their busy agenda.

Fine with him, so long as the money made it into that box.

Griff removed the signature card and glanced at it. "What about the physical? What if I flunk?"

The couple glanced at each other, but Foster spoke for both of them. "We'll take it on faith that you won't."

"That's a lot of faith."

"If we anticipated a problem, you wouldn't be here."

"Okay, I get my advance, and you get my clean bill of health. And then?"

"And then you wait to be notified of where you need to be and when. Laura's next ovulation."

Griff looked at her. She was gazing back at him calmly, apparently not caring that her ovulation was being discussed. He would have liked some clarification on exactly what ovulation entailed, but he wasn't going to ask. He didn't need to know. He knew how to fuck, and that was all they were requiring of him.

"You'll meet once a month for as long as it takes to conceive," Speakman explained. He lifted his wife's hand to his mouth and kissed the palm. "Hopefully it won't take too many cycles."

"Yeah, I hope that, too," Griff said. "I'll be half a million dollars richer."

Feeling restless again, he got up and moved to one of the bookcases. He read a few of the titles, those that were in English, but they didn't register with him. They sounded like philosophy and boring stuff. Not an Elmore Leonard or Carl Hiaasen among them.

"Something troubling you, Griff?"

He turned back to the couple. "Why me?"

"I explained that," Speakman replied.

"There are a lot of blond, blue-eyed guys around."

"But none with your particular genetic makeup. You have everything we could wish for our child. Strength, amazing stamina, speed, agility, even perfect eyesight and uncanny coordination. I could go on. There were articles written about you, published not just in sports magazines but in medical journals, about what an incredible specimen of the human male body you are."

Griff remembered the articles, written by trainers and sports medicine experts, one of whom had dubbed him "a biologic masterpiece." He'd caught hell over that in the locker room, his teammates taunting him about his so-called perfection and wanting to test it with the crudest physical contests they could devise. It was another matter when he took chicks to bed. They really got off on screwing a "masterpiece."

But he also remembered the scathing editorials that had followed his fall from grace. In them he had been lambasted not only for his crime but for squandering his God-given attributes.

God-given, my ass, he thought.

Those who had marveled over him wouldn't have thought he was so bloody perfect if they'd known the two who'd spawned him. If Mr. and Mrs. Speakman could have seen what he'd come from, they would have had second thoughts, too. Did they really want the blood of his parents flowing through the veins of their kid?

"You don't know anything about my origins. Maybe I just lucked out, got a few good genes that stacked up right by sheer accident. My gene pool could be mucked up with any number of bad seeds."

"We would take that chance no matter who the sperm donor was, even myself," Speakman said. "Why are you trying to talk us out of this, Griff?"

"I'm not." Actually, to some extent, he was. He'd spent five years in prison thinking about the bad choices he'd made. If he'd learned nothing else, he'd learned not to jump in headfirst until he knew exactly how deep the water was.

He said, "I just don't want to get into the middle of this and then have something go wrong that I'll be blamed for."

"What could go wrong?" Laura asked.

He laughed bitterly. "You haven't been around much, have you? Believe me, things can go wrong. For instance, what if I fire blanks?"

"You mean, what if you have a low sperm count?" Speakman asked.

Griff gave a brusque nod.

"Do you have reason to suspect that's the case?"

"No. But I don't know. I'm just asking, What if?"

"When you go for your medical exam, have it tested." Speakman paused, then said, "I believe you're experiencing a carryover of prison paranoia."

"You're goddamn right I am."

A heavy silence followed. Speakman rubbed his jaw as though

sorting through words to find the right ones. "Now that the subject has been broached, let's talk about your incarceration."

"What about it?"

"I'll admit that it factored into our choosing you."

Griff covered his heart with his hand, pretending to have had his feelings hurt. "You mean there was more to it than my being the ideal physical specimen?"

Speakman ignored his sarcasm. "You cheated your team, the league, and most of all your fans. Making you a persona non grata, Griff. I'm afraid you'll be subject to insults."

"I haven't had any confrontations."

"There hasn't been time for any," Laura said.

Her reasonable tone irritated him. "I'm not expecting to win any popularity contests, okay? I cheated and broke the law. I was punished for my crime. All that's behind me."

"But there's also the matter of the bookmaker who died."

Griff had wondered when that would come up. If they had any smarts at all, and he believed both did, they would inevitably have asked about Bandy. He was surprised only that it was the wife who had cracked open the delicate topic.

"Bill Bandy didn't *die*, Mrs. Speakman. He was murdered."

"You were a suspect."

"I was questioned."

"You were arrested."

"But never charged."

"Neither was anyone else."

"So?"

"So the murder remains unsolved."

"Not my problem."

"I hope not."

"What the hell—"

"Did you do it?"

"No!"

Their exchange was heated and rapid, followed by a tense silence that Griff refused to break. He'd said what he had to say. He didn't kill Bill Bandy. Period. The end.

"However," Speakman said in the soft and conciliatory tone of an undertaker, "the shadow of suspicion *was* cast on you, Griff. You were eventually released for lack of evidence, but that doesn't vindicate you."

"Look, if you think I killed Bandy, then what the hell am I doing here?" He flung his arms wide to encompass the room, the house. "Why would you want me to father your kid?"

"We don't think you committed murder," Speakman said. "Absolutely not."

Griff shifted his angry gaze over to Laura to see if she shared her husband's belief in his innocence. Her expression remained impassive, not accusatory, but sure as hell not exonerating.

Then why was she hiring him to go to bed with her? Did he really need this kind of abuse?

Yeah, unfortunately he did. He needed the money. He had to get back on his feet, and six hundred grand was a better than fair shot at doing so. To hell with them, with her, if she thought he'd clobbered Bandy. They must not have felt too ambiguous about it, either way, or he wouldn't be here. On top of being crazy, they were hypocrites.

"The matter of Bandy's homicide as well as the federal crimes for which you were convicted remain black marks against your name, Griff," Speakman said.

"I'm aware of that."

"So how realistic is it that someone around here will hire you? How realistic is it that someone will hire you for any amount, much less for what Laura and I are offering?"

The answer was obvious. When Griff declined to waste his breath on it, Speakman continued. "Your prospects are bleak. You can't play football. You can't coach football. You can't write about or talk about football, because none of the media outlets will hire you to do so. You admitted having to liquidate all your assets to pay your debts, indicating to me that you didn't save for a rainy day."

Speakman seemed to enjoy highlighting his shortcomings. Maybe, Griff thought, he should challenge him to a footrace. See who was better at that. "I made three million a year from the Cowboys, plus endorsements," he said tightly. "Everybody got a chunk of it, starting with my agent and the IRS, but what I got to keep, I spent, and had a whale of a great time doing it. What's your point?"

"My point is that you seem to have no head for business or you would have appropriated your income differently. It also appears you had no talent for larceny, or you wouldn't have got caught."

"A trap was laid for me. I walked into it."

"Nevertheless." After a beat, Speakman said, "I'm not trying to insult you, Griff."

"Really?"

Again Speakman ignored his caustic tone. "You asked why you were chosen."

"I'd almost forgotten the question."

"It required a long explanation. And I wanted to be brutally honest about our reasons for extending you this offer. Primarily, you have the genetic makeup to create the child we desire. Second, for reasons just discussed, you're in urgent need of the money we're offering to pay. Last, you're totally independent.

"You have no family, no real friends, no attachments, no one to whom you must account, and that is a tremendous benefit to us. We've emphasized the confidentiality this arrangement demands. We're the only three people who will ever know that I didn't sire the child Laura will conceive."

Griff was somewhat placated. Besides, he couldn't afford to get huffy. Especially over the bald truth. He moved to the desk, picked up a crystal paperweight, weighed it in his palm. "You're putting a lot of trust in me to keep my mouth shut."

Speakman chuckled. "Actually, we're not. We're putting a lot of trust in greed."

"Six hundred thousand?" Griff set down the paperweight and grinned at Speakman. "Not all that much when you think about it. Not what I'd call greedy."

Laura looked at her husband. "You haven't told him the rest?"

"We hadn't got that far," Speakman replied.

Griff said, "The rest?"

Speakman rolled his chair over to the desk and picked up the paperweight. Taking a handkerchief from his pants pocket, he used it to polish the crystal as he smiled up at Griff. "It's not that we question your integrity."

"Bullshit. You'd be fools not to question it."

"Right," Speakman said, laughing softly. "We would." With the handkerchief still wrapped around the paperweight, he replaced it on the desk, moved it an eighth of an inch to the left, then slowly withdrew the handkerchief, which he refolded into a perfect square before returning it to his pocket.

"So, for my and Laura's peace of mind, and to ensure your silence, you'll be paid one million dollars upon the birth of our child. Additionally, you'll receive one million dollars each year on his birthday. And all you have to do in return is forget you ever knew us."

CHAPTER

5

GRIFF TOSSED THE HONDA'S KEYS TO THE VALET PARKING attendant and walked briskly into the sleek lobby of the upscale building. A swank hotel occupied the lower twelve floors, condos the top twelve.

The lobby bar was relatively quiet on this midweek evening. A pianist was playing Sinatra-type standards on a white baby grand. Most of the tables were occupied by businessmen, nursing cocktails while they played one-upmanship.

The bar accessed a lighted patio where seating was available, but Griff chose to stay indoors, where he could enjoy the air-conditioning while keeping an eye on the entrance. He claimed a free table, signaled the waitress, and ordered a bourbon.

"House or label?"

"House is fine."

"Water?"

"Rocks."

"Want to start a tab?"

"Please."

"Will anyone be joining you?"

"No."

"I'll be right back."

Although the occasion—getting out of prison—and the day he'd had—his bizarre meeting with the Speakmans—seemed to call for a highball or two, Griff didn't really like to drink. Since he'd had to mop up regurgitated booze so often as a kid, he'd never really developed a taste for it.

But the drink the waitress delivered to him looked and smelled good. The first sip went down smoothly, although he could tell by the instant fire it ignited in his belly that it had been over five years since he'd had spirits of any kind. He cautioned himself to go slowly. He wasn't sure how long he'd have to wait.

A million dollars.

"You'll be paid in cash," Speakman had told him. "It will be placed in the safe-deposit box, and only you, I, and Laura will be signatories. There will be no records kept, no paperwork of any kind. Once Laura conceives, absolutely no connection can ever be made between you and us. If our paths happen to cross, which will be unlikely, you won't recognize us. We'll be meeting for the first time. Understood?"

"Understood."

Conversation was suspended when Manuelo came in to deliver a phone message to Mrs. Speakman. She read it, then excused herself, saying she would be back shortly. She left, Manuelo trailing her.

Speakman noticed Griff watching the manservant as he silently closed the double doors behind himself. "Don't worry about Manuelo," he said. "He speaks only a few words of English. I told him that you were an old school chum who was passing through. He wouldn't have recognized you from your football days. By the time he reached the U.S., you were in Big Spring."

Laura Speakman returned almost immediately. Her husband asked, "Anything important?"

"Joe McDonald with a quick question that he didn't think could wait till morning."

Foster laughed. "That's Joe. Always in a hurry."

While they were chatting about the impatient Joe, Griff thought of another problem. "Cash will be hard to spend," he said abruptly.

After a slight hesitation, Foster said, "Yes, I'm afraid that will present some difficulties. I imagine that you'll be under close scrutiny by the IRS and the FBI, since there was some speculation about your empty bank accounts at the time of your arrest."

"It was assumed you had money tucked away somewhere."

Beneath Laura Speakman's cool statement, he heard an implied question mark. "Just like it was assumed I knocked off Bandy," he said tightly. "I didn't, and I didn't."

She held his stare for several moments, then said, "All right."

But she said it like she was only half convinced, and that pissed him off. Even though he was going to bed her, he didn't think he would ever like her. She was good to look at, but he'd never been attracted to the ball-breaker type. And why was she busting his when they were vital to what she needed him for? He considered bringing this irony to her attention, then decided not to. He doubted she would see the humor in it.

He said, "I need the money, Mrs. Speakman. The money is the only reason I would even consider doing this. At least I've been honest about it."

His implication was clear—that they were being less than honest about their reasons. She was about to take issue when her husband intervened. "You haven't asked me for financial advice, Griff, but I'll offer some. Get a job that earns you a paycheck. Have a checking account, credit cards. Normal things. If you do get audited, how you'll explain your millionaire's lifestyle will be up to you. Probably for the rest of your life, they'll be looking for a source of your income."

He raised an eyebrow, adding, "Perhaps some of your former business associates can assist you with the matter. I'm sure that on occasion they use banking facilities abroad that don't question the source of great sums of cash."

"I wouldn't know," Griff said. "But even if they do, I won't be associating with them anymore." He looked over at Laura and added, "Ever." He emphasized it with a curt bob of his head.

Speakman asked Griff if he had any more questions. They cleared up some minor points. And then Griff raised one that turned out to be major. It concerned a potential problem with the long-term payout. Ten, fifteen, twenty years down the road, he didn't want to encounter a dilemma for which a solution hadn't been worked out ahead of time.

A heated discussion ensued. No solution was reached, but Speakman promised to think hard on it and get back to Griff with a resolution as soon as possible. Could Griff live with that? he asked. Grudgingly, Griff said he could. That settled, Speakman suggested they seal their deal with a handshake, which they did.

Speakman then invited him to stay for dinner.

Before Griff could accept or decline, Mrs. Speakman said, "Oh, darling, I'm sorry, but I didn't notify Mrs. Dobbins that we'd have a guest and she's already left for the day. I thought the idea was to keep Mr. Burkett's visit here a secret. Manuelo is one thing, but . . ."

Looking flustered for the first time since she joined them, she searched for excuses not to sit at the table with him. Apparently she had no qualms over having carnal knowledge of him, so long as she didn't have to eat with him. "Besides," she added lamely, "I've got a massive amount of work waiting for me upstairs."

"Doesn't matter," Griff said. "I've got plans. In fact, I'm already late."

"Then don't let us keep you any longer," Speakman said.

Laura Speakman stood up. She seemed relieved that he was leaving, and possibly just a bit ashamed over her inhospitality. "You should be hearing from me in about two weeks, Mr. Burkett. How can I reach you?"

He gave her his phone number, the one Turner had connected in the shabby apartment. She wrote it down on a slip of paper. "I'll call and tell you where to meet me."

"In two weeks?"

"Thereabouts. It could vary a day or two either way. I'll be using an ovulation predictor kit to test for an LH surge."

"LH . . . ?"

"Luteinizing hormone."

"Ah." As in "I see," when actually he didn't have a clue.

"Hopefully I'll be able to predict the day, but it might be short notice."

"Fine. Whatever."

Her eyes skittered away from his, and that was when Griff figured her out. She could play hardball with the big boys up to a point. She could have her menstrual cycle, and ovulation, and his sperm count talked about freely in technical and practical terms. But when it came down to the nitty-gritty, to actually climbing into bed with a stranger, she turned pure female. Which to him was reassuring.

She said good-bye and excused herself. Speakman offered to escort him to the front door. When they reached it, he said, "I'm curious, Griff."

"About?"

"What you'll be thinking about as you leave here. Will you be considering what to buy first?"

Actually, what he'd thought as he'd driven away from the gray stone mansion was that, even though they looked like reasonable and intelligent people, it was probably a good thing that Foster and Laura Speakman couldn't reproduce, because both of them were fucking nuts.

Who would do this? Nobody, that's who. Not when there were scientific methods of fertilization available. Not when you had the money to pay for those methods. Maybe in Bible days this was the way to go when you couldn't have a kid. But not today, when there were options.

By the time he'd reached his destination, he'd almost convinced himself that he would never hear from the couple again.

Almost.

"Another?"

He glanced up. The cocktail waitress had returned. He was surprised to find the glass of bourbon empty. "No thanks. A Perrier, please."

"Sure. I'll be right back."

I'll be right back. She had used that expression twice, not knowing that the seemingly harmless phrase was like salt on an open wound to him.

His mother had said those words to him the night she left. For good that time.

She'd often stayed away for days at a stretch, leaving without so much as a "so long," returning without explanation or excuse for her absence. He never got too upset or worried when she wasn't around. He knew that when she got tired of the current boyfriend or vice versa, and the guy either kicked her out or simply moved on, she would come home.

When she did, she never asked how he'd been, or what he'd been doing while she was away. Was he okay? Had he gone to school? Had he eaten? Had he been frightened by the storm? Had he been sick?

One time, he had been. Sick. He got food poisoning from eating an opened can of beef stew that had been left out too long. He puked till he passed out, then came to on the bathroom floor, lying faceup in diarrhea and vomit, a knot as big as his fist on the back of his head from the fall.

He was eight years old.

After that, he took more notice of what he ate when his mother was gone. He learned to fend pretty well for himself until she re-appeared.

On the night she left for good, he knew she wasn't coming back. All day, she'd been sneaking things from the house when she thought he wasn't looking. Clothes. Shoes. A satin pillow a guy had won for her at the state fair. She slept on it every night because she said it pre-served her hairdo. When he saw her stuff that pillow into a paper grocery sack and take it out to her present boyfriend's car, he knew this absence would be permanent.

The last time Griff saw his father, he'd been in handcuffs, being shoved into the back of a police car. A neighbor had called the cops, reporting the domestic dispute.

Dispute. A polite name for his father beating the shit out of his mother after coming home and finding her in bed with a guy she'd met the night before.

His mother went to the hospital. His daddy went to jail. He was placed with a foster family until his mother had recovered from her injuries. When the case came to trial, the DA explained to the six-year-old Griff that maybe he would be called on to tell the judge what had happened that night because he'd witnessed the assault. He lived in dread of that. If his old man got off, he would make Griff pay for tattling on him. The retribution would include a beating with his belt. It wouldn't be the first, but it promised to be the worst.

And he honestly couldn't say he blamed his dad. Griff knew words like *whore, slut,* and *cunt* meant ugly things about his mom, and he figured she deserved to be called those bad names.

As it turned out, there was no trial. His father entered a guilty plea to a lesser charge and was sentenced. Griff never knew when he got out of jail. Whenever it was, he didn't contact them. Griff never saw him again.

From then on, it was just his mother and him.

And the men she brought home. Some moved in for extended periods of time, a week, maybe two. Others were guests who hit the door as soon as they got their pants back on.

Griff remembered, not long after his dad had been put in jail, crying because his mom had locked the door to his bedroom and he couldn't get out, couldn't get away from the spider that had crawled onto his bed. The guy she was with that night had finally come into his room, killed the spider, patted him on his towhead, and told him it was all right, he could go back to sleep now.

When he was old enough to be sent outside to play, some of his mother's men friends had looked at him with apology, even guilt. Especially if the weather was bad. Others didn't like having him around at all. That was when his mother told him to get lost and stay lost for a few hours. Sometimes he was given money so he could go to a movie. Most often when banished from the house, he would wander the neighborhood alone, looking for something to occupy him, later looking for mischief.

Some of his mother's friends had given him no more notice than they would a seam in the faded wallpaper. Not many, but a few, were actually nice to him. Like the guy who'd killed the spider. But, unfortunately, he'd never come back. One guy, Neal something, had stayed a month or so. Griff got along with him okay. He could do a couple of magic tricks with cards and showed Griff how they were done. He came into the house one day with a shopping bag and handed it to Griff saying, "Here, kid. This is for you."

Inside the bag was a football.

Years later, Griff wondered if Neal had recognized him when he got to be a pro player. Did he remember giving him his first football? Probably not. He probably didn't remember Griff or his mother at all.

Men came and went. Years passed. His mother would leave. But she would always return.

And then that day came when she was covertly packing the car that belonged to a guy who'd shown up with her a few weeks before and had stayed. His name was Ray, and he'd taken an instant dislike to Griff, who would snort skeptically whenever Ray launched into a story about his phenomenal record as a rodeo cowboy before a bronco stepped on his back and ruined him for the arena. Apparently the bronco ruined him for everything else, too, because as far as Griff could tell, Ray had no visible means of support.

Ray didn't like Griff, and he made no bones about it. But Griff wasn't very likable, either. By the time Ray appeared on the scene, Griff was fifteen, full of himself, full of anger and rebellion. He'd been busted for shoplifting and for vandalizing a car, but mercifully got probation both times. He'd been suspended from school twice for fighting. He carried a chip on his shoulder that begged to be knocked off. Over the years, his hair had darkened, and so had his outlook on life.

So that evening when his mother followed Ray to the front door and turned back to tell him good-bye, Griff feigned indifference and kept his eyes trained on the TV. It was secondhand, and the picture was snowy, but it was better than nothing.

"See you later, baby."

He hated it when she called him baby. If she'd ever babied him, it was so far back he couldn't recall it.

"Griff, did you hear me?"

"I'm not deaf."

She heaved a dramatic sigh. "Why are you being so pissy tonight? I'll be right back."

He turned his head, and they looked at each other, and she knew that he knew.

"You coming, or what?" Ray bellowed from the front yard.

The look Griff exchanged with his mother lasted a few seconds longer. Maybe she appeared a little sorry for what she was about to do. He wanted to think she was. But probably she wasn't. Then she turned quickly and left. The door slammed shut behind her.

Griff didn't leave the house for three days. On the fourth day, he heard a car pull into the driveway. He hated himself for feeling a surge of hope that he'd been wrong and she'd come back after all. Maybe she'd seen through Ray and his bullshit. Maybe Ray had seen her for the whore she was and was bringing her back.

But the footsteps on the porch were too heavy to be hers.

"Griff?"

Shit! Coach.

Griff hoped he couldn't be seen where he was slouched on the ratty sofa watching TV. But no such luck. The door squeaked when it was pushed open, and he cursed himself for not having locked it. In his peripheral vision, Coach appeared at the end of the sofa. Hands on hips, he stood looking down at Griff with disapproval.

"I missed you at practice. School office tells me you've been absent from classes the last three days. Where've you been?"

"Here," Griff said, continuing to stare at the TV.

"You sick?"

"No."

A pause. "Where's your mom?"

"Fuck I know?" he grumbled.

"I'm gonna ask you again. Where's your mom?"

Griff looked up at him then and with exaggerated innocence said, "I think she's at the PTA meeting. Either that or the church ladies' sewing group."

Coach walked over to the TV. He didn't turn it off; he yanked the plug from the wall outlet. "Get your stuff."

"Huh?"

"Get your stuff."

Griff didn't move. Coach walked toward him, his footfalls rattling the empty cereal bowls and soda cans littering the TV tray Griff had placed in front of the sofa. "Gather up your stuff. Right now."

"What for? Where am I going?"

"To my house."

"Like hell."

"Or cop an attitude with me, and I'll call CPS." Coach placed his meaty fists on his hips again and glared down at him. "You've got one second to choose."

Laughter from a nearby table jerked Griff back into the present. At some point during his reverie, the waitress had brought his Perrier. He drank it like a man dying of thirst. He was covering a soft belch when the woman he'd been waiting for came through the revolving entrance door. He stood up and waved at the waitress to bring his check, and by doing so attracted the woman's attention.

Upon seeing him, she stopped suddenly, obviously surprised.

He signaled for her to wait while he took care of his tab. He did that with dispatch, then walked toward the woman where she still stood halfway between the entrance and the elevators.

"Hey, Marcia."

"Griff. I heard you were getting out."

"Bad news travels fast."

"No, it's wonderful to see you." She smiled and looked him over. "You look good."

He drank in the sight of her, from the top of her tousled auburn hair to her high-heeled sandals. The curvy terrain in between made him light-headed with lust. Laughing softly, he said, "Not as good as you."

"Thank you."

He held her gaze for several moments, then asked, "Are you available?"

Her smile faltered. She glanced around the lobby, her unease showing.

He took a step closer and said in a low voice, "It's been a long five years, Marcia."

She considered a moment longer, then, reaching a decision, said, "I have someone at midnight."

"It won't take me near that long."

He took her elbow, and they walked to the elevators, saying nothing until they were inside one of the mirrored cubicles. She inserted a small key into a discreet slot in the mechanical panel. Responding to his quizzical look, she said, "I've moved up a couple of floors, into the penthouse."

"Business must be good."

"I have three girls working for me now."

He whistled. "Business is *really* good."

"The market for my product never goes soft." Laughing, she added, "So to speak."

Griff was even more impressed by her success when they stepped out of the elevator into a lobby with a marble floor and a clear skylight for a ceiling that provided a view of a quarter moon and a sprinkling of stars bright enough to defy the skyline lights.

Three doors opened into the private lobby. "Are you friendly with your neighbors?"

"One is a Japanese businessman. He's rarely here, but when he is, he finds the proximity very convenient."

Griff chuckled. "He comes over to borrow sugar?"

"At least once while he's in town," she said demurely. "The other is a friend, a gay decorator who envies me my clientele."

She unlocked her front door. Griff followed her inside. The interior looked like a picture in a magazine, probably would be her gay neighbor's wet dream. Griff gave it a cursory glance, said a polite "Very nice," then reached for her and pulled her against him.

He hadn't kissed a woman in five years, and the sex was going to have to be damn good to top the pleasure he derived from pushing his tongue into her mouth. He kissed her like a horny kid whose prom date was easy. Too eager, too greedy, too sloppy. His hands were everywhere at once.

After a minute of his mauling her, she pushed him away, laughing. "You know the rules, Griff. No kissing. And I'm the initiator."

His sports jacket was fighting to stay on while he was frantically trying to shake it off. "Give me a break."

"This once. But some rules must apply."

"Right. I pay up front."

"Hmm."

The sleeves of his jacket were turned inside out when he finally was able to fling the thing to the floor. He dug into his pants pocket for the money clip of cash Wyatt Turner had given him. The tight-ass would have conniptions if he knew his client was spending his food and gas money on a prostitute. Speaking for himself, Griff didn't begrudge a penny of Marcia's fee. If he had to, he'd skip a few meals.

"How much?"

"Two thousand. For an hour. Straight sex."

He gaped at her and swallowed the golf ball now lodged in his throat. "Two *thousand*? You've gone up. A lot."

"So has the cost of living," she replied coolly. "And business expenses."

He expelled a gusty breath of disappointment, then bent down and retrieved his jacket from the floor. "I don't have it. Maybe tomorrow night," he said wryly.

"How much have you got?"

He held out the money clip. She took it and pulled out two hundred-dollar bills, then gave the clip back to him. "Don't tell anybody."

Griff thought he might weep out of gratitude. "I'll be eternally in your debt."

Marcia was the most select prostitute in Dallas, and it was strict business practices that had put her there. She was a businesswoman all the way. Through the grapevine, Griff had heard that she, acting on tips from clients, had invested wisely in real estate. She'd bought up farmland north of Dallas, and when the city expanded in that direction, she had scored huge. It was also said she had a stock portfolio worth millions.

All that could have been rumor, but he wouldn't have been surprised if it was true. It was said she'd started "escorting" to help finance dental hygiene school but had soon realized that she was better at polishing knobs than she was at polishing teeth. And she could make a hell of a lot more money at it.

Soon after he'd signed with the Cowboys, Griff had learned of her through a teammate, being told that Marcia was the best if you could afford her, because even then she'd been expensive. He preferred a professional to the team groupies who threw themselves at him and, once he'd slept with them, inevitably caused hassles he didn't need.

Marcia was discreet. She was clean. She was scrupulous when it came to prequalifying her clients, making sure they were disease free, financially stable, and safe. She never took walk-ins. She'd made an exception for him tonight.

She had the wholesome face of a church choir soloist, paired with a voluptuous body that invited sin. Somehow, despite her occupation, she managed to remain a lady, and if a client didn't treat her as such, he didn't remain a client.

Five years hadn't left any noticeable damage, Griff was pleased to discover as she undressed. She was lush, but firm where she ought to be. He couldn't get his clothes off fast enough. Knowing him, remembering his preferences, she didn't assist him but idly touched herself while she watched him peel off garments and toss them aside. When her fingers disappeared between her thighs, he made an involuntary gurgling sound but was too far gone to care how gauche he seemed.

When he was undressed, she went to him and gently pushed him back until he was seated on the edge of the bed. He pressed his face into her deep cleavage, mashed her heavy breasts against his cheeks. She handed him a condom; he rolled it on. "What do you want to do, Griff?"

"At this point . . . Doesn't matter."

She lowered herself to her knees between his thighs and bent her head toward him, whispering, "Enjoy."

"Griff?"

"Hmm?"

"It's after eleven. You need to go."

He'd been sleeping on his stomach, his head buried in the soft, scented pillow, virtually comatose. He turned onto his back. Marcia had showered and was wrapped in a robe. "You went out like a light," she said. "I didn't have the heart to wake you sooner, but you have to go now."

He stretched luxuriantly. "Felt good, sleeping naked, sleeping on sheets that don't smell like industrial-strength detergent." He arched his back and stretched again. "Do I gotta?"

"You gotta."

She said it with a smile, but he knew she meant it. He couldn't argue after she'd already been so charitable. He sat up and swung his feet to the floor. She had his clothes waiting for him, actually hurried him along without seeming to as he pulled them on. She held his jacket for him, then placed her hand on the center of his back and propelled him toward the door.

When they reached it, he turned to her. "Thank you. You made a huge concession, and I appreciate it more than you know."

"Coming-home present." She kissed her finger, then pressed it against his lips. "But next time, it has to be by appointment and full fare."

"My financial situation should improve substantially by tomorrow." But remembering how uneasy she'd been to be seen with him in the lobby, he added, "If you still want me for a client, that is. I could be bad for your business."

"Every business requires a little finessing now and then." She was making light of it, but he knew the thought had crossed her mind. "You might want to try one of the new girls. They're young and gorgeous, and I trained them personally."

"Satisfaction guaranteed?"

"Always. Want me to set something up for you?"

A mental image of Laura Speakman flashed through his mind. "I'm not sure what I'll be doing, where I'll be. Let me call you. But I tried the old number. Got a recording that it had been disconnected."

She passed him a business card. "I have to change it periodically. To keep the vice cops honest," she added, smiling.

He kissed her on the cheek, thanked her again, and they exchanged a good-bye. She closed the door, quietly but firmly. Getting into the elevator, Griff met the gay decorator getting out. The man looked him up and down, then closed his eyes and gave a soft, swooning moan. "Too, too cute," he murmured as he glided past.

The lobby bar was doing less business now than earlier. The girl who had waited on him was chatting with one of the idle bellmen. The pianist had been replaced with canned music.

The doorman was greeting an arriving guest when Griff pushed through the revolving doors. Outside, the air had softened, but it was still hot enough to steal his breath until he acclimated. He stood there, sweating, for a full sixty seconds, waiting for the parking attendant to show. When he didn't, Griff went looking for him. He walked the length of the porte cochere and rounded the corner into the parking garage.

Where he ran into a fist.

It connected with his cheekbone like a jackhammer. One jab. Two. Then another.

He staggered back, swearing loudly, swinging wildly in uncoordinated self-defense, trying to bring his assailant into focus.

Rodarte.

CHAPTER
6

R ODARTE'S GRIN TURNED HIS FACE INTO A HALLOWEEN MASK.
"Oh, I'm sorry. Did that hurt?"

Griff's indrawn breath whistled through his teeth, which were clenched in pain. He dabbed at his cheekbone, and his fingers came away red. *"Son of a bitch!"*

Rodarte lit a cigarette, laughing as he fanned out the match. "That's what I heard, too."

Griff glowered at him.

"I heard your mother would screw a dog if nothing else was around. Poor little Griff. You had it rough, didn't you? Till Coach Miller and his wife took you in."

When Griff had been indicted, overnight going from poster boy to pariah, a lot of his ugly past had been exposed. Neither Coach nor Ellie had been a source of information. Griff would have bet his life on that. But a hotshot reporter from the *Morning News* had dug until he'd excavated just enough facts to hold together his speculations. They made for a sensational exposé. In conclusion, the writer had implied that Griff Burkett's fall had been predestined from birth, that he'd been bred to transgress, and that the crime he'd committed should have been foreseeable.

Rodarte leered at him. "Tell me, how did it feel to throw the big game? Honestly, now. Just between us. Did you have any twinge of conscience? Or not?"

Wyatt Turner's warnings rang in Griff's ears. *Do not cross him. Turn the other cheek.* Which seemed an ironic admonition at this particular moment, when his cheekbone was throbbing and the entire side of his head was hurting so bad he thought he might throw up.

Griff wanted to grab Rodarte by his greasy hair and smash his face against the concrete wall of the parking garage, again and again until his ugly features had been pulverized to mush.

But Griff couldn't do a goddamn thing without bringing trouble down on himself, and Rodarte knew that. Nothing would have given the bastard more pleasure than seeing Griff locked up again on the very day he'd been released.

Muttering an invective, Griff turned away, but Rodarte grabbed him by the shoulder, brought him back around, and shoved him up hard against the wall. "Don't turn your back on me, you cocky fucker."

More than the name-calling, being manhandled like that cleared Griff's head of sharp pains and made his anger as brittle and cold as glass. He could kill this bastard. Easy. Being tackled in a game was one thing. Being touched by Rodarte was quite another. "Take your hands off me."

Either his steely tone, or maybe his eyes, telegraphed the murderous fury he felt, because Rodarte let go and shuffled back several steps. "You were owed that," he said, hitching his chin up toward Griff's bleeding cheekbone. "For flipping me off today. I drove all the way out to jackrabbit country to commemorate your release, and that's the thanks I got for my thoughtfulness."

"Thanks. Now we're square." Griff brushed past him.

"I had an interesting conversation with some former associates of yours yesterday."

Griff stopped and turned.

Rodarte took a deep pull off his cigarette, then dropped it on the garage floor and ground it out with the toe of his shoe while he blew smoke upward. "I don't need to name names, do I? You know who I'm talking about. Your former business partners."

"They went slumming?" Griff asked.

Rodarte merely grinned.

The three bosses of the organized crime group—the Vista boys, as Griff thought of them. That was who Rodarte was talking about. The men in the five-thousand-dollar suits. The trio Bill Bandy had introduced Griff to when he needed a quick fix to a big gambling debt.

The Vista triumvirate had been obliging, and then some. They'd opened wide the doors of their luxury offices in the high-rise building they owned in Las Colinas overlooking the golf course. And that was just the beginning. There were lavish dinners in the private dining rooms of five-star restaurants. Private jet trips to Vegas, the Bahamas, New York, San Francisco. Limousines. Girls.

Seduction in its purest form.

The only thing he'd turned down was the drugs, although at any given time, he'd had access to any and all he wanted.

"Those guys know you're out," Rodarte was saying. His smile was dangerous and insinuating, a jackal's grin. "They're not all that glad about it. They thought for sure you'd get nailed for doing Bill Bandy."

"I had nothing to do with Bandy."

"Riiiight."

Griff would be damned before he stood here pleading his innocence to this asshole. "You see the Vista boys again, tell them I said they can go fuck themselves."

Rodarte winced. "Oooh, they're not gonna like that. First you kill their key bookmaker—"

"I didn't kill Bandy."

"See? I don't think they buy that, Griff. You were so pissed at him for ratting you out to the FBI, of course you killed him. You had a right to. Almost an *obligation*. Look, I understand. And so do they. A rat's a rat. If you hadn't snuffed him, Bandy might have given them up next."

"So what's their gripe?"

"They'll never know for sure whether or not Bandy would have betrayed them. While you," he said, poking Griff in the chest with his index finger, "you actually named names to the FBI. *Their* names. You see the problem? Their thinking is that Bandy would have remained loyal to them if it hadn't been for you. Regardless of how it all came down, they blame you for fucking up their smooth operation."

"Gee, this is a sad story."

Ignoring the remark, Rodarte went on. "You were bad for their business. For years after you got sent to Big Spring, they found it harder to entice a professional athlete anywhere in the southern United States. Players of every sport were nervous, afraid that if they cheated, they'd get caught like you did."

Rodarte took a breath, and when he spoke again, his voice was softer. "The Vista boys, as you affectionately call them, haven't fully recovered from the grief you caused them."

"The grief *I* caused *them*?" Griff finally gave vent to the angry pressure that had been building inside him. "None of them served a day of time."

"Only because the FBI was building their racketeering case around your testimony alone." Rodarte gave a rueful shrug over the flaws in that strategy. "Your story didn't fly with the federal grand jury. They figured you were trying to point the finger at others to take the heat off yourself."

He poked Griff again. "That's the only reason the Vista boys weren't also indicted. But they came close. They haven't forgotten how close. And all thanks to you. They're sorta holding a grudge."

"The feeling is mutual. Now, get out of my way."

When Rodarte failed to back away, Griff tried to go around him. Rodarte sidestepped, blocking him. "But basically these are nice guys we're talking about. They might welcome you back into the fold—on one condition."

"Are you their recruiter now?"

Rodarte winked. "Let's just say a word from me could grease the skids for you."

"I'm not interested in getting back into the fold."

"You haven't heard me out."

"I don't need to."

Rodarte dusted an imaginary speck off the lapel of Griff's jacket. If the man touched him again, Griff thought he might have to break every bone in his hand.

"Take a piece of advice, Griff. Think about it."

"I had five years to think about it."

"So you won't be working with them again?"

"No."

"What about their competitors? The Vista boys are business-men, after all. They're nervous—just a little—over what you might do now that you're out."

"I'm thinking of opening a lemonade stand."

Rodarte's frown said that crack was unworthy of him.

"It's none of their goddamn business, or yours, what I do," Griff said.

"They beg to differ. Especially if you're planning to link up with one of their competitors."

"Relieve them on that score. They've got nothing to be nervous about. See ya, Rodarte."

Again Griff moved away, but Rodarte scrambled and planted himself in his path. He moved in close and lowered his voice again, this time to a conspiratorial whisper. "Then there's the matter of the money."

"What money?"

"Come on, Griff," he said in a singsongy, wheedling tone. "The money you stole from Bandy."

"There was no money."

"Maybe not cash. A safe-deposit box key, maybe? Foreign bank account numbers? The combination to a safe. Stamp collection."

"Nothing."

"Bullshit!" Rodarte stabbed Griff in the chest with his finger once again, harder, angrier.

Griff saw red, but despite his wish to break bones, he couldn't touch the man. One touch would be all the provocation Rodarte needed to engage him in a fight. If he got into a fight with Rodarte, even if he won, he'd spend the night in the Dallas County Deten-tion Center. Bad as his new apartment was, he preferred it over a jail cell.

"Hear me, Rodarte. If Bandy had any money squirreled away, the secret died with him. I sure as hell didn't get it."

"Pull my other leg." Rodarte slammed him back against the wall and moved in close, baring his teeth. "A hot hustler like you would have made sure he didn't come away empty-handed. You've got expensive tastes. Cars. Clothes. Pussy. If you didn't tuck away some of Bandy's money, how are you going to finance all those luxuries?"

"Don't worry your pretty head about it, Rodarte. I've got it covered."

"Yeah?"

"Yeah."

"Doing what?"

Griff didn't reply.

Rodarte said, "I'll find out, you know."

"Good luck. Now get the fuck out of my way."

They shared a long, hostile stare. It took every ounce of willpower Griff had not to knee the guy in the balls and throw him off. But he stood his ground and his gaze didn't flinch. Eventually Rodarte dropped his hands from Griff's shoulders and took a step back. But he wasn't admitting defeat.

"Okay, Number Ten," he said softly. "You want to make this hard on yourself, fine by me. In fact, I prefer that you do." He whispered as though making a malevolent promise.

Griff went past him and had made it to the corner of the garage when Rodarte called him back. "Hey, answer me one question."

"Yes, I think you're ugly."

Rodarte laughed. "Good one. But, seriously, when you snapped Bandy's neck, did you come? I know that happens sometimes."

"What do you think?"

Laura didn't have to ask *About what?* She and Foster hadn't talked about Griff Burkett yet, but he might just as well have been the centerpiece on the dining table. His presence between them seemed almost that tangible.

She set down her fork and reached for her wineglass. Cradling the bowl of it between her hands, she thoughtfully stared at the ruby-colored contents. "My first impression is that he's angry."

"At?"

"Life."

The formal dining room, which accommodated thirty or more,

was used only for entertaining. The first twelve months of their marriage, they'd hosted numerous dinner parties. In the past two years, there had been only one—at Christmas for SunSouth's board of directors and their spouses.

This evening, as on most evenings, they were having their dinner in the family dining room. Much cozier, it was separated from the commercial-size kitchen by a single door. The housekeeper-cook got off at six o'clock each day. Her last duty was to leave dinner in a warming tray. Since Laura had assumed much of Foster's workload, she usually stayed at the corporate offices until seven-thirty or eight, making their dinner hour late. Foster refused to eat before she got home.

Tonight their dinner had been delayed by the interview with Griff Burkett. Laura had lost her appetite, but Foster seemed to be enjoying the beef Wellington. He cut off a bite and chewed it exactly twelve times, four series of three, swallowed, took a sip of his wine, blotted his mouth with his napkin. "Spending five years in prison would put any man in a bad humor."

"I think Mr. Burkett would be angry under any circumstances."

"That anger having been ingrained into his personality?"

"Well, you read the newspaper story about how he grew up," she said. "Granted, his early years were a nightmare. But that doesn't excuse what he's done as an adult. He broke the law. He deserved his punishment. Possibly more than he received."

"Remind me never to get on your fighting side, Mrs. Speakman. You're ruthless."

She didn't take offense, knowing he was teasing her. "I just have no tolerance for grown-ups who blame their shortcomings, even their lawlessness, on a disadvantaged childhood. Mr. Burkett alone is accountable for his actions."

"For which he has atoned," her husband reminded her gently. Lightening the mood, he added, "I promise to do my part to see that our baby doesn't have a disadvantaged childhood."

She smiled. "Left alone, I think you'd spoil him rotten."

" 'Him'?"

"Or her."

"I'd love a little girl who looks just like you."

"And I'd be over the moon to have a boy."

Their smiles remained in place, but the unspoken words hung there above the dining table. Neither a son nor a daughter would have Foster's features. Similar, perhaps, but not his.

Laura took another sip of wine. "Foster . . ."

"No."

"Why 'no'? You don't know what I'm going to say."

"Yes, I do." He indicated her plate. "Finished?" She nodded. He laid his knife and fork at a precise diagonal across his plate and folded his napkin beside it.

She stood up as he backed his wheelchair away from the table. "I'll ask Manuelo to clear the table while I get the coffee."

"Let's have it in the den."

In the kitchen she filled a carafe with coffee, which she'd set to brew while they were having dinner. She placed it on a tray with cups and saucers, cream pitcher, and sugar bowl. She carried the tray into the den. Foster was washing his hands with bottled sanitizer. When he was done, he placed the bottle in a drawer.

She fixed his coffee and carried it to him. He thanked her, then waited until she had hers and was seated on one of the leather love seats, her feet tucked beneath her.

He continued the conversation as though there hadn't been an interruption. "You were going to say that we could take the more conventional route. Have artificial insemination with an anonymous donor."

That was exactly what she'd been about to say. "They keep sperm donors anonymous for a very good reason, Foster. We would never know his identity, never have a mental image of him. The child would be ours. We'd never be studying his or her features, looking for similarities to . . . to someone we'd met."

"Do you object to Griff Burkett's features?"

"You're missing the point."

He laughed and rolled his chair over to the love seat. "No I'm not, I'm teasing you."

"I guess I'm not in a teasing mood tonight."

"I'm sorry." He reached up and ruffled her hair.

But she wouldn't be placated so easily. "This is probably the most important decision we'll ever have to make."

"We've already made it. We've been over this a thousand times, studying it from every angle. We've discussed it for months. We talked it to death, and then talked it some more, and finally agreed it's the right path for us."

For *you,* she started to say but didn't. "I know I agreed, but—"

"What?"

"I don't know. In theory . . ." She let the sentence trail. What worked in theory didn't necessarily translate well into flesh-and-blood reality. Particularly since it was *her* flesh and blood that would be affected.

"I'm only asking for one child," he said, stroking her cheek. "If I could, I'd give you the three or four children we planned on. Before."

Before. There it was, that giant qualifier. That six-letter word was weighty with its significance to them. It was the line of demarcation in their lives. Before.

His eyes moved over her face lovingly. "I still dream about making love to you."

"You do make love to me."

He smiled wanly. "Of a sort. Not the real thing."

"It's real to me."

"But it's not the same."

She leaned forward and kissed him intimately on the mouth, then nuzzled her face into his neck. He held her close, smoothing his hands over her back. During her busy workdays, hours would go by when she would forget his condition and the drastic effect it had had on their lives, their marriage.

Mean reminders of it would strike her unaware, coming from nowhere like blow darts, giving her no warning, making them impossible to dodge. During a meeting, or while she was on the telephone, or when she was conducting a brainstorming session, one would hit, numbing her for a millisecond before the pain set in.

But these quiet evenings at home were the worst. When they were alone, like this, each remembered how it used to be, how they used to make love when the mood struck them, laughing at their passionate haste, collapsing in happy satiation afterward.

Now she occasionally went to the room where he slept in a hospital bed, rigged with every modern contrivance to maximize his comfort. She would undress and lie with him, her body pressed against his. They kissed. He caressed her, and sometimes just the intimacy of that was enough. Other nights, she would reach orgasm, which wasn't really satisfying because she always felt selfish afterward. When she expressed this, he comforted her by saying that his completion was derived from knowing that he could still give her physical pleasure.

But if she left his bed feeling like an exhibitionist, she knew he must feel like a voyeur. Because it wasn't mutually fulfilling, it was . . . well, as he'd said, it wasn't the same.

They rarely talked about their life together before the night it was turned upside down. Memories of that first year of their marriage were indulged privately, neither wanting to cause the other heartbreak by reminiscing aloud. The memories were agonizing for her. They must have been even more terrible for Foster. She was still whole and healthy. He wasn't. He didn't seem to harbor any resentment or bitterness toward fate, or God. Or her.

But how could he not?

Taking her shoulders between his hands now, he eased her away from him. "Do you have any misgivings, Laura? About using Burkett or anyone else. Any hesitation at all? If so, we'll call it off."

Did she have any misgivings? She had thousands. But this was the way Foster insisted it be done, so this was the way it must be done. "I want to see the results of a complete medical checkup."

"He promised to act on that quickly and mail us the report. As soon as we've looked it over, we'll burn it."

"I don't think there will be a problem. He appears to be as physically ideal as we believed."

"What about his character?"

She scoffed at that. "Less than ideal. He proved that five years ago."

"His crime doesn't concern me. What I meant was, do you think we can count on his discretion?"

"I think the money will be incentive for him to keep our confidence."

"I made the conditions as simple for him as I could."

He had explained to Griff Burkett that he was never to make any claims toward the child, never to contact them, never to acknowledge their existence. If Griff kept to those conditions, he would receive one million dollars a year.

Burkett had asked, "For how long?"

"For the rest of your life."

He'd divided an incredulous look between them. "Seriously?"

"Seriously."

Regarding them as though they had both lost their minds, he said, "Having a kid, and keeping its conception a secret, is that important to you?"

The question sounded like a prelude to extortion. Laura wouldn't have been surprised if at that point he'd demanded twice the amount they were offering. But when Foster said, "Yes, it's that important to us," Burkett chuckled and shook his head, as though finding such an ideal incomprehensible. Obviously he had never felt that strongly about anything or held anything that dear. Not even his career.

"Well, it's not like I want a kid," he said. "In fact, since puberty I've been damn careful to guarantee that I didn't father one. So you can relieve yourself of the worry that I'll show up someday to claim him. Or her," he said, addressing that to Laura.

"What about the confidentiality issue?" Foster asked.

"There is no issue. I get it. I keep my mouth shut. We run into each other by accident, I look right through you with no recognition whatsoever. For a million dollars a year, I can lose my memory. Like that." He snapped his fingers. "One thing, though."

"What?"

"What happens if you . . . if I outlive you?"

"Laura would uphold our obligation to you."

"What if she's not around?"

That was one question they hadn't anticipated. They'd never considered the possibility that he would survive both of them. She and Foster looked at each other, and she knew they were thinking the same thing. If Griff Burkett outlived them, they were leaving their child and heir vulnerable to extortion, financial as well as emotional. They had agreed that their child would never know how he came to be. They would let him assume, as everyone else would, that Foster had fathered him.

"That's a scenario that hadn't occurred to us," Foster admitted.

"Well, now that it's occurred to me, it needs to be addressed."

Laura said, "By that point in time, you would be extremely well off."

"You're well off now," Griff retorted. "You wouldn't enter into a contract with a contingency as important as this left unsettled. Would you?"

He was right, but she was reluctant to concede the point. "I'm sure that over time we can work something out."

"Un-huh. Not over time. Now."

"He's right, Laura. The timeliness is critical. I'm proof that our lives can change in a heartbeat. It's better that we resolve this issue now, rather than leave it dangling." Foster thought on it for a moment, then said, "Unfortunately, every solution that comes immediately to mind would involve paperwork, and it's essential that we avoid that." He spread his arms, palms up. "Griff, either you'll have to trust me to come up with a workable solution, or—"

"When?"

"I'll give it top priority."

Burkett frowned as though that weren't good enough. "What's the *or*?"

"Or, what I'm reading from you is that it's a deal breaker."

Laura noted that he didn't have to think about it for long. "Okay, I'll trust you to work something out. After all, you're putting your trust in me, and I'm the convicted felon."

"I'm glad you're the one who cited that, Mr. Burkett."

Laura had spoken before thinking, but she didn't regret saying it. He'd needed to be reminded that the risk they were taking far outweighed his. He moved nothing except his eyes, but she felt their angry impact when they connected with hers.

"You mean so you wouldn't have to," he said. "So you wouldn't have to point out that if anybody in this room is untrustworthy, it's me."

"Laura meant no offense, Griff," Foster said.

Continuing to hold her stare, he said, "No. Of course not. None taken."

But she knew he didn't mean it, just like he knew that she *had* meant what she'd said.

"Risk on both sides is inherent to any business partnership." Foster spoke from experience. He was also an excellent mediator, who always tried to defuse a disagreement before it got out of hand. "I think shared risk is a positive thing. It leaves everybody vulnerable to some extent and keeps everyone honest." He turned to Laura. "Anything else?"

She shook her head.

"Excellent," he said, slapping his hands on the arms of his chair three times. "Let's shake on it."

Now Foster was saying, "You told him you'd be in touch within two weeks."

"I'll be monitoring my cycle, taking my temperature each morning, so that hopefully I'll know the day I ovulate."

"And how long after that before you'd know if you conceived?"

"Two weeks."

"I get giddy thinking about it."

"Get giddy when I pee on a stick and it turns pink. Or blue. Or whatever it's supposed to turn."

Laughing, he kissed her soundly, then by tacit agreement, they headed for the elevator tucked discreetly under the stairs. "Race you to the top," he said as he rolled his chair into the metal cage.

She jogged up the curving staircase and was there to meet him when he arrived. "You always win," he grumbled.

"Those sprints up the stairs keep me in good shape."

"I'll say." He reached around and smacked her on the butt.

Hearing their approach, Manuelo opened the door from inside Foster's bedroom. "Can we skip the therapy tonight?" Foster asked. The aide smiled and shrugged, indicating he didn't understand the question. "He's faking that. I know he is. He knows damn well I'm talking about the therapy he puts me through and how I feel about it." He clasped her hand tightly. "Spare me, Laura. Please."

"Hey, I've got it just as tough tonight. I've got to review that union contract again. But I'll come and tuck you in." She kissed him lightly on the lips and continued down the wide hallway to her office.

But an hour later, when she went into Foster's bedroom, Manuelo had done everything that needed doing. The drapes were drawn. The thermostat was set to his preferred temperature. There was a carafe of ice water and a drinking glass on his nightstand. The call button was within reach. He was sleeping, a book resting on his lap.

She turned off the bedside lamp and for the longest time sat there in the darkness, in the chair beside his bed, listening to his breathing. He didn't stir, and she was grateful that he was able to sleep so well.

Eventually, she left him and went alone to the bed they used to share, wishing that her sleep could be that sound.

CHAPTER

7

THE FOLLOWING MORNING, GRIFF HAD A HITCH IN HIS BACK from sleeping on the soft mattress, which sagged in the middle. He denied that the chronic pain was a holdover from thirteen years of getting slammed into by tacklers—eighth grade through his years with the Cowboys.

His right shoulder also bothered him more than he wanted to admit. Over the course of his playing days, he'd had four fingers broken, one of his small fingers broken in the same place twice. The second time, he hadn't bothered to have it set, so it had healed crooked. Assorted other gridiron mishaps and melees made getting out of bed every morning a slow process.

Fondly recalling the comfort of Marcia's perfumed and silky sheets, he limped into the drab kitchen, boiled water for instant coffee, toasted a piece of bread, and washed it down with a glass of milk to chase the bitter pseudo-coffee taste from his mouth.

Before he forgot, he called the probation officer assigned to him. Jerry Arnold's voice-mail recording had made him sound like a likable enough guy, and now his live voice sounded even friendlier and nonthreatening. "I was just calling to make sure you got the message I left yesterday," Griff said after an exchange of hello-how-are-yous.

"Sure did. But let me repeat the info back to you, check to see

I got it right." He recited the address and phone number Griff had left.

"That's right."

"How about a job, Griff? Anything yet?"

"I'm seeing about that today."

"Good, good. Keep me posted on any progress."

"Will do."

"Well, you know the conditions of your probation, so I won't bore you with them again."

"They're etched onto my brain. I don't want to go back to prison."

"And I don't want you to." The bureaucrat hesitated, then said, "You were a hell of a ballplayer, Griff. A thrill to watch."

"Thanks."

"Well, good luck today."

That chore out of the way, Griff headed for the shower. It had furry black stuff growing on the tile grout, but to his surprise the hot water was plentiful. He dressed quickly but carefully, choosing the best from the clothing Wyatt Turner had left in the apartment for him. He made a mental note to ask his lawyer where the rest of his stuff was being stored and how he could go about retrieving it.

Then he remembered that if the Speakmans came through with their down payment, he could go out and buy all new stuff. The thought made his gut purl with happy anticipation.

However, he wouldn't know until after two o'clock today if they'd come through as promised. In the meantime, he had other errands to run.

He got to the walk-in medical clinic at eight-thirty and was out in under an hour. "How soon before I can pick up the lab results?"

"Three to five days."

"Make it three," he said, giving the nurse a wink and his best smile. Simpering, she promised to try. Obviously she didn't follow Cowboys football.

From the clinic he drove to a branch of the public library—the one nearest his former Turtle Creek address. He doubted there was one in the neighborhood of his present apartment, doubted many of the residents in the area could read.

He arrived at the library only to discover it didn't open until ten. A cluster of toddlers and young mothers—when had young mothers got so damn good looking?—had congregated at the doors waiting for them to open.

Moms and kids alike regarded him curiously. At six feet four he towered over all of them. The cut and bruise on his cheekbone, Rodarte's contribution, drew their attention, too, making him feel particularly conspicuous among the Thursday Morning Story Time at the Library crowd.

Once the doors were unlocked, the moms herded their children to a far corner while he went to the information desk. The librarian smiled pleasantly and asked what she could do for him. "I need to use a computer. And I'll probably need some help."

Five years of advancement in computer technology equaled aeons. But the librarian patiently showed him how to access the Internet and do a Google search, and soon he was knee-deep in information on SunSouth Airlines and, more specifically, its owner.

First, he got an overview of Foster Speakman's background. Starting in the 1920s with his great-great-grandfather, his family had amassed a fortune from oil and natural gas. As sole heir, Foster was bequeathed megamillions in addition to vast parcels of land in New Mexico, Colorado, and Alaska.

He held an MBA from Harvard Business School and was a polo player of renown. He had received countless citations and awards from business and civic groups for community service. Economic analysts lauded his courageous takeover and turnaround of the foundering airline.

If he'd been a football player, Speakman would have been the starting quarterback for the Super Bowl champs and voted MVP.

He and Mrs. Speakman—not Laura—were photographed attending various charity and social functions. One photograph accompanying an article in *Forbes* showed Foster standing tall and proud in front of a SunSouth jet, arms crossed over his chest, looking like a man who'd just conquered the world. He appeared robust and strong.

Which meant that somewhere between the time he'd bought the airline several years ago and now, he'd become paraplegic. Illness? Cataclysmic event?

While pondering the possibilities, Griff came across Elaine Speakman's lengthy obituary. She had died after a valorous and lengthy battle with leukemia. No children had come from the marriage.

The widower had married Laura Speakman one year and five months following Elaine's death.

Foster and Elaine had been well represented in the press. But Foster and Mrs. Speakman II were featured nearly daily—which explained his allusion to their being celebrities.

Then Griff found what he'd been looking for. One year and seventy days into their marriage, Foster and Laura Speakman's lives were irrevocably changed. The story made the front page of *The Dallas Morning News* under a banner headline and a graphic photograph. The news hadn't reached Big Spring. Or if it had, he'd missed it. Or if he had heard about it, he'd forgotten it because it didn't pertain to him and he'd had no interest.

Griff read the story twice. There were links to numerous follow-up stories. He read them all, then, using the back icon, returned to the original story and read it yet again. And when for the third time he reached that telling sentence, which explained so much, he sat back in his chair and said, "Huh."

It was a nice neighborhood. Unlike the one he'd grown up in, there were no loose shutters or curling window screens on these houses. Lawns were mowed, hedges were clipped, and flower beds were weeded. The basketball hoops actually had baskets, and if the driveways were littered with anything, it was shiny bikes and skateboards, not rusted-out cars sitting on blocks.

Although this neighborhood was younger by twenty years, it had the same kind of "family" feel as the one where Coach and Ellie Miller lived. Where *he'd* lived from the day Coach had removed him from his mother's ramshackle place. Coach had contacted Child Protective Services and handled the legalities, which were incomprehensible and uninteresting to Griff as a fifteen-year-old. He supposed Coach got himself appointed his guardian. In any case, he'd stayed with the Millers until he graduated high school and went away to play football for the University of Texas.

He located the address he sought and drove past the house slowly, checking it out. On either side of the front door was a pot of white flowers. Above the backyard fence, Griff could see the top of a swimming pool slide. Two kids were tossing a football back and forth on the front lawn. They were old enough to be cautious of strangers and eyed Griff warily as he slowly rolled past.

He went to the end of the block and turned the corner. He realized his palms were damp with apprehension. And that made him angry at himself. Why the hell should his palms be sweating? He had as much right as anybody to be on these nicely maintained streets. The people who lived here were no better than he was.

But he'd felt the same anxiety that day when Coach Joe Miller had pulled into his driveway and said, "Here it is." Griff had looked at the house with the welcome mat on the threshold and the blooming ivy crawling up a trellis and felt as out of place as a turd in a punch bowl. He didn't belong here. But he'd die before he let on that he felt inferior.

Sullenly, feet shuffling, he'd followed Coach up the steps and through the front door. "Ellie?"

"In here."

Griff had seen Coach's wife at the games. From a distance, she looked okay, he guessed. He'd never really given her a second thought.

She turned to them as they entered the kitchen. Her hair was in curlers, and she had bright yellow rubber gloves on her hands.

"This is Griff," Coach said.

She smiled at him. "Hi, Griff. I'm Ellie."

He kept his like-I-give-a-shit frown in place so they wouldn't guess that his heart was beating harder than it did before a fourth-and-goal play, and in the hope they wouldn't hear his stomach growling. He'd glanced through the open door of the pantry. Besides at the supermarket, he'd never seen so much food stored in one place. On the counter was a pie with a golden crust, oozing cherry juice. The aroma was making Griff's mouth water.

Coach said, "He's going to be staying with us for a while."

If this news came as a shock to Ellie Miller, she hid it. "Oh, well, good," she said. "Welcome. Now, can you give me a hand, Griff?

That pie leaked sticky stuff all over this oven. I'm trying to get the racks out so I can clean it while it's still warm, but my gloves will melt if I grab hold. Pot holders are there in the top drawer."

Not knowing what else to do, he'd got the pot holders and removed the hot metal racks from the oven. With no more ceremony than that, he moved into the Millers' house and into their lives.

He always suspected that Coach and Ellie had discussed the possibility of this before Coach came to get him that morning. Because he was shown into a room set up for an adolescent boy. It had a double bed covered by a red-and-white blanket with the image of the high school team mascot on it—a fiercely scowling Viking. Other sports pennants were tacked to the wall.

"That's the closet. Let me know if you need more hangers." Ellie glanced down at the small duffel bag Griff had brought with him but didn't comment on how little it would hold, how little he had. "You can keep your folding clothes in this chest. If anything needs washing, the hamper is in the bathroom. Oh, goodness, I haven't shown you the bathroom." It was so clean, he was afraid to pee in the toilet.

They all went to Sears that afternoon so Ellie could "pick up some things," but what they came home with was new clothes for him. He'd never had food like Ellie cooked, including the pie they ate for dessert that night. He'd never been inside a house that smelled good, that had books on shelves and pictures on the walls.

But he learned from the oven-cleaning experience that such luxuries didn't come free. He was expected to do chores. Never having been required to do a damn thing in his life except stay out of the way when a man was in the bedroom with his mother, Griff found that this aspect of family life took some getting used to.

Ellie's rebukes were gentle and usually included some reproach to herself. "You forgot to make your bed this morning, Griff. Or did I forget to tell you that sheets aren't changed till Friday?" "You won't be able to wear that favorite T-shirt tomorrow, because I didn't find it under the bed until after I'd done the laundry. Be sure it gets in the hamper next time."

Coach was less subtle. "Have you finished your history paper?"

"No."

"Isn't it due tomorrow?"

He knew it was. One of his assistant coaches was Griff's history teacher. "I'll get it done."

Coach turned off the TV. "Right. You will. Now."

Whenever he was disciplined, Griff muttered rebellious plans to leave. He was sick and tired of their harping. Do this, do that, clean up this, carry out that. Only dorks went to church on Sundays, but had he been given a choice? No. It was just expected. And what did he care if the car was washed and the lawn mowed?

But he never followed through on any of his threats to leave. Besides, his muttering was largely ignored. Ellie chatted over it, and Coach either turned his back or left the room.

Coach didn't go soft on him at practice, either. If anything, he was tougher on him, as though to assure the other players that Griff was nothing special to him just because he was lodged under his roof.

One afternoon, still mad over being denied access to the TV the night before, Griff sloughed off during drills. He didn't connect a single pass to the receivers. Running backs had to come take the ball from him because he didn't scramble to get it to them. He fumbled a snap.

Coach watched him; despite his scowl, he didn't blow the whistle on him, give him a pointer, or chew him out.

But at the end of practice, when everyone else headed for the locker room, Coach ordered him to stay where he was. He placed a blocking dummy thirty yards away and tossed Griff the football. "Hit it."

Griff threw the ball with no more effort than he had put into the rest of the practice and missed the dummy. Coach glared at him. "Try again," he said, tossing him another football. Again he missed.

Coach handed him a third football. "Hit the damn thing."

"I'm having an off day. What's the big deal?"

"The big deal is that you're a chickenshit."

Griff threw the ball then, straight at Coach. The ball bounced off his barrel chest. Griff turned toward the locker room.

When Coach grabbed him by the shoulder and whipped him around, his helmet nearly flew off, taking his head with it. Before

Griff could recover, Coach planted his wide, leathery hand in the center of his chest and shoved. He landed hard on his ass. Pain shimmied up from his tailbone, straight along his spine, and directly into his brain. It hurt so bad, he caught his breath and tears came to his eyes. They were more mortifying than his position on the ground.

"I'm not scared of you!" he shouted up at Coach.

"Do I have your attention now?"

"Why don't you pick on somebody else for a change? Phillips missed ten of ten today. I don't see you making him kick till he gets one between the frigging uprights. How many times did Reynolds fumble during the last game? Three? Four? Why aren't you on his ass? Why is it always mine?"

"Because Phillips and Reynolds don't have any talent!" Coach seemed to use up all his breath in that one roar. His voice was much softer when he said, "And you do."

He flicked sweat off his forehead with the back of his thumb. He looked away, then back at Griff, who was still sitting in the dirt because his butt bone hurt too bad to try to stand.

Coach said, "Not another player on this team, not another one in this school, or in any of our rival schools, has talent to match yours, Griff. And you're *pissing* it away, feeling sorry for yourself and carrying a chip on your shoulder because your mother was a whore. You've had a lousy life up till now, no denying that. But if you let it ruin the rest of your life, who's the fool? Who will you be spiting? You, that's who.

"You may not be scared of me, but you're scared shitless of yourself," he said, jabbing the space between them with his finger. "Because in spite of yourself, you're better than the two who made you. You're smart and good looking. You've got more natural athletic ability than I've ever seen in any sport. And because of those gifts, you just might make something of yourself.

"And that scares you, 'cause then you wouldn't be able to wallow in your goddamn self-pity. You wouldn't be able to hate the world and everybody in it for the shitty hand you were dealt. You wouldn't have an excuse for being the self-centered, self-absorbed, complete and total jerk that you are."

Speech over, he stood looking down at Griff a moment longer, then turned away in disgust. "If you've got the guts for it, suit up tomorrow and be ready to apply yourself. If not, stay the hell off my team."

Griff was at practice the following day and for every day after that, and that season he led the team to the state championship, as he did for the three following years. Neither the incident nor Coach's lecture was ever referred to again. But Griff didn't forget it, and he knew Coach didn't.

Their relationship improved. They had ups and downs because Griff constantly pushed him and Ellie to see just how far he could go before they got sick of him and kicked him out.

When he defied his weekend curfew and came in an hour and a half late, they didn't kick him out, but Coach imposed the worst punishment fathomable—making him wait two months beyond his sixteenth birthday to take his driver's test and get his license.

They encouraged him to invite friends over, but he never did. He'd never developed friend-making skills and didn't really have the desire to. Overtures by classmates were rebuffed. Sooner or later people abandoned you, so why bother? In the long run, you were better off keeping to yourself.

Sometimes he caught Ellie looking at him sadly and knew she harbored unspoken worries about him. Maybe she sensed, even then, that the worst was yet to come.

Things rocked along pretty well. Then, early in his junior year, an incident in the locker room got Griff suspended from school for three days. It hadn't been a fair fight—Griff against five other athletes, three football players and two on the basketball team.

When they were pulled apart by assistant coaches, two of the boys were taken to the emergency room, one with a broken nose, the other needing stitches in his lower lip. The other three had bloody noses and bruised torsos but didn't require hospitalization.

Griff, instigator of the seemingly unprovoked fight, suffered no more than a few scrapes and a black eye.

"We have no choice, Coach Miller," the school principal said as he relinquished Griff to him. "Just be glad the parents of the other boys declined to press assault charges. They could have," he added, glaring at Griff.

Coach took him home, marched him past a subdued Ellie, and confined him to his room for the duration of his suspension. On the evening of the second day, Coach walked into his room unannounced. Griff was lying on his back on the bed, idly tossing a football into the air.

Coach pulled up his desk chair and straddled it backward. "I heard something interesting today."

Griff continued tossing the football, keeping his eyes on it and the ceiling beyond. His tongue would rot out before he would ask.

"From Robbie Lancelot."

Griff caught the football against his chest and turned his head toward Coach.

"Robbie asked me to thank you for what you did. And especially for not telling."

Griff remained silent.

"He figured I was in on whatever it is that you're not telling. I'm asking you to tell me now."

Griff pressed the football between his strong fingers, studied the laces, avoided looking at Coach.

"Griff."

He dropped the football. Sighed. "Lancelot weighs what? A hundred twenty-five, maybe? He's a nerd, a geek. A pest, you know? People cheat off him during chemistry tests, but otherwise . . ." He looked over at Coach, who nodded understanding.

"I had finished my workout with weights and went into the locker room. I heard this commotion back by the showers. Those five guys had Robbie backed into a corner. They had his underwear. He was standing there without anything on, and they were making him . . . you know. Work it. Saying stuff like 'Are you really, Lance a lot?' 'Let's see this big lance of yours.' 'Too bad your lance isn't as big as your brain.' Stuff like that."

He glanced at Coach, then away. "He was crying. Snot was running out his nose. His dick was . . . he was yanking on it something fierce, but it wasn't . . . doing anything."

"Okay."

"These guys were giving him hell. So I plowed through them and pulled him away from the wall, walked him to his locker, told him to get his clothes on, wipe his nose for God's sake, and get the hell out of there."

"And then went back and beat the crap out of his tormentors."

"Tried anyhow," Griff mumbled.

Coach watched him for a long moment, then stood up, replaced the chair beneath the desk, and went to the door. "Ellie says dinner's in half an hour. You'd better wash up."

"Coach?" He turned back. "Don't tell anybody, okay? I've only got one more day of suspension, and . . . and I promised Lancelot."

"I won't tell anybody, Griff."

"Thanks."

To this day Griff remembered the expression on Coach's face as he left his room that evening. He was never able to define it, but he knew that something important had happened, that some sort of understanding had passed between them. As far as he knew, Coach had never betrayed his confidence about the incident.

By now he'd made the neighborhood block and for the second time approached the house with the white flowers on either side of the front door and the backyard pool with the slide. He'd wasted enough time. It was do or die.

The two kids with the football were still throwing passes to each other when Griff parked at the curb and got out.

CHAPTER

8

THE BOYS STOPPED THEIR PLAY, WATCHING AS HE WALKED TO-
ward them. "Hey," he said.

"Hey." They said it in unison, cautiously.

"Is this Bolly Rich's house?"

"He's inside," replied the taller of the two. "He's my dad."

"What's your name?" Griff asked.

"Jason."

"You play ball?"

Jason nodded.

"What position?"

"Quarterback."

"Yeah?"

"Second string," Jason confessed self-consciously.

"Want to play first string?"

Jason looked at his friend, then back at Griff. "Sure."

"Give me the ball."

Again Jason first consulted his friend with a look, then passed
the football to Griff, keeping himself at arm's length. "I'm throwing
ducks."

Griff grinned at his use of the term for a slow and wobbly pass.
"That happens to everybody once in a while, but you can avoid it."
He took the ball in his right hand, pressed his fingertips against the

laces. "See this?" He held the ball for Jason and his friend to observe.

"You've gotta keep the pads of your fingers tight, like you're trying to squeeze the air out of it. So when you let it go . . ." He motioned for Jason's friend to run out for a pass. The kid went willingly. Griff drew back his arm. "You've got control, better aim, and speed."

He threw the ball. It sailed straight and sure. The kid caught it and beamed. Griff gave him a thumbs-up, then turned to Jason. "A bullet instead of a duck."

Jason raised his hand to shade his eyes against the sun. "You're Griff Burkett."

"That's right."

"I had a poster of you in my room, but my dad made me take it down."

Griff snuffled a laugh. "I'm not surprised."

"Griff?"

He turned. A slight man, wearing cargo shorts, a holey T-shirt, and old sneakers, had opened the front door and was standing on the threshold between the flowerpots. He was balder, but his eyeglasses were the same ones Griff remembered from the last time Bolly had interviewed him.

"Hello, Bolly." He looked down at the boy. "Keep practicing, Jason." The youngster nodded respectfully. Then Griff joined Bolly at the door and extended his hand. To the man's credit he shook hands with him—after only a second or two of hesitation. But the eyes behind the wire frames weren't exactly glowing with happiness to see the most hated man in Dallas at his front door.

"I think Jason has the potential of being good one of these days."

Bolly nodded absently, still trying to recover from his shock. "What are you doing here, Griff?"

"Can I have a minute or two of your time?"

"What for?"

He glanced over his shoulder at the two boys, who were watching this exchange with undivided attention. Coming back around, Griff said, "I promise not to abscond with the family silver."

The sportswriter hesitated for several seconds more, then went into the house and motioned for Griff to follow him. Off the entryway, Bolly led him down a short hallway and into a compact, paneled room. Shelving was jam-packed—even overflowing—with sports memorabilia. Framed photographs of Bolly with star athletes took up most of the wall space. There was an untidy desk in the corner dominated by a telephone and a computer. The monitor was on. The screen saver showed fireworks blossoming in multicolored silence.

"Sit down if you can find a spot," Bolly said as he squeezed himself behind the desk.

Griff removed a stack of newspapers from the only other chair in the room and sat down. "I called the sports desk at the *News*. The guy who answered said you were working from home today."

"I do most days now. Go into the office only a couple days a week, if that much. If you've got e-mail, you can conduct just about any business from home."

"I used a computer in the library this morning. Felt like a caveman looking at the control panel of a 747."

"They build in obsolescence. Keep you buying upgrades."

"Yeah."

An uncomfortable silence followed. Bolly picked up a stray tennis ball on his desk and rolled it between his palms. "Listen, Griff, I want you to know I didn't contribute anything to that piece about you that came out during your trial."

"I didn't think you did."

"Well, good. But I wanted you to know. That writer— You know he's in Chicago now."

"Good riddance."

"Amen. Anyway, he pumped me for information on your background. Your folks. Coach Miller. All that. All I told him, the *only* thing I told him, was that you had the best arm and best hustle of any quarterback I'd ever seen. Topping Montana, Staubach, Favre, Marino, Elway, Unitas. You name me one, you were better. I mean that."

"Thanks."

"Which makes me all the more pissed off at you for what you did."

Bolly Rich, a sports columnist for *The Dallas Morning News*, had always been fair to him. Even when he didn't perform well, like one *Monday Night Football* game against Pittsburgh. It was his rookie year, his first time playing the Steelers on their turf. He played the worst game of his career. Bolly's column the next morning had been critical, but he'd placed part of the blame for the humiliating loss on the offensive line, which had done precious little to protect the new quarterback. He hadn't crucified Griff the way other sportswriters had. That wasn't Bolly's style.

Griff was hoping to appeal to Bolly's sense of fair play now. "I fucked up," he said. "Huge."

"How could you do it, Griff? Especially after such an outstanding season. You were one game away from the Super Bowl. All you had to do was win that game against Washington."

"Yep."

"No way Oakland could have defeated the Cowboys that year. Y'all would have waltzed through the Super Bowl game against them."

"I know that, too."

"You only had to get the ball to Whitethorn, who was standing on the two. The two! Nobody near him."

Bolly didn't have to recount the play for him. He'd replayed it in his mind a thousand times since he threw that pass while the final seconds of the game ticked off the clock.

Fourth and goal on the Redskins'—*it would be the goddamn Redskins*—ten-yard line. Cowboys trail by four. A field goal won't do it.

The center snapped the ball into Griff's hands.

Whitethorn shot forward off the line of scrimmage.

A Redskins lineman slipped, missed the tackle. Whitethorn got to the five.

Skins defenders trying to blitz were stopped dead. They couldn't climb or penetrate Dallas's line, collectively named "Stonewall" that season.

A Skins linebacker was charging toward Whitethorn, but Whitethorn was now on the two with space around him. The team was only one step shy of the goal, of victory, of the Super Bowl.

All Griff had to do was lob a short screen pass over the line into Whitethorn's hands.

Or miss him, and get paid a cool two million by the Vista boys.

Cowboys lost 14–10.

"It was a crushing loss," Bolly was saying, "but I remember how the fans still cheered you as you left the field that day. They didn't turn against you until later, when it came out that you'd missed Whitethorn on purpose. And who could blame them? Their Super Bowl–bound star turned out to be a cheat, a crook."

Talking about it five years after the fact still made Bolly angry. He dropped the tennis ball, which bounced off his desk onto the floor, ignored. He took off his glasses, rubbed his eyes with agitation, and asked brusquely, "What do you want, Griff?"

"A job."

Bolly replaced his glasses and looked at him as though waiting for the punch line. Eventually, realizing that Griff was serious, he said, "What?"

"You heard right."

"A *job*? Doing what?"

"I thought a paper route might be available. Could you put in a good word for me with someone in that department?" Bolly continued to stare at him; he didn't smile. "That was a joke, Bolly."

"Is it? Because beyond that, I can't imagine why you've come to me asking about a job. You go anywhere near the sports desk at the newspaper and you'll probably be tarred and feathered. If you're lucky."

"I wouldn't have to go near the sports desk. I could work directly for you."

Bolly frowned. "What'd you have in mind? Not that I think there's a chance in hell of this going anywhere. I'm just curious to see how your mind is working."

"You can't be everywhere at once, Bolly. You can't cover more than one game at a time. I know you use people to cover games for you. Provide the color only someone who is actually at the game can get."

"I use some stringers, yeah."

"Let me be one. I majored in English. I have a fair command of the language. As much as anybody in Texas." His quick grin wasn't returned. "I can at least put two sentences together. Most important, I know the game. I *lived* the game. I could give you insightful play-by-plays that nobody else could, add a perspective that would be unique, based on actual experience. Years of it."

He'd rehearsed the pitch, and to his ears it sounded good. "I could describe how great it feels to win. How lousy it feels to lose. How much worse it feels to win when you know you've played like shit and the win was a fluke." He paused, then asked, "What do you think?"

Bolly studied him a moment. "Yeah, I think you could give an accurate account of wins and losses with some original flavoring thrown in. You'd probably be pretty good at it. But even with terrific language skills, you couldn't come close to describing what it's like to be a team player, Griff. Because you don't know."

"What do you mean?" But he didn't have to ask. He knew what Bolly meant.

"You were a one-man show, Griff. You always were. Going all the way back to high school, when you first started gaining notice from college recruiters, it was all about you, never the team. You led your teams to victory after victory with your amazing ability on the field, but you were a piss-poor leader off it.

"Far as I know, you were never voted a team captain, which doesn't surprise me. Because the only thing that made you part of any team was wearing the same color jersey. You made no friends. Teammates admired your game. Those who didn't envy you idolized you. But they didn't like you, and that was okay with you. You didn't give a damn so long as they carried out the plays you called.

"I never saw you encourage another player who'd made a mistake, never saw you congratulate one for making a good play. I never saw you extend your hand in friendship or lend a helping hand to anyone. What I did see was you giving back Dorsey's Christmas present unopened, saying, 'I don't do that crap.'

"I saw you rebuke Chester when he invited you to a men's prayer breakfast for his wife, who was going through horrible chemo and radiation. When Lambert's fiancée was killed in that car wreck, you were the only one on the team who didn't attend the funeral.

"You were an outstanding athlete, Griff, but a sorry excuse for a friend. I guess that's why I'm surprised, and slightly offended, that you would come to me now, like we'd been good buddies, and ask for my help."

It wasn't easy to hear those things about himself, especially since they were true. Quietly, humbly, Griff said, "I need the work, Bolly."

Bolly took off his glasses to rub his eyes again, and Griff knew he was about to turn him down. "I hate what you did, but everybody can make a mistake and deserves a second chance. It's just . . . Hell, Griff, I couldn't get you into any press box in the league."

"I'd cover college ball. High school."

Bolly was shaking his head. "You'd be met with the same animosity there. Maybe even more. You cheated. First you broke the rules by gambling. Then you threw a game. You fucking threw a game," he said with heat. "For money. You robbed your own team of a sure-win Super Bowl. You were in bed with . . . with *gangsters,* for crissake. Do you think anybody would allow you near kids, young players?" He shook his head and stood up. "I'm sorry, Griff. I can't help you."

He had lunch at a Sonic drive-in. Sitting in the borrowed Honda, he gorged on a jalapeño cheeseburger, a Frito pie, two orders of Tater Tots, and a strawberry-lemonade slush. It had been five years since he'd had junk food. Besides, he figured that if he was going to be a despised outcast, he might just as well be a fat one.

On the drive out to Bolly's neighborhood and up till the time Bolly had told him not only *no* but *hell, no,* Griff had congratulated himself for having the character to seek a job when, by two-thirty this afternoon, his immediate money problems would be solved. He'd sought work *before* going to the bank to check the contents of that safe-deposit box. In his opinion, it had taken a lot of integrity to humble himself and appeal for a job, hat in hand, when after today he wouldn't have to do any labor, ever, if he didn't want to. He'd even endured Bolly's sermon, and the sportswriter hadn't gone easy on his personality flaws.

Although he had to admit that Bolly's memory was sound. The

man also had a keen insight into his nature. That was why he hadn't asked forgiveness or tried to justify himself. He'd never been the touchy-feely type. He'd never wanted to pat his teammates on the ass after a big play, and he sure as hell hadn't wanted any of them patting his. He'd left all that rah-rah bullshit to the benchwarmers, while he was out there on the field doing the bone-breaking, bloody work, getting creamed by tacklers who got marks on their helmets if they sacked him.

But why was he stewing about Bolly's censure? None of that mattered. Now he had only two teammates, and all he had to do to make them happy was get one of them pregnant. Easy enough.

He had indigestion as he walked inside the bank building. He blamed it on the jalapeños, not nerves. He looked about him, as though expecting to be spotlighted and exposed for the most gullible fool ever to walk the planet.

But it went exactly as Foster Speakman had told him it would. No muss, no fuss. He made an inquiry at the information desk, then was escorted to an elevator that went into a subterranean part of the bank, where a polite, grandmotherly type asked him to sign a card. She compared it with the signature card that Foster Speakman had filed, as promised. Satisfied, the grandmother showed Griff into a cubicle.

His heart was knocking in a beat out of time with the Yanni filtering through the overhead speakers. Grandmother delivered the box, told him to take his time and to press the button on the wall when finished, then withdrew. The key Speakman had given him last night was in the pocket of his jeans. He fished it out and unlocked the box.

From the bank, Griff drove straight to NorthPark for a shopping spree. He liked his jeans old and "worked in," but he bought two new pairs anyway—because he could. His boots were too comfortable to replace, but he had them shined. He found three designer shirts in Neiman's that didn't look too faggy. He changed in the dressing room and wore one of them out of the store.

None of the sports jackets in the Armani boutique were wide enough in the shoulders for him, but he found one that would work with some tailoring. He was told he could pick it up in a few days.

He bought a four-hundred-dollar pair of sunglasses. Odd that styles of sunglasses had changed more than anything in the past five years. He also bought a cell phone. It probably wouldn't have taken as long to buy a house. By the time all the added features had been demonstrated to him, and the calling plan options explained, and his voice-mail retrieval set up for one-digit dialing, he was impatient to get out of there and actually use the damn thing to make a call.

Which was to Marcia. He dialed the first number listed on the card she had given him and got an anonymous, innocuous recording asking him to leave a message, which he did. Waiting on her to return his call, he drove around the area, taking in all the commerce, going past his old haunts and favorite restaurants. Some were still in business, others had given way to new.

When, after an hour, Marcia still hadn't called, he dialed a number that belonged to one of her girls. Young, gorgeous, satisfaction guaranteed.

"Hello?"

She had a husky, sexy voice. He liked her already. "Hi. My name is Griff Burkett. I'm a client of Marcia's. She recommended I call you."

At first he thought she'd hiccuped, but then he realized she was crying. "Marcia—" She got choked up and couldn't finish. Then she wailed, "Oh, God! It's just so awful!"

"What's so awful?"

"Marcia's in the hospital."

Presbyterian Hospital was surrounded by a network of roads under repair. By the time he wound his way through the construction zones and the detours they imposed, Griff was swearing as profusely as he was sweating.

He jogged across the seeming miles of parking lot and, after finally reaching the main entrance lobby, had to wait his turn at the information booth. He was raw with impatience by the time the attendant gave him Marcia's room number.

Standing outside her door, leaning against the wall, was the neighbor Griff had seen last night getting off the elevator. When he noticed Griff striding down the corridor toward him, he jumped as if he'd been struck with a cattle prod and positioned himself in front of the hospital room door.

Frantically, he waved his hands in front of his face. "No, no. Go away. She won't want you to see her like this."

"Why is she here?" Griff hadn't got anything out of the hysterical girl on the phone.

The man stopped his protestations and lowered his hands. His sharp, foxy face contorted into a mask of misery. His eyes were already red from crying. They began to leak fresh tears. "I can't believe this happened to her. At first I thought it was you, although you didn't look the type. The savagery of it was—"

"Savagery?"

The man started waving his hands in front of his face again, this time in embarrassment over his emotion. Frustrated, Griff moved him aside, ignored the No Visitors sign, and went into the room. The blinds were drawn against the glare of the afternoon sun, and all the lights were off. But he could see well enough, and what he saw caused him to halt midway between the door and the hospital bed.

"Oh, Jesus."

"I told you it was savage." The neighbor had followed him in. "I'm Dwight, by the way."

"Griff. And I didn't do this to her."

"I realize that. Now."

"What happened?"

"About an hour after I saw you in the lobby, my doorbell rang. I wasn't expecting a guest, and the concierge hadn't announced anyone. I looked at the security monitor and saw Marcia, standing there in the foyer, only sort of . . . doubled over. She was . . . like this."

She'd had the living daylights beat out of her. Griff couldn't see all of her, of course, but there were bruises and swelling on every inch of exposed skin. If the rest of her looked like her face, she was lucky to be alive. Several cuts had been closed with butterfly clips. Blood had matted her hair to her head. Her face was so misshapen with swelling that if he hadn't known who she was, he would never have recognized her.

"Her jaw was broken," Dwight whispered. "They did surgery

this morning to wire it together. Last night, no amount of morphine could dull the pain."

Griff lowered his head and took several deep breaths. When he raised his head, he asked with deadly calm, "Who was her next client? After me. Someone was coming at midnight. She hustled me out so she could get ready for him. Do you know his name?" He turned to Dwight suddenly, and his expression caused the man to back away in fear. "Do you know his name?" he repeated angrily.

A moan from the bed drew their attention to Marcia. In two strides Griff was at her side. Being careful of the IV needle taped to her hand, he gently pressed it between his. "Hey there," he said softly.

Both eyes were swollen shut, but she managed to pry one of them open. The lovely green iris was floating in a lake of bright red. Since she couldn't move her jaw to speak, she merely made a whimpering sound in her throat.

"Shh." He bent down and kissed her forehead, barely letting his lips touch for fear of hurting her. "Take advantage of the drugs. Rest." He kissed her forehead again, then straightened up and turned to Dwight, who was standing at the foot of her bed, sniffling softly.

"Did you call the police?"

Dwight shook his head.

"Why the hell not?"

"She couldn't talk because of her jaw, but she became hysterical when I mentioned calling the police. I guess . . ." He glanced over his shoulder to make sure there were no eavesdroppers about. "Because of her profession, she didn't want the police involved."

"But you called 911."

"Immediately. Paramedics were there within minutes."

"How did you explain her condition?"

"I have a circular staircase in my apartment. I told them she'd gone up to use the powder room and had fallen on her way down."

"And they believed that?"

"Probably not. But they left it to the ER staff to summon a policeman. He didn't believe the staircase story either and urged Marcia to identify her attacker by writing down his name. She refused."

With limited strength, Marcia squeezed Griff's hand. He leaned down over her again and gently lifted a strand of hair away from a patch of her scalp that had been shaved to allow for sutures. "Who was it, Marcia? Who were you seeing after me?"

Barely moving, she shook her head. She applied more pressure to his hand, and he realized she wanted him to lean in close enough to hear her speak. He bent low, placing his ear just above her lips.

When he heard the single word she whispered, he jerked his head up and looked down into the single eye she could hold open. She closed it for several seconds, letting him know that he'd heard correctly.

"This was about *me*?"

She nodded.

Rage surged through him. His veins swelled and pulsed with it. But his voice remained remarkably calm. "He's going to die." He said it as a fact, meaning it unequivocally, telling her that she could bank on it. "Stanley Rodarte is going to die."

Now he understood why she had refused to call the police. Rodarte would have made it understood that accusing him would bring on a reprisal even worse than the beating he'd already given her.

Most sickening was knowing that the only reason Rodarte had victimized Marcia was to send a message to Griff. In that, he'd succeeded. Griff read the message loud and clear. Rodarte wasn't finished with him yet.

Well, guess what, cocksucker, Griff thought. *I've only begun with you.*

"I'll make him pay for this," he vowed to Marcia in a whisper. "I swear to you."

She pressed his hand. He bent down to her lips again. The garbled sounds came from the back of her throat, but she managed to make her warning understood. "Be careful of him."

CHAPTER

9

THE CALL CAME EARLY ON A MONDAY MORNING, JUST AS HE was waking up, but before he'd got out of bed. He rolled over, sleepily groped for his new cell phone on the nightstand, and flipped it open. "Hello?"

"Mr. Burkett?"

That woke him up. "Yeah. Here."

She didn't identify herself. She didn't have to. "Would one o'clock today be convenient for you?"

"One o'clock?" Like he had to think about it. Like he might have a conflict. Like he had something else to do. "One o'clock's fine."

"Here's the address." She gave him a number on Windsor Street. "Got it?"

"Got it."

She hung up. Griff snapped his phone shut, then lay there clutching it, clutching the fact that they were really going through with it. Then he sat bolt upright. The hitch in his back protested loudly enough to cause him to catch his breath. He threw off the sheet, got out of bed, and, buck naked, went clambering through his apartment until he found a pen and paper to write down the address. He was certain he'd committed it to memory, but he was taking no chances.

He went into the bathroom. Standing at the toilet, he looked down at himself and muttered, "Don't even think about getting stage fright."

As expected, he'd passed the physical exam with flying colors. The nurse had come through for him in only two days. The report showed his EKG to be normal, his lungs clear. He had low blood pressure, low cholesterol, and a low PSA—he thought that had something to do with his prostate. His sperm count, by contrast, was high. Excellent.

He'd put the report, along with his cell phone number, in the addressed and stamped envelope Speakman had given him for this purpose, and dropped it into the nearest mailbox.

That had been two weeks ago. Since then, he'd moved to another apartment and acquired a tan.

Using his newfound cash, he had abandoned the roach-infested place and moved into a duplex. Living strictly on a cash basis presented the expected problems. Eyebrows were raised when he signed his lease, but the management of the complex took the cash without asking too many questions. His new place wasn't in the ritziest of neighborhoods, which would have required letters of recommendation and closer scrutiny, but it was worlds above where he'd been.

The complex had a security gate, well-kept grounds, a gym, and a pool—which accounted for his tan. After moving in his new furniture and setting up a sound system and plasma-screen, high-definition TV (the best invention ever), he didn't have much else to do except work out—it had been during a moment of pique that he had considered getting fat—and lounge by the pool.

He also went to the hospital nearly every day to visit Marcia, and he always took something with him. He'd taken flowers until the nursing staff complained that the room was becoming a greenhouse. Dwight, who'd proved to be a steadfast and attentive friend to her, chided Griff for not being more creative. So one day he took her a teddy bear. The next day he carried in a goofy hat. "To wear until you can get out of here and have your hair done," he told her as he gently placed it on her head.

She still couldn't speak, but she communicated her gratitude for his visits with her expressive eyes. By now she could take short strolls down the corridor. Dwight had referred a plastic surgeon who, ac-

cording to Dwight's affluent and well-preserved clientele, was a genius. After examining Marcia, the surgeon promised to do great things
but said he couldn't even begin until she had completely healed.

She still sipped her meals through a straw, and every time Griff
witnessed that, his fury resurfaced. What he conjectured was that
Rodarte had gone up to Marcia's penthouse immediately after their
encounter in the garage. Expecting her client, she'd opened the door
to him. He'd pumped her for information about Griff, and when
she didn't—actually couldn't—divulge any, he'd tried beating it out
of her.

From Rodarte's standpoint, it was a failed mission only insofar
as he still didn't know what Griff's future plans were. But he'd had
the satisfaction of terrorizing and disfiguring a beautiful woman who
was an acquaintance of Griff's. Knowing he could get away with it
because of her profession was a bonus. Rodarte was a lowlife, a bully
who would enjoy inflicting pain just for the hell of it. Gratifying his
mean streak was really all the motivation he needed.

Griff couldn't think about it without becoming enraged. On one
of his visits to the hospital, he again broached the subject of reporting Rodarte to the police, but the fear and anguish that filled Marcia's
eyes dissuaded him.

"He won't get away with it," he told her. "I promise you."

There had been no sign of Rodarte since the assault. Griff knew
where to find him, but he didn't dare go looking. Rodarte would love
for him to come crashing down doors threatening bloodshed. No
doubt that was the kind of reckless reaction he had hoped to provoke.

Griff wouldn't give Rodarte the satisfaction of getting his butt
thrown in jail again, nor did he wish to make matters worse for his
suffering friend. So for the time being, he honored Marcia's silent
pleas and didn't seek retribution.

Today thoughts of Rodarte were obscured by Laura Speakman's
call. Having had two weeks to prepare for it mentally, he was surprised by how nervous he was. To distract himself until the appointed
time, he went for a five-mile run, then worked out with weights in
the gym. His goal wasn't to build himself back up to his football
playing size but to maintain the lean, strong form he had now.

He followed the weights session with laps in the pool. But when it occurred to him that too much exertion might be detrimental to his sexual performance, he immediately got out.

He flossed before he brushed. He clipped his fingernails. He put on his new Armani sports jacket. He left his apartment at twelve-thirty. He arrived at the address at twelve thirty-seven. He had twenty-three minutes to kill.

The house was in an established area that had a Neighborhood Crime Watch, where residents were on the alert for people who lurked about and looked suspicious. He decided it would be better not to wait parked on the tree-lined street where he would fit that description to a tee.

Instead, he pulled into the narrow driveway and followed it around to the rear of the house, where there was a sheltered parking area and a neat backyard, made shady by two venerable sycamore trees. A privacy fence separated the property from the houses on either side.

In this older neighborhood, people were buying the houses and either razing them to rebuild on the coveted wooded lots or completely renovating. Griff guessed this was one of the latter, because it appeared as though what had once been the garage had been converted into a room. But it had been done well, and the house had retained its character and charm.

He'd bought the red Honda from Wyatt Turner. It wasn't what he wanted to drive, but it ran okay and he figured that paying cash for a flashy new car—soon after shelling out a deposit on the duplex—would send up all kinds of red flags to his probation officer, the IRS, the FBI. Even his lawyer eyed him suspiciously when Griff asked how much he wanted for the car and then counted out hundred-dollar bills to pay for it. Turner didn't ask how he'd come by the cash. Griff didn't volunteer the information.

Now he kept the Honda's motor running so he could leave the air conditioner on. He drummed his thumbs on the steering wheel and hummed accompaniment to the country song playing on the radio. The artist had sung the national anthem to open one of the Cowboys' home games, then, at the invitation of the owner, had watched all four quarters from the sideline.

After an easy win against Tampa Bay, he'd asked Griff for his autograph. This guy was a hot new star. He'd won several Grammy Awards, but he'd hem-hawed and stammered, tongue-tied and starstruck, as he extended Griff his program and a Bic pen.

Today that singer wouldn't piss on him if he was on fire.

He heard her car over the radio and his own humming. He shut down the Honda, took a deep breath, exhaled, and got out.

He followed the driveway along the west side of the house and came up behind her on the small porch as she was unlocking the front door. Sensing him there, she turned, startled. "Oh."

"Hi."

"I didn't realize you were already here."

"I parked around back."

"Oh," she said again, then hurriedly unlocked the door and went in ahead of him. She closed the door as soon as he'd cleared the threshold. A short entry hall opened into a living area. Louvered shutters were closed over the wide windows, so the room was dim. It was basically square, with a small fireplace in the center of one wall, a hardwood floor, standard pieces of furniture.

She lowered the strap of her handbag from her shoulder but clutched the bag against her chest, as if she was afraid he might grab it from her. "I thought I'd got here ahead of you."

"I don't live far."

"I see."

"Couple of miles. I got here sooner than I expected."

"Have you been waiting long?"

"Not too long. But you're not late. You're right on time."

During this scintillating conversation, she had adjusted the wall thermostat. Cool air began whirring through the ceiling vents. Griff was grateful. He'd begun to perspire. He wanted to take off his sports jacket but thought she might read something suggestive into the removal of a garment, any garment. Since he didn't have a clue how this was supposed to go, he figured he'd follow her lead, even though doing so involved some sweating.

She was dressed for the office. Her suit was black, but the fabric was summer weight. Linen, he thought. The skirt came to the tops of her knees, the jacket was nipped in at the waist. Under it was a pale pink top that draped across her chest and looked soft. Same jewelry as before. Black high-heeled sandals. Her toenails were painted a pearly ivory color.

He'd noticed all this as he came up behind her on the porch. He didn't dare scope her out now, because she was drawn as taut as a piano wire, acting uptight and all business. If she'd had DO NOT TOUCH tattooed on her forehead, it couldn't have been any plainer how she felt about being alone with him.

"There are some magazines in there." She pointed out an armoire in the corner. "And a TV with . . . with videos." Simultaneously they looked at the closed doors of the armoire, then back at each other.

"Okay," he said.

"Give me a few minutes. Then, whenever you're ready, I'll be in the bedroom."

And with that, she walked across the living room, down a hallway, turned in to a room at the end of it, and closed the door.

Well, at least now he knew how it was going to be. They'd do it like porcupines.

He shrugged off his sports jacket and folded it over the back of a chair. He went to the armoire and opened the double doors. It contained a treasure trove of pornography. He sorted through the stack of magazines. A panoply of possibilities. Something for everybody. Same with the collection of videos.

Who had stocked this stuff? he wondered. Foster? Her? Somehow he couldn't see them visiting a triple-X video store, browsing among the titles for something that would turn him on. "What do you think he'd like, honey? *Twixt Twins* or *Euro Snatch*?

Maybe they'd sent Manuelo on that errand; one of the magazines was in Spanish. Maybe Manuelo was into porno. Maybe that accounted for his vacuous smile.

Griff recognized his musing for what it was: stalling.

He wandered into the kitchen at the back of the house. There was bottled water and a six-pack of Diet Coke in the fridge. He took a bottle of water, twisted off the cap, drank some as he went into the former garage, which was now a sunroom, although not that much sunlight was coming in through the drawn blinds. The house was as sealed off as Mrs. Speakman.

He returned to the living room and sat down on the sofa that faced the armoire. He tugged off his boots, wiggled his toes, and tried telling himself he was comfortable and relaxed. He sorted through the magazines again, and the glossy photos on the covers got things started. But, deciding he preferred his own imagination, he set the magazines aside, pulled his shirttail out, and unbuttoned his jeans.

He leaned back against the sofa cushions, closed his eyes, and recalled the night he'd been with Marcia. But erotic images of her were instantly obliterated by those of her lying in her hospital bed looking like something out of a war zone.

Shit!

Before he lost what he had, he searched his mind for something to think about that would keep it up. What had recently tickled his fancy or even sparked his curiosity? That mind search took only a few seconds, but it was the real deal, all right. He became instantly aroused.

And once he really focused on it . . .

He tapped on the closed door.

"You can come in."

He opened the door and stepped into the bedroom. It was completely furnished, although later he couldn't remember a damn thing about it except the pastel sheet that covered her to her waist. She was lying on her back, a pillow beneath her head, her hands clasped over her stomach. She still had on the pink top, and he could see a sliver of bra strap at her shoulder.

And under the sheet?

Her jacket and skirt were folded on a chair. Shoes were beside the bed.

Panties? He didn't see them. On or off?

In any case, he was glad he'd followed a hunch and kept his clothes on. Obviously getting naked wasn't part of the program.

But out of necessity his jeans were unbuttoned. Her glance in that vicinity was so fleeting he wondered if what she saw even registered before she looked up toward the ceiling and kept her eyes trained on a spot there.

He walked to the side of the bed and faced away from it. She didn't say anything, so neither did he. He took off his jeans but left his boxers on. For good measure—literally—he discreetly squeezed himself through his shorts and felt a reassuring bead of moisture dampen the cloth. Then keeping his back to her, he lifted the sheet and lay down. He felt ridiculous modestly pulling the sheet over his legs, but he did.

He lay there on his back, also staring at the ceiling, for thirty seconds or so. But this was a real mood killer, not to mention the jeopardy in which it was placing his ability to make a kid.

He turned onto his side to face her. She didn't speak, or even blink. But she opened her legs. The one nearest him made contact. The outside of her thigh glanced the top of his. Just that much skin-to-skin contact gave him the needed staying power.

He moved onto her, situated himself between her legs, and pushed his boxers past his hips. She raised her knees, not in a way that was particularly inviting, but at least they were anatomically positioned to have sexual intercourse. He probed where he was supposed to probe.

His heart bumped. No panties. Just . . . her.

She turned her head aside and closed her eyes.

Which made him angry. It was a given that this was going to be awkward. Difficult even. But she'd done nothing so far to make it any easier. While he'd been out there thinking dirty thoughts to get himself aroused, what had she been doing? Obviously nothing. Masturbation probably wasn't in her vocabulary, but couldn't she have done something to make herself more receptive? If not for his sake, then for her own? Couldn't she tilt her hips up just a little? Shift forward, shift back? Take him in her hand and guide him home? *Something?*

The only thing she did was to turn her face away.

The more he thought about it, the angrier he became. This was her idea, not his. She was orchestrating this, not him. She didn't want conversation beforehand? All right. He didn't have anything to say to her anyway.

She wanted to do it with their clothes on? Okay by him.

No foreplay? Who needed it? Not him.

She wanted to turn her head away like she was about to be sacrificed or something? Let her cope any ol' way she liked.

She wanted to lie as stiff and unyielding as a board? Fine.

But it wasn't fine, because it soon became apparent that he couldn't penetrate her without hurting her, and the thought of hurting her—

"Just do it," she said.

So he did it.

After that, biology and primal instinct took over. The tight resistance only compelled him to push harder, deeper. He closed his eyes, but only because he couldn't stand to watch her grimace. That was what he told himself anyway. He tried to empty his mind of all thought except the money he was going to have.

That's it, think about the money. Don't think about her. Don't think about how this feels or how snug . . . Shit! Don't think snug. Don't think . . . ah, hell . . .

With a long groan, he emptied himself, then forgot the rules and collapsed on top of her. His face remained pressed into the pillow, near her head, strands of her hair curling against his nose, until he could catch his breath.

She didn't move when he levered himself up and withdrew. She just lay there with her face still turned to the wall, eyes closed, a vertical frown between her eyebrows. He got out of bed, pulled up his boxers, and stepped into his jeans. When he finished buttoning up and buckling his belt, he looked over his shoulder. She had lowered her knees. The sheet had been pulled up to her waist again. She lay with one forearm across her eyes.

"Are you all right?"

She only nodded.

He stood there, feeling guilty, although he didn't know why. He felt like the time Ellie had caught him stealing a ten-dollar bill from her wallet and then had insisted that he keep it. He opened his mouth to say something, called it back, then finally said, "Look, you told me to—"

"I'm fine, Mr. Burkett." She lowered her arm and opened her

eyes, but she didn't look in his direction. "It betters my chances to conceive if I lie here for a half hour or so. That's all."

"Oh. So, you're okay?"

"Yes."

She didn't thank him. It sure as hell seemed inappropriate to thank her.

She was pulling on her suit jacket when she walked into the living room. Seeing him on the sofa, she stopped, shocked to find him still there. Gauging by her expression, she wasn't at all happy about it, either. She shoved her arm into the sleeve and wrestled the jacket into place. "Why didn't you leave?"

He stood up. "I—"

"You should be gone by now."

"I—"

"You shouldn't have waited, Mr. Burkett." Her voice sounded like tearing cloth. She was either mad as hell or on the edge of hysteria. He couldn't be sure which, but this was the most emotion he'd ever seen from her. Her cheeks were red. The calm, cool, and collected lady of the manor was about to lose it. "Why didn't you just *go*?"

Quietly he said, "Your car has mine blocked in."

In an instant, her posture went from rigid to limp. She released her breath slowly, touched her forehead with the tips of her fingers, then her flaming cheek with the backs of them, looked embarrassed. "Oh."

"I would have moved it myself, but you had the keys."

He gestured toward her handbag. She looked down where it hung at her side. "Right." Then, changing back into the got-it-together businesswoman persona, she said, "I apologize for holding you up."

"No problem."

"You should have come and told me."

"If it helps to keep lying down after . . . you know . . . I didn't mind waiting awhile. The whole point of this is to get you pregnant."

She nodded, then consulted her wristwatch. "I must go or I'm going to be late for a meeting. Will you reset the thermostat, please?"

"Sure."

"Just pull the door closed after you. It will lock. I'll be in touch, one way or the other."

She couldn't get out of there fast enough, and her haste to leave made him feel ornery. He had decided he wasn't going to say anything. If he was smart, he wouldn't.

But.

He said, "I wondered why you would go along with this, Mrs. Speakman."

Already halfway through the entry, she halted, turned, looked at him. "You know why, Mr. Burkett. I want a child."

"But *this*?" He tapped his fly, then motioned toward her middle. The gesture caused a frisson in her cool bearing. Some of the high color came back into her cheeks. He went to her, stopping only a few steps away. "After meeting both of you, I could almost understand your husband."

"Your understanding isn't important to us. Or necessary."

"Okay. Say I wanted to understand for my own peace of mind. Your husband is eccentric, maybe even altogether crazy, but looking at this child and heir thing from his point of view, from a rich man's point of view, I could sorta get it. *Sorta*." He shook his head, frowning with perplexity. "But you, I just couldn't figure."

"So don't bother trying."

He took another step closer, crowding her, making her uncomfortable, wanting to because in the bedroom she had made him feel like a vandal ravaging the village virgin. "Why, I asked myself, would you agree to making a baby this way?" His eyes held hers. He lowered his voice. "And now I know."

Coldly, she said, "*Now?*"

"Now that I know why your husband is in that wheelchair."

I can do this, Laura asserted to herself as she entered the conference room. Everyone else had assembled. She moved to the head of the table. "Sorry I'm late."

"We promise not to tell Foster," one of the department heads quipped.

"Thank you. We all know that punctuality is a religion to him."

"Long lunch?" someone teased.

Her hand faltered just a bit as she reached for the water carafe. "No, just an errand that took longer than I anticipated."

The errand hadn't taken that long. Her recovery from it had. She wondered how women who had extramarital affairs in the middle of the day completed their afternoons with any level of composure. She'd been certain that when she returned to her office, her assistant, Kay, would look at her with accusation and say, "You've just had sex."

But apparently there were no visible signs of how she'd spent her lunch hour. Kay had treated her as she always did, efficiently reminding her of the meeting as she handed her a stack of phone messages in the order of their priority.

To everyone else, this was any ordinary Monday. To Foster, it was a day of monumental importance. For her, one of substantial ambiguity. Foster was spending the day at home. She didn't have that luxury. She had to face this assembly of corporate heads while, less than an hour ago, she'd had sex with a stranger.

Yes, it was strictly for the purpose of procreation, and, yes, she'd done it with her husband's blessing, and, yes, for the sake of their future together she could do it again until they were successful. She *would* do it.

She sipped from her water glass, then smiled down the length of the conference table. "Who's up first?"

"Me," said the man in charge of baggage handling. "Unfortunately, we've had an incident in Austin. Foster isn't going to like it."

Foster was still very much a presence, but lately she had been his proxy for some of the executive meetings. The daily commute to the office, short as it was and with Manuelo along to facilitate it, had proved to be too much. So Foster had limited his days in the office to two per week. On days when it was mandatory for the department heads to meet, Laura presided, then in the evening she would give him a detailed recounting of what had been discussed.

In only a few short years she'd gone from asking passengers "Coffee or tea?" to serving as the CEO's understudy. When Foster had hired her as Hazel Cooper's replacement, her transition into management had gone smoothly. For years, she had been preparing herself for such a position. It was what she had aspired to and, having been given the opportunity, she felt confident she could meet the challenges.

But when her job description suddenly expanded to include dealing with a disabled husband as well as assuming many of his corporate responsibilities, the transition wasn't quite so seamless. Up until that point in her life, she'd been resistant to delegating any responsibility. Now she had no choice. Minor and routine jobs that she had formerly insisted on doing herself, she began assigning to subordinates.

Even so, the largest share of the workload remained hers. Nor could the tasks she did for Foster be turned over to someone else. Only she could do them because Foster demanded they be done in a particular order and in a particular way, *his* particular way, which was a way far more meticulous than anyone else's. His insistence on perfection put a strain on her time.

But no matter how difficult and demanding her schedule became, she refused to buckle under. Quitting, or even slacking off, wasn't an option. She was doing what must be done, and she would continue to.

However, she had begun to fear the impact motherhood would have on the careful balance she was maintaining. How could she possibly be a full-time mother, which she wanted to be, without detracting from her duties as wife, department head, and stand-in CEO? The prospect of juggling that additional responsibility was daunting. But if—*when*—she was forced to confront it, she would.

At present there were other matters demanding her attention, such as this one involving baggage handling. "What kind of incident?" she asked that department head.

"The worst. Stolen bags."

"You're right. Foster isn't going to like it. Details?"

The explanation was lengthy and involved, and generated discussion around the table. Laura tried to concentrate on what was being said, but her mind wandered. Her ability to focus simply wasn't there. She'd left it behind in that small, tidy house on Windsor Street, along with her dignity.

Why, I asked myself, would you agree to making a baby this way?

"Laura?"

She yanked her mind back to the business at hand. Everyone was looking at her, and she wondered how many times she'd been addressed before she realized it. "I'm sorry. My mind drifted for a moment."

The question was repeated. Laura answered. The meeting continued. While she wasn't wholly attuned, she wasn't caught again being inattentive. But as soon as there was a convenient point to adjourn, she did so. "We'll pick up the rest at the next meeting, okay? I've got a killer schedule this afternoon."

As the others filed out, no one seemed especially curious about her absentmindedness or abrupt adjournment. Joe McDonald did stop on his way to the door. "Hard day?"

"Harder than most."

"Maybe this will cheer you up." From behind his back, he produced a large white envelope and, with a flourish, laid it on the table in front of her. "Ta-da!"

"What's this?"

"Your baby."

"My *what*?"

"Uh . . ." Obviously taken aback by her stunned reaction, he said, "What I mean is, you've been waiting a long time for it. Check it out."

Having recovered from his choice of words, she opened the envelope and slid the contents onto the table. It was an eleven-by-fourteen artist's rendering of a SunSouth jet with a new and distinctive logo on the fuselage.

"Oh, my God!" Laura exclaimed. "This looks great, Joe! Truly great!"

He hooked his thumbs into his suspenders. "I thought you'd like it."

"Like it?" she said, unable to contain her excitement. "I *love* it." She ran her finger over the artwork as she read the words printed on the airplane. "SunSouth Select."

Joe beamed. "As I said, your baby."

CHAPTER

10

JOE LEFT HER, AND LAURA DECIDED TO TAKE ADVANTAGE OF THE solitude in the conference room. She remained seated in the tall leather chair at the head of the table—the one in which Foster had sat the first time she saw him—and looked again at the four-color rendering of the sleek jet.

SunSouth Select was a concept that she'd been working on for more than a year. It was a service-oriented innovation for the business traveler that she hoped to implement before SunSouth's competitors did something similar. She wanted SunSouth to be the initiator, not an imitator.

Joe seemed surprised that Foster hadn't yet seen the syllabus. Laura had worked on it for months, and once it was done, Joe had assumed she would take it straight to Foster. "No," she told him. "I want SunSouth Select to be a surprise. I want to present it to him as a complete package."

"You want to have all your ducks in a row."

"Exactly. And I'm still waiting on some market analyses and cost projections. When they're ready and I've had a chance to study them, I'll lay out the entire plan for him."

This was uncustomary. Always before, she and Foster had worked in tandem. One rarely made a move without the other knowing about it. While it was true that she wanted to surprise him with a kit-and-caboodle proposal, it was also true that, when she did, she wanted his undivided attention. She hadn't had that in months. He'd been preoccupied with finding the right man to sire their child.

He thought of little else, talked of little else. Every conversation included at least one reference to a child and its conception. That was the prevailing issue of their lives now. If she became pregnant, she knew that Foster would become an expert on prenatal care, diet, exercise. He would spend hours researching and committing to memory every aspect of pregnancy. No doubt he would chart their child's development on a daily basis.

He had once been quoted in *Business Week* as saying that his airline's success was in large part due to his OCD—obsessive-compulsive disorder. The interviewer thought he was joking. He wasn't.

He had been diagnosed as an adolescent, although he had exhibited the symptoms in early childhood. His parents had thought his compulsions went hand in glove with his brilliant mind and were nothing to worry about. But when those compulsions began to interfere with normal function and everyday life, his parents had sought psychiatric help.

Foster was put on medication to keep the disorder under control. He wasn't "healed," however, and so in a very real sense his obsessiveness was indeed responsible for his fanatic attention to detail, and therefore for SunSouth's extraordinary success.

Unless the weather was prohibitive, late arrivals and departures were not tolerated at SunSouth Airlines.

Each packet of peanuts contained exactly the same number. One too few, the customer was cheated. One too many cost the airline money.

Flight attendants and pilots did not alter their uniforms, not even by wearing nonregulation cuff links or an unapproved shade of panty hose.

If he'd had less charisma, Foster's obsessiveness would have incited mutiny by subordinates. But he was so personally disarming that it was indulged. Most regarded it with amusement instead of impatience. He was even teased about it. It was looked upon as an idiosyncrasy, an endearing one at that. And no one, not even his sternest critics, could argue with his success.

But Laura had a different perspective on Foster's OCD because she lived with it. She covered for him to keep it less noticeable to colleagues. Only she knew how much it governed his life. Increasingly so, it seemed. His compulsions were an integral part of him. Because she loved him, she accepted and tolerated them. But doing so had once been easier. Before.

Laura got up and walked to the window, rubbing her arms to ward off the chill of the air-conditioning. She twirled the wand on the blinds and looked through the slats at the traffic speeding along the expressway. A SunSouth jet, only minutes into its flight, was banking toward the west. The 3:45 to Denver, she thought automatically.

She watched the jet as it climbed, the sun reflecting off its silver fuselage, hurting her eyes when the shaft of light pierced them. But then she realized that her eyes stung with the need to cry. Resting her head against the window frame, she closed her eyes tightly, squeezing out tears. She whispered, "I want my life back."

Foster had waited one year after Elaine's death before asking Laura out. Initially Laura had misinterpreted the invitation, believing he had invited her to attend a black-tie charity event with him for some business purpose. But when several dozen white roses were delivered to her apartment in advance of his picking her up, she began to think perhaps there was more to it. Undeniably, the thought of that made her feel bubbly on the inside.

By the end of the evening there was no question that it had been a bona fide date. If Foster had asked any other executive—say, the CFO—to accompany him, he wouldn't have taken hold of both his hands and kissed his cheek good night.

Their evenings out became more frequent. There were dinners together after work, sailing on area lakes on Saturday afternoons, and Sunday suppers, which she cooked at her place. She attended his polo matches, and he had no compunction about kissing her in front of his teammates after a victory. She became his regular date to private dinner parties and public events. She stopped accepting other dates, even invitations from her tennis buddy, who began teasing her about her new beau.

She couldn't apply such a frivolous moniker to Foster Speakman, but away from the office he acted like one. The more time they spent alone together, the less chaste their embraces became. She had started devoting a lot of thought to him, his smile, his eyes, his mannerisms. She found herself engaging in gauzy daydreams about him unlike any she'd had about other men, not even in adolescence. She'd always enjoyed an active social life. She'd had a generous number of boyfriends, and enough lovers to be confident of her allure, but not so many that she need be embarrassed by the number.

But among them there were no standouts, no disappointing heartbreaks, or near-miss commitments. Because every romantic relationship she'd ever had, from the first car date to the last man she'd slept with, had been qualified. It could not interfere with her ambition.

Which now placed her in a real conundrum with Foster. Because of the professional implications, neither acknowledged their increasing intimacy and longing for more. Their kissing and groping left them fevered and frustrated, but each was determined to preserve their working relationship.

One evening while they were cuddled on the sofa in her den, watching a movie on TV, he suddenly reached for the remote and turned it off. "Thank you," she said. "I was finding it hard to get into, too."

"I loved Elaine with all my heart, Laura."

Recognizing the seriousness of his tone, she sat up and looked into his face. "Yes, you did. I know that."

"If she had lived, I would have loved her forever."

"I don't doubt that."

"I'll always cherish her memory and the years we had together."

None of this came as a surprise to Laura. She'd seen them together on numerous occasions following that first time at their home. It was obvious how deeply they had loved each other. Since Elaine's death, Foster had honored her by establishing a foundation to raise money for leukemia research. He wasn't just a mouthpiece with a checkbook, either, but a crusading advocate and hands-on fund-raiser. In death, as in life, Elaine was a vital part of him.

He stroked Laura's cheek. "But Elaine is no longer here. You are. And I'm in love with you."

He spent that night with her. Most nights following that, they spent together. In the office, they continued as they always had done, performing their individual jobs, conducting themselves in a professional manner, treating each other no differently than they treated their colleagues. They were confident no one knew about their personal relationship, but Laura learned later that they had fooled only themselves. Everyone knew.

One morning, she walked into his office unannounced and laid an envelope on his desk. "What's that?"

"My resignation."

He struggled to contain his smile. "We're not paying you enough? You've had a better offer?"

She sat down in the chair facing his desk. "Foster, the last four months have been the happiest of my life. Also the most miserable."

"Well, I hope that being with me has been the happy part."

She gave him a soft look. "You know how happy I am to be with you. But the secrecy makes it seem . . ."

"Sordid?"

"Yes. And sleazy. I'm sleeping with my boss. As a career woman, I don't like what that suggests about me. I don't like the connotation co-workers would apply to it. I don't want to give up my job. It's what I've worked so hard to attain. You know how much I love it.

"But I can't possibly give you up," she said, her voice turning husky with emotion. "Between the two, I love you more than I love my job. So . . ." She gestured toward the envelope lying on his desk. "I must leave SunSouth."

He picked up the envelope then and looked at it, turning it this way and that as though contemplating the contents. "Or," he said, "you could marry me."

Elaine Speakman had set a precedent by serving on the board of directors, so no one cried nepotism. No one wanted to anyway. When

Foster and Laura announced their plans to the other executives and the board members, the only discussion was the date the nuptials would take place and if they would be taking a SunSouth jet on their honeymoon.

If there was watercooler talk about her marrying Foster for his money, or any other self-serving reason, Laura never knew of it. Even if she had been aware of such scuttlebutt, she would have ignored it. While some may have regarded what had happened as a Cinderella story—in those very words it had been hinted at in a newspaper column—she knew her only reason for marrying him was that she loved him wholly and completely. She couldn't be bothered by the conjectures of mean-spirited people.

Their marriage was covered extensively in the press, although there were no pictures accompanying the stories. They kept the wedding itself private, inviting only their most intimate friends to the chapel service and the dinner following it.

Foster paid lip service to moving from his family estate, but Laura realized what a sacrifice that would be for him. He loved his family home and hugged her tightly when she told him she loved it, too, and that that was where they would stay and make their life together.

She moved in, changing very little of Elaine's decor. Like his wealth, his love for Elaine was only another aspect of him. Laura didn't feel threatened by his late wife's memory, any more than she was intimidated by his fortune.

Foster would have preferred her to be pregnant by the time they returned from their honeymoon in Fiji. When she demurred, he had teased her about her biological clock. "I'm thirty-one!" she exclaimed.

He placed his ear against her lower body. "But I can hear it ticking."

Even so, she had begged for time to be a bride before she became a mother. It was a decision that later seemed terribly selfish, and one she would always regret.

That first year they were kept busy with the burgeoning airline and settling into married life. Although Laura was to learn that "settling" was a foreign concept to her husband. The man never rested.

The more he had to do, the more he got done. He was a tireless, in-cessant generator of energy. He had the work ethic of a Trojan but was also a proponent of la dolce vita. His enthusiasm for life and liv-ing was contagious. Laura reveled in the whirlwind of their life.

Foster used the media to his advantage, regularly feeding them tidbits of information about his airline even when there was no ac-tual news to report, so that SunSouth was kept constantly in the minds of the public. His name, along with Laura's, appeared fre-quently in the business sections of the newspapers.

They received national magazine coverage, once pictured play-ing doubles tennis with the president and first lady. The televi-sion newsmagazine *20/20* did a segment on them, touting them as the team that had, despite industry naysayers, resurrected a failed airline. They appeared on *Good Morning America* to talk about the Elaine Speakman Foundation and the medical research it was funding.

The gossip columnists who had snidely implied that Laura was a gold digger were soon extolling her intelligence, business acumen, impeccable taste, and unaffected charm. The Speakmans became the darlings of the local society pages, and their photographs began appearing regularly as hosts, guests, or sponsors of one event or another.

As they were leaving one such event, a decision was made that would change the course of their lives forever.

It was a Tuesday night. They had attended a retirement dinner for a notable Dallasite. The hotel where the dinner had been held and the Speakman estate were separated by only three miles of city streets.

When the parking valet brought up Foster's car, Laura went around to the driver's side. "You toasted him more times than I did," she said.

"I'm fine to drive."

"Why chance it?"

She got behind the wheel. He sat in the passenger seat. They were talking about the next day's agenda. She had just reminded him of a meeting the following afternoon. "I have a busy day," he remarked. "Any chance we could change that?"

Then everything changed.

The driver of a delivery truck ran a red light, an error that cost him his life. Opposed to wearing a seat belt, he was ejected from his truck through the windshield.

Otherwise he might have had to be cut from the mishmash of metal caused by the collision, as Foster had been. The cab of the truck fused with the passenger side of Foster's sedan. It took rescue workers over four hours to extricate him from the wreckage.

Laura was rendered unconscious by the impact. She came to in the ambulance, and her first thought was of her husband. Her rising hysteria concerned the paramedics treating her. They answered honestly, "We don't know about your husband, ma'am."

It was agonizing hours before she was told that he was alive but that his condition was critical. She learned later that he underwent emergency surgery to repair extensive internal injuries causing life-threatening hemorrhage. Because she had sustained only a concussion, a broken arm, some scrapes and bruising, she was finally permitted into the ICU, where Foster struggled to survive. Specialists came and went. In hushed voices they conferred. None looked optimistic.

Days passed; Foster clung to life. Laura kept vigil at his bedside while monitors telegraphed in blips and beeps his extraordinary will to live.

In all, he had six operations. From the outset, she realized that the orthopedists knew he would never walk again, but they performed the surgeries as though there was hope. They used pins and screws to reattach bones that would never move unless someone moved them for him. Other specialists spliced blood vessels to provide better circulation. He underwent a second abdominal surgery to repair a tear in his colon that had gone undetected during the first.

She couldn't remember what the other surgeries were for.

It wasn't until weeks after the accident that Foster was fully apprised of his condition and prognosis. He took the news with remarkable aplomb, courage, and confidence.

When they were alone, he reached for Laura's hand, pressed it between his, and reassured her that everything would be all right. He looked at her with unqualified love and repeatedly expressed his gratitude to God that she had escaped the accident without serious injury.

He never implied that she was responsible. But as she gazed down at him through her tears that day, she said what she knew must have crossed his mind, as it had hers a thousand times. "I should have let you drive."

Two years later, staring sightlessly through the window in Sun-South's conference room, she was still anguishing over her decision to drive that night. Would Foster have driven a bit faster, a bit slower, preventing them from being in the center of the intersection when the truck failed to stop? Would he have seen it ahead of time and swerved to avoid the collision? Would he have done something she hadn't?

Or, if fate had dictated that they were in that spot at that precise moment, she should have been the one sitting in the passenger seat.

Foster had never suggested she was to blame. He had never even referenced their brief conversation about how much each had had to drink and who should drive. But, although it remained unspoken, the question was always there between them: Would this have happened if he'd been behind the wheel?

Laura acknowledged how pointless it was to ask. Even so, the suppositions tortured her, as she knew they must Foster. They would go to their graves asking, *What if?*

Griff Burkett had somehow learned about the accident. She hadn't stayed to have a conversation with him about it, but if he knew the details of why Foster was in his wheelchair, he surely understood why she would go along with this or any plan Foster devised.

Foster hadn't died, but his previous life had ended the night of the wreck. And Laura was left guilt-ridden.

Having a child, conceiving it in the way Foster wished, demanded very little of her, considering everything he'd had to give up. A child and heir was one of the dreams that had been snatched from him that night. Maybe by granting him that dream, she would relieve her guilt and, by doing so, get back a portion of her former life.

Impatient with her self-pity, she turned away from the window. As she did so, a pinching sensation between her legs caused her to wince, as much from the memory it evoked as from the physical discomfort.

It had been difficult for Griff Burkett to penetrate her. That she was dry and inflexible said much about the status of her private life, and that had been mortifying. But at least he'd had the sensitivity to realize her condition and to hesitate. He'd even seemed reluctant to proceed, knowing it would hurt her. In fact, he had . . .

No. She wouldn't think about it. Wouldn't think about him. Doing so would make it personal. If it became personal, her argument wouldn't hold. The argument she'd used to convince herself to go along with Foster's plan was that *using a surrogate father to conceive was just as clinical as, and no more emotionally involving than, undergoing artificial insemination in the sterile environment of a doctor's office.*

But the tenderness between her thighs was a taunting reminder that she had been with a man. A man moving inside her. Climaxing inside her.

How could she have thought for one foolish moment that it would feel clinical?

CHAPTER

11

THE SPORTS BAR WAS CROWDED AND NOISY, BUT GRIFF HAD thought if he spent one more evening cooped up inside his apartment, he was going to go round the bend.

Without anything constructive to do during the day, the evenings were particularly long. His tan was already too deep to be healthy. Although he kept to a strict exercise regimen, he was bored with working out. He'd seen all the current movies, some more than once. He'd caught up on his reading. Everything he found entertaining anyway.

Marcia was completing her recuperation at home, and via Dwight, she had asked Griff not to visit her there. "She's dealing with a lot just to recover. Then she's facing the plastic surgery," Dwight had told him. "She needs some space. I'm sure she'll contact you when she's back to her glorious self."

The message had been polite enough, but Griff could read between the lines. He was an additional complication she didn't need. She didn't blame him for what had happened, but distancing herself from him would be safer and healthier, for herself and for her business.

Consequently, he didn't even have his daily trips to the hospital to look forward to. He was bored. And, possibly for the first time in his life, lonely. Being a social outcast was different from choosing to be alone.

One of the things he'd hated most about his incarceration was the lack of privacy. During those five years, he'd yearned for solitude, and swore that when he got out, he was never going to take it for granted again. But at least when he was in the mood to talk, there were other prisoners to shoot the bull with. His meals were eaten in the company of other people.

Now he had nobody with whom to do anything. Days would pass when he didn't exchange a single word with another person.

Not that he was gregarious by nature. As Bolly had so candidly pointed out, he'd always been a loner. No doubt that tendency was a holdover from his childhood. His mother's neglect had taught him to be self-sufficient. He'd relied only on himself for everything— sustenance, pacification, and entertainment.

That mandatory self-reliance developed into a personality trait. It also became a weapon he used to keep other people at arm's length, out of either dislike or mistrust. He didn't see the percentage in letting anyone hold sway over him. Even the most casual friendship required too much. To be a friend, one must give as well as accept. Griff found both equally difficult. Coach and Ellie had finally figured that out and had stopped pressuring him to make friends, resigning themselves to his preference for his own company over anyone else's.

But in his former life he'd at least been around other people even if he didn't mingle with them. At school, with the Cowboys, at Big Spring. Now he was actually lonely. So a few days ago, out of desperation, he'd called one of his former teammates, one with whom he'd been comparatively friendly.

The former tight end, who owned a successful software company now, congratulated him on getting released and lied by saying that it was great to hear from him. But when Griff suggested they get together for a beer, the guy ticked off a dozen excuses in the span of thirty seconds, one being that he'd gotten married.

"She's a great lady, don't get me wrong. But she keeps me on a tight leash. You know how it is."

Actually, he didn't. But what he did know was that this big, tough former NFL player would rather Griff think he was a henpecked husband than drink a beer with him.

Tonight, unwilling to spend another night in the solitary confinement of his apartment, Griff had dressed and gone looking for a crowd. He'd found one at an expensive sports bar in an upscale neighborhood. The place was sleek and snazzy, serving more fruit-flavored martinis than beer. It catered to the young, beautiful, and fit. Griff's was the palest tan among them.

He was ogled by the twenty-somethings in skimpy summertime tops and short skirts. He ogled back, but not ambitiously. Which was somewhat surprising, since he hadn't had sex with anyone since Marcia.

Well, and Laura Speakman.

Don't go there.

That was what he told himself every time his thoughts went there.

People were standing three deep at the circular bar. He had to wait almost half an hour before a barstool became available. He claimed it, ordered a beer and a burger. While he ate, he watched a baseball game on the large-screen TV suspended over the center of the bar.

He'd become aware of a brunette sitting on the far side of the bar, facing him. She flashed him a smile and a glimpse of tit every time her boyfriend—or husband or whatever he was—wasn't looking. Beyond that, Griff let the barroom dramas pulse around him without taking notice.

He stretched his meal out over five innings of the Rangers game. To maintain ownership of his barstool, and to keep from going back to the empty apartment, he ordered a second beer he didn't want.

The Rangers were up by three. They were having a good season. If they made it to the play-offs, he would become interested. Otherwise, he didn't much like baseball. He couldn't make sense of a sport where the perfect game was one in which nothing happened. Baseball aficionados would disagree, saying that plenty happened during a no-hitter, but he couldn't appreciate it.

Of course, it was a hell of a lot more fun to watch when you'd wagered on the outcome.

His gambling had started out as innocently as that. He did it for fun. Even while he was at UT, he would make calls, place bets on NCAA games, although he'd never bet on a Longhorns game. But he'd wanted to. He didn't yield to the temptation of betting on his own games until he was drafted by the Cowboys.

The shrink who'd counseled him at Big Spring had a theory. He said Griff had felt guilty over his good fortune. The Longhorns had won the national championship his senior year. He'd missed being awarded the Heisman by two votes. He was the number one pro draft pick that year and an enviable prize for the Cowboys, whose veteran quarterback had retired. When he signed with the team, his picture was on the cover of *Sports Illustrated*. Fame and fortune at twenty-three. Heady stuff.

The shrink's take on it was that he'd gambled in the subconscious hope of getting caught, being punished, and losing everything, including Coach and Ellie's affection. The shrink had emphasized that. "Coach Miller is perhaps the one individual in the world you respected and for whom you felt affection. Yet you deliberately did what you knew he couldn't forgive, the one act that would cause an irreparable breach in your relationship."

His summarizing analysis was that, subconsciously, Griff felt he should be penalized for all the good things that had happened to him—beginning with Coach giving him a home and ending with him becoming starting quarterback for the Dallas Cowboys—because in his deepest, darkest self, he'd felt these boons were undeserved. His ruin had become a self-fulfilled prophecy.

Maybe that was right.

Or maybe that was horseshit.

He'd gambled because it was fun and because he could get away with it.

Then, when he got deep in hock, it stopped being fun. And he couldn't get away with it anymore.

As he sat sipping his second beer, trying to make it last, he idly wondered how much money had been gambled on the outcome of this Rangers game. How much would his former business associates in the fancy Las Colinas office make off these nine innings? Plenty, you could be sure. The Vista boys had bookmakers all over the country working for them.

One less, now that Bill Bandy was no longer in their employ.

Griff hoped that sniveling little snitch was being slowly turned on a spit over the fieriest fire in hell.

"You got any money on it?"

Having been lost in thought, Griff turned his head to his right, to make sure he was the one being addressed. The man on the next stool was glaring at him, his upper lip raised in a belligerent smirk.

"Pardon?" Griff said.

"Ask him again." A second man was standing behind the first. His truculent expression matched that of his friend, and his eyes were equally bloodshot from too much drink.

Calmly Griff said, "Ask me what?"

"I asked if you put any money on this game." The one on the stool hitched his thumb toward the TV screen.

"No. I didn't." Griff turned away, hoping that would be the end of it.

"You don't gamble anymore?"

Ignoring him, Griff reached for his beer.

The one on the stool jabbed his arm, causing him to slosh beer onto the bar. "Hey, asshole. Didn't you hear me? I asked you a question."

By now, those nearest to them had become aware of the cross words being exchanged. The music continued to blare through the speakers with palpable percussion. Action continued on the TV screen, but conversations were suspended as attention was directed toward them.

"I don't want any trouble," Griff said under his breath. "Why don't you guys just back off, go somewhere and sober up, okay?" But he knew they weren't going to simply walk away. The second one had moved up behind his barstool, crowding in close. Griff's back was to him, but he sensed the man's hostile, challenging stance.

He made eye contact with the bartender and motioned that he wanted his check. The bartender hastened over to a computerized

cash register. Griff glanced across at the brunette who'd been flashing him. She was sucking her drink through a straw, watching him
over the frosted glass. Her escort was looking at him, too.

The guy standing behind Griff's barstool said, "I guess he only
bets on the games he throws."

"Fucking cheater." The first guy jabbed his arm again, hard.
"Fucking, fucking cheat—"

Griff's hand shot out with the speed of a striking snake, grabbed
the man's wrist, and slammed it down onto the bar like the coup de
grâce of an arm-wrestling match.

He howled in pain. The second one landed on Griff's back like a
mattress stuffed with lead. Griff came off his barstool and tried to
shake the guy off. There was a noisy shuffling of feet as people hastily backed away. Somewhere a glass broke. Two bouncer types appeared and pulled the guy off Griff's back. "Break it up."

One of the bouncers pushed Griff's shoulder, shoving him back
several steps. Griff put up no resistance. He raised his hands. "I
didn't ask for any trouble. I didn't want it."

The two bouncers took firm hold of his hecklers and escorted
them away. They protested drunkenly but were taken outside. But
the show wasn't over. All eyes remained on Griff, especially now that
he'd been recognized. His whispered name moved through the crowd
like a spreading stain.

The bartender presented his check. Before he could count out the
bills to pay it, a young man in a fashionable suit materialized beside
him. He was obviously the man in charge. "It's on the house," he
said to the bartender, who nodded and retrieved the check.

Griff said, "Thanks."

But the young man's expression wasn't hospitable. "I'm asking
you to leave and not come back."

Anger and embarrassment caused Griff's face to grow hot. "I
didn't do anything."

"I'm asking you to leave and not come back," the young man
repeated.

Griff stared at him for several seconds more, then pushed him
aside and strode past. The crowd parted to clear a path. When he

reached the door, one of the bouncers held it open for him. As Griff walked through, the bouncer muttered, "Cocksucking cheat."

Outside, the air wrapped around Griff like a damp shroud. However, he would have had better luck throwing off the cloying, humid atmosphere than he would his anger. He'd been minding his own business, hurting nobody, and he'd been asked to leave and not come back by a guy wearing one of the shirts he'd passed over at Neiman's because it looked too faggy.

Screw 'em. He'd had better burgers at Dairy Queen for a fraction of the cost, so what the fuck did he care, anyhow?

He cared because he'd been humiliated in front of people who used to cheer him. And going from a superstar of the Dallas Cowboys, surrounded by media photographers and screaming fans, to being escorted out of a glorified burger joint was quite a comedown.

He got to his car and unlocked it. Before he had time to open the door, he was grabbed from behind and flung against the rear quarter panel.

"We're not finished with you." It was the guy from the bar, the one who'd first spoken to him. His buddy was standing right beside him. They weren't drunk. They were stone-cold sober. And, Griff realized with a blast of clarity, they weren't disgruntled fans, either.

"This is for my wrist," the guy snarled. He buried his fist in Griff's stomach.

No, Griff thought as his knees liquefied, *these guys aren't sports fans with too many beers under their belts. They're pros.*

CHAPTER

12

"Foster?"

"Hmm?"

"Will you come to the office tomorrow?"

He set down the book he'd been reading and looked across at Laura. She'd brought home paperwork from the office. Since dinner, she had been sitting on the sofa in the library, riffling through various reports. "If you want me to."

"Some of this stuff is over my head," she said. "It's technical and requires your input. It's been almost a week since you were there. I think it's important for you to go to the office whenever you can."

"You think the mice are playing?"

She smiled. "No, because they know I would tattle on anyone slacking off." She hesitated, then said, "I think it's important to *you* that you go."

"Oh, so you think that *I'm* slacking off."

She placed her hands on her hips in feigned exasperation. "Are you trying to pick a fight?"

"Okay, no more teasing. But you do understand, don't you, that just because I'm not physically at the office doesn't mean I'm not working."

"I know that your mind is always busy, but there's an energizing quality about actually being in the office."

He considered her for a moment. "You're doing your job as well as covering for me. Have the dual responsibilities become too much for you?"

He'd touched a sensitive spot, and she reacted. "Do *you* think they have?"

"Not at all. I've just noticed that you seem tired."

She let that go for the moment. "I'm concerned for you, not me. You love SunSouth. It's your lifeblood. You need that airline as much as it needs you. And when was the last time we went out to dinner?"

His head went back a fraction. "Sorry. I must have missed the segue. When did we switch subjects?"

"We didn't. It's the same subject."

"It is?"

"We rarely see our friends anymore. I can't remember when we last went out or had a couple over for cards or Sunday brunch. You stay here most days. All I do is work. I love it, and I'm not complaining, but . . ." She stopped, dropped her chin, and let the sentence trail off.

"You got your period."

She raised her head, met his gaze, and as her shoulders gradually sank, she nodded. "I'm sorry."

He frowned with regret. "I knew it."

"By my whining?"

"No. This was the first morning that I didn't ask about your period."

"Foster." She'd been mistaken. It wasn't regret behind his expression but self-reproach. He'd been tracking her cycle diligently, asking about it every day, sometimes several times a day.

"I jinxed it this morning by not getting up in time to see you off before you left for your breakfast meeting. I always ask you about your period first thing in the morning. This morning, I didn't ask."

"Foster, believe it or not, my menstrual cycle doesn't depend on your asking about it."

"You were late."

"Only two days."

"Why were you late?"

"I don't know."

"You've never been late before."

"Not usually, no."

"Then why now?"

"I don't know, Foster," she said, trying to contain her impatience. "Stress, maybe."

"Dammit!" He struck the arms of his wheelchair three times. "When you didn't start two days ago, I let myself begin to hope. I should have asked. If I'd have asked—"

"I would have menstruated anyway."

"We'll never know."

"*I* know. My temperature had dropped, indicating I wasn't pregnant. I've felt premenstrual for days. That's why I've been draggy and tired. I hoped I was wrong but . . ." She shook her head wistfully. "I dreaded telling you."

"It's not your fault. Come here."

His soft tone compelled her to set aside the paperwork. When she reached him, he guided her onto his lap. She sat down gingerly. "Don't let me hurt you."

"If only you could." They smiled at each other but left unsaid the many things they always left unsaid about the accident and its residual effect on their lives. He squeezed her shoulder affectionately. "This is a letdown, but it's not a defeat. You did everything you could."

"Which obviously wasn't enough."

"Success has been delayed. That doesn't equate to failure."

She ducked her head, murmuring, "You know me so well."

"I know how your overachiever's mind works. Sometimes to a disadvantage."

Both being type A personalities, they had compared their childhoods and discovered that, despite the sizable financial gap between the two families, they had been reared similarly. Her parents, like his, had expected much from their only child.

Both their fathers had been dominant but not unloving. The pressure to succeed that they had placed on their children was more implied than overt, but that didn't make it any less effective.

Her father had been career Air Force, a bomber pilot who'd

served two tours of duty in Vietnam. After the war, he was a test pilot and trainer. A natural daredevil and risk taker, he rode his motorcycle without a helmet, slalomed on both water and snow, went skydiving and bungee jumping.

He died in his sleep. A cerebral aneurysm burst. He never knew what hit him.

Laura had adored him and took his death hard, not only because of the bizarre unfairness of it but because he hadn't lived to see her achieve all the goals she'd set for herself.

Her mother had considered her dashing husband an unparalleled hero. She worshiped him and never recovered from the shock of finding him lying dead beside her. Grief deteriorated into depression. Laura was helpless to stop its inexorable pull until eventually it claimed her mother's life.

Laura had been a straight-A student, valedictorian, Phi Beta Kappa. She had achieved every goal she'd ever set for herself. Her parents had openly showed their pride. They'd called her their crowning achievement. But their deaths, both tragic and premature, had left her feeling that she had failed them miserably.

Foster knew this. She pointed her finger at him now, saying, "Don't start with that psychobabble about me not wanting to disappoint my parents."

"Okay."

"But that's what you're thinking," she accused. "Just like you're thinking that this is your fault because you didn't ask me about my period this morning."

He laughed. "Who knows whom well?"

She ran her fingers through his hair. "I know that you don't like changing your routine, because if you do, terrible things will happen. Isn't that the principle by which you live, Foster Speakman?"

"And now here's proof of how sound that principle is."

"The laws of nature are also sound." She shrugged. "An egg wasn't fertilized. It's as simple as that."

He shook his head stubbornly. "Nothing's that simple."

"Foster—"

"It's indisputable, Laura. Unwritten laws govern our lives."

"To some extent, possibly, but—"

"No but. There are cosmic patterns in place that one should not violate. If one does, the consequences can be severe."

Lowering her head, she said softly, "Like switching drivers at the last minute."

"Oh, Christ. Now I've made you even more unhappy." He pulled her head down onto his chest and stroked her back.

She couldn't argue this with him. To try to do so would be futile. Shortly after they were married, in an effort to better understand his OCD, she had talked with his psychiatrist. He had explained Foster's conviction that disorder predestined disaster. Patterns could not be broken. Series could not be interrupted. Foster believed this with his heart, mind, and soul, and the doctor had told her that trying to convince him otherwise was a waste of breath. "He copes with it extremely well," he'd told her. "But you would do well to remember that what to you is a hitch, is chaos to him."

Tacitly agreeing to let the matter drop, they sat quietly. After a time, Foster said, "Griff Burkett will be disappointed, too."

"Yes. He'll have to wait at least another month for his half million."

He hadn't asked her anything specific about her first meeting with Burkett. When she came home that evening, she'd given him a detailed account of everything that had taken place in the office, but she'd told him nothing about that until he asked. "How was your appointment with Burkett?"

"Brief. He did what he needed to do and left."

She hadn't elaborated, and he hadn't asked for more information, perhaps sensing that going into detail would make her uncomfortable.

"So you'll be calling him again in a couple of weeks?" he asked now.

She sat up and looked deeply into his eyes. "Do you want me to, Foster?"

"Yes. Unless it was unbearable to you."

She shook her head but looked away. "If you can bear it, I can."

"Isn't this what we agreed?"

"Yes."

"It's what we want."

"I know. I just hope it happens soon."

"It's what we want."

"I love you, Foster."

"And I love you." Then he drew her head to his chest again, saying, "It's what we want."

A week after the beating, Griff began to think he would live. For the previous six days, he hadn't been so sure.

The sons of bitches hadn't even been kind enough to beat him unconscious. And that had been deliberate. They'd wanted him awake to feel every punch, grind, and gouge. They'd wanted him conscious so that when they lifted up his head by his hair and pointed out to him a car parked nearby, he would recognize it as Rodarte's olive drab sedan and see the cute flashing of its headlights. They didn't want him muzzy or confused. They wanted him to remember the beating and who was behind it.

They'd given him a concussion. He'd suffered a couple in football, so he recognized the symptoms. Even though he didn't experience the amnesia that sometimes accompanies a concussion, the nausea, dizziness, and blurred vision had plagued him for twenty-four hours.

By rights, he shouldn't have moved, except to use his cell phone to call 911, summoning an ambulance to the parking lot. But a trip to the emergency room would have involved paperwork, the police. God only knew what else.

Somehow he'd managed to climb into his car and drive himself home before his eyes swelled shut. Since then, he'd been popping ibuprofen tablets every couple hours and trying to find one position in which to lie that didn't cause throbbing pain. He didn't worry about internal injuries. The pros knew how to damage him so he would feel it, but they didn't want a murder on their hands. If they did, he'd be dead. They'd only wanted him praying for death so he'd feel better.

He got up solely to pee, and not until his bladder was full to bursting. When he did leave the bed, he walked like an old man, bent at the waist, shuffling because every time he tried to lift his feet, a knifing pain in his lower back brought tears to his eyes.

Yesterday his mobility had improved a bit. This morning, he'd worked up enough courage to get in the shower. The hot water had actually felt good, easing some of the aches and pains.

The bedroom stank of him because he hadn't been up to the task of changing the sheets. Sick of looking at the same four walls, he left the room for the first time in a week. Coffee sounded good. He realized he was ravenously hungry. Things were looking up.

He was scooping scrambled eggs straight from the skillet into his mouth when his doorbell rang. "Who the hell?" He couldn't think of anyone who would come calling.

He made it to his front door and looked through the peephole. "You gotta be kidding," he muttered. Then, *"Shit!"*

"Griff?"

Griff hung his head, shaking it in wonderment at his fuck-all rotten luck. "Yeah. Just a minute." He fumbled with the locks, which he'd had the wherewithal to secure when he returned home the night of the beating, fearing that Rodarte's thugs might show up for round two.

He pulled the door open. "Hi."

His probation officer gaped at him. "Holy shit. What happened to you?"

He'd met Jerry Arnold in his office a week after speaking to him on the telephone. Griff had figured that a person-to-person meeting might win him some favor. When he'd left the ten-minute meeting, he knew he'd earned a few points.

Now Arnold's good opinion of him was in jeopardy. Ordinarily Griff would tower over the short, stocky black man. Today, since Griff was standing at a sixty-degree angle at best, they were roughly eye to eye. "What happened?" Arnold repeated.

This being the longest time Griff had been out of bed in a week, he'd begun to feel light-headed and shaky. "Come in." Turning his back on his guest, he slowly made his way to the nearest chair and lowered himself into it as carefully as possible. Even so, every ache and pain that had been lulled by his hot shower was jarred awake again. "Take a load off, Jerry," he said, indicating another chair.

Arnold dressed and conducted himself like a bureaucrat and

looked like a man with huge responsibilities and a lot on his mind—a wife, a mortgage, a few kids to rear on a government employee's salary. And unreliable ex-cons to babysit. He placed his hands on his hips, reminiscent of Coach. "You gonna tell me, or what?"

"I got thrown into the gorilla cage at the zoo. Those fuckers can get testy."

Arnold wasn't amused.

Griff sighed, in resignation and pain. "I ran into some former fans. Last, hmm, Thursday, I think."

"And you still look this bad?"

"Don't worry. It hurts a lot worse than it looks." He grinned, but the other man's frown stayed in place.

"Did you go to the emergency room? Has a doctor seen you?"

Griff shook his head. "I didn't report it to the police, either. It was just a couple of drunks. They jumped me in the parking lot of a restaurant." He made a gesture that dismissed the incident's importance. "I didn't fight back, so you don't have to worry about them filing assault charges against me."

Finally Arnold sat down. "Is this kind of thing happening a lot?"

"I get dirty looks, but this is the first time the hostility has turned physical. As I said, they were drunk." He gave a sanitized version of what had happened.

"Do you think Vista was behind it?"

"Vista?" Griff snorted. "If Vista was behind it, I wouldn't be here to tell you about it. It's nothing, Jerry. Swear to God. I'm feeling much better."

Arnold made a point of looking at the cold sweat Griff could feel beading on his forehead, but he didn't comment further. "How are you doing otherwise?"

"Good."

Arnold looked around the apartment, taking in the fancy TV, the new furnishings. "This is a nice place."

"Thanks."

The man's eyes moved back to him. "How'd you pay for it?"

"Cash. Which I came by legally."

"How?"

"It has nothing to do with Vista, none of that. I haven't broken any laws. I haven't placed a bet."

"Do you have a job yet?"

"I'm looking into a couple of things."

"You were going for an interview . . ."

"It didn't pan out."

"What was it?"

"I didn't get the job, so what difference does it make?"

Arnold didn't get visibly ruffled over the attitude behind the question, but he repeated in a no-bullshit tone, "What was it?"

Resigned, Griff said, "I asked a sportswriter if I could do legwork for him. You know Bolly Rich?"

"I read his column."

"I proposed becoming one of his stringers. He turned me down." Actually, Griff was glad Arnold had pressed him about this. He hoped the probation officer would call Bolly for verification. Bolly would confirm that Griff had tried in earnest to secure employment.

"Anything else?"

"Nothing concrete." Griff hoped Arnold would let it go at that, because basically Griff liked the guy. He had a rotten job, but somebody had to do it. Griff had nothing personal against him, and he'd have hated lying to him.

"Let me know soon as you land something. It'll look good on your record."

"Will do. Soon as I land something."

"In the meantime, no bookies, no Vista."

"Hell, I know that."

"No matter how discouraged you become."

"Believe me, Jerry, I want nothing to do with them."

"I do believe you." He said it like he wanted to but didn't. "Try to stay out of places where you might run into football fans."

Griff gave him a look.

Abashed, he said, "Hard to do, I know, but try not to provoke another incident."

"I didn't provoke this one."

"I believe that, too." And this time he sounded sincere. He stood up to leave. Griff tried not to let his relief show. "Stay where you are," Arnold said when Griff made to get up. "I'll see myself out." He turned to go, then came back around. "Have you heard anything from Stanley Rodarte?"

Griff was glad for the concealing effect the swelling and bruising had on his expression. "Actually, he showed up at the prison the day of my release." He admitted it in case this was a trick question. Arnold might have been in contact with Wyatt Turner, who could have mentioned Rodarte's unwelcome appearance.

"Did you talk to him there?"

"No." Again, the truth.

"He'd mean trouble for you. The last person you'd want to see coming."

"You can say that again."

"I'd like to know if he comes around. In fact, I need to know."

"Absolutely."

"You'd be dumb to take him on alone, Griff."

"I won't."

Thoughtfully Arnold threaded his clip-on necktie through his fingers. "His reputation being what it is, I'm a bit surprised he's keeping his distance. Nothing from him since that day at the prison, huh?"

"Nope. Nothing."

So much for not lying to his probation officer.

Griff's physical strength and conditioning served him well, and he mended. During the week following the surprise visit from Jerry Arnold, the swelling around his eyes and mouth subsided and his face began to look familiar.

The bruises faded to an ugly greenish yellow, then the green began to go away, leaving him with only an overall jaundiced look. The gash above his eyebrow was reduced to a faint pink line. It matched the faint pink line across his cheekbone, a lasting gift Rodarte had delivered himself that night in the parking garage.

Rodarte had a shitload of grief to answer for. Despite what he'd told his probation officer, Griff couldn't wait for the opportunity to pay the bastard back.

He hadn't resumed his multi-mile runs yet, but he had swum laps the past two days. His muscles were sore, but in the good way that came from exercise, not from being pounded on by fists that had felt like meat tenderizers.

He wasn't up to full speed, but he no longer moved like a ninety-year-old with arthritis in every joint. He was feeling more like himself. Which was good. Because Laura Speakman called one morning as he was stepping out of the shower.

"One o'clock?"

"That's good for me."

"I'll see you then."

He looked at himself in the full-length mirror on the back of his bathroom door. If she had turned her head away from him before, she might go into a full-fledged cower at the sight of him today. His appearance had improved, but he still looked like he'd taken a sound beating.

He gave himself another critical once-over in the mirror, front and back. *One good thing*, he thought, *she won't be seeing me naked*.

CHAPTER

13

LAURA OPENED THE DOOR FOR HIM, THEN STOOD ASIDE AND motioned him into the house. No sports jacket this time, she noted. He was wearing a white oxford cloth Polo shirt tucked into his jeans, and brown cowboy boots, which he'd been wearing the other two times she'd seen him. He was carrying a small white paper sack.

She closed the door and joined him in the living area just as he was taking off his sunglasses. She managed to keep from gasping but just barely. His face, particularly around his eyes and along his jaw, was bruised.

Gauging by the sickly color of the bruises, they were a week or so old. They must have looked much worse when fresh. The cut above his eyebrow was new. The one on his cheekbone was fainter than it had been a month ago.

Either he was accident prone or . . .

She didn't want to speculate on the *or*. None of the possibilities that came immediately to mind were good.

He noticed her staring, but since he neither acknowledged nor explained his battered appearance, she didn't ask about it. He set his sunglasses and the sack on the coffee table, then stood looking at the closed doors of the armoire for several moments before turning back to her. "It didn't take?"

Because she was still wondering under what circumstances his face had become so bruised, it took a second or two for his question to sink in. Looking away, she shook her head. "If it had, we wouldn't be here."

"Right."

The a/c cycled off. Without its soft whir, the house seemed abnormally quiet.

"Well—"

"I—"

They began at the same time. Laura motioned for him to go ahead.

He reached for the small sack he had carried in with him and passed it to her. "I brought this."

She looked at him curiously, then opened the sack and peered inside. When she saw the box, her heart gave a little jump.

"It's, uh, it's not the kind that has a spermicide," he said. "I double-checked, 'cause some of them do. Have it, I mean."

Not trusting her voice to speak, she nodded.

The cowboy boots shifted slightly. "I just thought since—"

"Yes. Thank you." Before any more could be said, she hurried toward the bedroom.

Once inside, she closed the door and leaned against it. She had the sack clutched in a death grip. Her palms were actually damp. This was silly, getting so flustered. But what flustered her more than the tube of lubricant was that he had thought to bring it. That he had thought at all about what they would do today.

She set her handbag on the dresser and went into the bathroom. The mirror above the sink reflected an image that looked surprisingly normal. Dark hair. Gray eyes that verged on green, a distinctive black spot in the right one. A triangle-shaped face, the brow slightly wider than the jaw. It was saved from being too prim by her lips, which were full and—she'd been told—sexy.

Her color was a little high. She attributed that to the midday heat.

A month ago, as well as today, she had carefully selected what to wear, dressing in her most structured business suits. Nothing too feminine, certainly nothing provocative. She took off her suit jacket, skirt, and shoes. As before, she left on her top, which today was an unadorned V-necked T-shirt, light blue, not too fitted. She also left on the three strands of silver chain around her neck, which somehow made her feel more dressed than *un*.

She took the box out of the sack, opened it, removed the tube. Just in case he was wrong, she read every word on the label. Twice.

Afraid that she'd taken too long, she hurried from the bathroom, folded back the covers, and got into bed. She removed her panties and tucked them between the mattresses, as she had done last time. She raised the sheet to her waist, then a bit higher.

She closed her eyes and tried to relax and control her hectic breathing. Her heart was beating way too fast. This waiting for him was agonizing.

What was he doing out there?

Well, of course she knew what he was doing. She just wondered *what* he was doing. Was he sitting up? Lying down on the sofa? Did he feel any self-consciousness at all? Was he the least bit anxious about his ability to perform? Had it occurred to him to wonder what she was thinking about while she waited for him?

She hadn't heard any sound coming from the living room either the last time or today, so she imagined he had decided against the videos in favor of the magazines.

Or maybe he didn't need either and was simply fantasizing, conjuring up his own prurient images. Surely he'd been with countless women. When he was a football star, women would have thrown themselves at him. Undoubtedly many still would. He would have had hundreds of erotic experiences from which to draw.

What kind of woman appealed to him? Tall or petite, slender and athletic or curvy and buxom, blond or redhead? Brunette?

His knock was soft, but it still gave her a start. She took a deep breath. "Come in."

He stepped into the room. Although they were the only two in the house, he closed the door. Even without his boots he seemed towering in the confines of the bedroom. Their eyes connected for a nanosecond as he walked toward the bed. He sat down on the edge of it, his back to her.

He hesitated for several beats, then raised his hips only high enough to push off his jeans. He worked them down his legs and left them lying on the floor. She thought he removed his socks, too, but she couldn't be sure.

He started to get between the sheets, then muttered something she didn't catch. She cut her eyes to him, about to ask what he'd said, when he hooked his thumbs into the waistband of his boxers and pulled them off.

She glimpsed a tan line at his waist. There was a stark contrast between the brown skin above it and the white skin—*dear God*— below. And then his shirttail dropped back into place.

He raised the sheet and slid in beside her. "Did you use it?"

"Yes."

With no more preamble than that, he rolled onto her and separated her knees with his. His first thrust lodged the head of his penis inside her. But just. She closed her eyes and turned her head aside, but she could sense him looking down at her with dismay and anger.

Using one straight arm to support himself, he worked his other hand between their bodies. She tensed. But he didn't touch her, he stroked himself in short, rapid tugs. A few times his knuckles brushed against her.

Soon, she sensed the tightening of his muscles. His breath became uneven and hot against her face. He gave a soft groan a heartbeat before he removed his hand, pushed himself into her fully, and came.

The arm he'd used to bear his weight gave way. He settled on her heavily, all six feet four of him. Tanned skin and white skin. He pulled in a deep breath and let it out slowly. He rearranged his right leg. It felt muscular and hard against the inside of her thigh, and rough with hair. His shirt was slightly damp with perspiration. The dampness seeped through her T-shirt, into her skin. She could smell his sweat. Soap. Semen.

When he moved, he moved suddenly, as one does when on the verge of sleep and muscles are seized with a violent twitch. He raised his head and levered himself up but was yanked back down on top of her. Laura, not realizing what had happened, tried to push him off.

"Relax!" he growled.

Then she saw the problem. One of her chains had looped itself around a button of his shirt. He fumbled with it, cursing under his breath, until he worked it free.

Less than five minutes after pulling off his boxers, he was pulling them back on. Laura kept her eyes averted, but in her peripheral vision, she followed his motions, which were jerky and abrupt, those of an angry man barely holding on to his temper.

He stuffed his shirttail into his jeans as though he was furious at it. He buttoned up his fly with dispatch, but his belt buckle presented a challenge. When he finally managed it, he slapped it lightly into place and turned to face her.

"Why did you lie to me?"

"I didn't use it because I was afraid it would make a difference."

"You're damn right it would have made a difference. That's why I brought it."

"I mean I was afraid it would prevent conception."

"I told you it wouldn't."

"It might have affected the motility of the sperm. Something. I don't know," she said defensively. "I just didn't want to take a chance."

"Well, I didn't want to hurt you again." His loud vehemence seemed to surprise him as much as it did her. It rendered them both silent. Finally he said, "Look, I know you have a low opinion of me. You think I'm an outlaw. A criminal. A big, dumb football player. Well, fine. Think whatever you want to. I really don't give a rat's ass so long as your money's good."

He paused for breath, and when he spoke again, his voice was gruff. "But I hurt you. Twice now. And I resent you thinking that would be okay with me. Because it isn't."

She sat up but kept the sheet pulled to her waist. "It shouldn't make any difference to you."

"It does."

"Well, it shouldn't!" He was provoking an emotional response from her, and she didn't want to feel any emotion, even anger. "This isn't about how you feel or how I feel."

"I understand that. But if you've gotta do it this way, you could at least make it easier on yourself. Why don't *you* watch the dirty movies?" He raised his hands to stop her from commenting. "Forget it, forget it."

Again, he paused to take several deep breaths, then said, "No touchy-feely. Fine. I'm not into all that, either. No kissing or foreplay because that would . . . Because . . . I get why there's no kissing or foreplay, okay? But couldn't we at least have a conversation first?"

"What for?"

"Because maybe that would stop you from cringing, and I wouldn't feel like I was violating you."

"I don't think of it as a violation."

He snorted in disagreement. "Could have fooled me. You don't even look at me."

She gave him a meaningful look then, but she didn't dare verbalize what she was thinking—that looking at each other would make it harder, not easier.

He seemed to realize that, too, because he turned away and mumbled a string of swearwords. He tilted his face up toward the ceiling, placed his hands on his hips, and blew out a gust of breath. He ran his fingers through his hair. "Christ." After a time, he looked at her again. "I walk in here, we've barely made eye contact. You're lying there, still and silent, resigned to a fate worse than death. How do you think that makes me feel?"

"I don't care how it makes you feel."

She did, but she couldn't let him know that. Actually, his concern touched her, and that was a dangerous sentiment. They couldn't be friends. Or enemies. They could be nothing to each other. Between them there must be nothing except total indifference, or she could never return to this house.

Her features impassive, her tone cool, she said, "This is biology, Mr. Burkett. Nothing more."

"Then why don't you just have me jerk off into a bottle and hand it over? You've made it plain how distasteful it is to have me on you. Admit it, you came unglued when I put my hand down there. Hell, you panicked when your chain got caught on my button. If it's so god-awful, why do you put yourself through it?"

"I thought you had that figured out."

"You were driving the night your husband lost his manhood. Poor you. You've got that cross to bear the rest of your life. This is your penance, I guess. Screwing a lowlife like me. Is that it?"

He'd scoured an open wound, and she lashed back in self-defense. "If I can stand it, surely you can."

His expression changed to match hers. The skin of his face was pulled tight, actually changing the configuration of the bruises. "I didn't sign on to be insulted."

"And I didn't promise to make polite conversation. Stop worrying about how I feel and just—"

"Play stud."

"That's what you agreed to do."

"Well, I'm rethinking our agreement. I don't need this shit."

"No. Just our millions."

He glared at her for several seconds, then turned. He reached the door in two long strides and flung it open so hard it bounced back when it hit the wall. "I'd say 'Fuck you, lady,' but I already did."

He slammed the front door on his way out, thinking he was leaving for the last time. Even if he wanted to come back, which he didn't, his exit line was reason enough for them to fire him.

Fire him? Like this was a normal job. Like the terms of his employment would ever be a matter of record. He could just imagine some time in the future being interviewed by a prospective employer.

What was your last job, Mr. Burkett?

I was paid to fuck this rich wacko's wife.

Uh-huh. And you failed to perform the task?

Oh no, I performed just fine.

Then what was the cause of your dismissal?

I lost my temper and told her off.

I see. And all you had to do was show up, keep your mouth shut, and just fuck her?

That's right.

You're not very bright, are you, Mr. Burkett?

Apparently not.

It sounded like a third-rate joke.

She must have parked around back, where he'd parked the first time, because the red Honda was the only car in the driveway. In the time it took him to reach it, he was already considering going back inside to apologize. He was still mad as hell, but he couldn't afford his anger. The price tag of it was half a million now, and millions more to come. Not worth it. Not by a long shot.

He turned on his heel and had started back toward the house when he spotted something that drew him up short.

CHAPTER

14

RODARTE WAS PARKED HALFWAY DOWN THE BLOCK. THE WINDshield of his car reflected the leafy trees above it, so Griff couldn't see him. But he stuck his hand out the driver's window and gave a friendly little wave.

Griff forgot about his apology to Laura Speakman. He jogged to the Honda, scrambled in, and cranked the motor. The tires left rubber in the driveway as he backed out. He sped the short distance and came to a squealing stop a half inch from the grille of Rodarte's sedan. He was out of the Honda before inertia settled in.

Rodarte was waiting for him. His car engine was idling, but the driver's window was down. It took all Griff's self-control not to grab him by the neck and haul him out through that window. "You're a goddamn coward, Rodarte."

"Are you trying to hurt my feelings?"

"You hire goons to do your dirty work on men. Women you beat up yourself."

"Speaking of, how is your favorite whore?" Rodarte laughed at Griff's expression of rage. "Okay, so I got a little carried away. Why didn't you report me to the police?"

"That was Marcia's decision."

"But I bet you didn't argue against it, did you? The very thought of police involvement puckers your sphincter, doesn't it? As for the working over you took, I heard you got jumped by a couple of former fans."

"They were pros."

"You know this?"

"You were behind it."

Rodarte wagged his finger at him. "But you didn't file a police report. I'll bet you didn't tell your lawyer, either. Or your probation officer. Jerry Arnold, right?"

"You know who my probation officer is?" Griff regretted the question as soon as he asked it. It revealed how surprised and alarmed he was to learn that Rodarte was so well acquainted with his life.

Rodarte grinned. "I know lots about you, Number Ten."

He must. He must have been tailing him or he wouldn't have known that Griff would be in that particular sports bar the night he sicced the brutes on him. He also wouldn't have known to find him here, on this street, today. Right now.

Jesus.

And before Griff could even fully process the worrisome implications of that, Rodarte said, "One thing I don't know is the name of your new gash there."

Griff turned his head quickly to see Laura Speakman backing her car out of the driveway. Fortunately, she drove away in the opposite direction.

"Real estate agent," Griff said. "She was showing me the house."

Rodarte snickered. "You're looking for a house just after getting settled into your duplex?"

"Turns out I'm not crazy about the neighborhood."

"Where did you get the money to buy all those fancy toys? Sound system. Big-screen TV. All that."

Griff's mind was spinning. He wanted to cram his fist into Rodarte's mouth because every word from it increased his alarm. Rodarte knew where he lived. He knew how he spent his money. And now he knew about this house. Most alarming was that he might learn about Griff's arrangement with the Speakmans.

"See," Rodarte said conversationally, "what I think is, is that before you used your big, strong quarterback's hands to snap Bill Bandy's neck, you dipped those hands into his private till."

"That's crap and you know it. How could I have taken any money? I was arrested at the scene."

"A technicality," Rodarte said with a dismissive gesture. "Before the real heat came down on you, you managed to stash the ill-gotten funds where nobody could find them. They've been sitting somewhere, earning interest, waiting on you to get out. Now they're coming in handy. Just as you planned."

He paused, frowned, and said sadly, "Only thing is, Griff, the way those Vista boys see it, it's their money, not yours. They would be real grateful to anybody who could recover it and bring it home to them."

"In other words, you."

"I'm just trying to make things easier for you, is all. I'm doing everybody a favor. These guys get their money back, and they just might forget about what you did to poor ol' Bandy. You see where this is going? How nice it would be for everybody?" His ingratiating smile collapsed. "Where's the money?"

"You're delusional. About Bandy. About ill-gotten funds. About every frigging thing. You think if I had money, I'd be driving this piece of shit?" He raised his arm toward the Honda. "A secondhand car I bought from my lawyer?"

Rodarte regarded him for a moment, then said smoothly, "You cut quite a figure in that new Armani jacket."

Griff tried to keep his expression neutral. "Thanks. It would look like shit on you."

Rodarte chuckled. "I'm afraid you're right. I haven't got the figure."

"You haven't got the balls, either. If you did, you'd get out of that butt-ugly car, stop making veiled threats, and fight me like a man."

Rodarte pulled a face as though considering it. "You sure you want me to do that, Griff? Think hard now."

Griff was seething, but he knew he could not give vent to his rage. If he laid into Rodarte, he'd be giving the woman-beating son of a bitch exactly what he wanted. "Marcia didn't have anything to tell you," he said. "You ruined her face for nothing."

Rodarte shrugged. "I guess. She didn't tell me anything useful, and from what I understand she won't be telling anybody anything for a long time. Wonder if she's able to give blow jobs, what with her jaw wired shut and all. And something else . . ." Griff didn't bite, but Rodarte told him anyway. "You'd think a whore wouldn't make such fuss over getting it in the ass."

A tide of red-hot fury washed through Griff.

Rodarte sensed it and grinned. "You ever had her that way?"

Griff had wondered if Rodarte's assault included rape. He hadn't asked Marcia because he hadn't wanted to cause her further distress. And, possibly, he just didn't want to know exactly how badly she'd suffered on his account. Now that he did, he wanted even more badly to kill the man grinning up at him.

Rodarte nodded toward the house midway down the block. "And what about her? Even from this distance, I could tell your new lady friend has a sassy little butt. Just as well tell me her name. I'll find out anyway."

Griff's outrage went from fiercely hot to icy cold in seconds. The degree of his rage frightened him, and it should have frightened Rodarte. "One of these days," he said softly, with conviction, with promise, "I'm gonna have to kill you."

Rodarte dropped the gearshift into reverse and smiled as he backed the car away. "I have wet dreams about the day you try."

Reluctantly, the concierge rang Marcia's penthouse. With his back turned to Griff, he spoke in whispers into the telephone until Griff reached across the counter and tapped him on the shoulder.

"Give me the phone. Please," he added but with impatience. Reluctantly, the man passed Griff the receiver. "Marcia?"

"Actually, it's Dwight."

"Hey, Dwight. Griff Burkett. I want to come up."

"I'm sorry, you can't."

"Who says?"

"She doesn't want company."

"I need to see her."

"She's resting."

"I'll wait."

There was a dramatic sigh, followed by "She'll probably kill me, but okay."

Dwight answered the door to the penthouse and stood aside to admit Griff. "This isn't one of her good days."

"Mine, either," Griff returned grimly as he followed Marcia's neighbor into the spacious living room, where Marcia was reclined on her sofa. She appeared to be sleeping, although it was hard to tell because her head was swathed in bandages.

"She had surgery?"

"The first of many. Three days ago. Her nose had to be rebroken. She's still got a lot of pain, but they said she was well enough to come home."

"Generally, how's she doing?"

"Not very well. She—"

"I can hear you, you know." Her voice was muffled by the bandages and her jaw still had limited range of motion, but she was her droll self, and Griff took heart in that.

Injecting some levity into his voice, he said, "Hark! The mummy speaks!"

"I've got lobster bisque simmering on the stove," Dwight said. "She's cranky as a mama bear, but be sweet to her." He patted Griff on the arm as he passed on his way into the kitchen.

Griff pulled an armchair closer to the sofa and placed it where Marcia could see him without having to turn her head. She said, "If you think I look bad now, just wait till the bandages come off. I'll be a real freak show."

She was wrapped neck to ankles in a bathrobe, but he could tell that her lush curves had been diminished. He wondered how much weight she'd lost just since he'd last seen her. He reached for her hand and pressed a kiss onto the back of it. "You couldn't be a freak show no matter how hard you tried."

"I'd hate for my own mother to see me like this. Not that she will, since she disowned me years ago."

"So much for how you look, how do you feel?"

"Stoned."

He laughed. "Good drugs?"

"I could make a fortune selling this stuff. If only it weren't against the law. But then so is prostitution."

"Speaking of breaking the law . . ." He looked directly into her eyes, which peered at him through a slit in the bandage. "I'm going to the police about Rodarte."

Her reaction was immediate. "No!"

"Listen to me, Marcia. I know what he did to you. He bragged to me about it not an hour ago."

She stared up at him for a long moment, then closed her eyes as though to shut out him, her memory, everything. Griff felt the shudder that went through her.

"Why didn't you tell me?"

"I didn't want to talk about it."

"He hurt you."

"Yes."

"Bad."

She opened her eyes then. "I'm a whore. I've done everything. But always when I was in control. Having it forced on you is different." She closed her eyes again. "Believe me." When she reopened her eyes, she said, "Try explaining that to a cop."

"I will. You were raped."

"And he'll say it doesn't matter."

"It matters to me!" He shot up from his chair, sending it over backward. Dwight came running, wearing an apron, a dripping spoon in his hand. "Get back to your bisque," Griff ordered. Dwight hesitated, then cupped the spoon with his free hand and, walking backward, retreated into the kitchen. The decorator's almost comical rush to her rescue had defused Griff's temper. He righted the chair and sat down, taking Marcia's hand again.

"Rodarte's not going to give up. The son of a bitch has been stalking me. He knows everything going on in my life. But all that's nothing compared to sodomy. I'd like to kill him for that. But I can't, and he knows it. I can't do anything without violating my probation. He's going to stay after me, Marcia. Pushing. He'll continue hurting people close to me. The only option left is to take it to the police."

"I'm begging you, Griff, don't."

"But—"

"Look at me!" Tears filled her eyes. "If you do this, I'll have a huge spotlight focused on me and my business. Every Bible-thumping Holy Roller—some of whom are clients, by the way—will come out of the woodwork, condemning me and my occupation. It wouldn't matter to my self-righteous critics that I went to the emergency room, torn and bleeding. They'd say it was punishment befitting my sins.

"If Rodarte is made to answer for himself at all, which is doubtful, he'll deny the beating and blame it on a customer or boyfriend who was there after him. Probably you. There's no DNA. He used a condom." Sourly, she added, "I'm glad of that at least."

"Christ," Griff swore, knowing that what she said was probably right. "So you expect me to do nothing?"

"I'm *asking* you to do nothing. I avoided public scrutiny when I was my gorgeous, voluptuous self. Do you think I could endure it looking like *this*? I couldn't, Griff. I'd jump off the roof first." She said it in such a way that he believed she would. "The threat of exposure would frighten my clientele away for good. I'd lose everything. If you have any regard or feeling for me at all, let it go. Let it go." She withdrew her hand from his and closed her eyes.

"I think you should leave now. She needs to sleep." Dwight had slipped back into the room. His tone wasn't unkind, but unquestionably he was Marcia's self-appointed advocate and protector.

Griff nodded and came to his feet. Before turning away, he bent down and kissed Marcia's closed eyes.

Dwight saw him to the door. "I suggest you call before you come here again." Griff gave his silent consent with a nod.

In the foyer, he punched the button for the elevator but was so lost in thought, he stood looking into the empty cubicle for several moments before it registered with him that it had arrived.

On the descent, he realized that further argument wasn't going to change Marcia's mind. Pressuring her would only add to her mental anguish. He had already inflicted enough suffering on her, and when all was said and done, she was right. Taking this matter to the police would fix a spotlight not only on Marcia but on him. He didn't want that any more than she did.

No, he would have to solve his Rodarte problem alone, one-on-one with the son of a bitch.

He stopped at the florist's in the lobby and ordered an orchid plant to be delivered to Marcia's penthouse. On the enclosure card, he wrote, "Okay. It stays our secret. But he *will* pay."

He didn't sign it.

CHAPTER

15

GRIFF HEARD THE DOORBELL CHIME INSIDE THE HOUSE AND then approaching footsteps. His gut tightened with apprehension over how he would be greeted. Maybe with the door slammed in his face.

Was coming here a bad idea?

Too late to change his mind now. Because the door was pulled open and he was looking into Ellie Miller's smiling face.

He waited in dread to see her smile dissolve. Instead, it brightened. "Griff!"

She looked ready to launch herself against him and give him a big hug but checked the impulse and instead reached across the threshold and grabbed his hand with a strength surprising for a woman so petite. She looked him over from head to toe. "You're thinner."

"I've been doing a lot of swimming, less weights."

She hadn't stopped smiling yet. "Come in, come in, we're standing here letting cold air out, and our electric bill is sky-high as it is."

He stepped into the house and was instantly enveloped in its familiar scents and sights and textures. He paused to take a look around. The hall tree was where it had always been. The wallpaper hadn't changed. The framed mirror, which to him had always seemed a little too small for that particular spot, was still there.

"I replaced the living room carpet last year."

"It's nice."

Beyond the carpet, everything was exactly as it had been the last time he was here. Except that the picture of the three of them was no longer on the end table. The photo had been taken minutes after the NCAA national championship victory, he still in his grass- and bloodstained jersey, hair matted down by sweat and the weight of his helmet, standing between Ellie and Coach. Three beaming smiles. Ellie had had the picture framed and prominently displayed within days of the game.

The Millers had never been happier or more proud of him than after that Orange Bowl victory, except maybe the day he signed his letter of intent with the University of Texas. That day this house had been filled to capacity with sportswriters from all over the state. Ellie had fussed over the mess they were making, dropping cookie crumbs and spilling punch. Coach had complained when the TV lights blew out a fuse.

But their grumbling wasn't taken seriously. It was obvious to everyone there that the couple was bursting with pride over Griff. Not only had he been offered a full scholarship to play football for the university but he was graduating cum laude from high school. Coach's decision to take him in had been validated. His investment in that recalcitrant fifteen-year-old had paid off, and in ways beyond Griff's athletic ability.

The four years Griff had played for UT, he was coached by some of the most respected and knowledgeable men in the game. But he still had relied on Coach Miller's advice. He took everything he'd learned from Coach into that Orange Bowl game with him. It was Coach's triumph as much as his.

It was later, after signing on with the Cowboys, that Griff stopped listening to his mentor's advice and started thinking of Coach as a nuisance rather than a sensible guiding hand. The absence of that framed photo on the living room end table spoke volumes about Coach's feelings toward him now.

"Come on back," Ellie said, shooing him into the kitchen. "I'm shelling peas. You can buy them already shelled, but they don't taste as good to me. Want some iced tea?"

"Please."

"Pound cake?"

"If you've got it."

She frowned at him as though her not having pound cake on hand would happen the day hell froze over. She cleared her pea-shelling project off the kitchen table. He sat down in the chair that had been designated his after his first dinner here and was embarrassed by the unmanly nostalgia that made his throat seize up. This was the only real home he'd ever known. And he'd brought disgrace to it.

"Coach isn't here?"

"He's playing golf," Ellie said with vexation. "I told him it was too blamed hot to play at this time of day, but he hasn't grown any less hardheaded. In fact, he just gets worse."

She served the tea and pound cake, and sat down across from him, clasping her hands on the table. He looked at those tiny hands, remembering the bright yellow rubber gloves she'd had on the day he moved in and recalling one of the rare times he hadn't avoided her touch. He'd had the flu. Sitting on the edge of his bed, she'd laid her palm against his forehead, testing it for fever. Her hand had been soft and cool, and to this day he remembered how good it had felt against his burning skin. To her it had been an instinctual thing to do, but until then, Griff hadn't known that was what moms did when children complained of feeling sick.

Ellie and Coach had never had children. The reason for that was never explained to him, and even as a teenager he'd had the sensitivity not to ask. Maybe her childlessness had factored into her welcoming that surly and sarcastic boy into her home.

She hadn't smothered him with motherly affection, which she'd sensed, correctly, that he would have rejected. But with the merest signal from him, she made herself available. She would lend an ear if he wanted to talk through a problem. In a thousand small and subtle ways she had demonstrated the maternal tenderness she obviously felt for him. He could see it in her eyes now.

"It's good to see you, Ellie. Good to be here."

"I'm so glad you came. Did you get my letters?"

"Yes, and I appreciated them. More than you know."

"Why didn't you write back?"

"I couldn't find the words. I—" He shrugged helplessly. "I just couldn't, Ellie. And I didn't want to cause a rift between Coach and you. He didn't know you wrote to me, did he?"

She sat up straighter and said smartly, "It's not up to him what I do or don't do. I make up my own mind about things."

Griff smiled. "I know you do, but I also know you support Coach. The two of you are a team."

She had the grace not to argue that.

"I knew how pissed he was," Griff said. "He tried to warn me against setting myself up for a big fall. I didn't listen."

He distinctly remembered the day that their steadily declining relationship was finally severed. Coach had been waiting for him at his car after practice. The Cowboys' coaching staff knew Coach Miller well, knew how influential he'd been on their starting quarterback, and always welcomed seeing him.

Griff didn't. Their conversations had grown increasingly contentious. Coach had no quarrel with his performance on the football field, but he didn't approve of much else, such as the rate at which Griff went through money.

Griff wanted to know the point of having it if you couldn't spend it. "You'd be wise to put aside some for a rainy day," Coach told him. Griff ignored the advice.

Coach also disapproved of the pace of his life. He cautioned Griff against burning the candle at both ends, particularly during the off-season, when he got sloppy with his workouts and kept late hours in the glossy nightclubs of Dallas and Miami, where he'd bought a beachfront condo.

"Discipline got you where you are," Coach said. "You'll sink fast if you don't maintain that discipline. In fact, it should be more rigid now than before."

Yeah, yeah, Griff thought. He figured Coach's dissatisfaction was based on jealousy. He no longer had control over the decisions Griff made or the way he lived his life, and that rankled the older man. While Griff appreciated everything Coach had done for him, he was old school in his thinking. His strict lessons no longer applied. Coach had got him where he was, but now that he was here, it was time to cut the apron strings.

Griff began distancing himself. Their visits became less frequent. He rarely returned his mentor's phone calls. So he wasn't happy to see Coach that day he ambushed Griff at his car. With his typical tactlessness, Coach came straight to the point. "I'm worried about your new associates."

" 'New associates'?"

"Don't play dumb with me, Griff."

He could only have been talking about the Vista boys, and Griff wondered how Coach knew about them. But then, he'd rarely been able to sneak something past the man. Coach's vigilance had been a pain in the butt when Griff was a teenager. It was a bigger pain now that he was a grown-up. "You're the one always harping on me to make friends. I've made some friends. Now you don't like them."

"I don't like you getting too friendly with these guys."

"Why? What's wrong with them?"

"In my view, they're a little too shiny."

Griff guffawed. " 'Shiny'?"

"Slick. Slippery. I don't trust them. You should check them out."

"I don't snoop on my friends." Looking Coach straight in the eye, he said what he hoped would end the discussion. "I don't go poking my nose into other people's business."

Coach didn't take the hint. "Make an exception. Do some snooping."

"What for?"

"See what they're really about. How do they pay for those fancy limos and chauffeurs?"

"They're businessmen."

"What's their business?"

"A tin mine in South America."

"Tin mine, my ass. No miner I ever knew needed a bodyguard."

Griff had heard enough. "Look, I don't care how they pay for the limos. I like the limos and the chauffeurs, not to mention the private jets and the pussy they get me free for the asking. So why don't you go away and leave me the hell alone? Okay?"

Coach did just that. It was the last conversation they'd had.

Griff looked at Ellie now and shook his head sadly. "I thought I was smarter than him. Smarter than everybody. When I got caught, Coach denounced me. I didn't blame him. I understood why he washed his hands of me."

"You broke his heart."

He gave her a sharp look. She nodded and repeated solemnly, "You broke his heart, Griff." Then she laughed lightly. "Of course, he was pissed, too."

"Yeah, well, it's probably just as well he's not here. If he was, I doubt I'd have been invited in for cake."

"Honestly, I doubt it, too."

"I knew I took a chance by coming."

"Why did you? I'm delighted. But why did you come?"

He left the table and moved to the counter. He took a black-eyed pea from the brown paper sack, held the pod between his thumbs and split it open, then shook the peas into the stainless steel bowl. He tossed the empty pod back into the sack.

"I keep hurting people, and I don't want to."

"Then stop doing it."

"I don't mean to. I just do."

"How?"

"Just by being me, Ellie. Just by being me." He turned and rested his hips against the counter, crossed his ankles, folded his arms over his chest, and studied the toes of his boots. They needed another shine. "I'm destructive. It seems to be the curse of my life."

"Stop feeling sorry for yourself."

His head came up, and he looked across at her.

"Stop crying in your beer and tell me what's going on. Who's been hurt?"

"An acquaintance. She was hurt bad on account of me. No other reason, just because of her association with me."

"I'm sorry for that, but it doesn't sound like it was your fault."

"Feels like it was. It goes back to . . ." He gestured as though saying, *back then*. "There's this guy. Ever since my release, he's been right here," he said, holding his palm inches from his nose. "He's got it in for me, and he's not going to go away until I'm dust under his heel."

Griff had kept one eye on his rearview mirror the whole time he'd been driving here. He'd taken a circuitous route, too, doubling back several times, to make certain he wasn't being tailed by either Rodarte or somebody Rodarte had hired to follow him.

Of course Rodarte would know where the Millers lived. If he'd wanted to get to Griff by harming them, he would have done so. Griff supposed Rodarte didn't consider Coach as vulnerable as Marcia. The idea of coming up against Coach might even scare him. And it should.

"Are you in trouble, Griff?"

He knew she was asking if he was involved in something illegal again. "No. I swear it."

"I believe you. So go to the authorities and tell them about this person who's hounding you and—"

"I can't, Ellie."

"Why not?"

"Because he's not acting strictly on his own."

"You mean—"

"Vista. The same men Coach called slippery, and he didn't know the half of it."

"Then you certainly need to talk to the authorities."

He shook his head, thinking back to what he'd resolved yesterday as he left Marcia's penthouse. "I've been up to my eyebrows in the 'authorities' for the past five years. I don't want anything to do with the authorities."

He couldn't report Rodarte's crime without bringing a lot of shit down on himself and Marcia. The hell of it was, their silence gave Rodarte protection and room to maneuver. Rodarte could make a real menace of himself, and Griff was hamstrung.

"But the police or the FBI need to know if—"

"I no longer trust the system, Ellie. I'm doing what I'm supposed to do. I've formed a good relationship with my probation officer. I think he's on my side. I want to stay under the radar, do nothing that would call attention to me."

"And to that murder."

"And to that murder," he admitted.

"They never caught the person who killed that Bandy character, did they?"

"No, they never did."

The silence became dense, stretched out. She didn't come right out and ask. She didn't want to insult him by asking. Or maybe she didn't want to hear the answer. She took a sip of tea, returning the glass to the table with more care than necessary.

"You can't live your life dodging the bad guys, Griff. You'll just have to ignore them."

"I've tried. It's not that easy. In fact, it's impossible. Ignoring them only makes them more determined to get my attention. And they'll use other people to do it, to bend me to their way of thinking. I won't play with them, Ellie. I won't break the law again. But I don't want other people getting hurt."

Specifically, the Speakmans. If Rodarte found out about Griff's deal with them, he could ruin it, and it was the only thing Griff had going. Beyond that, Rodarte could do irreparable damage to the couple's reputation. Speakman might be as crazy as a loon, but he seemed like a decent enough guy. He was respected for his community service and for giving away barrels of money to charity.

And it made Griff queasy to think of Laura Speakman being subjected to Rodarte's violence as Marcia had been. Given half a chance, Rodarte would hurt her and not think twice about it. He'd already noticed her, spoken of her in terms that enraged Griff.

Noticing Ellie's look of concern, Griff relaxed his stance and smiled. "I didn't come here to worry you. I just needed a sounding board, and you've always been a good one."

She got up and took his hand again. "More than anything, I want you to be happy, Griff."

"Happy?" He repeated the word as though it was of another language. Happy seemed an unattainable goal.

"Have you got a job yet?"

"I'm looking into some things. One will open up soon."

"In the meantime, what are you doing for money?"

"My lawyer sold all my stuff. There was a little left after he paid the fines and such. What wasn't sold he put in a warehouse. I cleared it out a few weeks ago. Sold a few things on eBay. I'm doing okay."

She pulled her handbag off the peg near the back door and took a fifty-dollar bill from her wallet. "Here."

He staved her off. "Ellie, I can't take that."

"Yes you can. I insist. It's part of my Hawaii money."

"Hawaii money?"

"After years of my pestering him about it, Joe's finally consented to take me to Hawaii later this summer. I've saved some spending money. If you don't take this, I'll buy fifty dollars' worth of tacky souvenirs I don't need and will never want to look at again. Take it."

He took it. Not because he wanted to or needed it but because she wanted to give it to him, and she needed him to accept it. "I'll pay you back."

They heard the car at the same time. She looked up at him, gave him a very weak smile of reassurance, and turned to face the back door as Coach came in. "Whose car—"

That was as far as he got. Seeing Griff in his kitchen stopped him in his tracks. His sparse hair had gone grayer. He'd put on maybe ten pounds, but he was still as solid as a brick wall, not fat. There were more squint lines extending from the corners of his eyes, showing up white against his perpetually sunburned face. Otherwise he looked much the same as he had the day he'd brought Griff to this house almost twenty years ago.

Griff registered all this within the span of a second, which was only as long as Coach stood still before continuing on his lumbering way through the kitchen, past the living room, and down the hall. The slamming bedroom door echoed loudly through the house.

It was a while before Ellie spoke. "I'm sorry, Griff."

"I didn't expect him to be glad to see me."

"He is. He just can't show it."

Griff didn't have the heart to disabuse her. "I've gotta go."

She didn't argue. At the door, she looked at him with concern. "Take care of yourself."

"I will."

"You promise?"

"I promise."

"I never got an opportunity to tell you this, but when all that happened five years ago, I hurt for you. What you did was wrong, Griff. Very wrong, and you have no excuse for doing it. But I couldn't have hurt more for you if you'd been my own flesh and blood."

"I know that." His voice was dangerously rough.

"Don't get discouraged." She patted the back of his hand. "The best for you is yet to be. I'm certain of it."

He didn't disabuse her of that, either.

"Need help with that, ma'am?"

Laura turned, ready to accept the kind offer of assistance. But when she saw Griff Burkett, her smile froze in place as her eyes filled with alarm. "What are you doing here?"

He lifted the large box she was carrying out of her arms, which seemed to have gone boneless at the sight of him. "Where were you taking this?"

She continued to gape at him.

"You keep looking at me like that, you're going to attract attention," he said. "Where were you taking the box?"

"To my car." She nodded in the direction of the reserved spaces in the executive parking lot, not too far from the employee entrance from which she had emerged. She glanced around nervously. Rows of cars baked beneath the blazing sun, but there was no one else around, which was why she'd been carrying the box in the first place.

The building that housed the corporate offices of SunSouth Airlines was one of Dallas's famed contemporary structures, built basically of glass held together by a framework of steel. So anyone looking out from this side of the building had an unrestricted view of the parking lot and could see her with him, possibly even recognize him.

However, if he hadn't been this close, she probably couldn't have identified him herself. He'd altered his appearance with a baseball cap and sunglasses. He had on a faded T-shirt that was nearly threadbare, knee-length shorts with a ragged hem, and sneakers instead of cowboy boots. But his height and the width of his shoulders were impossible to disguise, although he attempted to by walking in a slouch.

"What are you doing here?" she repeated.

"I know it's against the rules."

"Foster would—"

"Go apeshit, I know. But it was important that I see you."

"You could have called."

"Would you have taken the call?"

Probably not, she thought. "Okay, you're here. What's so urgent? Are you backing out?"

He stopped, turned to her. "Do you want me to?"

"You left saying you didn't need this shit, remember?"

"And you reminded me how much I do."

They looked at each other for several seconds, then simultaneously remembered how vulnerable they were to being seen together and resumed walking in the direction of the reserved spaces.

"Which one's yours?"

"The black BMW."

"Hit the trunk button."

She juggled her keys, depressed the button, and the lid of her trunk automatically opened. He lowered the cumbersome box and placed it inside. "What's in here? For being so bulky, it's light."

"An airplane model. I'm taking it home."

"To Speakman? I notice he didn't come to work today."

He was still bent at the waist, fiddling with the box. To a casual observer it would have looked as though he was situating it in the trunk to prevent damage during transport.

"How do you know that?"

"Because that first parking slot has his name stenciled on it, and it's empty. I know he wasn't here earlier because I've been staked out across the street—"

"Staked out?"

"At that pizza place. For hours. Watching this door, waiting for an opportunity to talk to you."

"What's so important that it couldn't wait until the next time we meet?"

"Will there be a next time?" He straightened up and turned to face her.

She gave a small bob of her head.

"You, uh—"

"Yes. Day before yesterday."

"Oh."

He just stood there.

She examined her keys.

Forever.

Then he said, "You must've been disappointed."

"Of course I was. *We* were. Foster and I." Drawing a quick breath, she said, "So, you and I must meet again." Having avoided looking at him except peripherally, she tilted her head back and looked directly into the opaque lenses of his sunglasses. "Unless you resign."

"We've been over that."

"Then what's so important that you came here?"

"I came to warn you."

She had expected a demand for more advance money. Maybe even an apology for what he'd said to her before he left last time. But a warning? "Warn me about what?"

"A couple weeks ago. When we were together. You saw the bruises on my face?"

"And your hip."

He tilted his head, and she knew that if she could see into his eyes they would be looking at her curiously. There was only one way she would have known about the bruises on his butt, and she'd given herself away. But to try to maneuver herself out of the blunder would only make it more awkward.

"What about the bruises?" she asked impatiently.

"I wish I could say the other guys looked worse."

"Guys? More than one?"

"Two. I was jumped in a restaurant parking lot and beaten up. A few weeks before that, a friend of mine got it even worse." His lips formed a hard, thin line. "Much worse. And hasn't recovered yet."

Laura couldn't believe what she was hearing. "What are you into?"

"Nothing!"

"You and your friend got beaten up over *nothing*?"

"Listen to me," he said, bending nearer, talking quickly and softly. "It goes back to five years ago, but it has nothing to do with me now. Except that there's this asshole who's made it his life's mission to ruin my life. His name is Stanley Rodarte. He drives an ugly, olive green car. If you see him, stay out of his way. Under no circumstances let him get near you while you're alone. Are you hearing me?"

"I'm rarely alone."

"You were just now. Look how easy it was for me to get close to you." As though to emphasize that, he looked down at the space between them, which was less than a foot.

"I appreciate the warning," Laura said, distancing herself, and more than just physically. "But your extracurricular activities have nothing to do with Foster and me. This Stanley whatever poses no threat to us."

"Rodarte, and the hell he doesn't," he said, pushing the words out. "Listen to me. He's dangerous. Given a chance, he would hurt you, in ways you probably can't even imagine. This is no bullshit. He—"

"Laura?"

They jumped guiltily at the sound of another voice. She turned and spotted Joe McDonald approaching them from the next row over. "Hi, Joe," she called, trying to sound normal and glad to see him.

"Remember what I told you," Griff said in an undertone, then he walked quickly away.

Forcing herself to move, Laura headed off the marketing head, who was looking curiously after Griff's tall figure as he wove between the rows of cars. "Who was that?"

"Someone cutting across our parking lot. Lucky for me. He saw me lugging the box with the Select model in it and offered to carry it for me."

"Where was the guard at the door?"

"He wasn't there when I came through, and I didn't want to wait." Without it being obvious, she steered Joe toward the entrance. "I'm eager to get the model home and show Foster."

"So tonight's the big night?"

"It is. Wish me luck."

As they approached the entrance, she glanced casually over her shoulder. Griff Burkett had disappeared.

CHAPTER

16

Laura didn't tell Foster about Griff Burkett's unexpected appearance.

Ordinarily she didn't keep anything from her husband. But she was reluctant to share Burkett's warning about a man in a green car because even a hint of her being in danger would send Foster into a tailspin. He would respond in typical Foster fashion; she would have armed guards within an hour.

Furthermore, she wanted nothing else competing for Foster's attention tonight.

She changed clothes before coming down to dinner, putting on a simple black dress that was one of his favorites. She took extra time with her hair and makeup. She applied fragrance.

Descending the staircase, she realized she had butterflies, and that nervousness surprised her. But then, she reminded herself, she'd been preparing for this night for months. A little stage fright was understandable.

She barely touched her meal, but Foster didn't notice because he was enthusiastically telling her about a new exercise Manuelo had incorporated into his physical therapy sessions.

"It's helping to strengthen my back and arms. I've noticed a big improvement already."

"Did he learn the technique at that seminar you enrolled him in last month?"

"Yes. Obviously he's a quick study."

"He would be even quicker if he knew English."

"He's a very proud man."

"How would learning English damage his pride?"

"He would regard it as a betrayal of his heritage."

Before she could comment further, he asked about her day at the office. "I'm glad you mentioned it," she said, giving him a mischievous smile. "I have a surprise for you after dinner."

When they were done with the meal, she asked him to follow her from the dining room. He rolled the wheels of his chair forward and backward three times before moving ahead. He'd adopted that habit a few weeks ago.

Also, plastic containers of hand sanitizer had begun showing up everywhere. Initially he'd used them when he thought she wasn't looking. Now dozens of them were scattered throughout the house so that one was always within Foster's reach. Cleanliness and germ killing had always been obsessions, but these recent signs of his OCD disturbed her. She would insist he speak with his psychiatrist about these manifestations.

But tonight they would not address his disorder or anything else negative. Besides, once Foster was focused on the project she was about to introduce, his symptoms would probably recede again.

She'd set up everything in the den beforehand. Leading him to the closed door, she pushed it open and dramatically intoned, "Introducing SunSouth Select." She stepped aside so he could see the prominently displayed artist's rendering, the banner she'd had made bearing the new logo, the graphs and charts standing on easels for quick reference, and the model.

Looking a bit overwhelmed by the visuals, Foster did the three-times back-and-forth routine, then slowly rolled his chair into the room. "What's all this?"

"An innovation in airline service, conceived with frequent fliers and business travelers in mind," she said, as though addressing a room full of people from a podium. "Allow me?"

"By all means."

She stood before him as though assuming center stage. "Sun-South Select will offer red-carpet treatment on a limited number of flights from Dallas to high-density destinations. Houston, Atlanta, Denver, Los Angeles, Washington, D.C., New York. One early morning flight. One late evening.

"Select will be for members only. Fliers will be prescreened and registered. They will have passes enabling them to avoid the normal airport security checks. Select will provide white-glove baggage handling. Car service to and from the airport would be optional but recommended to guarantee even better service and fewer of the hassles normally associated with business travel.

"Airplanes designed for one hundred thirty passengers would be reconfigured to accommodate fifty. Even the overseas carriers who cater to their first-class passengers would pale in comparison to the pampering given the subscribers to SunSouth Select.

"Expensive? Definitely. But less expensive than owning even a fractional share of a private jet, and much more leg- and headroom," she added with a smile. "For what a business executive would spend chartering a private jet to these destinations, he could fly in much more comfort with specially trained flight attendants waiting on him. Or her."

So far Foster had said nothing, but he was listening.

She continued. "Because it would operate under the auspices of SunSouth Airlines, the traveler would be assured of Select's dependability, stringent safety standards, and incomparable efficiency.

"That efficiency is SunSouth's trademark, but it hasn't come without a price. The one criticism often heard, especially from the frequent business passenger, is that SunSouth is equivalent to traveling in a Greyhound bus. Ten months ago, the airline began offering a reserved seat as opposed to first-come-first-served. That's proven to be a hugely successful option.

"Eighteen point three percent of our passengers are willing to pay the additional twenty dollars per ticket to guarantee a reserved seat and have the convenience of boarding first. Extrapolating, if even one half of one percent of those eighteen point three percent buy a membership in SunSouth Select, the airplanes will fly full.

"In recent years, private jet ownership has become extremely competitive, but this mode of transportation is still affordable to only a minuscule percentage of travelers. On the one hand, you have no-frills airlines, like SunSouth and Southwest. On the other, private jets.

"SunSouth Select would fill the gap in between. That gap is projected to widen as carriers decrease first-class service in favor of economy travel. Granted, it's a narrow margin of the marketplace, but a vital one because it caters to those who *must* and *do* fly tens of thousands of miles each year. Fortunately, those fliers are also the ones who have the funds to spend on air travel. If SunSouth doesn't claim that niche in the marketplace, a competing airline will. Select will ensure that SunSouth maintains its position as a leader in the airline industry."

It was the planned wrap-up to her pitch. When Foster was certain she had concluded, he rolled his chair forward and back three times, then moved to the table where she had placed the model. One side of the fuselage had been made of clear plastic so that the interior, which far surpassed even the most luxurious and roomy first-class cabins, was visible. He studied it for what to Laura seemed an interminably long time.

Finally he spoke. "It's been tried before. Rolls-Royce service for Rolls-Royce prices. Those airlines didn't last long."

She had an answer for that argument. "They didn't sell memberships. They relied on single bookings, so they ran into cash-flow problems. We would sell memberships, renewable annually. Before the first plane ever took off, we'd have operating capital to sustain the service for at least a year. And earning interest at the same time."

"The membership would entitle the passenger to fly a given number of segments?"

"Miles, actually, since some of the segments are longer than others. We're thinking in the neighborhood of seventy-five thousand miles. If the member doesn't fly them all, he forfeits them. If he flies above that number, for each additional flight, he pays a fee equivalent to the price of a first-class ticket on another airline."

"And those numbers work?"

"It's in the syllabus." She passed him a three-ring binder with the SunSouth Select logo embossed on the leather cover. He studied the logo but returned the binder to the table unopened.

"How much would we have to charge for the memberships?"

"As I said, the syllabus contains several financial projections. If we charge this much, our margin of profit would be larger than if we charged that much."

"I know what a financial projection is, Laura."

Taken aback by his tone, she murmured, "Of course you do. I just wanted you to understand that this is all preliminary."

"Really? It seems so well thought out."

"I've worked on it long and hard, Foster. I've tried to think through every aspect and contingency."

"Who else has been in on it?"

She laughed. "That makes it sound like a conspiracy."

"It sort of looks like a conspiracy. A few weeks ago when I asked you if the mice were playing while the cat was away, I meant it as a joke."

"Are you angry?"

Forward, back, forward, back, forward, back, then over to the bar, where he poured himself a shot of scotch. He didn't offer to pour her one. "What does the TSA say about these special passes issued to members?"

"It isn't a new idea. Passes for frequent fliers is a topic already on the table. Some are already in use at selected airports."

"Where would the planes come from?"

"With so many airlines reducing flights for economic reasons, we could buy the grounded planes for pennies on the dollar."

"It would still cost millions. Millions more to convert them to that," he said, gesturing toward the model.

"SunSouth has an extensive line of credit. We borrow the money—"

"And if this concept fails, we're stuck with a huge debt and no way to pay it back."

"We would incorporate those newly purchased planes into our normal operation. Our planes always fly full, usually they're oversold, and we were planning to expand the fleet next year anyway."

He finished his scotch in one swallow, then went back to the bar, took a cocktail napkin, and wiped the rim of his empty glass, circling it three times, before placing it in the rack beneath the sink. He replaced the stopper in the crystal decanter and put it back exactly where it had been. He used one of the bottles of hand sanitizer.

Finally he said, "It's all very speculative, Laura."

"And preliminary. I said as much. It needs a lot of fine tuning. I'm relying on you for that."

He didn't address that. "The likelihood of it succeeding is slim."

"So was the likelihood of SunSouth's making it when you took over. Everyone told you there wasn't room for another commercial airline based in Dallas. Economists said you were crazy. Business analysts laughed in your face. You didn't listen. You steamrolled over the skeptics. You didn't let anything keep you from realizing your dream."

"I wasn't a cripple then."

If he'd slapped her, she couldn't have been more shocked. Indeed, he had struck her where he knew it would hurt the most. She stared at him, then, recovering from her initial astonishment, turned and headed for the door.

"Laura. Laura, wait! I'm sorry." She paused, her hand on the doorknob. He came up behind her and reached for her hand. "God, I'm so sorry. Forgive me."

He pulled her down onto his lap, took her head between his hands, forcing it around so she would have to look at him. "I'm sorry." He kissed her cheek, then her lips. "I'm sorry. Forgive me."

Hearing genuine regret in his voice, she relaxed her posture. "Why would you say something like that, Foster?"

"It was uncalled for. Completely."

She looked over his shoulder at the display, which represented so many hours of labor for her and many others. "I thought this would excite and invigorate you."

He stroked her hair. "I ruined your surprise with my negativity. I apologize for that. Especially since you've already had one letdown this week."

He was talking about her period. True, that was a letdown, but she wouldn't be distracted from this subject by talking about that. "Do you hate the idea of SunSouth Select?"

"It's a lot to absorb in fifteen minutes." His gentle smile was an attempt to soften the blow, as were his carefully chosen words. "You've had months to fuel your enthusiasm. I was blindsided. Give me some time to mull it over."

"But your initial reaction is thumbs down."

"Not at all. It's cautiously favorable to an idea that needs further study."

Which translated to thumbs down.

He guided her head to his shoulder. "In the meantime, congratulations on a job well done. It's one of the best presentations I've ever heard."

He was rejecting the idea but giving her an A for effort. She hated being patronized but was too downcast to take issue with it tonight. She'd poured all her energy into the presentation. Now that it was over, and hadn't yielded the result she'd wished for, she felt hollow and depleted.

"Now," he said, as though a minor matter had been dealt with and dismissed, "tell me what else happened today."

CHAPTER

17

BOLLY RICH CLIMBED THE BLEACHERS AND SAT DOWN BESIDE Griff. For a full sixty seconds they sat there in identical poses—forearms braced on their thighs, hands clasped between their knees—staring at the players on the field.

Bolly was the first to break the silence. "What the hell are you doing, Griff?"

"I'm watching practice."

"This is the third day in a row you've been here."

"You're counting?"

"Yeah, I'm counting. What's the deal?"

"Well, in my learned opinion, Jason is as good as any other player on this team. They don't have a strong running back. Their safety's for shit. Jason's scrambling, but he's—"

"Cut the crap, Griff," Bolly said, even angrier than before. "What are you doing watching a middle school's football practice?"

Griff turned his head then and looked at him. "Killing time, Bolly. 'Cause I've got nothing else to do. Last time I checked, this was public property, giving me as much right to be here as you. You don't like it, you don't have to speak to me. I didn't invite you up here. So why don't you go back down there and rejoin the decent folk before I rub off on you and you get ousted from the Booster Club?"

Down on the field, the coaches had the boys huddled, letting them drink from their water bottles while talking them through plays. The boys looked too small for their wide shoulder pads. From this distance they looked like bobble-head dolls, all out of proportion. Griff had started playing football at about Jason's age. He supposed he had looked small then, too.

Bolly stayed where he was. He said, "My kid idolizes you."

"I make a sorry hero."

"I told him as much."

They watched as the coaches divided the offensive players from the defensive and herded the two groups to opposite ends of the field to run practice drills. Five minutes passed. Ten.

Then Bolly cleared his throat. "That night in Buffalo?"

Griff didn't acknowledge that he'd heard him, although he knew immediately the particular night he was referring to.

"Never been so cold in my life."

"Ten below at game time," Griff said. "Or so they told me later. They didn't have the heart to tell us in the locker room before the game. Sixty minutes of football played in blowing snow, and at the final whistle, all we had to show for it was a freaking field goal. The kicker, wrapped in Mylar and sipping hot drinks on the bench the whole game, trots his skinny ass out there and makes the only three points of the game. My fingers are bleeding from some Bills lineman digging his cleats in. They're so cold I can't even bend them. That runty kicker gets all the glory."

Bolly snuffled a laugh. "He was a cocky bastard to start with."

"Tell me. Where was he from anyway? There were no vowels in his last name."

"One of those eastern European countries. Switched from soccer to football so he could come to the States and make more money. Cowboys are well rid of him."

It had been an inglorious win to a game that came late in the season, its outcome irrelevant to the play-offs. The airport was closed because of the blizzard, so the team couldn't fly home. No one was in a party mood as they returned to the hotel for another night. Most went straight to their rooms.

"You and I wound up the last ones in the bar," Bolly said, as though following Griff's thoughts. "I got wasted."

"Bolly—"

"No, no, this needs to be said, Griff. I got drunk on my ass and blubbered like a baby about my marital problems."

Best Griff could recall, Bolly's wife had packed up and moved out on him, saying she was sick of staying at home with their young son while he was away having fun with the guys, covering one sporting event or another.

"It worked out okay, apparently," Griff said.

"Lucky for me."

As drunk as Bolly had been that night, Griff was surprised that he even remembered his emotional meltdown. Maybe he'd needed that catharsis to make things right at home. He and his wife were still together. He had a nice house, a kid with a reasonable haircut and no visible body piercings. Why bring it up now?

"I never thanked you for keeping my confidence," Bolly said quietly.

Griff looked over at him.

Shrugging self-consciously, Bolly removed his tinted eyeglasses and twirled them by the stem. "A lot of my colleagues cheat on their wives when they're on the road. They sure as hell don't cry over them. I'd given you plenty to talk about in the locker room. But you never breathed a word of it to anybody."

"I didn't have any friends, remember? Nobody to tell."

Bolly gave him a wry look. "But you never brought it up to me, either. Held it over me. You know. In fact, you pretended it hadn't happened." He ducked his head and squinted down at his sneakers. "And you never called in the favor, not even when you came asking me for a job. That's been eating at me ever since."

Bolly replaced his glasses. Several minutes passed while they watched as Jason's coach gave him some pointers on taking the snap. Finally Bolly said, "This guy's okay for a middle school coach, but Jason could use some extra help. I realize it's not much of a job. In fact, Griff, it's not—"

"I accept."

"Hold on. Any offer of payment I make will be insulting."

"You don't have to pay me. I need something constructive to do. Buy a dozen footballs for me to use, and we'll call it square."

Bolly considered him a moment, then seemed to reach a decision. "How about here, an hour before practice each day?"

"Suits me." They shook hands. "Tell Jason to come prepared to work his butt off."

"He'll be thrilled. Start tomorrow?"

"I'll be here."

Bolly stood and clumped down several of the bleachers, then stopped and turned back. "This doesn't mean I excuse what you did, Griff. You're still on probation, with me as well as with the court. The least hint of trouble, you're outta here."

"There won't be any trouble. I swear."

Bolly nodded, then continued down the bleachers to join the other dads who were standing on the sideline watching practice.

Griff wasn't invited to join them, and wouldn't be, but that was all right. He felt better than he had in a long while. He had a project now, something to look forward to, a reason for getting out of bed in the morning. And for coaching an aspiring quarterback, no one was better qualified. Knowing that made him feel good.

He was smiling when his cell phone rang.

He arrived ahead of her and parked in back. A few minutes later, she pulled her car in behind his.

"A meeting ran long," she said as she got out.

"I just got here myself."

Together they walked toward the front of the house. While she was unlocking the door, he looked in both directions along the street. No olive sedan. He'd come straight from the middle school practice field and knew he hadn't been followed there. In fact, he hadn't seen Rodarte or anyone suspicious since their last confrontation—a month ago, he realized.

But he didn't think for a moment that Rodarte had been scared off. In fact, his noticeable absence was unnerving. Griff would prefer him to stay visible, at least occasionally. With that in mind, as soon as they got inside, he asked Laura if she'd seen the guy he'd warned her about.

"In the ugly green car?" One of her eyebrows arched slightly.

"Why are you looking at me like that? Do you think I made him up?"

"What I think is that you took an unnecessary risk of being seen with me."

"I know the rules, but you needed to know about Rodarte."

"I doubt it."

"Look—"

"I don't want to argue about it," she snapped. Then she rubbed her forehead and sighed wearily. "I haven't seen a man in a green car lurking about."

"Good. Thank you. That's all I wanted to know. Why didn't you just say that and save us the argument?"

She looked ready to take issue, than changed her mind and started toward the bedroom.

"What was the model?"

"What?"

"The model. In the box I carried to your car."

"It was an airplane model."

"I figured that much. You were taking it home to show your husband. What for?"

"For a presentation."

"Yeah? How'd it go?"

Avoiding eye contact, she combed her fingers through her hair. "It doesn't matter now." Before giving him an opportunity to say more about it, she walked down the hallway and disappeared into the bedroom.

Griff stood looking after her, wondering what had caused her to be in such a snit. A quarrel at home? Bad day at the office? Or just put out that she had to endure him again.

Screw it. Let her be snippy. Let her sulk. Whatever. He didn't care. He only hoped to God it worked this time. He was ready to cash in and blow.

He tugged his shirttail from his waistband and pulled off his boots. He checked the wall thermostat and lowered it several degrees. He went into the kitchen and checked the fridge. Same bottled water, same six-pack of Diet Coke. He didn't want either, but he unbuttoned his shirt and stood in the open door of the fridge, fanning the cold air onto his chest.

Back in the living room, he opened the armoire and scanned the titles of the videos. Maybe he should check one out, just for variety. Let's see. Men with women. Women with women. *A Tail of Two Cities.* Hmm. *Which two cities?* he wondered. On one cover a chick wearing nothing but strips of black leather was straddling a motorcycle. Her snarl and sharp red fingernails turned him off, not on.

He closed the armoire doors, once again rejecting the videos and magazines in favor of his own imagination.

"Come in."

He went into the bedroom and closed the door. Midway across the room, he stopped. She was lying as before, staring at the ceiling, covered to her waist by the sheet. Above it, she was fully dressed.

But this time there were tear tracks on her cheeks.

When he didn't immediately move to the bed, she glanced at him, then back at the ceiling.

He walked to the foot of the bed. "What's the matter?"

"Nothing."

"You've been crying."

"I'm just tired."

"You cry when you're tired?"

She looked at him and said testily, "Sometimes. Now, can we please just get this over with?"

Pissed off by her tone and the condescension behind it, he muttered, "At your service, ma'am," and shoved down his jeans, actually hoping the sight of his tented boxers would offend her. It did. She turned her head aside.

He kicked off his jeans, peeled off his shorts, and crawled onto the bed, stretching out on top of her. He wrestled with the sheet, cursing its tenacity, before he got it out of the way. Her legs parted. He moved into position, thrust, missed, thrust again.

It was easier than the first two times. Faster, too. Quickly over. If you looked up *slam-bam-thank-you-ma'am* in the dictionary . . .

He didn't even give himself time to catch his breath before levering himself up. As he did, he glanced at her averted face. And froze. Fresh tears were rolling down her cheeks like silent admonitions. Her lower lip was clamped between her teeth as though to keep it from trembling.

Well, shit. How bad could it have been?

Apparently pretty bad, because her chest hitched on a sob.

"Hell, did I hurt you?"

She shook her head.

"You said you wanted it over with."

She tried to say something, but the words got lodged in her throat. She swallowed convulsively.

Griff, at a loss, didn't say anything. Instead, he laid his hand against her wet cheek. At his touch, she tensed beneath him. When she raised her hand, he expected her to remove his from her face. Instead, she covered his hand with hers, then turned her face into his palm so that the heel of his hand was under her chin and the tips of his fingers were curved up over her hairline.

Her breath struck with hot gusts of emotion. Tears were captured in his palm. He watched her throat as she struggled to contain the choppy sounds of weeping. And then, when she couldn't hold them back anymore, she clamped her teeth again. Except this time it wasn't her lip that was caught between them. It was the meaty pad at the base of his thumb. She sank her teeth into it.

The effect on Griff was instantaneous. He sucked in a quick, audible breath.

Her teeth let go immediately. He lifted his hand off her face. Their eyes connected with an impact as startling as the bite. Her eyes, swimming in tears, widened fractionally when she felt what he couldn't control. Didn't want to control. He swelled inside her with an infusion of blood so hot and insistent, he had neither the time, the willpower, nor the desire to withdraw.

He filled her completely. Or was she shrinking around him? It was difficult to tell. And it didn't matter. Because, God, it was a rush, the most erotic damn thing ever to happen to him.

He pressed his hips forward, tentatively, testing her reaction. Her eyes closed briefly, then reopened. Her eyelashes were wet, forming spiky clumps, very pretty. There was a black speck in the iris of her right eye that he'd never noticed before, but he'd never been this close to her before. He had never really looked into her eyes. He hadn't allowed himself to look into them.

Still tentative, he angled his hips forward and up. Her breath made a soft hissing sound as she inhaled through her teeth. Her eyes closed. Encouraged, he slid his arm beneath her, scooped her ass into his hand, and tilted her up at the same time he pressed deep. A hungry sound vibrated in her throat, because by now her lips were rolled inward, tightly compressed. She was breathing rapidly through her nose.

He pulled back, almost out, then sank into her again. She groaned. He did it again. His strokes were long, slow, and deep, and she responded with corresponding movements that soon had him calling on deities in mindless gasps.

Her hands, which before had always stayed motionless at her sides, were moving restlessly. She took fistfuls of the sheet, twisted it, then released it and reached for more, for something, and found the front panels of his shirt, still unbuttoned. She clutched the fabric, tugging until he could feel it pull taut across his back. Her throat arched as her head dug into the pillow. Her hips lifted to meet his thrusts, more shallow now, and faster.

Then holding her tightly to him, grinding against her, he came hard, and so did she. Even when he was spent, lying on her like a dead man, her tiny orgasmic aftershocks nipped at him. It was like being kissed right on the tip of his cock. He was too whipped even to smile, but in his mind he did.

Eventually they were still.

He cupped the back of her head in his hand and rolled onto his side, carrying her with him. And he held her like that, one hand securing her head beneath his chin, the other still firmly on her ass, holding her in place, keeping him inside her. The sensations were indescribable. He was torn between wanting to stay there like that until they petrified, and looking at her.

He wished there was a way to get out of their clothes without moving. He was suddenly desperate to be skin to skin. He wanted to look at her breasts. At all of her. To touch, explore, nuzzle, and pet all those tantalizing spots he hadn't let himself even think about.

Later. Right now, her lethargy was so absolute, she appeared to be asleep. He angled his head back so he could look into her face. Her lips were slightly parted, damp and soft looking, swollen and red from her biting them. Where the fuller lower lip met the upper one, there was a shallow dimple. Jesus, that was a sexy spot, begging to be caressed by the tip of his tongue.

He was lowering his head to do just that when her body went rigid. Her eyes sprang open, and in a flurry of thrashing limbs she separated them and sat up. "Oh, God." She buried her face in her hands. "Ohgodohgodohgod."

"Laura—"

"Don't say anything! Just please don't . . . don't . . . Oh, God." She was groping for something at the side of the bed, and he saw it was her underwear. She wrestled the panties on and left the bed, disappearing into the bathroom and soundly closing the door behind her.

He got up and clumsily pulled on his boxers, went to the bathroom door, and knocked. "Laura." Without waiting for permission, he opened the door.

She was working her skirt up over her hips and shoving her feet into her shoes at the same time. Once she had the skirt fastened, she grabbed her jacket off a hook on the back of the door. In perpetual motion, she pushed him aside and went past, snatched her handbag from the top of the bureau, and flung open the bedroom door.

"Laura, wait!" He trailed her down the hall. Halfway across the living room, he hooked her elbow with his hand to bring her around. "Will you wait a damn minute? Talk to me."

She yanked her arm free, wouldn't look at him. "There's nothing to talk about."

"Only everything."

"That didn't happen." She patted the air with both hands, emphasizing each word. "It did not happen."

"It happened."

Squeezing her eyes shut, she shook her head furiously. "No, it didn't. I—" She covered her mouth with her hand to catch a sob.

"Oh, my God." Spinning away from him, she walked quickly to the door.

He lunged after her, but she was out like a flash.

"Laura!" he shouted.

She didn't look back.

CHAPTER
18

FOSTER WAS ON THE TELEPHONE WHEN LAURA CAME INTO HIS office. She hesitated on the threshold, but he waved her in. Her arrival gave him a welcome excuse to conclude his conversation with one of the board members. It had begun to bore him.

Running the airline wasn't as much fun as it used to be. Key personnel were so good at their jobs, they could do them without his supervision. From a management standpoint, it was gratifying to know he'd made wise choices in hiring them. But their reliability made him superfluous.

These days he often felt like the token handicapped employee.

He wrapped up his phone conversation with a promise to continue it soon. Laura was standing with her back to him, staring out the window. "To what do I owe this honor?" he asked. "You're usually too busy to pay me a call during business hours. Or *is* this business? Are you here as department head or wife?"

"Wife. Do you have time for me now?"

"Always."

She'd taken his rejection of SunSouth Select hard, harder than he would have guessed. Since joining the executive ranks of the airline, she had been overruled and outvoted on numerous issues, but she took those small defeats in stride and ultimately gave wholehearted support to the majority rule.

Not this time, and with reason. Although she'd given others credit for creative and informative input, Select had been her vision, and he had essentially squelched it. Judging from her mood over the past couple of weeks, she had regarded it as a personal rejection.

The subject had come up only once in the meantime. Last week during an executive meeting, Joe McDonald had mentioned Select in passing. Laura had shot him a warning look that said: *Don't talk about that.* It hadn't been spoken of again, at least not in Foster's presence, and he didn't think it was being whispered about behind his back. Nowhere in the building had he seen any of the materials Laura had used for her presentation. He got a sense that, since he hadn't taken up the baton, everyone considered it a dead issue.

He had snuffed SunSouth Select while, actually, the prospect of offering alternative carrier service was exciting. Unbeknownst to Laura, he had been thinking about it himself and doing his own research into that growing market, assessing how he might claim a large segment of it.

He'd studied the new superlight jets and considered ordering a fleet of them with which to begin a top-notch charter service. He'd even given thought to doing as Laura suggested and starting an offshoot of SunSouth.

But whatever form the innovation took, it would be his conception and his design. Not hers or anyone else's. He would be the leader, not the crippled has-been.

He'd given her space and time to nurse her wounded pride, basically by pretending not to notice her dejection. Was this unscheduled visit to his office a sign that she was finally climbing out of her funk? One could hope.

He said, "You didn't bring wine this time."

She turned around and looked at him quizzically.

"Has it been so long ago that you've forgotten? You surprised me with lunch here in this office. To celebrate our three-month anniversary."

"Four-month. And it was champagne."

"Was it? What we drank isn't the part I remember. However, I vividly recall dessert."

She smiled and modestly ducked her head. "Fun times."

"I miss them."

After several beats, she raised her head and looked at him, all seriousness now. "We could still have fun times, Foster."

"Not like that."

"Not *exactly* like that. Different. But just as good."

He gave a mirthless laugh. "Not from my standpoint."

She held his gaze for a moment, then declared, "I'm not going back."

"Back?"

"To the house. To Griff Burkett. I'm not doing it again."

So. This was how she was going to pay him back for hurting her feelings. Keeping his expression impassive, he folded his hands in his lap, clasping them loosely. "Oh?"

"No."

"Why this sudden—"

"It's not sudden. I've thought about little else since . . . since the last time. I'm not going back."

"You said that. I think I deserve to know why."

"Because it's wrong."

"Wrong by what standard? How can it be wrong if I sanction it?"

"*I* don't. It's wrong by *my* standard."

"I see. When did you decide it was wrong?"

She looked away, saying in an undertone, "When you first proposed it." Then, more staunchly, she said, "I was against it from the beginning. I consented to it only because I love you and wanted to give you anything you asked of me. But I can't do this. I won't."

"I thought you wanted a child as much as I do."

"That hasn't changed," she exclaimed. "I *do* want a baby. I want that for us. Very much. But we have options. I can be artificially inseminated using an anonymous sperm donor."

"You know how I feel about that."

She hesitated, then said, "All right. I'll make that concession. Since Griff Burkett is already in our confidence, we can use his semen. He suggested that at our first meeting with him, remember? That way he wouldn't lose out on his money. We'd take his specimens to the doctor's office and claim they were yours. No one would know the difference."

"I'd rather not resort to that method."

"I don't see it as resorting."

"I do. And, anyway, isn't it too soon to go to plan B? It's only been three cycles."

"I know how many it's been," she said curtly. "But even if it was only one, I'm not doing it again."

"Is it Burkett you find objectionable? Does he treat you badly?"

"No."

"Rudely, roughly?"

"No."

"Because if he does—"

"He *doesn't*."

"Okay." He let that lie without further comment, giving her time to collect herself.

She took a deep breath and let it out slowly. "My decision has nothing to do with him. This is about me. And the whole idea of it."

"We discussed the idea for months, Laura. We went over every aspect of it, time and again."

"I'm aware of that."

"And you agreed."

"Yes. But talking about it in the abstract and actually . . ." Suddenly she drew herself up to her full height. "I shouldn't have to justify the way I feel. Or try to explain it. I don't want to do it," she said with emphasis. "That should be the end of it."

He let several moments elapse, then said, "This surprises me. It's not like you to leave a job unfinished."

"True."

"You've never walked away from a commitment."

"No, and I didn't plan to break this one. I thought I could approach it like any other challenge. But I can't."

"I didn't think it would cause you this much emotional distress."

"Well, it does."

"Perhaps you're taking it too personally."

She looked at him aghast. "I'm your *wife*. I'm having sexual intercourse with another man. How in God's name can it not be personal?"

"You're becoming hysterical, Laura." He cast a cautious glance toward his office door.

She hugged her elbows and turned her back on him. He rolled forward and back three times, then wheeled his chair away from his desk and moved up behind her. He reached out and placed his hands on either side of her waist. She flinched and tried to move away, but he held her firmly. "I miscalculated. I didn't think it would offend your sense of right and wrong."

"I hate disappointing you, Foster. I know how much this means to you. But there's a moral ambiguity that I cannot get past."

"I honor your feelings, of course. As well as your decision."

She expelled a soft breath. "Thank you."

He applied enough pressure to turn her around to face him. "You've been morose for weeks. I haven't remarked on it, but I've noticed."

"I admit I haven't been myself. This has been weighing heavily on my mind. It was distracting me from work. Worse, it was creating a barrier between us. Knowing it would be a disappointment, I put off telling you, but had to before it was time to meet Burkett again. The dread of telling you has been nerve-racking. I'm glad to have this conversation behind us." She gave him a tremulous smile, then leaned down and kissed his lips.

When she pulled away, he said, "It's been fifteen days since you were last with Burkett, correct?"

She nodded.

"Then this discussion may have been for nothing," he said with a bright smile. "You may be pregnant already."

What if she's pregnant?

It was the big what-if in Griff's life now. Each morning he woke up wondering if this would be the day he'd get the congratulatory call.

Of course, that was their goal, wasn't it? A fertilized egg would be the answer to all their troubles. It would make the childless couple happy, and make him a millionaire for the rest of his life.

But if Laura had conceived, he would never see her again.

Which was no cause for celebration.

"Griff?"

He was startled to find Bolly standing elbow to elbow with him on the practice field sideline. The sportswriter was looking at him strangely.

"Sorry. I was—"

"A million miles away. I had to say your name three times. Were you asleep?"

Griff removed his sunglasses and blinked against the blistering sun. "In this heat? Hardly. I was concentrating on Jason. He's showing some good hustle out there today."

"Thanks to you."

"No, he's applying himself. Credit belongs to him."

"The boy is obsessed with football. Worries his mom."

"How come?"

"She's afraid he'll go whole hog and get hurt."

"Moms are like that." He supposed.

"She'd rather he play badminton."

Griff winced and Bolly laughed. "My sentiments exactly. Say, listen, I just got a call. I've been granted an interview with that new goalie the Stars signed yesterday, but it's a narrow window of opportunity before he flies home to Detroit. If I rush, I can catch him at DFW before his flight. I hate to pull Jason out of practice. Would you mind driving him home?"

"Of course not."

"I wouldn't ask, but my mother-in-law had to go to the podiatrist, and my wife volunteered to drive her, so—"

"Bolly, go. Should I stay with Jason till you get home?"

"No, just see him into the house, make sure he locks the door. He knows the rules of staying by himself."

"Okay. No problem."

Bolly looked toward the field and picked out his son, who barely had time to hand the ball off to a halfback before being slammed to the ground by a tackle. But he wasn't down for long. He was back on his feet in time to see the halfback make a first down. He jumped straight up into the air, raised his fist, and whooped with joy.

Bolly, still watching, smiled, but then a worry line formed between his brows. "Griff, on second thought, maybe—"

"You can trust him with me, Bolly."

Bolly turned back to him and held his gaze for several seconds while silently debating the advisability of asking for this favor. Then he nodded. "I appreciate it, Griff. Thanks."

When practice was over, Jason jogged off the field toward Griff, who gave him a high five. "Great practice, QB. Especially that last offensive series."

"Thanks." The boy was red in the face, and sweat had plastered his hair to his head beneath his helmet, but he was basking in the praise.

Griff told him about Bolly's unexpected errand. "Which leaves me your ride home today."

"You mean it?"

"Don't get excited. My car's crap."

On the way, Griff pulled into a Braum's. "I could use a milk shake. How 'bout you?"

As long as they were there, they decided they might just as well have burgers and fries to go with their shakes. They were seated in a booth, talking amiably about Jason's team and the strengths and weaknesses of various players, when Griff became aware of a trio of construction workers. He'd noticed them when they came in but had given them only a passing glance before returning his attention to Jason.

Now he realized that he'd been spotted and recognized. The workmen kept their voices low, but the looks they directed at him sizzled with hostility. Others began to notice. Griff could feel a dozen pairs of eyes fixed on him.

Jason, who'd been chatting nonstop, barely pausing long enough to fill his mouth with food, became aware of the charged atmosphere. His chatter slowed down and then stopped altogether. He looked toward the three men, then across at Griff, his eyes clouded with concern.

"It's okay, Jason."

But it wasn't. Because when the men got their carryout orders and were on their way to the exit, they had to pass the booth in which Griff and Jason sat. As the last one filed past, he said, "You suck, Burkett." Then he hawked up a gob of phlegm and spat it at

Griff. It missed, smacking into the vinyl upholstery inches from Griff's shoulder.

Their departure left a vacuum. No one moved. Griff figured everyone was waiting to see what he would do. What he wanted to do was follow the guy out and kick his ass up into his hard hat. Had he been alone, he would have.

But with Jason there, he couldn't. He didn't mind the embarrassing scene for himself nearly as much as he minded it for the boy, who was sitting with his head down, his hands in his lap beneath the table.

Soon the clerks and other customers resumed their business. Everyone but Jason. "You finished?" Griff asked.

The boy raised his head. "It's not fair!"

Griff was surprised to see that he wasn't embarrassed but angry. "What's not fair?"

"What that man did just now. What people say about you."

Griff pushed aside his plate and propped his forearms on the edge of the table. "Listen to me, Jason. Spitting like that was disgusting. It only made him look like an asshole, but what I did five years ago was much, much worse." He looked through the window at the three, who were climbing back into their utility truck. "How much do you think that guy earns in a year?"

Jason raised his shoulder in a disinterested shrug.

"A fraction of what I made when I was playing football. A tiny fraction. That guy works hard and doesn't earn as much as I spent on having my tailored shirts laundered. He doesn't hate me for making more money than him. What he hates is that I was living the life every guy dreams of, and I threw it away. I took money for cheating. I was stupid and selfish, and I broke the law. There's no getting around that."

"But you're not bad now."

He was screwing a paraplegic's wife for money. That was pretty damn bad. The only thing worse would be to want to screw her whether he was being paid to or not.

He'd tried not to think at all about what had happened. When he did, he tried passing it off as physiological cause and effect, sexual mechanics that, with all the gears oiled and working, had produced a predictable result.

Or as caprice. A fluke. Stars had collided, but it wouldn't happen again for another million years.

But in whatever terms he tried to explain it, it stayed on his mind. Constantly. Every time he thought about her teeth sinking into the bottom of his thumb, he got hard, his gut tightened with longing, and all he wanted was to be inside her again.

"I'm nobody's hero, Jason. Don't make me into one. You want a hero, look at your dad."

"My dad?" Jason scoffed. "What's he do that's heroic?"

"He loves your mom. He loves you. He takes care of you, worries about you."

Jason, still sullen, said, "That's nothing."

"That's huge." Then, to keep from sounding too preachy, he added, "But he can't throw a football for shit. And don't tell him I said *shit* in front of you."

"He says it all the time."

Griff laughed. "Then he's *my* hero."

Jason started smiling again.

The following day started out like every other. Griff got out of bed and went into the bathroom. As soon as he'd peed, he consulted the calendar he'd tacked to the wall. This was his routine now. He was marking off the days, for crissake.

He'd bought a computer and taught himself to use it. After extensive Internet research, he thought he had a fairly comprehensive overview of the female reproductive system and how it worked, more than he had learned from basic biology in school.

Some of the message boards he'd logged on to gave him more information than he wanted—did he really need to know about mucus plugs and yolk sacs?—but he'd learned a lot about timing and what happened within that twenty-eight-day cycle. He'd learned what an LH surge was.

If he'd been with Laura on the day she ovulated, he approximated when she would have menstruated—if she was going to. Those five days had come and gone. If she'd had a period, and if his calculations were correct, he should have heard from her three days ago, when she should have been ovulating again.

But she hadn't summoned him back to the house on Windsor Street. So did that mean she hadn't had a period and therefore had conceived? Maybe she was holding off breaking the glad news until she'd had her pregnancy confirmed by a doctor. Or maybe, because of what had happened the last time, she didn't intend to call him, ever again. But wouldn't he have been notified that the deal was off?

Not knowing was making him crazy, but all he could do was wait.

As he did every morning, he made a notation on the calendar, then showered. When he stepped out of the tub, he heard his newspaper being thunked against his front door. Disinclined to dress yet, he wrapped a towel around his waist. He retrieved the paper from his small porch, went into the kitchen, and started a pot of coffee.

While waiting for it to brew, he perused the front page and drank orange juice from the carton. He flipped the paper over, read the headlines beneath the fold, and finding them relating to the same world crises that they'd related to yesterday, he pulled out the sports section.

The headline caused his heart to stutter. Blood rushed to his head and made him momentarily dizzy. "The fuck is this?"

BURKETT QUESTIONED IN DEATH OF BOOKMAKER, the headline read.

FURTHER WOES FOR FORMER COWBOY?

VETERAN COACH DENOUNCES FALLEN STAR.

Recognizing the stories, he looked at the dateline. Not this morning's issue. It was five years old, and though it was well preserved, he saw now that the paper on which the sports section was printed didn't match the rest of the newspaper. It had yellowed some with age.

Rodarte.

He knocked over a kitchen chair in his rush. In seconds, he was out of the kitchen, through the living area, and flinging open his front door. He charged out onto his narrow patch of yard and scanned the street. He didn't really expect to see the green sedan, and he didn't. Rodarte had given himself time to get away.

"Son of a bitch!" Griff grabbed the towel, which was slipping off his waist, and stormed back inside, slamming the door behind him. Rodarte hadn't reappeared in almost two months. Now, just when

Griff had begun to think—hope—the bastard had given up and gone away, this.

Clever of him, planting this old sports section in today's newspaper where Griff was certain to find it. Rodarte was rubbing his nose in the shit he'd made of his life five years ago.

When he felt composed enough to confront the fine print, he righted the chair and poured himself a cup of coffee, then sat down at the kitchen table and began to read. Every word was like a blow, hurtful because it was true.

Not since Pete Rose's gambling and Jose Canseco's admission to using steroids had a professional athlete scandalized himself as much as the record-breaking, all-star quarterback Griff Burkett had. Media coverage had been extensive and pervasive. The story had made headlines internationally. ESPN had dedicated hours of programming to it.

But Rodarte had done well to choose this particular issue of *The Dallas Morning News,* because these stories were summarizing chronicles of his long, inexorable fall.

The gambling had started small, but it grew like a creeping vine he couldn't kill or control, until it dominated, becoming more exciting for him than the Sunday games. Winning big on a wager was more thrilling than winning big on the gridiron.

It had evolved into an addiction. Before it had got out of hand, he should have been smart enough to recognize the danger signs. Maybe he had. Maybe he had just ignored them.

He got caught up in a dangerous but exhilarating spiral. If he won, he raised the stakes of the next bet in order to win more. If he lost, he raised the stakes to recover the loss. The spiral became a maelstrom that eventually sucked him under.

Bill Bandy looked more like a tax accountant than one's idea of a bookie. He was a slightly built man who probably had weighed no more on the day he died than on the day he graduated high school. He had thinning brown hair, a small face with a pointed chin, and a sharp nose. His pinched nostrils and pale blue eyes waged a constant war with airborne allergens. His hands were as soft and white as a woman's, and one got the sense they would feel moist if touched.

No one would have pegged him for a mobster. Yet that was exactly what he was. It was rumored that, back in St. Louis, before he'd been relocated to Dallas, he had poisoned an uncle who had double-crossed him. Griff never knew if that was fact or fiction.

Bandy worked for Vista, the syndicate's dummy corporation that ostensibly ran a tin-mining operation somewhere in South America. The actual location and other details were vague. Vista's real enterprises were high-stakes gambling, money laundering, and, Griff suspected, drug trafficking.

Vista's *miners* in the Las Colinas high-rise wore designer suits and diamond-studded Rolexes. They packed heat even when they went to the men's room. They had bodyguards with automatic pistols and cars with bulletproof windows.

You did not fuck with them.

That was what Bill Bandy had told Griff over a plate of chicken enchiladas one night at his favorite Mexican restaurant. Griff was midway into his fourth season with the Cowboys. Bandy had invited him to dinner to discuss business, specifically the repayment of his gambling debt, which was now three hundred thousand and change.

"You don't fuck with these guys, Griff. If it was me, I'd extend you some more credit. Hell, you make millions. I know you'll be good for the money in a few months. But these guys?" He blotted his dripping nose with a damp white handkerchief. "There's no charity in their hearts. Believe me."

Griff dunked a tortilla chip into the salsa and munched it noisily. He took a sip of frozen margarita and winked at the starstruck teenage girls staring at him from the next table. "What are they going to do? Send some guy with hairy knuckles to break both my legs?"

"You think this is funny?"

"I think you're about to panic when panic isn't called for. They compound the interest every week, making me a profit center for them. So what's their problem?"

"They want their money."

Finally Bandy's funereal tone captured Griff's attention. No longer nervous or fidgety, Bandy's pale gaze was rock steady. Even his nose had dried up temporarily. Griff thought maybe the fable of his poisoning an elderly uncle was true.

Maintaining that cold expression, he continued. "Be glad they sent me as the messenger, or you might not be starting on Sunday, or any Sunday for the remainder of the season. Make no mistake, they can inflict serious injury on you, Griff. They *will*."

"It wouldn't make sense for them to injure me. If I can't play, they'll never get their money."

The argument didn't make a dent in Bandy's resolute expression. Griff pushed aside his plate and sighed with disgust that he had to deal with this now. The team was facing the Falcons on Sunday in Atlanta. The Cowboys were favored, but not by much. It wasn't going to be a cakewalk by any stretch. He should have been psyching himself up for a tough game, studying the playbook, not pandering to gangsters.

"Okay. Give me a few days," he told Bandy. "I'll liquidate something. A car. My condo in Florida. Something. What's the minimum amount that would temporarily satisfy them? Two hundred thousand? That's more than half what I owe them. Would that buy me some grace?"

Bandy dabbed his leaking eyes with a corner of his handkerchief. "There may be another way."

"To buy me time?"

"To cancel the debt."

Griff gaped at him as if he'd said that he could have a week on a desert island with every Playmate of the Month for the past year, that they were all nymphomaniacs with the hots for him, and that no clothes were allowed.

Bandy asked, "Are you willing to meet with them? Discuss options?"

"Where and what time?"

The "them" Bandy had referred to were three men, who welcomed Griff into Vista's opulent offices with hearty handshakes and unlimited hospitality. *What would you like to drink? Help yourself to the tray of sandwiches there. I highly recommend the beef tenderloin with the horseradish sauce. How about a massage after the meeting? We've got a girl on staff who'll give you a massage with a happy ending.* Wink, wink. *If you get my meaning.* Which Griff did.

You'd never know by the reception they gave him that he owed them over a quarter million dollars and that they were making threats against his person if he didn't pay this debt immediately.

The only native Texan was tall, trim, darkly tanned, with large and very white teeth. He was an avid golfer who talked loudly, lewdly, and nonstop. It was he who placed his arm across Griff's shoulders and told him about the masseuse with the magic hands and mouth. Larry was the guy's name.

Martin had a swarthy, Mediterranean look. He was obese. He didn't breathe, he wheezed like an off-key bagpipe, and looked like he could go into cardiac arrest at any moment if only his heart could work up the energy.

The third, Bennett, was quiet and unobtrusive. Balding and fair skinned, he sat apart, contributing little but studying Griff with the unblinking, lashless stare of something scaly and venomous.

After the initial greetings, they got down to business. The terms of their proposal were simple: Throw the Atlanta game on Sunday, and his debt would disappear. That was not how they put it, but that was the bottom line.

Martin told him they didn't expect him to try to lose. "Just don't play up to your full potential."

Larry winked again. "Give the fucking Falcons a fucking chance. That's all."

"And who knows," Martin wheezed, "if the Falcons pull out a win, we could throw a little extra bonus your way, in addition to clearing your debt." Gasp. "Right, Bennett?"

Bennett the Silent nodded his stiff comb-over.

Griff told them he'd think about it.

Fine, they said. He had till Sunday to make up his mind. And just to show their goodwill, they insisted that he avail himself of the massage with the girl, who capped off the fifty-minute rubdown with a blow job. Not that he couldn't get head whenever he wanted it. There were always girls just dying to notch their bedposts with the Lone Star logo of the Dallas Cowboys. But this girl was exceptional.

On Sunday, while he was suiting up, during the singing of the national anthem, even as he took the field following the opening kickoff, he was still wrestling with his decision. He didn't know what he would do until late in the fourth quarter, with a 10–10 score, when Dallas was deep in their own territory and it was third and twelve.

He took the snap. Dallas linemen went down like bowling pins under a Falcons blitz. His fastest, strongest running back got blocked by two linebackers. The third one was chugging toward Griff, smelling blood. Scrambling, looking for an open receiver, Griff realized how easy—and convincing—it would be to throw an interception.

Atlanta won 17 to 10.

The partnership was forged.

CHAPTER

19

I F YOU WANT TO PUT SPIN ON IT, YOU GOTTA GET YOUR THUMB under it." Griff demonstrated the rotating hand motion to Jason Rich. "See? You gotta whip your thumb under just as you release the ball. Now try again."

He handed over the football. Jason's face was tense with concentration as he gripped the ball the way Griff had demonstrated and threw a pass. "Much better."

"One more time, Griff? I think I let go a little too late."

"Okay, but only one. Practice is about to start."

Griff saw improvement in the second pass. "Good work, Jason. You're getting the hang of it. Throw a few thousand more and you'll have it down pat. You'll be breaking records."

Behind his mask, Jason's sweaty face broke into a grin. "Yesterday was fun. Except for . . . you know."

"Yeah, I'm sorry you had to see that."

"I told my dad. He said you handled it the only way you could. If you had fought them, it would've made it worse."

"I'll say. Did you see the size of those guys?"

Jason laughed, then said tentatively, "Maybe we could go for milk shakes again sometime."

"I'd like that."

"Me, too. See you tomorrow."

Griff knocked on the top of the boy's helmet, two taps. "I'll be here."

Jason trotted off to join his teammates, who were assembling on the sideline of the practice field. Bolly was among the other dads. Griff raised his hand in greeting, and Bolly waved back.

Griff jogged across the field to retrieve the footballs Jason had thrown and stuffed them into the cloth bag he kept in the trunk of his car. He pulled the drawstring to close the bag and slung it over his shoulder.

That was when he saw Rodarte, standing outside the chain-link fence, watching him.

Griff was already hot from being in the sun for the hour with Jason. When he saw Rodarte, it seemed his blood reached the boiling point in seconds. He had to force himself not to charge the fence.

Unhurried, he went through the gate and joined Rodarte on the other side. The son of a bitch didn't even deign to look at him. Instead, he stared across the field to the far sideline, where the middle school head coach was cautioning his young team not to let themselves become overheated or dehydrated during practice.

"You're pathetic, Rodarte," Griff said. "Collecting old newspapers like a bag lady."

Rodarte chuckled but still didn't turn to face him. "Fun reading. I hated keeping it to myself."

Griff started to grab him by the shoulder and force him around, but he didn't dare lay a hand on the man. Rodarte would fight back. And if it got ugly, which it inevitably would, there were too many witnesses. In particular Bolly. Griff had promised him there wouldn't be any trouble. Yesterday the sportswriter had entrusted his son to him. Griff would have hated like hell to betray that trust now.

He could tell Rodarte to go to hell and simply walk away. Let him stand there and dissolve from the heat till he was nothing but a puddle of sweat being absorbed by the hard, baked ground.

But ignoring him wouldn't be smart. Rodarte's being there wasn't coincidence, any more than this morning's incident with the newspaper was a harmless prank. After staying invisible for weeks, Rodarte had resurfaced. Until Griff knew why, he wouldn't turn his back on him.

Rodarte reached into his pocket and took out a pack of gum. "I'm trying to quit smoking."

"Good luck with that. It would be just awful if you got sick and died."

Rodarte gave him a sly grin as he unwrapped a stick of gum and put it in his mouth. "You still banging that broad?"

Griff's jaw tensed.

"I suppose since your favorite whore is still out of commission, you gotta get it somewhere." His grin got slier. "You could do a lot worse. Not only has Mrs. Speakman got a sweet ass but she's loaded. But I'm sure you know that. Nobody ever called you stupid, Number Ten. A lot of other ugly names, but never stupid."

Griff didn't rise to the bait.

"Is she footing your bills these days? Buying you all that neat new stuff?" Rodarte laughed that nasty laugh again and noisily smacked his chewing gum. "Sure she is. And glad to do it. Stuck with a husband who's only half a man, I'll bet she's willing to pay any price to ride a big, strong football hero like you."

Griff didn't move, even though he craved to see Rodarte bleed.

Lowering his voice to a suggestive whisper, Rodarte said, "I'll bet she's one of those no-nonsense businesswoman types who goes absolutely wild in the sack. Am I right? She works out all her career insecurities on your dick, and she likes to be on top. Come on, Burkett, share. Is she one of those?"

"You're maggot shit."

Rodarte barked a laugh. "You're fucking a paraplegic's wife and *I'm* maggot shit?"

"What do you want?"

"Want? Nothing," Rodarte said innocently. "Just thought I'd drop by, say hi. Didn't want you to think I'd forgotten you. I wanted to reassure you that when you self-destruct—and you will, you know—I'm gonna be there to see it, and hopefully to help bring it about. I'm so far up your ass, Burkett. You have no idea."

Griff feared if he stayed any longer he was going to take the first step toward the predicted self-destruction. Which was precisely what Rodarte wanted. Despite his resolve not to turn his back on the man, he did so and began walking away.

"Jason's showing progress."

Griff whipped back around. Rodarte, laughing softly, spat his wad of gum into the dirt. "The boy hasn't got much natural talent, but he works hard. Plain to see he worships the ground you walk on. Probably wants to follow in your footsteps. Well, not the cheating and murdering path you took, but your football glory days."

Squinting at Griff across the space separating them, Rodarte let his evil grin spread across his acne-cratered face. "Be a shame if something were to happen to the boy. A crippling accident or something that would prevent him from following his dream. He might even die."

Griff took the steps necessary to close the distance between them. "You lay one hand on that kid and—"

"Calm down," Rodarte said in a cajoling voice. "I was just speculating on the fickle finger of fate. Jesus, you're a hothead. I try to have a friendly little chat here at the middle school athletic field and you—"

"What do you want, Rodarte?"

He dropped his saccharine pretense, and his eyes turned flinty. "You know what I want."

"I don't have any of Vista's money."

"They're not convinced. I'm sure as hell not. And I'm not going to stop with you till I break you and you give it up. I'm as permanent as a birthmark."

Griff aimed his index finger at him and began backing away. "You stay away from me. You stay away from everyone around me."

Rodarte laughed. "Or what, Number Ten? Or what?"

Griff violated a condition of his probation, the primo one that Jerry Arnold continually reminded him of: *Don't go near your former associates.*

The way Griff saw it, he had no choice. Rodarte had threatened Jason. And the way he'd talked about Laura . . . The implied threat, which went beyond the nasty stuff, had raised the hair on the back of Griff's neck. Rodarte wouldn't have a qualm against harming either of them. Even Laura's money couldn't protect her. He would hurt her and Jason without a blink, and would enjoy the hell out of doing it.

To prevent that, Griff must confront this issue head-on, now. He wasn't willing to live with the constant threat of Rodarte. He certainly didn't want to inflict it on two people who were entirely innocent. He couldn't bear the guilt of someone else falling victim to Rodarte's brutality the way Marcia had.

Griff drove straight home from the practice field, rushed through a shower, and dressed. He left behind his new Armani jacket in favor of one he'd had before his incarceration, not wanting to look too well heeled.

It was nervy to arrive at Vista's offices unannounced, but he was betting that the triumvirate would agree to see him, out of curiosity if for no other reason. He was right. After waiting in a reception area for almost half an hour, he was summoned into the inner sanctum where he'd met with them the first time.

Same paneled walls, indirect lighting, and sound-absorbing rugs, but the hospitality was noticeably lacking. No sandwich tray, no open bar. Larry's tan was just as bronze, but it appeared that more time may have been spent in the club bar than on the links. He'd gone a little soft around the middle.

Griff was surprised to see that Martin could still breathe without some form of respiratory apparatus. But he was now relying heavily on a cane to help support his immense body.

Bennett had given up on the comb-over and shaved his head. It was perfectly white and round, and from the back looked like an overgrown billiard ball sitting on his shoulders. With even fewer lashes now, his eyes were more reptilian than before.

Larry had one hip propped on the corner of a desk. Bennett was in an armchair, legs crossed. As Griff walked in, Martin collapsed onto a short leather sofa that was barely wide enough to accommodate him. Both his lungs and the seat cushions emitted a whoosh of air as he settled.

Griff wasn't invited to sit.

Martin began. "What do you want?"

Griff responded just as bluntly. "Call off Rodarte."

No one said anything for a full thirty seconds. Finally Larry broke the taut silence. "Would that be Stanley Rodarte you're talking about?"

Griff didn't buy the dumb act. "You'll be glad to know your watchdog is persistent. He was in Big Spring the day I got out, and he's been making a nuisance of himself ever since. He assaulted a friend of mine. A woman. Sodomized her and ruined her face. When that failed to win me over, he set two guys on me. For a week after, I could barely walk and my pee ran red."

"Gee, Griff, we're sorry to hear that," Larry said, his voice dripping sarcasm. "And this would be our problem . . . why?"

Griff resented their playing innocent. He wasn't telling them anything they didn't already know, so he'd rather they just own up to it and tell him that he and Marcia had it coming.

"Look, it sucks for you if Bill Bandy hid money where you can't find it. But get off my back about it. I didn't take anything from him. And you know damn well I didn't kill him."

"You had motive."

"So did you."

The FBI had arrested Bandy on charges of illegal gambling. Facing several years in federal prison, Bandy had played his bargaining chip—Griff Burkett. He told the feds about Griff's association with Vista, specifically about the upcoming play-off game against Washington. No one in Dallas was happy about the loss that day, except the federal agents who were building a strong racketeering case against the Cowboys' QB.

The deal Bandy had struck worked out great for him. Griff got caught; all charges against Bandy were dropped. But this exchange had made the Vista men nervous. What if the FBI wanted more from Bill Bandy than a cheating football player? The bookie might have been tempted to use them as another free pass at some point in the future.

The Vista trio had removed the temptation from Bandy by killing him.

At least that was what Griff had surmised and now had essentially accused them of. Unfazed, their stares remained unblinking.

"Maybe there was some secret stash," he continued, "but I

haven't spent the last five years on a treasure hunt. I don't want back in your operation, and I'm not working for a competing outfit. You can threaten me till doomsday, and you'll still come up empty. So whatever you're paying Rodarte to put pressure on me is money wasted. Call him off."

Several moments passed. They sat like statues. Eventually Martin looked over at Larry, Larry looked over at Bennett, and Bennett continued to stare at Griff.

If Griff had still been a wagering man, he'd have put his money on Bennett as the enforcer of the group. Larry was the windbag, the people person, the public relations guy. Martin was the brains and the puppet master. Bennett, silent and stationary Bennett, who seemed to have ice water in his veins, was responsible for damage control.

It was Martin who finally spoke. "What makes you think . . ." Wheeze. ". . . that we'd have dealings . . ." Gasp. ". . . with a scumbag like Rodarte?"

"He told me himself. He said he'd talked to you. He passed along your message that there might be a way for me to make amends. That you might be willing to forgive and forget."

"Forgive and forget?"

This was the first and only time Griff had actually seen Martin smile, and it made his balls contract.

"Is Rodarte delusional, or are you?" Larry asked. "After you gave the grand jury the juice on us, you think we'd ever welcome you back?" He snorted his opinion on the chances of that. "First of all, asshole, we're not forgiving or forgetful. Number two, you're the last person we want in our operation. We're not slow learners. Once you screw us over, *you're* screwed. Third, if one of our competitors—not that we have any that matter—takes you in, that's good news to us. It only shows that they're fucking ignoramuses.

"Lastly, you're actually right about one thing. Rodarte did come sniffing around just before your release. He's always had the mistaken idea that he's a hotshot and that we're impressed by him. We're not. He's a lowlife thug, is all.

"But, hey, we don't want to appear unfriendly, especially to someone so inferior. So we dazzled him with bullshit and a couple shots of eighteen-year-old scotch, then sent him on his way. If he's squeezing you, he's doing it on his own time and for his own reasons."

"And more power to him," Martin wheezed.

"Amen to that," Larry said. "More power to him. We won't be brokenhearted the day you die, Burkett. The only reason you're still breathing is because you deserve no better than Rodarte. We'd rather somebody of his caliber handle an asswipe like you, save us having to get our hands dirty. Now get the fuck out of here before we remember just how pissed off we really are."

On his drive back from Las Colinas, Griff got stuck in a traffic jam behind a freeway accident that had two lanes closed. Staring into the brake lights of the car ahead of him, he ruminated over what Larry had told him. It felt like the truth. They wouldn't mourn his passing, but if they'd wanted him dead, he'd be dead.

The Vista boys were scary, but Rodarte, acting on his own behalf, was even scarier. Griff wasn't comforted by the knowledge that Rodarte was working independently.

That thought was interrupted by his cell phone's chirp. He flipped it open. "Hello?"

"Are you free?"

CHAPTER

20

H IS HEART SKIPPED. "When?"

"Now."

"I'm fifteen minutes out." Thirty at least, but he didn't want her to change her mind.

"I'll see you then."

It took five minutes for him to get past the accident; then he herded the Honda as though driving in the Le Mans and reached the house twenty-two minutes after getting her call. He went in through the unlocked front door and found her standing in the center of the living room.

She was wearing a snug white skirt and a sleeveless red top with white buttons down the front and wide straps over her shoulders. She looked great.

"Hi," he said.

"Hi."

"I was on 114 when you called. There was an accident."

"I didn't give you much notice."

He shrugged off his jacket and laid it over the back of the nearest chair. "How have you been?"

"Fine. What about you?"

"I've been okay. Airline keeping you busy?"

"Always."

"This heat sucks."

"I can't remember when it last rained."

"That time of year, I guess."

Up to that point, they hadn't broken eye contact. Now she did. She looked toward the window, where the louvered shutters let in only slivers of sunlight. "I asked you to meet me today so I could tell you in person."

His stomach dropped. "You're pregnant."

She shook her head.

"No?" he asked, making sure.

"No."

"I thought maybe you would be. We doubled the chances last time."

Her eyes flicked back to him briefly, then away. "I'm not pregnant. But I . . . we, Foster and I, have decided to try A.I."

His encounter with Rodarte, his meeting with the Vista boys, her call, the wild drive here, seeing her, all had combined to jumble his brain. Her words didn't compute. He shook his head slightly. "Sorry?"

"Artificial insemination."

"Oh. Right." Again his stomach took a dive. "Instead of us—"

"Yes."

"Huh."

There was a significantly long pause before she continued. "We realize the financial implications that our decision will have on you."

"Uh-huh."

"So we'd like for you to remain the donor." Nervously she wet her lips. "If you're willing, that is. And if you are, and the insemination is successful, the terms of the payout will stay the same."

He searched her face, but she avoided looking directly at him. After a moment, he went over to the sofa, sat down on the edge of it, and stared into near space, thinking what a bitch of a day this was turning out to be.

She must have taken his silence for either reluctance or indecision. She said, "You don't have to give me your answer today. You have time to think about it. I have to set up appointments with a specialist. I'm sure there will be tests. I think I have to go on supplemental hormones. So it could be a while before we needed you. Weeks, I would guess."

He looked over at her.

"Once the procedure is scheduled," she went on, sounding rushed, "I'll contact you and we'll work out a time and place for me to pick up the specimen. It'll have to be retrieved on the actual day. I'll give you as much notice as I can. A day, possibly two."

"All right."

"Between now and then, if you decide you don't want to . . . to participate, we'll pay you five hundred thousand anyway. For the times you've . . . for your trouble."

"Generous of you."

"Naturally, whether you opt to continue or cancel the arrangement here and now, it goes without saying that I expect the absolute confidentiality you agreed to."

Finally, something he wanted to address. "You don't want anybody to know about . . ." He tilted his head in the direction of the bedroom. "What happened in there last time."

"About any of it, Mr. Burkett."

"No, I'm sure you don't, Mrs. Speakman."

She drew herself up straight and retrieved her handbag from an armchair. "Well, I think that covers everything. Thank you for coming on such short notice."

"There's a double entendre if I ever heard one." He'd spoken in a mutter, but intentionally loud enough for her to hear.

Ignoring the remark, she moved toward the door. "I have to go. I have a meeting in half an hour."

"Liar."

She came around quickly.

"You don't have a meeting. You're running off." He left the sofa and started walking toward her. "You're scared. You don't trust yourself to be here. Did you confess to your husband that you really got into it last time?"

"What Foster and I talk about—"

"Is that why he changed his mind about our little arrangement?"

"*He* didn't. I did."

Up till then, he'd been growing steadily angrier. But that stopped it. This was her decision, not Speakman's, and not one they'd reached as a couple. He said the first thing that popped into his mind, the first thing he wanted to know. "Why?"

"I can't . . ." She faltered, then started again. "I can't continue with you like this, that's all. I agreed to it only because it was what Foster wanted. And I love him. I do. I love my husband."

"All right."

"That's the only reason I consented to this."

"So you said."

"But I can't be with you anymore."

"I got that, too. And when it comes right down to it, that's all you had to say. You don't owe me an explanation."

She looked at him strangely, then lowered her head. Neither of them moved. Seconds ticked by while he stared at the way her hair grew in a swirling pattern around the crown of her head. Finally he said, "When did you decide?"

"I knew when I left here last time that I wouldn't come back. But I fretted over it, and didn't tell Foster of my decision until two weeks ago."

"Why didn't you call to tell me then?"

"We decided to wait and see if I was pregnant before we told you. If I was, it would be a moot point. I thought the matter was settled." The red top expanded with the deep breath she took, straining the white buttons. "But Foster has spent the past two weeks trying to change my mind."

"He still wants his baby conceived the natural way."

"Yes. He hasn't really applied pressure, but he's made his wishes known. He's made it clear how disappointed he'll be if we change course now. He's used every tactic he knows to try to persuade me that we should continue as planned, at least through several more cycles."

"Only he didn't persuade you."

"No."

"Then why didn't you call and tell me the deal was off? Why are you here?"

"Because I let Foster think he finally wore me down." Her gaze moved around the room, then came to rest for several seconds on the third button of his shirt before moving up to meet his eyes. "He kept after me until I agreed to meet you one last time. If I don't conceive today, he said, he *promised,* he would never ask me to come here again and will agree to switching to a clinical method."

Griff assimilated that. "One last time."

"Yes."

"Today."

"Yes."

"So he thinks we're—"

"Yes."

"But we're not."

"He'll never know, will he? He'll think this time had the same result as the previous three."

"Only the two of us will know different."

"Unless you tell him."

"Your secret is safe with me."

"I hate that word," she said with obvious anguish. "I don't like keeping secrets from my husband."

She looked beyond him toward the hallway that led to the bedroom, and her gaze stayed fixed on it so long that Griff looked over his shoulder to see what could possibly be holding her attention. The hallway was empty. He thought she might be seeing into the bedroom, seeing them moving together, seeing herself coming. That would be a secret she would want to keep from her husband.

He came back around just as she looked up at him. Their gazes held for several long moments, then she gestured at the front door. "Well . . ."

"Your meeting."

She gave a wan smile. "There's no meeting."

"I know." He returned her smile, but he didn't feel it.

She reached behind her back for the doorknob. "Don't forget your jacket."

"Right."

"Be sure the door is securely closed so it will lock."

"Of course."

She pulled open the door, and they were struck with a blast of hot air. She said, "Depending on circumstances, this could be the last time I'll see you."

"Could be."

She paused, then gave a self-conscious shrug. "I can't think of anything to say that seems appropriate."

"Small talk seems smaller."

She smiled faintly at the reminder of her words to him the night they'd met.

"You don't have to say anything, Laura."

"Then . . ." She stuck out her right hand. "Good-bye."

He took her hand. They looked down at their clasped hands, then at each other. She released his hand and his gaze simultaneously, and turned toward the open door.

But she did only that. Turned and stopped.

Griff hesitated only heartbeats before acting. He moved in close behind her, reached over her shoulder, put his hand flat against the door, and slowly pushed it shut.

Laura stared at herself in the vanity mirror. The reflection looking back seemed to be of someone else. The woman in the mirror was disheveled, not as meticulously turned out as usual. Most disturbing, her eyes were filled with uncertainty. Where was the characteristic self-confidence? What had happened to the surety that she had a grip on the situation? Who was this tremulous stranger?

She ran her fingertips across her lips and dabbed at the smudge of mascara at the corner of her eye. No question, the image in the mirror was hers.

"Laura?"

She spun around, flattening her hand against her chest. "Foster. I didn't hear you."

"Obviously not. You nearly jumped out of your skin." His wheelchair was straddling the threshold between bedroom and bath. "Manuelo told me you were home."

She had parked in the detached garage, entered the house through the mudroom, and used the back staircase. "He said you were on the telephone." She forced a light laugh. "At least I think that's what he said. I didn't want to interrupt your call. I'm glad you chose to stay at home today. The heat is unbearable. It's making everyone cranky. People were driving like maniacs, so rush hour was more hazardous than usual."

Realizing that she was talking too much and too fast, she forced herself to slow down. "All this to say, I'm a mess and wanted to take a quick shower before seeing you. How was your day?"

"Uneventful. Besides the weather and the traffic, how was yours?"

"I had back-to-back appointments this morning, including the one with the reps from the FAA to discuss Southwest's and American's complaints."

"You'll have to be more specific. Southwest and American are always filing complaints against us."

"Highest form of flattery."

He grinned. "If we were failing, we'd never hear a peep out of them. How did your appointment with Griff Burkett go?"

The question came so suddenly and out of context, it took her off guard. "The same as before. Briefly. Efficiently."

"I thought he might be the reason you're so late getting home."

"Why would you think that?"

"No reason."

She let it drop. "I hope you didn't wait dinner on me."

"Mrs. Dobbins made a sandwich to tide me over."

"Good."

"So why are you late?"

"I was almost home when I remembered something I'd left at the office and had to go all the way back for it. Myrna was still there."

"My assistant is usually the last to leave. Unless it's you."

"She was finishing up some business letters and asked if I would wait on them so I could bring them home for you to sign. I have them right here."

She tried to squeeze past his chair into the bedroom, but he caught her hand. "The letters can wait. I want to know Burkett's reaction when you told him this was the last time you'd be meeting him. Or did you tell him?"

"I told him as soon as he arrived."

"And?"

"And nothing, really. Once I assured him that we would adhere to the original terms if he remained the donor, he said it was all the same to him. Something like that."

"He's not backing out then?"

"I didn't get that impression, no."

"I didn't think he would. Did you discuss how we would retrieve the semen?"

"Only in the most general terms. I told him I had to consult a specialist first. Then when he's needed, he'd be notified."

"Maybe the A.I. won't be necessary. Let's hope."

"That's what we all hope, Foster."

He surprised her by pressing his hand against her lower abdomen. "I feel good about this time. Karma. Something. It just feels different, like something significant happened."

She smiled, hoping it didn't look shaky. "Hold that thought." Stepping away, she said, "I really would like to get out of these clothes. You're welcome to stay."

"No, I'll leave you to your shower. I'd only stay if I could offer to wash your back."

"You can pour me a glass of wine instead. I won't be long."

"How about club soda? Just in case."

"Okay."

He kissed the air, then maneuvered his wheelchair across the adjacent bedroom and through the door, each of his motions done in a sequence of three.

Laura waited until she was alone, then closed the door to her bathroom and hastily removed her clothes. Before stepping into the shower, she worked up enough courage to examine herself in the full-length mirror. Her eyes were still glassy and dazed looking, her lips slightly abraded. She touched her nipples, navel, pubic hair.

Holding back a guilty whimper, she placed her fingers vertically against her lips and whispered, "Oh, God." But she wasn't certain for what, specifically, she prayed.

CHAPTER

21

THE MONTH WAS LONGER EVEN THAN ANY HE'D SPENT IN prison. Compared with this, those months had whizzed past like comets.

He'd held out for three days before doing the forbidden. He'd called the SunSouth offices. After listening to a seemingly endless menu of confusing options that required pushing a series of digits, he finally reached a human being who told him in a polite but busy-sounding voice that he had reached Ms. Speakman's office. "Kay Stafford speaking, how can I help you?"

"I need to talk to Ms. Speakman."

"In regard to what?"

He wondered what the cool, well-trained Kay Stafford would say if he told her the unmitigated truth. Instead, he replied, "Foster is a former college buddy of mine. I met with the two of them a few months back."

"Your name?"

"Ms. Speakman will remember."

She put him on hold and was gone for an interminable time. When she finally came back on the line, she said, "I'm sorry, Ms. Speakman isn't available to take your call. Would you care to leave a message?"

She asked by rote. If Laura had refused his call, chances were good that her assistant would deep-six any message he left. Besides, what could he say?

Leave your rich husband and be with me.

Or don't leave him and be with me.

I don't care what the hell you do, just be with me.

"No message," he said brusquely and hung up.

He charted her menstrual cycle even more diligently than before, marking the days off on his calendar.

He got hooked on a soap opera.

He watched senior tour golf tournaments and chess matches on the sports networks, and they moved even more slowly than his days.

He perused the classified ads daily, but unless he wanted to be a telemarketer, he found nothing he could do anonymously, and he knew before trying that no one would hire the infamous Griff Burkett.

Desperately lonely one afternoon, he called Marcia and invited himself for dinner. "I'll bring the dinner and the wine. How can you pass up a deal like that?"

"I appreciate the offer. But give me a bit more time, Griff."

Time. It had become his enemy.

By way of consolation, Marcia offered to set him up with one of her girls. He declined, which brought on her husky, sexy laugh. It was good to hear her laughing again, a sign that the old Marcia was emerging from the bandages and the trauma. "You don't want a date with one of my talented girls? That's interesting. Are you seeing someone?"

He experienced a vivid flashback to Laura, moving beneath him, purring that low, sexy sound that he now heard in his dreams. "Yeah. I'm seeing someone."

He spent most of his time restlessly pacing the rooms of his condo, wondering when he would hear from her, *if* he would hear from her, *what* he would hear.

Rodarte didn't reappear. Griff could only hope the Vista boys had strongly advised him against hassling Griff further. But that was naïvely optimistic. Contrary to what Rodarte had implied, he wasn't in league with Vista or answerable to them. And even if he had been, they would have supported any bad ending he had planned for Griff Burkett.

He considered warning Bolly and Jason of an ugly man in an ugly car, but he was afraid that would spook Bolly and he would scotch the coaching sessions, and that one hour each day was the only hour during which Griff was marginally distracted.

He called Laura twice more at her office, without success. After the second time, he brazenly called her cell phone. Knowing that she would recognize his number on caller ID, he was surprised but elated when she answered. But all she said before hanging up was "Stop calling me. You can't call me."

He tried to exhaust himself by swimming laps. On the days he didn't swim, he ran miles. He worked out in the gym as though he were still in training. He went to multiscreen cinemas and saw every movie on the marquee.

He killed time.

Finally, while waiting inside a fruit smoothie store for his yogurt-and-berry blend, the call came. He almost dropped his cell phone as he snapped it off his belt and flipped up the cover. "Hello?"

"Griff, Foster Speakman. Congratulations."

His field of vision shrank to a pinpoint, consumed by onrushing blackness. The clerk behind the counter signaled to him that his drink was ready. Griff looked at him with misapprehension. He turned and left the store. Out on the sidewalk, he stood in the shade, but heat had been trapped beneath the canvas awning. It was like being inside an oven. He was suffocating.

"Griff? Did you hear me?"

"Uh, yeah, I'm just . . ." His hand had grown slippery with sweat. He switched his phone to the other. "I guess 'congratulations' means you've got good news for me."

"We've been successful." The millionaire didn't even try to contain his jubilation. "Laura's pregnant."

The disgruntled clerk came out of the store, bringing Griff's smoothie with him. He had a silver bar piercing his eyebrow and yellow teeth that needed orthodontia. "You can't just order something and then walk out."

Ignoring him, Griff asked, "Are you sure?"

"Three home pregnancy tests this morning were all positive. That's pretty much indisputable."

"Hey, I'm talking to you," the clerk said. "You're gonna pay for this." He thrust the drink at Griff.

"Hold on a minute," he said to Speakman. Covering the phone, he grabbed the drink, which looked nauseatingly frothy and rich, and hurled it into the nearby trash can. He stuffed a five-dollar bill into the pocket of the clerk's shirt. "Now get the fuck out of my face before I rip that thing out of your eyebrow."

"They should've left you in prison to rot." Sneering, the clerk shot Griff the finger and went back inside the store.

Griff took several deep breaths, and all that did was inflate his lungs with scorching air.

"Apparently I caught you at a bad time," Speakman said.

"Not really. I was paying out at a store. I apologize. How reliable are those home pregnancy tests?"

"I shared your skepticism. Laura, too. She was reluctant to take the tests in the first place, afraid that doing so might jinx it." He laughed. "But once the third one came out positive, she began to believe it was true. A test at the doctor's office confirmed it."

"She's already gone to a doctor?"

"This morning. She pleaded with her gynecologist's office to work her in. They did a blood test. They just called her with the happy news that her hormone level indicates that she's pregnant."

"Is she there with you?" Griff imagined them hugging each other, laughing, crying with joy.

"She was at the office, but she's on her way home now. I've iced down the champagne. Well, *I'll* have champagne. Laura, of course, can no longer drink, so I've got club soda on ice for her." Speakman laughed. Griff forced himself to join in. "I wanted to share the news with you immediately. You've just become a very rich man."

"Yeah. It's kinda hard to take in."

"Would it be convenient for you to come to the house tomorrow evening? I've worked out the details of that hitch."

"Hitch?"

"How you would continue to be paid in the event that neither Laura nor I outlived you."

"Oh, that."

It seemed like a long time ago since he had been in the library of the mansion, sipping Coke from cut crystal, talking about deal points, hammering out the details of this bizarre arrangement. Now that he thought back on it, it seemed like a dream. And only now did he realize that he'd never thought it would actually work out as planned. He hadn't counted on it ending to everyone's satisfaction. But it had. The Speakmans were going to have the child they wanted. He was going to be a millionaire again. He was set for life.

He felt like he'd been hit with a sack of shit.

"It's an unlikely scenario," Speakman was saying, "but I've worked out a contingency for it. Also, we'd like to pay you your half million in person."

"I thought we weren't supposed to ever see each other again."

"Just this once. This is a special occasion, and I want to give it the ceremony it deserves. A gesture of our eternal gratitude. Will you come?"

"Sure," Griff heard himself say. "What time?"

He arrived at eight-thirty on the dot. He dialed the house from the gate, identified himself to Manuelo, and the gate swung open. The aide opened the door even before Griff rang the bell. He was wearing his customary black, his smile as vacuous as before. He didn't say a word before ushering Griff through the vaulted entry and into the familiar library, where Foster was waiting. Alone.

"Griff!" he exclaimed happily. He did a funny thing with his chair before wheeling it forward. Smiling ear to ear, he clasped Griff's right hand between both of his and pumped it enthusiastically. "I'm so glad you could come."

"Wouldn't have missed it."

"Worth the errand, huh? Five hundred thousand in cash. Do you have an armored truck to go home in?"

Griff laughed as expected.

"What would you like to drink?"

He nodded at the highball glass sitting on the end table at Speakman's elbow. "One of those will be fine."

"*Uno más,*" Speakman told Manuelo, who went immediately to

the bar and poured Griff a drink from a decanter. As soon as he delivered it, Speakman motioned that the aide could leave. Manuelo pulled the double doors closed behind him.

Speakman retrieved his drink from the table. "I drank an entire bottle of champagne last night and woke up with a terrible headache this morning. But you can toast with good bourbon, too, can't you?" He raised his glass. "To our success."

"To our success," Griff echoed. He took a hefty swig of the whiskey, which burned all the way down. "Mrs. Speakman isn't joining us?"

"Unfortunately, no. A matter has been brewing in Austin for several months. A baggage handling problem that needed her attention. Or so she thought. I tried to talk her out of going, but she insisted that one of us needed to see to the resolution, and she thought the quick round-trip would be too much for me."

Griff figured that was the excuse she'd given her husband. The truth of it was that she had hightailed it to Austin because she didn't want to see *him*. Her absence sent a clear message that caused him to waver somewhere between longing to lay eyes on her again and anger over her cowardice about meeting him face-to-face after that last afternoon together.

"I won't let her take on that extra work for much longer," Speakman said. "From now until the baby is born, my hardest job will be getting her to delegate responsibility. She's stubborn when it comes to turning a chore over to someone else." He chuckled with self-deprecation. "Of course, so am I. But we both want to be full-time parents. When the baby arrives, I have no doubt she'll devote herself to mothering."

Of course, that was what this had been about, wasn't it? Laura wanted a baby. She wanted to give her husband a baby. A few orgasms had been a bonus, but they sure as hell hadn't changed her agenda, and he'd been a damn fool to think they might.

He was no different than a sperm bank, except that he had party favors—a hard dick, fingers, a tongue. He'd got her off a few times. So? So, nothing. She belonged to Foster Speakman, and so did the baby she would have. Bingo. Mission accomplished. Time to pop corks.

So long, Griff Burkett. It was nice knowing you. Nice fucking you. Nice fucking you over.

And if he had any doubt of that, he had only to listen to her husband's gushing monologue. "You should have seen her this morning when that third test was positive." He placed his fist over his mouth to contain his rising emotion. "Her face . . . I've never seen her look more beautiful than when she smiled at me and said, 'We have a baby.' *We.* That two-letter word was extremely meaningful to a man in my condition."

"I'll bet."

Speakman didn't seem to pick up on Griff's snideness. He was too caught up in his euphoria. "Even before she took the test, I knew she was pregnant. Her breasts are already fuller. So tender she won't let me touch them." He laughed. "It would embarrass her, my telling you this. Forgive me for going on and on. I can't help it. My heart is full to overflowing. And I'm still a bit drunk, I think."

That reminded him to offer Griff another drink. Griff declined with a shake of his head. At the mention of Laura's breasts, he'd shot the remainder of his whiskey. It had made his ears ring and his heart beat fast. He felt clammy and a little nauseated.

"Do you have any inclinations toward what it is?" Foster asked.

"What what is?"

"The baby. Did you feel particularly abundant in X's or Y's the day it was conceived?"

On the day it was conceived, what he'd felt was Laura. Her skin. Her heat. Her passion. The whiskey had caused his throat to sting, but he managed to say, "No. I never thought about it one way or the other."

"I think about it constantly," Speakman admitted sheepishly. "Our child's sex—in fact, all its characteristics—were determined the instant the egg was fertilized. Isn't that amazing?"

"Amazing." *Amazing how many times I came inside her.*

"I can't wait to know whether it's a boy or a girl, but we can't find out till the fifth month."

Amazing how many times we came together.

Speakman chuckled. "Five months from now you'll probably be

lying on the beach of some Caribbean island with a cold drink in one hand and a hot chick in the other."

Griff forced a smile. "Sounds good."

"I guess you'll eventually know about the baby. What it is. What we named it. You'll probably read the announcement in the newspaper."

"If that Caribbean island gets newspapers."

Speakman grinned. "You're sure you won't have another drink?"

"No thanks."

Speakman reached for Griff's glass and carried it with him to the bar. As before, he went through a ritual of placing their glasses in the rack beneath the sink, wiping the spotless countertop, and folding the towel until all the edges were even. After he'd hung it in the towel ring, he adjusted the hem again. When it finally met with his satisfaction, he washed his hands with sanitizer.

Then he lightly slapped the arms of his wheelchair three times. "Now, down to business." He did that weird back-and-forth thing with his chair, then rolled over to the desk. On top was what appeared to be a box of stationery. Indicating it, he said, "Your money."

Griff made no move toward it.

Speakman, misreading his hesitancy, laughed. "Go ahead. It's yours. Look in the box."

Griff approached the desk and indifferently lifted the lid off the box. Inside it were stacks of hundred-dollar bills, neatly banded with paper strips.

"Pretty, isn't it?"

Griff gnawed the inside of his cheek, saying nothing. He was afraid of what he would say if he spoke, afraid he would tell Speakman the low opinion he had of a man who would pay another to have sex with his wife, no matter how lofty the reason.

Out of curiosity, he'd looked up that Bible story. It was the wife, Sarah, who had sent another woman to her husband, but basically the situation was the same. It hadn't worked out too well in Genesis. In fact, things had got real mucked up. And all because this Sarah had wanted a baby, and wanted it her way.

You could tell yourself it was only biology, but it was still sex. It was still a man and woman lying down together and using equipment that was functional but also pleasure giving. Nobody had yet invented anything more intimate.

What he wanted to know was: How could any man ask that of his *wife*? Contempt for Foster Speakman roiled inside his gut along with the whiskey, along with his jealousy.

Of course, he was no prince of virtue. He was taking the man's cash. He would deal with his disgust for himself later. But right now, he was revolted by Speakman, who was smiling at him like he'd won a jackpot, smiling without giving a thought to the emotional turmoil Griff and Laura had suffered for the sake of his foolish, selfish, stubborn demand.

"I won't be insulted if you want to count it."

Griff shook his head.

Speakman looked at him curiously. "Frankly, I'm surprised."

"By?"

"Your reserve. Have you gone shy on me?"

"What did you expect?"

"More . . ." He made a rolling motion with his hands. "Reaction. Exuberance. You act almost reluctant to take your pay, like you're sorry—" He broke off and studied Griff for a moment, then began to laugh. "Oh, dear."

"What?"

"You don't want it to end, do you? That's it, isn't it? You're sorry those afternoon interludes with Laura are at an end."

"That's nuts."

Speakman shook his index finger at him. "I don't think so."

"Let's just settle our business so I can get outta here." Even to his own pounding ears, his voice sounded like a growl.

"Ah, Griff, don't be embarrassed. Making love to my wife is no hardship duty. Well I know. How could you help but get a crush on her? Like your gambling, you developed a taste for her, didn't you? The more you had, the more you wanted. Now it's hard to give her up. I understand. Truly I do."

Griff clenched his fists.

Speakman chuckled again, then held up both hands, palms out.

"I'm sorry, I'm sorry, I'm sorry. I apologize for laughing at you, but it's just so damn amusing. Your job is over and you've earned your money, but you're heartbroken about it. Can't you appreciate the irony?" Speakman winked up at him. "You're so downcast, I think you must have *really* enjoyed doing her."

That clipped the last tenuous thread of Griff's restraint. He gave vent to his disgust. "You sick fuck."

"Possibly," Speakman said affably. "But at least I'm not horny for another man's wife, for a woman I can never, ever have again. Poor Griff, poor Griff, poor Griff."

Griff glared down at him through a red mist of rage, then turned his head away and searched the desktop, looking for something, anything, that would silence that maddening, taunting chant.

"Mrs. Speakman?"

Laura had been staring through the airplane window as the jet made its final approach into Dallas. She'd been addressed by a flight attendant leaning across the empty aisle seat.

"When we get to the gate, I'll be escorting you off ahead of the other passengers."

"Oh, no, please don't." She disliked being given any special treatment when on a SunSouth flight.

The young woman smiled. "Sorry, orders from the cockpit."

"Why?"

"The tower informed the pilot that you were being met immediately upon arrival."

"Met? By whom?"

The attendant lowered her voice to a whisper. "Maybe by that handsome husband of yours. I remember that time on your birthday when he set up a string orchestra in baggage claim. Such a romantic surprise. Anyway, you're to obey captain's orders and disembark first."

She hoped that Foster didn't have an elaborate homecoming planned for her tonight. It had been an exhausting day, starting early and ending much later than it should have. All she wanted to do was go home, take a quick shower, and then have a long night's sleep.

The pilots made a perfect landing, right on time. She made a mental note to report that to Foster.

After a short taxi to the gate, a flight attendant got on the PA and asked the other passengers to remain seated. Laura felt self-conscious as she was ushered up the aisle. She smiled an apology to passengers with whom she made eye contact.

When she reached the cockpit door, the captain was standing there. He doffed the bill of his hat. "Mrs. Speakman."

"Flawless flight, Captain Morris," she said, reading his name tag with peripheral vision, a knack she'd developed over the years.

"Thank you."

But his expression was grave, and because he didn't engage her in conversation, she felt a prickle of apprehension. "Is something the matter?"

"Please." He gestured toward the open aircraft door. She stepped into the Jetway and was surprised that the pilot accompanied her. Even more surprising, he placed his hand beneath her elbow. Before she could react to that, she noticed two men coming toward them.

They were wearing the dress uniforms of senior police officers. Upon seeing her, they respectfully removed their hats.

Her footsteps faltered. The pilot's hand tightened around her elbow.

"What's happened?" The words came out drily, scratchily, barely audible. Then she cried out, *"What's happened?"*

The homicide detective stared down at the corpse and blew out a gust of air. "Jesus Christ."

His partner, a man of few words, grunted assent.

A member of the Crime Scene Response team, who for the past hour had been collecting evidence, agreed with a sad shake of his head. "Bad, huh? Bad as I've ever seen. Maybe not as gruesome as some murders, but . . . well, only a real cold-blooded bastard could do this."

"Or a real *hot*-blooded one," the first detective remarked.

"Crime of passion, you think?"

"Maybe. Whatever, the son of a bitch deserves to get the needle."

His partner harrumphed again.

"Excuse me, Detectives?" A uniformed officer appeared in the open double doors of the library. "You said to let you know as soon as Mrs. Speakman got here. They're taking her into the living room now. That way." He motioned in the general direction.

When the pair of investigators entered the room, Laura Speakman was standing between two police chaplains. One gave them a surreptitious nod, letting them know that she'd been told, but that was obvious. She was as pale as the dead body.

The taciturn detective took up a position against the wall. The other advanced into the room. "Mrs. Speakman?"

"My husband's dead? There's no mistake?"

"No mistake. I'm sorry."

Her knees buckled. The chaplains guided her down onto a sofa. One sat near her, placing his arm protectively along the back of the seat. The other asked a uniformed officer to get her a glass of water.

As the detective approached, he withdrew his card from the breast pocket of his jacket and extended it to her. "Stanley Rodarte, ma'am. Homicide detective, Dallas PD."

CHAPTER

22

L AURA, HE'S HERE."

Kay Stafford had appeared in the doorway of Laura's bedroom, where she was reclined on a chaise. The draperies were drawn. The room was cool and dim. Her assistant spoke quietly and slowly, the way everyone was addressing her today, as though fearing a sudden noise might cause her to shatter like crystal. They could have been right.

"I put him in the den," Kay said. "Take your time coming down. He said he would wait."

Laura sat up and slipped her feet into her shoes. "I might just as well talk to him now, although I don't know what I can tell him today that I couldn't tell him last night."

Detective Rodarte had stayed until almost midnight. He'd spent some of that time questioning her. The rest of the time he, his silent partner, and other police personnel had moved in and out of the library, doing whatever it was they did at the scene of an apparent murder.

They consulted in hushed voices, casting looks in her direction, occasionally asking her for information. She was asked by a solicitous policewoman if there was someone she should call. "Someone to stay with you tonight."

Neither she nor Foster had family. Since the accident, they hadn't kept close contact with friends. "My assistant," she replied.

She'd given the policewoman Kay's home number. Kay had arrived within a half hour, sharing Laura's shock but somehow managing to perform the simple tasks that Laura seemed incapable of doing. She gave directions, supplied answers to practical questions, and dealt with the telephone, which had begun to ring with irritating frequency.

Kay had a notepad in her hand as they walked downstairs together. "I hate to bother you with all this now, Laura."

"Go ahead. I don't have the luxury of collapsing. That will come later, when . . . when everything's settled. What do you need?"

A proviso of Foster's will, which he'd altered when they married, was that, in the event of his death, Laura would serve as head of Sun-South until the board could elect another. She'd been granted power of attorney to make decisions and conduct business. So, in addition to becoming a widow last night, she'd stepped into the role of CEO.

Kay said, "The media are camped outside the entrance of our building, awaiting a statement."

"Ask Joe to write something generic. 'Everyone at SunSouth is stunned by this tragic event, et cetera.' But ask him not to release it before faxing it here for my approval." She trusted her marketing head to write an appropriate press release, but it was her practice, as well as Foster's, to sign off on everything. "Tell him not to conduct a formal press conference or respond to any questions about the . . . the crime. We'll leave that to the police."

Kay checked that item off her list. "Operations has asked if they should coordinate a minute of silence in memory of Foster. Anything like that?"

Laura smiled wanly and shook her head. "Foster wouldn't allow the schedule to be interrupted even by one minute. But the thought is appreciated. Make sure everyone knows that."

"Have you given any thought to funeral arrangements?"

Laura, having reached the bottom of the staircase, stopped and turned to her. "I can't schedule the funeral until the body has been released."

Unexpectedly, tears filled her eyes. Two years ago, following the car accident, Foster had lain in an ICU clinging to life. She'd feared that each breath would be his last and that soon she would be organizing his funeral. But she hadn't had time to prepare for talking in those terms now. This time it was a sudden reality. There would be a funeral. When it would be she didn't yet know.

Last night she had been advised not to go into the library. She had taken that advice. What had been described to her was grotesque, and she hadn't wanted that to be her last image of Foster. It had been jolting enough to see the zippered body bag as it was wheeled out on a gurney. Inside the bag was her husband's body, but to the police, it was evidence.

Sensing her employer's distress, Kay said, "I apologize for having to mention it. But people are keeping the phone lines hot, here at the house and at our offices, asking when the service will be and where. The lobby is already full to overflowing with flowers."

Laura touched her assistant's hand. "I'll let you know as soon as I know something. In the meantime, ask Joe to include in the press release that in lieu of flowers, people could make donations to Elaine's foundation. Foster would prefer that."

"Of course. One last thing. The governor issued a statement this morning, extolling Foster as an entrepreneur, model Texan, and human being. Then she called to ask if there was anything she could do on a personal level, as a friend to you both."

"I'll respond personally as soon as I can. In the meantime, tell her how much I appreciate her thoughtfulness."

Kay accompanied her as far as the den, where Detective Stanley Rodarte was waiting. *Rodarte.* Laura had recognized the name instantly from Griff Burkett's warning. He'd been sure to include mention of an olive drab sedan but had failed to tell her that Rodarte was a homicide detective with the Dallas Police Department.

Rodarte was studying a painting of an English hunting scene. He turned when she walked in. "Is this an original?"

"I believe so."

"Hmm," he said, sounding impressed. "Must have cost a bundle."

She didn't honor that with a response.

"Sure is a beautiful home, Mrs. Speakman."

"Thank you."

"Did you redecorate when you moved in after marrying Mr. Speakman?"

"Elaine Speakman had done such an excellent job with the decor, I saw no need to change it."

Oddly, his smile didn't improve his looks. It made him uglier. "Most second wives want to rub out all traces of the first."

The statement was inappropriate and irrelevant. She thought he'd said it only to see how she would react. She hadn't warmed to him last night, sensing immediately that he was crass and sly. Now she decided she disliked him intensely.

"I'm being asked about funeral arrangements," she said.

"The ME is performing the autopsy this afternoon. Depending on what it shows, we should be able to release the body to you either tomorrow or the next day. But I advise against making any definite plans without clearing them with me."

"I understand."

Turning her back on him, she moved to one of the leather sofas and was about to sit down when he stopped her. "If you wouldn't mind, I'd like you to look at the library now. See if you notice anything out of kilter. Beyond the obvious, that is."

She'd known that sooner or later she would be required to go in. She was torn, one part of her needing to see the spot where Foster had died, another resistant to ever entering the room again. Given a choice, she might have postponed it for as long as possible, making the dread of it torturous. In a way, she was glad Rodarte had relieved her of having to make the decision on her own.

Woodenly, she left the den and led the way across the vestibule to the double doors of the library. The hardware on them had been dusted for fingerprints. Seeing that she noticed the smudged dark powder, Rodarte said, "Murder is messy business."

He pushed the doors open, and she stepped into the room. "You remember Carter," Rodarte said.

His partner detective, whom she recognized from the night before, was standing in front of a wall of bookshelves, silent and grim as a sentinel. Neither his stance nor his expression changed when she came in.

Except for him, most of the room looked surprisingly normal. Only one area near the desk was in disarray. The desk itself and everything on it had been dusted for fingerprints. An end table lay on its side. The lamp and everything else that had been on the table were scattered across the rug, most broken. The rug itself was buckled. Foster had never allowed even the fringe of it to be mussed, insisting that it be raked several times a day.

She made an involuntary hiccuping sound when she saw his wheelchair.

And there was blood. On the wheelchair. On the rug. On the desk.

Rodarte touched her elbow. "Would you like to do this later?"

What she would have liked was for him not to touch her. She removed her elbow from his hand. "Other than what is obvious, it doesn't appear that anything has been disturbed."

"Good." He pointed her toward a seating group. "Let's sit down."

"In here?"

He shrugged and made a face that asked, *Why not?*

Either he was stupid and insensitive, a jerk, or just plain cruel. Laura suspected the latter, but she didn't want to take issue with him over where he would conduct this interview. "I've been sitting or lying down all day. I'd rather stand." She went over to the wall of windows, keeping her back to the room.

Forgoing a graceful lead-in, Rodarte asked, "Why did you go to Austin yesterday?"

Out of the corner of her eye, she noted that Carter had finally moved. He took a small notebook and pen from his breast pocket. But it was apparent that he was merely reinforcement. Rodarte was the lead investigator.

"At my husband's request, I went to handle a problem. There had been reports of luggage theft. Our handlers had been accused. One, as it turned out, was guilty. The Austin police have the reports if you care to check."

"You took a SunSouth flight back?"

"The nine o'clock, last of the evening. On final approach for landing, the flight attendant notified me that I would be escorted off the aircraft. Your chaplains met me in the Jetway. They took me to a private lounge in the airport and told me that my husband had died. I didn't learn that he'd been murdered until you told me."

"Up to the point when you were escorted off the plane, you didn't know that anything was amiss here at home?"

"How could I?"

"Phone call? Text message?"

"I didn't know anything was amiss."

"You'd been gone all day. Did you talk to your husband yesterday at any time?"

"Around noon, he called my cell to ask how things were going. Then I called him around six to tell him that the matter had been settled and that I would be on the nine o'clock flight back and not to wait dinner on me."

"Just those two calls?"

"Yes."

"Did Mr. Speakman have any appointments scheduled last night?"

"None I was aware of."

"Well, apparently he did meet with someone here."

She turned and looked at him.

"There was no sign of a break-in," he said by way of explanation. "Whoever killed your husband was let into the house."

"Manuelo would have answered the door."

He frowned. "We still can't find him, Mrs. Speakman."

Last night when Rodarte had asked her help in reconstructing the crime scene, she had mentioned the aide. Rodarte had written down his full name. When she explained what Manuelo's duties encompassed, the detective had ordered that the entire estate be searched. There had been no sign of the man.

"His room over the garage is still empty," he told her now. "Bed is made, no dishes in the sink. Clothes in the closet. He doesn't own a car, right?"

"Not to my knowledge."

"And none of the vehicles belonging to you and Mr. Speakman is missing. So how did Mr. Ruiz leave and where did he go?"

"I have no idea. The only thing I know with certainty is that he wouldn't have left Foster alone."

"Does he have relatives?"

"I don't believe so. At least none I know of."

"You're sure he was on duty last night?"

"He's always on duty, Mr. Rodarte."

"Twenty-four/seven?"

"Yes."

"Your housekeeper-cook, Mrs. uh—"

"Dobbins."

"Right. She said she leaves at six o'clock."

"As soon as dinner is prepared. I can't imagine why there would have been a change in that schedule. Have you questioned Mrs. Dobbins about last night?"

"She put a roasted chicken in the warming tray and left at six. She said Manuelo Ruiz was here when she left. She's sure of that because she told him she was leaving. So it's assumed he was here."

"I'm certain he was. He wouldn't have left Foster alone," she repeated. "Never."

Rodarte walked over to the area in front of the desk where the rug was bunched up. He squatted down as though to study the dark stains on it. "Much as I hate to, we need to talk about the actual slaying."

"Must we? You were so descriptive last night. It sounded very . . . horrible."

"It was. That's why I advised you against looking at your husband's body. It was nothing you wanted to see, believe me. He was still in his wheelchair with a letter opener sticking out the side of his neck."

She hugged her elbows tightly against her torso. "I'm certain by your description that it was Foster's letter opener. It was a replica of Excalibur. I gave it to him for Christmas because he loved the Arthurian legend. It stayed on his desk there."

"Mrs. Dobbins confirmed that. But once I get it from the ME, I'll have you identify it so there'll be absolutely no doubt."

Something else to dread, she thought.

Rodarte said, "What it looks like is, the killer pushed it in to the hilt, then tried to pull it out. But the blade had severed the artery, so when he tried to remove the weapon from your husband's neck, the wound started gushing blood. I guess he panicked and decided to leave it."

"And my husband bled to death."

"Right." Rodarte stood up. "We found two blood types on the rug. One was your husband's."

"Two?" She looked at the bloodstains, then at Carter, finally back at Rodarte.

He shrugged. "We don't know who the second type belongs to. Could be Manuelo Ruiz's, but we have nothing to match it with. Except for the DMV, Ruiz isn't in any database we've run him through. He has a current Texas driver's license. That's it."

"He drove Foster in a customized van."

"Did Ruiz have papers?"

"Immigration papers? I assume so."

"He didn't."

Her temper sparked. "If you knew that, why did you ask?"

He gave her what he probably mistook for a disarming grin. "Habit. Always trying to trap somebody in a lie. Hazard of my job."

"I'll tell you the truth, Detective."

His face brightened. "Will you?"

"Yes."

"Good. Tell me about you and Griff Burkett."

She hadn't seen that coming. A wave of dizziness assailed her.

Noticing her instability, Rodarte motioned her toward a sofa. "This may take awhile. Want to rethink sitting down?"

She hated conceding that she needed to, but she did. She sat down in an armchair. Rodarte offered to get her a glass of water. She declined with a shake of her head. He sat in the chair facing hers and, leaning toward her, clasped his hands between his widespread knees. She noticed that his fingernails needed trimming.

"I'll save us both some time here, Mrs. Speakman. Griff Burkett's fingerprints were all over the letter opener that killed your husband."

CHAPTER
23

LAURA COVERED HER MOUTH WITH HER HAND, AFRAID SHE would be ill in front of the two detectives.

"Are you okay?" Rodarte asked.

She shook her head, surged to her feet, and ran from the room. She barely made it into the powder room in time to retch into the toilet. Because she hadn't eaten anything since dinner the evening before, there wasn't much to empty. But the bile was bitter and continued to make her gag for several minutes. When the spasms finally ceased, her clothing was drenched with sweat. Her ears buzzed, her extremities tingled, and she was trembling uncontrollably.

She covered her face with her hands. From the moment she saw the police chaplains in the Jetway, she'd known that what they were about to tell her was catastrophic and that, whatever it was, Griff Burkett was involved. That overwhelming intuition had now been confirmed, and she wasn't sure she could survive it. Knowing that he'd killed Foster might very well be the death of her, the death of the child she carried.

But she couldn't think of the baby now or she truly would go mad.

"Laura?" Kay was knocking on the door. "Laura?"

"Just a moment." She rinsed her mouth out and splashed cold water over her face, which was as pale as chalk. She ran her fingers through her hair, then, forcibly composing herself, opened the powder room door.

Kay was there, Rodarte just behind her. His expression was more inquisitive than concerned. Kay said, "I'm taking you upstairs and putting you to bed."

"No. I'm better now. But could you please bring me a glass of Coke, Sprite, something fizzy?"

Kay was reluctant to leave her, but she went to fix the drink. Laura brushed past Rodarte and led him back into the library. Her knees were rubbery. Her damp clothes made her chilled in the air-conditioning. She wrapped herself in a throw before returning to the chair she had so quickly vacated.

The other detective hadn't left his post, or even moved as far as Laura could tell. The three remained in silence until Kay delivered her the requested drink. "Call me if you need me," she said, shot Rodarte a baleful look, and gave Laura's arm a reassuring squeeze.

"Thank you, Kay. Please close the doors as you leave."

Laura sipped her glass of soda, hoping it would settle her stomach and not come right back up.

Again Rodarte began without preamble. "Did you know him before he went to prison?"

She shook her head.

"Only since he got out?"

She nodded.

"How did you meet? Where?"

"In this room." She could tell that surprised him. "Foster was interested in him. He'd heard on the news that he was being released. He wrote to him, asked him to meet with him here."

"Interested in him, how? What was it about a criminal football player that interested your husband?"

Looking him right in the eye, she lied. "I don't know." Telling the truth wasn't an option. She had to protect her child's future. She also had to protect the secrecy that Foster had insisted upon. "Mr. Burkett was only here that one time. By the time I was asked to join them for an introduction, they had concluded the business part of their meeting and were having a drink together."

"It was friendly?"

"Very. At least it seemed so."

He studied her a moment. She wasn't sure he believed her. In fact, she was almost certain he didn't. But there was no one to dispute her. "Was it during this friendly get-together that sparks ignited between you and Burkett?"

"Excuse me?"

"How soon after that did you two start hooking up at that house on Windsor?"

The glass of soda almost slipped from her unsteady hand.

He grinned. "I bet you're wondering how I know about your romance. Well, see, I've had my eye on Burkett ever since the day he got out of Big Spring."

"Why?"

"I investigated the murder of Bill Bandy. Does that name mean anything to you?"

"Griff Burkett was implicated in his murder."

"He *committed* the murder, Mrs. Speakman. No question in my mind. But he was clever, didn't leave any hard evidence, not enough for me to get an indictment from the grand jury. But there's no statute of limitations on homicide. If it's the last thing I do, I'll see justice done for the late Bill Bandy."

Griff had known the detective was following him. It was clear now why he hadn't wanted her talking to Rodarte, why he had used scare tactics to warn her against being alone with him. He hadn't wanted her to hear the conviction in Rodarte's voice when he said, *He committed the murder.*

"He was more careless this time," Rodarte was saying. "Or more arrogant. Leaving behind the murder weapon. Fingerprints."

"Why do you think he did that?"

"First thing I intend to ask him when we find him."

She raised her head and looked over at him. He read the question in her eyes.

"No, we haven't located him yet. He's gone underground. We've got cops staking out his apartment, but there's been no sign of him. That old Honda he's been driving? We found it in a strip center parking lot up in Addison. Lab guys are going over it now. I've got men watching the house on Windsor, too, but he hasn't been there. By the way, the yard service came this morning and mowed the grass, edged the sidewalk. Who pays for the upkeep on that house?"

"I do. I lease it."

He glanced around the luxurious surroundings, making a silent comparison between the two houses. When he came back to her, he said bluntly, "What for?"

She gave him a look full of meaning.

He studied her for a moment, then flashed that revolting grin. "I already knew you rented the house."

"I know," she said coldly.

He spread his hands wide. "Sorry. It was my duty to check it out, Mrs. Speakman. The lease isn't in your name, but I traced it back through that corporate name to you."

"It wouldn't have been that difficult to do." It was a subtle insult to his investigative skills, but if he caught the slight, he didn't take issue with it.

"When's the last time you saw Burkett?"

She dropped her gaze to her hands, moistly clenched in her lap. She knew the cagey detective would pick up on the body language, but she couldn't help herself. "Almost six weeks ago."

"Six weeks? That long?"

"Yes."

"You're sure?"

She gave him the exact date and saw that Carter wrote it down in his small spiral notebook.

"What made the date memorable?" Rodarte asked.

"I told him that I wouldn't be coming back."

He whistled softly. "How'd he take it?"

"He understood and accepted my decision."

"Really?" he asked skeptically.

"Really."

"Why did you end the affair?"

"I don't see the relevance of that."

"There may be none. Or it could be extremely relevant."

She lost the staring contest. "What we were doing was wrong. I couldn't do it anymore. I told him we couldn't see each other again."

"Before him, had you had other affairs?"

"No."

"No one would blame you. In light of Mr. Speakman's . . ."

"Mr. Speakman's what?" she demanded frostily.

He backed down. "Burkett was your first and only affair since you married Speakman?"

"That's what I said."

"And when you broke it off, Burkett didn't argue, put up a fuss, beg you to reconsider?"

"No."

"Huh." Thoughtfully, he scratched his acne-scarred cheek. "That doesn't sound like the Griff Burkett I know."

Coolly she said, "Then perhaps you don't know him very well."

"Apparently you don't, either, Mrs. Speakman. Because when you called off your affair, Burkett didn't take it lying down. Not at all. He's been simmering over it. Last night he came here, overpowered Manuelo Ruiz, then drove a letter opener into your husband's neck. Classic crime of a jilted lover."

She forced herself not to look away from him. She deserved his implied scorn, she supposed, although in light of her grief, and guilt, it seemed unusually cruel punishment. It was one thing to endure the censure of people you respected. It was quite another to bear the scorn of someone you held in low esteem.

He got up and walked to the desk. "You're sure nothing is missing from this room?"

"I don't believe so. I can't be sure until I've looked more thoroughly."

"When you feel like it, please do."

"Certainly."

"Does this mean anything to you?"

He'd pulled on a pair of latex gloves to pick a single sheet of paper up off the desk. He carried it over to her. "I wanted you to see this before I bagged it as evidence."

He held the sheet so she could read the typewritten paragraphs. There were three of them. After several tries to get through the first sentence with any degree of comprehension, she looked up at him with puzzlement. "It's nonsense."

He laughed shortly. "I'm glad you said that. I thought I was losing it. It made no sense to me, either. It's just a bunch of big words strung together, right?"

"Just a bunch of big words."

"Any explanation?"

"No."

"Do you think your husband typed these paragraphs?"

"Why would he?"

"Beats me. I wondered if maybe he'd lost some of his mental faculties, too."

She was affronted by the question, and she let it show. " 'Too'?"

"If I seem insensitive, I'm sorry. Your husband's physical condition was obvious. How was he mentally? A lot of people depended on him being Foster Speakman, CEO. Employees. Stockholders. Even passengers who fly SunSouth relied on him being all there."

"Let me assure you that he was *all there,* Mr. Rodarte. Foster was in full command of his faculties."

"I thought maybe his car accident had jarred something loose." He tapped the side of his head. "Maybe you hadn't even noticed."

"I would have noticed."

"Well, the signs could've slipped past you. You've been awfully busy."

He paused strategically. *Busy with your lover.* That was the implication. She refused to take the bait and only stared at him with a passivity she was far from feeling.

"Your husband took medication."

"Yes. Drugs to strengthen his immune system. Others for the health of his digestive tract, which was severely damaged in his accident. Sometimes a sleep medication."

"Along with those, he took prescriptions for acute anxiety. I'll spare us some more time here, Mrs. Speakman. I've already talked to your husband's psychiatrist."

Laura drew a deep breath. "As an adolescent Foster was diagnosed with OCD. Obsessive—"

"I know what it is."

"Then you also know that it can be controlled with medication."

"I believe you." He chuckled. "I'm a little obsessive myself. You poll a hundred people on the street, nearly all are crazy in one way or another."

Such an inane remark didn't warrant a response.

"Would you say your husband's OCD was under control?"

"Yes."

"Was he depressed?"

"No."

"Not even just a little?" the detective wheedled. "For instance, he might have been a little depressed over your affair with Burkett. The guy turns my stomach for what he did, but even I gotta admit, he's got a face the ladies go for. The height. The hair. The gladiator's body. To a man who's disabled, like your husband was, that in particular would be a slap in the face. Did he know about Burkett and you?"

She shook her head.

He cupped his ear.

"No," she said tersely. "He didn't. Not to my knowledge." She stood up. "Is that all, Detective?"

"Not quite. Did Burkett try to contact you after the breakup?"

She considered lying, then thought better of it on the chance Rodarte already knew the answer to this question, too. "A couple of times, he called the SunSouth offices and tried to talk his way past Kay. I never took his calls."

"You haven't seen him since that day you told him it was over between you?"

"No."

"Or talked to him?"

"The one time he reached me, I hung up on him."

"Did he ever issue threats against your husband?"

"Of course not!"

"Did he ever suggest to you that if your handicapped husband was out of the picture, you'd be free to come back to him? Instant divorce. That kind of thing. Did he ever suggest that he might remove your husband?"

She looked at him aghast. "If he had, don't you think I would have acted on it? Reported it?"

His smirk insinuated much.

She drew herself up straight. "No, Mr. Rodarte. Griff Burkett never posed a threat to either Foster or me."

"That you know of."

She was about to speak when she realized that it was a valid speculation. Hedging, she said, "He never threatened me."

"But he could have threatened your husband without your knowledge."

"Foster never said—"

"But Burkett *could* have."

Reluctantly, she nodded.

Rodarte glanced at his mute partner, his expression tongue-in-cheek. When his attention came back to Laura, he said, "Did Burkett ever mention a hideaway? Ever talk about a friend with a lake cabin, or a private getaway, someplace he may be laying low now?"

"Nothing like that. He didn't confide in me. We didn't talk much at all."

Too late she realized she'd walked right into that one. "No, I guess not," Rodarte said, leering and casting his partner another glance. "Mrs. Speakman, it goes without saying that if you hear from Burkett, you'll contact me immediately."

"Of course."

"I'm posting some men here at the house."

"Is that necessary?"

"Burkett may have come here last night for the two of you," he said quietly. "He didn't know you were going to be in Austin, did he?"

She shook her head slowly, stunned by the thought that Griff would want to harm her. "It wasn't decided that I would go until early yesterday morning."

"So when Burkett came here last night, he expected you to be here, too."

"I suppose." She closed her eyes, trying to imagine Griff in a murderous rage. His hands were large and strong, but they could be gentle. Were they also capable of violence? She couldn't imagine that. Could she?

"I advise you to keep someone with you," Rodarte said. "Actually, I'd rather you move to an undisclosed location until Burkett is apprehended."

"I'll think about it."

"Do." He looked around the room and silently consulted Carter, who closed his notebook and slid it back into his breast pocket. "I guess that's all for now. Unless you can think of anything else that might be pertinent."

She shook her head absently. Then she remembered a question she had wanted to ask him. "Who reported the murder?"

"Nine-one-one got a call."

"From Foster?"

Rodarte shook his head. "The ME said he wouldn't have had time. He wouldn't have been able. And there was no phone near him."

"Manuelo doesn't speak English."

"No, the caller definitely spoke English."

"So it was Griff Burkett."

Rodarte shrugged. "Looks like."

CHAPTER
24

GRIFF WOKE UP WONDERING WHERE THE HELL HE WAS.
And then he remembered, and wished he had remained asleep.

Foster Speakman's blood was on his hands. The man had died fighting for his life, blood gushing from his neck, his terrified eyes fixed on Griff.

Griff sat up and buried his face in his hands. "Fuck me."

If not already, then very soon, every cop in Texas and neighboring states was going to be looking for him. When the fingerprints on the letter opener in Foster Speakman's neck were run through databases and matched to Griff's, Rodarte would feel like he'd won the lottery. Better.

He hadn't got Griff for Bill Bandy. But this time there was so much physical evidence placing Griff in the Speakmans' library at the time of Foster's death, they probably wouldn't even bother with a trial.

Nor was there any question of motive. Rodarte knew about Griff's rendezvous with Laura and had determined they were for sex. All the elements stacked up. Griff Burkett would go straight to death row. He might just as well start swabbing his arm in preparation for the needle.

Rodarte would go on TV and say that Griff Burkett, already

a convicted felon who had been implicated in one murder, had gone to the Speakman mansion, argued with the defenseless, cuckolded husband—who was confined to a wheelchair, for crissake—and savagely stabbed him. No doubt he would emphasize the savagery of the crime by throwing in a few more adverbs, like *ruthlessly, brutally,* and *heinously.*

The media would lick their chops. The story contained the juicy ingredients that make a reporter salivate: A victim already stricken with tragedy. Money. Sex. A cozy rendezvous. A ne'er-do-well who had seduced the beautiful wife into an affair that ultimately led to the violent death of her husband.

It was the stuff that could win a Pulitzer for a journalist who didn't mind wallowing in slime.

Griff sat on the edge of the sagging mattress and looked at the bloodstains embedded in the creases of his hands. He'd scrubbed them until the small bar of soap was a sliver, and the stains were still there, an indelible part of his hand print.

Things couldn't possibly get worse.

Well, actually, they could. Laura would be told that he had killed her husband.

Last night, after fleeing the Speakmans' estate, he'd driven to his apartment and hastily packed several changes of clothing. But he didn't tarry there, knowing that would be the starting point of the search for him. He'd been at home when he was arrested the first time, dragged out in handcuffs, shamed before his neighbors, his disgrace spotlighted in the media. He didn't want a repeat of that humiliating scene, so he left hastily, taking only what he could carry, knowing he might never set foot inside the place again.

He drove to a shopping center and abandoned the red Honda in the parking lot. Soon an APB would be issued. Every law enforcement officer would be on the lookout for it, so he had to put distance between himself and the car.

He'd walked for miles, keeping to dark streets, no particular destination in mind. Just walking. Trying to figure out what the hell he was going to do now. First order of business was to find a place to hole up until he could get his head on straight.

He'd reached the motel by coming up on the back side of it. It faced an interstate highway but was set well back from it on the access road, a low-slung row of rooms squatting between a pawnshop and a store that sold retread tires for as low as $14.99. The businesses were closed, their doors bolted for the night.

It was a low-rent, hasty-tasty motel with a flickering red-neon Vacancy sign in the office window. Actually befitting him. It was the kind of place his mother would have gone to with a man she met in a bar. The kind of place where Griff might have been conceived.

The clerk was glassy-eyed from the joint he was sucking on when Griff walked in. Griff asked how much for a night, laid cash on the counter, and picked up the key that was wordlessly slid toward him. He wasn't even required to sign a register. If the junkie noticed the bloodstains, he was indifferent to them.

Griff let himself into the room, dropped his duffel bag, and went directly into the phone-booth-size bathroom. The toilet was stained. It smelled of piss. The whole room stank of other bodies, mildew, lives in ruin. He stepped into the shower fully clothed, washing himself and his clothes, letting the water run until the red current swirling around his feet faded to pink and finally became clear.

The bedspread was stained, but he was too exhausted to care. The amorous grunts and groans coming through the thin wall from the room next door kept him awake, but the rhythmic knocking of the headboard lulled him into an uneasy doze just as the sun was coming up.

Now, though, he was fully awake. It was going on noon, and he had to know just how grim his situation was. He switched on the TV that was bolted to the wall. Local stations were beginning their midday newscasts, and, as expected, Foster Speakman's murder was the lead story on every one.

They showed live video pictures of the estate's perimeter wall, police cars blocking the gated entrance. One station had its helicopter circling the property, although there wasn't a good view of the house because of the trees. A file photo of "this prominent Dallas businessman and distinguished citizen" appeared on the screen. The picture of Speakman was several years old, taken, Griff guessed, before the car accident, when he was more robust.

The governor, speaking from her office in Austin, solemnly hailed

Foster Speakman as a man who had been, and would remain, an inspiration to all who knew him. She commended him for the courage with which he had faced his personal tragedy. His murder was shocking. Her heart went out to his widow, Laura Speakman, who had demonstrated a courage and poise that matched those of her late husband. She vowed the full assistance of her office and every state agency in the apprehension and conviction of Speakman's murderer. "The perpetrator of this egregious crime will answer for it," she pledged.

A Joe somebody, whom Griff remembered from the SunSouth office parking lot, was identified as the airline's spokesperson. He resolutely dodged microphones and cameras as he waded through reporters on his way into the corporate building.

"He's promised a statement will be forthcoming shortly," the anchorwoman told her viewers. "We'll get that to you as soon as possible. Greg, you interviewed investigators at the scene. What have you learned from them?"

Greg, the field reporter, had taken up a position outside the ivy-draped estate wall. He said the police were reluctant to discuss the details of the case at this time. "One interesting aspect to this mystery," he said, "is that the victim's aide, Manuelo Ruiz, who was constantly at Mr. Speakman's side, apparently wasn't in the home last night. His absence is unexplained."

"That is interesting," the anchorwoman said without interest.

The well-coiffed anchorwoman didn't attach any importance to Manuelo's disappearance, but it was damn important to Griff that the aide hadn't yet been found.

He continued to flip through the channels until all the stations moved on to other stories. He hadn't been named as a suspect, but neither had anyone else. Only that one reporter had mentioned Manuelo. And Rodarte hadn't appeared in any of the reports Griff saw.

"Has his nose to the ground looking for me," he muttered, switching off the set.

Griff's involvement was still unknown by the general public, so that bought him a little time. He had a hiding place. It was unlikely the motel clerk would remember the guest in room number seven,

even when Griff's face started appearing on TV screens. So he had some breathing room.

His primary worry was finding Manuelo—Ruiz, was it?—before Rodarte did. But in order to do that, he needed a car.

He located a Dallas telephone directory under the bed, along with a dusty Gideon Bible. The directory had seen more use, but not by much. It was several years old, and bugs had left droppings on the pages, but it had business listings as well as residential. He used the motel's phone to place the call.

"Hunnicutt Motors."

"Is Glen there?"

"Hold please, I'll see."

He was subjected to elevator music for several minutes.

"Glen Hunnicutt." It was a booming voice as large as the man who possessed it.

"Comfort Inn. You said it could just as well have been the honeymoon suite at the Paris Ritz."

Only another ex-con, even one incarcerated in a minimum-security facility, would recognize the tone and know what it signified, would know not to blurt out a name or say too much. Following a significant pause, the car dealer said, "Hold on."

Griff heard the receiver being set down, movement, a door closing, more movement. When he came back to the phone, Glen Hunnicutt spoke in a low rumble. "How're you doin'?"

"I was doing great."

"Was?"

"Now I'm screwed. I need to borrow a car, and nobody can know about it."

Glen Hunnicutt was a successful used-car dealer. By his own admission, he'd got greedy. For several years he'd cooked his books, fudging heavily on the income he reported to the IRS. He got caught and was sent to Big Spring to repent.

Being away from his wife had been torture for him. She was all he talked about. With every breath, he bemoaned his homesickness for her and their marriage bed. One evening Hunnicutt really got the doldrums, droning on and on about his celibate misery.

"And it's not just getting laid I miss. She's special. I mean it, really. She puts up with me, and that's saying a lot. I love her so much. That may sound sappy, but it's the God's truth. I don't know if I can take being away from her. I really don't. She—"

Griff, who'd been an unwilling audience for this lament, sent his chair over backward as he lunged toward Hunnicutt. "Jesus Christ, will you shut the fuck up?"

Then he hit Hunnicutt in the mouth as hard as he could, his famous throwing arm behind the punch. His knuckles connected with Hunnicutt's perfect caps, cleanly separating them from his gums.

Hunnicutt, spitting chipped porcelain and blood, was helped to his feet by other prisoners who rushed to his aid while hurling recriminations and insults at Griff. As one held a towel to Hunnicutt's bleeding mouth, he said, "Joke's on you, asshole. You've just done Hunnicutt here a favor."

Above the heads of the others, Hunnicutt and Griff made eye contact. Griff held it for several beats before turning away.

It was possible for prisoners in minimum security to obtain furloughs—temporary, unescorted releases from the prison. They were granted for limited and specific purposes, such as a family crisis, a funeral, or specialized medical treatment. Including dentistry.

The next morning, Hunnicutt filed a formal request for a release to have his teeth fixed. He met the requirements. He was given a form that cited all the rules and restrictions of the furlough. He affixed his signature to the bottom, promising to uphold them. A few days later the warden granted him the temporary release.

In between trips to the dentist's office, Hunnicutt and his wife kept the sheets hot at the Comfort Inn in Big Spring.

For slugging his fellow prisoner, Griff was reprimanded and his privileges were temporarily revoked.

When the car dealer returned, sparkling new caps well cemented, he'd sidled up to Griff and thanked him. "What the hell are you talking about?" Griff grumbled. "I just wanted you to put a lid on it."

Knowing better, Hunnicutt said, "I owe you one. A big one."

Griff hoped Hunnicutt remembered that IOU. He was cashing it now. "Nothing fancy or flashy," he said into the greasy telephone receiver. "Just a reliable set of wheels. Will you help me?"

Following another long hesitation, Hunnicutt said, "I've got a boy now."

Griff's shoulders slumped with disappointment. He could press the issue. He could remind Hunnicutt that while he and his wife had been screwing each other blind, he'd been doing a series of menial and unpleasant tasks as punishment.

But what right did he have to drag this likable guy, a husband and now a father, into the tub of shit he was in? Hunnicutt would be guilty of aiding and abetting. He'd be violating his probation. It was a lot to ask of him. Too much.

"I understand," Griff said.

"He just turned four."

"It's okay. Forget I asked."

"He was conceived at the Comfort Inn."

Griff's heart skipped a beat. He held his breath.

Hunnicutt said, "Last row of the lot. Third car in from Lemmon Avenue. Keys will be under the mat."

Griff gripped the phone, squeezed his eyes shut, and what came from his lips might have been a silent prayer of thanks. Then he said, "If you're asked, I stole the car, okay? Don't get into trouble over this. Tell them I stole it."

Hunnicutt said nothing.

"Did you hear me?"

Hunnicutt hung up.

On foot, Griff estimated it would take him a couple hours to walk to Hunnicutt Motors. He couldn't leave until after dark. Twilight came late this time of year. He had approximately nine hours to kill.

He was hungry, but his stomach would have to wait till he could use a drive-through and decrease the chances of being recognized.

Trying to ignore the hunger pangs, he lay on the bed and stared at the dirty ceiling. He thought about Laura, the hell she must be going through, the emotional pain, the guilt.

Because by now, she would know about his fingerprints on the murder weapon. Rodarte, in his insidious way, would have told her he knew about their affair. It was a classic case of jealous outrage, almost a cliché. Her lover had killed her husband.

And how would Laura have responded? How could she have responded? Would she tell Rodarte about their contract? No. Griff couldn't see her telling all for Rodarte's avid ears. She would omit that part. Not for Griff's protection, or even her own. But for Foster Speakman's. And the child's. She might be painted a scarlet woman, but at all costs, she would preserve Foster's reputation and secure the future of her baby.

If only he could talk to her . . .

But that wasn't going to happen, so he might just as well stop wishing for it.

He opened the telephone directory again and looked for listings under Ruiz. There wasn't one for a Manuelo. He hadn't expected that kind of luck. But maybe the Salvadoran had relatives. Using the motel phone, Griff dialed the first number.

"Hola?"

"Manuelo, por favor."

His grasp of Spanish was limited to what he'd learned in two years of high school, but he gathered by what the woman said that he had the wrong number.

He went down the list, calling every Ruiz. No Manuelos. And even if he had run down the one he sought, Manuelo wouldn't have stuck around waiting for Griff to show up. He would've run like hell.

The man was no fool.

Without a car, there was nothing more Griff could do until dark. He had no choice but to wait out the long hours of the afternoon.

CHAPTER

25

I T'S NICE OUT HERE."

At the sound of his voice, Laura jumped and turned around suddenly. "Oh, Detective. Hello."

Rodarte had crept up on her deliberately, wanting to get an honest reaction out of her, not one she had time to rehearse. He climbed the steps and joined her in the gazebo. "You don't see many of these anymore." He pretended to admire the lacy woodwork trim on the circular roof.

"Foster's grandmother had it built even before the house was completed. Foster told me she wanted someplace where she could sit and watch the swans. They always had swans in the pond."

The gazebo sat on a rise overlooking a pond where a pair of honest-to-God swans were gliding across the mirrored surface of the water. *Rich folk,* he thought scornfully. If he had their money, he'd spend it on something better than gazebos and swans.

"You mind?" He nodded at one of the vacant wicker chairs. She shook her head, and he sat down. She was wearing sunglasses, so he couldn't see her eyes to tell if she'd been crying. He guessed she had because she was twisting a damp Kleenex between her fingers. *Tears of grief or guilt?* he wondered. He really didn't care. Not unless she'd plotted with Griff Burkett to kill her husband.

Now, *that* would be a story, wouldn't it? It would be written up in *People* magazine; *20/20* would do a segment on it. They'd make a movie of the week out of it. Maybe they'd cast him in a bit part, or he could serve as technical adviser to the producers, get movie credit.

But first he had to prove it.

"More peaceful out here than inside," he remarked as he settled against the floral-print chair cushion.

Mrs. Speakman's assistant had been joined by Mr. Speakman's, a woman named Myrna something, who vacillated between crying like a baby and issuing orders like a drill sergeant. Together with Mrs. Dobbins, the housekeeper, they were manning the telephone, finding places for the floral arrangements and fruit baskets that were delivered by the truckload, cleaning up after all the cops who had been in the house last night, and making lists. They made endless lists.

A homicide generated a lot of busywork for everybody but the corpse.

"I had to get some fresh air," Laura Speakman said. "And away from the telephone."

"Who's called?"

Behind the opaque lenses he figured she was giving him one of her haughty, condescending looks. "People conveying their condolences."

"Anybody I should know about?"

"Griff Burkett. That's who you mean."

He grinned as though to say, *You know me too well.* "It's my duty to check. Has he tried to contact you?"

"No. He wouldn't."

"You sure about that?"

"He wouldn't." She went back to looking at the swans. One had buried its face beneath its wing.

"I got the autopsy report from the ME." Her only response to that was to roll her lips inward and compress them into a hard line. "Your car accident two years ago? Besides the obvious damage to his spinal column and legs, your husband suffered a lot of internal injury."

"I mentioned that this morning when we talked about his medication."

"It was pretty bad."

"Yes, it was."

"Some of his organs were friable. That's the word the ME used. Weak. Eventually he would have died from one of those organs giving out. Probably sooner than later. That also according to the ME." He paused on purpose. "But what killed him was a severed artery."

She swallowed. "How long would it have taken?"

"Hmm, not long. But there was blood on his hands, tissue under his fingernails."

She snapped her head around to look at him.

"That's right, Mrs. Speakman. Your husband fought for his life."

Rodarte actually enjoyed telling her that. Finally he got a reaction out of her. Her chest rose and fell on a quick little breath. She pressed the Kleenex against her mouth.

"He lived long enough to struggle with his attacker," he continued. "Have to admire him for that. Him, paralyzed from the waist down, battling a guy with Burkett's size and strength. He never had a chance, but he put up a brave fight." Leaning forward, he placed his hand over hers. "Are you all right?"

She yanked her hand from beneath his. "I'll be fine."

"I know this is hard for you."

"Is there anything else, Detective?"

"You can make arrangements for burial now."

"Thank you."

"Just contact the funeral home. They'll know what to do."

She nodded.

He stood up and moved to the railing that enclosed the gazebo. Staring out across the well-manicured landscape, he said thoughtfully, "Do you think Burkett attacked your husband suddenly, in a jealous rage? Or do you think they quarreled over the money?"

"Money?"

When he came around, she had removed her sunglasses and was staring up at him inquisitively.

"Didn't I mention the money to you?"

"What are you talking about, Detective? What money?"

"The cash. In the navy blue box. It was on your husband's desk in plain sight when the crime scene unit got here. They nearly shit when they— I'm sorry. Pardon the expletive." He gave her a feeble smile. "See? Just thinking about it rattled me. It's not every day you see that kind of money all heaped together. Half a million in one-hundred-dollar bills."

Her lips parted soundlessly. She stared into near space for several moments, then shifted her gaze to a shrub loaded with big blue flowers that looked like pom-poms. He didn't know what you called the flowers, but he knew how to define Mrs. Speakman's reaction. She was stunned to hear about the half mil. More specifically, she was stunned to learn he knew about it.

"Half a million dollars in cash," he said. "Sitting right there. It's under lock and key in the evidence room now. You'll get it back. Unless it turns out to be ill-gotten funds of some kind."

"Ill-gotten?"

"Drug money, something like that."

She turned back to him and stood up suddenly. "Listen to me, Detective Rodarte. My husband wasn't involved in anything illegal, and if you were to check his financial portfolio, you'd realize just how ludicrous that allegation is."

"You said he had a meeting with Griff Burkett here in your home. That's how you two met."

"What bearing does that have on this?"

"You said you didn't know what they talked about."

"I still don't see the relevance of—"

"Burkett was found guilty of racketeering, Mrs. Speakman. So I was thinking that—"

"Whatever you're thinking, you're wrong."

"Then how do you explain the cash?"

She folded her arms across her middle and tilted her head to one side. "Why are you just now mentioning this box of money to me?"

"With everything else, it slipped my mind," he lied.

Their mutual stare held for several seconds, then she shrugged. "Foster kept large amounts of cash in the safe here at home, and in another at his office."

"You don't say. Why?"

"He liked to pass it around."

"Pass it around?"

"It was a trait of his. An idiosyncrasy. He was a lavish tipper. He enjoyed leaving huge gratuities to waiters, hotel maids, the toll-booth attendant, anyone who did a service for him. Sometimes he would go out to the airport and hand out cash gifts to SunSouth ticket agents, baggage handlers, people who worked for him and were rarely thanked for the jobs they did. He did things like that often. Ask anybody."

He raised his hands in surrender. "I believe you. It's just a strange hobby. Never heard of such."

"Foster didn't advertise it. He did it for the pleasure he derived from doing it, not for self-aggrandizement."

"Thank you for telling me," Rodarte said, faking sincerity. "That could be one explanation for the box of cash. Except . . ."

"What?"

"Burkett's prints were on the lid of the box. How do you explain that?"

"I can't. But it proves that Griff Burkett isn't a thief."

He chuckled. "Well, the Department of Justice, gamblers nationwide, and the Cowboys organization would disagree. He took them for plenty every time he shaved points. I guess he didn't need your husband's half million."

She pounced on his remark as though about to contradict it, then closed her mouth quickly and put her sunglasses back on. Whatever she had been about to say, she'd thought better of it. "If that's all, I'd like to go in now and place that call to the funeral director."

"Sure," he said, waving her toward the steps. He walked along beside her as they crossed the expansive lawn. Whenever he got too close, she moved away, which amused him. "Oh, I forgot to tell you. We found two different blood types in Burkett's Honda. One, of course, was your husband's. Burkett must've had his blood all over him."

The sunglasses weren't large enough to conceal her grimace, but she didn't address the issue of her husband's blood being on her lover. "The other is probably his," she said. "If there was tissue beneath Foster's fingernails, he probably scratched him."

Rodarte said, "I would think that, too, except we've already tested it. Doesn't match Burkett's blood type. So what I think is, it's

Manuelo Ruiz's blood. Because it's the same blood type as what we got off your library rug."

"Implying what?"

"That Manuelo Ruiz was bleeding, too." Rodarte tugged on his earlobe as though thinking it through. "The man's vanished. I got in touch with Immigration to try to track him down. Guess what? Ruiz didn't have papers. Your husband hired him illegally."

"That's academic now, isn't it?"

This rich bitch was one cool broad, staring up at him through her dark sunglasses, her body language a dead giveaway to her contempt for him. He'd like to have done something to shake her up, something to crack that smooth mask she wore whenever she was talking to him. Twist her nipple, maybe. Push his hand between her legs. Something that would shock and frighten her.

"I guess it's beside the point now." He smiled amiably, even as he was thinking how much pleasure he would derive from humiliating her.

"Then what is the point, Detective?"

"Griff Burkett knocked off the wetback, too."

Well, at least that elicited an honest reaction. He wasn't sure if she flinched away from the racial slur or from his allegation that Burkett had committed double murder. It was hard not to look smug, but he kept his stoniest cop expression in place. "I don't know if he got rid of Manuelo before or after he killed your husband, but it's almost a certainty that he's responsible for Ruiz's unexplained disappearance."

She wet her lips, pulled the lower one through her teeth, and he understood why Burkett liked fucking her enough to kill for it.

"Maybe Manuelo was frightened away by what he saw," she said. "He ran."

"Without taking any clothes or personal belongings? Without a car? Without the half million cash? Unlikely, Mrs. Speakman. But, on the outside chance that he ran from something that scared him out of his wits, I've had cops calling on every Ruiz in the Dallas phone book. Fort Worth, too." He leaned forward and whispered, "Want to know something funny? We weren't the first to call those folks today, asking did they know Manuelo."

"No?"

"No. Come to find out, somebody beat us to the punch. A man has been calling the same people, looking for Manuelo Ruiz."

"Griff Burkett?"

He spread his hands at his sides and smiled.

She removed her sunglasses, carefully folded down the stems, and studied them for several moments before lifting her head and looking up at him. "Well, which is it, Detective Rodarte?"

"Which is what?"

"If Griff Burkett killed Manuelo, as you allege, then why has he been calling people named Ruiz, looking for him?"

She held his gaze for several moments, then turned her back to him and started walking toward the house.

Rodarte stared after her, trying to control the anger pulsing through him. All right, she'd got him on that one, and he had no one to blame but himself for the blunder.

Truth be told, he hadn't dwelled a lot on the fate of Manuelo Ruiz because he didn't give a flying fuck what had happened to him. Whether Burkett had killed him or was trying to chase him down because he had witnessed a murder and needed to be silenced, it mattered not in the least to Rodarte.

He would either find the wetback's body or run him down and get him to testify against Burkett. Whichever, he had Burkett for Foster Speakman's murder. Burkett's ass belonged to Stanley Rodarte.

And so does the widow's.

Chuckling to himself, he thought of the payback he'd extract for her snooty condescension. After the funeral. After the folderol had died down. After Burkett was locked behind bars. Using the prison grapevine, he'd make sure Number Ten heard about his attentions to the lady. Every salacious detail.

Jesus, was that gonna be fun, or what?

CHAPTER
26

FOR THE REMAINDER OF THE AFTERNOON, GRIFF PACED THE dismal room, wondering how in hell he'd sunk so low. When had this unstoppable decline started? When he accepted Vista's first bribe? Or before that, when he began placing bets while at UT? Or had he been irreversibly ill-fated when his mother had abandoned him to run off with her boyfriend Ray?

Sometimes he thought he'd been doomed even before he was born.

During the weeks between his conviction and the day he reported to Big Spring to begin his sentence, he'd conducted a search for his parents. Wasn't it natural for a child to turn to his parents when he was in trouble?

Thanks to the Internet and websites dedicated to linking lost relatives, it hadn't taken him long to track down his father. After serving his jail sentence in Texas, he'd left the state, alighting several places but never staying anywhere for long, until he eventually wound up in Laramie, Wyoming. He died there in a local hospital at the age of forty-nine. Hospital records said he suffered from several maladies related to alcoholism.

It took more time to locate his mother. She had either committed bigamy and married men without first securing divorces or simply assumed the names of the various men she lived with.

As the day of Griff's incarceration approached, he frequently asked himself why he was bothering to try to find her, why he was even curious about her life now, when she'd left him without a shred of remorse. To his knowledge she had never tried to learn what happened to him, so why was reconnecting with her so important?

He didn't know what drove him. It was a compulsion he couldn't explain, even to himself, so he gave up and just went with it.

His doggedness paid off. On the day before he was to begin serving his sentence, he found her in Omaha. He obtained an address and a telephone number. Before he could talk himself out of it, he called the number.

It was a decision he came to regret.

Quite a send-off to prison, he thought now, caustically.

Why today, when he was in worse trouble than ever, was he conjuring up all this crap about his parents? Maybe because thinking about them reinforced what he strongly suspected: He had been on this path to self-destruction before he even left the womb.

Which didn't bode well for the eventual outcome.

Depressed, he lay down on the ratty bed and actually slept for a while. Perhaps that was his body's way of letting him temporarily escape from his reality. Even kinder was his subconscious, which let him dream about Laura. His hands were on her. He was moving inside her. She was clutching his ass, arching up to receive him, moaning his name. Heartbeats away from coming, he woke up, her name on his lips, soaked in sweat, sporting a painful erection.

He got up, showered, and turned on the TV in time for the local evening newscasts. As he'd feared, a smug-looking anchorman with bad hair announced that the police were seeking Griff Burkett for "questioning in the brutal slaying of Foster Speakman."

This came as no surprise, of course, but Griff sat dazed, immobilized by the sudden appearance of Stanley Rodarte on the screen. He was standing in the glare of video lights, which intensified his ugliness. "At this point, Mr. Burkett is only a person of interest. All we know at present is that he was inside the Speakmans' mansion last evening."

This statement of fact caused a feeding frenzy among the reporters, who began firing questions at him. Full of self-importance,

Rodarte denied them answers, saying only "Burkett's involvement warrants further investigation. That's all I have for you right now." He turned his back on them and walked through the iron gates onto the Speakman estate.

Rodarte was there. Inside the ivy-covered walls. With Laura. She would revile Griff Burkett now. Rodarte would stoke that, use it to win her to his side. The thought of her and Rodarte breathing the same air made his empty stomach clench as tight as a fist.

Darkness finally fell. Even with the temperature hovering in the low nineties, it felt good to be outdoors, away from the lingering odors in his motel room. But it took Griff nearly two hours to walk to Hunnicutt Motors, and by that time the heat was taking its toll. He hadn't dared stop to buy a bottle of water, so he arrived at the car lot gritty with dried sweat and dehydrated.

But the hike had been worth it. The car had been left as promised.

It was a nondescript sedan somewhere between brown and gray. The model name on the trunk lid was unfamiliar to him, and he couldn't even identify the car's maker. Pontiac? Ford maybe? The cloth upholstery gave off the musty smell of stale tobacco smoke when he warily opened the unlocked door. No alarm went off.

The keys were beneath the floor mat, the gas tank was full, and the engine fired as soon as he turned the ignition. Conveniently, the chain that was usually stretched across the driveway as a security measure was lying on the pavement. Hunnicutt had thought of everything.

Wyatt Turner, attorney-at-law, lived in one of the nouveau riche neighborhoods of North Dallas. Every house had a swimming pool in the backyard, golf clubs in the garage, and inside, an upwardly mobile couple trying to keep up with the Joneses. Pets were optional. Most had children.

The Turners had only one. Griff had never seen Wyatt Junior in person, but he'd seen his picture on Wyatt's desk. He was a fifty-fifty blend of his parents, which was unfortunate for the kid. Griff had met Susan Turner only once, at a social function long before he was in need of Wyatt's services. She was a pallid woman, virtually colorless, with a personality to match. She practiced law also, but not criminal law like her husband. Taxes, corporate, probate, something dull like that. And Griff bet she was good at it. She was uptight, unfriendly, and unattractive. Compared with her, Wyatt was the life of the party.

Griff cruised past their house and saw that there was only one light on inside. He hoped it was Wyatt burning the midnight oil and not Susan. He parked two streets over and conscientiously locked the car door when he got out. He had dressed in shorts and T-shirt, running shoes, ball cap. In a neighborhood of yuppies like this one, people ran at all hours, whenever they could wedge the workout into their busy schedules. He hoped that if he was seen, he'd be mistaken for a guy who had time to exercise only late at night.

He jogged the two blocks. One dog barked at him from behind a wood fence, but otherwise he went unnoticed. At least he hoped so. Someone inside one of these upscale homes could have spotted him and called a neighborhood security watch or the police. That was a risk he had to take.

He had noticed that the house next door to the Turners' had a For Sale sign out front. The property was dark, inside and out, which was to his advantage. When he reached it now, he detoured off the sidewalk into the shadows of the yard. He went around to the side yard that abutted the Turners' driveway. There he crouched in the shrubbery to catch his breath and plan his next move.

Through open blinds, he could see into the lighted room of the Turners' house. It was a home office, reminiscent of Bolly's except much neater. A stuffed deer head mounted on the wall. Framed diplomas. Law books on the shelves. A computer monitor was on, casting a bluish light onto the desk and several open files.

The lawyer appeared, coming into the room carrying a glass of milk and what looked like a sandwich on a plate. He was wearing a white T-shirt and a pair of pajama bottoms. The tail of the T-shirt was tucked into the elastic waistband of the pajamas. *Tucked in.* In spite of his situation, Griff had to smile at his lawyer's sleeping attire. But he shared a bed with Mrs. Turner, so that explained it. Griff would have sooner made love to a corn husk.

Turner sat down at the desk, took a bite of the sandwich, and as he chewed, he gazed into his computer monitor. Griff took a deep breath and stepped out of the shrubbery. He crossed the driveway and walked up to the pair of French doors that opened directly into the office. He tapped lightly on a pane of glass.

Startled, Turner looked in his direction. When he saw Griff, his face registered a series of expressions—astonishment, apprehension, finally anger.

Griff tried the door handle. It was locked. He jiggled it several times, making metal rattle against metal. He read the curse on Turner's lips as he got out of his chair. He glanced cautiously into what Griff presumed was a hallway, then quickly came to the door and opened it.

Angrily he whispered, "Do you know that every cop within five hundred miles is after you?"

"Then you'd better let me in before one of them spots me on your doorstep."

Turner motioned him in, then stepped outside and looked down his driveway into the street. Satisfied that there were no wolves at the gate, he shut the door, after which he went around the room hastily drawing the blinds closed.

Griff picked up the sandwich and began wolfing it down. Between the car lot and here, he'd used the drive-through window to pick up a Whataburger and demolished it as he drove. It had taken the edge off his hunger but hadn't appeased it. Peanut butter and jelly had never been his favorite, but right now it tasted delicious. He drank the milk, too. Turner was watching him, seething.

"I need this more than you do," Griff said through a mouthful. Then, motioning toward his lawyer's paunch, he added, "A lot more."

"I want you out of here."

"I need information."

"I'm not CNN."

"You're my lawyer."

"Not anymore."

Griff stopped chewing. "Since when?"

"Since you—" Turner's loud voice startled even him. He froze, listening, then went to the door and looked into the hallway again.

"Don't move," he whispered to Griff over his shoulder. "Don't make a sound."

The lawyer disappeared into the dark hallway. Griff could hear doors—he assumed to bedrooms—being softly closed. Despite Turner's warning, he went to the French doors and separated the slats of the blinds to peer out, wondering if Hunnicutt's car parked two streets over had aroused a watchful homeowner's suspicion. Had anybody noticed a jogger at midnight suddenly disappearing into the dark shadows surrounding a vacant house?

Turner returned, walking on tiptoe. Quietly he pulled the door closed behind himself. "Susan's a light sleeper."

"Since when aren't you my lawyer?"

"Since you murdered Foster Speakman," the lawyer returned, matching Griff's angry stage whisper. "Christ, Griff. Foster Speakman! You could just as well have killed the president. Is it true you were screwing his wife?"

Griff held his accusatory stare for several seconds, then crammed the last of the sandwich into his mouth, muttering, "You should be so lucky."

"What?"

"Nothing." He finished the milk, then wiped his mouth with the back of his hand. "I didn't know a lawyer could fire a client."

"I don't want anything to do with you. You're too dangerous."

"Dangerous?" Griff spread his arms wide. All he had on him was the car key and his cell phone clipped to the elastic waistband of his running shorts.

"I'd call you dangerous," Turner said. "He said you stabbed Speakman in the neck with his letter opener. A paraplegic, Griff. He said Speakman tried to fight back, tried to protect himself from you, but—"

"He who? Who said? Rodarte?"

"Of course Rodarte. He and that silent partner of his came to my office this morning. Rodarte did all the talking. He asked if I knew where you were, and fortunately I could honestly say no." Turner frowned, unhappy over knowing Griff's whereabouts now. "Rodarte is having a field day. This time, make no mistake, he's got you."

"I don't get my day in court?"

Turner gnawed the inside of his cheek and cast a worried glance toward the closed door. "Make it quick." He sat down in his desk chair and tried to look lawyerly—a role hard to pull off in the pajama outfit. "How'd you meet the Speakmans?"

"I was invited to their home. Speakman proposed a business deal."

Turner looked dubious. "What kind of business?"

"We talked about me doing some ads for his airline." That wasn't exactly a lie. It wasn't exactly the truth, but he couldn't tell Turner the truth. Not yet. Foster Speakman's reputation be damned. As far as keeping his secret was concerned, all bets were off. But Laura shared that secret. Griff would keep it for her sake.

"That's nuts," Turner remarked.

"That's what I told him. But, come to find out, he had a lot of idiosyncrasies and weird ideas. Anyway, he told me to think it over, he would, too, so forth."

"The wife? Laura?"

"I met her that same night."

"Instant lust, Rodarte said."

"Rodarte said that?"

"Words to that effect. He said the two of you had a hot and heavy affair."

Griff wondered where Rodarte was getting his information. Probably he was merely speculating and making it sound like fact. "She and I got together. Four times to be exact. Over a period of months. The last time we saw each other, she called it off."

"Why?"

Disinclined to tell Turner more than that, he shrugged. "Typical reasons. Guilt mostly. I thought I'd never see her again."

"But you wanted to."

He didn't answer, but his expression must have given him away.

Turner groaned. "You just handed Rodarte motivation on a silver platter. To get the girl, you bumped off her husband. You don't even need a criminal law degree to see that, Griff."

"Besides motivation—"

"And opportunity."

"I didn't barge in on Speakman last night. I went to the mansion at his invitation."

"He *invited* you?"

"He invited me."

"What for? Did he confront you about the affair? Had the wife felt so guilty she confessed all?"

"I don't know. I don't know how much Laura told him about us." In all honesty, he didn't.

"Have you been in touch with her?"

He shook his head.

"I advise you not to try."

"As my former lawyer?"

Ignoring the sarcastic dig, Foster asked, "Can you prove Speakman invited you to the mansion last night?"

"Not yet."

"What does that mean?"

Losing patience, Griff said, "Besides motive and opportunity, what's Rodarte got on me?"

The lawyer hesitated.

"Come on, Turner. You owe me at least that much. What am I up against?"

Turner snorted. "Well, there's the murder weapon covered with your fingerprints. Your DNA will match the tissue they dug out from under Speakman's fingernails." He pointed toward the bloody scratches on the backs of Griff's hands. "Correct?"

"Correct."

"Hell, Griff," he said, wincing, "Rodarte doesn't need anything else to nail you for Speakman. But there's also this guy named Ruiz."

"Manuelo. Speakman's aide. Looks like a South American head-hunter with a pleasant but empty smile."

"Nobody's seen him." Turner paused and looked at him expectantly. When Griff didn't say anything, he continued. "Rodarte checked with Immigration. No file on him. He was an illegal."

"You're using the past tense."

"Was he there last night?"

Again Griff refrained from saying anything.

"Don't bother lying," the lawyer said. "They found blood on the rug and in your car. My old Honda. The blood wasn't yours or Speakman's. Rodarte surmises it's Ruiz's. He's searching for his remains."

Beneath his breath, Griff said, "Fuck!"

"Well finally, the oracle speaks. And isn't that an eloquent statement?" the lawyer said with asperity. "Was he alive when you left him?"

"Which?"

Turner rubbed his high forehead as though to smooth out the worry lines. "Either."

"Speakman was dead. Ruiz was *adiós*."

"He escaped you?"

"He ran."

"Did he see Speakman get stabbed?"

Griff didn't respond.

"Did you . . . Was Ruiz also injured? *Was* that his blood on the rug and in the Honda?"

Griff was about to answer, then checked himself. "Are you my lawyer or not?"

Turner studied him for a moment, than asked quietly, "What about the money, Griff? The half million. And don't play dumb, because your fingerprints were on the lid of the box. So, what was that about?"

"Beats me," he replied laconically, with a shrug. "Speakman says, 'Look in the box.' I looked in the box. I guess he was showing off how rich he was."

"It wasn't for you?"

Griff looked at him as though that was the most preposterous thing he'd ever heard in his life.

"Rodarte suggested that Speakman was paying you off for something."

Griff's gut tightened. "Like what?"

"Something you had delivered. Or a service you'd performed for him."

"Shit, Turner, where's your brain? Where's Rodarte's? If that money had been for me, I sure as hell wouldn't have left it behind. I'd have it and be living it up in some exotic locale, not bumming peanut butter sandwiches off you."

The lawyer wasn't fazed. "Lotta money, Griff. Large bills banded together. Stacked neatly in a box. Kind of like the take you got from Bandy for throwing the play-off game against the Skins."

"I'm telling you—"

"Okay, okay. For now let's say Speakman just liked keeping boxes of cash around and it had nothing to do with his murder. Rodarte doesn't even need that element to get a conviction." Turner stood, circled his chair, placed his hands on the back of it, as though he were about to address the court. "Listen to me, Griff. This is a prosecutor's dream case. They've got hard evidence. They've got your DNA. And if Ruiz is alive—"

"He is. Or was last time I saw him."

"And if he isn't already back in Honduras—"

"El Salvador."

"Whatever. If they can catch him, they'll have an eyewitness in addition to the incriminating evidence. But," he said, lightly slapping the leather chair back for emphasis, "on the positive side, you placed the 911 call, right?" Griff nodded. "So that suggests you didn't want Speakman to die. It can be argued that Speakman invited you there, and if the jury buys that, then the next step is their believing that there was no premeditation on your part. You went to Speakman's house at his invitation. He confronted you with the affair you were having—"

"Had."

"Had with his wife. You argued. Something he said lit your fuse, next thing you know—"

"I picked up the letter opener on his desk and plunged it into his neck."

Turner actually looked sad about it. "You've got a good chance of being charged with manslaughter, instead of murder one. That's probably the best you'll do on this one, and I'm telling you that both as counsel and as a friend." He paused to let that sink in.

"I hate to paint such a bleak picture, but that's how it is, Griff. And you're only making yourself look guiltier by running. Turning yourself in to Rodarte will be rough. I'm not saying it won't. But it'll be much harder for you if you don't."

"I'm not turning myself in."

"If you do—tonight, *now*—I'll represent you. I'll be right there with you every step of the way. Let them conduct their investigation, and then we'll see just how badly the evidence is stacked against you. Rodarte has been known to exaggerate, to insinuate that he has more than he actually does, but we *know* he has the weapon and, coupled with the motive, it's damn incriminating.

"It actually works in our favor that you left the money behind. You didn't commit robbery, so it's not a capital murder. I'll argue like hell for the manslaughter charge. I'll also file for change of venue. Get the trial out of Dallas.

"But wherever it's conducted, you can bet the prosecutor will hammer home how defenseless Speakman was against you. He'll paint you as a brute who attacked a man who couldn't possibly fight back and win. He'll make the jurors despise you, and any argument you put forth won't change the indisputable fact that you were a football player and he was a paraplegic.

"Turn yourself in and let me take over your defense. The only time you have to speak is at your arraignment, when you plead not guilty. You don't have to breathe a bloody word to Rodarte, the jury, nobody."

Griff had listened patiently, but now he said, "And you think *not* talking will make me look innocent? Come on, Wyatt."

"I believe in jurisprudence, in our system of justice."

"Well, your perspective on it is different from mine. You promised me I'd get off with probation if I cooperated with the feds and told them what I knew about Vista's operation. Look what happened to that."

"That was different."

"Right. We were dealing with the federal grand jury and what-ifs. This time Rodarte's got my prints on the instrument that killed my lover's husband."

Turner's head dropped forward. He stood, a frown creasing his brow. Finally he raised his head. "I appeal to you once more, Griff. Give yourself up."

"That's the best you can do?"

"That's it."

Griff studied him a moment, then said softly, "You haven't even asked me."

"Asked you what?"

Snuffling a rueful laugh, Griff said, "Never mind. Have you heard from Jerry Arnold?"

"He called this afternoon. Kept saying, 'Why would he do something like this?' Stuff like that. You've lost another fan."

Griff wasn't surprised. "Well, thanks for the info. And the sandwich." He turned toward the French doors.

"Griff, wait."

"See ya, Turner." He opened the door.

He heard the squeal of brakes as though a car had taken a corner too fast. He heard gunning engines, the *whish* of rubber on hot pavement. And in the house across the street, the front windows reflected colored lights. Red. Blue. White.

CHAPTER

27

TURNER RAISED HIS HANDS IN SURRENDER. SELF-DEFENSE maybe. "I had to call them, Griff. It's for your own good."

Griff sneered. "As counsel and friend, go fuck yourself."

Then he was out the door. He skirted the swimming pool and used a lawn chair to help him vault the privacy fence. His knees took the brunt of the eight-foot drop to the ground on the other side. Another swimming pool. This one had the underwater light on. It felt like a searchlight, directed on him.

A searchlight made him think of a police helicopter, and that gave him the impetus to bust through the gate without fiddling with the latch. He ran through that yard, across the street, into the front yard of another house, where the sprinklers were on. His thrashing legs got wet, and so did the soles of his shoes, making them slippery.

Another freaking fence. "Shit!" Didn't these people trust their own neighbors? He searched for the gate, which was hard to detect in the darkness. He found it, but it was locked from the inside. He backed up, threw himself against it. It didn't budge.

He heard tires screeching, close enough for him to smell the smoking rubber.

He ran through the sprinklers again to the neighboring house. Finally, a house with no fence, only a hedge. He plunged through it. The thorny holly plants clawed at his bare legs, tearing skin, but he didn't let that slow him down. He ran between that house and the one behind it, which put him on the street where he'd left the borrowed car.

He paused in the darkness between two houses, his lungs a bellows, his heart a jackhammer. He could hear shouting, tires squealing, car doors slamming. Hunnicutt's car was three houses from where he stood. Nothing here was moving. Yet. He couldn't delay. The search for him would soon spread to this street. He had to risk exposure.

He stepped from between the two houses, primed to sprint.

A police car, lit up like a Christmas tree, took the nearest corner on two wheels.

Griff ducked back into the shadows. Cursed Turner. Cursed his luck. Cursed his whole frigging life.

Then he ran.

Later, he would wonder how in hell he had got out of there. His escape almost made him a believer in divine intervention. Maybe for once in his life, God had suited up to play on his team.

He zigzagged through the neighborhood, moving from one patch of darkness to another. The chopper did appear with its searchlight, which was more powerful than the beam of any lighthouse. For hours he dodged it and the squad cars that either sped or crawled through the streets. Policemen on foot searched, practically going door to door.

He took a few minutes' refuge in an open garage, where he found a rag to blot the streams of blood off his legs. Sweat made the wounds sting mercilessly. Once, when he got trapped between the approaching chopper's searchlight and a policeman on foot, he slid into the deep end of a swimming pool. Luckily there was no underwater light, and the pool was one of the pretentious ones, designed to replicate a tropical lagoon formed by lava rock, so it was dark.

He held his breath until he thought his lungs would burst, but because of all the swimming he'd done recently, he was better conditioned than he would have been normally. Looking up through the surface, he could see the chopper's light sweeping the area. The policeman came so close, Griff could hear him muttering to himself.

Finally both the officer and the helicopter moved on. Griff's head cleared the surface, and he gulped oxygen. He climbed out of the pool, pruney but revived. His legs weren't stinging anymore. He didn't even attempt to return to the car. Cops would have been all over it once they ran the tag number through the DMV and discovered it didn't belong to anyone living on that street.

He still had his cell phone. Thank God he'd taken it with him. He thought about dialing Glen Hunnicutt, asking him to meet somewhere and pick him up. But he didn't want to involve the man any more than he already had.

He had no one else to call. No one he could trust. No one who trusted him.

He felt safer when he was out of Wyatt Turner's neighborhood, but only a bit, because he still had a long way to go to reach the motel. Cops all over the city would now be on the lookout for a man of his description on foot. There would be a lot of harassed joggers in Dallas that morning. Those who ran before daylight were sure to be stopped and scrutinized.

When he walked beneath the freeway overpass and saw the neon vacancy light flickering in the motel office window, he wanted to weep with relief. It wasn't much, but it was the only hiding place he had. Dawn was just breaking.

He needed to lie down. Close his eyes. Breathe easily. Rest.

But as he neared the parking lot, he noticed that the dope-smoking night clerk was no longer on duty. His replacement was dressed casually, but he looked too clean-cut to work in a place like this.

Griff ducked behind the used-tire store's portable marquee. From that tenuous hiding place, he watched the guy come out from behind the check-in desk. He left the office and started down the breezeway. He was carrying a foam cup. Steam was rising from it. The aroma of freshly brewed coffee made Griff's mouth water. But his heart began to feel very heavy when he saw the guy stop at room number seven and knock three times on the door.

It was opened by a man who was as clean-cut as the one manning the office. He took the coffee from his buddy and savored his first sip with a long "Ahhh." They had a brief exchange, then the office guy left the other inside the room and walked back to the office.

Griff crouched behind the sign advertising the special on retreads and bent his head over his knees.

How the hell had they found him? Was Rodarte fucking clairvoyant?

He remained hunkered down behind the sign for a while, until his overtaxed leg muscles began to cramp, his knees to grow stiff, and the eastern horizon to become limned with orange.

Knowing he had to relocate, he reached into his sock for the bills he'd tucked there before going to Turner's. The currency was wet from his time in the pool, but it was spendable. He'd hid his cell phone beneath the diving board of the swimming pool, out of sight, before he'd slipped into the water, then retrieved it when he got out. The battery still had juice.

That paltry amount of cash and the phone were the only resources left to him. He didn't even have a dry change of clothes. But he couldn't stay here. He had to move. He forced his aching legs to unfold and began walking, being careful to keep something between himself and the office of the motel.

As he walked, he flipped open his phone and placed one short call.

Glen Hunnicutt was in his office, drinking coffee and shooting the breeze with a customer, when the dealership's receptionist tapped on his open office door. "Excuse the interruption, Mr. Hunnicutt. There's someone here to see you. A detective with the police department. He says it's important."

"Come in." Hunnicutt rolled his hand, motioning the man into his office.

"Stanley Rodarte, DPD." He extended Hunnicutt his card.

"Have a seat, Detective," Hunnicutt said expansively, pointing him toward a chair. "You want some coffee?"

"No thanks."

"You sure? Our coffee's as good as our auto-*mo*-biles."

"No thanks."

"Maybe a nice, cold Dr Pepper?"

"Nothing, thanks," Rodarte said, showing his impatience.

"You shopping cars this morning, Detective?"

"No." Rodarte nodded toward the other man in the room, who was seated across from Hunnicutt's desk. "Could we have a minute alone? This is a police matter."

"Meet James McAlister. Jim's my lawyer, so I have no secrets from him." The look on Rodarte's face was priceless. It was all Hunnicutt could do not to chuckle. The detective hadn't expected a lawyer to be present.

Hunnicutt had arrived at the dealership shortly after daybreak so he could replace the security chain before his employees began reporting for work. He'd been at his desk catching up on paperwork when Griff's warning call came through the main phone line. Fortunately, he'd answered.

Upon hearing his voice, Griff said, "It's hit the fan. I'm sorry. You'll be hearing from a cop named Rodarte. Stanley Rodarte. He gives you grief, you say this to him. You listening?"

"I'm listening."

Griff had left Hunnicutt with the message, then hung up.

Addressing Rodarte now, Hunnicutt said, "Jim's here to buy a car for his daughter who's turning sixteen next week. He expects a discount from me. Like hell, I said. He never gave me a discount on legal fees. I told him—"

"We found a car belonging to you," Rodarte said, brusquely cutting in. "It was found abandoned on a neighborhood street a few miles from here."

Hunnicutt looked at McAlister, registering surprise. "You found it? Already?" He whistled. "I'm impressed. We only reported it stolen, when, Jim? Eight, nine this morning? You guys in the DPD are good!"

Rodarte had received his second blow. "You reported the car stolen?"

McAlister snapped open the briefcase resting on his lap and took a form from it. It had been filled out by the policeman who'd responded to Hunnicutt's call, reporting that a car was missing from his inventory. Rodarte yanked the form from McAlister, glanced at it, and verified its accuracy, down to the car's make and model, license plate, and VIN. Hunnicutt got the impression Rodarte was about to wad up the form and hurl it to the floor. McAlister rescued it just in time and replaced it in his briefcase.

"When was it stolen?" the detective asked tightly.

"Don't know. I didn't notice it missing until this morning. Cars get shifted around all day, every day. It could have been missing a couple weeks, a couple days, or a couple hours. No way of telling."

"Griff Burkett's prints are all over that car," Rodarte growled, looking like a man barely in control of his temper.

"Griff Burkett? *The* Griff Burkett? No shit! You sure?"

"Oh, yeah. I'm sure."

"Well, I'll be. Imagine that. Hmm. Wonders never cease."

Rodarte's glower turned darker. "He left it parked two streets from his lawyer's house, where he went last night asking for information that would help him elude arrest for the murder of Foster Speakman. Turner called us instead."

Hunnicutt looked over at McAlister. "Lucky I've got you."

"Burkett managed to get away on foot," Rodarte said.

"The boy has talent," Hunnicutt said. "Fastest quarterback I've ever seen. That fancy footwork of his was something to watch, wasn't it?"

Rodarte looked ready to explode. "You gave that car to him, which amounts to aiding and abetting a murder suspect."

"That's an awfully ugly allegation," McAlister said calmly. "I'm hereby instructing my client not to answer any further questions, Detective."

Ignoring the lawyer, Rodarte kept his eyes on Hunnicutt. "When did Burkett call you? Yesterday? Last night?"

Hunnicutt said nothing.

"Obviously you admire him, but he's no hero. Yesterday he made a bunch of calls to area families named Ruiz. I had cops calling those same families, searching for clues into the disappearance of Manuelo Ruiz, who we believe witnessed Foster Speakman's murder. We compared notes. Same phone number showed up on several caller IDs. We traced that number to a fleabag motel out on 635. I've got men staking out the place, waiting for him to slink back to where his stuff's at.

"And when he does, I'm going to put him through the wringer. Your name's bound to come up. He'll give you up, Hunnicutt. Burkett doesn't have friends, only people he uses then shits on. He has loyalty to no one except himself. You talk to me now or face indictment later."

Rodarte paused, took a breath. "Now, where is he? If you know, and you don't tell me, you're obstructing justice. *Where is he?*"

Hunnicutt calmly lit a cigarette. "You sure you couldn't use a Dr Pepper?"

Rodarte banged his fist on Hunnicutt's desk. "Tell me, goddammit!"

"Detective Rodarte, you're harassing my client," McAlister said.

Rodarte stood up and leaned far across Hunnicutt's desk, thrusting his face close. "I can get your phone records for this place, prove he called here."

"You'd need a search warrant," the lawyer said. "I doubt any judge in the county would grant you one for such a flimsy reason, but if one did, and if you found a number belonging to Mr. Burkett on those records, it still wouldn't prove that he spoke with Mr. Hunnicutt.

"How many calls a day do you estimate come into this busy car dealership? Hundreds, right? My client can't be responsible for any of them. And if you did manage to prove that my client talked to Mr. Burkett, that doesn't prove that he provided him a car or assisted him in any way."

Rodarte, still ignoring the attorney, glared into Hunnicutt's guileless face.

"I think you've run out of ammunition to back up your threats, Mr. Rodarte." Hunnicutt placed his cigarette in the hollow belly of his armadillo-shaped ashtray and stood up. He moved to his office door and opened it.

Rodarte disregarded the blatant suggestion that he leave. He asked, "How'd Burkett get the key to that car if you didn't give it to him?"

Hunnicutt yelled through the open doorway, "Sweetheart, come on in here a sec."

The receptionist who'd ushered Rodarte in reappeared, asking brightly, "Did he change his mind about the coffee?"

"What's my pet peeve?" Hunnicutt asked her. "What do I get onto the salespeople about more than anything?"

"Letting customers leave without buying a car."

Hunnicutt boomed a laugh. "Second to that."

"Leaving the keys under the floor mats."

"Thank you, honey."

She left, and Hunnicutt turned back to Rodarte. "Leaving the keys under the floor mats. They do it for convenience's sake, always meaning to go back later and properly lock the cars they've taken out on demonstration drives. They plan to go back when they don't have customers stacked up. But—thank God, and I ain't complaining— sometimes they've got customers waiting. So they just slide the ignition key under the mat. Then they get distracted or busy and forget." He shrugged his burly shoulders. "I chew ass about it all the time, but what can you do? They're selling cars like hotcakes."

He shared a long look with Rodarte, who glanced over at the unflappable lawyer. McAlister raised his eyebrows eloquently. Rodarte stalked through the office door. When he pushed past Hunnicutt, he said in a malevolent undertone, "You haven't heard the last of me."

Hunnicutt said to his lawyer, "Excuse me, Jim. I'm gonna walk him out."

"Glen—"

"It's cool."

He moved quickly for a man his size and caught up with Rodarte as the detective was climbing into his car. Rodarte rounded on him. "I know you provided Burkett that car. You were jailbirds together at Big Spring. Next time, you'll go to Huntsville, and let me tell you, that ain't no country-club prison like the one you're used to. Your big white ass would be a turn-on to lots of queers I've put there." His eyes glinted with malice. "You've made an enemy today, Hunnicutt. Nobody makes a fool of me and gets away with it. You wait and see."

Hunnicutt leaned in. He was a head taller than Rodarte and seventy pounds heavier. "Don't threaten me. I know about you. You're a bully. The worst kind. You got a badge to back it up. But if you even think about hurting me or a member of my family, you remember what I told you today."

"Yeah, what's that?"

Hunnicutt leaned down even closer and whispered, "Marcia's got a lot of friends." As he straightened up, he had the pleasure of watching Rodarte's eyes turn wary. Griff had known what he was talking about. The name meant something to Rodarte, and so did the implied threat. It instilled, if not fear, at least reservation.

Hunnicutt held the detective's stare, then stepped back and flashed a wide smile. "If you're ever in the market for a used car, come see me." He walked to the front of the olive green sedan and kicked the tire. "But I'll tell you right off, I wouldn't take this for a trade-in."

What was he going to do?

Where could he hide?

Surrendering, as his turncoat lawyer had urged him to, wasn't an option. Even if he wanted to entrust himself to the legal system again, which he didn't, Turner had deserted him, and, by the sound of it, so had his probation officer. There was no one in his corner.

No, he could not turn himself in. But while dodging capture, he could be gunned down in the street, if not by someone wearing a badge, then by a citizen with a vigilante mentality.

Taking temporary shelter in a cement culvert, he flipped open his phone and punched in the familiar number, only because there was absolutely no one else he could call.

It rang six times before it went to voice mail. "Thank you for calling the Millers. Please leave a message." Griff hung up and immediately redialed, more from a desire to hear Ellie's cheerful voice than with the hope of his call being answered. He listened to the recording again, wondering where Coach and Ellie could be this early in the morning.

But if one of them had answered, what would he have said? What could he say that they would believe?

He punched in another number he had committed to memory. Jason Rich answered. "Hey, Jason, it's Griff." He tried to sound like nothing out of the ordinary had happened. "I called to apologize for not making it to our workout yesterday. And looks like I won't be there today, either."

"How come?"

"I've come down with some kind of stomach flu. I think I got hold of some bad tamales. I've been puking my guts up." A short pause, then, "Is your dad around? I'd like to talk to him, please."

"You're sick?"

"Yeah."

"Then it's not true, what he said?"

"What who said?"

"That policeman."

Griff pinched the bridge of his nose, hard. "Was his name Rodarte? A detective?"

"A man with scars on his face. He came here yesterday and talked to my dad and me."

Griff had hoped that Rodarte would forget his tie to the Riches, but Rodarte never forgot anything. He had made a veiled threat to harm Jason. Yesterday he had questioned him, probably put pressure on the kid to tell him everything he knew about Griff Burkett. He would have frightened the boy. Griff could have killed the son of a bitch for that.

"He said you—" Jason's voice cracked. "He said you—"

"Jason!"

Bolly's voice, coming out of the background. Sharp. Intrusive. "Who are you talking to? Jason, *who is that*?"

Then Jason, in a pleading voice, said, "Dad, he's—"

"Give me the phone." Scuffling sounds. Then directly into Griff's ear, Bolly snarled, "I should have known better than to trust you."

"Bolly, listen, I—"

"No, *you* listen. The cops have been here twice. My wife freaked out, especially when this Detective Rodarte told her what you did."

"Bolly—"

"I don't want you calling here. I don't want you near my family. I trusted you with my son. Jesus, when I think—"

"I wouldn't lay a hand on Jason. You know that."

"No, killing your lover's paraplegic husband is more your speed."

Griff squeezed his eyes shut, trying to block out the accusation and the image it conjured. "I called to tell you to be careful of Rodarte. Keep Jason away—"

"Don't dare even speak my son's name."

"Listen to me!"

"I'm over listening."

"Don't leave Jason alone with Rodarte. Don't leave Jason alone, period. I know what you think of me—"

"You don't know the half of what I think of you. I hope this Rodarte finally nails your ass. And when he does, I hope they fry it."

CHAPTER

28

FOSTER SPEAKMAN'S FUNERAL BEFITTED A HEAD OF STATE.
Prestonwood Baptist Church had the only sanctuary large
enough to accommodate the crowd, and the membership gra-
ciously offered it and their choir for the service. The auditorium was
filled to capacity. The overflow were seated in annex buildings, where
the service was telecast on closed-circuit TV.

Secret Service agents ensured the safety of the first lady, who attended on behalf of the president, who was out of the country. Several congressmen were also there. The governor of Texas delivered
the eulogy. A notable clergyman delivered the homily. A Tony-
winning Broadway star with whom Foster had attended prep school
led the congregation in singing "Amazing Grace." To conclude the
service, the Lord's Prayer was led by the senior pilot of SunSouth
Airlines, leaving not a dry eye in the church.

The cortege stretched for miles.

The event was well documented by the media, from the arrival of
dignitaries and celebrities at the church until the crowd at the ceme-
tery dispersed. Most of the television coverage ended on a poignant
image, the same heartrending tableau that was captured by a still
photographer and published in the newspaper: Laura Speakman silhouetted against the cloudless sky, standing alone with head bowed
beside the casket of her husband.

As Laura stood there, she didn't realize that cameras with tele-photo lenses were clicking away fast and furious from a respectful distance. In fact, that was the first moment she'd felt truly alone since Foster's death, five days earlier.

Finding privacy in which to grieve had been near impossible be-cause she'd been surrounded by people. There were duties and re-sponsibilities that only she, as his sole survivor, could handle. Performing these tasks had, by necessity, kept her grief at bay during the day.

At night, when she retired to her bedroom, she was still aware of the other people inside her house. Kay had ensconced herself in one of the guest bedrooms, Myrna in another, both refusing to leave Laura alone overnight. Policemen were at the gate. Others patrolled the acreage within the estate wall.

Consequently, she hadn't yet indulged her sorrow or fully grasped that Foster was gone. Not until this quiet, solitary moment, when the reality came crashing down on her.

Kay had accompanied her to the funeral home to select the cas-ket. She remembered going, looking at the choices, listening to the funeral director's recommendations. But she hadn't really looked at the casket until now. It was handsome and simple. Foster would have approved.

For the spray, she had ordered white calla lilies, a flower he particularly favored because of its clean and uncluttered form. She reached out and touched one of the blossoms, rubbing it between her fingers, registering both its creamy texture and what that tangibility signified. This was real. This was permanent. Foster was not coming back. She would never see him again. She had so many questions to ask him, so many things to say, but they would remain unasked and unsaid.

"I loved you, Foster," she whispered.

Her heart was convinced that he knew that. At least the old Fos-ter had known how much she loved him. Strange, but since his death, when she thought about him, she didn't see the man in the wheel-chair, behaving oddly, saying things he knew would wound her.

Instead she saw him as he'd been before the accident. She envi-sioned the Foster who'd been vital and bursting with energy, his body as strong and vivacious as his personality, his humor and optimism infectious to everyone with whom he came into contact.

That was the Foster Speakman she mourned.

By the time the limousine arrived at the mansion, the place was already packed with guests who'd been invited to eat, drink, and share memories of Foster. It was expected that she host such a reception, but the very idea of enduring it had exhausted her. She'd delegated the planning to Kay and Myrna. In the formal dining room was an unsparing buffet. Waiters passed through the crowd with trays of canapés. People were queued at the bar. A harpist provided background music.

Laura mingled with the guests, accepting their condolences, crying with some, laughing with others, who told anecdotes about Foster. During the telling of one story, out of the corner of her eye, Laura noted that the double doors to the library remained closed. She had learned through Kay that the police had released it as a crime scene and that she was free to use it again. Mrs. Dobbins had arranged for it to be thoroughly cleaned.

Nevertheless, no one went near that room. Nor did anyone mention the circumstances of Foster's death.

Detective Rodarte was a grim reminder of them. He arrived late and kept to the edges of the crowd. Laura tried pretending he wasn't there, but she was constantly aware of him. She would turn and catch him disdainfully scanning the crowd, or staring at her with unnerving concentration.

The house was almost clear of guests when Laura drew Kay aside. "I want you to call a meeting for two o'clock tomorrow."

"What kind of meeting?"

"Executive council and board members."

"Laura, surely you're not thinking of coming into the office tomorrow," she exclaimed. "No one expects you to plunge right back in."

"Foster would," she said with a brief smile. "Two o'clock. Please, Kay," she added when she saw that her assistant was about to protest. "Make my excuses now. I must go upstairs. Let me know when everyone's gone."

Half an hour later Kay tapped on her bedroom door. "It's me," she said, stepping into the room. "Everyone's gone except the caterer's crew. They're loading up their vans now and will soon be out." She glanced at the suitcase lying open on Laura's bed. "Explain to me again why you're being moved out of your own home?"

"Detective Rodarte believes I'll be safer in a hotel."

"Safer from whom? Griff Burkett?" Kay scoffed. "He's probably in Mexico or someplace by now. You've got twenty-four-hour guards here. He couldn't get to you if he wanted to, and he would be crazy to try."

"Well, the detective believes he might be just that crazy. And Burkett hasn't left the area. At least he was still around three days ago. He went to his attorney's house in the middle of the night. The attorney called the police. Burkett managed to get away. But on foot." She zipped the suitcase closed and pulled it off the bed. "Detective Rodarte is of the mind that he's desperate and dangerous, and until he's captured, he poses a threat to my safety."

And, she thought, *he's afraid I'll protect my lover from capture.* He hadn't said as much, but his insinuations hadn't required any guesswork.

Kay said, "I think it's criminal that you're being forced out of your home, particularly now, when you need a haven."

Laura looked at the beautiful surroundings wistfully. "Actually, Kay, I probably wouldn't stay here anyway. It's an awfully large house for one person. Anyway, it never really was mine."

She didn't explain the statement. She wasn't certain she could. Over the course of the past few days, she'd come to realize that she felt like a visitor here. A welcome visitor, but a visitor all the same. Foster had never treated her as such. In fact, he had encouraged her to change the decor to her liking, to make it her house. But she'd felt it would be improper to do so. It had been his family's home for much longer than she'd been a member of his family. He was her only reason for being here and her only connection to the house. His death had severed that connection.

Besides, she wasn't sure she could ever go into the library again.

Kay took the suitcase from her. "Let me carry that. You look like you're about to collapse. Did you eat anything?"

"A little," she lied. She'd thrown up the English muffin she forced down for breakfast. As for the carafe of coffee that had been on the tray, she couldn't bear the smell of it and had poured it down the bathroom sink. So far, no one knew about her morning sickness.

She and Kay descended the sweeping staircase. Rodarte was waiting at the bottom of it, leaning against the carved newel post, cleaning his fingernails with the tip of a pocketknife that he should have been using to pare them.

"Ready?" He closed the knife and slipped it into his pants pocket, pushed himself away from the banister, and headed for the front door. There was a squad car waiting just beyond the entrance.

When Laura saw it, she drew up short. "I'm driving myself."

"Are you sure you're up to it, Mrs. Speakman? The DPD would like to extend you the courtesy of—"

"Thank you, but I prefer taking my own car."

"You won't be needing it," Rodarte argued. "You'll be driven wherever you want to go."

"Are you placing me under arrest, Detective?" It was the first direct challenge she'd issued him.

"Nothing of the sort."

"Because if that's your intention, do it properly. I want to be read my rights, and then I want to call my attorney." Probably she should have sought legal counsel already, but doing so would have implied guilt. At least she feared that's how Rodarte would see it. It was equally possible that by not calling in an attorney she was playing right into the detective's hands. The car issue was a means of testing the nature of the "protection" he insisted on extending her.

Rodarte looked over at Kay and shook his head with regret, as though to say that Laura was becoming hysterical and that under the circumstances her fraying nerves were understandable. Looking back at Laura, he spoke to her as though she were mentally unstable. "These measures are for your protection, Mrs. Speakman."

"I'm taking my car," she declared, enunciating each word.

He tried to stare her down, but she didn't budge. Finally he heaved a theatrical sigh and said to one of the uniformed policemen loitering near the patrol car, "Go get her car."

Laura passed the policeman her keys. No one said anything until he returned driving the car. He climbed out, and Laura took his place behind the wheel. Before she shut the door, Kay leaned in.

"I'll finish here and help Mrs. Dobbins lock up. After that, you can reach me at home." She scanned Laura's face, looking worried about what she saw. "Order room service. Take a long bath. Promise me you'll get some rest."

"I promise. Don't forget to schedule the meeting. You should call everyone tonight."

"I will."

Laura closed the car door and reached for her seat belt.

Rodarte opened the passenger door and got in. Smiling, he said, "I thought you might want company."

Certainly not yours, she thought. But she said nothing as she started the car, drove down the long drive, and passed through the gate. A squad car that had been parked on the street pulled out in front of her. Rodarte's partner, Carter, was driving the green sedan, riding her rear bumper. The other squad car followed him.

She complained of the police escort. "We look like a parade."

Rodarte merely harrumphed, flipped open his cell phone, and reported to whomever he called that they were under way.

Their destination turned out to be a luxury downtown hotel where he'd registered her under an assumed name. Accompanied by Carter and two uniformed policemen, they went in through the service entrance and used the service elevator to reach the top floor.

"You have it all to yourself," Rodarte told her as they alighted from the elevator. Two policemen were waiting outside a room at the far end of a long hallway. Rodarte unlocked the door to the room and ushered her in. Carter remained outside.

It was a well-appointed, spacious room. Rodarte placed her suitcase on the luggage rack inside the closet, poked his head into the bathroom, checked the view of the Dallas skyline beyond the wide windows, then let the sheer drape fall back into place as he turned to face her. "I hope you'll be comfortable here."

"It's very nice."

"There'll be a policeman stationed outside your door, whether you're in the room or not. Another will be at the end of the hall, where he can monitor the stairwell and both elevators. They'll be in radio contact with guards at various posts downstairs, inside and outside the building."

"Is all this precaution necessary?"

"I'm making sure that nobody gets in."

And that I don't get out.

As though underscoring her thought, he extended his hand. "Can I have your car keys, please?"

"What for?"

"Safekeeping. We'll be watching your car, too."

Despite everything he'd said, this room was essentially a holding cell. Until he was convinced that Burkett had acted alone in killing her husband, she would remain under suspicion and, it appeared, under lock and key.

She folded her arms across her chest and assumed a stance. "I'd be interested to hear what my attorney has to say about your authority to confiscate my car keys."

He grinned, and with a wide sweep of his arm motioned toward the nightstand. "There's the phone."

His smirk, the challenge in his expression, said he knew she was bluffing.

"What if I need to go somewhere?"

"Oh, I'll leave the keys with the cop outside your door here. If you need to go somewhere, just ask him. He'll clear it with the cops downstairs. You'll be either accompanied in your car or followed." He touched her arm with the backs of his fingers, almost like a caress. "Your safety is our top priority."

She pulled her arm away from his touch, which made her skin crawl. "I feel well protected."

"Good."

She hoped he would go then. Instead, he sat down on the end of the bed. She remained standing.

He grinned, as though knowing how repulsed she was by his sitting on the bed she would sleep in. Then his smile inverted into a frown. He said, "You've been so busy with all the funeral arrangements I haven't wanted to bother you with the investigation. But just to give you an update, there's been no trace of Manuelo Ruiz. No leads, even."

"I'm sorry to hear that," she said, meaning it. "I'd like to learn what Manuelo knows about that night."

"I don't think we'll ever know what he saw or heard. I think Burkett made sure of that."

She turned away and moved to the window. Lights were just beginning to come on against a twilight sky. There was a lot of traffic on the expressway, moving in both directions. People were going about their lives. Having dinner out. Attending baseball games. Grilling burgers in the backyard with friends. She envied that normalcy. It had been missing from her life since the night of the car accident.

That fateful crash was the pivotal event of her life, even more so than she had realized at the time. If not for it, Foster and she might be going to a movie tonight. They would have conceived their children naturally, out of love for each other. There would have been no need to seek alternative methods. They wouldn't have met Griff Burkett. He wouldn't be a fugitive, Foster would be alive, and she wouldn't be wishing that this loathsome detective would go away and leave her in peace.

"So far, I've been able to keep your affair with Burkett out of the press."

She hadn't heard him move up behind her. He was standing so close she could smell his aftershave and feel his humid breath on the back of her neck.

"But I don't know how long I can keep it under wraps, Laura."

It was inappropriate and unprofessional for him to use her first name. Yet to correct him would only call more attention to it, and she preferred to appear indifferent. He wanted her edgy and uneasy, even fearful of him. So she let it pass and kept her back to him.

"Reporters want to know what business Burkett and your husband . . . late husband . . . had with each other. What was Burkett's motive for killing him? That's what they're clamoring to know.

"Now, strictly as a favor to you," he said, lowering his voice to an intimate pitch, "I haven't revealed that, haven't even acted like I know what could have possessed Burkett to do such a terrible thing. But when he's caught, well, that'll be another kettle of fish. When he's indicted, this thing is going to blow wide open, more than it already has. There's no way I can conceal your adultery."

That word brought her around. But unable to stand being that close to him face-to-face, she moved away. "I'm prepared for that."

"Really? Are you sure you're prepared for the beating you're going to take? Right now you're regarded as a tragic figure, the bereaved widow of a murder victim. The media is sensitive to your feelings, treating you with kid gloves. But I don't have to tell you how nasty reporters can get, especially when they feel like they've been deceived. They can turn on you." He snapped his fingers loudly. "Like that. You'll need protection from that onslaught."

"I appreciate your concern."

"Someone at your back, acting as a buffer."

"Thank you."

"You'll be glad to have me close. Protecting you like a . . ." He waited a beat, then said, "brother."

Inwardly she shuddered. "I'm very tired. If there's nothing else—"

"The car keys?"

She retrieved them from her handbag and reluctantly handed them over, being careful not to touch him. "Thanks." He bounced the keys in his palm and looked smug to have them in his possession. "Order anything you like from room service. The DPD is taking care of the charges."

"How long are you going to extend me this hospitality?"

"Till Burkett is in custody."

"That could be a while."

He grinned. "I don't think so. But you'll be our guest till then, whenever it is. In the meantime, don't worry. He can't get near you." Having made clear his message, he went to the door and placed his hand on the knob. "If you need anything, call me. Anytime." He glanced beyond her toward the bed, then his gaze slid back to her, and he smiled. "Nighty-night."

CHAPTER
29

As soon as Rodarte was through the door, Laura turned the dead bolt. She heard him confer with Carter and the policeman outside, then the soft *ping* of the elevator when it arrived.

But even after she knew he was gone, she stood hugging herself. She would ask housekeeping to bring her a can of air freshener so she could rid the room of his scent. But later. She didn't have the wherewithal to talk to anyone just now. She was weary of words.

She unzipped her suitcase and began unpacking it. But halfway through the chore, she ran out of energy. Even the will to move deserted her. She lay down on the bed. Tears came easily. They ran unchecked from the corners of her closed eyelids, trickled down her temples and into her hair.

Just as they had that day when Griff Burkett had brushed her tears away, the day it all had changed, the day—*face it, Laura*—he had reawakened her to feelings and sensations she hadn't experienced in a very long time. She'd told herself she didn't miss them, didn't yearn for them. How foolish she'd been. How wrong.

But she'd been particularly susceptible to tenderness that afternoon. Foster's indifference to her SunSouth Select proposal had cut her to the quick. It was worse than an outright rejection would have been. He simply had never acknowledged it again. He'd acted as though she'd never made the presentation. He'd killed the project with apathy, smothered it with his silence.

That afternoon, just before leaving to join Griff Burkett, she'd gone into Foster's office looking for something. What she'd found was the syllabus she had spent hundreds of hours preparing. It was in his wastepaper basket, along with the pieces of the airplane model. He'd disassembled it and tossed each component into the trash.

Even Griff Burkett had asked her about the model. He, a stranger, with no vested interest whatsoever in the airline industry, had been more curious about it than Foster.

Seeing the destroyed model had devastated her. It signified the death of her idea. Even though it was almost a certainty she would ovulate that day, she should have called Griff Burkett and canceled their appointment. She was too emotionally fragile to go, but she went, not wanting to explain to Foster why she had skipped a cycle and wasted an opportunity to make a baby for him.

While she lay beneath the sheet, waiting for their hired stud to come into the bedroom, she felt like a sacrifice on an altar. And it occurred to her then that that was precisely what she was, a sacrifice on the altar of Foster's ego. She'd been crying over that when Griff came into the room.

Neither had expected what happened next. She was certain that Griff hadn't intended it any more than she. Indeed, her tears had made him angry at first.

And then, with surprising gentleness, he had whisked them away. His caring had soothed the hurt of Foster's rejection. Instinctually she had grasped at it, clutched it with a desperate need for validation and tenderness, understanding and affection. Griff had responded to this reaction as most men would, sexually.

She had never joined him in that house seeking sexual satisfaction. Quite the opposite. She had fought the very idea of it. She went through her days, and nights, telling herself that she didn't feel deprived, that fulfillment came from other aspects of her life with Foster, that she didn't miss the weight of a man on her.

But feeling him swell inside her had been powerfully erotic. She was seized by a longing so acute, wasn't it natural, even excusable, that her body responded, and that, almost in spite of herself, she had given herself over to it?

She could almost justify what had happened between them that day.

But how could she excuse the afternoon four weeks later? She couldn't. What they'd done had been wrong, and ultimately calamitous.

Now she pressed her hand against her lower abdomen and wept for the child who would never know his father.

Either of them.

The next day she presided over the meeting she had called. All the department heads were there, as were all the board members.

She cut straight to the chase. "I won't hold you to the terms of Foster's will, automatically appointing me CEO. Foster wrote the proviso to prevent leaving the airline without a specified executive officer in the event of his sudden death. You know how he hated leaving anything to chance. However, he also ran this corporation as a democracy. I intend to carry on that tradition."

She reached for her water glass and took a sip. "Foster's manner of death will result in a trial. If not a trial, then at least there will be a formal inquiry and legal entanglements that can't be avoided. One way or another, I'll have to get through them, unsure of how or when they will be resolved. I want to prepare you for some unpleasantness. Allegations will be made, and I'll have to address them publicly.

"There will be an ongoing melee with the media. I hope to protect SunSouth from the worst of it, but Foster's and my names are synonymous with the airline. I beg your cooperation. If anyone from the media asks you for a comment, please refer them to our legal department. No matter how harmless a reporter may seem, please don't reply to any questions or make any statements or speculations. Anything you said could be used out of context."

"What unpleasantness do you predict?" one asked.

"The nature of our relationship with Griff Burkett may come into question. I confess it was intensely personal and private." An awkward silence descended over the room. Everyone focused on something other than her.

When no one spoke, she continued. "That brings me to my next point. If at any time you deem me unsuitable or incapable of carrying out my responsibilities to SunSouth Airlines and its employees, if you don't wish me to represent the airline as CEO or in any other capacity, request my resignation and I'll tender it immediately and without argument. I want you all to understand that."

Finally Joe McDonald raised his hand. "I've been appointed spokesperson for this meeting."

"All right." She braced herself. Perhaps they'd already decided that a woman whose husband had died under unexplained but violent circumstances, who was involved with a felonious ex–football player in any way, wasn't fit to be their CEO.

"We discussed this in advance of the meeting," Joe told her. "And we're in unanimous agreement that we want you to remain in your present position. That is, CEO."

"I'm very pleased to hear that," she said, struggling to keep her emotions under control. "I would hate to lose my husband and my job in the same week. But what I told you remains in effect. The continued success of SunSouth must be your priority. If ever you feel the future of the airline is in jeopardy, it's your *duty* to replace me."

"It's our duty to support our leader," Joe said. Several others said, "Hear, hear." Joe continued. "We stand with you, Laura. You have our complete trust in your integrity, as well as in your ability to run this airline."

"Thank you." She blinked away tears. "Now, with that matter settled, let's talk about Select." There were murmurs of surprise. "Are there still copies of the syllabus circulating?" she asked Joe.

"I collected them all. You told me that, for the time being, Select was tabled."

"For the time being, it was. I'm officially untabling it."

It was an exhausting day but a rewarding one. She accomplished much. The reintroduction of SunSouth Select had been received with the enthusiasm she had hoped for. Many commended her for moving ahead and focusing on the future, rather than dwelling on the unhappiness of the past.

Following that meeting, she had conferred with the senior partner of the law firm that handled Foster's personal affairs. In deference to her, the venerable gentleman had come to her office. They went over Foster's will, the various bequeathals he'd made to charity groups, and specifically to the foundation named after Elaine.

"I'd like to deliver that donation personally," Laura told him. "As you know, the foundation was very dear to Foster. In fact, once the estate is sold, I want all the proceeds to go to it."

"Sold?"

He was surprised that she wished to sell the estate and tried to dissuade her from making such a radical decision at a time when her emotions were running high.

She remained steadfast. "This isn't a rash decision. I've had two years to think about it. If Foster hadn't survived the car wreck, I would have put the estate on the market then. There are no surviving Speakmans. I don't want to live there alone, and it's too magnificent to stand empty. That would be a waste. So please make the necessary arrangements. I want the sale to be handled as discreetly as possible, with no fanfare, and no media. Those conditions must be specified in the contract with the realtor."

"Understood," the attorney said.

Rightfully, her unborn baby was heir to the estate. But she couldn't see herself bringing up a child in those vast, formal rooms. The child would never miss what he'd never known. No doubt the attorney would have argued the unfairness of her decision, but she didn't tell him she was pregnant.

He, as well as the SunSouth personnel, needed time to absorb the shock of Foster's death before being further shocked by his having left an heir. She needed time to absorb it herself.

Except for the police car following her back to the hotel, she felt more at peace than she had since Foster died. Her mood wasn't buoyant by any means, but she felt a sense of satisfaction for having endured the day without succumbing to the sorrow that had kept her inert the night before.

The police officer at the door of her room didn't forget to ask for her car keys. She relinquished them with a frown, which he pretended not to see. While she sipped a Coke from the minibar, she watched the six o'clock news. The manhunt for Griff Burkett was still the lead story.

Rodarte was on camera, talking about possible leads, but Laura didn't believe him, and the reporter interviewing him also looked skeptical. When asked about Manuelo Ruiz, he paused strategically, then said, "I'm afraid to speculate on Mr. Ruiz's fate, although we remain hopeful that he'll be found unharmed." His point was made by what he didn't say.

She switched off the TV and took a shower. She looked at the room service menu, because in spite of a mild residual nausea, she was hungry. She wondered how that could be. Nothing looked appetizing, but she ordered a club sandwich and asked that mashed potatoes be substituted for French fries. At least the potatoes and the toast on the sandwich might settle her stomach.

The food arrived. The policeman signed the tab, grudgingly adding the five-dollar tip she insisted he give the waiter in addition to the fixed service charge. She took the tray onto the bed with her and, while nibbling at the food, began making a list of Foster's possessions that she wanted to give to people who'd been special to him. There were items from his office, the house, and especially the library, that she knew he would want certain individuals to have.

That done, she started writing acknowledgments. Kay had already tackled that job, but some of the thank-you notes Laura thought it was only proper that she write personally.

The policeman knocked loudly on the door, startling her. "Mrs. Speakman? Are you all right?"

Setting aside the note cards, she got up, went to the door, and looked through the peephole. He almost filled the fish-eye lens, standing with his back to the door, arms extended at shoulder level, as though barring entrance.

"I'm fine, Officer."

"Good. Stay inside."

"What's the matter?"

"Don't open the door."

She unlatched the chain, unlocked the bolt, and opened the door.

The policeman turned and pushed her back into the room. He kicked the door shut with his heel at the same time he backed her into the wall.

"Never knew a woman yet who stayed put when told to."

It was Griff Burkett.

CHAPTER

30

"LET GO OF ME."

"Un-huh."

She tried to push him away. He tightened his grip on her shoulders, which only caused her to struggle harder. "Stop that!" he said.

"Then let me go."

"Not a chance."

She stopped trying to fight him off, but her eyes threw daggers. "How did you get past the guards?"

"They're in the stairwell. One of them's missing his hat, shirt, and gun belt," he said, nodding down at himself. The shirtsleeves were several inches too short, the buttons strained against his chest, and the fit across his shoulders wouldn't pass close inspection, but it had fooled Laura enough to get her to open the door. He hoped it would fool anyone who saw him escorting her from the building.

"I didn't hit them hard. They won't be out long. I've got to smuggle you out of here before someone realizes they're not at their posts." He pulled her away from the wall. "Get some clothes on."

She dug her heels in and tried to wrest her hand free from his grip. "I'll scream this building down before I go anywhere with you."

He took her by the shoulders again. "I did not kill your husband, Laura."

She closed her eyes and shook her head, refusing to hear.

"Listen to me. Manuelo Ruiz stabbed Foster, not me."

Her eyes popped open. She gaped at him. "Manuelo would never—"

"He did. And I'll give you a detailed account of what happened that night. Later. Right now, we're getting out of here. Now, dammit, get some clothes on." He said it with an undertone of threat, playing on her evident fear. He would make amends later, but he didn't have time for niceties now.

Coolly, she said, "I can't dress as long as you're holding on to me."

Gradually he removed his hands from her shoulders but was poised in case she tried to get to the door. She stepped around him and moved to the bureau. She took several articles of clothing from a drawer, considered them, exchanged them for others.

Impatiently, he yanked the items from her hand and threw them onto the bed, then jerked on the belt of her robe, untying it. "Get into them, and make it fast." She turned her back and let the robe slide off her onto the floor. She was naked. He was running for his life, but it was a sight that momentarily stopped him from thinking about anything else. She stepped into panties and worked a T-shirt over her head, then started moving toward the door. He grabbed her arm, halting her.

"There's a tracksuit in the closet."

The closet was adjacent to the door. He went to it, slid open the door, and sorted through the clothes.

"That," she said.

"This?" She nodded. He peeled the tracksuit off the hanger and thrust it at her. "Hurry."

She stepped into the stretchy pants and pulled them on. "If you force me to go with you—"

"I don't have a choice."

"Of course you do!"

"Shoes." He took a pair of sneakers from the closet and dropped them at her feet.

"You'll be adding kidnapping to your other crimes."

He helped her balance while she worked her feet into the sneakers. "Where's your purse?"

"Griff, I implore you."

"Are you wearing the jacket?"

She pulled it on. "Rodarte—"

"Will be checking with these guys any minute."

"That's right. You'll never get me out of this hotel. He has guards posted downstairs, too. They've got my car keys."

He fished her ring of keys out of his pants pocket and jangled it at her. "You're walking out of here, Laura. You and your *police escort.* Anyone challenges you, you say you need some things from the store, you have a hankering for Taco Bell, your grandmother is sick. I don't care what excuse you give, just make them believe it."

She looked him over. "Despite the getup, don't you think they'll recognize you?"

"For your own safety, you'd better hope they don't."

She glanced down at the holster on his hip. Rather than frightening her, it seemed to embolden her. Taking a stance, she folded her arms and looked up at him. "You wouldn't hurt me. I know you wouldn't."

"You don't think?"

Slowly, she shook her head.

He moved in close and lowered his face to within inches of hers. "I'm not going back to prison. So if I'm caught, all bets are off. I'll blare to the whole frigging world that Foster Speakman couldn't get it up. He was no longer a man, the marriage was a sham, and, in order to have a kid, he hired me to fuck his wife." Her face went slack with dismay.

"Yeah," Griff said, "think about that. I saw the pictures of his funeral, watched the stories about it on TV, saw you posed so pretty at his graveside. I've read his obituary and listened to politicians singing his praises. Everybody thought he was bloody wonderful, didn't they? What do you think their opinion of Foster the great is going to be when I tell them he paid me to play stud for him?

"And don't forget, to prove it's true, I've got a hundred grand in the bank with his name on the signature card." He encircled her biceps, forming an unbreakable grip with his strong fingers, and shoved her toward the door. "Now move it."

"Hey, Thomas?"

Griff pulled up short, and Laura with him. The sound came from the earpiece he'd stuck in his ear after putting on the cop's uniform. Thomas was being paged by one of his counterparts downstairs. Giving Laura a warning look, Griff clicked on the transmitter clipped to the shoulder seam of the shirt. "Go ahead," he mumbled.

"Where's Lane?"

"At the elevator with Mrs. Speakman," he whispered, as though not wanting to be overheard. "He's bringing Her Highness down."

"What for?"

"She wants some carryout."

"Sick of room service food?"

Griff grunted a noncommittal reply.

"Yeah, she's got it really tough," the cop said sarcastically. "Even with Lane tagging along, Rodarte isn't gonna like it, her going out after dark."

"Then Rodarte can come babysit her."

The other cop laughed. "I hear that." He clicked off.

Griff looked through the peephole, then pulled open the door and checked the hallway. He pulled Laura behind him as he ran toward the service elevator. He'd placed a dolly in the open door to keep it there. When they were inside, he dragged the dolly in and pushed the button for the ground floor.

"Where's your car?" he asked.

"In the employee parking lot."

"Once we're out of the building, where?"

"To the right."

"How far?"

"Fairly close." His eyes drilled into hers, demanding more. She said, "Within steps of the entrance. But we'll never get past the guard at that door."

"He's napping."

The cop was still out cold, right where Griff had left him, behind a Dumpster, out of sight of any hotel employee who happened to use that entrance. Griff had come dressed in a set of navy blue work pants and shirt, carrying a stack of empty boxes. The ruse had worked long enough for him to get close to the cop and knock him out.

The policeman on the top floor, guarding the stairwell and service elevator, had reacted with surprise when the elevator doors opened and Griff stepped off. "Hey, you're supposed to clear it downstairs before—" Griff had thrust the boxes at him and punched.

Hearing the commotion, the cop guarding Laura's door had come running. He'd rounded a corner and got clouted on the head with the butt of his buddy's service pistol. Of the two, he was the larger. Griff had hastily stripped him of his uniform shirt, hat, and gun belt.

He'd handcuffed each of them behind their backs, also linking the pairs of handcuffs together, then put duct tape over their mouths. Even when they regained consciousness, they'd make an awkward, mute, four-legged animal that would have trouble getting out of the stairwell and raising an alarm.

He was guilty of assault on three police officers. That was the least of his worries.

He knew there was another cop posted at the corner of the parking lot. It was just dark enough that Griff hoped from that distance the cop would see only a uniform shirt and hat and would mistake him for Lane. As he and Laura emerged from the service entrance, Griff kept his face averted but raised his arm and waved. The cop waved back.

Laura led him to her BMW. He unlocked the driver's side. Thinking of the horn, he said, "Remember what I told you upstairs. If you want to uphold your late husband's reputation, you do not want me to be caught."

He closed the door and quickly walked around to the passenger side. Once he was in, he put the key in the ignition and started the motor. "Take the freeway to Oak Lawn. Exit and head north until it merges with Preston."

She looked at him with surprise.

"That's right, Laura. We're going to your house."

Getting past the policeman at the gate was going to be the next tricky part. While Laura drove, Griff formulated a plan.

"You won't get away with this," she said.

"I have so far, haven't I?"

"Policemen in five states are looking for you."

"But they haven't found me."

"Where have you been hiding?"

He didn't answer that. "When we get to your place, make sure your headlights are on bright. Pull in so that they're shining directly into the windshield of the patrol car that's parked in front of the gate."

"Are you sure the gate is still being guarded?"

"I'm sure."

"How did you know where to find me?"

"Followed Rodarte."

She looked at him with astonishment. "You've been following Rodarte? How?"

"What's the code on your gate?"

She turned her head back to the road, and her hands tightened on the steering wheel. "I can't think of a single reason why I should tell you that."

"Can you think of a reason why your husband would have had half a million in cash at your house that night, stacked neatly in a stationery box?"

"I explained that to Rodarte." In nervous stops and starts, she told Griff about Foster's heavy tipping practice.

"Half a million dollars' worth?" Griff said, laughing. "Nobody's that generous."

"Rodarte believed me."

"I doubt it. In any case, I could throw a shitload of doubt on that explanation. Or"—he paused for emphasis—"you could give me the gate code." She gave him the code, and then he told her how it was going to play out when they reached the estate.

As instructed, when she turned in to the private drive, she pulled in so that her headlights shone directly into the squad car. Griff opened the passenger door. Before getting out, he said, "I could make mincemeat of Foster Speakman's reputation. Remember that."

He stepped out of the car, leaving the door open, and walked toward the keypad on the column near the gate.

The policeman had got out of the squad car and was approaching him, his hand raised, shielding his eyes against the glare of Laura's headlights. Griff kept moving, asking over his shoulder, "How's it going here? Everything quiet?"

"Yeah. What's up?"

"Officer?" Laura called out to him.

The cop turned toward her. Griff reached the column, punched in the sequence of numbers she had given him, holding his breath until the double gate began to swing open.

"Is everything all right here?" Laura had alighted and was standing in the open door of her car, talking to the policeman.

"Yes, ma'am."

"This additional security is so unnecessary."

"Better to be safe, ma'am."

"I need to pick up some things from the house. I shouldn't be long."

By now, Griff was back at the car, sliding into the passenger seat. She bent down and addressed him. "You don't have to go inside with me," she said, following the script he'd given her. "In fact, I'd rather you didn't. I'll be perfectly safe inside my own home."

"I'm supposed to stay with you, ma'am. Rodarte's orders," he said, making sure the other cop heard it.

She huffed as though vexed and looked back at the officer. "Could you move your car please, before the gate closes?"

Quickly he returned to his squad car, started it, and rolled it forward far enough to clear the gate. Laura drove through.

Griff didn't start breathing again until the gate closed automatically behind them. But if that officer was any kind of sharp, he'd be checking with Rodarte to see if Laura's visit to her home had been approved. Or he would soon be receiving a call from the hotel telling him that Mrs. Speakman had been abducted. Griff hoped to be in and out before either happened.

"Go in through the front door, where he can see us."

She followed the driveway and parked directly in front of the house. Griff got out and approached the mansion's grand entrance, looked around, played the role of bodyguard in case they were being observed. Laura used her key and opened the front door. The alarm started beeping. She made no move toward the keypad.

Griff said, "The house on Windsor Street would become a tourist attraction."

She understood the warning and punched in the code that silenced the alarm.

"Lights?"

She touched a switch that seemed to turn on every light in the house. "Fancy," he said, impressed.

"Now what?"

"Now we go to the garage. Specifically, to Manuelo Ruiz's apartment above the garage."

She looked at him with incredulity. "Is that what this is about?"

"That's what this is about. How do you get to the garage?"

Looking like she wanted to argue, she turned instead and walked stiffly across the foyer. He followed, relieved that she was leading him in the direction opposite the library.

The kitchen was three times larger than the house Griff had grown up in.

On the far side of it was a door. Laura walked toward it. "Wait," he said. "That goes outside?"

"Through the mudroom, then outside."

"Is the exterior door visible from the front gate?"

"No."

Griff went around her, opened the door, and saw a utility area that deserved a more glamorous name than mudroom. He opened the exterior door and looked out. There were no longer policemen patrolling the estate grounds. They'd been pulled off when Rodarte had moved Laura to the hotel yesterday evening. Griff had been watching, and he knew.

Nevertheless, he felt exposed as he and Laura crossed the motor court between the house and the detached garage. Laura indicated a door at the side of the building. "Manuelo's apartment is through that door and up the stairs, but you won't find him there."

"I don't expect to."

There was a keypad on the wall adjacent to the door. "Another freaking code?" Griff motioned to it impatiently, and Laura punched in a sequence of numbers. The door opened with a metallic click.

They slipped inside. Griff pulled the door closed behind them and heard the lock engage.

"No lights," he said, sensing that she was groping the wall for the switch plate. "You came to pick up stuff from the house, not the garage. The lights stay off."

He pulled a small flashlight from the policeman's belt and switched it on. He shone the beam down at their feet, but he could see her in the ambient light.

"Laura. Is there really a baby?"

CHAPTER

31

J UDGING FROM THE LOOK ON HER FACE, THE QUESTION HAD TAKEN her completely by surprise. She stared at him for several seconds, then made a small motion with her head.

He felt an expanding pressure inside his chest. He'd never felt anything like it before, so he couldn't put a name to it. It was a strange feeling, and yet a good one. Like supreme satisfaction. Like the total opposite of what he'd been feeling the other day in the motel when he'd reviewed his life history.

He looked down at her abdomen but couldn't detect any change. Of course there wouldn't be any yet.

He wondered if she was thinking, like he was, about their last afternoon together, when he'd reached around her and closed the front door. How could they have foreseen the cataclysmic impact that simple motion would have? Because of it, one life had ended. And another had begun.

His gaze tracked back up to her face. Their eyes met and held. This warm, closed space in which they were standing seemed suddenly to be very small and airless. He didn't dare take a deep breath for fear of breaking the silence that pressed in on them, teeming with implication.

He knew there must be something appropriate to say to a woman who had your baby inside her, but damned if he could think of what it might be, so he didn't say anything, just continued staring into her eyes, until she finally looked away.

He touched her chin and brought her head back around to face him. "I'll go to death row unless I find Manuelo Ruiz. Do you understand?"

She shook her head, slowly and then more adamantly. "No, I don't. It's not possible. Manuelo worshiped Foster. He wouldn't—"

"But I would?"

She searched his eyes, then made a motion with her head and shoulders that could have meant either yes or no. But even if she had the slightest doubt, it was crushing to him.

He dropped his hand. "I don't know why I hoped you would believe me when my own lawyer didn't even bother to ask whether or not I had killed your husband. He just assumed I had. I didn't. Manuelo did."

"He couldn't."

"It was a bizarre accident. Seeing what he'd done, the guy wigged out. He bolted. He's scared and may be halfway to El Salvador by now. But without him, I'm sunk."

He shone the flashlight beam on his wristwatch. They'd driven away from the hotel twenty-seven minutes ago. Thomas and Lane and the rest of them were probably catching hell from Rodarte by now. Soon a posse would be dispatched.

"My time's running out." He motioned her up the staircase.

On their way, she said, "If Manuelo is running, this is the last place he would be."

"Officially, there's no record of the man beyond a social security number, which was fake, and a Texas driver's license with a phony address."

"How do you know this?"

"Rodarte. He was quoted in the newspaper."

"If the police can't find him, how do you hope to?" By now she had reached the door at the top of the stairs. It was unlocked. Griff switched off the flashlight and followed Laura into the apartment.

"Where are the windows?"

"There aren't any. Only skylights on the back side of the roof."

Trusting her to be telling the truth, he turned the flashlight back on but kept it aimed at the floor. It was a spacious single room which, Griff estimated, covered half of the garage below. It was equipped with a small kitchen area with dormitory-size appliances, and a TV in a cabinet opposite the bed. The bathroom was compact.

The apartment had already been tossed by the police. Bureau drawers had been left open, the closet door stood ajar. The twin bed had been stripped. The mattress was askew.

"Hold the light." Griff passed her the flashlight, then started his search with the TV cabinet. "How did Manuelo come to be Foster's aide?"

"He was a janitor at the rehab center. Foster was there for several months after he got out of the hospital. One day after a strenuous therapy session, he experienced respiratory distress. He was no longer hooked to monitors, he couldn't reach the call button. Manuelo happened by. He didn't summon help but came in, lifted Foster out of bed, and carried him to the nurses' station. Foster credited him with saving his life. I think Manuelo felt the same about Foster. His life improved dramatically when Foster took him in."

The drawers of the cabinet had yielded nothing except some loose coins, a broken pair of sunglasses, nail clippers, underwear, folded T-shirts. "In from where?" Griff asked. "Where had he lived before?"

"Foster may have known. I never did," she replied, following his movements with the beam of the flashlight. "Manuelo showed up here with a small duffel bag of belongings and moved into this apartment. Foster bought him new clothes. He paid for his training as a nursing aide, on how to care for paraplegics. Manuelo was devoted to Foster."

Griff snuffled. "Yeah. I know."

Although the bed obviously had already been searched, he felt the mattress and box springs, looking for bumps where something could have been stashed. He moved the bed away from the wall and motioned for her to direct the flashlight onto the floor beneath it. Low-nap carpet. No sign that it had been sliced to form a secret pocket. "Did he have family? Friends?"

"Not to my knowledge. Griff, Rodarte has already asked me all this. The police have been searching for Manuelo since the night ... the night Foster died."

"The first time I saw him, Manuelo struck me as a survivor," Griff said. "Foster told me he'd walked to the U.S. from El Salvador." A small curtain hid the plumbing for the tiny kitchen sink. He parted it but found only pots and pans, some dishwashing liquid. He looked in the oven and microwave but came up empty. He checked the fridge but found nothing except a few canned drinks, condiments, three oranges.

"Walking through Guatemala and Mexico? That tells me that he was either very, very poor or running from something and didn't want to risk traveling on public transportation. Probably both."

In the bathroom, he looked in the tank of the toilet, then took the light from Laura and shone it down the shower drain.

She asked, "How do you know to do that?"

"Some things you learn in prison."

There was nothing in the medicine cabinet above the sink except shaving implements, toothpaste, toothbrush. He returned to the main room, hands on hips, looking about. The ceiling? He couldn't see any seams in the material where Manuelo might have cut out a section to form a hiding place.

Inside the closet were several pairs of black trousers, two pairs of black shoes, and a black baseball-style jacket. "Where's the duffel bag?" he asked rhetorically.

"The what?"

"You said he arrived with a small duffel bag of personal belongings. Where is it?"

"I suppose he took it with him."

"Trust me, he didn't stop to pack that night. He didn't take his clothes or his toiletries. It said in the newspaper that cash was found in his apartment. Nobody leaves money behind, unless they don't leave of their own accord."

"Which is why Rodarte suspects you of—"

"Killing Manuelo, too. I know. But I didn't. Laura, the man was hysterical. Out of his head. He ran like the devil was after him." He frowned at the look she gave him. "No, it wasn't me he was afraid of."

She didn't respond to that. Instead, she said, "He didn't pack, so you believe that his duffel bag is here somewhere. So what? What good would finding it do us?"

"Maybe none. But a top-notch rehab hospital wouldn't have hired even a janitor without immigration documents. If Manuelo sneaked into the country, he must have had help getting falsified papers so he could get work. He had to have had a contact. And I bet he would have stayed in touch with that contact in case he had to get the hell out of Dodge, quick. He would have—"

The wail of approaching sirens cut him off. "Shit!" He grabbed Laura's hand and pulled her through the door onto the landing of the stairwell. He switched off the flashlight, but just as he did, he noticed the door opposite the one to Ruiz's apartment. "What's that?"

"What? I can't see anything."

"That door. Where does it go?"

"It accesses the attic space above the other side of the garage. It's not finished out. Foster had talked about one day flooring it, but— What are you doing?"

Griff had pushed open the door, and the hot, contained air rushed out to envelop them. He switched on the flashlight and shone it into the large space, empty except for exposed insulation and joists, plumbing pipes, and electrical conduits.

About three feet in front of him, an air-conditioning duct stretched along the floor for the entire width of the attic; it was the duct that would have conveyed a/c and heat into Manuelo's apartment.

Griff aimed the flashlight beam on the silver tube and tracked it from the far wall forward.

The sirens were getting closer, louder.

He tried to block them out and concentrate on the duct, taking in every seam, every wrinkle in the material, looking—

He uttered a soft cry of elation when he saw the patch. "There it is!"

Wasting no time to think about it, he stepped out onto the two-by-four nearest him and inched along it toward the patch. If he slipped, he could drive his foot through the Sheetrock, which wouldn't support his weight. The only thing keeping him from fall-

ing through it and landing hard on the garage floor twenty feet below was his agility. And his will to find Manuelo Ruiz.

When he got even with the patch, he stuck the flashlight in his
mouth, and, balancing on the balls of his feet, leaned across the emptiness toward the duct.

The sirens had stopped. Not a good sign.

He ripped away the tape forming the patch and plunged his hand
into the hollow duct. His fingertips brushed something, but it was
just out of reach. The flashlight fell from his mouth onto the Sheetrock floor several inches below the two-by-four on which he bal-
anced. It rolled away, out of reach. He let it go.

He crabbed along the two-by-four until he could grasp the object
inside the duct. The attic space was as hot as an oven. Keeping his
balance while reaching into the duct was an extreme effort. His knees
were screaming. Sweat ran into his eyes, making them sting. The
policeman's shirt was too damn small. It was confining his shoulders, limiting his reach. He strained against it, ripping the shoulder
seams but gaining a longer reach.

Finally he got two fingers on the object, clamped them shut, and
pulled the object far enough forward for him to grab hold. He gave
it a hard yank, ripping the skin of the duct as he pulled it out. It was
a black duffel bag.

He stood up quickly and, with the deft steps of a tightrope walker,
made his way back to the door at the staircase landing. "I've got it!"
But he was talking to empty darkness. Laura had vanished.

CHAPTER
32

THE HOUSE WAS STILL ABLAZE, LIGHTS ON IN EVERY ROOM. Through windows where the drapes were open, Laura could see uniformed policemen searching the rooms for her and Griff.

She was halfway across the motor court when her elbow was hooked from behind. "This way," Griff said.

She tried to throw off his hand, but his hold was tenacious and she had to run to keep up with him. "Griff, this is insanity. Turn yourself in. Talk to Rodarte. Tell him what you told me about Manuelo."

By now they were on the far side of the garage, out of sight of the house, away from the landscape lighting, running pell-mell through the darkness. They went around the pond and then plunged down a natural berm. She lost her footing and would have fallen if he hadn't kept his tight grip on her. She stumbled along after him.

The ground leveled off at the estate wall. It didn't appear this tall from a distance. Now its twelve feet seemed awfully high. The vines and shrubbery covering it were dense but well maintained. Incongruously, there was a cold drink can standing upright at the twisted root system of a wisteria that was in full leaf and completely covering a section of the wall.

"Griff!" She pulled hard on his hand.

He turned to her. "Listen and believe, Laura. Rodarte is convinced that I killed Bill Bandy five years ago. Now he's convinced that I killed your husband. If I turn myself in, I'll be at the mercy of a legal system I no longer trust. Especially since Rodarte's on the case."

"Then turn yourself in to someone else."

He shook his head stubbornly. "Not until I can take Manuelo Ruiz in with me, ready and willing to corroborate my story. I've got to find him."

"Okay, I can see that," she said, breathless from their run. "But let me go back. Let me tell your side of it and explain why you're reluctant to surrender."

"No."

"If I say—"

"Why did Rodarte have you under lock and key?"

"To protect me from you."

"Right. So if I get backed into a corner, as long as I've got you as my hostage, I've got something to bargain with."

"You wouldn't hurt me."

"*You* know that. Rodarte doesn't. Now come on." He dragged her forward, toward the wisteria.

"Do you expect me to climb that?"

"Don't have to." Still keeping hold of her with one hand, he used the other to clear away some offshoots of the vine, revealing a metal grate at the base of the wall. He shoved it aside with the toe of his shoe. "Drainage," he said.

"How did you find this?"

"I came looking." He put his hand on her shoulder, forced her down. "Crawl through. I'm right behind you."

Lying down on her stomach, she wiggled through the opening. The ground was damp, but because of the drought, it wasn't muddy. The wall was about a foot thick. On the other side was a twenty-acre greenbelt that served as a buffer between the elite private properties that backed up to it, like the Speakmans', and the commercial district on the far side.

By the time she was on her feet, Griff had pushed the duffel bag through the opening. It was a squeeze to get his shoulders through, but he did and sprang up on the other side. Taking her hand, he guided her across a rough and rocky creek bed. It was dry now, but when it rained, the runoff from the Speakman property would drain into it through the grate by which they'd made their escape.

Once across the creek bed, Griff took off running through the greenbelt. But as they approached the boulevard on the far side, he slowed to a walk. Across the wide street was a row of boutique shops and two popular restaurants. The shops were closed, but the restaurants were busy with the dinner crowd.

Pausing in the shadows of the park, he released her hand long enough to take off the uniform shirt, leaving him in a white T-shirt. He removed the pistol from the policeman's holster, then tossed the gun belt, shirt, hat, and cold drink can into the nearest trash receptacle. He zipped the pistol into Manuelo Ruiz's duffel bag.

Taking her hand again, he waited until the traffic thinned, then struck off across the divided street. He didn't run, which would have attracted attention, but walked swiftly toward the parking lot of the Indian restaurant. He wove them through the rows of cars until they reached the back of the lot, where it was dark.

He fished a remote key from his pants pocket and used it to unlock a car. He opened the passenger door and motioned her in. He walked around and got behind the wheel, closed the door, and tossed the duffel bag onto the backseat. The dome light dimmed and then went out, leaving them in darkness.

They sat still and silent, trying to catch their breath.

Not until now that they'd stopped did Laura realize how breathless she was, and how fast her heart was pounding, as much from adrenaline as from physical exertion. The palms of her hands were dirty. The front of her tracksuit was streaked with loose soil.

"I'm sorry about that," he said, when he noticed her palms.

"I'm a fugitive, too. I'm not worried about a little dirt."

"You're not the fugitive, I am. You're my hostage, remember."

She smiled ruefully. "You asked why Rodarte had placed me under lock and key? He claimed it was for my protection."

"But?"

"He was afraid I would help you escape." His gaze remained steady, but she could read the unasked questions in it. "He never said that, but I sensed that was why he put me in the hotel, under guard. And I suppose I have helped you escape, haven't I?"

"Does that mean you believe I'm innocent?"

Before she could answer, a police car screamed down the boulevard, its lights a wild kaleidoscope. Griff turned on the car's ignition. Grinning, he said, "Rough neighborhood. We'd better move to a safer one."

He had to wait for another oncoming police car to roar past before pulling out into the street. "You're thumbing your nose at them," she remarked.

"Nothing that brave. They won't be looking for this car."

"Whose is it?"

He drove, saying nothing.

"The visit to your lawyer's house made the news."

"Yeah, I saw. The media failed to mention what an untrustworthy son of a bitch my *former* attorney is."

"He said by turning you in he was trying to help."

"Bullshit. He was trying to cover his own ass."

"They searched for you for hours."

"I got lucky."

"How did you get away?"

He gave her a wry grin. "It wasn't easy. Sometime, when you've got a lot of time, maybe I'll tell you all the adventures I encountered that night."

She gave his clothing a once-over. "The police were looking for a man in running shorts and sneakers."

"Which were barely holding together by daylight the next day. I was traveling light, but luckily, before going to Turner's house, I'd put some cash in my sock. I used it the next day to buy some clothes at a big flea market." He glanced down at the T-shirt and work pants. "Selection was limited. I'm sure some of the goods were hot, so no one questioned the customer who looked like he'd been dunked in a polluted river and then run through a shredder."

"Were you recognized?"

"Doubtful. The market draws a large Hispanic crowd. Typically they follow soccer, not American football. I tried to be inconspicuous."

Her eyes shifted up to his blond hair. "That couldn't have been easy."

"Especially not when I started asking around about Manuelo Ruiz, looking for someone who might know him. Those inquiries aroused more suspicion than my ragtag appearance. I didn't stay long."

"Where have you been hiding?"

He didn't reply.

"You're not going to tell me, are you?"

"The less you know, the better. Rodarte can never accuse you of collaborating with me. You're my hostage. Got that?"

"I've got it. I don't think Rodarte will be convinced. When he introduced himself, I recognized his name immediately. Before, when you warned me about him, you didn't say he was a policeman. You made him sound like a criminal. You said he'd beat up a friend of yours."

"He did. And sodomized her. Ruined her face. Broke—"

"A *woman*?"

"Yeah, and Rodarte nearly killed her."

Laura had assumed Griff was referring to a male friend. Learning that Rodarte had assaulted a woman filled her with repugnance and fear. "He attacked her because of you?"

"Because she wouldn't give him any information."

"What kind of information?"

"About my past and present business dealings. Not that she knew anything, but it did her no good to tell Rodarte that."

"He must have thought she knew something. Is she a close friend?"

"I guess you could call it a friendship. Actually, I'm her client. She's a prostitute."

That piece of news took her aback. Had he been using the hundred thousand she and Foster had paid him to buy the services of a prostitute? Of course the money was his to spend, it was just that she had never known anyone, of either sex, who admitted going to a prostitute. Maybe that was why it was so startling to her that he had in such a matter-of-fact way.

Curiosity compelled her. "What's her name?"

"Marcia. She's not a street hooker. She has a penthouse. She's clean, classy, very expensive, beautiful. Or was. It's been months since the assault, and she's still recovering, going through a series of reconstructive surgeries on her face. She won't even talk to me about the other. Rodarte has a badge, but he uses it as a free pass to hurt people and get away with it." He shot her a glance. "You've been with him. Did he ever touch you?"

"Last night he stroked my arm. It made me shudder. I think he knew that, and that's why he did it. Behind everything he said was a sexual innuendo."

Griff's long fingers were flexing and contracting around the steering wheel as though preparing to pull it out of the dashboard. "It was only a matter of time before he hurt you. Which was another reason I wanted to get you out of there. Anything he did to you, he would have felt you had coming because of your affair with me."

She remembered Rodarte coming up close behind her, promising in an insinuating whisper to be her protector—or not—when her affair with Griff was exposed. Griff may indeed have rescued her. But there was still much he had to answer for. "So you had a car, and a hiding place, and you've been following Rodarte."

"You were my connection to Manuelo. I knew you'd be essential to finding him. But I also knew Rodarte would be keeping close watch on you, expecting me to turn up sooner or later.

"Yesterday evening, after the funeral and reception, I was parked on Preston Road, near where I left the car tonight. When I saw this caravan of police cars coming from the direction of the estate, I pulled out into traffic. So I was actually ahead of your police escort. I slowed, let you drive past, then followed you to the hotel."

"How'd you get the room number?"

"I didn't, but it was a logical guess that you'd be on the top floor."

"I had the floor to myself."

"I figured that, too. When I got up there tonight, I had a nanosecond to look down the hall and see which door the cop was guarding before throwing an armload of empty boxes at his buddy.

"Anyway, last night, once I knew where you would be when I needed you, I went back to the estate to try to find a way in. The guard never left the front gate, but the ones that had been patrolling the grounds were pulled off. No need for them since you were no longer there.

"I knew that the park behind the property was the only possible access. I combed every inch of that side of the estate wall, practically on hands and knees. In the dark, mind you. I was looking for a rear gate. Something. Took hours before I found the grate. I loosened it, crawled through."

"And left that drink can there so you could find it again from the inside."

"In a hurry. Just in case cops were in hot pursuit. The rest you more or less know." After a beat, he said, "Except this."

He turned in to the parking lot of a multiscreen movie theater and found an open slot between a van with a Garfield clinging to the rear window with suction cups on his paws and a pickup truck with tires taller than their car.

He cut the ignition and turned toward her. "The night I got out of prison, I was desperate to get laid. I went to Marcia. Just that once. There's been nobody since."

She took a breath, held it for several seconds before letting it out. "I wondered."

"Why didn't you ask?"

"I didn't have the right."

He moved suddenly, stretching his arm across the space separating them, curving his hand around the back of her neck and pulling her toward him. He kissed her hard, stamping his lips firmly against hers, pressing his tongue deep into her mouth. Then he pushed her away as suddenly as he'd grabbed her.

Hoarsely, he said, "You had every right."

He let go of the back of her neck and returned to his place behind the wheel. For several moments they sat in silence, hearing only the soft popping sounds made by the car's motor as it began to cool.

Finally he turned to her. "He called me. Foster. The day the pregnancy was confirmed. He invited me to your house the next night so he could thank me and pay me in person. Did you know any of this?"

"No."

"He also said he'd figured out how I would be paid if I outlived you both. Remember that hitch?"

She nodded.

"He said he'd worked out a solution. He used that and the promise of the half million to get me there. And while I was there, Manuelo tried to kill me."

"*What?*"

"You heard me."

"*Why?*"

"Because Foster ordered it."

She inclined away from him until she was pressed against the passenger door. "You're lying!"

"No, I'm not. And you know I'm not, Laura, or you'd have put up a bigger fight before leaving that hotel with me. You're not a pushover and you're no coward. If you'd wanted to get away from me, you'd have been screaming bloody murder every step of the way, because, as you said, you know I wouldn't carry out any threat to hurt you. You're here because you want to be. You want to hear the truth of what happened. In any case, you're going to listen."

He paused for breath and to organize his thoughts. Also to see if she would, after all, open the car door and run screaming across the parking lot. She didn't, so he began.

"Over the last several days, I've spent the daylight hours, and a lot of the nighttime, thinking. *Thinking.* And remembering. In my mind I've replayed every word, every small detail, from the first meeting till those last horrendous moments of Foster's life, and I can see now how well he planned it. It was a masterful game plan.

"It even occurred to me that he'd lied when he called to tell me you were pregnant. I hadn't heard it from you. I thought maybe that was the juiciest piece of bait for the trap he laid. That's why I asked you earlier if you were really pregnant."

"It was confirmed the day before he died."

"So that much was true. Once Foster knew he had his child and heir, he wasted no time setting me up to be silenced forever. Only his plan backfired, and he died instead."

"How? How, Griff? What happened when you got to the house?"

"Manuelo let me in like before. Poured me a drink, then left Foster and me alone in the library, behind closed doors. We toasted our success. He started talking . . . well, bullshit. About how delighted the two of you were over the pregnancy."

"That wasn't bullshit."

"Yeah, but . . . but it was the way he was telling it. He got choked up, or pretended to. He told me you'd never looked so beautiful as when you said, 'We have a baby,' and how meaningful that word *we* was to a man in his condition.

"He told me your breasts were tender, that you wouldn't let him touch them and how embarrassed you'd be to know he'd told me that. He talked about the baby. Could I guess what it would be? Had I thought about what it might be when we were making it? He reminded me that I'd have to read in the newspaper whether it was a boy or girl. I wouldn't know its name until I read about it."

Griff gave a bitter laugh. "Looking back, I can see that he was goading me. He was saying things he knew would get under my skin. At the time I just wanted him to shut up about you and the baby. I didn't want to hear what a happy little family the three of you would be."

He gave her a significant look, wondering if she could read between the lines. He guessed she could. She lowered her gaze to her hands, which were clasped tightly in her lap.

"He showed me my payoff money. The sight of it made me sick. Sick at my stomach, sick at myself. Marcia claims she never feels like a whore, but when I looked down into that box of money, I did. Our deal wasn't illegal, but I felt a lot guiltier taking Foster's money than I did taking the two million from Vista, and that's the God's truth, Laura.

"I didn't even want to touch it, and he sensed that. He said he was surprised by my restraint. I mumbled some excuse for it. Then he started laughing and said, 'Oh dear, you don't want it to end, do you?' "

Laura looked at him sharply. "What?"

"Something like that. He began gibing me about developing a taste for you like I had the gambling. He said I must have really enjoyed 'doing' you, and that's a quote. He was giving me this gloating smile. Thinking about it now makes me angry all over again."

At the risk of casting doubt on his innocence, he reined in his anger and stuck to the facts. "I called him a sick fuck. He wouldn't shut up about it and started saying over and over, 'Poor Griff.'

"The taunting made me irate, Laura. I admit that. I felt myself about to lose it. Wheelchair or not, I wanted to deck him. I wanted to so bad I had to turn away. When I did, I looked down at the desktop. Swear to God I didn't see the letter opener. Or if I did, it didn't register. What I noticed was this sheet of paper with official-looking writing on it.

"Foster backed down then. He stopped that hideous chanting. I don't know if he sensed how close I was to knocking him across the room, or if he saw what had caught my eye. But in any case, he said, 'Oh, that's why you're here, isn't it? That's my proposal for what should happen if both Laura and I die before you. Read it.'

"At that point, I just wanted to conclude our business and get the hell out of there before I did something I would regret. So I picked up the sheet of paper and began to read. Or tried."

"It was gibberish."

Surprised, he said, "You've seen it?"

"Rodarte gave it to me, asked if I knew what it meant."

"Okay, so you know it was a ruse. I'd belted the strong bourbon. And I was still seeing red over the things he'd said. I thought that was why I wasn't understanding what I was reading. I went back to the beginning and started over. And that's when I sensed movement behind me."

"Behind you?"

"Manuelo. I hadn't heard him return. Foster was probably doing that 'poor Griff' bit so I wouldn't. I caught a glimpse of Manuelo just in time."

Reflexes, honed by years of dodging tacklers, had kicked in. He'd moved sideways only a fraction of a foot, but it was enough to neutralize Manuelo's lunge toward him.

"Unfortunately, his reflexes were almost as quick as mine, and he was able to wrap his arms around me, one at my throat, the other around my rib cage. You know how wiry and strong he is."

She nodded.

"He began to squeeze. He felt like a python around me." Griff remembered struggling, clawing at the man's arms. He broke Manuelo's skin with his fingernails but achieved nothing else. For a man so short in stature, the aide had astonishing strength. His muscles had been conditioned to place pressure where pressure was desired, and to do so with absolute control.

They'd engaged in a macabre dance, going round and round, knocking over the end table, sending objects to the floor, breaking a lamp. "I tried like hell to break his stranglehold," Griff went on, "if only for a millisecond, long enough for me to take a breath. Nothing worked.

"Soon, I felt myself growing weaker. Black dots appeared in my field of vision. I'd had the wind knocked out of me and lost consciousness on the football field, so I recognized the signs and knew I was on my way under. But I could still see Foster sitting in his wheelchair, slapping the arms of it in sequences of three, muttering 'Do it, do it, do it,' also in sequences of three."

Laura pressed her fingertips against her lips.

"Are you believing any of this, or am I wasting my breath?" he asked.

"Go on."

"You're not gonna like what I'm about to say. I was on the brink of blacking out when I realized what I think I knew from the moment I met him. He was a lunatic."

"Don't—"

"No, Laura. You're going to hear this. He was insane. At least on some level. What man in his right mind, married to you, would ask another man to have sex with you? Pay him to. For *any* reason."

She didn't produce an answer, and Griff hadn't expected one. "I'm convinced now that doing away with me was his intention all along." She was about to protest, but he spoke before she could. "Think about it. He was fanatical about keeping our agreement a secret. In order to guarantee that, I had to die. Leaving me alive was untidy. For a compulsive cleaner, I was an unacceptable wrinkle in the bar towel, a water spot on the granite. He insisted on perfection, and for his plan to be perfect, I had to be eliminated." He paused, then said, "Him I could understand. But I wondered about you."

"Me?"

"Were you in on it, Laura? Was this your plan, too?"

"I'm not even going to honor that with a response."

"Why'd you go to Austin that day?"

He listened as she explained the circumstances. "Whatever happened that night, I wasn't a part of it," she said with heat. "I didn't even know you'd been to the mansion until Rodarte told me your fingerprints were on the murder weapon."

He dragged his hand down his face. "I didn't think you would plot my death, but when my lights were going out, the question did flash through my mind. Were you conveniently in Austin so you wouldn't have to witness my murder?"

"You truly thought that?"

"Uncanny how clearly you see things when you think you're about to die. You'd refused to talk to me after our last afternoon together."

"You know why I didn't, why I *couldn't,* talk to you, Griff."

"Guilt."

"Yes."

"So maybe the only way to rid yourself of your guilt was to do away with me."

She looked at him, her gaze unflinching.

He sighed. "Okay, I know better. But that's what went through my mind. But then, just as I was about to lose consciousness, a worse thought occurred to me. You were in on Foster's secret, too."

She looked at him without reaction for several seconds, then recoiled. "What are you saying?"

"After you gave birth to the child, what if he decided that you were a threat to his secrecy, too?"

"Foster loved me. I know that. He adored me."

"I don't doubt it, Laura. But his mind was more twisted than his body. What if he began seeing you as a flaw to his perfect plan? If you were out of the picture, he would be the only one on earth who knew the truth about his heir's parentage. You would be a living threat and, as such, would have to go."

"He would never!"

"Maybe," Griff said without conviction. "But it was the fear he would that saved my life. It gave me renewed strength. I started fighting that Salvadoran son of a bitch like something just let out of hell. I bucked. I kicked. I clawed. Even tried to bite him.

"But I was starved for oxygen. My coordination was for shit. I could barely think. All I accomplished was to use up my reserves. It was then I realized that the only way I'd survive was to pretend to succumb. I went limp.

" 'Good, good, good,' I heard Foster say. Manuelo let go. I had the presence of mind to fall facefirst onto the rug so I could hide that I was breathing. Foster said, *Muy bien, Manuelo. Muy bien. Muy bien.*

"I could hear Manuelo gasping for breath. He was standing close to me. I partially opened one eye and saw his right shoe inches from my head. I grabbed him around the ankle and yanked his foot out from under him. Gravity did the tough part."

Manuelo went down hard, landing on his back. Griff lunged on top of him and drove his fist into the man's nose, felt cartilage give way to the thrust, felt blood on his knuckles. But Manuelo wasn't dispatched. He placed the heel of his hand beneath Griff's chin and gave a push that could have snapped his neck if he hadn't averted his head in time.

Manuelo used that instant to throw Griff off. He sprang to his feet with the agility of a cat and kicked the side of Griff's head with his heel. Griff cried out as pain splintered through his skull. He felt a surge of nausea in the back of his throat but swallowed it as he staggered to his feet.

He managed to stand, but unsteadily. The room was spinning. To stave off the unconsciousness that threatened, he blinked rapidly and brought Manuelo into focus. The man's vacant smile had been replaced by a snarl.

"He had the letter opener in his hand," Griff told Laura. "Foster was saying, 'No blood, no blood, no blood.' But I don't think Manuelo heard him. He was past listening, past caring. The fight had become a matter of personal honor. He'd been ordered to kill me. To save face, that's what he was going to do."

Laura's eyes were wide. She hadn't moved or spoken in several minutes.

"When Manuelo sprang, I dodged." Griff had relied on his timing, the innate talent that had enabled him to throw a pass with a precision that defied physics a split second before he was tackled. He'd waited until Manuelo moved, then ducked, fallen to the floor, and rolled. "Manuelo couldn't stop his momentum. He broke his fall against Foster's wheelchair, landing hard."

"And the letter opener . . ."

"Yeah." It had been buried to the hilt in the side of Speakman's neck. "When Manuelo scrambled back and saw what he'd done, he screamed. Long as I live, I'll never forget that sound." Another sound Griff would never forget was the gurgling noise coming out of Speakman's mouth, which was opening and closing like that of a dying fish. But Laura didn't need to know the grisly details of how her husband had suffered before he died.

"It was a dreadful accident," he said to her now. "But to Rodarte it looks like the act of a jealous jilted lover."

For a long time, they sat in silence. Finally Laura took a deep breath, as though rousing herself from a sound sleep or a bad dream. "You're right. To Rodarte it looks exactly like that."

"What does it look like to *you*?"

CHAPTER
33

AFTER SEVERAL SILENT MINUTES, GRIFF SAID, "YOU MUST BE-lieve me, at least a little, or you wouldn't still be in this car."

Laura ran her fingers through her hair. She'd been trying to find words that would convey the doubts she'd been harboring without sounding disloyal to the husband she had just buried. But she wasn't sure that was possible.

"Foster was over the moon about the baby," she began, "but I begged him not to notify you until we'd had the pregnancy confirmed."

"He called right after you got the results of the blood test."

"That evening, he admitted speaking to you. He apologized for not waiting on me to be there when he called you but said he couldn't wait to share the happy news. He said that you wished us well, but that you were mostly interested in how soon you'd get your money."

"That's a lie. I—"

She held up her hand. "Let me tell it from my perspective. You can rebut it later." He nodded. "Foster and I celebrated that night. He'd had Mrs. Dobbins prepare a special dinner. He forced a second helping of potatoes on me, reminding me I was eating for two. He wouldn't let me out of his sight. He made me use his elevator rather than walk upstairs. He said the staircase was dangerous, that I could fall. I told him I would go insane if this was how the next nine months were going to be. But I was indulgent of his mood. We actually laughed about his overprotectiveness.

"When Manuelo had him settled for the night, I went to him. He held me and told me how much he loved me, how thrilled he was about the baby. Things like that." Her cheeks warmed with self-consciousness. "He was very tender and attentive, more affectionate than he'd been in months. I stayed with him until he was asleep." She was intensely aware of Griff's utter stillness, his unwavering gaze.

"His behavior being what it was that night, I couldn't understand his insistence that I go to Austin the following morning. It was an unnecessary trip. The incident could have been handled by the supervisor there, and should have been. It was an insult to him that Foster sent me as an overseer. That wasn't his usual style of management. Sending me didn't make any sense."

"It makes sense to me."

Reluctantly, she nodded. "We had wrapped up the problem in Austin by midafternoon. I could have been on an earlier flight back to Dallas, but, without consulting me, Foster had obligated me to have dinner with some of the key people in the Austin office. The meal dragged on forever. I barely made it to the airport in time for the nine o'clock flight, the last of the night."

"He didn't want you back before then. He wanted you out of the way. By the time you got back, I would be dead."

"I still can't believe that, Griff. I just can't. Despite what you think, he wasn't a lunatic. I'll admit he had grown increasingly obsessive. Doing things in sequences of three. The cleanliness. Did you notice the bottles of hand sanitizer?"

"Everywhere."

"Nothing could be soiled, nothing out of place, nothing left to chance. But it's unthinkable to me that he would order Manuelo to kill you with his bare hands."

"He didn't want my blood ruining his priceless rug."

She shot him a look. "You know what I mean. How did he plan on getting away with it?"

"He would claim I had stormed the castle and tried to kill him."

"Over what?"

"You. He would say that Manuelo had saved his life when I attacked him in a jealous rage."

"But Foster didn't know Rodarte. He certainly didn't know that he had discovered the Windsor Street house and had concluded we were having an affair. If you'd been killed instead, what motive would Foster have given the investigator—"

"Rodarte would have made damn sure he was put on the case. He'd promised to witness my self-destruction."

"Then what reason would Foster have given him for your attempt on his life?"

Griff thought about it. "Money. I went to the mansion and demanded more."

"Foster wouldn't have told anyone about our arrangement with you, especially not someone as slimy as Rodarte."

"Maybe he'd have said he offered me a job in advertising, then changed his mind and withdrew the offer."

"Plausible, I suppose."

"Knowing Rodarte as I do, I'm sure he eventually would have played his ace, broken the news to the poor cuckold that I'd been sneaking afternoons with his wife. Of course, Foster would have let him go on thinking I had acted out of jealousy. Our secret affair would have made him look more like a victim, and me a likelier murderer."

Laura silently conceded that it sounded logical, but she wasn't yet ready to fully accept it. "Why would Foster have that phony document? And the box of cash? How would he have explained them?"

"If Manuelo had killed me," he said, "they wouldn't have been there. Foster didn't expect anyone but me to see them."

There was no disputing that. "All right, I see how he could have given Rodarte a credible explanation, and Rodarte would have accepted it, believing Foster to be in the dark about us. But what would Foster have told me?"

"Probably that the confirmed pregnancy had made me greedy. I got to the mansion and demanded more than the half million. When he refused to pay more, I attacked him. Thank God for Manuelo. And thank God I'd done the job I'd been hired to do. You were pregnant. My death was a tragedy, but wasn't it lucky that I was no longer around, an ongoing threat to your secret and the well-being of your child." He paused, then added, "It would have been just as he wanted it, Laura. Neat and tidy."

They were quiet for a time. Movies ended. People trickled out of the theater and made their way to their cars. Others arrived. There was a line to purchase tickets. But the van and the pickup truck stayed, and no one paid attention to the couple sitting in the innocuous midsize car between them.

"Your fingerprints were on the hilt of the letter opener."

"So were Manuelo's."

"But he could have handled it at any time." She tried to make eye contact, but he avoided it. "Griff?"

"I didn't want you to know how he died."

"I have to know."

He looked away from her, out the windshield, his eyes following a family of four, mom and dad, two children, who'd just come out of a movie. The young son was rolling his eyes, flapping his arms, doing a disjointed jig, obviously imitating an animated character. They were laughing as they piled into their SUV and drove away.

"Why were your fingerprints on the letter opener?"

"I was trying to save his life," he replied in a quiet voice. "When I saw what had made Manuelo scream, I pushed him aside and shouted at him to call 911. But he was transfixed by the horror of what he'd done. So I placed the call. While I was doing that, Manuelo split.

"I bent over Speakman to see just how bad it was. My initial reaction was to try to pull the letter opener out of his neck. I took hold of it but almost immediately realized it would be better to leave the thing where it was. It was partially plugging the wound, and even at that it was gushing." He stopped, cursed softly. "Laura, you don't want to hear this."

"I must."

He hesitated, then continued. "There was nothing I could do but what I did, which was to apply pressure around the blade, try to slow down the bleeding."

She swallowed. "Rodarte said that there was blood on Foster's hands, tissue under his fingernails. That he had . . ."

Griff held out his hands to her, palms down, so that she could see the scratch marks on the backs of them. "He was trying to pull the letter opener out. I knew for certain he would die if he did, so, yeah, we fought over control of it."

He waited to see if she would respond to that, but when she didn't, he went on. "I talked to him, trying to calm him down and stop him from struggling. I told him that help was on the way. Told him to hold on, to hang in there. Stuff like that. But . . ." He shook his head. "I knew he wasn't going to make it, and I think he did, too."

"Did he say anything?"

He shook his head. "He couldn't articulate."

"Were you with him when—"

"Yes. I stayed."

"Thank you for that."

"Jesus, don't thank me," he said, sounding almost angry. "Believe me, as soon as he was gone, I was out of there. I knew what it would look like. I showed no more guts than Manuelo. I grabbed my ass and ran. And . . ." He stopped, looked away, toward the brightly lit entrance to the theater.

"What?"

He blew out a gust of breath. "There were plenty of times after that last afternoon with you when I wished he was dead." He looked directly into her eyes then. "Not dead specifically. Just . . . just *not*. In the depths of my rotten soul, I wished him away." He continued looking at her for ponderous seconds before speaking again. "But I didn't kill him. Do you believe that?"

She opened her mouth to speak but discovered she couldn't. His story was more credible than she wanted it to be. But she also remembered that afternoon of fevered lovemaking, the hunger and urgency of it. Her impassioned responses had unleashed from him a wild possessiveness. She remembered the way his large hands had moved over her body, claiming it, the intensity with which he had thrust into her, and how jealously he'd held her afterward.

She lowered her head and massaged her temples.

"Forget I asked," he said curtly. "You're not going to believe me until you have Manuelo Ruiz's sworn statement that he accidentally stabbed your husband. You and Rodarte."

She reached out and angrily grabbed his hand. "Don't you dare compare me to Rodarte. And don't give me attitude, either. You're asking me to believe in your innocence. I want to, Griff. But believing you also means accepting that my husband, the person I had loved and admired for years, was a madman who plotted your murder. It's a lot to absorb so soon after burying him. Forgive me if that's proving to be difficult."

She dropped his hand, and for several moments the atmosphere crackled. He was the first to relent. "Okay. No more attitude." He reached into the backseat and got the duffel, placed it in his lap, and unzipped it. "My only hope of exoneration—from anybody—is to find Manuelo Ruiz."

He rifled the bag, removing what appeared to be the aide's keepsakes from El Salvador. A rosary. A map of Mexico, with a red crayon line snaking up through it to a starred spot on the Texas border.

"His route," he said. There was an old photograph of a couple on their wedding day. "His parents, you think?" He passed her the picture.

"Possibly. Their age looks right."

That was it except for a few Spanish-language paperback books and an inexpensive wallet. Griff checked every compartment. In the last one he looked, he found a piece of stained paper. It had been folded so many times, the creases were dirty and almost worn through. Griff carefully spread it open on his thigh.

He read what was printed on it, then smiled and passed the sheet to her. Written in pencil were four digits and a name. She looked back at him. "An address?"

"Appears to be. It's a place to start looking."

"It could be right here in Dallas or in Eagle Pass."

"Yeah, but it's something." He seemed suddenly galvanized. "Do you have a cell phone?"

She reached into her handbag and withdrew it. Checking the readout, she saw that she'd missed several calls. "I had silenced it at the office and forgot to turn it back on. Kay called once. Rodarte's called three times. The last time was twelve minutes ago."

She handed the phone to Griff. He pressed the send button, so that Rodarte's number would be automatically dialed. It rang only once before he answered. "Mrs. Speakman?"

"Sorry to disappoint you, Rodarte. You've got me. And I've got her."

"You're a moron, Burkett. You're just digging yourself in deeper."

"Listen, I'm gonna make this quick, simple enough even for you. I did not kill Foster Speakman. Manuelo Ruiz did."

Rodarte laughed. "Right. The minion. The slave who idolized the guy. Yank somebody else's pod."

"It was an accident. Manuelo was fighting with me."

"Trying to protect Speakman from you."

"Wrong again, but we'll go into the details later. You and I both need Manuelo. You're right about him worshiping Speakman. That's why he was so horrified by what he'd done, he ran. Find him and all our problems will be over. I've got a lead for you." He read off the address. "We found it in Manuelo's belongings. He didn't have much, so this means something or he wouldn't have kept it."

"What city?"

"I don't know, but you've got resources."

"And he's got almost a week's head start."

"That's why you can't waste any time. If you find him, treat him kindly, and you'll get the truth of what happened that night. Nobody committed a murder. Manuelo will tell you that. He can tell you—"

Griff broke off suddenly, surprising Laura, who'd been following every word. One second he'd been speaking rapidly into the telephone, the next, he was silent, staring into near space. Through the phone, she could hear Rodarte saying, "Burkett? Burkett, are you there? Burkett!"

"Griff?" she whispered. "What?"

He focused on her sharply, then slapped the phone closed, abruptly ending his call. He opened the car door and dropped the phone onto the pavement. As he turned on the car's ignition, he said,

"Rodarte's probably put a satellite track on your phone, so we've got to get the hell out of here."

"I don't understand." She clutched the hand grip as he backed out of the parking slot and wheeled the car sharply.

"Manuelo Ruiz can clear me."

"That's why you're desperate to find him."

"And why Rodarte is desperate *not* to."

CHAPTER

34

H E SPED OUT OF THE THEATER PARKING LOT, WOVE THROUGH the commercial complex, and took the first ramp he could onto Central Expressway, heading north, driving as fast as he dared but not so fast as to invite being stopped. He drove with one eye on the rearview mirror, afraid that, at any moment, he would see a pursuing squad car.

"Why wouldn't Rodarte want to find Manuelo Ruiz?" Laura asked.

"Think about it. He hasn't exactly launched a full-out manhunt for him, has he?"

"He thought that you had killed him, that all they would discover was a body. He was more interested in finding you."

"So he could indict me for murder. Best-case scenario for Rodarte would be for Manuelo to be across the border, well on his way back to the jungle, never to be seen or heard from again. Shit!" he hissed, thumping the steering wheel with his fist. "Do you think he got that address? Do you think he understood it?"

"I—"

"Because if he finds Manuelo before I do, the man will never make it into a court of law, probably not even into an interrogation room."

"You think Rodarte would help him escape?"

"If Manuelo's lucky, that's what he'll do. What scares me is that Rodarte will make sure no one hears Manuelo's account of what happened. Ever."

"You mean . . . he would kill him?"

Griff shrugged.

"Griff, he's a police detective."

"Who's dedicated himself to putting me on death row. To that end, Manuelo's easily dispensable."

"So what do we do? Call one of Rodarte's superiors, tell them your side?"

He shook his head. "I don't know who his friends are. He recruited two of them to beat me up. I wouldn't know who to trust."

"Then what?"

"We find Manuelo before Rodarte does."

"How are we going to do that?"

Swerving in front of a truck to take an exit, Griff muttered, "Wish the hell I knew."

The pancake house was open all night. At any hour it was well lighted and crowded, and so was the parking lot. A car left there didn't attract attention. Griff parked, and they got out.

"Welcome to the glamorous world of a fugitive." He took Laura's hand and led her around to the back of the building, where the odorous Dumpsters were open and overflowing.

"Where are we going?"

"It's a half-mile walk. Are you okay with that?"

"A half mile is a warm-up."

He smiled down at her, but his expression was grim. "I didn't say it was an easy half mile."

Leaving behind the commercial area, they entered a residential neighborhood. Over the past several days, through trial and error, he'd learned the safest route, if not the easiest. It took them through yards with dense shrubbery and large trees but no exterior lighting, fences, or barking dogs.

They came upon the house from the rear. Griff was relieved to see that no lights were on inside. Each time he came back to his refuge, he was afraid the owners had returned during his absence.

The backyard was enclosed by a stockade fence, but when they reached the gate, he opened the latch without difficulty. "It's never locked." He ushered Laura through the gate, then closed it silently.

"Who lives here?" she asked, speaking in a whisper. The houses on either side were obviously occupied. Lights shone through windows. Somewhere close a sprinkler was swishing. They could hear a television show's soundtrack.

"I used to." He led the way to a back door, opened it, and pulled her in behind him. The alarm system began to bleep, but he punched in a sequence of numbers and it went silent. "They never changed the code. All these years, it's been the same."

"This was your house?"

"My high school coach and his wife. They took me in when I was fifteen."

"The Millers." At his look of surprise, she added, "I read about you."

He didn't risk turning on any lights, but there was enough light from the neighbors' houses straining through the kitchen window curtain that he could make out her features as he searched her face. "You read about me?"

"When Foster recommended you to father the baby. I researched your background."

"Oh." He waited a beat, then said, "I guess I passed. In spite of the fact that my dad was a wife beater and my mother a whore."

"That wasn't your fault."

"People say the apple doesn't fall far from the tree."

"Generally speaking, people are unfair."

"Not in this case. I turned out rotten, too."

She shook her head and was about to say something when the refrigerator cycled on, creating a buzz that sounded as loud as a chain saw in the silent house. She jumped. He touched her arm. "It's just the fridge. It's okay. Come on." He took her hand and pulled her behind him as he made his way from the kitchen into the living area, where the drapes were drawn and it was much darker.

Still speaking in a whisper, she said, "So this is where you've been staying all this time?"

"Since my escape from Turner's house."

"They've been sheltering you?"

"Hardly. They don't know I'm here. I came to see Ellie not too long ago. She mentioned a trip to Hawaii. I guess that's where they are. Anyhow, I showed up here, prepared to throw myself on their mercy. I didn't have to."

"You may when they return."

"I may," he said ruefully. "I'm sure Coach will kick me out. But at least they can't be accused of sheltering me. I'm sorry I can't turn on any lights. The neighbors know they're away and will be keeping an eye on the house. It's that kind of neighborhood. Careful. I've got to close this door." He shut the door between the living room and the hallway, plunging them into total darkness.

"Didn't Rodarte think to look for you here?"

"I'm sure he did and probably still has a car doing periodic drive-bys. But when he discovered the Millers were out of state, he figured I wouldn't be here. Besides, he knows Coach can't stomach the sight of me now. He'd think if I showed my face around here, he'd be the first person Coach would call. I've been hoping that all this would be cleared up before they return from their vacation and they'd never know that I'd used their house." He laughed softly. "Ellie probably would figure it out, though. I've tried to clean up after myself, but she's an excellent housekeeper."

"Is that their car we were in?"

"Their second car. Not used much. I sneaked it out of the garage in the middle of the night, drove it to the parking lot of that restaurant, and left it. I've been coming and going from there. As far as the neighbors know, the car is still in the garage."

He felt his way along the wall till he reached the doorway to his bedroom. "In here."

When they were inside and the door closed behind them, he released her hand and felt his way over to the desk. He found the lamp by feel and turned it on. They blinked against the sudden light. He motioned toward the window that overlooked the front yard. "Crude but effective."

He'd stretched a dark blanket over the window frame and secured it all around with tape, so that not even a sliver of light would shine through. "From the outside all you see is drawn blinds."

"Genius."

"More like desperation."

A laptop computer was on the desk. He switched it on. He'd found it in the spare bedroom. Coach had always cursed computers, saying they were "too damn hard to operate," so Griff supposed it was Ellie who'd joined the age of electronics.

While it was booting, he watched Laura as she moved around the room, looking at photos, trophies, clippings, and other memorabilia of his life—starting at age fifteen.

"You began early."

She was looking at a photo of him taken before he was old enough to shave. He was kneeling with one knee on the turf, wearing a football uniform with full pads, his helmet tucked under his arm, his expression as badass as he could make it. The photos and awards in this room chronicled his football career from those adolescent teams up to that fateful play-off game with the Redskins.

"You loved it, didn't you?" she asked.

"Yes."

"Do you regret what you did?"

"You have no idea." He glanced at the computer monitor. It wasn't a speedy, streamlined new model. Programs were still loading. Laura sat down on the edge of the bed and folded her hands in her lap, like she was settling in to listen.

Griff looked at a framed photo of himself caught in the motion of throwing a pass. It had been taken during the game that had won his high school the state championship. Coach's team. The school district had held a victory parade upon their return from Houston, where the game had been played in the Astrodome. Up to that point, it had been the highlight of Griff's life.

"You know from the day you start that it can't last forever," he said. "Even if you go all the way to the pros, it's short term. Thirty is old. Thirty-five is ancient. And that's if you escape serious injury. You're never more than one play away from the end of your career. Or even the end of your life. Each time the ball is snapped, it's a tempt of fate."

He turned his head and looked at her. "But I wouldn't trade a day of it. Not a single day. I loved the buildup that was part of each game. By kickoff time, I'd have a knot in my gut harder than a fist, but it was a good kind of anxiety, you know?"

She nodded.

"I loved the snap, getting my hands around that ball. I loved the adrenaline rush I got every time I called a tricky play and it was perfectly executed. I received perks and favors all along the way, a college education, millions in salary. But the truth is, Laura, I'd have played for nothing.

"Because even on the worst days, I loved the game. I loved it even on the Monday mornings when I could barely get out of bed for the aches and pains." He smiled. "Most mornings it still takes me half an hour before I can stand up straight."

He looked at the computer. It was still grinding. "I remember one Sunday afternoon in Texas Stadium, lying on the turf after I'd been sacked by a thousand pounds of Broncos in front of a capacity home crowd. I looked up through that stupid hole in the ceiling of the stadium, and even then, knocked flat on my butt and having lost seven yards on the play, I was so goddamn happy to be there I laughed out loud. Everybody thought I'd had my bells rung, got a concussion, or just plain cracked under pressure. No one could guess I was laughing out of pure joy over the game. The *game*." He shook his head and snuffled a sad laugh. "Yeah, I loved it. God, I loved it."

Several moments elapsed. He heard Laura draw in a long breath and let it out slowly. "And they loved you."

When he looked back at her, she was staring at a photo of him with the Millers. "You mean Coach? Ellie?" He shrugged uneasily. "Emphasis on the past tense."

She indicated the walls, the full shelves, and said softly, "It's all still here, Griff."

He held her gaze for a moment, then turned back to the computer. "Finally." He moved the cursor to the icon that would link him to the Internet. He felt Laura move up behind him and look over his shoulder.

"What's your plan?"

"Haven't got one. Go on some kind of search engine, I guess. See if I can find this address. Start with city of Dallas, move to Dallas County, expand to the whole damn state if necessary."

"Is that your top speed?"

He typed by hunting and pecking. He looked up at her over his shoulder. "Are you faster?"

They switched places. She sat in the desk chair. He braced his arms on the back of it so he could see the monitor. She was a much more proficient typist. "Manuelo didn't write down whether it was Lavaca Street or Road or Lane," she remarked. "We'll have to try them all."

"How many Lavaca Streets, Roads, et cetera do you think there are in Texas?"

"Hundreds?"

"That's my guess, too. And Rodarte's got better computers and more people."

"Can I make a suggestion?"

"Be my guest."

"Tax records. Every property is taxed."

"You think a person who provides fake documents to illegal immigrants pays property taxes?"

"The taxes would be assessed. Whether or not they're paid is another matter."

"Okay. Are there tax records online?"

"We'll try. Tax assessor records for Dallas County?"

"Knock yourself out."

She began searching for such a website. "Tell me about Bill Bandy."

The request surprised him, and for a moment he didn't say anything. Then, "What do you want to know?"

"How you met. How you got involved with him."

He gave her a condensed version. "When I got in over my head, he introduced me to a syndicate. They canceled my debt, in exchange for a few interceptions, fumbles. Nothing that couldn't happen to any quarterback on any given Sunday."

"Bandy betrayed you."

"The feds offered him probation in exchange for setting me up, and I'll bet they didn't have to twist his arm too hard."

"There's a Lavaca Street in Dallas, but the addresses have three digits, not four," she reported.

"Try Lavaca Road."

"The newspapers said that Bandy delivered the two million to your Turtle Creek condo."

"True. He was wearing a wire. Second I took the box of cash from him, agents came busting through my front door, read me my rights."

"You were put in jail?"

"Yes," he said tightly, remembering the humiliation of that experience. "Wyatt Turner got me released on the condition that I give up my passport. Soon as I got out, I went looking for Bandy."

Laura stopped typing, turned and looked up at him.

"Right. It was a stupid thing to do. But I was furious. I guess I wanted to frighten him into thinking he was as good as dead for setting me up." He cursed himself under his breath. "What a goddamn fool I was. When I got to Bandy's place, the door was open. I went in. I almost walked out without seeing him. He'd been stuffed between the back of the sofa and the wall. His neck had been wrenched so hard his head was practically facing backward."

"Who killed him?"

"I'm sure the Vista boys were behind it. They wanted him silenced, so he couldn't give them up like he had me."

"They could've killed you, too."

"I think they thought it would be more fun to keep me alive, let me be charged with Bandy's murder. I'm sure it was them who tipped off the cops."

"How did they know you were going to be at Bandy's place?"

"I guess they figured I'd go after Bandy, at the very least to tell him how disappointed I was in him," he said with sarcasm. "I was still kneeling beside the body when two squad cars showed up, responding to an anonymous 911 call from a pay phone, they said."

"Vista was watching you."

"Obviously. And if you could see this guy called Bennett, you'd think he could sit through a tornado without blinking. Anyway, here I was, facing federal charges of racketeering and illegal gambling, and there was my bookie, the one who'd ratted me out, dead on the floor.

"Enter Detective Stanley Rodarte, who'd been dispatched to investigate the crime scene. He came in and introduced himself, told me what a great ballplayer I'd been, and what a shame it was that I'd turned crooked. Then he looked at the body, looked back at me, and started laughing. It seemed that open and shut."

"No address like this on Tarrant County's tax records, either," Laura said.

"Denton? What's on the western side of Tarrant?"

She consulted a map on the screen, where the counties were delineated. "Parker."

"Try that, too. Damn," he said, looking at the map and realizing the scope of this effort. "This could take all night." He consulted his watch, wondering if Rodarte had already isolated the address and was speeding toward it.

"It wasn't the open-and-shut case Rodarte thought it would be," Laura said.

"Bandy's back room had been torn all to hell. Ransacked. My prints were on the sofa, the wall behind it—hell, I was kneeling beside his body when the police arrived. But they couldn't place me in that back room, hard as Rodarte tried. The grand jury found it impossible to believe that I would avoid leaving prints or other evidence while ransacking the place, then take off gloves before killing Bandy. And if I had, where were the gloves?"

"Why was his back room ransacked?"

"Rodarte is of the opinion that Bandy had money squirreled away in there somewhere and that I helped myself to it."

Again she turned and looked up at him. "But you didn't have any cash stuffed in your pockets at the time, did you?"

"No. But it wouldn't necessarily have been cash I was looking for. It could have been a bank account number. A combination to a safe. Something I could commit to memory. Later, when I was out of prison, I'd have a treasure waiting for me." He looked at her hard. "Just so you know, I never went into Bandy's back room. I didn't know what was or wasn't in there. As far as I know, he didn't have any funds stashed away for a rainy day."

Quietly she said, "I didn't ask." She turned back around and, after scanning the information on the monitor, said, "There's no Lavaca anything in Parker County."

Griff opened the duffel bag and removed Manuelo's map. "Pull up that map of the state again." She did. When it appeared on the monitor, he tapped a spot. "That red crayon star is here." He pointed to the southern tip of the state. "Somewhere between Mission and Hidalgo."

"We assume that's where he entered the country. Lord, how far is that from here?"

"Four hundred miles at least. Probably closer to five."

"Lots of counties."

"Yeah, but I'd bet his contact wouldn't be too far from this area. Say Manuelo came north through San Antonio and Austin."

"Basically following I-35."

"Basically. Let's concentrate on the counties immediately to the south of Dallas–Fort Worth."

"Hood, Johnson, Ellis."

"Check those and work your way down."

They found it in Hill County. "Griff! There's a Lavaca Road in Hill County. On the outskirts of town it turns into FM 2010. We thought it was a house number!"

He leaned over her, and she pointed it out on the screen.

"What town is that?" he asked.

"Itasca."

"Repeat that," Rodarte said.

"Itasca."

"Where the hell is that?" He was driving with one hand, holding his cell phone to his ear with the other.

He'd had a desk cop back at the police station searching for the address Griff Burkett had rattled off to him before hanging up. Thanks to a satellite and technology he didn't understand, Laura Speakman's cell phone had been tracked to a movie theater. Before he could even get excited about it, they'd found the damn thing lying on the parking lot pavement.

From there the trail had gone cold because Mrs. Speakman's car had been left at the mansion, they didn't know what Burkett was driving now, and the moviegoers they'd questioned didn't know diddly. Rodarte had left Carter there to try to pick up the trail. Actually,

Rodarte was glad he could assign his partner another task. From here on, he preferred working alone.

Rodarte became furious thinking about Griff Burkett and his adulterous lover—had she plotted her husband's murder with him?—laughing up their sleeves at him. The idiots he'd posted to guard her were going to be looking for jobs tomorrow. Then he was going to hurt them. And their wives. And their kids. They would come to regret the day they were born.

And that didn't begin to cover what he had planned for Griff Burkett and the poor, innocent, grieving widow. He wished he'd fucked her when he had a chance. *Who would she have told? The cops?* he thought, scoffing. *No way.* Not when he could turn it around and tell them about her illicit affair with her husband's killer. Yeah, he should have responded to the impulse he'd had there in her hotel room, bent her over and fucked her. His problem was he was just too nice a guy.

The desk cop was rattling off directions. "From where you're at, go south on 35 E till you get to I-20 and head west. Then out of Fort Worth, take 35 dubya south. Watch for the exit."

"So where's this Lavaca Road or whatever?"

"Runs out the east side of town and turns into farm-to-market 2010. We reckon that's where the numbers came from. It's not exactly a street address, but it makes sense."

"I guess," Rodarte said, unconvinced. "But stand by in case I need to call you again."

"I already called the local *po*-lice down there. Chief's name is Marion."

"First?"

"Last. Plus I alerted the Hill County SO. Marion's sending a squad car to scout out the area, see if his boys can pick up anything. When you get there, you'll have plenty of backup."

"Is there still an APB out for Manuelo Ruiz down there?"

"I asked Marion to jog everybody's memory."

"And one for Griff Burkett?"

"Considered armed and dangerous. Just like you said, Detective."

"He's got a cop's service weapon."

"Told Marion that, too. Pissed him off." After a pause, he added, "And to think we used to cheer the son of a bitch."

"Yeah, to think."

The best that could happen would be for Burkett to be spotted and plugged by an underpaid, overanxious Hicksville cop, a Cowboys fan who bore a grudge based on principle.

Someone else killing Burkett would remove any suspicion from him. But there was a distinct downside: it would deprive him of taking down that bastard himself, and that was something he very much looked forward to.

"What's the number of the police station down there?" Rodarte asked the desk cop. Once he had it, he clicked off and called that number. He identified himself and was soon patched in to Chief Marion. "Rodarte, Dallas PD."

"Yes, sir," he said crisply.

"Just calling to follow up. What's happening down there?"

"There's nothing on FM 2010 except an old farmhouse. Vacant. Looks like it was abandoned a long time ago. My men said a strong wind would knock it down."

"No shit?"

"The place was deserted. We'll keep looking, but among my officers and the sheriff's deputies, they don't know of anything else out that way. Not for miles."

"Okay. Keep me posted."

"Sure thing, Detective."

Rodarte closed his phone and tossed it onto the passenger seat, cursing his culpability. Had Burkett sent him on a wild-goose chase? Given him some busywork to keep him occupied while he and his ladylove got away?

He pulled his car to the shoulder of the freeway, rolled down the window, and lit a cigarette. He kept the motor idling while he considered his options.

"Itasca," Laura repeated. "Ever heard of it?"

"No, but I'll find it." He gave her shoulders a squeeze. "Great work. Thanks." He moved toward the door. "Switch out the light till

I'm gone. And remember not to turn any lights on unless the door to this room is closed."

"You're going now?"

"Right now. I just hope Rodarte doesn't have too much of a lead."

"But we don't know if that's it, Griff. And even if it is, Manuelo may be long gone."

"I've gotta try. He's my last hope."

"I'm coming, too," she said decisively.

"Un-huh. No way. I don't know what I—"

"I'm coming with you." She stood up, but when she did, a strange look came over her face and she pushed her hands between her thighs.

"What's the matter?"

She just stood there, looking at him with alarm. Then her face crumpled, and she groaned, "Oh, no."

CHAPTER
35

EVEN WHEN HE SAW THE BLOOD ON HER HANDS, SAW THE streaks of it on the legs of her tracksuit, Griff didn't comprehend what was happening until he looked into her eyes and saw the anguish in them. "Oh, Jesus."

In a keening voice she said, "My baby."

He reached for her, but she backed away. "Laura, I gotta get you to a hospital."

"There's nothing to be done."

"You don't know that."

"Yes, I do." Her eyes filled with tears. "It's lost."

"No, no, we'll stop it. We can. We will."

She looked around frantically. "Where's the bathroom?"

He got to the door ahead of her and reached inside to switch on the light. She slipped around him and closed the door behind her.

"Laura?"

"Don't come in."

He placed both palms on the door and, leaning into it, ground his forehead hard against the wood, never in his life having felt so useless. Miscarriage. He'd heard the word, knew what it meant, but had never realized that it entailed that much blood, or caused this much despair. He felt pointless, superfluous, and helpless. The laws of nature had emasculated him.

He stood outside the bathroom door for what seemed forever. Several times he knocked, asked how she was doing, asked if there was something he could do. She replied in monosyllabic mumbles that told him nothing.

The toilet flushed numerous times. Water ran in the sink. Eventually he heard the shower. Shortly after it stopped running, she opened the door. She was wrapped in a towel. His eyes moved over her from the top of her wet hair to her toes and back up, stopping on her eyes, red-rimmed and tearful.

"Is it hopeless?"

She nodded.

He assimilated that, marveled at the anguish it caused him. "Does it hurt?"

"A little. Like really bad cramps."

"Um-hmm," he said, as though he had any idea what menstrual cramps felt like.

"I need something to put on."

He looked beyond her. Her tracksuit was in a sodden heap on the floor of the shower. "I'll find something."

"Do you think Mrs. Miller has some pads?"

Pads? His mind scrambled. Pads. Right. Ask him about Tiger Balm or jock itch remedies and he was conversant. Athlete's foot? On it. But he'd never even walked down the feminine hygiene aisle of a supermarket. Not on purpose anyway. He'd never bought a product for a girlfriend, wife, daughter. His knowledge of such things was limited to the box of tampons his mother had kept beneath the bathroom sink. He knew they were necessary, but that's all.

"I'll be right back."

He didn't even think about the lights he was turning on as he went banging through the house, bumping into walls, flinging open doors he'd left closed the last few days. In the Millers' bedroom he opened the closet they shared. Coach's clothes hung on one side, Ellie's on the other, shoes lined up neatly beneath.

He yanked a robe off a hanger, then began rifling bureau drawers until he found her underwear. Not the skimpier, lacier kind he'd seen Laura in, but what he came up with would do.

Pads. Wouldn't Ellie be past menopause? Hell if he knew. He

searched their bathroom but didn't find any personal products in any of the cabinets. The guest bath? Ellie had nieces who came to visit occasionally. Maybe . . .

In the guest bath closet he found extra toilet tissue, toothpaste and soap, disposable razors, even cellophane-wrapped toothbrushes. Pads and tampons. Thank God for Ellie. He grabbed the box of pads.

Laura was sitting on the lid of the toilet, hugging her waistline, staring into near space, rocking back and forth. He set the items on the counter, then crouched in front of her. She was still wrapped in the towel. He saw the goose bumps on her bare arms and legs. "I'm sorry I took so long."

"You didn't. It's all right."

"You're cold." He placed the thick robe around her shoulders. "Put your arms in." He guided her arms into the sleeves, then pulled the robe together over her chest, towel and all.

"Thank you."

"What else can I do?"

"Nothing."

He remained squatted down in front of her, staring into her face. "Are you sure . . . Maybe . . ." She shook her head, cutting him off, severing his hope.

Fresh tears spilled over her eyelids and rolled down her cheeks. "There was a lot. Too much for it to be a false alarm."

"You should go to the hospital. Call your doctor at least."

"In a day or so, I'll go to the doctor. I know they have to make sure that it all came out." She swallowed hard, he thought probably to hold back sobs. "I'll be okay. I have to get through this part. It's not pleasant, but . . ." She swiped at the tears on her cheeks. "This happens all the time. One out of every ten pregnancies. Something like that."

But it doesn't happen to you. And not to me. This was a sorrow they shared. He touched her cheek, but she yanked her head back and stood up. "I need privacy now."

"Can't I—"

"No. There's nothing you can do. Just . . ." She motioned for him to leave.

Her rejection made him feel like he had fangs and claws. His merest touch was a violation to her tender, feminine flesh. His size and sex suddenly felt incriminatory. He didn't know why that was, but he felt burly and awkward and blameworthy as he stood up and backed into the open doorway. He went out and pulled the door closed behind himself.

When she came out, Griff was sitting on the edge of the bed, his elbows on his knees, his head in his hands, his fingers making tunnels through his hair.

Hearing her, he looked up, his expression bleak. She felt self-conscious, wrapped from chin to ankles in the pink terry-cloth robe that belonged to a woman she'd never met. He'd found underwear for her. Sanitary pads. Even with her husband, she'd never shared moments as personal as the last few she'd shared with Griff Burkett.

He said, "It's my fault, isn't it?"

"Your fault?"

He came to his feet. "In the hotel, I was rough with you."

"No, you weren't."

"Yes, I was. I manhandled you. Then I forced you to run, made you crawl through a wall on your belly, dragged you—"

"It wasn't your fault, Griff."

"Like hell! It wouldn't have happened if I'd left you alone. You'd still have your baby if you were safe inside your hotel room, not on this damn fool's mission of mine."

"Listen," she said softly, hoping to calm him. "I've been feeling twinges for several days. I was spotting on the morning of Foster's funeral. That's normal during early pregnancy. I thought it was caused by stress, the shock of his death. I ignored it. But the cramps and spotting were signals. It would have happened no matter what, Griff." She could tell by his expression that she hadn't persuaded him.

"Are you still bleeding?"

"Some. I think I've already expelled the . . ." Unable to bring herself to say it, she ended with "I think the worst of it is over."

"So, you're going to be okay?"

"Don't worry about me. I'm sorry I caused you this delay."

"Delay?"

"Manuelo."

"Oh. Right."

"Do you know how to get to Itasca?"

He looked at her like he didn't understand the question, then said, "South on 35 out of Fort Worth. I'll find it."

"How long will it take you?"

"I don't know. Hour and a half maybe."

"And if you do find Manuelo, how are you going to convince him to come back with you? He doesn't even speak English."

"I'll make myself understood."

"He'll be scared. When he sees you, God knows what he'll do."

"I can take care of myself. Can you?"

"I'll be all right."

"Can I get you anything before I go?"

"I can't think of anything."

He turned his head away. "Yeah, okay." He was speaking in a clipped voice, lightly slapping his palms against the outsides of his thighs, anxious to be away. "I would stay, except—"

"No, you must go. Actually, I'd prefer to be alone right now."

"Sure. Understandable." He plowed his fingers through his hair and walked in a tight circle, then whipped the bedspread back. "Lie down. Sleep."

"I will. Be careful."

"Yeah."

He turned abruptly and left the room, pulling the door closed, not loudly but soundly. She heard the door connecting the hallway to the living room being opened, then shut.

Knowing she was finally alone, she sagged under the weight of her heartache. She lay down on the bed, turned onto her side, and drew herself into a tight ball. Then, burying her face in the pillow, she opened the floodgate that had been tenuously holding back her emotions.

Her sobs were so intense, they shook her whole body. So when the mattress dipped, she didn't trust herself to believe that he had come back. She didn't let herself accept it until she felt his hand stroking her shoulder and heard his whispered "Shh, shh."

He'd made it as far as the back door. He'd even taken hold of the doorknob. His future, possibly his life, depended on finding Manuelo Ruiz before Rodarte did. It was in his best interest to leave now, drive as fast as he could to that dot on the map, and rout out the only individual in the world who could save him from being convicted of murdering Foster Speakman.

Besides that, Laura had rejected his help. She'd practically pushed him out the door. No mystery there. It was his fault that she'd lost the baby. Earlier tonight, when she told him it was for real, that she was pregnant, he'd thought: *Finally.* For the first time in his life, he'd done something right and good.

He should have known that it wouldn't last, that he would somehow mess it up. Anyway, it was over. The baby was lost, and there was nothing he could do about it now.

Go! Go! Turn the freaking doorknob.

He was moving back through the living room before he fully realized he'd made an about-face. He heard her sobs when he opened the door into the hallway. The sight of her huddled inside the pink robe, weeping into the pillow, made his heart feel like something had pinched it, hard.

He lay down behind her and touched her shoulder. "Shh, shh."

"You need to go," she moaned.

"No, I need to be here with you. I want to be." Placing his arm across her waist, he scooped her back against him.

"You can't let Rodarte—"

"I can't leave you. I won't." He pressed his face into the nape of her neck. "I'm sorry, Laura. God, I'm so sorry."

"Please stop saying that, Griff. Stop thinking it. This wasn't your fault. It wasn't anyone's fault. It was nature's way of saying something wasn't right. I was only seven weeks pregnant. It wasn't even a baby yet."

"It was to me."

She raised her head. Her swimming eyes found his. Then with a long, mournful sound, she turned toward him and pressed her face against his chest. His arms went around her, drawing her to him, holding her close, tucking her head beneath his chin. He sank his fingers into her hair and massaged her scalp.

She wept and he let her. It was a female thing, a maternal thing. The tears were essential, cleansing, as necessary for healing as the bleeding. He didn't know how in hell he knew that. He just did. Maybe in times of crisis, you were graced with superior insight like that.

When her crying finally subsided, she tilted her head back against his biceps. "Thank you for coming back."

"I couldn't leave."

"I didn't want you to."

"You pushed me away."

"To keep myself from begging you to stay."

"Honestly?"

"Honestly."

He looked deeply into her eyes. "They're pretty."

"What?"

"Your eyes. When you cry, your eyelashes stick together in dark spikes. They're pretty."

She gave a soft laugh and sniffed. "Yes, I'm sure I look radiant right now. But I appreciate the sweet talk anyway."

"It's not sweet talk. I don't make sweet talk."

She hesitated a moment, then tucked her face back into his neck. "You've never had to. Have you?"

"I never wanted to."

"With Marcia?"

"She was paid to sweet-talk me."

"And with me, it certainly wasn't necessary. With or without it, you were being paid."

He placed his finger beneath her chin, forcing her to look at him. "Do you think that on that last day I was thinking about the money? Or making a baby? No. I broke every speed limit to get there for only one reason, to see you. That afternoon had nothing to do with anything except you and me. You know that, Laura. I know you do."

Slowly, she nodded.

"Well, good." They smiled gently at each other.

She was the first to speak. "You're not rotten."

He laughed. "We're back to that?"

"Did you ever look for your parents? What happened to them after they abandoned you? Do you know?" He didn't say anything for such a long time that she said, "Forgive the questions. You don't have to talk about it."

"No, it's okay. It's just ugly."

But she continued to look into his eyes, hers inquiring.

He supposed she was entitled to know just how ugly it was. "My old man died of alcoholism before he was fifty. I tracked my mother to Omaha. Right before I checked in to Big Spring to start serving my sentence, I worked up enough nerve to call her. She answered. I heard her voice for the first time in, hmm, fifteen years.

"She said hello again. Impatiently, like you do when you answer the phone and the caller doesn't say anything but you can hear them breathing. I said, 'Hey, Mom. It's Griff.' Soon as I said that, she hung up." Although he'd tried to form a callus around it, the pain of that rejection was still sharp.

"It's funny. When I was playing ball, I used to wonder if she knew I'd become famous. Had she caught me on TV, seen my picture on a product or in a magazine? I wondered if she watched the games and told her friends, 'That's my son. That Pro Bowl quarterback is my kid.' After that call, I didn't have to wonder anymore."

"Your call caught her off guard. Maybe she just needed some time to—"

"I thought the same thing. Glutton for punishment, I guess. So I hung on to that phone number. For five years. I called it a few weeks ago. This guy answered, and when I asked for her, he told me she'd died two years ago. She had a lot of pulmonary problems, he said. Died slow. Even knowing she was going to die, she made no attempt to contact me. Truth is, she simply never gave a shit about me. Not ever."

"I'm sorry, Griff."

He shrugged. "Doesn't matter."

"Of course it matters. I know how bad it hurts. My mother abandoned me, too." She told him about her father. "He was a real-life hero, like a character in the movies. His death shattered Mom and me, but eventually I recovered. She didn't. Her depression became debilitating, to the point where she wouldn't even get out of bed. Nothing I said or did made her better. She didn't want to get better. One day she put herself out of her misery. She'd used one of Daddy's pistols and left herself for me to find."

"Jesus." He pulled her close and kissed her hair.

"For the longest time, I felt that I had failed her. But now I realize that she failed me. Even though this baby was infinitesimal, only weeks from conception, I felt fiercely protective of it, Griff. I wanted to guard it from being hurt, emotionally as well as physically. How could a parent, any parent, relinquish the parental instinct to nourish and protect her child?"

He drew a deep breath and let it out slowly. He didn't have an answer. He'd been asking that about his mother for as far back as he could remember. "I should have been up-front with you about my background. But I was afraid that if I was, you'd think I was the bad seed and choose someone else as a surrogate."

"I admit I didn't think too highly of you at first."

"Tell me," he said, a smile behind his voice.

"My opinion of you changed when you brought the lubricant."

"You're kidding."

"No."

"I didn't want to hurt you again."

"Hmm, and got very upset when you discovered I hadn't used it."

"Yeah, but what really made me mad was that you thought I wouldn't mind hurting you."

"So you said. Your angry reaction changed my opinion of you. You cared much more than you wanted to show. I saw that you weren't nearly as rotten as people think. As *you* think."

"Don't go pinning any medals on me, Laura. You were still another man's wife, but I started looking forward to being with you. I wouldn't admit it, even to myself. But I did. It was his idea, and every time you met me, it was because he insisted on it. But after that day you had the orgasm, I stopped kidding myself."

"So did I," she confessed softly. "I knew it would be dangerous to be alone with you again. That's why I told Foster I wouldn't go back. But I did. And, despite everything that's happened, I can't honestly say I'm sorry I did."

He came close to saying something then, making some kind of profession, the likes of which he'd never thought he would make to another human being. But the timing was off. Way off.

Instead, he took her hand and laid it against his chest, pressing it close to his heart. She wouldn't know, couldn't know—for him, who never invited a touch—how significant that small gesture was. But he knew.

She said, "I always wondered . . ."

"What?"

Looking chagrined, she shook her head. "Never mind."

"What?"

"What you used."

"Used?"

"To . . . you know. While I was in the bedroom, waiting. I always wondered what you did, what you used to get aroused."

"Oh," he said around a soft laugh. "I used you."

"Me?"

"The first time we met there, you had on a soft pink top under your ball-breaker's suit."

"I beg your pardon."

"You were wearing the kind of business suit that said you wanted to be taken seriously. Seen as an equal in the workplace, not as a woman. But it didn't work, because to me you still looked like somebody I wanted to have sex with. Especially that top. It was about the color of this robe."

"I know the one."

"So to get it up, I thought about your breasts under the top, all soft and warm. Thought about sliding my hands up under your top and touching them. And that did it."

"Just that?"

"Well, there may have been some flashes of tongue against nipple," he added, grinning unrepentantly. "And the times after that, I thought about you, lying in there, prim on the top, nothing on the bottom, waiting for me. Worked every time. Of course, that last day was different."

"Yes."

He touched her lips with the backs of his fingers. "The hardest thing I've ever had to do was let you leave and go back to him."

"I think he knew something had happened that afternoon. Something shattering for me. When I got home that evening, he acted strangely. I was undone, and he knew it. He was almost taunting me."

Easing him away from her, she turned onto her back and stared up at the ceiling. "I've come to realize that all this—you, the baby, all of it—was Foster's way of punishing me for being at the wheel when he was injured."

"How could he blame you? It was an accident."

"That's just it, Griff. He didn't believe in accidents. You have to understand his OCD. Everything had to be done in sequence and in a particular way. No deviation whatsoever. He believed that any change in the order of things resulted in calamity.

"He wanted to drive home that night because he'd driven us there. But I said no because he'd had more to drink than I had. I interrupted the sequence, and what happened was a consequence of that. He never blamed me out loud. But I think now that he did inside. He must have harbored a deep resentment that became corrosive."

Griff was glad she was talking this through. She needed to, more for herself than for him.

"I could have conceived a child by going the clinical route, using a donor. Foster used his OCD as an excuse not to. But that wasn't the reason. I see that now. I loved him purely and exclusively, and he knew that. Our marriage was sacred and precious to me. I valued it above everything. So he devised a way to weaken it, if not destroy it altogether."

"Like his legs."

"Like his legs. Morally, he knew how I felt about his plan. I told him time and again I thought it was wrong, but he wouldn't take no for an answer. He played upon my being an overachiever, never backing away from a challenge or task. I can see now how deftly he manipulated me. He appealed to what he knew would get me to agree."

"Then he put you in bed with me, a pariah, a man you couldn't admire and wouldn't like."

"No," she said with a sad smile. "There you're wrong. He chose you because you were handsome and strong, unquestionably masculine. You'd been abstinent for five years. I'd been for two. How could each of us not become attracted to the individual who was giving us what we'd been missing? He *wanted* us to be attracted. Especially me. So that, in my heart, I would be committing adultery, violating the marriage vows I'd held so dear."

What she was saying made sense. Or it would have to the twisted mind of Foster Speakman. "Once the child was conceived and I was dead, you would feel the loss, along with the guilt."

"I think that's what he had in mind."

"You believe me? Everything I told you about how he died? Without question?"

"It's hard to think this way about my husband, but yes, Griff, I believe you. Your death was part of his plan. The perfect punishment. I would never be able to look at the child without thinking of you and remembering my sin. My infidelity would never have been acknowledged as such, but I would have spent the entirety of my life trying to make up for it." After a long moment, she turned on her side again to face him. "We dragged you into a terrible mess. I apologize for that."

"You didn't drag me, I jumped in willingly, with far fewer scruples than you. I was after the easy money. Lots of it. Even Rodarte said that a hustler like me would—"

"Rodarte!" She sat bolt upright and gave him a shove. "You've got to go now."

"I can't leave you."

"You have to, Griff. I'm fine. But I won't be if you stay with me instead of finding Manuelo. You must go. You know I'm right."

He did know that. Regretfully, he got off the bed, then bent down to stroke her hair. "You're sure you'll be okay with . . . everything." He motioned toward her middle.

"I'll be fine."

"Stay in bed. Try to sleep." He kissed her lips lightly. "I'll be back as soon as I can." Before he could talk himself out of going, he turned.

Coach and Ellie were standing in the open doorway. In his loudest sideline voice, Coach bellowed, "What the hell are you doing in my house?"

CHAPTER
36

HERE'S THE THING, RODARTE TOLD HIMSELF. GRIFF BURKETT had successfully (a) lured or (b) kidnapped Laura Speakman from the hotel. He had escaped arrest at her mansion. He was driving an unknown vehicle. Basically, he was in pretty good shape to elude capture for a while longer, maybe even enough to get far away.

So why had he used the Speakman broad's cell phone to call him, knowing that Rodarte would be able to track the call and mark their location? Sure, Burkett had been smart enough to leave the phone in that theater parking lot, but why take such a risk in the first place?

Burkett wouldn't. Not unless he had something to say that was mighty important, something that he felt would get him off the hook completely.

Rodarte sat in his car on the shoulder of the interstate and smoked half a pack—fuck quitting—before determining that Burkett hadn't been playacting. He'd sounded excited and definitive. Burkett believed that Lavaca Road in Itasca was a link to Manuelo Ruiz, whom he claimed had killed Speakman accidentally. Meaning Burkett was innocent.

It must be true. If Ruiz *had* witnessed Burkett murdering Speakman, Burkett would be racing down to Itasca to silence the man, not calling Rodarte and telling him where to find him.

Conclusion: Manuelo Ruiz was no longer a footnote in the case. He'd been bumped up to a principal player. His new status called for action.

Rodarte used the redial button on his cell phone. It rang only once before being answered. "Itasca PD."

"This is Rodarte again. Put Chief Marion on."

A few clicks, then, "Detective Rodarte?"

"Anything?"

"Nothing. I got two men still watching the house, though."

"Call them back and cancel the APB on Manuelo Ruiz."

Rodarte sensed Marion's surprise. "Why's that?"

"Somebody screwed up," Rodarte said, faking exasperation. "Dumb computer geeks. Looking for a house address and came up with a route number instead. Got y'all hyped up for nothing. I hope to God they never issue those guys guns."

The other cop chuckled. "Thanks for the call, Detective. I'll pull everybody in, including the sheriff's office. My officers will be disappointed. They thought they were going to get in on something big."

"Not tonight."

"What about Burkett?"

"Still at large."

"Big guy like him, you'd think he'd be easy to spot."

"You'd think."

"Well, we'll keep an eye out."

Rodarte apologized again for the mix-up, said he hoped he hadn't kept Marion and his officers up too late, and told him good-bye. He flicked his cigarette butt out the window, then, smiling, pulled his car onto the interstate and headed toward Itasca.

When he saw the Millers, Griff thought, *The surprises just keep on coming.*

Both had on sandals, shorts, and florid Hawaiian-print shirts. Ellie was wearing a straw hat. A wilted lei drooped from her neck. She looked flummoxed. Coach, in spite of his ridiculous attire, was seething.

Hoping to defuse the impending explosion, Griff said, "Coach, Ellie, this is Laura Speakman."

Coach nudged Ellie aside and bore down on Griff. "The widow? Yeah, we know who she is. We read about Foster Speakman's murder in *The Wall Street Journal* while we were in Hawaii." He shot Laura a look, then his hard gaze swung back to Griff. "Next thing I know, I'm getting a call from a Dallas detective, apologizing for bothering me while I was on vacation, but it was important, he said."

"Rodarte?"

"That's right. Stanley Rodarte. He asked if we knew where you were. Had we had any contact with you? Would we know where he should start looking for you? Why? I asked. Did this have to do with Bill Bandy? Oh no, he said. That's old news. He's looking for you in connection with the Speakman murder. Your fingerprints were on the murder weapon."

"Joe, your blood pressure," Ellie said quietly.

"I told him I didn't know anything about you, what you were doing, where you were, and I didn't want to know. Now I come home and find you all cozy *in bed* with the late millionaire's wife. And it doesn't look to me like she's in mourning."

"Well, you're wrong!" Griff shouted, going toe-to-toe with Coach's anger. "She's mourning the loss of her baby. *My* baby," he said, thumping his chest. "She miscarried it tonight there in your bathroom."

Ellie made a sorrowful, wounded sound.

"Laura was pregnant by me, but I didn't kill her husband." Griff looked beyond Coach at Ellie. "You've got to believe that." To Coach he said, "It's up to Laura how much she confides in you, but she can tell you that I did not commit murder. I'm on my way now to find the only man who knows that for certain and can keep Rodarte from putting me on death row."

Griff moved toward the door, but Coach planted his hands firmly on Griff's chest, stopping him. "You're not going anywhere. I'm turning you in."

"You can't stop me."

"Oh yeah?" Coach shoved him backward.

"He has to go, Mr. Miller." Laura swung her feet to the floor and got off the bed. "I'll tell you everything you want to know. But Griff didn't kill Foster. In order to prove it, he must leave now."

The older man divided a look between her and Ellie, whose expression indicated that, this once, she had sided against him. He came back around to Griff, who could tell Coach was warring with himself for reasons he believed to be right and just. "If you're innocent—"

"I am."

"Then turn yourself in."

"I can't. While I'm wading through the formalities, Rodarte might eliminate this other guy."

"Eliminate? What do you mean?"

"Exactly what you think I mean."

"Who is this other guy?"

"Speakman's aide, who's been missing. Coach, there's no time to explain it all now. I've got to go."

Coach stepped back and raised both his hands. "Dig yourself in deeper. See if I care. I wash my hands of you."

"You already did, five years ago."

"Long before that!"

The words hurt, but Griff couldn't dwell on them now. He picked up Manuelo's duffel bag. When he looked back at Laura, he didn't say anything, but he hoped she knew what he felt.

Then he brushed past Coach and left the house in a dead run.

Rodarte located the abandoned farmhouse while dawn was still several hours away. As described, it was the only structure he'd seen since he left town central, and it was practically falling down. He hadn't passed any patrol cars, and none were in sight. Chief Marion, good as his word, had called back the posse.

Rodarte slid his nine-millimeter from his shoulder holster and chambered a bullet, took a flashlight from his glove box, then cautiously got out of his car. He made a circuit around the house, shining the flashlight on the unstable piers holding up the structure and onto the roof, which not only sagged but had large holes. Most of the windows had been broken out. The place was a shambles.

It was surrounded by fallow cotton fields, the earth as flat and black as a griddle. The air was hot and still, and so quiet he could have heard a gnat fart. Neither the approach of his car nor his prowling had flushed out Ruiz or anybody else who might have been hiding inside. He didn't get the feeling that he was being watched through one of the busted windows, either, and his instinct for that kind of thing was excellent.

Minding his step for fear of falling through the rotted planks, he walked across the porch and tried the front door. It swung open on rusted hinges that squeaked. Standing on the threshold, pistol in his right hand, he shone the flashlight around the interior. It stank of mice, living and dead.

There was one main room, with a fireplace full of litter and old ash. Opening off this room were several doorways. He crept to them one by one. Bedrooms. One bathroom. A kitchen. All vacant. No sign of occupancy for at least a decade.

"Fucking waste of time," he muttered. So Burkett had been yanking his chain after all, sending him on a wild-goose chase while he was hustling the widow down to Mexico for some R&R, romance and rutting.

He switched off the flashlight, sat down on a windowsill, and lit a cigarette to smoke while he ruminated on his next move. He blew a plume of smoke through the vacant window frame. Without any wind, the smoke hovered in the air like a ghost. Rodarte stared through it across a yard of hard-packed, parched earth.

There was a pen that probably had been home to a hog, a goat maybe. Too small for a horse. The posts of a barbed-wire fence either were listing or had already toppled. The wire lay in rusty coils on the ground. Thirty yards or so beyond the fallen fence was a barn that appeared in even worse condition than the house.

The barn.

Rodarte stuck the cigarette between his lips and squinted through the smoke rising off it. He checked his flashlight to see how the battery was holding out. Getting dimmer, but still working. He dropped the cigarette onto the bare wood floor and ground it out.

Outside, he could see well enough without the flashlight. But he kept it in one hand, his pistol in the other, as he went around the house to the back. The yard was an obstacle course. An abandoned wheelbarrow lay on its side. A tree stump obviously used as a chopping block still had the hatchet embedded in it. The shadowed hulk under an attached lean-to turned out to be a disemboweled tractor.

He stepped over the fence, carefully avoiding the lines of barbed wire, and walked toward the barn. The double doors were closed but held together only by a wooden latch that pivoted on a nail. He flipped it up and pushed the door open just wide enough for him to peer inside. The darkness was penetrating. The stifling air smelled of manure and soured hay.

Sensing no movement or sound, he opened the door wider and slipped inside. He switched the flashlight on and shone it around. His knowledge of barns was limited to what he'd seen in movies, but in his uneducated opinion, this one was fairly standard. A loft running the length of one side. Horse stalls. Tack and farm implements.

And Manuelo Ruiz.

Or somebody.

Instinctually, Rodarte knew he wasn't alone. And for one split second, he felt a pang of fear. *It could be Burkett.* Burkett might have set him up. Burkett might have sent him here to be ambushed. Had he been outsmarted by that cagey son of a bitch?

Before Rodarte could complete the thought, he sensed movement behind him. As he turned, a hard blow landed on his shoulder, numbing his arm and hand. He dropped the flashlight. With his other arm, he swung a wide arc that ended abruptly when his palmed pistol connected with the side of his attacker's head.

It wasn't Burkett. Too short, too dark, too thick through the middle. And Rodarte hated himself for the relief that came from knowing that.

But he still had a fight on his hands. The man was stunned and staggering but not downed. He ducked his head and lunged toward Rodarte. The detective got a knee up in time to catch the man beneath his chin and practically shoved it up his nostrils. Rodarte heard teeth clack together and figured that some of them had broken. With a grunt of pain, the man fell to the earthen floor.

Rodarte, his momentary fear now replaced by anger, grabbed the flashlight and shone it down, directly into the man's face. It was swarthy, broad, the features flat. The eyes blinking against the beam of light were inky black. They widened marginally when they saw the barrel of Rodarte's pistol aimed directly at them.

"*Hola*, Man-u-el-o."

The man showed a flicker of surprise.

"Yeah, I know your name. We've got a mutual friend. Griff Burkett."

At that, Ruiz rattled off a barrage of Spanish.

"Shut up!" Rodarte barked. Ruiz fell silent. "I'm not interested in anything you have to say. Anyhow, you should save your strength for the job you've got coming up."

Reaching down, he grabbed the man's shirtfront and hauled him to his feet. "See that shovel over there?" He directed the flashlight's beam at the pile of tools he'd spotted earlier. "Get it." Ruiz just stood there looking at him vacantly. "Don't pull that *no comprendo* bullshit on me." He hefted the pistol and clearly enunciated, "Go and get the fucking shovel."

Ruiz's obsidian eyes glittered in the flashlight's beam, but he did as he was told. "Don't even think of trying to clobber me with it," Rodarte said when Ruiz turned with the shovel's handle gripped in both hands. "I'll shoot you right now if you do."

He motioned for Ruiz to go ahead of him through the barn door. Rodarte followed at a cautious distance, the nine-millimeter aimed at the man's spine.

The eastern horizon was turning gray. "Get a move on, Man-uelo." Planting his foot against the other man's buttocks, Rodarte pushed him hard enough to cause him to stumble and fall.

Ruiz rolled over onto his back and glared up at Rodarte in a way that made the detective glad he had a gun trained on him. "We'll see how feisty you're feeling after you've put that shovel to good use." Ruiz looked at the shovel, then back at Rodarte, seeming puzzled. "What?" Rodarte asked around a chuckle. "You didn't expect *me* to dig your grave, did you?"

CHAPTER
37

LAURA STARED BACK AT THE TWO PEOPLE STARING AT HER.
She could smell the plumeria blossoms of Ellie Miller's wilting lei. The odor was heavy and sweet. "You just returned from vacation?" she asked.

Ellie replied. "We got into DFW a half hour early. Around four-thirty."

"I'm sorry you had to come back after a long flight to find a stranger in your bed." She gave a soft, humorless laugh. "Like the three bears. How was your flight?"

Ellie crossed to Laura and took her hand. "You're the one who's had a rough night. How're you feeling?"

"I'll be all right."

"Sure you will. But right now it's bad. Cramping?"

"Hmm."

"I know. I went through this four times."

"I'm sorry."

Ellie shrugged philosophically. "Wasn't meant to be." She patted Laura's hand. "I'll get you something for those cramps."

She went out, leaving Laura alone with Coach Joe Miller. He was an intimidating presence. He stared at her, his expression judgmental. Yet he also seemed curious about her, in spite of himself.

"I'm sorry about your baby." He nodded toward the door

through which his wife had passed. "Ellie shrugs it off, but her heart broke each time."

"I'm sure it did."

"You're sure it was Griff's baby?"

"No question. My husband was incapable."

"Sterile?"

"Incapable," she repeated.

"Huh." He digested that, then asked, "Is that why you took up with Griff?"

Before she could answer, Ellie returned carrying a bottle of ibuprofen and a glass of water. "Take two."

Laura had already sworn off analgesics that pregnant women were advised not to take. Swallowing the capsules was a painful reminder that the precaution was no longer necessary.

"What are you doing?"

That from Ellie, whose voice was sharp, imperious, and directed toward her husband, who had picked up the telephone on the desk.

"Calling the police."

"You're going to sic the police on that boy?"

"He's not a boy, Ellie. He's a man. He has to be held accountable."

"Please, don't call Rodarte," Laura said. "He's Griff's sworn enemy."

"Because he's a homicide detective and Griff is a . . . a . . ."

"See?" Ellie said, planting her fists on her narrow hips. "You can't even bring yourself to say it because you know it isn't true."

"If it's not true, why's he running?" Coach asked. "Why doesn't he turn himself in?"

Ellie, having no answer, looked helplessly toward Laura, who implored Coach to hang up the phone. "Please don't make that call. At least not until I've told you about Griff and me. And Foster. All of it. Please, Mr. Miller."

He considered her for several moments, then reluctantly replaced the phone and folded his thick arms across his barrel chest. "Well?"

She began with the day Foster first told her of his plan and left nothing out except the most intimate details of the four times she and Griff had been together.

"I never heard anything so outlandish," Coach said. "You're telling me that your husband *paid* Griff to . . . to do that?"

"Regrettably, I went along, for reasons that are too complex to explain now. After I learned I was pregnant, I didn't expect ever to see Griff again."

While she was listening to Laura's story, Ellie's eyes had turned moist. "How did you feel about that? About never seeing Griff again?"

Laura hesitated, then said, "I was conflicted. And because I was, I would never have *allowed* myself to see him again."

Ellie nodded, understanding.

"I would have stayed with my husband forever," Laura continued. "Rearing the child as his, exactly as he wanted."

"So what made it all go south?" Coach asked. "Let me guess. Griff."

"Actually, Foster. I blame myself for not seeing how severe his OCD had become. I think I didn't want to see it. Anyway, it, coupled with the accident, had changed him. He was no longer the Foster I fell in love with. I hoped a baby would bring that Foster back.

"In any case, I was committed to our marriage and our life together. If he hadn't attempted to kill Griff, I would be with him tonight. And Griff wouldn't be a fugitive." She divided a look between them. "I swear everything I've told you is the truth."

She had no doubt that Ellie believed her. Coach was gnawing the inside of his cheek, apparently unconvinced. Suddenly he turned and picked up the telephone.

"Joe, didn't you hear a single word she's said?"

"There's nothing wrong with my ears, Ellie."

"Then how can you—"

"Because I know Griff," he said. "He's always looked out for number one. He's never given a damn about anyone except himself. You, me, his teammates. Nobody."

"You're wrong," Laura said.

"He may have been a little selfish before," Ellie said. "But he's different now. I saw the change in him when he was here. And if you weren't so damn stubborn, Joe Miller, you'd—"

"Mr. Miller, please," Laura said. "You'll regret—"

"I'm calling the police." He shouted it over their chorused protests, slicing his hand through the air. "Now that's all there is to it."

There wasn't much traffic to slow Griff down. Rush hour at its heaviest was a couple hours away. He made good time to the Itasca exit. The town still slumbered, but he crawled through it, heeding speed limit signs, not wanting to get stopped now.

It wasn't difficult to find Lavaca Road. He continued along it until it turned into FM 2010, a narrow, rutted road that seemed to have been traveled so infrequently as to have become completely overlooked.

After a couple miles, he began to fear that he and Laura had been wrong. But then he spotted a dilapidated farmhouse and barn, showing up as smudged shadows against a sky just turning pastel with the rising sun. But he knew he had the right place.

Rodarte's car was parked in front.

Griff slowed and turned in to the gravel driveway, spotting them instantly—two dark figures silhouetted against the glow in the eastern horizon. He rolled to a stop, turned off the engine, and opened the car door. The early morning atmosphere was soft and silent, deceptively benign.

Keeping the two men in sight, he reached into the duffel bag and took out the policeman's pistol. Impersonating a deliveryman, incapacitating the cops, his and Laura's madcap escape from the estate, all seemed a long time ago. Those recollections were blurred.

But vivid in his memory was the look on her face when she realized that the baby was lost.

If . . . if . . . if . . .

There were so many of them, he didn't even know where to begin regretting.

But one big *if* remained: if he didn't live through this, he hoped Laura knew that he loved her. Bad timing or not, he wished he'd said it when he'd had the chance.

He stuffed the pistol into the back waistband of the navy blue work pants he was still wearing. When he got out, he left the car door open, just in case he had to make a quick getaway. He walked along the exterior wall of the house toward the rear, realizing what a large and easy target his white T-shirt made against the faded clapboard. Rodarte and Manuelo Ruiz stood as still as scarecrows in the fallow field.

But then Rodarte raised his arm and waved. "Hiya, Griff."

Griff disliked guns. Didn't know much about them. Knew even less about police-issue pistols. But as he crossed the littered yard and walked toward the other two men, he was comforted by the weight of the pistol at the small of his back.

He had to step over a barbed-wire fence that had been knocked down. Dirt clods and fossilized tractor tracks made the ground uneven. But he didn't look down. He kept his gaze fixed on Rodarte. When he got close enough to make out the detective's features, Griff saw that he was smiling with amusement as he held his pistol aimed at Manuelo.

The tableau confirmed what Griff had feared—Rodarte didn't plan to use Manuelo Ruiz as an eyewitness. Even if Griff allayed Manuelo's fear and persuaded him to return to Dallas and tell the truth about Foster Speakman's accidental death, Rodarte would never permit it. Because Rodarte didn't want Griff to be exonerated. He didn't even want him locked away for good. He wanted him dead.

And now Griff understood why. He knew why Rodarte had been waiting for him outside Big Spring FCI. He understood why he'd been tailing him and monitoring his every move since his release. He'd thought Rodarte was trying to scare him into making either a mistake or a confession. Fact was, Rodarte was scared of him.

The ground at Rodarte's feet was littered with cigarette butts. At Manuelo's feet lay a shovel. Behind him were a mound of freshly turned dirt and a wide hole. The implication sickened Griff. The bastard had made the Salvadoran dig his own grave while he stood there, smoking and smiling.

Probably, Griff thought, he and Manuelo would share the grave.

Manuelo stood as still as a statue carved of teak. His eyes were as hard and impenetrable as polished stones. Griff couldn't tell if he was afraid, resigned, or waiting for an opportunity to pounce. He had no idea what his arrival would signify to the Salvadoran. He wished he had the Spanish-language skills to tell him that Rodarte was their common enemy, *not each other*.

"I was beginning to think you weren't coming," Rodarte said when Griff halted about ten yards away from him.

"You were expecting me?"

"Hoping. What kept you? Bet I know." He winked. "The widow's hot snatch. Hope you got a piece of it, 'cause it'll be your last." Leer still in place, he said pleasantly, "Hand over the pistol."

"Pistol?"

"You want a knee blown out?"

"You can't aim at both of us at the same time. If you take your gun off Manuelo, he'll be on you before you can blink."

"Okay. What say I shoot him first, then blow your knee out just for giving me lip?"

Griff reached behind his back.

"Easy."

With exaggerated slowness, Griff pulled the pistol from his waistband. He could kill Rodarte without remorse. Marcia was reason enough, not to mention the rest of it. But even with a fatal wound, Rodarte might have time to get off one shot. Griff couldn't risk Manuelo dying. He still needed the aide's testimony about Speakman. He held the pistol far out to his side.

"Toss it over."

Griff did as told. The pistol landed among the butts at Rodarte's feet. "Thanks. Now we can all relax."

Nodding in Manuelo's direction, Griff said, "Let him go."

"No, I don't think so."

"He'll head straight for El Salvador. You'll never see him again."

"Probably. But why should I lose sleep over it? He might develop a guilty conscience about running out on you."

"So you know he killed Speakman?"

"Must have, or you wouldn't have told me where he was at."

"I realized that mistake too late."

"Lost your famous timing, Number Ten?" The detective formed a sad face. "Gee, that's too bad. And just when you needed it most."

"Let him go. Your quarrel is with me, not him."

Rodarte chuckled. "Well, you've got that right."

"You want me to go down."

"What gave me away?"

"You want me to go down for Bill Bandy. But not because you think I killed him. You know I didn't."

Rodarte grinned. "You're getting warmer."

"You know I didn't because you did."

"And they call jocks dumb." He snorted. "Of course, it did take you five years to figure it out."

"The Vista boys hired you to muzzle him permanently."

"It was sort of an audition. There was word going around that Bandy's days were numbered. The Vista trio were afraid he was going to turn them over like he did you. I'd been wanting to do some moonlighting for them, but they're a tight little clique. It's hard to win their trust."

"So you seized an opportunity."

"I offered my services."

"Thinking that if you rid them of Bandy, they'd welcome you into their fold and put you on their payroll."

Rodarte beamed his ugly smile. "Who better to help out with problems like Bandy than a homicide detective who can steer murder investigations in the wrong direction?" He began to laugh, deep inside his chest, then out loud. "It was a great plan, and then it got even better. Swear to God, Burkett, when you showed up at Bandy's place, I nearly pissed my pants. I couldn't have planned it any better."

"You were there when I arrived."

"In the back room. Before I snapped his neck, he swore up and down he didn't have a secret stash, but have you ever known a bookie who didn't lie? If I returned some skimmed funds to Vista in addition to getting rid of Bandy, think how pleased they'd be.

"So I was back there tossing the place when I heard the door. You came barging in like a bull elephant with a grudge to settle. When I realized it was you, I could barely contain a fit of the giggles. While you were woe-is-me-ing over Bandy's body, I sneaked out back."

"And called in an anonymous nine-one-one."

"At a pay phone around the corner. Soon as it went out over dispatch, I radioed in, said I was in the neighborhood, volunteered to check out the alleged homicide." He grinned. "You know the rest."

"You had a golden opportunity to kill me, too. Why didn't you?"

"I was afraid to, afraid that would piss off the Vista boys. I thought they might have special plans for you, and it wouldn't sit too well if I robbed them of the pleasure. In hindsight, I should have taken you out."

"Those five years were awfully long for me, but they must have been torture for you," Griff said. "As long as I was alive, you were vulnerable. You've been scared shitless I would figure it out. That's why you've been hassling me, pretending you were acting on behalf of Vista, knowing all along I hadn't stolen from Bandy. You didn't find anything in his back room, did you?"

Rodarte shrugged. "Maybe he wasn't lying after all."

"You're still not in Vista's fold. Apparently they weren't impressed."

"Not yet."

"But you're hoping that killing me now will win their approval."

"It can't hurt. They don't like you."

"They like you even less."

"We'll see." He laughed abruptly. "You know what's really funny? I didn't even have to bring about your downfall. You did that all by yourself. Fucking a paraplegic's wife. That's low, Burkett. Even for the likes of you. The only thing," he said, pulling his face into a pucker of concentration. "What was that half mil for? Was he trying to buy you off?"

Griff just stood, glaring at him.

"Not going to tell me? Okay. Doesn't matter anyway." He leaned forward and casually picked the pistol off the ground, then turned and fired a bullet directly into Manuelo's chest.

Without a sound, the Salvadoran fell backward into the make-shift grave.

CHAPTER
38

G RIFF GAVE A STRANGLED CRY AND LURCHED FORWARD. "You killed him!"

"Not me, Burkett. You." Rodarte pitched the pistol toward the open grave, where it landed in the dirt. "You ran the man down. By the way, remind me to ask Mrs. Speakman how you learned about this place. Anyway, you ran Ruiz down here, forced him to dig his own grave, then, using the weapon of a policeman you assaulted, you shot Ruiz in cold blood so he couldn't testify against you at Foster Speakman's murder trial."

Griff was still staring at the empty spot where Manuelo had been standing seconds before. He looked at the pistol, much too far away to retrieve. His gaze coming back to Rodarte, he held up his clean hands. "They'll know I didn't fire the pistol."

"Oh, you will. After you're dead. Don't worry. I'll set it up to look convincing."

"Laura knows the truth."

Rodarte winked. "I have ways that'll convince her otherwise."

Forgetting every rule of self-preservation, Griff lunged.

Rodarte reacted, getting off two shots before Griff grabbed the wrist of his gun hand and wrenched it. Rodarte screamed in pain and dropped the pistol.

Payback time, Griff thought as he slugged Rodarte hard in the mouth. He swung his left fist at the detective's cheekbone and felt the skin split. But his satisfaction was short-lived because of the pain in his left shoulder, like a branding iron being gouged deep into the flesh. Only then did he realize that he'd been struck by one of Rodarte's bullets. However, the pain only fueled his rage. He struck mercilessly.

Rodarte fought back with a vengeance. He landed a punch in Griff's gut, and when Griff staggered back, Rodarte sidestepped and threw another at his kidney. The angle wasn't good, so the blow didn't have full impact, but it was enough to cause Griff's knees to buckle.

He caught himself before he fell and, acting reflexively, kicked backward, connecting solidly with Rodarte's shinbone. That slowed the detective down long enough for Griff to come around to face him again and catch a fist in his ribs rather than his kidney.

They hammered at each other until Griff lost all sense of time and place, till his hands hurt almost more than the bullet wound, more than any other bleeding part of him. Rodarte's mouth was a ghoulish maw, from which he continually spat blood. His eyes were crazed with hatred. And Griff knew that Rodarte would fight till one of them was dead.

Not long ago, he would have thought, *Fine. I'll kill the bastard, or he'll kill me, and either way it won't matter much*. But now he wanted to live. He wanted to live for a long time, and with Laura. That hope kept him fighting even after the fight had gone out of him and every effort was tremendous.

The sweetest sound he'd ever heard was the wail of sirens. They were coming from far away but rapidly approaching. While they were a relief to Griff, they seemed to madden Rodarte and renew his flagging strength and determination.

He bared his blood-covered teeth and charged. Griff feinted left, then right. Rodarte plunged forward headlong, tripped over a deep rut made by a tractor tire, and fell facefirst into a nest of coiled barbed wire.

He shrieked like a banshee, but later Griff wondered if it was from the pain caused by the vicious barbs, or from fury over being defeated.

Griff stood watching as Rodarte struggled to free himself, but his frantic attempts to escape the wire only increased its hold on him. The barbs became embedded in his clothing, his flesh.

The sirens were closer now. Griff shouted down at Rodarte. "Stop fighting it! It's over!"

"Fuck you!"

Miraculously, the detective managed to roll onto his back, but he was wrapped in wire. Strands of it were stretched taut across his face, the barbs digging deeply into his contorted features. Still his arms and legs thrashed. He managed to get a knee up, although his shoe was trapped in a snare of wire.

"Give it up, Rodarte," Griff gasped as he wiped his bleeding nose. "For God's sake."

The sirens couldn't have been more than half a mile away. Griff scanned the road for the approaching police cars. Across the flat, fallow fields, he saw the flash of colored lights. One minute, two at the outside and—

"Kiss your ass good-bye, Number Ten."

Rodarte was aiming a small pistol up at him; only now Griff could see the ankle holster beneath his pants leg. The detective was bleeding from countless puncture wounds, but he seemed unaware of them. The hand holding the pistol was scraped and bleeding. But the finger around the trigger was steady, and so was his aim. The wire across his face made his ugliness even more grotesque. Although it had pinned down one side of his mouth, he still managed a distorted smile.

Griff registered all this in a millisecond. He knew this was his last heartbeat. His final thought was of Laura.

And then Rodarte's smile went slack. He gave a short cry at the same instant Griff was knocked to the ground. Manuelo Ruiz was a blur moving past him, and so was the edge of the shovel as it arced down from high above the Salvadoran's head directly into Rodarte's cranium, cleaving it in two.

After talking almost nonstop for an hour, Griff settled tiredly against the hospital pillow and stared at the acoustical ceiling tiles. His new lawyer, who'd come recommended by Glen Hunnicutt, spoke from

across the room. "Gentlemen, my client has answered all your questions. I suggest you leave now and let him get some rest."

The two Dallas detectives ignored the lawyer and remained
where they were. Griff supposed they were waiting to see if he had
anything to add. One of them was gray haired, taciturn, and weary
looking, a veteran. The other was younger than Griff. More aggres-
sive and edgy than his partner, he'd done most of the talking.

Griff couldn't remember their names. He wasn't real sure about
the attorney's. Hunnicutt had made arrangements with him while
Griff was still in surgery to repair the bullet wound in his shoulder,
which had been nasty and painful but not too damaging, certainly
not life threatening.

After a lengthy silence, he asked, "Is Ruiz gonna make it?"

"Seems so," the younger detective replied. "He's a tough customer, I'll say that for him."

"He is that." Griff could remember how it had felt having the
life squeezed out of him. "He won't be charged for killing Rodarte,
will he?"

The detectives shook their heads in unison. The younger said, "If
he hadn't, Rodarte would have shot you."

Griff acknowledged that with a small nod.

"That old barn is used as sort of a halfway house for aliens
coming in. When he entered the country, Ruiz was directed there,
told he could obtain false documents from a guy who'd meet him
there. The papers cost him all the money he had, but with them
he could get work immediately. Immigration officials are looking
for the guys who run that operation." He paused, then added,
"Through the interpreter, Ruiz also admitted to killing Foster Speakman."

"It was an accident," Griff said.

"That's what he claims."

"It's the truth."

"He said you and he were fighting. Is that correct?"

"Yes."

Since Griff and McAlister—that was his name, Jim McAlister—
hadn't had time to confer privately before this interrogation, the
lawyer cautioned him now with a soft clearing of his throat. Not that

Griff would have blurted out the truth, the whole truth, and nothing but the truth.

The younger detective continued. "Ruiz was a bit sketchy about the cause of that altercation."

Manuelo was being loyal to his late boss. He wouldn't incriminate Speakman by telling the police that he had been ordered by him to kill Griff. Griff saw no point in telling them, either. He kept his poker face.

"You want to shed any light on that, Mr. Burkett?" the younger detective prodded.

"I can't."

"Was there some kind of *thing* between you and Speakman?"

"Before that night, I'd met him only once, and it was a friendly meeting."

"You had no cross words that night?"

"No."

"Did you provoke Ruiz?"

"No. Not intentionally anyway. He attacked me from behind."

"He admitted that," the older detective grumbled. He was frowning, as though confused. Or highly skeptical. "Still doesn't explain why he attacked you."

"I don't know why."

"Come on, Burkett," the younger detective said. "Of course you know. What were you doing there?"

The lawyer cut in. "I'd like a private word with my client before he answers that."

"No, it's okay, Mr. McAlister. I can answer." Griff was betting that the police didn't know about his relationship with Laura. He was gambling that Rodarte had kept that like an ace tucked inside his sleeve, waiting to play it when it would be most advantageous to him and most detrimental to Griff and Laura. He said, "The meeting that night was a second job interview."

"Job?"

"To do endorsements for SunSouth." It was an implausible claim but also impossible for them to disprove.

"What about all that money?"

"Beats me," Griff lied, speaking before McAlister could stop him. "The box was sitting on the desk in plain sight. Speakman told me to open it and look inside. I did. About that time is when Ruiz attacked me. Maybe he thought I was about to steal the cash from his boss. As I said, I don't know what set him off. Whatever it was, he'll regret it for the rest of his life. He worshiped Speakman."

Clearly the detectives believed there was more to it, but that was all they were going to get from him.

Grudgingly, the younger detective said that Ruiz had told them the same story. "He admitted to killing his boss accidentally during his struggle with you, and said that when he ran from the house, you were trying to save Speakman's life. All of which clears you."

Jim McAlister sat back in the vinyl chair, looking complacent.

"Did he also corroborate everything I told you about Rodarte?"

The younger detective nodded. "He didn't understand what the beef was between you and Rodarte, but everything else he told us matches what you said went down at the old farm."

"What about Bill Bandy's murder?" McAlister asked.

"What about it?" asked the older detective.

"For five years suspicion has been cast on my client. He has steadfastly denied any involvement beyond discovering the body."

The detectives glanced at each other in silent consultation over how much they should tell. Finally the younger detective said, "We're inclined to believe Mr. Burkett's allegation against Rodarte. He's been under investigation by Internal Affairs for a while. Many complaints have been filed against him and some of his pals within the department. Too many to ignore. Serious stuff, like harassment, brutality, corruption. One woman suspect claimed Rodarte fondled her while she was in his custody and then got rough with her when she protested."

"Sounds like him," Griff growled. He had hoped to keep Marcia's encounter with Rodarte out of the fray and was now glad to know she could be left in peace.

The younger detective was saying, "Anyhow, Bandy's murder case will be reopened and investigated from a different perspective."

"Am I under arrest?" Griff nodded toward the door of his hospital room, where a uniformed policeman had been posted.

"For the assault on the three police officers in the hotel, as well as for impersonating an officer."

"There were mitigating circumstances," McAlister said.

"Save 'em for the judge at his arraignment," the older officer said. He seemed to hold defense attorneys in no higher esteem than he did the lawbreakers they represented.

"Just be glad you're not being charged with kidnapping," the younger detective chimed in. "According to Mrs. Speakman, when you explained to her that Rodarte was impeding justice, she went willingly to help you locate Ruiz."

Three pairs of eyes were fixed on Griff, waiting to see how he would respond. He said, "Without Mrs. Speakman I would never have found him, and without him I would have been falsely charged with murdering her husband. I'll never be able to repay her trust in me." He paused, then asked what was in store for Manuelo Ruiz.

"Soon as we clear things up with him, and he's well enough to travel, he'll be sent back to El Salvador. He faces charges there. Killed a guy who'd allegedly raped his sister. We figure, let the authorities down there have him. They've got first dibs."

"I wish him well," Griff said, almost to himself.

"Generous of you," the older cop said. "If he hadn't attacked you, you wouldn't be in this mess."

"He also saved my life." Taking a deep breath, Griff closed his eyes and asked tiredly, "Is that it?"

CHAPTER

39

HIS NEW LAWYER TOOK IT FROM THERE. MCALISTER USHERED the detectives out. He instructed Griff to stay in contact and not to answer any further questions without him present, told him to rest, and then he too left.

Griff closed his eyes, but rest eluded him. Although his body was battered and he was exhausted, his mind wouldn't shut down. Yesterday, he, along with Manuelo, had been transported by helicopter to the trauma center at Parkland Hospital, where both had undergone surgery.

He had vague recollections of being prepped and a few drug-blurred memories of the recovery room. This morning he had awakened in this private room, a little more than twenty-four hours after he saw Rodarte's skull split open with the sharp edge of a shovel.

James McAlister, attorney-at-law, had shown up only minutes ahead of the Dallas detectives. He'd barely had time to introduce himself and tell Griff that as soon as Glen Hunnicutt had heard about the events in Itasca, he'd called him on Griff's behalf.

Now Griff was relieved to have the interrogation behind him. But it had left him more exhausted than before. His body ached from his fight with Rodarte. His shoulder throbbed. But his mind was unsettled over Laura.

As Foster Speakman's widow, she would once again be in the

spotlight while the police and media sorted through the legal detritus left by Burkett, Ruiz, and Rodarte. The speculation that would swirl around her was inevitable. He could only hope for a bigger story to come along that would supplant them as the lead on the nightly news.

But in the meantime, how was she bearing up? Was she well? Beyond the obvious, had she suffered from the miscarriage?

He blamed himself for whatever suffering she had to endure. Things might have turned out differently, her heartbreak might have been avoided entirely, if not for their last afternoon together. If he hadn't stopped her from leaving, as she'd been about to, could everything that had happened since have been prevented?

But—and now was the time for brutal honesty—if he'd had it to do over, would he have let her leave? Or, acting on her hesitation, would he have reached around her and closed the door as he'd done? Thinking back on it, he wondered, would he have let her go? Even knowing what he did now, would he?

He closed his eyes and let his mind drift back to that afternoon, to the sick disappointment he'd felt when she told him she was leaving and never coming back. He hadn't tried to persuade her otherwise. How could he? He had no rights to her. None.

He'd had to stand by helplessly, hopelessly, and watch as she pulled open the door and said, "Depending on circumstances, this could be the last time I'll see you."

"Could be."

"I can't think of anything to say that seems appropriate."

"Small talk seems smaller." Her smile told him she remembered when she'd said those same words to him. "You don't have to say anything, Laura."

"Then, good-bye."

They'd shaken hands, and he'd got the sense that she was as reluctant to let go of his as he was of hers. But she did let go and turned toward the door. When she made no move to go through it, he reached past her and pushed it shut.

He left his hand there for several seconds, giving her time to protest, giving her time to say, *What the hell do you think you're doing? Open the door. I'm leaving.*

When she didn't, he drew his hand back and placed it beneath her chin. With the merest pressure, he brought her around to face him. He looked deeply into her eyes and saw in them the same unspoken, desperate longing he felt, and when he did, he fell on her hungrily, pressing his open mouth against her neck, pinning her to the door with his body. She gave a low moan and reached for him. They kissed wildly, recklessly, with abandon and without finesse.

They brought one month of mental foreplay to this moment.

Her skirt was tight fitting, but he managed to work it up over her hips. He pulled down her panties as far as her knees; then she took over and got rid of them while he dealt with his belt and fly. Cupping her bottom in his hands, he lifted her and positioned her open thighs over his. He touched her. She was ready. In one fluid thrust, he was buried in her completely.

She wrapped her arms around his head and held fast as he fucked her, as much with his mind as with his body. Because of their position, it was impossible to move much, but he rocked against her, pressing as high and hard as he could. *Thinking about* what they were doing, *knowing* that he was at last inside her again, made him burn. And the angle was perfect for her. With each stroke, he grazed the erogenous spot. When he came, so did she. And it was crashing.

For what seemed endless minutes, they clung to each other, their breathing loud in the empty house, their bodies giving off incredible heat. Finally he withdrew and gently set her on her feet. Her arms remained wound around his head, his mouth on her neck. Slowly he kissed his way up to her chin and then let his lips hover above hers for agonizing seconds before settling against them. Her lips parted, accepting his tongue.

It was their first real kiss. It was a perfect kiss. Silky and wet and sweet. Intense. Very sexy. When finally they drew apart, he placed his palms on the door on either side of her head, and rested his fevered forehead against hers. "The past thirty days have been the longest of my life," he said, his voice raspy. "I lived in fear of you calling and saying we wouldn't need to meet again. I was afraid I would never get to kiss you."

She placed her fingers lengthwise over his lips. "If we talk, I have to go," she whispered. "You can't say anything. I can't hear anything."

He pulled back, about to argue, but her expression begged him to understand. And he did. They had to pretend this wasn't personal. Each knew better. They weren't fooling themselves. What had just happened had nothing to do with making a baby or anything else except raw desire. But they could not acknowledge it out loud. The only way she could stay was to pretend that she was doing this because her husband demanded it.

Saying nothing more, they went into the bedroom and began removing their clothes. By the time she got out of her shoes and had taken off her top, he was down to his skin. Unwilling to wait another moment to lie down with her, he stretched out on the bed and pulled her down beside him. Gathering her against him, he held the back of her head in his palm and kissed her until they were breathless.

He undid the front fastener of her lacy bra. Her breasts were lovely, soft, natural. He took the weight of one in his palm, brushed his thumb across the nipple until it was very stiff, then caressed it with his tongue. When he drew it into his mouth, she arched her back and whimpered with pleasure.

Blindly he sought her hand and guided it down. He sighed raggedly when her fingers closed around him, then her thumb, discovering a drop of moisture in the slit, spread it around the glans in slow, mind-blowing circles that were nearly his undoing.

Reaching around her, he unfastened her skirt and pushed it past her hips and down her legs. Naked now, she modestly lay back with her thighs closed, forming a perfect, enchanting V. He leaned down and gently blew on her, then pressed a kiss into the damp curls, teasing, teasing until her thighs relaxed. He moved between them and made slow love to her with his mouth.

It was she who drew her knees back and tugged on his hair until he was lying on top of her and his sex was deep inside her again. This time it was unhurried, more emotional than passionate. He savored each sensation and made certain she did. When he felt himself getting close, he took her face between his hands and looked down into her eyes, wanting there to be no question that it was he, only he, making love to her, and for only one reason.

He lost count of the number of times they made love that afternoon, because it was one long act, one erotic exchange melding into the next. Though they weren't free to speak, they allowed each other unlimited access.

His lips touched each feature of her beautiful face again and again. He was at liberty to stroke every inch of her skin, to kiss the backs of her knees. He slid his thumb down the groove of her spine all the way to the cleft of her hips, then lay with his cheek resting in the small of her back.

Equally curious, she examined his large hands, tracing the heavy veins on the backs of them, sucking his crooked little finger into her mouth. She seemed to like his chest hair. A lot. She nuzzled it frequently. He loved the feel of her breath ruffling through it, loved feeling her fingertips exploring his navel and her knee tucked snugly under his balls, loved feeling her mouth's wet tug until he thought he would die of pleasure.

They were lying quietly, fondling and kissing idly, as satiated lovers do, when she looked at him sadly and pulled away. And he'd had to let her go. There was so much he wanted to say, but he was forbidden to. He wanted to tell her that, for the first time in his whole, misbegotten life, he was in love. He loved, period. He loved her.

"God help me," he whispered now to the walls of his hospital room, "I did from the start."

He must have slept. A slight shift of air roused him. He opened his eyes. Coach was standing just inside the door. He said, "Were you asleep?"

"Just resting my eyes."

He hesitated, then walked to the side of the bed and looked Griff over, his gaze settling on his bandaged shoulder. "How is it?"

"I'll live. Hurts like hell."

"They don't have any pain medication in this hospital?"

"I'm getting it." He raised his hand with the IV port. "It still hurts."

"Any permanent damage?"

"The surgeon says there shouldn't be. If I do my physical therapy."

"Yeah, well, I wish him luck. You always shirked on that."

"She."

"Huh?"

"The orthopedic surgeon is a she."

"Oh." Coach looked around the room, took note of the TV suspended from the ceiling, the wide window. "Nice room."

"Can't complain."

"Food okay?"

"All I've had is beef broth and lime Jell-O."

"You hungry?"

"Not really."

Having run out of small talk, they were quiet for a time. Then Griff said, "Thank you for not calling the cops on me the other night."

"I did."

Griff looked at him with surprise.

"Despite Ellie's yammering, I put in a call. But not to Rodarte. After being passed around to several detectives, I finally landed one who sounded like he had some sense. I told him what was what, where you were headed, and that the situation had all the makings for becoming dangerous, possibly lethal to somebody. He got in touch with the police department in Itasca and mobilized them immediately."

"So you believed me."

"I believed her."

"Laura."

"I believed every word out of her mouth. You, I still know to be a liar."

"I was not lying! I did not—"

"Hell, I know you didn't kill Foster Speakman or that Bandy lowlife. That's not what I'm talking about."

"Then give me a hint."

"You lied about that game against Washington."

Griff's heart skipped a beat or two. He hadn't seen that coming. He stared at Coach for a moment, then averted his head and mumbled, "What are you talking about?"

"You know goddamn well what I'm talking about." His face red with anger, Coach bent over him until Griff was forced to look him in the eye. "That pass to Whitethorn. That game-throwing pass that got you sent to prison." Coach jabbed the edge of the hospital bed with his index finger. "I know the truth, Griff, but I want to hear you say it, and then I want to know why."

"Say what? Why what?"

Coach fumed. "I've looked at the video of that play till I'm cross-eyed. From every possible angle. In slow motion and fast forward. Time after time after time. A thousand times."

"So has everybody and his grandmother."

"But everybody and his grandmother don't know the game like I do. And not everybody knows *you* like I do. Nobody taught you and coached you like I did. Griff." His voice had turned husky, and if Griff hadn't known better, he would have thought he saw tears starting to form in the older man's eyes. "You couldn't have thrown a better, more accurate pass. You practically walked the football to the two-yard line and laid it in Whitethorn's hands. You put it right between the numbers on his jersey."

He straightened and turned away for a moment, and when he came back around, he said simply, "He didn't catch it."

Griff remained silent.

Coach said, "Whitethorn didn't catch it, but not because you threw a bad pass. He simply dropped the damn ball."

Griff, feeling the pressure of his own emotions, nodded. "He dropped the damn ball."

Breath streamed out of Coach's mouth, sounding like a plug had been pulled on an inflatable toy. It even seemed to Griff that he deflated. "So why in God's name did you lie about throwing that game? Why did you admit to a crime you didn't commit?"

"Because I was guilty. I was guilty as hell. I had every intention of screwing up and losing that game for my own profit. For two million dollars, I was gonna see to it that we lost. But . . ."

He broke off, unable to continue for several moments. When he did, his voice was gravelly. "But when it came right down to it, I couldn't do it. I wanted to win that game. I had to." His hand formed a fist as though trying to grasp the unattainable. "The only hope I had of saving myself was to win that game."

He lay back and closed his eyes, placing himself there on the field. He heard the roar of the crowd, smelled the sweaty jerseys of his teammates as they huddled, felt the tension compressed into a stadium of seventy thousand screaming spectators.

"We're down by four. A field goal won't do. The clock is running out. No time-outs remaining. It's the worst-case scenario, and if that isn't enough, the Super Bowl is riding on this game. We've got time for one more play.

"To cash in from Vista, all I really had to do was let the clock run out, and Washington would have had it. But, coming out of that last huddle, I thought, Fuck those Vista bastards. Fuck their dollars. They may break both my legs, but I'm going to win this championship.

"It all came down to that one play, Coach. One pass. One *choice* that would make me better than the sludge I'd come from. What I did on that play would define my character. My life, actually."

After a moment, he opened his eyes and laughed at the irony. "Then Whitethorn dropped the pass. He *dropped* it!" He scrubbed his face with his hand as though to rub out the memory of seeing his receiver lying on his back in the end zone, his hands empty as the game clock ticked down to double zeros.

"But it really didn't matter. I had sold my soul to the devil anyway. After the loss, I figured I might just as well get paid for it. So when Bandy showed up with my cash, I took it.

"Sometimes I think that maybe the shrink at Big Spring was right, that maybe I wanted to get caught. Anyway, after I was busted, people assumed I'd thrown a pass that was impossible to catch. Whitethorn let them think it. And I let them think it. I was guilty of everything else. I had lied, gambled, cheated, broken the law, pissed on the rules and ethics of professional sports." He smiled wryly. "But I didn't throw that game."

Coach dragged his fists across his damp eyes. "I've waited a long time to hear you say it."

"It feels good to say it. Because the worst part of it, the very worst thing of the whole experience, prison, everything, was knowing how badly I had shamed you and Ellie."

Coach cleared his throat and said gruffly, "We lived through it."

He said it in an offhand manner, as though this moment didn't have any significance. It did, though, and it was huge. Griff hadn't begged his forgiveness, and Coach hadn't granted it. Not in so many words. But that was the understanding that passed between them without it getting sloppy and sentimental. He was in Coach's favor once again. He had his pardon. Maybe even—dare he think it?—his love.

"It would mean a lot to Ellie if you came around more often, let her cook you a meal, fuss over you some, sneak you money she thinks I don't know about."

Griff smiled. "I will. I promise. If I'm not in jail."

Coach frowned. "Over what you did to get Laura away from Rodarte?"

"She told you about that?"

"Yeah, and it's all over the news today. But I don't think the assault charges will stick. Not when it comes out what a threat Rodarte posed, and she'll make sure everyone knows."

Mention of her name brought Laura into the room with them, an intangible but conspicuous presence. Griff looked hard at Coach, who read the unasked questions in his eyes. "She can't come to see you, Griff." He spoke in as soft a voice as he could manage. "Press would be on it like flies on dogshit. There's already been speculation. Raised eyebrows. You know what I'm talking about. Nothing specific, just the suggestion that something between the three of y'all was a little shady.

"Don't forget, it's only been days since she held a very public funeral for her husband. Joe Q. Public doesn't know that Speakman had gone off his rocker, and, for the future of the airline, she'd like to keep it that way. She certainly doesn't want anybody to know what you were hired to do for them."

"She told you about that, too?"

"All of it." Coach shook his head in bewilderment. "Hell of a thing. Never heard of such."

"It's in the Bible."

"Yeah, but Moses also wore a beard to his navel and ate locusts."

"Abraham."

"Well, anyway, Laura said you would understand why she can't come to you now."

"I do understand." Then after a beat. "I love her, Coach."

"I know." At Griff's surprised look, the older man nodded. "The other night, when your whole future depended on chasing down Rodarte and Ruiz, you stayed with her. That wasn't like you, putting somebody else's welfare ahead of your own. You've got to make another sacrifice now, Griff. If you truly care about this lady, you've got to give her time. Distance. Absence from you."

Griff knew that. He understood the necessity. But that didn't make it any easier to accept. "Is she all right?"

"Doing fine. Her worst problem is Ellie."

"Ellie?"

"She's in her mother hen mode. Practically smothering the girl."

Griff smiled and closed his eyes. "She's in good hands."

He must have dozed off again, because when he woke up, Coach was gone. The room was empty. He was alone.

EPILOGUE

GRIFF ANSWERED HIS CELL PHONE ON THE SECOND RING. "Hello?"

"One o'clock today?"

His heart stopped before stuttering into a dangerously rapid beat.

"Can you be there?"

"Uh, yeah. Yes. Yes."

"I'll see you then."

He held the phone to his ear for another thirty seconds before snapping it closed. Then he stood there in the shopping mall, letting other shoppers eddy around him while he reassured himself that he was awake, that he wasn't dreaming, that it had actually been Laura calling.

As with the first time, he arrived at the house easily twenty minutes early. He drove around the neighborhood till twelve fifty-eight. When he got back, her car was in the driveway. He parked behind it. It seemed a long walk to the front door. He was reaching for the bell when the door opened and she was standing there.

"I heard your car."

For a long time, he didn't speak, just stood there, taking in the sight of her. Finally his joy pushed its way out of his tight chest in the form of a light laugh. "You look terrific."

"Thank you."

"No, I mean it." She was wearing a pink, body-hugging sweater and a pair of black slacks. Simple, elegant, sexy as hell. "Really terrific."

She blushed at the compliment and stepped aside, motioning him in. He walked into the living area that was so familiar, yet completely altered since the last time he'd been here. The house had been transformed into an inviting home.

The armoire he recognized, but the sofa was new. There were additional pieces of furniture, artwork on the walls, magazines and books and an area rug, a bowl of white tulips on the coffee table. For the first time, the shutters were opened, letting in sunlight. It wasn't that cold out, so the low fire in the fireplace was more for ambience than for heat.

He turned to Laura, knowing what she was going to say before she said it. "I live here now."

"I read that you'd sold the mansion. Do you like it here?"

"I love it."

They exchanged a long stare, finally broken when she motioned him toward the sofa. "Would you like some tea?"

"Sure."

"Hot or cold?"

"Cold, please."

He sat down, and she disappeared into the kitchen. Curious, he leaned forward and opened one of the doors to the armoire. There was a TV, some reading material, and recent movies on DVD. Nothing X-rated. He closed the doors and settled against the sofa cushions in what he hoped looked like a relaxed position. In the two hours and eighteen minutes between her call and his arrival, he hadn't known a moment of easy breathing.

She returned carrying a tray with a pitcher of tea and two glasses. She set it on the coffee table and filled a glass for each of them. "Sugar?"

"I'm okay."

She passed him a glass, then carried hers to an armchair where she sat down facing him.

He sipped his tea. She took a sip of hers. But they drank in the sight of each other. He was afraid of starting the conversation, afraid of saying the wrong thing. He didn't know why she had invited him here today. The familiar manner in which she'd called, and the time of day she'd specified, couldn't have been coincidental. Yet she'd done nothing to suggest that this would end the way their past meetings in this house had. She may have simply invited him over for tea.

Eventually he said, "Your airline is going gangbusters. That new Select thing sounds interesting."

"It's scheduled to launch in three months." She laughed as she shook her head. "It's hectic and crazy. So much to do. A million decisions. Daily deadlines."

He smiled over her apparent exuberance. "But you're enjoying it."

"Every minute," she admitted. "I'm very optimistic for its success. We've already sold seventy-eight percent of our membership goal. Through the industry grapevine, I've heard that our competitors are scrambling to initiate similar services."

"Imitation is the sincerest form of flattery."

"Absolutely. But it's still *imitation*. We'll be first."

Her enthusiasm was evident in the way her whole face lit up. Her eyes sparkled. Her smile was so beautiful and uninhibited, it made his heart ache. And he realized this was the first time he'd ever seen her look really happy. Ever.

He raised his glass in a mock toast. "Good luck to you and Select. Not that you need luck. SunSouth's stock is at an all-time high."

"You're monitoring the stock?"

"I'm an investor."

"Truly?"

"Yep. Whatever you're doing, keep it up. It's working."

"I'm very busy and working hard, but I'm also maintaining some balance in my life. I give myself Wednesday afternoons off."

That explained her casual outfit. She wasn't going back to work later. He tried not to read anything into that. Tried but failed.

She watched him closely as she said, "Those Wednesdays off allow me time to devote to other things that are important to me. Like the Elaine Speakman Foundation."

He shifted in his seat. "The foundation. Right. I saw your picture in the newspaper recently. At some black-tie fund-raising event. How'd it go?"

"Very well."

"That's good."

"Beyond the money raised that night, the foundation recently received a sizable donation."

"Oh, yeah?"

"One hundred thousand dollars."

"You don't say."

"Hmm, but it was a rather unusual donation."

"In what way?"

"For one thing, it was made in cash. Hundred-dollar bills deposited directly into the foundation's account."

"Huh."

"Anonymously."

"Huh."

"And the bank handling the deposit said the donor insisted on remaining anonymous."

Griff kept his expression impassive.

"I respect him for keeping such a generous donation private," Laura said. "I only hope he knows how much his gift is appreciated."

"I'm sure he does."

After what seemed to Griff an endless suspension in conversation, she relented with a gentle smile and changed the subject. "You've been staying busy, too."

"You heard about the program?"

"I saw you interviewed about it on TV."

"It's catching on, working out really well."

"You sound surprised," she remarked.

"I am. It just sorta dropped into my lap."

Upon his discharge from the hospital, he had appeared in court and pleaded guilty to the assault charges. Jim McAlister got him released on bail and at his sentencing hearing argued brilliantly on his behalf. His arguments were supported by Laura Speakman's deposition, presented in her absence by her attorney, as well as by the testimony of Internal Affairs officers who had been investigating Stanley Rodarte.

Griff received a stern reprimand from the judge and had a year of probation tacked onto the ones he was already serving. Jerry Arnold remained his probation officer. McAlister and Glen Hunnicutt, who had proved to be a true friend, took Griff out for dinner to celebrate what they considered a victory.

Shortly after that, Bolly Rich had surprised him by inviting him for lunch. He apologized for refusing to listen when Griff tried to warn him about Rodarte. He said he was sorry for refusing to give Griff aid when he most needed it, but mostly for not giving him the benefit of the doubt. "It was two weeks before Jason would speak to me again."

Griff waved off the apology. "Don't worry about it, Bolly."

"You're letting me off the hook too easily."

"I've been let off easily, too."

Then Bolly told him of a program he and other sportswriters across the country had been discussing for a long while. They felt the time had come to implement it. "We're tired of the negativity surrounding sports, college and professional. As much as we write about slam dunks, touchdowns, and home runs, we're forced to report on drug abuse, steroid use, guns and violent behavior, rape—"

"Gambling," Griff said.

"Gambling. We're sick of all that crap. We want to turn it around, put honor and the ideals of good sportsmanship back into sports. But we're just a bunch of wordsmiths, and I'm the most colorful of the group, if that gives you any idea. What we need is a spokesperson." Uneasily, he added, "And somebody who is squeaky clean wouldn't have much impact."

"You need a poster boy with a catchy slogan like 'Don't fuck up like I did.'"

Bolly grinned. "That sorta captures the gist of our thinking."

"They needed a bad boy like me to talk to young athletes," he explained to Laura now. "With the voice of experience, I warn them against common pitfalls. Bolly and his colleagues rounded up some corporate sponsors to fund the program. The NCAA has lent its full-fledged support. Fellowship of Christian Athletes. Alumni organizations. Sports associations all over the country have scheduled me to speak." He shrugged. "Maybe the talks I give are doing some good."

"You're being modest, Griff. I read just this week in Mr. Rich's column that already they've collected thousands of pledges signed by athletes swearing off steroids, et cetera. Including his own son."

"Jason's a good kid. He probably wouldn't get into all that anyway."

"But others would. Your speeches are making a huge impact."

"We'll see." He grinned at her. "At the very least, I'm chalking up a hell of a lot of frequent flier miles on SunSouth."

"You should sign up for Select."

"Can't afford it. My expenses are covered, and I get a more than decent salary, but I'm not going to get rich, Laura. Ever." He would never be rich like Foster Speakman. Like her. That was what he was telling her. "But I'm working in sports, on the periphery at least. And I'm doing something worthwhile." He smiled. "Sometimes, after I give a speech, they even ask me to toss the football a time or two. Give them pointers. Stuff like that."

"I'm sure those young athletes are dazzled."

"I don't know about that. But I enjoy it."

They were quiet for a time. She glanced out the window, into the fireplace, at the bowl of tulips. "Would you like some more tea?"

"No thanks."

"How is your friend Marcia?"

He was surprised she remembered Marcia. "Doing good. I saw her just last week."

"Oh."

At that Laura's polite smile wavered just a bit. Or maybe he imagined it. "She's got one more surgery scheduled, but it's only for fine tuning."

"The operations were successful, then."

"She looks fantastic. Better than ever."

"That's good. Is she . . . has she returned to . . . work?"

"Full-time."

"Really."

"Yep. Business as usual."

"Hmm."

If she was wondering about the nature of his visit to Marcia, why didn't she come right out and ask? He was hoping she would. He could tell her they were strictly friends now, but at least Laura's asking would indicate she cared about whether he was satisfying his sexual urges with a professional.

Instead, she said, "How were your holidays?"

"Fattening. Ellie cooked like there was no tomorrow. Yours?"

"I went away. Stayed in a bed-and-breakfast in Vermont, drove back roads, read a lot."

"Sounds nice." Sounded lonely.

"Would you like some more tea?"

"You asked me that already, and I said no."

"Sorry. How is your shoulder?"

"Fine."

"All healed?"

"Laura, why did you call me?"

His abruptness surprised her, then she looked chagrined for being caught stalling. She took a deep breath and said quietly, "I wanted to thank you."

His heart plummeted. She really had invited him just for tea. "What for?"

"For keeping our secret. You had so many opportunities to tell the whole sordid story. You didn't. You protected Foster, as well as me. He certainly hadn't earned your confidence. I wanted to tell you how much I appreciated it."

"Well, I didn't exactly want the world to know I'd been your stud for hire."

"Whatever your reason, thank you."

"You're welcome."

He didn't want her goddamn *gratitude*. He had honored his promise to Coach and to himself not to contact her, although not a day had gone by that he hadn't wanted to. So today, after months, when she'd called, he'd thought maybe . . .

But no. While he was sitting here making polite conversation, aching to touch her, wanting to taste her mouth, all she'd wanted was to say *thank you*. He couldn't take any more.

Agitated, he rubbed his palms against his thighs, then abruptly stood up. "Look, I need to run. I've got a . . . thing."

"Oh, I'm sorry." She stood as well. "I didn't mean to keep you."

"No, it's okay. It was good to see you."

"It was good to see you, too."

"Right. Thanks for the tea."

As he turned toward the door, he lightly slapped his side, which served as a reminder. "Oh, I almost forgot. I brought you something." Reaching into the flap pocket of his sports jacket, he took out a small box.

She looked at him quizzically as he passed it to her. "What's this?"

"One way to find out."

She held it, hesitating a moment before pulling the end of the ribbon to untie the bow. He realized he was holding his breath as she removed the lid. Lying on a bed of satin was a tiny gold star with an infinitesimal diamond in its center. She kept her head down, staring at the charm, so he couldn't see her reaction. But she remained so still he began to think this had been a lousy idea.

When another moment passed and she still didn't say anything, he tried to justify himself. "It wasn't very far along, I know. Probably no bigger than that diamond. But . . ." He ran his fingers through his hair. "But there's no marker, you know? Nothing to show that it ever existed. And it did. At least for a few weeks."

She kept her head down, didn't move. *Shit! Bad idea. Really, really bad*. He should just shut up about it and leave. Instead, he said, "I thought you might like to have something to remember it by."

When she finally raised her head, her face was wet with tears. "I'll always remember it. I'll hold it in my heart for as long as I live."

They moved simultaneously. His arms enfolded her, and he held on like he would never let her go. He might have vowed as much. Afterward, he couldn't remember for sure what declarations he'd made at some later time and which ones he'd made right then, just before cupping her face in his hands and lifting it to his. He did remember telling her he loved her, repeating it as he kissed her lips, her eyes, cheeks, and brow. Finally their lips met and they kissed deeply and ardently.

And then for the longest time, as afternoon turned to evening, they sat on the sofa together, enjoying the fire, holding hands, and talking. They talked about nothing that was too serious. They swapped anecdotes. They exchanged frivolous information. They laughed often.

It was their first date.

praise for *hurt people*

"Cote Smith writes characters that are beautifully, viciously alive. *Hurt People* is the supremely rare kind of novel that will crawl inside your heart and live there forever."

—Laura van den Berg, author of *Find Me*

"Cote Smith's debut novel is a wonderfully vivid evocation of childhood in the 1980s, as well as a page-turning noir thriller. It's amazing how beautifully these two flavors work together!" **—Dan Chaon, author of *Await Your Reply***

"Cote Smith's *Hurt People* is a jackknife of a novel: it's sharp and it plunges deep. The book beautifully captures the menacing atmosphere of a prison town and the intense bond between two brothers."

—Elliott Holt, author of *You Are One of Them*

"At the center of *Hurt People*, a young boy grows up in the shadow of four prisons and his malcontent older brother. When his unquestioning loyalty is challenged, he is forced through a one-way gate to the adult world of secrets. Quiet and moving, *Hurt People* is a scorching meditation on childhood in a prison town, where irresponsible adults, poverty, and dark intentions threaten a young boy's innocence at every turn."

**—Marie-Helene Bertino, author of
*2 A.M. at The Cat's Pajamas***

HURT PEOPLE

HURT PEOPLE

Cote Smith

FARRAR, STRAUS AND GIROUX   NEW YORK

Farrar, Straus and Giroux
18 West 18th Street, New York 10011

Library of Congress Cataloging-in-Publication Data
Names: Smith, Cote, 1982–
Title: Hurt people : a novel / Cote Smith.
Description: First edition. | New York : FSG Originals, 2016.
Identifiers: LCCN 2015035376 | ISBN 9780374535889 (paperback) |
    ISBN 9780374714628 (e-book)
Subjects: LCSH: Brothers—Fiction. | Escaped prisoners—Fiction. | BISAC:
    FICTION / Literary. | FICTION / General. | FICTION / Psychological. |
    GSAFD: Psychological fiction
Classification: LCC PS3619.M5735 H87 2016 | DDC 813/.6—dc23
LC record available at http://lccn.loc.gov/2015035376

Designed by Abby Kagan

Our books may be purchased in bulk for promotional, educational,
or business use. Please contact your local bookseller or the Macmillan
Corporate and Premium Sales Department at 1-800-221-7945,
extension 5442, or by e-mail at
MacmillanSpecialMarkets@macmillan.com.

www.fsgbooks.com • www.fsgoriginals.com
www.twitter.com/fsgbooks • www.facebook.com/fsgbooks

1   3   5   7   9   10   8   6   4   2

For Brett

HURT PEOPLE

one

ALL WE WANTED was the pool. It waited in the center of our apartment complex, sleeping beneath a blue tarp. Sometimes the wind snuck under the tarp and puffed it up as it passed, giving the pool an irregular, visible pulse.

My brother and I walked by the pool every spring day after school. This was in 1988. He would grab the gate's bars and stare. I touched the bars too. I wanted the pool because I wanted whatever my brother wanted, whether anyone said I could have it or not.

Now it was summer. School was out, the tarp was off, and the rest was up to our mother. We asked to swim every day after Memorial Day. Our mother hadn't said yes yet. It's too cold, she said. I'm too tired. You just ate.

We didn't give up.

We pressed her in every way we could. My brother was a real good arguer. A teacher once told my mother he would

make a good lawyer someday, and in a city where there were more prisons than restaurants, that could be a good thing.

We lived in Leavenworth, a city famous for its prisons. My brother and I could name all four. There was the county jail, where the local felons lived; the women's prison, where all the bad wives and mothers went; and there was the juvenile correctional facility, home to the troubled young. But it was the federal penitentiary, stuck on a hill between Leavenworth and Fort Leavenworth, that loomed over everything. At school I'd seen pictures of palaces of kings and queens. This prison was bigger than all of them. Tall walls of concrete a mile long. Layers of barbed-wire fences. Guards perched in scattered sniper towers, in case anyone tried to escape. This, our mother told us, is where the country's worst wind up. This is what happens. She liked to remind us that when someone did something wrong, they were always punished, one way or another. And in our case, she said, living where we did, the punishment was always close. Waiting.

"I'll make you boys a deal," my mother said one morning. The three of us were in the kitchen, sitting at our small square table. Sitting down, our mother towered over us. She was taller than most women, even minus her huge head of hair. But she was also very skinny, something she passed on to me. Random people told us we needed to eat.

My mother leaned over her plate of french-toast sticks, waved us in conspiratorially. "If the temperature hits seventy-five," she said, "then we'll all go to the pool." She got up with her cup of coffee and left the kitchen, not waiting to field any questions. A moment later, we heard her bedroom door close, and then nothing, though I knew if I crept up and put my ear to the door, I would hear the soft hum of her rotating

fan. She always slept with it on, a habit from the days with our dad.

It had been more than a year since our parents split, but we saw leftovers of our old life everywhere. A nasty wash-cloth, soggy under the sink, was actually our dad's old tank top. A wineglass hidden in the cupboard at our dad's duplex had the faint stain of our mother's lips. If, when playing a game with my brother, I accused him of cheating, a tension stung the air.

Our dad was a cop for the city, and had been since before I was born. He was a popular policeman, so popular that it was hard to go do something quick like get gas or groceries without a stranger stopping him for small talk. They would ask about a missing person, news of the latest escape, or, with head down and eyes to the side, about the possible leniency of the law. But our dad never appeared put out, not to the people anyway, and they really liked him for this. His boss was to retire any time now, and in their heads the people had already ordained my dad their next chief.

Our mother never discussed our dad, other than to say, It's Friday, go pack your bag. I guess she didn't want us to know what she thought of him. There were times, though, when she was too tired or frustrated to filter her thoughts. One morning, for example, we were late to school because my brother spent too long getting ready in the bathroom. You're ten, my mother said to him as she turned into the school parking lot. What do you care how you look? God, you're just like your dad. Another time, while walking downtown with our mother, we saw a picture of our dad on the front page of the local newspaper. But when we asked our mother if we could buy the paper, cut out the picture, and give it to

our dad, she sighed and told us no. Believe me, she said, he already knows.

It was normal for our mother to go back to sleep after breakfast. She did this when it was her turn to work the late shift at the golf course on post. She worked there six days a week and a lot of those days she worked nights too, manning the pro shop while Army men, reluctant to return to their tiny quarters, hit bucket after bucket at the driving range. If she wasn't home by our assigned bedtime, my brother and I dragged our blankets to the living room to camp out for the night. We borrowed couch cushions and made a makeshift bed on the floor, next to the box fan. We tucked ourselves in and slept close.

We put our plates away and started dialing Time and Temperature. My brother said, "You can dial first because you are the youngest." Time and Temp was the only number I was allowed to dial. I had it memorized. I grabbed the phone off the wall, stretched the cord to the floor, and dialed. The tone purred once before the robot lady answered. She said hello to me and that the time was too early, the temperature too low.

I waited three minutes and tried again. This was our plan. After ten disappointing dials, I pulled the phone out of the kitchen to see what my brother was doing. I caught him on the couch, looking at the naked ladies in our mother's encyclopedias. The encyclopedias were an anniversary gift to my mother from my dad. Before they had separated, my mother often talked about going back to school to become a teacher. She was a big fan of history, she once told me, of learning from the mistakes of the past, including her own.

"You shouldn't be doing that," I said, though I had seen these naked ladies too. My brother had shown them to me.

"It was OK the other day," he said, "when you were looking." I hugged the phone against my ear with my shoulder, to look like an adult.

"You told me to come see. I didn't know what it was going to be."

"It's a book. I'm learning," he said. "It's OK. I'm older."

I couldn't think of a way to argue with him. My brother was older than me, by twenty-two months, a fact he was always throwing in my face. And it *was* a book, something about the human body. But the lady pictured, who was half skin, half insides, looked too much like our mother, making me uncomfortable. Her fully skinned half was model beautiful with blond hair. She had big blue eyes, twig legs like me.

I hung the phone up and went over to my brother, sitting with the book on his lap. I sat next to him so our knees touched, and looked at the lady. She wasn't looking back. Her face was turned to the side, flushed with red. I could see one breast.

"Mom wouldn't like this," I said. My brother closed the book but didn't move to put it away.

"If you don't dial," he said, "there's no pool."

My mother must have woken to the loud thumping. She came into the living room and saw my brother giving a cushion a flying elbow drop off the couch. I was in the kitchen with a beach towel tied around my neck like a cape. I was doing a running man dance. The phone was in my hand.

"Stop," my mother said. "Have you lost your mind?" She

had a hand in her big hair. I gave her the phone and let her hear the robot lady speak.

The time is twelve fifteen p.m. and the temperature is seventy-six degrees.

She held the phone away from her face and frowned.

"You guys, you're going to hate me for this, but I'm just too tired," she said. I stopped running in place. My brother stood on the couch with his shirt off.

"I don't understand," he said.

"There's nothing to understand. We need a new weather-woman." My brother jumped down. "It was only supposed to get up to seventy," our mother said. She held the phone by its cord now. The receiver banged the floor. "And I have to work tonight."

I took my towel off and sulked out of the kitchen. I moped past my brother and fell face-first into the couch.

"I'm sorry," my mother said, "I'm just too tired."

I held my breath and pretended I was doing a dead man's float.

"I can take him," my brother said, "if that's what this is all about." I pushed my face deeper into the crack between the couch cushions. My eyes were open but everything was black.

"You don't have to come," my brother said.

There was a pause. "Hmm," my mother said. In the blackness I could almost hear her think. "How old are you?" she asked my brother.

"Almost eleven."

"That's right. And you're going into what grade?"

"Fifth."

"Just fifth?"

"But I'm old for my grade. Plus I'm smarter than the other kids at school. When the teacher has to leave the room, I'm the one put in charge."

"I don't care about those kids," my mother said. "This is you and my baby boy we're talking about. Will you keep your eye on him?"

"Yes," my brother said. "He's my brother." This statement made me smile. I lifted my face out of the cushions. My mother looked like she wanted to give in.

"Fine," she finally said. "But in for dinner before it gets dark." We nodded. I could hear the phone's dead dial tone, beeping at us like a quiet alarm. Our mother picked up the receiver and pointed it at us. "You guys watch out for each other, OK?"

My brother put his arm around me.

"Strangers," my mother said.

It was just us at the pool. This was not a rare thing, though when we first moved to the complex late last spring, our mother had promised we would make new friends. She said there was a field behind our building, a nice open space good for any game. But the day we arrived, all we saw were hints of kids. A turned-over tricycle, flat-tired in the grass. A frayed jump rope, hung from an unreachable branch. All signs of potential, long-gone friends. When we asked our mother, she said they must have moved to the new complex that opened up the town over. When we asked why we couldn't stay in our old house, she told us to figure out a way to afford it. Plus, she said, sure that place was nice, but there was no pool.

As soon as we were through the gate I ran and jumped into the water like a crazy person. My brother took his time.

He walked to the diving board and pulled out a list of aerial moves brainstormed over spring. They had names like the Jellybean (a balled-up boy rolled headfirst off the edge), the Secret Serviceman (a bullet-stopping sideways dive), and the Elántra (to be determined). The water was not warm, so the first half hour we spent getting our bodies used to it. The second we played monkey see, monkey do. My brother did moves he knew I could safely do in the shallow end of the pool.

"I like this," I said.

"Yes," my brother said, "me too." He was on the diving board, deciding what move to do next. The sky behind him was blue, the same as the pool, and my brother smirked as an idea dawned. But when he was ready to jump, a siren sounded.

We looked up at the clear sky. Our city had only one siren, with only one sound, which it used for all its warnings.

"Is it a tornado?" I asked.

"Or a prison bust," my brother said.

"A test?"

"I don't think we should worry. I've heard it louder before." I said OK and watched him cannonball off. I crossed my legs Indian style and went underwater, sinking myself to the bottom. There I pretended I was having tea with a stranger. I opened my eyes and saw my brother blurred underwater, still grasping his knees into a cannonball. When we popped up the siren was no longer sounding.

Regular pool activities resumed. My brother asked if I wanted to race. Most races began in the shallow end and required the racer to do something like hold one leg and hop

to the border of the deep end and back. The loser received a playful dunk as reward. The winner got to gloat. My brother was doing a victory underwater handstand when a cop ran by.

"A policeman ran by," I said to him when he popped up. He pinched his nose and shot out the water.

"When?"

"Just now. When you were underwater."

"Was it Tony?" Tony was the cop who would sometimes drive by our apartment, give us knockoff baseball cards. I liked to think that my dad sent him, to check on us when he couldn't.

"I couldn't tell," I said. "He was moving too fast. What does it mean?"

My brother spun in the pool, looking around, but there was nothing to see. It was like nothing had happened. "I guess it means we're safe."

We were having so much fun that I wanted to believe him. For caution, we agreed that we would go in ten minutes early. This would make our mother proud. She would realize that my brother and I were responsible, that we were capable of good judgment. We could take ourselves to the pool every day if we wanted, not have to tag along with her to work. We could spend our summer like this.

We went back to racing. I lost a bunch and took in a lot of water when dunked. I had to get out and pee.

"Don't go inside," my brother said.

"I won't." We both knew if we went inside our mother might see us shivering in our soaked trunks and change her mind.

"Go behind the shed," my brother said.

"OK."

The shed was far from the pool, next to the woods. Our complex was at the edge of the city and was bordered by woods on three sides. I always thought of the woods as the deep end of the nonpool world and avoided going into them. My brother was the one who retrieved an overthrown ball, a misbehaving boomerang.

I stepped to the trees and pulled down the front of my trunks. My pee was the clear color of our mother's home-made lemonade.

I tiptoed my way back to the sidewalk to avoid the grass. I had to watch my feet to do this. When I looked up, I saw a man talking to my brother at the pool. At first I thought it was Rick, an ex-con my mother worked with at the golf course on post. Rick was the meanest person I knew. He always made fun of my brother and me, and when he took us on long rides in his special golf cart, whose engine he had messed with to make the cart go faster, Rick would do this thing where he would pinch our entire thigh with his thumb and pointer finger. We called it the Rick Pinch. We never knew when it was coming and could never be at ease.

But the man was not Rick. This man had a smoother, whiter face. He probably didn't smell of gasoline and grass like Rick always did. The man sat on the edge of the shallow end with his jeans rolled up. His legs were hairy and his toes skimmed the water's surface like mosquitoes. I didn't want to walk very fast to this man and my brother, but the cement was hot. I sat by my brother and cooled my feet in the pool.

"This is Chris," my brother said.

"Hey, what's up, little man?" Chris said.

"Hi," I said. I kept my head down, focused on my feet. I wished my brother would tell this man to go to the deep end. Sorry, he could say, we're using this end for racing. Just us two.

"Man," Chris said, "this sure is the place to be. You guys have it made, don't you think?" My brother agreed, and Chris started talking about how much he missed the pool. How it was good to be back and why did he ever leave this in the first place? My brother smiled and said he didn't know. It was pretty great. I didn't want to deal with this, so I went underwater. When I opened my eyes I saw my brother's legs next to Chris's legs. Chris had a tattoo on his left ankle. Some symbol or shape. I couldn't tell what it was. My lungs started to burn, so I floated to the top.

"What does your tattoo mean?" I said. Chris and my brother turned to me. My brother seemed mad that I'd interrupted. He always said I asked too many dumb questions.

"Hey, he talks," Chris said.

"What does it mean?" I said. Chris pulled the leg out of the pool and stared at it like it was a new fake limb.

"Oh, that? That's a secret only my friends know. I already told my man here, didn't I?"

"He told me part of it," my brother said. "He wouldn't tell the rest."

"I want to know," I said. "Tell me."

"Can't," Chris said. "Not unless we're friends. What do you say, little man? Want to be my friend?" I nodded instantly. I did not like the idea of being left out of a secret kept by my brother.

"Good," Chris said, "but let's hear you say it, so the whole

world can witness. Go ahead, say you're my friend." I looked at my brother, who shrugged one shoulder as if to say hey, why not. "Well, little man?"

"Yes," I said, "I am your friend."

Chris clapped his hand. "Nice," he said. Then he twisted his neck and glanced around.

"Are you looking for spies?" I said. I also had a problem where I said the first thing I thought. My brother looked at me like I was a new breed of idiot.

"Yes!" Chris said in a loud whisper. "We don't want this getting out, do we?" I shook my head. "OK," Chris said. He put his finger on the symbol, parting the wet hairs around it. His nail looked chewed on, dark with dirt underneath. "Well, the first thing you need to know is that it's Chinese."

There was a disappointing pause. A pool pump clicked on. "That's all he told me," my brother said, "and I pretty much already guessed that."

"Hey, guys," Chris said. "This thing hurt. It's a part of my body. I'm not going to give it away for free." I began to float on my back. Water found my ears, wooshed sounds around. I knew as much as my brother and no longer cared what the rest of the symbol meant.

"We don't have any money," my brother said.

Chris laughed. "I don't want your money. I have my own means." I swam to the side, hung off the shallow ladder. Chris wiped the sweat from his forehead. "Man, is it supposed to be this hot?"

"It was only supposed to be seventy," I said.

"Is that right?" Chris said. "Hmm. You know, my mother used to give us something special on days like these. You know

those popsicles that come in plastic strips? You ever have anything like that?"

"Yes," my brother said, "we have those."

"You do?" Chris said. "Let's do this, then. How about one of you gets us some treats, and when you get back, we'll all share. You share the popsicles, I'll share my secret."

My brother turned to me with his thinking face on. "We'll both go," he said, meaning me and him.

Chris raised his hands like he was being held up. "No, no, no. That won't work. If both of you leave, I'll get lonely. I need someone to keep me company. Plus, I don't live here. I'm not allowed at this pool by myself."

My brother's thinking face grew more serious; lines showed up on his forehead. "He'll go," my brother said. "I'll stay with you."

"Why can't we both go?" I said to him.

Chris sighed.

"It'll be quicker this way," my brother said. "You're small and fast. I'll be right here. I'm not going anywhere."

"Fine," I said.

"And don't wake Mom."

"I know," I said, standing up. Chris's sigh changed into a smile. The sun beamed on his face, coloring his teeth yellow.

"Hey, little man," Chris said. "Make mine a red."

Inside our apartment, my feet were quiet on the carpet. I got down and crawled into the kitchen, like an Army man. I stood up at the fridge and hoped my mother wouldn't hear when I opened the freezer and ripped three popsicle strips out of the box. When I stepped out of the kitchen, I saw her

sleeping silently on the couch. She was still in her robe, which hung loose off her chest and shoulder. I took a few steps to see if she had her swimming suit on, if she had changed her mind and planned to keep her promise. I couldn't tell until I was at the arm of the couch. From the side, I got a good angle into her robe. I saw the curves of her body. She had nothing on underneath.

By the time I got back to the pool, my body was dry and cold, and my palm was nearly numb from the popsicles. My brother opened his blue one with his fingers; Chris and I ripped ours with our teeth. We did not talk while we ate. We kept the plastic strips in our mouths and pushed the frozen chunks up from the bottom like toothpaste. For the first time, I was able to stare at Chris. His hair was a lighter version of my dad's. It was dirty blond and long enough that he had to brush it off his forehead. His body was thin and pale, like his face, but not so skinny that his ribs showed, like mine did. He scratched the trail of hair on his stomach, and I wondered if his hands were rough or not.

When all the ice chunks were gone, we drank the melted stuff left behind. I could feel the sugar on my tongue.

"Will you tell us about the tattoo now?" my brother said. Chris was leaning back in the pool chair. He sat up after a few seconds, his face scrunched up in pain. He put two fingers to his forehead, between his eyebrows.

"Ow," Chris said. "Ow, ow, ow."

"What's wrong?" my brother said.

"It hurts." Chris stood up and started stumbling around. "Hurts so bad."

"What does? Are you OK?"

Chris didn't answer. He dropped his popsicle wrapper and a small breeze took it. Now he had both hands on his head. He pulled his hair and yelled, "Ah! I got the brain pain!"

"What do we do?" my brother said.

Chris yelled again in response. His mouth stayed open in pain, showing all the fake red inside, outlining and tinting his teeth. Then, suddenly, he stopped moaning and spit a red pool. My brother and I looked at each other, confused.

"OK," Chris said, "it's passed. The pain has passed." He was smiling again. It was all an act.

My brother sat back down. "The tattoo," he said. He looked at Chris like he looked at me when we were running someplace and he had to stop and wait for me to catch up. Chris stood up and shook his head like a wet dog.

"Patience, my man. It's all about patience."

"But he got you a popsicle," my brother said, pointing to me.

"Yes, *he* did. But what have you ever done for me?" Chris looked away from both of us and into the woods. My brother didn't respond. I thought he was thinking of an argument. I knew he had an amazing one in him somewhere. It would be something Chris wouldn't have an answer for. Chris would open his mouth to say something back, but his brain wouldn't be able to help. He would apologize and have to tell us what we wanted to know. We would hear what the tattoo meant, say big deal, and return to our mother, victorious.

"You guys ever heard of the Gainer?" Chris said.

My brother looked confused. "Is that your tattoo?"

"No, this is something else." Chris stepped toward us. "This is my secret pool move." He lowered his voice and

looked at each of us seriously. "You want to see it?" My brother glanced at his list of moves, pinned down by a pool chair, the names written in big bubble letters.

"Trust me, this isn't on your little list," Chris said. "Do you want to see it or not?"

"I guess," my brother said.

"You guess. Well, OK, then get ready." Chris ran around the pool and jumped on the diving board. He lifted both of his hands to the sky and yelled, "For the Gainer!"

My brother and I stayed close to each other. The sun shone on Chris, who with his arms raised looked like one of our dad's old softball trophies, now boxed away in the dark part of his basement. We watched Chris unbutton his fly and drop his jeans. It was the first time I had seen boxer shorts in person. They were as white as his body, and I felt like I should look away, but I didn't. I was eager to see the move, to be there when the secret was revealed.

Chris stepped to the edge of the board and rubbed his hands together. A V of birds glided the sky, calling out to one another. Chris took a step back and raised his arms like he was holding a rifle. He mock-shot each bird, one after another, *pow!* bursting from his lips.

"Don't want them telling their little bird buddies, do we?" he said, and laughed. He stepped to the edge again. "OK," he said, and took a deep breath. "Here we go."

I grabbed my brother's arm, and we watched as Chris bounced once on the board and sprang into the air in a motion we had never seen before. He jumped forward but did a backflip, his body somehow upright as he entered the water. There was a big splash. When it died my brother and I looked

at each other like what was that. I wanted to say that that was the most amazing thing I had ever seen.

A large fly drummed my ear as we stood by the shallow end, waiting for Chris to pop up. After a few seconds, we started to worry. Maybe that super move had taken everything Chris had. Maybe he was a goner.

My brother fast walked to the deep end. He got up on the diving board and peered into the water below. The trees shook. My brother looked at me like he was about to do something he didn't want to do.

"Don't," I said.

"He needs help," my brother said, and did a few baby bounces on the board.

"Please don't." I had to pee again, even though I just went.

"I'll be right back." He put his arms out to the side, ready to dive. But as he took the final step to the board's edge, Chris's head popped up. He shot water from his mouth like a fountain and turned to my brother.

"You ready to try it?" he said, as if nothing had happened. He swam to the side and got out of the pool, his soaked shorts nearly see-through.

"I can't do that," my brother said.

"Sure you can. You can do anything, my man, because you've got me for a teacher."

"What about the tattoo?"

"Forget the tattoo. This is bigger than that. You get this down, nobody will mess with you. Can't you see that?" My brother appeared unconvinced. "Fine," Chris said. "Come here." My brother walked away from me and stood next to

Chris, who put his hand on my brother's shoulder and whispered something into his ear. I watched my brother's face change, saw him smile. Chris pulled away and my brother nodded. If a stranger were to drive by, they might think the two were father and son.

"Now," Chris said, "are you ready to try it?" Chris patted him on the butt. "OK, then get on up there."

My brother hopped on the board. I jumped into the shallow end, to get a better view, and because I was cold and felt far away.

"You're not going to master it in one day," Chris said, "but that's OK. We got all the time in the world, my man. None of us are going anywhere."

Our mother never came to the pool. The rest of that day my brother worked on learning the Gainer. Well, Chris made him work on the front dive first. He said my brother had to crawl before he could walk, which meant he had to dive before he could flip. I watched from the border of the shallow and the deep, and throughout the day, stepped closer and closer to where my toes could no longer touch.

On our way home, my brother and I walked side by side. My towel was wrapped around me like a skirt. My brother's hung on his shoulders like he was a prizefighter.

"Did he tell you what the tattoo meant?" I said.

"Yes."

"Will you tell me?"

"Maybe."

"Did he tell you not to tell me?"

"No, he didn't."

"Tell me." I had stopped but my brother kept walking. He was almost at our building's pea-green door.

"OK," he said. "But you can't tell Mom."

"I wouldn't."

"Or Dad. Not about Chris, either. That's part of it."

"I won't."

"And you have to make me a sandwich."

"OK." My brother waved me to the door. He cupped my ear and whispered what the tattoo meant, but I didn't know what that word was. I asked him to explain. He stood up straighter. He said, "You'll understand when you're older."

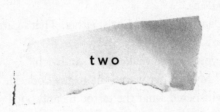

two

I DON'T THINK he knew either. I don't think my brother knew what the tattoo meant. But we agreed not to tell our mother about Chris. So I couldn't ask her. When questioned at dinner, over a plate of beans and toast, how was the pool, my brother said "fun" and "good." I bathed my toast in baked beans and kept my mouth shut. I thought someday I would be able to lie to my mother, but in the meantime I was glad I had a brother.

The next few days our mother said the weather was bad and unsuitable for the pool. At night, on the local channels, our county was displayed on a small map at the bottom right corner of the screen. We were warned about severe thunderstorms, flash flooding, and told to watch out for the occasional tornado. My mother would stare out our sliding glass door, which led to our small third-floor patio, and say, "Bad weather," like the weather had purposely done something

wrong, broken some rule. This happened so much that week I started to get mad at the weather with my mother. We would boo the weatherwoman when she gave us bad news. And when she dared show her face the day after a mistaken forecast, we pointed our fingers at the TV and said, "You've got some nerve."

My mother had to work the last night of that bad weather run. She ordered us to stay in and lock the doors. We're under a tornado watch the entire night, she said, so no going outside. After she left, I took her spot at the glass door and whispered, "This is bad. This is bad." I tried to make my voice sound like my mother's, but I actually liked it when there was a big flash of lightning. When, if I was looking in the right direction, the world shined a brief light on the pool.

My brother came out of our room for a big bowl of cereal. He poured what had to be half the box into a large Tupperware bowl. He opened the fridge but I already knew we were out of milk. "Did you drink the last of the milk?" he said.

I was staring out our sliding glass door, thinking of Chris and watching the rain beat the glass in sheets. "You did," I said. "You and your huge bowls."

My brother came to the door and stood by me. We stared at the darkness together. "Make us some milk," he said.

"No," I said. "You do it."

I hated mixing the milk. My mother never said we were poor, now that we were living alone in this apartment, in this part of the city, but certain situations said it for her. Whenever we couldn't do something it was because there wasn't the money. And when at school I remarked that the

milk in the carton tasted better than the stuff I had to mix at home, I got looks.

"What if I pitch to you tomorrow?" my brother said.

"You won't."

"I will. I swear."

I didn't answer him. My brother was always promising things, things that rarely came true, and used those promises to get what he wanted.

"Fine," I said. "But you also have to teach me the Gainer, once Chris teaches you."

"No way. You can't even dive." I walked away and sat on the couch, and let my brother think about how he hurt me. "OK," he said, "but it might be a while."

"Promise on Baron," I said. That was the name of our dead dog. He had lived with us at our old house when our parents were together. I didn't remember getting Baron but I remembered losing him. I remembered him limping a lot for weeks. Then one day, after school, I came home and he simply wasn't there. My brother knew I loved that dog. When Baron was alive, my brother made fun of me for treating a dog like a person, for tucking him in at night, telling him about my day at school when I got home. But the day Baron went, it was my brother who, against our dad's orders, fetched Baron's old toys out of the trash and gave them to me. To keep in secret.

"Promise on him," I said.

"I promise."

After cereal, we played with our G.I. Joes, something my brother was excellent at. While my playing was based on plots from cartoons or movies, my brother created his own stories,

which lasted hours, took over the entire apartment, and contained several startling plot twists. I tried to copy what my brother did, but my characters never sounded real, and quickly ran out of things to say. I could never tell as good a story as my brother. Days after we played, I would find men hiding in the cracks between the couch cushions, or dangling from a shower curtain ring. These men, my brother would explain, were the last survivors of a clan long thought dead, who when the time was right would rise out of the shadows and avenge the murder of their people.

I finished my playing early like usual so I could watch the rising action of my brother's plot. A good guy hung by one hand from the edge of a dresser while the head bad guy stepped on his toes. The villain looked on and laughed.

"Why do you let the bad guys win?" I asked him.

"Because you never see that," he said.

We went to bed an hour after we should have gone to bed. We tried to sleep in our room but it was too hot without the A/C on. It was off because it was broken. In the meantime, we had the box fan in the corner of the living room. So we slept out there with the big fan inches from our faces. At the bottom of the fan were three roaches. Two were dead and one had one leg. I felt bad for them, but my brother said there were worse places to die.

"Remember," I said, "you promised."

"So did you," he said. He was talking about Chris, how I said I wouldn't tell anyone, no matter what. "Now go to sleep."

I had forgotten that the next day was the weekend, which meant we would be going to our dad's duplex. My mother drove us across the city in the morning, on her way to work.

Some weeks, for easiness I guess, our dad would meet her at a halfway point, a corner station or public park. It was like a prisoner exchange. Our mother would stay in the car, windows up, and watch us walk from her van to our dad's police cruiser. Our dad, still in uniform, would stand behind the open driver's door and when we got close, say, "My boys."

This day our mother dropped us off at the duplex and drove away when she saw that we got in OK. Our dad was not inside. We called for him and ran upstairs to his bathroom, his shut bedroom door. We froze and listened for movement, heard nothing. My dad's bedroom, like the woods, like the pool at nighttime, was off limits.

We retreated from the room and checked the refrigerator for something to snack on, knowing there would be little. Our dad never planned ahead. Our mother said he once read somewhere to live each day like it's your last, and took it a bit too literally. A pound of beef thawed on the fridge's middle rack. A sports drink stood next to the meat, with maybe a sip left. In the crisper there were eight cans of beer, three slices of cheese, and two packets of fast-food ketchup. That was it. If this was the last day on earth, why stock up on groceries?

We shut the fridge door and the whole place felt empty.

"Hey, I'll pitch to you," my brother said. "Remember our promises?"

Our dad didn't come home until after dinnertime, after my brother and I played outside for over an hour. There was an old people's home across the street, and we liked to use its chain-link fence when we played home run derby. We liked to smash the ball over the fence and imagine we were real

stars. Later, when we were back in the duplex, hopping on the couches and pretending the carpet was lava, my brother reminded me that he had kept his promise. About pitching. And that I'd better keep mine. Or what? I had joked, but before my brother could make any threats, empty or otherwise, the storm door creaked open, announcing the arrival of our dad.

We jumped off the couches, and when he came into the living room, we pretended that we weren't out of breath, that we hadn't just been breaking the rules. Our dad, in his all-black police uniform, looked at the crooked cushions and smiled. "Boys," he said, as if this were an old western and he was greeting us in a saloon. He went upstairs to change. As soon as his door shut, we quickly put the couch and love seat back in order, so that when our dad came back downstairs— this time wearing running shorts with paint on them and a T-shirt older than my brother—the living room showed no signs of foul play. This made our dad smile even wider. "The perfect crime, eh, boys?" he said, and went out back to start the grill.

Our dad grilled out every time we were over there. Steaks. Pork chops. Hot dogs. Chicken legs. He had a microwave that I unplugged once to see if he would notice. He did, but only because he needed to thaw out some buns for burgers.

When the food was ready, he made us eat at the table while he ate in the living room and watched TV. It was like eating by a radio. We once asked him why we couldn't eat in there with him. He said he needed time to unwind after work, and that good folk sit at the table for dinner. It was one of those rules he made us follow but didn't follow himself.

"What are we doing tonight?" my brother yelled from the table. "Renting movies?"

"Only if you eat," my dad said.

"Are you going out?"

"Yes. But don't worry, you'll be asleep."

He had been going out most weekends we stayed with him, to the bar to throw darts. That's what he told us, anyway. I tried not to mind because, like he said, we were always asleep by the time he left, and he was usually there by the time we woke. And I never wanted to go with him—though my brother had mentioned it more than once—because I didn't like the way my dad smelled when he got back, when we saw him in the morning before he showered. I think the smell was what kept my mom in the van when she picked us up on Sunday.

My brother flashed his teeth at me. "We heard a siren a few days ago. Did any prisoners escape?"

"Yes," our dad said. "But only one. Now eat."

Escapes were not uncommon. With so many prisons, so many prisoners, and so few guards, people were bound to get out. That's what our dad said. He said the state never had enough money, and the city had even less. So, escapes would happen. My brother and I, we loved it when they did. Even though we knew it meant more work for our dad, more stress at his job, which he would take out on us, we didn't care. Because it also meant the sounding of the siren. The flashing of cruiser lights. It meant our city, for once, was exciting.

After dinner our dad drove us down to the local video store, and the entire ride my brother pestered him with questions. Who was the prisoner? What crimes did he commit?

How did he escape? As usual, our dad either gave no answers, or funny ones. *Who was the prisoner?* A criminal. *What crimes did he commit?* The illegal kind. *How did he escape?* Undetected.

A chime rang when we entered the store, and the lady at the counter, who had a thin body and long, pointy face like a witch, lifted her head with a smile and said, Oh, hello. This lady owned the store, and although she had plenty of hired help, still worked every Friday and Saturday night, and always talked to my dad at length, sometimes touching his wrist to drive her point home. She was older than my dad, but didn't dress like it. Tonight, she was wearing a black T-shirt of some rock band I remembered she and my dad talking about our last time here. The shirt was faded and full of big holes where her pale skin peeked through, and the store smelled different, like strawberries.

"Hey, I like that shirt," my dad said.

"I thought you would," the witch lady said. She opened her mouth and showed pointy but straight teeth. "I see you brought backup."

"Yeah, they love it here," he said. "Can't get enough."

The witch lady thumbed the fat ring on her pointer finger. "Must run in the family," she said.

My dad turned to us. "All right, boys, go pick some good ones."

"Yes," the witch lady said, "and take your time."

My brother and I went straight to the horror section. Now that our mother wasn't around to judge, our dad let us rent any movie we wanted, regardless of rating. The only catch was that we were not allowed to watch the movies alone. Our dad wanted to be there when a mummy gnawed an arm off

or a hostage got dropped off a skyscraper. He wanted to remind us that none of it was real, and that if things turned
too scary, he was just a couch cushion away.

My brother chose his movie carefully, sounding out the
plot summaries on the backs of the boxes, while I picked
mine based on the cover. Tonight, I selected the one where a
green, bald-headed monster was popping out of a toilet.
My brother's pick, which he settled on ten minutes later,
featured a southern black vampire who "enlists with a heavy
heart to fight for the North."

We brought our picks to our dad, who was leaning over
the counter, still chatting with the witch lady. "These look
like winners," he said, and returned to his conversation. The
witch lady took the tie out of her hair, let the black mess fall
down. She stretched the tie around her hand and slid it up
her skinny arm.

"What we need is more officers like you," she said. "Good
men. Men who spend time with their boys"—she winked at
my brother—"even with a nut on the loose. All the prisoners
in the world could escape. They could all do their worst, but
if we had more men like you, it wouldn't matter a bit."

"Oh, I don't know about that," my dad said.

"I do. And I know you'll nab this latest guy too. You
grabbed him before and you'll grab him again. Only a matter of time."

"Well," my dad said, "we'll certainly do our best."

The witch lady nodded and took the boxes into the back
to retrieve the tapes. As soon as she disappeared, my dad
checked his reflection in the counter's glass candy case.

"You put the prisoner away?" my brother said.

"Yes."

"Were you the one who caught him?"

"Yeah," my dad said, fluffing his hair. "The first time. But it's not a big deal. Nothing to worry about."

The witch lady returned. She rang up our videos, but only charged us for one.

"Oh, is there a deal going on?" my dad said.

"Yes," the witch lady said, sliding the videos to my dad. "The deal is if I ever need help, you better come running."

My dad put his head down and laughed. There was a weird pause as he pulled out his wallet and paid, and by the time he finally said something back, I had stopped listening. I was staring at my reflection, imprisoned in the glass, studying my features and imagining what it would be like to be older. I tried to imagine what I would look like all grown up. Would I take after my dad, or my mother? Or maybe, when I hit a growth spurt, I would look just like my brother. Maybe people would mistake us for twins.

"I'll see you out tonight?" the witch lady said.

"I will see you out tonight," my dad repeated, as if when I wasn't paying attention, he had fallen under her spell.

"We'll have a good time?"

"We will have a good time."

My dad said 'bye to the witch lady and wished her a good night. The witch lady touched my dad's hand with her hand.

"Let's both have a good night," she said, adding something like *sugar* or *sweetheart* at the end.

I put my movie in and took my place at my dad's side. Almost all of the movies we picked had cops in them—usually the stupid victim of some supervillain—and our dad liked

to point out each thing the police did wrong. *That's not how you hold a gun*, he would say. Or, *You can't just barge into someone's house like that.* He would then explain how things were really done, which was always boring and forgettable.

Tonight, after one bad cop got wasted by a hobgoblin, my dad let out a frustrated smile. My brother and I looked at each other and grinned, waiting for the lecture.

"Well what did he expect?" our dad said. "Entering a dark room without clearing it. Slice the pie!"

My brother and I rolled on our sides and laughed. Slicing the pie was one of our dad's favorites. Any time a cop went running into a warehouse, chasing a criminal or monster, our dad would yell, Slice the pie! Slice the pie! And even though my brother and I knew this was a real police technique, used by policemen to clear an area before entering, we still liked to laugh. At the way it sounded, at how mad the movie made our dad. At the idea that if the policeman had just followed procedure, things would have ended better. You never know, my brother joked. Maybe the goblin would have surrendered, come out claws up.

When the goblin was done feasting on the cop's insides, and my brother and I were spent from laughing, a sex scene came on. At this point, like usual, my dad covered our eyes with his hands, but didn't turn the volume down. I heard a doomed couple exchange deep kisses. I heard saxophones and the tearing of clothes. I heard my dad say, "Kissy kissy."

I woke up alone and out of place. The TV screen was black, and a pillow had replaced my dad's chest. I sat up and tried to remember where I was. My dad came out of the kitchen.

He had changed clothes. His shirt was tucked in. A button-up. He smelled different.

"Sleepy time," he said. "Your brother is downstairs."

As he reached out toward me, the dream I'd just had flashed in my mind. The escaped prisoner was on the loose and was coming after my dad. I was dressed as a cop and had been sent to investigate the video store, where the prisoner was last spotted. But I did everything wrong. I didn't slice the pie or hold my gun right, and the entire time my dad shouted, What are you doing? That's not what I taught you. You're going to get yourself killed. Oh no, here he comes. Here comes the bad man.

I sat up and tried to forget about the dream world. I asked my dad if he had to go.

"Yes," my dad said. "People are counting on me."

I pictured the witch lady, leaning against a jukebox. I pictured the prisoner, sneaking around town, a shadow creeping closer and closer.

"Did we finish the movie?"

"I put it away," he said. "We'll watch the rest tomorrow. Now go be with your brother. Boys sleep in beds." My dad and my mother both had sayings like these, things they said to us over and over. When my brother and I were mad at either of our parents, we used these sayings to make fun of them.

Downstairs, the only light came from a lamp I had to feel my way to in the dark. I clicked it once for its lowest setting so I wouldn't wake my brother. He was sleeping with his mouth open. I wondered if I slept that way and decided to ask my brother tomorrow if he would draw a picture of

me while I slept. I worried about swallowing spiders. We had seen lots when our dad first introduced us to the basement. He had a second bedroom but it was too small, and my dad said he didn't want his boys living in a closet, even if it was just for the weekends. Boys don't sleep in closets. Boys sleep in beds.

I turned off the lamp and tried hard to sleep with my mouth shut. I closed my eyes and saw visions of Chris, spiders, prisons. I saw my mom and dad and ghosts and ghouls.

My brother snored me awake. He was a super-loud snorer. I didn't know what time it was, but whenever I woke up in the middle of the night I made myself go look around wherever I was. I thought that then, when the world didn't expect me to be awake, I could catch the world doing something it didn't want me to see. A secret only I would know.

I used my brother's snores as cover for me upping the creaky steps. At the top I put my head to the door, like I'd seen in movies. I heard giggling. I opened the door a sliver and saw my dad, slouched, shirt off, snoring on the living room couch. The TV was on and a half-eaten block of cheese sat gross on the coffee table. The room smelled familiar, fruity, like our city's one department store.

I waited for my dad to wake and do something strange, a weird act I would relay to my brother the following morning. He would give me his full attention and say, And you actually saw that with your own two eyes? Yes, I would say, I was very lucky.

My dad dropped to his side on the couch and hugged his body. He did not shiver, but he looked small and cold. I wanted to cover him up with a blanket, but there were no

extra blankets in the house, only the one in his bedroom, where I was forbidden.

The air conditioner shut off. At the same time the TV cut away from its sitcom family to dead air. The new silence made me feel exposed, so I took a step back and crouched on the basement stairs. The stairs were made of a plastic wood and dug into my bony knees. I poked my head around the doorframe to continue watching my dad. I didn't want to miss the revelation.

The air conditioner clicked on and off several more times and still nothing happened. I made my arms into a pillow and rested my head. My mind started to wander. It went back to all the other moments I had crept on stairs, spied on people. Reflecting, I ended up falling asleep, dreaming of my parents fighting.

We are living in our old nice house.

I am watching TV downstairs with my brother, my elbows on my pillow, hands holding my head. It's late and the TV is the only light. We are watching his favorite game show. The one where the host makes the contestants do filthy things like bathe in beans if they can't answer a question correctly. The host is always smiling, but also likes to zing the contestants when they give answers that aren't even close.

I am not really watching the show; I just want to be with my brother.

The show ends. Without a word, my brother turns the TV off. The room goes dark. Before my eyes can adjust, my brother runs upstairs, taking them two at a time. I am left in the dark and my heart beats panicked. Down the hall is my dad's office. The door is halfway open when it's supposed to be closed. Red curtains cover the office window well, level

with the earth. When the moon is bright, like it is in this dream, it shines through these curtains and colors the entire room blood-red.

In the dream I shield myself with my pillow and run upstairs as fast as I can. I try to take two stairs at a time like my brother but fall and burn my knee on the carpet. In a movie I am for sure dead. But in my dream I am OK. I put the pillow on my shoulders, and take it easy taking the rest of the stairs.

When my head is almost level with the second floor of our house, I hear my mother's voice. She is loudly whispering an argument. I flatten my body on the stairs, my eyes peeking over the floor's horizon. My mother is standing at the sink, her back to my dad, who is sitting on a stool at the kitchen bar. He is wearing a softball cap, and his head is up, waiting for its turn to talk. It is clear they have been arguing for some time now.

"It's this place," my mother says. "These prisons. I feel like I can never get away."

"Away?" my dad says. "Is that what you want? You want to get away from me?"

"No," she says, though in the dream her voice is unsure. "That's . . . that's not what I want." She shuts the sink off and dries her hands, holding on to the rag long after the wet is gone. "I just need to do something."

"Oh, what. What could you possibly need?"

My mother throws the rag at my dad, but it's mostly dry and falls short of his face. "Don't talk to me like that," she says. "You're not here. You're out there. And you come home and I ask where have you been and you say at work."

"So," my dad says. "I have two jobs. Where else would I be?"

"Oh, c'mon. You smell all beery when you get home. And then you try to roll on top of me?"

"So sometimes I go throw darts."

"See. You're fuzzy with details."

"Details."

"You know what talking to you is like?" my mother says. "It's like, it's like when I ask one of the boys to do something simple, and I can tell that they understand, they understand what I want them to do, but they don't do it. Instead, they do something very similar, but not quite right, just to show me that they have power too. Like the other day, I asked your eldest to draw a tree before we left for the park. But he doesn't really care if we go to the park. He kind of wants to play in the backyard by himself. So you know what he draws? He doesn't draw a tree. He draws a bush."

My dad takes his hat off and throws it at the stove, right by where my mother is standing.

"You want me to draw you a tree? I'll draw you a god-damn tree." He is no longer pretending to whisper. "Hand me that marker. I'll draw right on my arm. See? Here. Look. This way everybody knows that even after I work all day at two different jobs, when I come home I still do whatever my wife wants." He stabs a marker I recognize as my own into his upper arm. He grips it with all of his fingers, like a kinder-gartener, or like a felon holds a knife.

"That's not what I want," my mother says. "That's not what I want."

"Then I don't know what you want," my dad says.

"Everybody wants something. I see that every day. Speeders want off with a warning. The Chief wants more tickets on Main Street." He doesn't look at her while he talks. He draws on his arm, filling in the shapes. "You're the only person I don't know. I don't know what you want anymore. I don't know what you could possibly want. We have two good boys. We have a house. I am working. I don't know what you want."

"That's not what I want. That's not what I want."

"Maybe I have to tell you," my dad says. "You can't decide for yourself, so I have to tell you." He slowly walks around the kitchen counter displaying his colored arm. "Look at this. This is what you want." He comes too close to my mother and she puts out her hand. He flexes his drawn-on arm at her. "Is this what you want? This is what you want."

My mother turns away. She grabs the rag off the kitchen floor. She runs water over it and, at first, holds it against her forehead. After a moment, she looks at my dad. "Come here," she says. My dad looks at his arm like he doesn't understand what it's doing there, flexed and floating in the air. He drops it and steps toward my mother, close enough their hips can touch. My mother holds my dad's arm and wipes at the marker. The rag is now a beach towel.

"This tree is really stuck," she says. She laughs, though without a smile. She scrunches her face and scrubs the arm harder. "I don't know if we'll ever get it out."

She laughs some more and my dad starts laughing too. Their laughter grows louder and louder, until I realized it was not their laughter anymore. The TV had finished its spell of dead air. The happy family was back, and I was awake.

I opened my eyes and remembered where I was, what I

was doing. My dad was still asleep on the couch, his back now facing me. So far in my life, I had never seen any markings on either of his arms, but I wondered if I looked now, when the world was asleep, if I might see something different. If his skin might be indented where he once etched a tree.

I waited for the TV people to laugh before I took each step. When I was finally standing over the couch, I paused and stared at my dad, sleeping in the television's glow. I studied his dirty blond hair, darker than Chris's and shaggy around the ears; his tan body, thin with muscle all over. He looked like a taller, thicker version of my brother, but with a mustache.

I waited for more laughter from the TV, but it didn't come. The sitcom was having its serious moment. A family was healing itself, a rift was resolved. I reached out anyway and touched my dad's naked chest. It was warm like a golf cart seat in the sun. He turned over on his back, but his eyes remained shut. I stepped back. When his breathing settled, I closed in and peered at his other arm. Near the shoulder was a small circle of pockmarks. I ran my finger over his skin. I smiled.

"What are you still doing here?" my dad said.

I didn't know what he was talking about, but I felt like he was waiting for an answer, for me to say something. "What is that?" I said, pointing to his arm.

My dad rubbed his eyes, put a hand down his pants and scratched. "What is what?"

I touched the pocked spot. It was weirdly soft. "That. Is that a tree?"

"A what?" he said. "No, it's a scar. From a shot I got when I was a kid. Never went away."

"Oh," I said, and we both went silent. My dad squinted his eyes open. I didn't know what he was expecting, but he seemed surprised, or confused, seeing me, his youngest son, in the living room with him, up when I shouldn't have been. His brow furrowed.

"You should be in bed," he said. He grabbed my wrist and pulled me near him. He smelled of beer and other things I didn't know. "Why aren't you sleeping?"

"I . . ."

"Explain yourself."

"I wanted to watch the rest of the movie?"

"The movie's in my room. You're not allowed in my room. You know that. Try again."

Afterward, when I was back in bed with my brother, I thought of a million different lies I could have told my dad. I had to use the bathroom. I was thirsty. You looked cold. But with his hand tight around me, I panicked, and told a truth.

"We made a new friend," I said. "At the pool."

Behind me, the TV went to a loud commercial, something about knives that could cut through marble. My dad sat up, releasing my wrist, and turned the TV down.

"What did you say? Who?" He rubbed his forehead like he had Chris's brain pain, pinching the gulf between his brows.

"His name is Chris," I said.

My dad sank back into the couch. "Oh," he said. "Great. That's great. And that's why you're up?"

I thought of the dream, pictured myself explaining about the tree, my theory about the world's secrets. "I don't know," I said. "I guess."

"OK," my dad said, "but you can tell me more tomorrow. Go back to bed." He pulled me down to him and kissed me on the head.

Something familiar caught my nose. "You smell like strawberries," I said.

He laughed. "Thank you. Now I'll see you in the morning."

I said good night, and my dad closed his eyes. A few seconds later he was breathing heavily.

On the way to the basement door, I stopped by the TV. A man was taking turns slicing through sheet metal and tomatoes. A pretty blond woman stood at his side, her face amazed. She was blown away by the man, his knives, and kept shaking her head in disbelief. But the man played it cool. He didn't glance up to smile or wink at the camera. He cut through one thing after another, only pausing to hold up the halved material. To show the whole world what he had done.

three

A SECRET, CHRIS SAID, is worth keeping. A secret has the potential to hurt. That's why you can't tell everyone everything. That's why some things must be locked up inside you, he said, touching my brother over his heart. Right here, the only place that is truly safe.

We learned the secret to secrets after our mother picked us up the next morning. After my dad made us eggs and burned us stacks of toast with jelly and apple butter. My brother and I had already been up for hours watching cartoons, waiting for my dad to wake and take the stairs slowly to the kitchen. When he came down, he still wasn't wearing a shirt. Some days I think my dad tried to see how long he could go without a shirt. I think this was a game he played. Today was Sunday, though, and I knew that by the time my mother knocked on the front door, my dad would be wearing his favorite yellow softball tank top, faded and full of holes.

After eggs and between shows my brother and I changed into our church clothes. I wore blue corduroy pants and a striped polo given to my mother by a military wife who golfed at my mother's work, and who pitied her. It was a terrible outfit. So was my brother's. But I paid attention to his, because I knew I would be wearing the same thing in twenty-two months, when the clothes were handed down. Thus, on Sundays, more than any other day, I looked at my brother like he was the future me. The compliments he got from strangers I got, and I felt bad when he said something mean to my mother, or when he was slapped on his knee for not paying attention in church. Every moment, I hoped for him to do great things.

When my mother rang the doorbell, my brother ran to get his bag from the basement. My dad did not get off the couch. And when I opened the door with a smile, my mother did not step inside. She looked down at where a doormat should have been.

"Do you want to come in for a second, Ag?" my dad called from the couch. Ag was for Aggie, which was for Agatha. "Made some eggs. I ran out of milk, so they're kind of bush league."

"No thanks," my mother said. She took a few steps and stood awkwardly in the entryway. "Already late for church. What's that smell?"

She smells the strawberries, I thought. I could still smell them too.

"Apple butter," my dad said.

My mother looked unconvinced, but she came into the living room anyway. She looked around at the blank walls, the low lighting. "How's the Chief?"

"Still at it," my dad said.

"Of course he is."

"What's that supposed to mean?"

My mother's nose was still at work, wiggling at the smell. She seemed to realize something and she blinked a long disappointed blink. "It means some people don't know how to quit."

My dad coated his eggs with ketchup, pushed them around with his fork. "I think he's almost ready."

"You've been saying that for years."

"Aggie . . . ," my dad started. The rhythm of their speech reminded me of my dream, except here my dad wasn't as quick with his answers.

My brother returned from the basement and turned off the television. My dad stood up. "Same thing next weekend, then?"

"Mm-hm," my mother said. We hugged our dad.

"Bye, Dad," my brother said.

"Bye, sons."

Our mother pushed us out the door.

We were quiet the drive home. My brother rode up front in our minivan, a purple-and-gray Ford Aerostar. It was the last big purchase we made as a family. I sat in back in silence, staring out the window, imagining myself a serious thinker, but really I just watched the city pass by with no deep thoughts.

We cut through the heart of downtown, which was designed to echo a time no one I knew could remember. The streets were narrow, built out of brick, and had names like Delaware and Cherokee, in honor of the people the settlers

had captured and killed. They were dotted with the same old lights that first lit the city when it wasn't a city, when it was just a nice town growing fat with hope. On each side there were small-time shops and the occasional bank, and when the streets were empty, like they were this morning, I liked to imagine them as the site of a showdown, an old western gunfight. I could almost see the old-time outlaws terrorizing the town until my dad rode in, the new sheriff, and put every trouble to bed.

Once out of downtown, we drove past the city's park. It was windy and gray, and there were no kids playing. There were men in orange jumpsuits, however, prisoners, spearing trash as armed guards looked on. This sort of sight wasn't uncommon. Whenever we drove through the city, I couldn't count to ten without seeing some sign of a prison: the big billboard at the end of the city that read, "Come Do Some Time in Leavenworth"; the guards in uniform who crawled out of their houses at all hours and unlocked their cars with countless keys attached to the hip, the teary-eyed out-of-towners who asked for directions to a given prison, where they would visit their locked-up loved ones. It was all part of where we lived. Still, common as it was, sometimes, if my brother and I had been bad that morning or the day before, our mother might slow the van down, point at the men in jumpsuits, and say something like, "See, that's why you do what I tell you. You don't want to end up like that, do you?" Today she drove by without a word.

Past the park we turned onto Tenth Avenue, and from there to Limit Street, which stretched the entire city and had its west end at our apartment. When we first moved in, our complex was called Oak Valley. But a month later,

before he left us for a different, safer city, the owner changed the name. He tried to spin the fact that we lived on a street called Limit at the limit of a sad city, and renamed the complex the Frontiers, as if the world around us were wide open and not surrounded by prisons.

At home we all took our after-church hangovers our separate ways. My mother went to her room and shut her door for a nap. She had to work that evening and tomorrow at noon, and wasn't to be disturbed. Unless someone is bleeding, she said, let me be. My brother had a contest with himself to see how many push-ups he could do. I wasn't sure why he did this, but guessed that a kid at school had teased him about being a taller, nearly as skinny version of me. My brother didn't say it, but I think he had visions of showing up to school in the fall a newer, better version of his spring self.

I lay in bed with a pillow over my head and fell asleep. It was a hard sleep but no dreams stuck around my brain. In the real world, a rustling sound found my ear. Something tickled. I felt my body start to wiggle. I opened my eyes and my brother was sitting over me, dangling my swim shorts.

He was singing a jingle. *"Let's go to the pool. Let's go to the pool."*

"Mom?"

"Mom," he said, still singing, *"Mom is gone."*

We had never gone to the pool while our mother was gone. We had never gone without her giving us the OK to go. I thought about mentioning this to my brother while we changed into our trunks, but was certain he would beat my

point with his own better point that I could not predict. This was why I never could argue with him. The times I tried, when I thought my thoughts were good, he would put my point in some other light, and soon I would be on his side.

I was able to stay quiet until we reached the bottom of the stairs, where the guilt caught up.

"Does Mom know?" I said.

"Does Mom know what?"

"You know."

"Mom knows lots of things," he said. He pulled out a sheet of paper he had folded in his trunks and pretended to read. I imagined the paper had a detailed drawing of a diver doing a Gainer, and wondered if he would ever let me see it.

"The pool," I said. "Did you ask her if we could go to the pool?"

"I did ask her."

"You did?"

"Yes." He put the sheet back in his pocket and held open the pea-green door. "Can we go?"

It took me until the pool gate before I realized my brother had not said whether my mother had said yes or no.

"Of course she said no," my brother said. He laughed at me, and opened the gate. It felt like we were breaking in, like we were sneaking into a prison, instead of escaping with everyone else. I stayed in the shallow end and watched my brother do move after move. Before each bounce off the board, he looked around to see if anyone was watching. A guard. A cop. Chris. The pool was silent. There was no one but us.

"I guess I'll work on my front flip," my brother said. "You

should work on it with me. That way, when Chris comes back, he'll be like, 'You guys have gotten good!'" That argument didn't appeal to me, but I liked the idea of doing something with my brother, and him inviting me.

Though I had only been off the diving board once before. And I was real scared then. We had just moved into the apartment. Our mother was with us, but she had gone inside to get a book and never came back. To get me to jump, my brother had to narrate a long tale of the sea, starring himself as a famous pirate captain whose waters stretched the entire pool. I was the former best friend who had betrayed the captain by breaking the one rule obeyed by all of the sea's wayward criminals: Thou shall not covet thy captain's wife (a take on the commandments my brother was forced to memorize back when we still suffered Sunday school). The story ended with me, the first mate, having to walk the plank. My brother let me keep my eyes open then, which he said real pirates wouldn't do. I think he felt the eyes of the few adults who were watching the entire performance from pool chairs.

I felt that memory in my stomach when I stepped onto the board.

"First, let's try a dive," my brother said. I could tell he was enjoying the role he was playing, the substitute Chris. I stepped to the edge of the board and looked out over the deep end. The sun hung low over the tops of the trees. My brother stood as close to me as he could without being on the diving board. So this is what it was like.

"Put your arms up," he said. "Hands together."

I did.

"Squeeze your head."

What?

"Pinch your head with your arms. Like this."

Oh.

"Now jump."

Um.

"Fall."

Well.

"Do something!"

His last shout pushed me off, though I didn't jump. I just kind of fell, and as I fell I saw my brother's face— surprised, but also smirking.

There was a loud pop, a punch in the stomach. I didn't go into the water right. The world around me became a blue dream. Water rushed up my nose and into my lungs, but I couldn't make it stop, or tell my body to float to the top. I hung underwater, thinking of nothing, feeling the same.

Chris was the one who pulled me to the pool ladder, after I don't know how long. All I knew was that I was in a pool chair and Chris's hands were all over me, pressing my chest, cupping my face.

"Just checking for leaks, little man," he said. "Nope, no holes. She'll float."

He sat me up. My brother stood behind him, wearing his concerned face, the one that also said he was annoyed.

"What were you doing down there?" he said. "Why didn't you come up?"

"I don't know. I thought I would."

"You thought you would? What does that mean?"

Chris stood up, put his hand to his chin. "Hmm," he said, "I think I know what this is about."

"He's an idiot," my brother said. "That's what it is. An idiot baby. A baby idiot."

"No," Chris said. "It's much worse than that." He folded his arms and his face fell, almost into a scowl. "You told someone, didn't you, little man? About me, about our secret?"

I thought of my dad the night before, what I said.

"No," I said.

"Are you sure? Are you sure you didn't accidentally let our secret slip, then try to take your shame to a watery grave?"

I looked at my brother, whose concerned face now widened with worry.

"No," I said. "I didn't tell anyone. I promise."

Chris's eyes narrowed, until the blue, the best part, disappeared. He laughed. "Just kidding, little man. I trust you. You and your bro, I know you wouldn't tell a soul." He took off his shirt and headed toward the diving board. "I know you know what makes a secret secret. And how to keep it."

He hopped on the board and stepped to the edge. My brother and I, confused as we were, expected him to do the Gainer. Instead, Chris twirled on one foot and fell backward, his hands behind his head like he was lounging on a couch. He seemed to hover there, parallel to the pool, his body floating like magic. Only at the last possible second did he throw his arms out and arch his body into a back dive. When he came up he said, "You two do know about secrets, don't you?"

My brother nodded.

"You do? Then tell me."

"A secret," my brother said, "a secret is something . . . is something you don't tell anyone. Even if they beg."

"Go on," Chris said.

"And . . . you keep it to yourself. No matter what. Even if you're tortured."

"Yes, of course," Chris said, backstroking to the shallow end. "Everyone knows that. But there's more."

A secret, Chris explained, can't be spoken. Put into words. A secret is a place, or an action. A symbol. Secrets aren't told. They are shown. Revealed. When you share a secret with someone, they look at you confused—like us with the tattoo, the Gainer. They get mad that they can't understand. Or they feel hurt that you kept something from them, even though it was for their own good, even though they weren't ready. That's why it's best not to tell. Even the people you love. *Especially* the people you love. If a secret is a secret, when it's revealed, it hurts people.

"What about us?" my brother said. "You told us about the Gainer."

"I did," Chris said. "And the first time you try it will not be pleasant." Chris walked out of the shallow end, body dripping, emerging like a swamp monster. "But that's just a little secret. There are much bigger ones. Greater, yes, but more dangerous. Secrets like that should never get out. Do you understand?" he said. "Do you understand what I'm talking about?" My brother looked at me as if I could help, then back at Chris. "So, then," Chris said, speaking directly to my brother. "If I was to show you more, could you keep it a secret?"

This time my brother didn't bother checking with me first. He nodded in silence, as if he too had fallen under the witch lady's spell. As if she had cast a curse that made him mute.

"That's right," Chris said. "No words."

Then he mouthed the Gainer. Then he touched his lips, curved into a grin.

The next morning my brother and I were eating cereal at the table. Our mother came into the kitchen in her lace pajamas. She had her big blond hair in a ponytail and I wanted to yank on it, like I wanted to do to the girls at school. She went straight for the coffee. She kept her back toward us while she waited for the brewer.

"So what did you boys do last night?" my mother said. My whole body flinched, but my brother responded naturally, like he was the best actor in one of the bad films we watched with our dad.

"Not a lot. We played hide-and-go-seek for a bit, messed around with toys."

My mother let his answer sit there for a while. "That sounds like fun. And you didn't go to the pool?"

"No."

"I noticed your trunks seem rather wet. Hanging in the tub."

Sometimes, Chris said, secrets are hard to keep. Sometimes the truth and secrets don't get along.

"Oh, that," my brother said. He looked down at his cereal, and for a moment I thought my mother had him. But he was just pausing for effect. "I left them there when I took a shower."

"Shower," our mother said. She poured her coffee and mixed in some mixed milk. "OK, good. Because you shouldn't be out there while I'm gone."

"We know," my brother said.

"I heard from somebody at work they still haven't got that prisoner guy," our mother said. Her voice had the same tone as when our county was under a tornado warning.

"How did he escape?" my brother said.

Our mother sat down at the table, her face hovering over her coffee. "What does that matter?"

"I don't know. I guess it doesn't."

"If you're so interested, ask your dad," she said. "Or read the paper."

Our mother often said this if we were asking too many questions, concerning things she didn't know about or didn't want to discuss. Pick up a book, she would say, the wannabe teacher. Go read the paper. Never mind that we couldn't afford a subscription, or that our dad brought a paper home only when he was quoted or pictured. Still, there were other ways. Papers were left behind in public places. If we were lucky, we would find one that way, discover the true story. We had done the same thing after the last breakout, which was only a year ago. We found a paper at the park, and my brother snuck it home under his shirt. After our dad had fallen asleep, my brother took the newspaper downstairs and read the article out loud. It became one of his favorite stories. The escapee was aided by a lady who ran a voluntary inmate dog-training program at the prison. Pups for Perps, my dad called it. The lady would bring in dogs from the city's animal shelter and pair them with inmates. The inmates would walk, feed, and pet the animals on a weekly basis. The idea was to have both dog and inmate practice being with others before they got out of their prisons and found a new home. But the more time the lady spent with the prisoners, the more she liked them, and the more she became attached, to

one man in particular. Soon she found herself shuttling him out of prison, stashing him in the back of the dog shelter's van, hidden in a kennel. She drove him a hundred miles to his home city, where he picked up some guns and drugs from old friends. But the police were waiting for him. They locked him back up, this time for longer. The lady was also put away, and the article featured her mug shot, above which read the headline "Man's Best Fiend."

"Who knows?" my mother said. "Who knows how these things happen? Who cares? You don't need to know." She refused to tell us more. She thought the details would give us very specific nightmares. "Anyway," she said. "You're coming to work with me this morning. I don't want you guys here by yourself. I worry sometimes."

I liked the golf course. Before I started school, when my mother first got the job because she felt bad that my dad had two jobs, she always took me to work with her. She would buy me fast-food french-toast sticks and tell me not to tell my brother. When I got bored playing with the putting machine in the pro shop, I watched TV in the club's dining hall under the loose care of the cook, Sandy. She was a middle-aged ex-con secretly dating a large black man named Cornbread, another ex-con, who was in charge of the course's greens. I had seen them hug once when they thought no one was looking. Whenever I came into the cafeteria, Sandy dropped whatever she was doing and gave all of her attention to me. "There he is!" she would say, in a way that tingled my neck. "Your VIP table is waiting, sir." Then she would sit me down with a free grilled cheese, pinch my ear, and say, "Anything

you need, you let me know. I'll do my best to keep out the riffraff."

When we got to the club that afternoon, Rick was waiting for my mother in the shop. He tapped the imaginary watch on his wrist.

"Look who decided to show," Rick said, his lips stretching across his tan face. Rick's entire body was a dark tan, from spending entire summers taking care of the golf course. He had a thin build, similar to my dad's, except his came with more of a gut, from all the years he pissed away on whiskey, he once said. Nowadays he drank beer.

He didn't see my brother or me at first, but when he did, Rick's smile went wider.

"Hey, everybody, look here, it's the Gabor sisters." I didn't understand the reference, but got that the sisters part wasn't supposed to be flattering. Still, I had to look at Rick's blond knees because I knew if I looked directly at him my face would start to reflect his smile. I don't know why. I knew I didn't like Rick.

A dying light flashed over our heads.

"Dammit," Rick said, "I told Cornbread to change that stupid thing." I counted the blinks of the light. My dad once told me to count the seconds between the flash of the lightning and the pop of the thunder—that's how many miles danger was away from me. I tried to do the same thing with the golf shop light. There were big gaps in the flickers. I counted the danger far away.

"So, girls, what's the lady outlook look like?" Rick said.

"OK, I guess," my brother said, just to give Rick an answer.

"Just OK? Listen, you maroons." He squatted down so our faces were even. His blond mustache sat straight, serious, telling us to pay attention. "You can't settle for OK in life. Haven't I told you that? You gotta always be looking, keeping your eye out for hot opportunities. They're not gonna just stroll by your lazy ass and grab you." He stood back up, and lunged at our mother. "You have to grab them!"

Our mother shrieked. She punched Rick's hands away from her ribs. "Hey, cut it out," she said, but with a smile. The two looked at each other, and the light above their heads flickered off, flickered on. "Boys, why don't you see what Sandy's up to?"

"Yeah," Rick said, holding on to our mother. "Why don't you go someplace that isn't here. Your mother and I have a game to play."

"Rick," our mother said.

"Oh, sorry. I forgot. We're saving that for tomorrow."

"That's not what I meant."

"What's tomorrow?" I said.

An Army man came into the clubhouse and wandered into the pro shop. My mother broke free from Rick. "Go help," she said.

"Fine, but tell these two goons I'll be watching them. They better not mess up my course." He pinched our mother on the elbow and walked away, a greasy handkerchief dangling out of his back pocket.

"Anyway," our mother said, "tomorrow is my birthday. The day you two treat me like a queen." She circled around my brother and me, slowly, giving her words an air of importance. "And to commemorate this historical moment, we'll

be having a party. At our place. What do you think about that?"

"Is Rick going to be there?" my brother asked.

Our mother stopped her circling and looked at the shop. Rick was cleaning the Army man's club, and the two were sharing a loud laugh. "Of course he is," my mother said. "All our friends will be there."

"Rick's not my friend," my brother said.

"Sure he is."

"No, he's not," I said. "He pinches people."

Our mother laughed. She didn't understand that we were serious. She didn't know him like we did.

"Well, he's my friend," our mother said. "And he's coming over. So you better learn to like it. OK?"

My brother threw his hands up. "Fine. What do I care."

"What do you care? You care because this is my special day, a chance for your mother to have fun. Well-deserved, long-waited-for fun. I think I've earned it, don't you?"

For a moment her eyes pleaded with my brother, but her mouth twisted into a smirk, like she knew what all her presents were before they were unwrapped.

"Sure," my brother said. "Now can we go?"

"Wait," she said, and for a moment she stared at us intensely, as if trying to memorize our faces. Finally, her eyes softened. "Yes, you may go." She dug a hand into her shorts pockets. "Do you want tokens for the range?"

"No," my brother said, pulling me away. "We're fine on our own."

Sandy had just returned from her break. She smelled of cigarettes and the citrusy perfume she used to cover up the

smoke. She was taking inventory. Towers of wax-paper cups were stacked all over the counter. As we made our way across the cafeteria, Sandy unwrapped a sleeve of smalls and started counting out loud. She was up to thirty when she saw us and lost her place.

"There they are!" she said, throwing her hands up like it was a parade. "Hip hip hooray! Hip hip hooray!"

My brother rolled his eyes, but my face smiled big. I couldn't imagine this ever getting old. Sandy pushed the tower of cups to the side of the counter so we could see her better. She was barely taller than my brother, even with her balloon hairdo, a brown and curly perm that stayed the shape of a hairnet at all times. She was a few years older than my mother, and sometimes I liked to pretend Sandy was my mother's big sister, my favorite aunt. I also liked her because she didn't like Rick, which I could tell by the way her face changed when his name came up, and by the way the two talked about each other behind their backs. (Sandy was the office gossip, according to Rick, even though the golf course didn't have an office; Rick, on the other hand, wasn't given a mean name, but Sandy would plug her nose and wave away stink lines when he walked by.) Whenever the two had to talk to each other, their words were filled with leftover anger. It was like me talking to my brother an hour after a fight.

Sandy took a small cup and filled it with orange soda. She gave it to us to share.

"So," she said, "what are the best boys up to today?"

She rested her elbows on the counter and put her head in her hands, very interested. We took turns taking sips and

told her a little about our plans. The old spots we would hit. The new places we hoped to find. Now that we were older, my mother let us explore the course by ourselves. My brother took this new ability very seriously at first and brought a large sheet of sketch paper to map out the entire confines of the Fort Leavenworth Country Club. I eventually spilled red Kool-Aid on the map while my brother was coloring an oak tree. For that, I did time locked in our toy trunk. With my brother sitting on the top. The map was never mentioned again.

"Fun," Sandy said. "That sounds like fun. Just be careful. I don't want anything happening to the best. Without the best, what would we be?"

Sandy gave us a refill with a to-go lid and we went out the side door, forgetting to thank her. The side door led to a large practice green we knew to keep off of. We ran around the course, stomping holes where we pleased before catching our breath at a women's tee. My brother asked if I wanted the last sip of the soda. I said sure, but when he handed me the cup it was empty, and my brother was laughing. Throw it away, he said. You touched it last.

The trash can was on the other side of nine's green, which I crept across, praying no golf balls fell from the sky and struck me down—punishment from the golf gods for desecrating their land. What I found wasn't punishment. It was a gift. On the lid of the trash can was a copy of the city newspaper, the *Leavenworth Times*. The weekend edition. I threw my cup away and tried to make sense of its stories, but the sections were disheveled and the pages out of order. Then someone yelled fore from far off. Seconds later a white dot

thudded at my feet. I tucked the paper under my arm and ran off the green to my brother. Moses coming down the mountain.

"What's that?" my brother asked. He took the paper from me and quickly solved its puzzle, putting the pages in their proper order. "Whoa. You see this?"

He held the paper up, but I didn't see what was so special.

"This." He pointed at the bottom right of the page, at a small article continued from 1A, which was missing.

" 'Stranger' Still on the Loose."

"Is that the prisoner?" I said. But before he could answer me, we heard the rumble of a familiar motor.

"Oh no," my brother said. "Rick."

We looked up the hill, but didn't see him. All we saw were the holes in the ground, the destruction we'd done.

"Quick!" my brother said. "This way!" He grabbed my wrist and pulled me along, shouting more action language. "Run for your life!" he said, and we ran all the way to the end of the rough, where the course met the woods. We stopped. A barbed-wire fence stood in our way: on it a cracked sign read KE P OUT.

At our feet several golf balls stained yellow with rain and age sat forgotten, waiting for their owners, who would never come.

"C'mon," my brother said. "We have to keep going."

We ducked under the barbed wire and disappeared into the woods. The trees were thick, and we struggled to find a path. Half-leafed limbs scratched back as we swam in. The little trees held hands and fought back like their parents.

The woods don't want us here, I thought. This isn't a place we should be.

After a few minutes of wandering, we came to a small clearing. I looked up at the trees that towered above us, at the sun, whose rays couldn't find the ground. This was not a comforting spot. There weren't any old tires to sit on, no stumps or sizable logs. So I stood there, waiting for my brother to pull out the paper and read what it said. To reveal the story of the Stranger.

Instead, he snapped off a dead branch and pretended to fence a bush.

"What do you think about what Chris said?" he said. "About secrets."

I stared at the unarmed bush and felt sorry for it. "I don't know. It's kinda cool."

"Yeah," he said. "Kinda cool. Kinda dumb, but kinda cool." He stepped back from the bush and tilted his head, considering the best way to kill it. "You didn't tell Mom, did you? About Chris?"

"I already told you. You told me not to."

"Good," he said. "Because it would only hurt her. And you don't want that."

He plunged his stick sword into the bush and let out a loud moan, making the dying sounds for his victim. He wiped his hands on his shorts and admired his work. "I've taken care of this villain. Now let's find someplace to read this in secret."

We left the clearing. I followed my brother back the way we came. Some of the branches were still bent, others had returned to their old selves. We took a random right and

came upon a creek, and my brother and I stood side by side on the little bank. I noticed a gang of tadpoles swimming above the clay-colored creek bed. I crouched to get a better view. The tadpoles chased one another in circles. They had games of their own. I put my hand in the water where the tadpoles played, and they shot away from my fingers like fireworks.

". . . is also known as the Stranger," my brother said. He had begun reading the article about the prisoner, which apparently continued mid-sentence.

Kern has been a Kansas prison inmate since 1985, when he was found guilty of the first-degree murder of Morgan Wells.

In December 1984, Leavenworth police responded to an eyewitness report of a woman being dragged into her home by a white male. Upon arriving at the scene and entering the house, police found Kern with a gun to his head, standing over the deceased Wells and a camcorder. Authorities alleged Kern had set up a camcorder to record the murder of Wells, and planned to kill himself immediately afterward. Authorities arrested Kern before he could shoot himself, however, and he was convicted in March 1985. He was sentenced to life imprisonment for first-degree murder.

Leavenworth Police and the Kansas Department of Public Safety are assisting the Department of Corrections with the search. Prison officials declined to comment on how Kern escaped, but say he is considered dangerous. Anyone with information on Kern should call the police immediately.

My brother tore out the article and put it in his pocket. Later it would sleep beneath his bunk bed, hidden with the rest. "The Stranger," he said.

"The Stranger," I said, to hear how it sounded from my mouth.

"The Stranger," my brother said. "The Stranger . . . *is coming to get you.*"

He turned his hands into claws and jumped at me, like Rick grabbed my mom. I tried to fight him off but he was bigger and quicker.

"Don't fight it," he said, squeezing me into a suffocating bear hug. "You'll only make it worse."

Let me go, I told him, please let me go. But when I heard my words they weren't my own. They were softer, more desperate, the words of Morgan Wells.

"Relax," my brother said. "Honey, relax." He put his finger to my head in the shape of a gun. "It'll all be over soon."

I closed my eyes. It would be easier to let him do what he wanted, to let him play out his plot. This I knew from suffering before. So I let my body sink into his—*Don't do it, baby, please don't do it*—and wondered what it felt like to die. I imagined my brain shutting off like a television, the picture of the world beaming large and colorful, then, in an instant, shrinking to a single dot of white. I closed my eyes and felt my brother drag his finger up and down the length of my cheek. I felt his breath in my ear. *This is what you get,* he said. *For talking to strangers. For sharing our secrets.* He cocked the gun with a click of his tongue. *Now smile for the camera, brother.*

"Stop!" I yelled, as much in my own voice as I knew how.

"Sorry," the Stranger said. "I can't."

"I'm not playing!

"Good, because this isn't a game."

"I mean it! Stop!"

The woods echoed with the alarm of my voice, loud enough for the whole course to hear. I felt my brother's grip tighten, then loosen. "What?" he said. "OK, fine." He let me go, but with a hard shove that nearly sent me into the creek. "I was just playing."

"That wasn't funny," I said. "Why'd you do that?"

"Do what?"

"Why'd you say that, about secrets? I didn't tell Mom about Chris."

"I know," he said. "You told Dad."

He pushed me aside and washed his hands in the creek.

"No, I didn't."

"Yes, you did. You did and I know you did."

"I didn't mean to. How did you know?"

"Because you're my brother. And I would have done the same thing if I was your age."

"Stop acting like you're that much older than me."

"I am."

"We're only two grades apart."

"Yeah, but I'm smarter."

"I'll be just as smart when I'm your age," I said. "No, I'll be smarter. So I told Dad. It was at night. He was asleep. He doesn't remember."

"Good."

"So you should have already known that. If you're so smart."

My brother shrugged. "When a secret is shared, people get hurt. That's what we said." He kicked a rock into the creek. "And Dad wasn't asleep. He was drunk." He walked away, leaving me by the water. I saw my wet reflection and thought of my dad. How he looked that night. The crooked shape his mouth took when I said he smelled like strawberries.

"I hate you," I said to my brother.

"No, you don't," he said, examining the woods, looking for the right way to go. "I'm not what you hate."

"Yes you are. And I'm going to tell Mom what you did."

"No, you won't," my brother said. "You don't know your way back. Or who's out there."

He crooked his hands into hooks, the same shapes he made a moment ago, playing the Stranger. I turned away and looked into the woods, the sea of trees before me. Nothing was familiar. But I told my brother I knew where I was going, and so what if I didn't. What did he care? I brushed past him and stepped into the woods, thinking of the scene where I told my mother what my brother did, the terrible things he said to me, and how he wouldn't let me go. My mother would stop helping whatever dumb customer was at the counter and storm after my brother. She would catch him under the arm and drag him to a dark corner. She would have hooks of her own. How does it feel? I would say as my mother slapped him, or hit him with her shoe. She would scold him and ask what kind of brother are you anyway? What kind of brother does this? And my brother would cry, but I wouldn't. I'd be sitting next to Sandy, Rick out of the

picture. I'd be drinking a soda all by myself. I'd have the last sip. I'd have the last word. I'd say, Who's laughing now?

I smiled to myself and took five steps into the woods before my brother stopped me. "Hey, dummy," he said. "This way."

I turned around and followed.

four

OUR MOTHER HAD TO WORK the following morning. We reminded her that it was her birthday, her special day, but she said we needed the money, so she picked up an extra shift. Before she left, she pulled my brother and me out of bed and gave us our orders for the day. We were to ready the apartment for her party. This meant we had to clean the place up, make it presentable for others. I asked what about decorations, and she said we didn't have the time or resources to worry about that.

"And don't even think about going to the pool," she said. "We're supposed to be under a tornado watch all day." She threw her keys in her purse and her purse over her shoulder. "Remember, if you hear the siren, you know what to do."

Yes, we told her. Go downstairs to our building's bottom level, where the washers and dryers lived. Crouch down and

cover our heads until the siren is silent, the danger is gone. We had practiced this many times.

"And just in case," our mother said, "I've asked our neighbor to check in on you. So you better be here when she comes by. Got it?" We nodded. "Think of the neighbor as your guard," our mother said. "And I'm the warden. I don't want any pool activity in the guard's report."

She kissed us on our cheeks, and a moment later we heard the van come to life, whine out of the parking lot, and sputter down Limit Street.

"OK, she's gone," my brother said. "Time for the pool."

He disappeared from the kitchen and came back with two towels and my trunks. He was already wearing his.

"What about the guard?" I said.

"If you believe that, you really are as dumb as Rick says," my brother said. "When's the last time you saw Mom talk to anyone around here besides us?" He threw my trunks at my face. "She doesn't know anybody. The only friends she's got are at work, and who knows how much she even likes those people." He paused, perhaps thinking about what we'd seen yesterday, the way our mother and Rick looked at each other. "Now go change."

We locked the door on the way out and my brother put the key in his fanny pack. We didn't keep the key under our doormat anymore because of the prison break. The mat was left over from our family life. It read, "Wipe Your Paws," and there were dog prints on it.

As we stepped out into the hallway so did a neighbor lady I'd never seen before. She had long greasy hair, and her body was drowned in baggy sweatpants and an oversized

T-shirt. I looked away. Later, my brother said the mistake we made was we didn't make eye contact. He said if you want to get away with something you have to act like the thing you're doing is something you do every day.

"Hey there," the lady said. "What are you two up to?" She fished for a pack of cigarettes in her sweatpants and waited for our answer. On the hallway walls were poorly framed pictures of painted flowers. "Well? Do they speak?"

"We were just going to wait outside," my brother said, "for our mother."

The lady exhaled her smoke, a wispy cloud that reminded me of the tornado watch. "Well, here's an idea. Wait inside."

She smiled at her response. We couldn't think of anything smart to say back, and the lady didn't wait for us to say OK or sorry. She snuffed out her cigarette in a Coke can cut in half, and went into her apartment. My brother pushed me back inside. We leaned against the door and slid down on our butts. I asked my brother what do we do now.

"We're trapped," he said. "We wait."

We spent the rest of the morning prisoners of the smoking lady. My brother took turns bad-mouthing her, our mom. That's the lady she gets to watch us? Gross. We thought of different ways we, or some higher power, might rid us of the smoking lady. Next time our mother took us on a trip I would "accidentally" leave a toy at the top of the stairs by the smoking lady's door, and then let's see what happens. Or she would go into the hospital for a typical physical and find out she had cancer all around her lungs and bones. That was how our mom's dad died.

While my brother made a list of all the ways the smoking

lady could die, I started cleaning the apartment. The first thing I had to do was pick up all our toys. There were fighting men everywhere, all left behind by my brother, all players in his never-ending plots. I had wanted to pick up many of these toys before, but knew if I did, my brother would yell at me. That guy needs to be there, he would say. No, don't move him. You'll ruin the ending.

Once all the men were put away in our room, I wiped everything down. I dusted the bookcase with the encyclopedias, not peeking in the book with the naked lady, the one who looked like my mother. I moved quickly to the TV, writing my name in the dust blanketing the screen, before wiping it all away. When I was done, I reported to my brother, who was up now, doing push-ups in his room. He told me great, good job; now do the floors.

We didn't have a vacuum, not anymore. Before we moved into the apartment, our parents sat down in our old house's empty living room and divided their things. My brother and I were supposed to be outside playing, but we'd gotten too hot and come in early, plopping ourselves tiredly on the floor. After little discussion, it was decided that my mother, the cleaner of the two, would keep the vacuum, and my dad would get the grill. Other items—the microwave, the record player, the VCR—were not as easily agreed upon. But they never really fought over anything either, like I imagined my brother and I would have if we had to split up the Christmas gifts addressed to both of us. In the end, my mother sat comfortably next to her pile of stuff, and my dad his, while my brother and I sat strangely in the middle, under the cool of the ceiling fan, unsure what pile our things belonged to.

But that vacuum had broken, had gotten clogged with too much dog hair. Now all we had was the carpet sweeper my mother borrowed from work. There wasn't any fur to worry about anymore, but there were a few roaches. Dead and alive alike. I found one under the couch, another behind the end table, and two in the box fan. I piled the dead on a paper towel and threw them away. The two live ones I kept in an old, lidless coffee can, which already had a roach in it to begin with.

I took the can to our room and asked my brother what should I do with it. He was on the floor resting from his routine, and it would have been easy to simply turn the coffee can over and watch the roaches fall on his face, dart in all directions over his squirming body.

My brother peered into the can. "Jesus," he said, and put his hand over his mouth. "Get that thing away from me."

"What do I do with them?"

"I don't know," he said, backing farther and farther away. "Take them outside or something . . ." My brother's words trailed off and his face suddenly changed. He had an idea. I could tell by the way his eyes shifted upward, moved far away, and his eyebrows curled into thinking mode. When it came to my brother's faces, I thought of myself as something of an expert.

"Quick," he said. "Grab your trunks."

"I'm wearing them."

"Let's go, then."

"What about the neighbor?"

"It's fine," my brother said. He pointed at the coffee can. "Now we have a reason."

———

My brother made me cover up the can with my pool towel. When we left the apartment this time, the smoking lady wasn't waiting, though the hallway still smelled like smoke. I told my brother I didn't think we should be gone long, in case she came back. He agreed. He just wanted to check something.

First, we released the roaches into the woods and watched them stumble around, confused by their new surroundings.

"I'm starting to hate this place," my brother said. "Gross roaches."

On our way back in we saw someone by the pool's front gate. It was Chris. He was lounging in a desk chair, wearing a T-shirt with the sleeves torn off, so we could see his armpit hair dangle like a sweaty vine. The chair he sat in had wheels, and to stop from rolling away Chris had tied a neon rope from an arm of the chair to a chink in the fence.

"Uh-oh," Chris said. "Here comes trouble."

I turned around expecting to see someone bad behind us, but saw no one. When I faced front, my brother and Chris were shaking hands, sharing a smile. The two talked about the weather, how clear the sky was, how it was the perfect day for the pool. Chris said he wished every day was like this, that they would last forever. Wouldn't that be great? he said. Just the two of us, catching some rays and hanging by the water? My brother agreed. That would be the best. Both of them seemed to forget that I was there.

A woman walked by with a dog and a kid. She was wearing cut-off shorts and a loose tank top. I didn't remember seeing her around the complex before, but the kid was too

young to be a friend, so maybe I just never noticed. He ran around in circles, holding a fat piece of pink chalk. I wanted it.

"Hey, I've got a question for you two," Chris said.

The woman stopped. "I'm sorry?" she said.

Chris sat up straighter. "Oh, not you, ma'am. I was talking to these two gentlemen. But don't worry, I'll let you know if I want your ear."

He pushed his sunglasses back up, and the woman smiled with her eyes down. She returned to pretending her kid was very interesting. The two walked a few steps until the kid crouched down to draw on the sidewalk, a large shape that didn't make any sense to me. The woman waited. Chris folded his arms behind his head and stared at the woman, watching her kid make art. He leaned over to my brother and spoke quietly.

"What do you think?" he said.

"About what?"

"The kid. Should we recruit him? Think he's old enough to learn you know what?"

My brother shook his head, returned Chris's hushed voice. Too young. Practically a baby. Babies can't swim.

"Yeah, you're right," Chris said. "He looks like a bit of a mama's boy. Probably a blabbermouth, too."

The kid finished shading in his odd shape and stood up proud. Chris's eyes followed them until they disappeared around a building. My brother and I stood there waiting for Chris to come up from his thoughts.

"Chris," my brother said.

"Yes."

"Can we go in the pool now?"

"Hmm," Chris said. "Oh, sorry, of course we can. Just had to wait until that lady left. Never know who she might know." He stood up and pulled off his shirt. His body looked tanner than last time, and there were mosquito bites where there weren't bites before, nestled into the blond hair below his belly button. The hair that ran into his shorts.

"Hey," Chris said. He had caught me looking at his hair. He put his hand under my chin and lifted my head until my eyes met his. I thought he was going to be mad, but all he did was smile. "Remember," he said, "we don't want any word getting out about this, do we? About the Gainer?"

I shook my head, but Chris didn't let me go.

"No," my brother said. "That's how you ruin a secret."

The water looked warm in the June sun. But before I could swim, my brother and Chris said I had to run inside and grab them popsicle strips. My brother didn't care what color, but Chris wanted a blue. When he finished his strip, Chris leaned over and without warning licked my brother on the face, leaving a long streak of blue across his cheek. My brother looked at Chris with shock.

"Gross," he said, and wiped off Chris's spit with the back of his hand. He stood up and backed away. "What was that for?"

"That was for your own good," Chris said, and laughed a little. "For your protection." He drank the rest of his strip and gargled the blue like mouthwash, swishing it around with fat cheeks before swallowing. "Did you know," he said, "that a giraffe's tongue is completely blue? Top to bottom." My brother asked a quiet why, his hand still touching his sticky face. "Well, they're out in the sun every day, aren't they?

Licking leaves off trees and stuff, their tongues just hanging out. The blue prevents them from getting burned. It's like their sunscreen."

Chris stuck out his tongue, which was coated a deep blue, darker than the pool, and extended farther than any tongue I'd seen before. I bet he could lick his own nose if he wanted, but instead he pretended he was stripping an invisible tree of its leaves, taking each leaf into his mouth and saying yum after.

My brother dipped his hand in the water and wiped off the rest of his face. "Giraffes don't do that," he said. "That's not true."

"Oh, it's not?" Chris said. "You don't think so?" He stood up and started toward my brother. "You know, your face is starting to look a bit pink, big man. I think you could use another coat!" He grabbed my brother and my brother squirmed, but only half trying to get away, his face open with laughter as Chris tickled his ribs and wagged his long blue tongue next to my brother's ear. Don't fight it, Chris kept saying. It's for your own good!

"All right, all right," Chris finally said. "Enough of that. No more messing around. We're here for serious business, right?" My brother dunked his head to get rid of the Chris spit. "Well, are we?"

"Yes," my brother said.

"That's right, the Gainer isn't some silly game. It's the real deal, so let's get ready."

They moved to the deep end, leaving me to throw away the popsicle wrappers.

"OK, show me what you got," he said. My brother stepped to the edge of the diving board, tested its spring with his

toes. I felt nervous for him, like the few times I remembered watching my dad's favorite football team on TV. He wanted his team to win so badly, and I did too, because the day's mood depended on how the game went. It decided if Dad might finish our swing set, or just sit in the grass, in a circle of empty cans and unused parts, clueless or careless about what went with what.

"Let's go, big brother," Chris said. "The world won't wait."

My brother jumped, and if I had let my mind think for a second about anything else, I would have missed the dive. It was that fast. And it produced little splash. In my mind Chris was already giving my brother a variety of high fives. In real life my brother came out of the water wearing his humble face. He swam over to the ladder and stepped out like an Olympic swimmer, so far in first he couldn't care less about the judge's score. Chris watched my brother wipe the water dripping off his body, pull the trunks away from his waist, so they didn't stick.

"You, sir, nailed it," Chris said. "You really nailed it, didn't you?" My brother looked up, but didn't even give a thank-you smile. Chris turned to me, still in the shallow water. "Hey, little man, look at this guy: Joe Cool."

I acted unimpressed.

"All right, Mr. Cool, let's step it up."

They moved on to the front flip, and Chris taught my brother all he needed to know to master the move. How before you jump, you have to tell yourself I won't jump until I'm committed. How after you jump, you have to throw your arms forward like you're inbounding a basketball. You have to let your arms take your body where your body wants to go, Chris said. Do that, and the rest will follow.

Just before my brother was about to flip, however, a car door slid shut. My brother jumped off the board, but not into the pool.

"Mom?" I said.

"No," my brother said, tilting his head toward the sound. "Just someone with a van, I think."

Chris swung his legs out of the water and ran over to the front fence. "Mom?" he said. "Who's this Mom character?"

The closeness of our apartment hit me in the head. I looked away from the pool to see if I could see the window from where we were.

"Is this Mom person someone we need to worry about?" Chris asked. "She's not a spy, is she?"

"No," my brother said, staring at the water. "She's not here. She doesn't matter."

He stepped on the board again, ready to get back to the flip, but Chris held his hands up. "Whoa. Pump the brakes, sir. What do you mean she doesn't matter? All moms matter."

My brother's face said he wanted to change the subject. "She doesn't know anything," he said. "That's all I meant."

He tried to step to the edge of the board, but Chris grabbed him by the trunks.

"Hey, not so fast. I want to hear more about your mom. I mean, we're friends, right?"

My brother looked down at Chris's hand, holding the butt of his trunks. I knew for a fact he didn't like when other people touched him. He hated shaking strangers' hands, didn't even like hugs from the people he was supposed to love.

"So tell me what's she like. Is she awesome? I bet she's awesome."

My brother tried to pull away from Chris. He twisted

around, but Chris had a Rick-like grip. "She's OK. Please let me go."

"Just OK?" Chris said. He pulled him closer, and my brother almost fell off the board, but Chris steadied him, his hand on my brother's naked side. "No way, this is your mom we're taking about. She's what made you, and you're something special, right?"

My brother grabbed Chris's wrist. "Let me go. I want to get in the pool."

"Hold on," Chris said. He scratched at the bites below his waist, spreading the red around. "So you live with your mom?"

"Yes."

"What about your dad?"

"No."

"No dad?"

"No."

"You don't have a dad?"

"No, I do. He just . . . he—"

"Left?"

"Yes."

"Is he coming back?"

"No. I don't know—"

"So she's by herself? What about suitors?" Chris said. A coy smile wiggled across his face. "Any love interests?"

My brother opened his mouth, stopped, and for a second, nothing came out. "I'm cold," he said. "Let me in the pool."

"You didn't answer me," Chris said.

"Yes I did. Let me go."

"Why won't you tell me? Is it a secret?"

"No," my brother said, raising his voice and squirming more violently. "Let go of me!"

For a flash, faster than my brother's dive, I saw Chris's face go angry. His eyes spiked down in a way we hadn't seen before. But like the dive's splash, the anger quickly disappeared, and Chris's face returned to its calm.

"Oh yeah," he said, releasing my brother's trunks. "Of course. Sorry."

My brother stepped off the diving board. He grabbed his towel from the pool chair and went to the shallow end to dry off.

"Get out of the pool," he said to me.

"What's wrong?" Chris said. "All right, all right. So you don't want to talk about your parents. I get it. But what about what I want? I've got a mom and dad too. C'mon, we can swap war stories."

"Hurry up," my brother told me. "Get your flip-flops."

"Oh, where are you going?" Chris said. "Don't be a couple of babies. The baby bros, everyone!" It was something Rick would have said.

"We have to go," my brother said, and pushed me toward the gate. "There's a lady watching us. We shouldn't be out here."

Chris ran ahead of us and blocked the entrance. "Guys, I apologize. I get it now. I went too far too fast." He stood with his arms crossed. "But I can't let you leave until you forgive me. It wouldn't be right."

"It's fine," my brother said, looking past Chris, to where we wanted to be. "We need to go."

Chris's face twitched, like a bug flew in his ear. He

slapped at the side of his head. "I don't know. That didn't feel right to me. That seem real to you, little man?"

"Don't ask him," my brother said. "He doesn't know what's going on."

"And what is going on?" Chris said.

"You were showing us pool moves."

"But then I ruined it, didn't I? I'm sorry." Chris put his head down. "What about this? What if next time we see each other, I share another secret? It can be anything you want. Another pool move. Something about *my* mom. Anything. I'll even take you somewhere, if that's what you want. Some cool place you've never been."

My brother draped his towel over his head, so I couldn't see his face, so I couldn't tell if he was thinking this last offer through.

"It's fine," he eventually said.

"Are you sure?"

"Yes. You said sorry."

"So we're square?" Chris said. We nodded. "Good."

He stepped aside and I followed my brother out the gate. Chris stayed behind the fence, and I was glad that he did. Though as we made our way around the corner to our building, we heard him call from the pool.

"Think about my offer, Mr. Cool!" Then, "I like that you stood up for yourself. You're on your way!"

I thought that my brother might smile at this, but he didn't. On his face I could still see a hint of blue.

five

THE QUEEN WAS almost late to her own party. The register at work broke and our mother was the only one who knew how to fix it. Ten minutes before people were supposed to show, she burst in the door, ink smudged on her fingers and face. Here she is, I thought, our majesty. Except she didn't look like any of the royal people I'd seen in books or on TV. Her work shirt was untucked and dirty, and instead of a crown, there was the large mound of her yellow hair, frizzled from the summer's humidity. She quickly surveyed the apartment, chewing nervously on a greasy lock. This was our queen.

"Good job, guys," she said. "The place looks good. Now let me go change."

She rushed back to her room and slammed the door, leaving my brother and me bored on the couch. We got on

the floor and had a foot war. I placed the bottoms of my feet against his and we pushed our feet back and forth like they were glued together. When our legs grew tired, my brother drew up a peace treaty that we signed with an imaginary feather pen. Our mother still hadn't come out of her room.

There was a knock at the door and the first thing I thought was Chris. My brother could read my mind. "It's not him," he said. "He wouldn't come up here."

Whoever it was knocked again.

"Maybe he wants to say sorry," I said. "Or maybe we forgot something."

"Maybe," my brother said, with his thinking face on. I could tell he didn't buy my idea, but like me, I think he was picturing what it would look like if Chris were in our apartment.

There was another knock, this one louder, less patient. My brother ran to the door.

It was Sandy and Cornbread. Sandy stood smiling with a cake. Carrot, she said. Your mother's favorite. Cornbread towered behind Sandy, twice her size, holding four boxes of wine, two under each arm. Both of them were wearing what they always wore, jeans and a hunter-green polo shirt from work. They smelled of grease and grass.

"How are my two favorite men?" Sandy said. She pushed her way past us, and Cornbread stooped his head to get in the door. We showed them to the kitchen, and Sandy set the cake on the empty table. She asked where our mother was and we pointed. "Oh, she must be getting pretty," Sandy said, and went down the hall to help her put on the final touches.

Cornbread put the wine on the counter and sat at the kitchen table, drumming his fingers. Like everything else he

touched, the table now looked like it was made for a small kid, the size of the child with the chalk. He tried to make conversation, but we only gave him one-word answers. Yes. No. Fine. When he ran out of questions, my brother and I returned to the couch and listened for our mother coming down the hall. Instead, we heard Cornbread checking the cupboard for cups. A moment later, he came out drinking from a glass dark with wine.

"That looks good," my brother said.

"It is good, but you can't have any." He came over to the couch and told us to scoot over. It was a tight squeeze. Even with his legs bent, Cornbread's knees still came up to my head. He asked if the TV worked and we said no, not really. "Well, we need something to look at."

And like a magic trick, Sandy came out with our mother, the two holding each other at the elbow. Sandy looked the same, face plain, head shaped like a hairnet, but our mother was changed. Her work clothes were gone, and so were the ink smudges. She was wearing a loose summer dress, yellow and flowing, and her wild hair fell completely straight, teasing her bare shoulders. She stepped closer, into the light, and I saw that her eyes looked different too—larger, her lashes longer, like they wanted to reach out and touch me.

"What do you think, boys?" she said.

"You look new," I said, and Cornbread laughed, causing the couch to shake. But I meant what I said. My mother was like a new mother. Bright, beautiful, she belonged to one of the royal families she liked to read about in history books. This was the queen she promised to be.

There was another knock, and Sandy threw her hands up. "Ooh, here they come," she said, and did a little dance to

the door. My brother rolled his eyes and went to the kitchen to grab a glass of mixed milk. But I stayed where I was, marveling at our mother. Her newness. For some reason, it felt wrong to do so, to look for so long. It felt like I was looking at the lady in the encyclopedia, the one who was half naked, half insides—but I couldn't help it.

A few seconds later, Sandy came back with new people, a man and a woman I'd never seen before. The man had his shirt tucked in when he probably shouldn't have. His belly ballooned over his belt like a waist floatie. The woman, less pretty than the witch lady, had brought party hats for everyone, and stuck close to the man until she saw how beautiful my mother was. Once the ladies were talking in a tight triangle, Cornbread got up and started talking to the man, leaving my brother and me alone.

Several more partygoers arrived over the next half hour, all with small presents in hand. I didn't recognize any of these people. They were not from my mother's work, and I had no idea where she had met them, where they had come from. They all waved hello, went to the kitchen, and returned with red plastic cups. The party had begun.

No one was talking to my brother or me, including our mother, so we went to our room. We shut the door behind us and that made things better for a while. But the party's murmur grew with each new guest. Someone brought speakers and a record player. The music went through our room's thin walls like they were made of paper, and the bass rattled our door. My brother said it was like there were zombies out there, pounding for us to let them in. Brains, my brother said. Brains. We made a game out of this, lying there in the

bottom bunk. We listed all the dumb things people did in the zombie films we'd seen with our dad. I said we should avoid shopping malls, which wasn't a problem in our city, since there were none. My brother suggested we hole up in the old people's home, because the zombies would probably come for the elderly last. Yes, I said, they would taste the worst. My brother laughed, said that wherever we go we should stick together. Of course, this was the first thing I thought of, but I didn't say anything because I knew if I really thought about the zombie scenario, I would do what I always did and think about what would happen if only one of us was bitten. What would I do if my brother began to turn? What then?

"It wouldn't matter anyway," he said. "Those movies always end horribly. Just when you think they're in the clear, another zombie appears and ruins everything. The undead mailman pops out of a dumpster."

I wished he would change the subject, but our door still thumped. The party was growing louder. Maybe I could call my dad and file a complaint. Or maybe the smoking lady would, unless she was out there too.

"What if one got into a prison?" my brother said. "All those guys would be eaten alive."

Somebody rapped at the door, making me jump. Sandy poked her head in, and the music followed. "Hey, guys, it's time for cake!" she said.

"Ah!" my brother screamed. "Zombie! Breach! Breach!" He rolled off the bed and grabbed a balled-up sock. "Head shot! Head shot! Shoot to kill!" He threw the sock ball at Sandy, just missing her face.

"Wow," Sandy said. "Well, OK, more for me, I guess."

She shut the door, leaving me to sit in the dark and think about zombies, me getting bitten and my brother being the one who had to put me down.

"I want some cake," I said.

"Are you crazy?" my brother said. "This place is crawling with brain-eaters."

"But I'm hungry," I said, which was true. In our mother's rush to get ready, she had forgotten to make us dinner.

My brother picked up the sock ball. "All right, I'll cover you. But watch out. If you see anybody you know, don't trust them. They're probably a zombie. They probably want your brains."

He opened the door to the loud music, and we pushed our way through a maze of adult legs, some attached to shaking hips. We didn't see any cake, only ironed pants and smooth dresses. Finally, the crowd parted and we could see what was going on. Someone had dragged the square kitchen table into the tiny dining room we never used, along with one chair. A moment later our mother emerged from the living room and sat at the table's only seat. The crowd closed around her. The music was muted and talk dwindled to a murmur. We were waiting.

The lights went off. But the room didn't fall completely dark. A man whose face I couldn't see, but who was wearing jeans, came from the kitchen holding Sandy's carrot cake, now a ball of light. Through a tangle of arms I saw the light make its way to my mother, who sat straight in her chair, head held high, like a queen perched on her throne.

The man set the cake in front of my mother, so that the spotlight was on her now. He started to sing in a low, even tone. I wanted to see who this person was, this man in jeans

with his shirt tucked in, but no belt. We pushed our way closer to the front, fighting through the drone of all the zombies. We finally made it to the table as the song wound down, but the singing man was nowhere to be seen. He must have slinked off into the darkness. Our mother was visible, though, and when she saw her two boys she raised her cup and nodded, an empty gesture to her loyal subjects.

The song ended, and someone said make a wish. My mother leaned over the cake. "I can't do this all by myself," she said. Sandy had used a candle for each year, instead of two wax numbers. "I need some help."

I felt my brother pulling away from me, drifting from the crowd to help my mother. Yes, I thought, it should be him. He's the stronger one, the one better at blowing up balloons. But before he made it to her side, another figure stepped into the light. It was the singing man. I could see the waist of his jeans floating by the candlelight, flickering by my mother's face. Though it wasn't until he bent down, grinned in the orange light, that I saw who it really was. That tan face. Those big teeth. Rick.

He put his hand on my mother's shoulder. "Don't worry, little lady, I'm real good at putting out fires." He poked my mother in her ribs, and her arm flew out, hitting my brother.

"Oh, I'm sorry. I didn't see you there," she said. "Would you like to help?"

My brother didn't answer. He was staring at the burning candles, watching their shape change with every breath. He put his hand over the fire, and slowly lowered it until the flame kissed his flesh.

Rick slapped my brother's hand away from the cake. "What are you doing, moron? Trying to kill yourself?"

My brother studied the palm he let burn.

"Relax," our mother said. She shifted in her seat so she was facing my brother. "You can help too, if you want. You and your brother."

"Yeah, good idea," Rick said. "For once the world could use your hot hair." He patted my brother on the back and I saw my brother's face immediately change.

"Don't touch me," he said. He blew on his burned hand, and looked at our mother. "Why would I want to help you?" he said. "Rick's a jerk. Why would I want to help a jerk?"

"Hey," our mother said, and the rest of the room went quiet, though none of the zombies moved.

"It's fine," Rick said. "I've been called worse. By worse." A few zombies chuckled, and my mother glanced around the room uneasily.

"You don't have to help," she said, "if you don't want to. You can just stand there and be quiet."

"I don't want to stand here. I don't even want to be here. Why can't we go to our dad's or something?"

Our mother sighed. Rick turned to one of the zombies to make what he must've thought would be an unheard remark. "Boy wants to run out on his mother. Must get that from the old man."

And true enough, my mother didn't hear Rick's comment. But my brother did. I saw his face, burning orange, change into a new kind of anger. Then he said something he'd never said before.

He said, "Hey, Rick, why don't you go to hell. Asshole."

My mother exploded from the table, knocking over her

cup of wine. "What did you just say?" She pushed Rick out of the way and grabbed my brother out of the crowd, dragged him into the hall. She must have not wanted everyone to see her scold my brother, though with the music off and the zombies silent, we could hear everything. Her hand smacking my brother's butt. Her saying, Look at me. Look at me. If you want to be rude, be rude from your room. My brother said fine. He would. He didn't want any stupid cake. What kind of cake was carrot cake anyway? A cake with a vegetable in it? Stupid. A second later we heard the bedroom door slam. My mother returned, apologized to Rick and the rest of the zombies. He's just mad about the pool or something, she said, and waved my brother's anger away like it was a housefly.

"That's no excuse," Rick said. "That boy needs to learn some manners."

My mother took her seat and looked around nervously until someone yelled for her to blow out the candles before the apartment burned down.

"Yeah," another zombie droned, "we want food!"

Rick got on his knees so he was level with my mother. He looked her in the eyes. "Go on," he said. "This is your birthday. Don't let anyone spoil it."

My mother took a breath. Rick put his hand on hers and they looked at each other the same way they had at the golf course. Like they had their own secret.

"Ready?" Rick said. "Make a wish."

My mother bent over the cake. I saw her thoughts go far away as she stared into the fire and visualized whatever it was she most wanted. She and Rick closed their eyes. They

opened their mouths and blew, their streams of air rushing the candles until every flame turned into smoke.

I returned to my room. When I opened the door, the lights were still off, but I could feel my brother's presence. He was seething on the bottom bunk.

"Leave me alone," he said, but I didn't move. I stood in the doorway, wanting to help, to cheer him up. "Didn't you hear me?" he said. "Get out of here." He threw something at the door, not soft like the sock ball. It clacked against the wall, and I picked it up off the floor. It was a toy man, one of the good guys. He told me to leave again, and this time I listened. But as I left I heard my brother talking to himself.

He said, "I hate him."

My mother opened her presents while Cornbread and Sandy passed around plates of cake. All of the gifts were bottles of booze, some guy's funny idea he got everyone to agree to. I took my cake to the sliding glass door, where it was just me. I had never had carrot cake before and didn't expect the inside to be the same color as the rust on our van. After forking the cake around and deciding I wouldn't like it, I stared out the door, thinking about the pool, Chris, the woods. I didn't have a particular thought, just a sinking feeling, like I got when we used to take trips to the lake. Back when we were a whole family, our dad would borrow a boat and we would drive it out to the middle of the lake and cut the engine. This was the only time we escaped Leavenworth. My brother and I would put on life vests and swim out while my

dad drank beer, argued with my mother. My brother would swim around, pretending to be an aquatic assassin, while I floated in the brown water, afraid to venture too far from the boat. I would lie on my back and stare at the sky, its gray as endless as the water around me, until the sinking feeling crept in. And in the middle of the lake, there were no sounds to comfort me, nothing except the water lapping in my ears. I realized I could stay out here all night and the waves would never stop lapping. I could take my vest off and sink to the bottom, the gray sky turning into a cold black, and still the lapping. My family would return to shore, hitch the boat to the van, and drive the long distance home. They would realize they had forgotten something, scratching their chins until my mother gasped when she realized what was missing. Me. They would speed back, search the spot I was last seen, but they wouldn't find me. All they would find was the lapping, the sound of the big scary world, the sound of me left behind, forgotten.

"I think it's time for bed," someone said. I looked up and saw that it was Sandy, standing above me with her hand out. She took my plate of cake and helped me up. "Pretty soon it won't be pretty."

I had no idea how much time had passed. The party had thinned, but there were still strange adults everywhere—sitting on the couch, standing by the bookcase, falling into each other with their words. I glanced around for people I knew. Cornbread had apparently left. My mother was nowhere I could see. Two men danced to a slow song and everyone laughed. One of the men grabbed the other man's butt and let out a scream. I looked down at my feet. I told myself I

could always count on my feet. I know these feet. These feet are familiar.

Sandy pushed me through the crowd. When we made it into the dim border of the hallway, I heard something familiar. It was my mother's voice. I stopped.

"I want to say good night," I said.

"Yes," Sandy said. "I think she might like that."

She guided me to our tiny dining room, where we had swarmed to sing "Happy Birthday." My mother was still sitting in her chair. There were three men standing over her, their shirts tucked under their fat belts. None of them were Rick, I saw, and I smiled. Sandy told me to go on, and I pushed through the men's legs, heavy as church doors. Hey, one man said. Watch it. My mother had her head down, slouched, and was laughing into her cup. She sloshed around whatever was left before gulping it down. The men kept talking. One cleared his throat, lifted his pants by his belt buckle. No one saw me.

I tapped my mother on her knee. Her dress was even softer than it looked. "Mom," I said.

Her eyes went big. They belonged to a pretty cartoon. "Hey! There you are!"

"I'm going to bed," I said.

One man said something and another laughed. My mother shooed them away. She put her arm around my waist, pulled me into her. "Was it a good time tonight?" she said, her thick breath lingering on my face. "Yeah, it was, wasn't it? I just wish your brother hadn't done what he did. You're not mad that Rick came, are you?"

I thought about it. I wasn't mad that he came; I was just

happier when he wasn't around. Though if it made my brother mad, I told myself that it should make me mad too. Finally I shrugged.

"Good," she said. "Good, good, good. Because I'm trying my best. I really am." She put her hand to my cheek and rubbed my ear. "He's not going to replace anyone."

I nodded again and looked at my feet. The summer had just begun, but sandal tan lines were already starting to form. A line of white surrounded by light brown started at my big toe, climbed the face of my foot, and forked into two faint paths. I knew as the summer wore on and the sun grew warmer, the contrast would strengthen. Soon the difference between the brown and white would be much sharper, the choices of the paths that much clearer.

"Hey," my mother said. "Hey, look at me. Look at your mother." She raised my head with her hand, and I thought of Chris. "You know, you were God's best surprise? Did I ever tell you that?" She grabbed my cheeks, brought me close, and gave me a kiss on the lips. Longer, wetter than usual. "Your dad and I, we didn't know you were coming, but we're both glad that you did."

She licked her thumb and wiped my lips. I could feel the red on my mouth.

"OK," Sandy said. "Visiting hours are over."

My mother laughed, and I saw where the wine had stained her teeth. "Uh-oh, you better listen to the guard here. For your own safety."

As Sandy pulled me away, my mother squeezed my hand a final time, her short fingers the same as mine.

"Good night," she said. "Good night, my cute boy."

————

I awoke from a pool dream. In the dream someone had taken my dad's favorite tank top and thrown it into the pool. Why don't you go get it, Dad? I asked. Just go get it. My dad chewed on the tips of his fingers before revealing that, the funny thing was, he never learned to swim. I reminded him about the lake and he said yes, but I never go in. I just drink beer. I got on the diving board and looked around. Where my brother was I did not know. He should be here. Where is he? He's playing in the woods, my dad said. Get the shirt and we'll go find him. Even in the dream I knew this was not a good thing. But it was a dream and I was not as scared. Standing on the diving board, I felt I belonged. I could live in the blue if I wanted, swim to any deep. I dove in. It was as easy as I thought it would be. The water didn't push back against me. It didn't pull me to the top, squeeze my lungs. I cut to the bottom, and when I opened my eyes, they didn't burn. I grabbed my dad's shirt and even though I knew it should have been heavy with water, it wasn't. I swam back up, effortlessly, and the sun shone around me, spotlighting the boy who could do anything.

I woke up laughing. The confidence from the dream carried over. I sat up in bed, fully alert, sure I was the best swimmer around. I threw the covers off and stood up, wet with sweat. But the wet didn't worry me. It made sense. I was a professional pool person. I was someone who wanted to be wet. Unlike others, I was better then.

I opened our bedroom door before I realized I was shirt-less. I didn't remember taking off my shirt before bed, but I took that as a sign. I stepped out and looked down our apartment hall. My mother's door was open, which it never was

when she slept. Her alarm flashed its red numbers at me, as if while I slept we'd lost power. As if a storm had passed unnoticed.

I snuck down the hall to peep into my mother's room, to see if she was sick. Maybe that's why she left the door open, in case she had to run to the bathroom and throw up the carrot cake. Her body wasn't there, though, no lumps in the covers.

I returned down the hall, curious. Maybe my mother fell asleep on the couch, like my dad had. Maybe I could get a good look at her while she slept. Maybe she had a secret mark too, something that would reveal itself to me. Would she still be wearing makeup, or was that something she washed off before bed? Would her hair be back to its old self, or would silently I feel its new soft?

I walked faster down the hall and peeked around the corner, eager to catch my mother, to see what she was like now. But what I saw was two people on the couch. My mother was there, yes, but she was not alone: Rick was there too, his hand on my mother's bare leg, a box of wine between them.

My mother sat in her bra. The top of her dress was pulled down to her waist.

"I can't," she said. "They're right around the corner."

She shivered, and Rick put his arm around her, brought her to him. "Is that it?" he said, and kissed her on the cheek. "Or is it something else?" He worked a finger under my mother's bra strap, teased it from her shoulder. "I think you're just not sure. I think that's what it is. And I get that. I do. Shit, I know what it's like to be alone." He turned two of his fingers into legs and walked them down my mother's thin arm. "But," he said, "I also think you owe it to yourself. Isn't that what you've been saying?"

He moved his hand farther up my mother's leg, until his arm disappeared completely beneath her dress.

"Stop," my mother said. "Rick," she said, "quit." But Rick didn't quit. He opened his mouth on my mother's shoulder, nipping at her with his teeth, and eventually my mother gave in. She leaned back into the couch and sighed, and Rick moved his face to my mother's, his back swallowing hers, eclipsing her body. I stood there and watched. I listened to them breathe through their noses, moan through shut mouths. I wanted to leave, but I also wanted to stay.

Rick pulled back and said something to my mother, gestured to someplace with his head. I could only see my mother's face. It moved side to side to say no, though it did so with a slight smile. "C'mon," Rick said. "I'll be real quiet. They won't hear a thing."

I didn't hear my mother answer him, but I imagined her shaking her head, saying no, this is not what I want.

"Wait, I've got it," Rick said. He stood up, still holding on to my mother's hand. "I'll grab that fan. It's so damn loud, it'll drown out anything."

And before my mother could say anything, he hopped across the room, desperately searching behind the TV for the fan's plug. He was so excited, so focused on the fan, he wasn't even thinking about my mother, who I could see for the first time since Rick had smothered her with his back. Now I could see everything. I saw the red on my mother's neck and shoulders where Rick's mouth had gone. I saw where Rick had pushed up the side of her dress, where he had walked his hard hand up her pale leg. And when I looked closely, as Rick finally found the plug and the room went

silent, I saw where my mother's bra had fallen. I saw the pink of her breast.

I looked away. I looked at my hand, which had been pressed against the back of the bookcase. It was covered in dust. Thick dust. I had missed this spot earlier in my cleaning. It hadn't been touched in months. I held my hand up to my face, this hand that didn't look like my own. I spread my fingers wide. I imagined my hands were webbed flippers, excellent for swimming. But unlike fish flippers, I could see through this webbing, and when I did, I saw my mother staring directly at me, her head tilted like our once-living dog. Her arm had fallen, revealing the rest of her breast. But she didn't cover herself up. And she didn't yell at me, or point above my head and mouth, Go to your room. This isn't a place you should be. Her neck kept crooked, and she looked right at me, through me, as if I wasn't there.

Finally, she shook her head, slowly, and without blinking. I turned and ran back to my room. I got in bed with my brother, who for once, and the one time I wished that he was, wasn't snoring. I could hear anything, everything. The apartment was all quiet. I lay there and I waited. I waited for my mother to walk back, to flip on the hall light, the yellow shining through our door's crack, forming a straight-edged capital C. I waited for the door to creak open, for my mother to say, hey, we need to talk. She would walk me to the bathroom and sit me in the bathtub, where I went when I was in the wrong. I would sit there, staring at the bath faucet, awaiting my execution. A moment later the lights would flicker in our bedroom, and that's how my brother would know I was a goner.

I waited for this all to happen. I waited in the dark. I put my brother's arm around me, my head on his chest, and waited. I waited and I waited, until dreams started to sneak into my head. I waited and waited, but my mother never came.

six

OUR DAD PICKED US UP the following morning. He actually
came to our door in uniform, and with a small box in hand.
He asked if our mother was around, but true to her word to
Rick, she was already at work.

I sat in the back of the cruiser, where the criminals went,
with my bag, which wasn't zipped up all the way. There was
a little hole at the end that gave the bag a mouth, and in my
mind I turned the bag into a person, someone I could talk
to. I asked the bag what was in the box my dad had brought.
Was it a gift? The bag didn't know, nor did it know why my
dad had come up and knocked, and not just waited outside,
like he normally did.

I thought about these questions until we passed a prison.
It hit me. My mother had told on me. She'd told him what I
had seen the night before, how I was up late spying on people
again. That was why he was here, to take me in. Don't be an

idiot, the bag said. He's got bigger fish to fry. There's a murderer on the loose. But as we drove around in the police cruiser, I couldn't help but feel like the lake again. I thought of all the things I was guilty of: two counts of spying, talking to a stranger, lying to my mother.

Oh, c'mon, the bag said. No one cares about that. You haven't done anything really wrong. Have you?

As we coasted by the second of three prisons we would pass driving through the city, I put my fingers in the wire screen behind the front seats, the barrier that separated the cops from the criminals, me from my brother and my dad. My dad's arm stretched across the passenger's seat headrest, a habit he picked up when he used to drive our family around. I shook the screen. I was the Stranger and my dad was the sheriff, my brother his deputy. I put my mouth right behind my dad's head, so close I could almost kiss him, so close that my breath brushed his hair. Hey, I whispered. Let me out. Let me out of here.

We didn't grill out that night. We went to my favorite fast-food restaurant, the one that served square burgers and soft-serve ice cream. The lobby was full of large men in prison-guard khaki who had just gotten off work. They stood in line, thumbs in pockets. There were also a few big-bellied men in dirty jeans—mechanics, struggling farmers. No matter who they were or what they did, my dad knew all of them. And they all knew my dad. Sometimes when we were in a crowded place like this, my brother and I would make bets on how long it would take before a stranger started a serious talk with our dad. But the time was never over thirty seconds and the game quickly lost the little fun it began with.

Today it didn't take long. The man in front of us turned and did a double take when he saw our dad. He was a younger man, with a small body and eyes as big as a squirrel's.

"How are you doing, sir?" the man said.

"Fine, Jason."

"Hey, can I talk to you about something, sir? Sue's got this lawyer, see . . . do you think we could . . ."

My dad sighed through his nose and scratched his mustache. He had a way of not letting his face change when he was annoyed with the public. I tried the same when dealing with my brother, but always broke down.

My dad turned to us. "You two know what you want?" he said. He gave my brother some money. "Order me whatever you get. Jason, let's warm up the table."

We stood in line and watched our dad lead the young man to a booth by a trash can. We didn't listen to what they were saying, because we knew the deal. Jason had done something stupid and now wanted our dad's help in fixing it.

My brother and I ordered our food, and the cashier gave us a number. Our dad was still talking to Jason, so we picked another booth by a window. We filled paper condiment cups with pools of ketchup for our fries to dive in. We set the table with yellow napkins and extra salt packets for our dad. We were proud and organized, but soon grew bored. We used the table as a football field and a salt packet as a football. By the time our dad came back, we still had no food and the table was a mess.

"Sit by your brother, son," my dad said to my brother.

"What did that guy want?"

"None of our business."

"Did he ask you about the prisoner?"

"He did."

"What'd you tell him?"

"I told him we're going to catch him."

"We are?" I said.

"Of course we are. We're the good guys, aren't we?"

"Yeah," my brother said.

"Yeah!" I said, a little too loudly.

My dad gave me a knowing squint, winked, and sat up a little straighter. I smiled back and sat on my feet, trying to be as tall as him.

"Find him yet?" a man said. Where he had come from I hadn't seen. He was an older man, wide in overalls, and with a gray beard down to his chest. I had seen him before and never liked him. He always talked to my dad with fake respect, like how my brother treated me the time I got to rule the apartment for a day as the result of a bet.

"Hi, Wayne," my dad said.

"You talk to his family?"

"Not yet."

"No?" Wayne took a sip from his gigantic chocolate milk shake, rested the cup on his stomach. "Well, I hope you hurry. You know, for your own sake. I mean, aren't you worried?"

"Nope," my dad said. "Not at all. There's nothing to worry about, right, boys?"

We nodded. Our dad was going to catch him. That was that.

"Oh, good," Wayne said. "That's real good." He shook his shake, loudly slurped what was left. "But, um, don't you think you should be worried? At least a little? I mean, if *I* was you, if I was the one—"

"Wayne, it's not a big deal. Escapes happen. Criminals get out."

"Yeah," Wayne said, "but not ones from around here." He looked around, as if the Stranger might be watching him. "Not ones everybody remembers."

"OK," my dad said. "We're trying to eat here."

Wayne laughed. Eat? Eat what? He didn't see nothing to eat. "You know, I've been around this city a long time," he said, leaning on our booth, addressing my brother and me. "I remember when your dad first showed up, just a young pup. A young pup in love. Puppy love," Wayne said, and wheezed at his own joke. "What I'm trying to say is that I know this city. I know how it works. And I'm telling you if you get this man before anything bad happens, you'll be chief in no time."

Yes. Chief. Our dad would be chief. The good guys would prevail.

"On the other hand, if you don't catch him, well, I guess you can always join the Army." I thought this was a joke too, and that Wayne would wheeze some more, but he didn't.

"All right, Wayne. That's fine."

"I'm just saying, it's one thing to say, it's another to do."

"I hear you. And we'll get him."

" 'We'? Ain't no 'we.' That's what I'm trying to tell you. You gotta do this. You do. Nobody cares about Tony or that Alan fellow. All eyes are on you."

"Wayne."

"Lives are on the line. Yours and your boys'."

"All right."

"You think they're safe, but I don't know. I don't know that anybody's safe. Hell, what about Aggie?"

My dad pounded the table.

"Wayne!"

The entire restaurant went quiet. Everyone stared at my dad, whose face turned red, like he'd held his breath too long underwater.

"Listen," he said, "my family is none of your business. We'll catch him, OK? Now please leave me and my boys alone."

Wayne put his hands up. "Hey, got it. Sorry, sorry. Didn't mean to disturb."

He waddled out the door and got in his big truck. The rest of the restaurant stopped staring.

"You should have told that guy to shut up," my brother said.

My dad put his head down, like he was looking through the table to see if his shoes were tied, to make sure everything was all right down there.

"We don't talk like that."

"Why not, he deserved it."

The cashier came to our table.

"I've been calling your number," she said, putting our trays down. "I've been calling your number and you never came."

My dad didn't look at her. I wondered if this would be one of those nights where he didn't talk to us, where he just popped in a movie and told us to be quiet.

"Make it to go," he said.

On the way home we stopped by the video store. Our dad stayed in the car while my brother and I ran in. The witch

lady was working and she gave us a big bad-toothed smile. We waved at her, but she stared above our heads like there was someone lurking behind us. We quickly moved into the horror section, where a short man with a buzzed head and a patchy beard stood in the way of the movies we wanted. The man thumbed a movie with a bikini-clad space alien on the cover. My brother said excuse me.

"You're excused," the man said. He looked us over, head to toe. "This a place for boys?" We tried to ignore him, his sweat-stained undershirt, his sour smell. My brother grabbed two movies without reading their summaries and pulled me from the aisle to the front counter. The witch lady looked at the movies, then out the store window, where the cruiser idled in the dark. She asked how our dad was doing, and what our plans were for the night. We said we were going to watch these movies with our dad, and would she mind hurrying? She pushed our change back. That sounds like a good time, she said. Enjoy it while it lasts. OK, we said, and we left.

Our dad didn't go out that night. We watched the first movie and I made it all the way through, head on his chest. The movie featured a pack of dogs that turned into unstoppable killers after drinking from a creek outside a small town's chemical plant. My dad said something about the environment, but the message was lost on me. After it ended, my dad stayed in his spot on the floor. He didn't get up and say it was time for bed, then change out of his tank top while we slow-marched to the basement. Instead, he said, "Who's up for another one?"

My brother was already walking to the basement door, and the question hit him in the back of the head. "Really?"

"Don't look so shocked, boys. Grab the pork rinds."

My brother ran into the kitchen, slid on his socks across the linoleum floor. He tossed the bag to my dad and we started the second film, *Lieutenant Lazarus*, about an Army man who died in the line of duty, only to be brought back to life by his wife, an amateur Wiccan, to fight and love again. I knew I wouldn't last past half an hour. I might see Lazarus die and be revived, but not the climax. I would miss the lessons learned.

An explosion woke me. I was somehow on the couch with my brother, lying head-to-toe, feet in each other's face. My brother snored. I did not remember moving or being moved. My dad was on the floor, sitting upright, the only one still watching the movie. It must have been near the end. Flames ate a bad guy's fort, coloring the screen orange from corner to corner. The screen was like the fireplace at our old house. It felt like Christmas and I did not want to move. When the credits came, my dad didn't get up or fast-forward to the end to make sure there were no bonus scenes hinting at a possible sequel. The name of every person who worked on the movie rolled by, one after the other, and there were no hidden scenes, no meanings tucked away.

The screen went black and my dad didn't move. My eyes adjusted and I could tell the difference between this black, where the film was still playing but had nothing to show, and the set's real black, when the TV was powered down or unplugged.

I slid off the couch and crawled to my dad.

"Are you spying on people again?" he said. I leaned against his shoulder and wondered how much he remembered from the other night. If I said the name Chris, would it mean anything?

My dad stared at the blank set. "Who's this guy your mother's seeing?" he said. He put his hand to the fake-black screen, and I could hear the pop of the TV's static. I knew he was talking about Rick, but I didn't want to say his name. "When I patrol late at night, I always swing by your guys' apartment. Sometimes I just sit there in the parking lot, watching, making sure everything's OK."

He didn't have to say the rest. I pictured my dad in the parking lot the night before, the night of the party. I saw Rick stumble out of our building in the dark, my mother close behind. I saw her walk him to his car, give him a kiss good night, as wet as the one she gave me. I saw my dad see all of this.

"Don't tell her," my dad said, "but sometimes I can't take the way your mother looks at me." He put his head on mine and I could taste his stale breath, battered with cheap beer. He must have started drinking as soon as my brother and I fell asleep.

"I don't like being in trouble either," I said.

"Well then, I guess we better change our ways," my dad said. "Otherwise we're no better than Lieutenant Lazarus, are we?"

I told him no, I guess not.

"It's funny, I kinda learned something from that stupid movie."

"What happened to him?"

My dad put his warm hand on my cold neck. "We'll find out tomorrow. Time for bed." He ejected the tape and pushed me toward the basement door.

"Are you going out?"

My dad kissed the top of my head. "Good night, you ghoul."

My brother wasn't asleep when I slid into bed. He couldn't, he said. He had Lazarus swimming laps in his brain.

"There was a spider," he said. "When I came downstairs. Right on my pillow."

"Did you kill it?"

I knew the answer was no. He hated bugs, so he wouldn't come close to touching it, not even through a shoe. He would have waited until the spider walked away. He would have crawled into bed and shut his eyes, hoping for sleep. But every time the sheet bristled his leg, he would think it was a spider. That's why he was still awake.

"Let's watch the rest of the movie," he said.

"We can't. Dad's gone."

"We can. Dad's gone."

He rolled over and turned on the lamp. "Fine, you can stay down here with the spiders."

He left me with the lamp, and I might have stayed down there if the biggest spider I'd ever seen hadn't crawled across the ceiling, right above our bed. I didn't bother closing my eyes, waiting for the spider to drop down a thread of web and land on my face. I ran upstairs to our empty living room, then up to my dad's room. The light was on but my dad was gone. My brother was rummaging through the trash on his dresser.

"How do you know it's in here?" I asked.

"Because it wasn't by the TV. And because this is the only room we're not allowed in."

As I stood in the doorway, I was very aware that the last time I'd been here, my dad had yelled at me. To never come back. This, shortly after he moved in. The first weekend my brother and I visited, when the basement was stacked with boxes and there was no bed for boys to sleep in. Our dad had gone out that night to have a few beers, to get a few buddies off his back. It would only be an hour or two, he told us, and set out pillows and sheets on the couch and floor. He left alone and returned otherwise. The next morning I snuck in after a bath, searching for a comb, and surprised a blob of blankets moving in unison. The hallway threw light on the headboard and a woman sighed a soft, spent breath. My dad's head emerged from the blob, his hair twisted and his face flushed. Get the hell out, he said. Don't ever come back.

"C'mon," I said. "It's not here."

"Maybe it's hidden," my brother said.

He opened a drawer, another, and combed through my dad's T-shirts and underwear. Nothing. He looked under the bed, felt under the mattress.

"Why would he hide it like this?" I said.

"Because he doesn't want it to hurt anyone," my brother said. "Duh."

I opened my mouth, but couldn't think of anything to say. It felt like we were talking about two different things, like my brother was after something other than the movie, though I couldn't imagine what.

I watched him wander to the closet, stand before its

closed doors like they were the entrance to a forbidden temple. He slowly slid one open. Nothing happened. There were no traps or poisonous darts. There were my dad's uniforms. There were dress shirts and a tangle of ties, none of which I'd ever seen him wear. My brother pushed the shirts apart. He got on his knees and picked through a pile of shoes.

"Check up top," I said. Above the hangers sat something shiny, though I couldn't tell what.

"Help me get it," my brother said. I shook my head. When my dad asked if I'd kept my promise, I wanted to answer him honestly.

My brother called me a baby, and removed the fan resting on a dining chair borrowed from downstairs. He dragged the chair to the closet, and in an instant was back on the floor, holding a metal box, the temple's long-lost treasure.

"Don't open it," I said. "That looks private."

"Not private," my brother said. "Secret."

The lid opened with a click, and I watched my brother's face change from wonder to something else.

"Found it," he said, and he held up a tape. I turned and ran downstairs, now that the search was over, just in case our dad returned. A moment later, my brother came downstairs, slowly.

"Hurry," I said.

"Relax. You know Dad."

He turned on the TV and put the tape in the VCR. A triangle appeared when he hit play, floating in a pool of blue. Then a person. No FBI warning. No rating or warning about the content to come.

"What is this?" I said.

"I don't know," my brother said. "It didn't say."

"What do you mean—"

A woman sat in a chair. Gagged but not blindfolded. Behind her a gray wall. A basement. Her wide eyes watched something off screen. Her face was something of shock and fear. Of begging and sorrow. Her body twisted, but was wrapped in rope. Her legs tied down, knotted together. All this and the hum of the room. No songs or effects. There was only what was real. A man appeared on screen, his back to the camera. Jeans and a T-shirt. Something in his hand. He took the gag out of the woman's mouth and let her scream. Until her voice grew to nothing, until she realized it was pointless. The man disappeared from the screen.

"You know what to say," he said, off camera. The woman didn't say anything. She put her head down and shook with tears. The camera zoomed in on the woman's face. She was young, not much older than a girl. The man backed the zoom out a bit, so we could see the woman's entire head, the bubble of space around her. We saw her head thrash. We saw her eyes beg. But she didn't speak, except to whisper please.

The screen went black, and I thought the movie was over. But it was just the man passing through the frame, standing in front of the woman before moving to the side, remembering that he wanted everyone to see. He put something to the woman's head. A toy gun. A real gun. The woman screamed please, she loved him. She wouldn't tell anyone. The man clicked off the safety and the woman shut her eyes impossibly tight.

"Go ahead," the man said. "Tell them why."

The woman put her head down. The man's voice was gravelly, strangely calm. He grabbed her by her hair, slowly tilted her head back.

"It's OK," he said. "I've already forgiven you. But you need to tell them. They need to understand that you deserve this."

The woman begged. Her brain wouldn't let her say anything but please. The man's hand combed her hair. He said it was OK. She didn't have to talk if she didn't want to.

The man put the gun to her head and, before I could shut my eyes, he fired.

The woman's body slumped limp. For a moment, the man simply stood there, staring with awe at what he'd done. The movie did not cut away. The camera would not move. The man touched the woman's shattered head. He rubbed the blood between his fingers, on his clothes. He removed the camera from its tripod and made us watch as he untied the woman and let her fall to the floor. The camera marveled at how lifeless something living could become. I felt sick. I tried to tell my brother to stop the tape, but the man started talking. He said things that didn't make sense. I didn't know this woman, he said, and zoomed in on her broken face, the dark pool it was drowned in. I didn't know her and she didn't know me. He said, Nobody knows anybody, and if you think you do, this is what you get. He grabbed her soaked hair and pushed the camera into her face. He zoomed in, tighter and tighter, closer and closer, until there was nothing but her big dead eye.

Do you know me? the man said. If you did, would you have done what you did? Would I be able to do this?

He shot her again. The woman's eye went a thousand directions.

This is what happens, the man said. Don't worry waiting. This is what we're all gonna get.

Then the screen went black, and there was nothing.

My brother wouldn't eject the tape. He sat on his knees, frozen. The TV was black, but I still saw the tape's images, over and over. Get it out of there, I tried to tell him, but a sob was stuck in my throat, hung there fat and dry. The tape wasn't going anywhere. It was here forever.

Who knows how long we would have stayed there if our dad hadn't come home. The cruiser's headlights washed over the front-door window, thawing out my brother. Without a word he ejected the tape and sprinted upstairs, returning it and the cursed box it came in. He flew back down the stairs and into the basement, forgetting that I was frozen too, so that when my dad came in, there I was, still sitting on the floor.

"I thought we had a deal," he said.

"I can't sleep."

He shook his head. "It's the movie, isn't it?"

My dad bent down and picked me up like I was nothing. He carried me downstairs, into the black of the basement, and tucked me in next to my brother, pretending to sleep.

"Don't worry," my dad said, "there's no such thing as a Lazarus. No one dead like that is ever coming back."

He started up the stairs and I tried to call after him.

"Dad," I said. But nothing more.

I rolled over and inched as close as I could to my brother, listening for his heartbeat in the dark.

seven

THE NEXT MORNING our mother picked us up for church again. When our dad answered the door, the sun was behind him, and he was wearing a new polo. It fit his arms well, but was too wide around the body. From the side he looked big and fit, but from the front a bit like a kid in his older brother's shirt.

He stepped to the side and told my mother to come in. "They're not ready," he said, and the entrance hall's linoleum creaked as my mother walked in, arms crossed like she forgot her jacket. She raised her shades and her face looked tired, her makeup faded.

"What are you watching?" she said.

"I don't know," I said as Lieutenant Lazarus mowed down a team of Soviets. My dad had put the tape in first thing this morning, and although I didn't want to watch the rest, I also didn't want to stare at a blank screen. Lazarus popped open

a Russian's skull like a can of cat food, started gnawing on his brain. He was a cannibal now. One of the ways his witch bride got the spell wrong.

My mom stopped the tape. "Where's your brother?"

I told her I didn't know that, either. I didn't tell her that he was still in bed, that he hadn't moved since last night. I'd wanted to stay with him, but as soon as I woke up he told me one of us needed to be upstairs.

My dad put the news on.

"Have you heard anything more about that guy?" my mother said, whispering too loudly.

"We've got a couple of ideas," my dad said. "It's not a big deal."

"A friend at work said his family still lives around here. Is that true?"

"A friend at work," my dad repeated. "Huh."

I turned from the TV and looked at my mom, who was picking at her hangnails, one of her bad habits she could never break. "Yes," she said. "Cornbread, I think it was."

"Right," my dad said. "Cornbread. Well, your friend is right. He still has family. Tony's already talked to them, but the Chief wants me to head out there today."

There was a short silence as the news went to the weather. I followed the weather report, waiting for the woman to tell me what today and tomorrow would be like.

"Anyway," my mother said, "thanks again for the phone."

"What phone?" I said.

"Your dad bought us a new phone. Dropped it off last night. Cordless, like something from the future."

"You're welcome," my dad said, mouth full of eggs. "Sorry I interrupted."

That's where he went. Why he didn't come home smelling like strawberries.

"Hey," my mother said, and I heard my dad drop his fork
on his empty plate. "Is everything OK?"

A graphic came on the TV. Five columns of clear skies, a
large orange ball in front of a pool of blue.

"Of course," my dad said. "You and your friend have nothing to worry about."

On the way home after church, my mother kept the radio
off. My brother sat up front, but still wasn't talking. Van
noises filled the void. Each sound was a symptom of the van's
larger illness, my mother said. The whining serpentine belt.
The thundering muffler. All point to old age, she said. All
hint that the van's best days are behind it.

At Eisenhower and Main, the vehicle idled oddly. My
mother petted the steering wheel. "I'll tell you guys, if I
found a way to escape this place, if I stumbled into some
money or something, I'd pack my bags and go right back to
school. You wouldn't catch me lurking around."

My mother let herself smile. I had never seen a college,
but I pictured my mother at my school, walking around,
hair bobbing, encyclopedia clutched to her chest.

"Of course, you guys would come with me. You know that,
right?"

I nodded my head. She turned on the radio. Over the
music, I could hear the van's engine ticking away.

We went to the pool every day that week, but we never saw
Chris. Or the smoking lady. We were careful to sneak out
each morning, sneak in each afternoon. When we left the
apartment, we sniffed the air for cigarettes, then poked our

eyes into the hallway, slicing the pie. The smoking lady was never there, though the hall still smelled of smoke. It became clear that our mother never checked with the smoking lady, to see how we were doing, or she did and the smoking lady lied and said we were good, then went back to sleeping or watching TV or whatever it was she did when she wasn't smoking. Either way, no one was watching my brother and me. Either way, we could do whatever we wanted.

Our dad had to work that Friday night, so instead of going to his duplex we went to work with our mother. There was something about the weekend, she said, that she didn't want us home alone. I thought her worry might have to do with the full moon floating in the sky, beaming like a silver coin, or the distant way my brother had been behaving.

At night we weren't allowed to explore the course like during the day. We had to stay indoors, which was incredibly boring. The cafeteria was closed, so Sandy was gone, as was Cornbread. There was just our mom, leaning against the counter in the pro shop, staring off into space, dreaming of what, I did not know.

When Rick showed, she perked up. He brought two greasy bags of food, one for him, one for her, none for us. Sorry, Rick said, I thought the mice were away. My mother took some change from the register and gave it to us for the vending machine. Make sure you each get something sweet, she said. Rick slid her a burger and pinched her by the elbow. He said, Don't mind if I do.

The vending machine was downstairs, next to the door that led to the golf cart garage, which was locked at night. The entire way down my brother mumbled mean things about Rick. Things like *God I hate that guy* and *Why can't he just*

die? I thought it would have been a perfect time for the candy bar my brother selected to fail to fall, to hang on its hook and refuse to dive. But the bar fell no problem, and when my brother handed me the leftover change, I was a nickel short of all the things I wanted.

Neither of us wanted to go back upstairs. Neither of us wanted to see our mother with Rick, even if it was just eating fries, or straightening the shop for the five customers who came at night after hitting a bucket at the driving range. My brother tried the garage door, just to make sure there was nowhere else we could go. When it didn't turn, he sat on the stairs and unfoiled his candy bar, eating the whole thing in three or four vicious chomps, not offering me a bite.

"Do you want to play a game?" I said.

"Do I look like I want to play a game?" He threw the candy wrapper on the floor.

Our mother came looking for us half an hour later. What were we doing, she wanted to know. She had a smirk on her face, seeing us there, alone but not complaining. It was as if she was proud that her two boys could go anywhere and have fun. Like she was happy knowing she could leave us anyplace and we would use our powerful imaginations to turn that place into a new and exciting world, alive with danger and possibility. She didn't seem to realize that my brother was angry, or upset, or something else. Since we'd watched the tape, it was hard to tell.

We didn't want to see Rick, I told her. That was all.

"You don't have to see anyone you don't want to see," our mother said. She stood there for a second, then sat down on the stairs, her knees popping as she crouched next to us. "You know, I'm not going to make you like anyone you don't

want to like. That wouldn't be fair." She picked up my brother's candy bar wrapper, turned it inside out. "But you won't be rude to anyone. And you'll do as I say or suffer the consequences."

She tried to put her arm around my brother but he brushed it off. *Suffer the consequences.* It was something a villain would say, a dungeon master, not a dungeon mate. Without a word my brother stood up and stomped up the stairs, leaving me with my mother.

"I guess he's still mad from the party," she said, and I felt her gaze drift toward me, as if to say, What do you think, cute boy? And even though I thought Rick was the biggest jerk alive, I still felt something for my mother. I still wanted to lean into her and smell her shirt and say I was sorry, for spying, for lying to her about Chris, for my brother. I wanted to tell her about the tape and for her to tell me it wasn't real.

But I didn't say anything, and after a minute of silence, my mother balled up the candy wrapper. She pushed the foil into her fist, like a magician would a handkerchief, until the whole thing disappeared.

My brother and I spent the rest of the night building a fort in the cafeteria. We dragged two tables together and hid underneath, behind the chairs that sat upside down on the tabletops. We didn't have a name for it, but our fort was someplace safe. No one could see us, we believed, but we could see everything. We saw Rick hang around, even though it was clear he wasn't here to work. We saw our mother help a man for fifteen minutes, showing him the different clubs available. We saw the man leave without buying anything, our mother and Rick shrugging and laughing.

When it became late, we fell asleep. We must have. Otherwise we would have seen it when our dad showed up. We wouldn't have missed him taking two chairs off our fort's table, turning them upright. We would've thought that after our dad sat down in one chair, it would have been our mother who sat in the other. We would've heard her thank him again for the phone, their voices warming in a way they hadn't in a while. We would have heard and seen all these things. We would have never guessed that the person who sat opposite our dad wouldn't be our mother. It would be Rick.

"Thanks for doing this," my dad said.

"Hey," Rick said, "anything for the po-lice."

It was my brother who poked me awake, I later realized. Who without a word told me to be quiet, and pointed at the chairs, the extra legs present. Our dad's were all black, draped in his uniform. Rick's were tight in light blue jeans, though we only saw one on the floor. He must have had his legs crossed, like talking to our dad the police officer was no big deal.

"You know why I'm here?" my dad said.

Rick laughed. "Yeah, I know why you're here. Because you missed the party."

"No," my dad said. "It has nothing to do with that."

"You sure? Sure you're not mad that you missed out?"

"Why don't you shut up and let me do the talking."

Rick uncrossed his legs. Now both feet were firmly on the floor. "How about you not talk to me like that," he said.

Or what? I would have said, my brother would have said, if one of us was playing the good guy, the other the bad. What are you going to do? We would have taken out our nightstick and showed it to Rick. Pulled out our gun if we

had one. I'm an officer of the law, we would have said. Now sit there, shut your mouth, and do as I say.

"Listen," my dad said. "I'm not here to get on your case. I know you jailed with Kern. That's all I want to talk about."

"Don't you mean the Stranger?" Rick said. "The big bad Stranger. Though I guess he's not a stranger to you."

I heard my dad sigh through his nose, perform his patience trick.

"Fine," Rick said. "What do you want to know?"

"I want to know anything I can use. Did he ever say anything to you?"

"Who? The Stranger? Oh yeah. All the time. Didn't you know, we were best buds?" Rick laughed. "Yep, we used to talk about all sorts of things. Sports, the weather. Our favorite movies. He liked those violent ones, you know, for mature audiences only."

"Rick," my dad said.

"Yeah, me, I'm more into comedies. But he was a real sick bastard. Said he liked making movies of his own. You know, homemade stuff. Real gory. You know anything about that?"

The tape. The woman.

"I'm being serious," my dad said.

"Good," Rick said. "That makes one of us."

"Did he ever say anything about what he wanted to do if he got out? Anyone he wanted to see?"

Rick laughed. "You mean other than you?" he said. "Nope, didn't say a thing." My brother and I looked at each other with confusion. "Seriously, are these the questions? You know we weren't in the same cell, right? Not even the same block. I barely saw the guy."

There was a pause in the interrogation. My dad crossed his legs at the ankle, making a diamond-shaped window, and through that window we saw my mother. She was still in the pro shop, no doubt curious what this talk was all about.

"Yes," my dad said. "I do know that."

"Oh," Rick said. "I get it." He stood up, and my brother and I retreated farther under the table so he couldn't see us. "I was right. This is about what you missed." He walked away from our dad and faced the pro shop. "Or, miss."

"I'm just trying to do my job," my dad said.

"Yeah," Rick said. "I know what you're trying to do." He watched my mother fish a misplaced shirt off a top rack, put it where it belonged. "You think you can scare her, is that it? Remind her who I am and she'll come running back?"

My dad shifted in his chair, and I heard the click of his pen as he put his pad away.

"That's it, isn't it?" Rick said. He laughed and my dad told him to shut up. That he didn't know what he was talking about. "Maybe," Rick said. "Maybe not. But I do know some things. Some things I know for sure."

Like what? my dad said. Oh, nothing much, Rick said. Just the threat Kern made that day in court, the day he was sentenced to life, with my dad, the arresting officer, watching. Rick pulled out a big dip of chew and tucked a chunk under his bottom lip, ballooning the lower half of his face into that of a deformed monster. *"You should have let me die,"* the monster said. *"You should have let me kill myself. Now someday I'm going to come for you. Someday I'll hurt the people you love."*

Rick dug an empty soda cup out of the trash, spit into it.

With the back of his hand he wiped away the monster drool dripping from his chin. "That about sum it up?" he said. "Or should we invite Aggie in here, reenact the whole thing?"

My dad stood up and put his finger in Rick's face. I always thought the two were the same height, but seeing them next to each other, it was clear Rick was taller, and more muscular.

"What?" Rick said, looking down at my dad. "What are you going to do? You touch me and I'll tell her all about what Kern said. You come near me again and good luck seeing your boys."

As if on cue, my mother entered the cafeteria. "What's going on?"

My dad paused. He looked at his finger like how did it get there, like a puppet finally becoming aware of its strings. "Nothing," he said.

"Is everything OK?"

"Yes." He smiled weakly. "He's all yours."

My mother watched him leave. "What was that all about?"

"He just had a few questions," Rick said. "That's all."

"Oh," my mother said. "What did you tell him?" There was worry in her voice, though I wasn't sure about what. Rick pulled my mother into him and stared at the cafeteria door, as if any moment my dad might return.

Rick said, "I told him what he needed to know."

The next day the van died. In the morning, my brother and I sat down for breakfast and watched our mother leave for work. We didn't talk about what we'd heard the night before.

What we learned, what it meant. How before our dad arrested the Stranger, he saved his life. That was the part of the tape we didn't see. But the Stranger hated our dad. The Stranger wished to die and our dad took that from him. Yes, and for that, the Stranger wanted our dad dead. He told him so. In court. And now the Stranger was out. Now the Stranger was coming for us all.

We didn't talk about these things the same way we didn't talk about the tape. We ate our cereal in silence until we heard the jangle of keys as our mother unlocked the door and stormed back into the apartment.

"The van is dead," she said. "Long live the van."

She grabbed the phone to dial for a ride. I had yet to use the new phone, with its long antenna, like something out of a spaceship. Our mother tried Rick first (no answer), then Sandy, then Cornbread (both stuck at work). She called Rick again and this time left a message. Come get me, she said. As soon as possible. Where are you?

"Call Dad," my brother said. "Make him help."

"Your father doesn't know a thing about cars," my mother said. "I wish that he did."

The phone rang. I thought it was our dad, calling to prove our mother wrong. But it was Rick. He would be here right away. Anything for a lady in distress.

When she finished talking to Rick, our mother found a tow man in the Yellow Pages. She wiped the sweat off her forehead and spoke into the phone, sayings things like "dead" and "estimate." Then she hung up the phone and spread her arms wide on the counter, like some busted perp. You're under arrest, I thought, and patted her down with my eyes. She let her head drop. "If I asked you two to wait for the tow

man," she said, "would you be able to do it? If I gave you the key, could you give it to the man and not mess it up?"

"Of course," my brother said. "We're not babies."

My mother worked the van key around the ring. "I don't like doing this, but I can't be late to work again. So it's up to you guys," she said, and when she placed the key in my brother's palm, she left her hand in his, like a low five gone wrong. "Don't talk to anybody and don't do anything stupid."

We waited with her until Rick finally showed up in what was a real nice sports car once upon a time. Two doors, faded black body, a ridge on its hood that looked like a nose. I pictured Rick driving my mom around the city in this car, fast and crazy, the way he raced around the golf course in his customized cart. I wanted to warn my mother. Watch his hands. Look out for the leg pinch.

Rick ran around the car to open the door for my mother.

"When will you be home?" my brother asked.

"Right after work." She buckled herself in, pulled the strap tight. "Take care of your brother, OK? You know the drill."

I stuck my head in the window so my mother could kiss my face, and saw Rick, grinning as always. "No need to worry, retard," he said. "Yours truly knows how to treat a lady."

My mother kissed me goodbye. "Go wait with your brother. Be good."

After they disappeared down our street, we opened the van doors to let the heat out, sat in some shade we found on the curb. It was early morning, but the day was an oven.

"We should be in the pool," I said, "where it's nice and

cool." If the pool wasn't a safe subject, I didn't know what was. "Are you mad?"

"No."

"Are we mad at Chris?"

"You want me to tell you how you feel? If you're not mad, then why be mad?"

The answer was that I hated myself for forgiving too easy, something I was known for. One summer my dad nicknamed me Marshmallow Man, because no matter what anyone did to me, especially my brother, I always forgave them and quickly returned to my original form.

"I don't like that he talked about Mom," my brother said, "or the way he talked about her, but he said he was sorry. So, I don't know."

A large truck turned onto our street, and we raised our heads with hope, but it wasn't the tow man. I got off the curb and hopped in the driver's seat to take my mind off things. I had sat here once before, up front with my dad, one night after a policeman's birthday barbecue, when my mother said my dad had had too much to drink. I scooted up to grab the wheel and put my hands where my dad had shown me. A dumber kid would have made driving noises with his mouth, bounced up and down like roads were nothing but speed bumps. But I was a real driver. I checked the side mirrors, shot my eyes to the blind spots. I put my blinker on when I wanted to turn and pumped the brakes when a kid chased a ball into the street.

I saw my brother approaching in the passenger mirror and nodded hello. His shirt was off, and he walked with his arms loose like boiled noodles. He got in the backseat like he was someone famous and I was his driver.

"Where to, sir?" I asked him.

"I'm here for the van. You called for a tow?"

"Oh, yes."

My brother stuck his foot in my face. "Well, here it is!"

"Cut it out."

"But it's me! The Toe Man!"

He pushed his stinky foot into my nose. "No you're not," I said. "You're gross." I fought his foot until finally I had to punch his leg to get his toes away from me. "I'm not playing that. I'm the taxi man. Now where to?"

My brother didn't answer, and when I looked into the rearview mirror I saw his face had changed. His eyes were slanted and menacing, and I knew right away he'd transformed into the Stranger, like he had in the woods.

"Sixth and Revolution," he said, giving our dad's address. *"And step on it. I've got a cop to kill."*

"Don't," I said.

He chuckled to himself.

"That's not funny," I said.

"I know," the Stranger said. *"I wasn't joking."*

I flicked on the imaginary meter and pretended to ignore him.

"But if you like jokes, I've got one for you. Why did the Stranger cross the road? To kill your entire family! Hahaha!"

He fell out of the mirror, rolling over in the backseat.

"Stop it," I said. "You shouldn't be laughing. You shouldn't play the Stranger anymore."

"Why not?"

"Because of the movie."

My brother stopped laughing.

"It wasn't a movie."

"Yes it was."

"No," my brother said. "Movies aren't real."

It took me a moment to understand what he meant. Because he didn't say any more, and I didn't either. Eventually my brother rose from the backseat, like a vampire rising from his tomb. For some reason, he looked as pale as one, too.

"Where are you going?" I said.

He handed me the keys and said, "I'm going to the pool."

The chain-link fence rattled, shaking under someone's weight. I rolled over in my pool chair, to find my brother, to ask where he was going, to yell at him for leaving me again. He had already left me in the van, where I waited for the tow man for what felt like forever before giving up and leaving the key in the ignition. But my brother was hovering in the pool, his eyes on the woods side of the fence.

"It is I," Chris said, "Sir Chris!" His voice boomed across the pool, in an unnecessarily grand way. I looked back at the front gate, which hadn't moved.

"Where did you come from?" I asked.

Chris gestured toward the woods, then bowed. "I have come from my secret kingdom, good sire, a place of magic and nobility." My brother swam to the side of the pool, rested his arms on the pool's lip. "Ah, this must be the fabled swimmer of the Frontiers," Chris said, "a serfdom famous for its watery ways. What say you, fellow nobleman?"

"What are you doing?" my brother said. "Why are you talking like that?"

"Talking like what?" Chris said. "Oh, dear sire, I apologize. You must forgive me if my words are colored with my native tongue. You see, I have just returned from conversing with my kin, whom I haven't seen in many a fortnight." *Kin. Fortnight.* I tried to lock these words in my brain, so I could look them up later. "You see, I sometimes forget we have our own way of speaking, to which others' ears may be unaccustomed."

"What's your kin?" my brother said.

Chris wagged his finger. "No, no, I cannot discuss them further. I will not."

"Why not?"

"Why, because of the charlatan." My brother looked as confused as I felt. "Have you gentlemen not heard? Oh, it's most terrible. There is a man, disguised as me, who travels from pool to pool, preying on innocent swimmers, ruffling their feathers by making unwanted small talk about their families. You know, mothers and the like." A small smile crept across Chris's face. "But that's not me. No, my cause is much nobler than petty gossip."

"Whatever," my brother said, and he pushed himself out of the pool.

"Dear sire, art thou questioning my purpose? Dost thou doubt my motives? If so, let me assure you, I come from an honest, polite people, mastered in the way of manners. Believe me, I will only broach the subjects deemed appropriate by you and your stableboy." No one looked in my direction, but it was clear they were talking about me. "While I can understand your hesitation, what with that big-mouthed fool on the loose, I promise, if you give me your trust, I will

not disappoint. I swear on my lineage, on the long list of my family's dead, you will be happy to see what I have traveled far and wide to show you."

He was obviously talking about the Gainer at this point, but it still piqued my interest. Maybe it was the language he was using, or maybe it was because Chris had only done the Gainer once, and although I had seen it performed in person, it didn't seem real. It existed in my mind as a blur, its unnatural motion part of an amazing, dying dream.

"What dost thou say?" Chris said, offering my brother his hand. "Can I count on your loyalty, as you surely can count on mine?"

My brother extended his arm and let Chris pull him out of the water. "Just the pool moves," my brother said. "Nothing else."

"I wouldn't dare of it, my liege," Chris said. He put his hand to his chest, which was much browner than when we had first seen him, though still flat and unmuscular, like mine. "We will speak of nothing else. You have my word, I will only take you as far as you want to go."

"Then I am yours, Sir Chris," my brother said, and bowed his wet head. "Now have my stableboy fetch me my towel."

"What do you think of my new trunks?" Chris said. He and my brother had dropped the medieval act and were now practicing pool moves. "Picked them up when I snuck by the old castle. Not too shabby, huh?" The trunks were blood-red and stopped well above his knees, much more suitable for swimming than the boxers he wore before. They're lifeguard shorts, Chris explained, though they didn't look new, as he

had described. The thick white cross on the left leg was cracked, and some of the lettering had peeled away, so that *life* was much more visible than *guard*.

"They're nice," my brother said, "now watch this." He flipped into the pool, crookedly and with a widely spraying splash, but landing upright. This was the first time I'd seen him flip.

"Whoa!" Chris said. "What in the world? When'd you get so good?"

My brother swam to the side. "I've been practicing, like you told me."

Chris gave him a high five, but I stayed where I was, sitting in the shallow end. That was awesome, Chris told him, but keep your body balled tight, my man. You're all over the place. Remember: one smooth, even motion. My brother nodded, listening to every word Chris said, and then he flipped again. This time a little straighter, a little less messy.

He flipped several more times, steadily improving, and soon he was running to the diving board instead of walking, becoming more confident the closer he came to perfection. Smiling wider the more Chris cheered him on, and for the first time since we'd watched the tape. I should have been happy for my brother, for his success. I should have been up there with Chris, cheering him along, instead of rooting against him, hoping he would hit his head on the board, just nick it, or fall flat on his stomach. But no one was paying attention to me. It was Chris and my brother, off on a wild adventure, while I was left to tend the horses.

I grew tired of playing by myself, and began walking around the inside of the fence, circling it again and again,

raking my hands against the chain link like I was the prisoner. Like I was the Stranger looking for a way out and they were the ones who should be afraid of me.

Still, no one noticed. After my brother mastered the front flip, he and Chris took a break. They stood next to the deep end and discussed what move my brother could do next. Had my brother ever tried a back dive? Chris wanted to know. No, my brother said. Chris put his hand on my brother's shoulder. He let it linger, and they didn't see me. They didn't see me sneak behind my brother, creep closer and closer until I was close enough to reach out and hug. They didn't see me slowly raise my arms, then with a flash throw them at my brother, shove him violently into the pool.

My brother fell on his face, and the water popped as it punched him in the stomach. He didn't sink, though, like part of me wanted him to. He thrashed in the water, immediately angry, immediately understanding what I had done. Before I thought to run, he was out of the water, his mouth open, his hands tensed into claws. He was the Stranger, only he wasn't playing. I hid behind Chris. I put his body in front of mine and held on to his waist. My brother's feet slapped the concrete, louder and louder, and I squeezed Chris and begged him to protect me.

"Whoa, whoa, whoa," Chris said. "Easy there, big man." He put his arms out like a protective gate, and my brother bounced around, telling Chris to move, to get out of the way.

"You think that's funny?" my brother said. "Do you?" His chest and stomach were red from falling on his front. "Get out of the way. I'll kill you!"

Chris held him back. "All right, all right. Let's take a breath. I'm sure it was an accident."

"Yeah right! You saw what he did!"

He kept hopping up and down, pointing at me. It wasn't until Chris grabbed him by his shoulders that he stopped jumping. He made my brother look him in the eye and said, OK, you're right. He saw. It wasn't an accident. But no need to get all hot and bothered about it. This is your brother. Surely he had a reason.

"Isn't that right, little man?" Chris said. "What, was there a bee on his head or something?"

I looked at my brother, dripping, his eyes fixed. Bee, he mumbled. Yeah right. Chris stared at me, waiting for an answer. But what could I tell him? What could I say that would make a difference?

"No?" Chris said. "Perhaps the bee was in your bonnet. Perhaps the stableboy needs a break. Some time away from his kingdom." He turned to my brother. "What sayest thou, good knight? Should we give your servant some time off? Send him on vacation?"

My brother leered at me. I could only imagine what he would do to me later, when he got me alone. "Yeah, why don't we send him far, far away. Like, forever."

I started toward the gate, keeping my distance from my brother. I'll wait by the van, I told them. For the tow man. Chris raised an eyebrow but didn't say anything. Just the pool moves.

"Good idea," my brother said. "And don't come back. Or you'll regret it."

———

The tow man was nothing like I pictured. I spent another hour waiting, trying not to think about my brother and Chris at the pool without me, trying to imagine the tow man instead. What he would look like, what he would say. But he wasn't the fat guy in overalls I imagined, a greasier version of that jerk Wayne, who hounded our dad at dinner. The tow man was skinny and wore pants. His face was clean-shaven minus a few hairs that hung from his chin like a frayed jump rope. He asked me where my mother was and when I said at work he didn't seem to care. He handed me the carbon paper to sign and didn't say anything when I wrote my name in print. He gave me my yellow copy, took the key out of the ignition, and a moment later the van was gone.

I thought about going to the apartment. I thought about sitting patiently on the couch, reading a book, and waiting for my brother. I thought about these things. Instead, I took a lap around our complex's other building, the building where the chalk kid and his mother lived. This way I could spy on the pool from a spot my brother wouldn't expect. I could watch my brother and Chris have fun without me, high five, share a joke at my expense. Whatever happened to that stableboy? one of them might say. Oh, who cares? the other would say. Let the baby have his horses.

I was sure I would see all of this.

But by the time I made it around the building, my brother and Chris were gone.

The pool was empty, the complex silent. I sat on the couch, waiting and hoping for my brother's return. I recalled the details: the pool gate swinging open with the wind; my

brother's towel heaped on a pool chair. This, I told myself, meant he wouldn't be gone long. He couldn't leave his towel out all night. He would have to bring it back or our mother would get mad.

But he wasn't back by lunch. Every ten minutes I went out onto the porch and looked for him, scanning the complex as far as I could, hearing nothing, seeing less. I took the kitchen timer into our room and set it to ten. As the timer ticked down, I tried to busy myself by playing with my brother's toy men. All the stories I told, however, turned into tales of two men turning against a third. I put away the toys and watched the timer ding.

Our mother would be home any minute. What would she say when she saw my brother wasn't here? Chris? Who is Chris? Some stranger? She would stare at me accusingly, as if I were the older brother, the responsible one. And you let him go by himself? I checked the time on the TV, reading between the blurry lines of the one channel we got. It was well past five. The TV's static distorted the man on the news, stretching his head, sucking it into some other dimension. What choice did I have? I had to go look for my brother before our mother found out. I had to leave the apartment and go into the world alone.

The smoking lady was waiting.

"Hey!" she yelled, much louder than she had to. "You! I see you!" She was wearing the same sweats as the last time we saw her, but her T-shirt was somewhat soaked, like part of her had fallen into the pool. She pointed her cigarette at me. Her hand was shaking.

"Yeah, yeah, yeah," she said. "You and your brother, think you're so smart. But I know kids. I've seen their tricks." She

took a long drag and ashed onto the hallway carpet. Orange flakes that could have started a fire, had she not smothered them with her bare feet. "Where is the other one? That, that big kid. I don't see him. Guess he's gone, maybe? Guess I tell your mother."

I felt a hand on my shoulder. "I'm right here," my brother said. I turned around and there he was, dry as the towel around his waist. "Just went to check the mail. That's not a crime, is it?"

The smoking lady finished her cigarette. She eyed us suspiciously and flicked the butt over the stairwell rail. She mumbled to herself. Something about no-good sons. Something like she'd be watching. She went into the apartment and slammed the door.

"She's the worst," my brother said.

I studied him for a moment. It was difficult to tell if he was still mad at me, if Chris was, too.

"I'm sorry," I said, "for what I did."

My brother frowned, as if he had forgotten about me pushing him into the pool until I reminded him. "Are you?" he said.

"Yes."

"Then show me," he said.

"How?"

"Don't tell Mom. About where I went. Where I go."

"Where did you go?"

"Just don't tell her, OK? Keep your mouth shut and you won't get hurt."

He went into our apartment, leaving the door open behind him. Through the doorway I could see the length of the apartment, down the hall and into our mother's room,

and through her window. I could see the long streaks on the windowpane where, on the day we moved in, my brother and I wrote secret messages to each other, using fingers coated with spit. What the messages were I could no longer remember. But I remembered pressing our wet fingers together and making a promise. To not tell our mother. To let her find the words on her own. That, we agreed, would be much more fun.

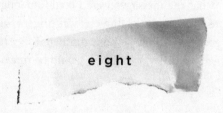

eight

MY MOTHER GOT rides from Rick the next couple of weeks, and there was no talk of fixing the van. Every morning Rick honked for my mother, a sharp blast that always made my heart leap. I began to hate his horn, unpredictable as his leg pinch, and so I asked my mother why she had to get rides from Rick. Why not Sandy or Cornbread? My brother and I were lying on the bathroom floor, curled near our mother's legs while she blow-dried her hair. This was something we did in the morning, if we were up early enough. We brought pillows from our room and put them at our mother's feet. In the winter, she would pass the dryer over our bodies, cold from the tile floor.

"We have similar schedules," my mother said. "It's easy."

But it didn't seem easy. Our mother was looking more and more tired after each shift, as if each ride with Rick drained

her face. She continually smelled like she did the night of her party, though not quite as strong. And if that wasn't enough, on the days she didn't work late, I would hear her take the cordless phone into her bedroom and shut the door. I would hear her talk, to Rick I guessed, and say things like *Oh stop* and *What a world*. In the morning she would emerge a cranky zombie who didn't want brains. Only silence. And coffee. She needs a day off, I thought, a day with her boys at the pool. Though I knew she wouldn't get one. If I asked, she would say if she didn't work, there wouldn't be any money. And if I asked couldn't Dad help out, she would say he certainly *could*, then let the dead air speak for itself.

So we went to the pool. We rarely saw the smoking lady, and when we did, she barely tried to stop us. She just stood in the hall, her cigarette fidgeting in her trembling hand, calling us no good and saying we'd be back.

The water was so warm we could jump in right away. Chris came most days, though he didn't talk to me much. In his eyes I went from pesky stableboy to traitor to the throne. Without a word I had been tried for treason, found guilty, and kicked out of the kingdom. I became mad at my brother for letting this happen, and each night I pictured myself in my mother's room, standing over her bed. I've got something to tell you, I would say. We've been keeping a secret. Or I pictured myself at the police station, in a gray room with my dad. He's at the pool, I would confess. The stranger you want.

But I couldn't make myself rat my brother out. Even though it increasingly felt like I was supposed to, like in the end it would be the right thing to do. Instead, we went to the pool, and when they told me to fetch them popsicle

strips, I did. When they told me to go home and leave them alone, I did that, too. It's fine, my brother would say, if I paused too long at the gate, I'll be home in a bit. And every day I was worried. And every day he stayed out longer. But he always came home, though what he did with Chris he would no longer say.

One morning we exited the apartment building and a police cruiser was parked in the spot reserved for our van. I though it was my dad at first, but the car light's bar was lit up, flashing bursts of red and blue. The officer stepped out of the car and I immediately saw that it was Alan, not my dad. He did a double take when he saw us. He must have not known we lived here, with our mother. Our dad must have never told him.

"Hey there," he said, and swallowed a breath, gathering himself. "Boy, you startled me. I thought you'd be with your pop." A lady came out of the building opposite ours, a small kid behind her. I didn't recognize the lady at first, but when I saw the kid I realized it was the mother and son we'd seen the day Chris was waiting in the chair outside the pool. The boy with the chalk. He was crying, and the mother was hugging him with one arm, rubbing his shoulder.

"I'll be with you in one second, ma'am," Alan said to the lady. He came over and walked us to our door. "I need you boys to go inside, OK? Is your mother home?" We told him no. It was just us. "OK, well, everything is fine," Alan said. "Just go inside, and I'll come check on you in a bit. Can you do that for me?"

We told him yes, of course we could, though we wanted to stay outside and hear what had happened, find out why

the kid was crying. Why Alan's police lights were on, but not his siren.

Alan opened the door and pushed us in, like two baby ducks. "Go on," he said. "You be good."

My brother marched upstairs, touched our doorknob, then marched back down to the pea-green door window. I followed him, and we took turns spying on Alan, the lady, and her kid, describing to each other what we were seeing. The lady is talking. Alan is nodding. He is jotting things down. Now the lady is pointing to her building, at a window on the second floor. Now she is crying. She is looking at the ground and shaking her head. Now she is taking her boy inside. Alan is right behind her. Now the door is closed. Now there is nothing.

"What are they doing now?" I asked my brother.

"He's probably checking out the crime scene. Taping it off."

I thought of the time our dad brought home the last few feet of a roll of yellow police tape. How I went upstairs one evening and found my room taped off, my brother guarding the door. Sorry, he said, can't let you in. Official crime scene. I pushed him out of the way and opened the door. Inside, Sparky, my favorite stuffed animal, was hanging from the ceiling fan, a suicide note taped to his chest. My condolences, my brother said. I'll notify the family.

"Do you think it's Chris?" I asked my brother.

"Do I think what's Chris?"

"Why Alan is here."

"What would he want with Chris? Chris hasn't done anything wrong."

"How do you know?"

"I just do."

"Right," I said. "Because you're best friends."

I shoved the pea-green door as hard as I could and went outside, stepping on every sidewalk crack and wishing it were my brother's or Chris's back.

"What's wrong with you?" my brother said. He had followed me outside and was puzzling at the weird way I was walking. "Do you want to ask Alan? I'll ask Alan."

I stopped my back-breaking. "What if it's the Stranger?"

"No," my brother said. "He wouldn't come here. I don't think it's anybody."

"How do you know?"

"Listen, if you want me to ask, I'll ask. I guess he could know something, probably more than Dad anyway. Not that that's hard."

He kicked a rock down the sidewalk, in the direction of the police cruiser.

"What are you so mad at Dad about?" I said. He shook his head, said isn't it obvious? The dull look on my face must've told him no, I didn't get it. So he ran through his list of grievances. It's Dad's fault we're here in the first place, and not in our big house. It's Dad's fault we have to see Rick every week. It's not Dad's fault the Stranger escaped, but Dad's not doing anything about it. The Stranger could be coming to kill us all and yet Dad does nothing. Dad has no leads. No clues. He says he's going to catch him, but then he goes out, leaves us alone. Dad doesn't care.

"He does too care," I said.

But when my words came out, they sounded shallow. They didn't come close to convincing myself, let alone my

brother. So we went inside, forgetting to ask Alan, and the cruiser's lights flashed behind us, without a wail, warning the Frontiers in silence.

By the time Alan came to check on us, our mother was home for what she called her mid-morning break. Really, she had stayed at Sandy's again and had come home to change clothes before heading back to work. She didn't ask what we'd done the night before. She didn't check to see if we had any food left, which we didn't. When Alan knocked on the door and my mother answered, my brother and I crept out of the room and spied. We heard Alan tell our mother about the break-in, how someone had entered a neighbor's (the chalk family's) apartment while they were gone. We learned what the burglar had taken: food, toiletries, nothing really valuable. They got in through the patio door, Alan said. Smashed the glass and walked right in. Actually, there had been a couple other break-ins around this area, our street and the street over. So make sure you lock up at night. Neither said what I was thinking, as I'm sure my brother was as well: What good is a lock if they throw a rock through the window?

After Alan left, our mother breezed past us into her room and changed into her work clothes. When she came back out, she had a bag like the ones we took with us to our dad's on the weekend. She seemed surprised to see us sitting in the hall, surprised we existed at all.

"I'm assuming you heard all that," she said. "Well." She looked at us and scratched her big hair, like we were two strays she'd found on the street. She put her bag down. "Well, so what. This is the city we live in. If it wasn't safe, your dad

would say something." She picked her bag back up and stood straight, as if by doing so she would prove the matter was settled. "I have plans," she said. "With Sandy. OK? I've already made plans and why is it every time I want—"

"Mom," my brother said. "No one is stopping you."

Our mother turned from the open door, the hallway light blanketing her in a faded halo. She frowned. She nodded. Then she left.

My brother went to visit Chris at the pool. It was sprinkling and he didn't invite me. I asked if he was going to ask Chris if he knew anything about the burglary, but he ignored me. After he left I locked the door and made a list. A list of things I didn't want anyone to take. Not the burglar, not Chris, not the Stranger. Not anyone. Sparky, I wrote. The G.I. Joes my brother didn't have and always wanted to borrow. I put my pencil down. I debated if I should add people to the list. I decided I should. At the top of the list, I wrote my brother's name, without thinking why I did this, why I picked him over everyone else.

That it wasn't Sandy my mother was staying with would have never occurred to me if not for my brother. Besides forgiving too easily, my other flaw, according to my brother, was that I believed whatever anyone said. So I believed it when my mother said she was sleeping at Sandy's, that she did so only because the van was broken and that she sure did miss us. I would have never guessed she was spending the night with Rick, re-creating, I guessed, my mother's birthday, their magical night on the couch.

My brother revealed this to me a few days later, one

evening when I wanted to call our mom and complain that we were hungry, that we were tired of eating watered-down flakes and heels of bread that had recently celebrated the one-month anniversary of their expiration date.

"Go ahead," my brother said, dangling a Joe from the fridge. "But she's not at Sandy's. She's with Rick."

I told him he was wrong. I asked him why Mom would leave Sandy's number for emergencies if she was with Rick.

"Try the number," my brother said. "You'll see."

I grabbed the new phone and dialed, and when Sandy answered after the first purr I turned to my brother to gloat. To say, In your stupid face. But then I thought of how Sandy had answered, what she had said: *Fort Leavenworth Country Club, may I help you?*

I pulled the phone away from my ear like it was a burning iron. I stared at it. On some faraway planet, Sandy said, *Hello? Is there anybody there? Hello?* Finally my brother took the phone out of my hands, smiled, and spoke into the receiver. *"Help us,"* he said, his voice slowing to an agonized groan. *"We're dying . . . The Stranger . . . He broke in . . . Please, somebody, help . . ."* He hung up and returned the phone to the wall. "See," he said. "It's one big lie."

Behind him, across the living/dining room, a late sun poured through the glass door. I thought about how easy it would be to climb up to our patio and break in. A lot of times the Stranger wouldn't even need a rock. A lot of times we forgot to lock the door, wedge the stick so the door couldn't slide.

"Why would she do that? What if something did happen?"

"You need to stop asking why," my brother said.

"Especially when it's obvious. She's a liar. Don't you get that? Just like Dad."

She may have been a liar, but thirty minutes later our mother did show up, bursting through the door in a sweaty panic. I was on the couch, trying to think of things to add to my most valuable items list.

"What the hell are you doing?" my mother said. "Are you all right?"

My brother came out of the kitchen, gnawing on the last stale cracker. "What are *you* doing? Shouldn't you be at work?"

My mother slapped the cracker out of his hand. "I mean it. Which one of you did it?"

"Did what?"

"It's not funny," my mother said. "I want an answer."

My brother picked up Sparky, who I had left in the living room after sleeping on the floor the night before, and held him up. "I'm sorry. On the advice of my lawyer here, I plead the fifth."

My mother grabbed my brother by the shoulders and shook him, slammed him against the back of the couch. "Stop it! This is serious! What if—"

"What if what?" my brother said. He shoved my mother off him and stood up. "What if something had happened? You wouldn't have been here. Or at Sandy's. Don't try and make us feel bad."

"For your information—"

"And we are dying here," my brother said. "We're starving and you won't even fix the van. You're off with Rick like an idiot."

"Hey!" my mother said. "You do not call me that." She

put her hands on her hips and started tapping her foot to some fast but silent rhythm, some angry rock song only she could hear. "Fine, you want the van back? Fine. I will get the van back. I will get the van back right now, if that's what you want. Is that what you want, or do you want to just keep annoying the hell out of me?" I want the van back, my brother said, trying to look defiant. But his face seemed unsure. "Good," my mother said, and she snatched Sparky from my brother's hand. "Then we'll start with this."

Holding Sparky by the neck, she left the living room and we heard her stomp down the hall and kick open her bedroom door. My brother and I glanced at each other, guessing. A minute later our mother returned carrying a pile of random things: a small box of jewelry, a hair straightener, an old radio that belonged to her dad. She dropped them all on the floor like they were junk.

"What's all that?" my brother said.

"This," my mother said. "This is what it's going to take. You think you're big enough to solve adult problems. Well, here's your chance. Go into your room and bring me your three most expensive toys."

"What? Why?"

My mother lowered her gaze. "Adults don't ask dumb questions. Now do it." We knew she was past the point of arguing, so we did as we were told. My brother brought back the action-figure fortress he rarely used, and never let me touch. I returned with a robotic dog I played with when I felt like I was forgetting Baron. The dog came with a two-button remote. The first button made the dog speak. The second, shake. It belonged on the list.

"What are you doing?" my brother said.

She took the toys from my brother and threw them in a bag. "Just what I said. I'm going to get the van back."

"Hey, you can't do that."

"This is what you wanted," my mother said. "Remember? Besides, aren't you getting too old for toys? You should be outside, exploring the world."

We followed her into the living room as she searched for her keys. "You won't let us," my brother said.

"Well, what do you need toys for? You have the pool."

"You won't take us. You only let us go once by ourselves." Even now my brother wouldn't reveal that we had been sneaking out to the pool against our mother's orders.

"Look, do you want to eat or what?" our mother said. "There they are." She threw her keys in her purse and grabbed her big sunglasses. She put them on inside, so we couldn't look her in the eye when she said goodbye, or maybe so she wouldn't have to look at us.

"This isn't fair," my brother said. "We didn't do anything."

"Well, sorry, but that's the way of the world. This is what has to be done. Now stay put. When I get back, we'll go for ice cream or something."

My brother tried to protest. "I don't want—"

"Be quiet!" my mother yelled. "OK? Stop being a brat! Nobody cares what you want. Not right now. Just wait here and shut up."

She stared at him hard, until my brother folded his arms and went to the couch, kicking it before he sat down. Yes, our mother said, kick the couch. Be like your dad. That'll help. Then she left, the bag of valuables thrown over her

shoulder like she'd got her wish and was leaving our city for good.

My brother and I didn't know how far away the auto shop was, so we didn't know what to do. Mad at my mother, he wanted to go to the pool, but did we have time, or would he be in the middle of a move when our mother returned and caught us outside with Chris? What lie would my brother tell? Chris could be a special swimming instructor, who traveled around to poor neighborhoods and gave out free lessons. He would teach a range of things. For the beginners, the swimming babies, he would demonstrate the basics—how to wade or float on your back. For the more advanced, like my brother, special meetings would be held at secret times, in private places, where Chris would show moves too tough for anyone but the gifted. The only things Chris would ask in return would be the occasional popsicle strip, and your faith, your commitment, to do whatever he asks, keep whatever secret. That's not too bad, Chris would say, when you think about all there is to gain.

We decided to wait inside.

My brother leaned against the porch's screen door, seeking relief from the heat, or maybe listening for the pool.

"What are we going to do?" I said. "We have nothing to do."

"You're going to shut up," my brother said, his tone taking on our mother's. "That's what you're going to do."

He got up and brushed by me, purposely nudging me with his knee as he passed. In the kitchen he took an ice tray out of the freezer and slammed it against the counter, much

harder than necessary. He dropped a few cubes into a glass, filled it with cloudy city water, and drank it all without coming up for air.

"I didn't do anything," I said. "Don't tell me to shut up." Outside, I heard sprinkles of rain. I slid the glass door shut and faced my brother. He came out of the kitchen with his glass of ice cubes.

"Oh yeah?" he said. "Watch this: Shut. Up." He crunched an ice cube with his mouth open. Broken bits littered the carpet.

"Fine," I said. "Be a jerk."

"I'm not the jerk," my brother said. "Mom's the jerk. You're the jerk. Baby."

"I'm not a baby," I said.

My brother laughed. "Hm, could've fooled me." He reared his head back to chomp more ice, his teeth gnashing it into chunk after chunk.

"You're the baby," I said.

"Oh yeah?" my brother said.

"Yeah. You won't even ask Chris anything. You're too afraid."

He stopped his chewing and set his glass down on the bookcase. The A book, which showed the woman's naked anatomy, was slightly pulled out from the last time my brother looked at it when our mother was gone. He took a step toward me and told me to apologize.

"For what," I said. "For you being a baby and a jerk? A baby jerk?"

My brother balled up his hand. "Say you're sorry."

"No," I said. "It's not my fault you're a jerk. A jerk worse than Ric—"

I didn't get to finish his name. My brother let out a yell and charged at me. I wasn't ready for him, and my body flew like my brother's did when I pushed him into the pool. I heard a loud thud and didn't realize it was my head hitting the glass door that went to our porch. I was on the floor with my hand held to my head but I didn't get why. I was crying but didn't understand that either. I wanted to sleep, but somewhere my dad wouldn't stop playing a record. The record was a country one and it kept skipping. The singer sang, *I'm sorry, darling, I'm sorry, I didn't mean to.* Over and over. It sounded like the singer could cry too. I opened my eyes and tried to focus them past the throbbing. The singer reached out to me, still singing *I'm sorry*, and rubbed my shoulder.

"I'm sorry," my brother said. "I didn't mean to."

My mother walked in at that moment and the record went away. She saw the living room, me on the floor and my brother standing over me, and gasped. It could have been a crime scene.

"What happened? What did you do to your brother?"

"We were playing is all," my brother lied. "He wanted to play."

"Stand up," she said to me. She didn't take out a small notebook to jot case notes down, like she should have. Her eyes were all over the room. "Is your brother telling the truth?" This wasn't good interrogation technique, our dad would say if this was a movie. You never interview suspects two at a time. Not at the crime scene. You pull them aside and shake them down one by one. Otherwise, one person's idea of the truth gets passed on to another, until everyone is remembering what happened the same way, even if that memory has big blind gaps, or is one large lie. "Is he?" she said.

Of course, there were other ways the interview could go wrong. One suspect could use another's story against him. In my case, I could listen patiently to everything my brother said, true or untrue, then tell my mother no, it happened just the opposite.

"Well?" my mother said.

I rubbed my head where a bump was coming up. "I wasn't playing," I said. "He shoved me for no reason."

"That's not true," my brother said. He looked at me like he couldn't believe I was lying, even if it was just a little bit. "He kept calling me names."

"No, I didn't," I lied. "He's been doing this for months. Hitting me all the time. Making me do things I don't want to do."

"Is that true?" my mother said.

"No!" my brother said. "He's making it up."

"It is too true. He said if I don't do everything he wants, Dad will never come back, and it will be all my fault."

"I never said that!" my brother said, so dumbfounded that he started to laugh.

"You think hurting your brother is funny?" my mother said.

"He's lying."

"What's wrong with his head?" my mother said. "Why is there a red spot? Is he making that up too?"

My brother turned away. He said he was sorry again, and for some reason didn't try to further explain himself with the truth. My mother said my brother would be sorry from his room tonight. That was her verdict. The interview was over. The case was closed.

"You know, I came back with good news," she said. "The

van is fixed. I left it running outside. I wanted to grab you boys and go out for ice cream." She looked at my brother. "But you made a mess of it, didn't you?"

"Who cares about ice cream?" my brother said. "You can't make everything better with ice cream. Dad sucks. You suck. This city sucks. I hate this damn family."

"Hey!" our mother said again, and she looked at me as if to confirm that it was my brother who just said these mean things. "You can go to your room right now," she said. "I'll tell you when it's time to come out."

My brother kicked the TV as he stormed back to our room. I didn't want to look at my mother. I was afraid if she took a good look, she would see right through me, the lies I had created.

"The van's still running," my mother said, her voice quiet. "How about we get some ice cream to put on that bump of yours."

I thought about my brother, alone in our room, using our toys to act out the pain he would later put on me. I turned and looked at the glass door. There was a small smudge where my face had hit.

"Don't worry," my mother said. "We'll get some for him, too. A peace offering."

I said OK and we went out to the van. It should have felt good to ride up front.

We went to the same fast-food place my dad took us to, though it was different after dinnertime. All the big men were out of uniform and in their stained jeans. They wore shirts that told you the kind of car they owned, or dreamed of driving. They brought their wives and kids with them,

and most didn't talk to either as they spooned scoop after scoop of ice cream. A few teens entered and exited, laughing, but the men kept straight faces.

My mother ordered two small cones for here and a sundae to go. The sundae came in a cup with a clear dome lid. I put my hand around the base to feel the warmth of the hot fudge racing to the bottom, melting the ice cream. There wouldn't be much left by the time we got home. "We should have gotten this to go," my mother said. "That would have been the smart thing." I nibbled away my cone's chocolate shell. "Though it's nice having some alone time with my baby boy. And I'm not sure your brother deserves much of anything tonight."

"He's not that bad," I said. I took a bite of my ice cream cone, leaning over the booth's table. The person before us had left an issue of the local newspaper, sports page up.

"You're just too sweet," my mother said. "Always have been. Mr. Marshmallow." Her words seemed like a trick. She was saying nice things to pile on the guilt, to make me confess about the lies I had told about my brother. But once this story was out, I knew I would only feel relieved until she asked what else I was hiding.

"How did you get the van back?" I said.

"I walked down there and gave them all the money I got for our stuff. And when that wasn't enough, I called your dad. He does owe us, you know. So he showed up and said he would pay the entire bill if I wanted. You know your dad, he has his good moments." She took a big bite of ice cream, let it melt in her mouth instead of swallowing it whole. "Your brother does too. He's just getting bigger, growing older, that's all." She took another bite and was already down

to the cone. "You know, that stuff your brother said about me and your dad . . ."

He didn't say anything. I made it up.

". . . some things are very tough to forgive, let alone forget."

My mother held up the remains of her cone. She seemed like she wanted to say more about my dad, but she didn't.

"I'm going to run to the ladies' room. You finish up."

She slid out of the booth, and to avoid her glance as she walked away, I studied the sports page in front of me. In the center was a baseball player at bat, swinging for the fences. I thought of the home run derbies my brother and I had, behind the old folks' home. I thought of my brother home alone, in the field out back, throwing the ball up to himself, hitting homers without me. Then I thought of him hitting with Chris.

I flipped over to the news. Our city was too small to have a paper with separate sections during the week. There was the news on the front, the sports on the back, and a glossy insert in the middle, advertising sales at Leavenworth's one grocery store. I licked my cone and scanned the headlines. The top story was on the proposal to build a new public library, a proposal voted down without a single yea. "We don't have the money," explained one councilman, whose face was pictured next to the quote bubble, like the whole thing was a cartoon, "not if we want to maintain the correctional facilities." And as if to further prove the councilman's point, below the quote was an editorial about the prison break, called "Nothing 'Strange' About Recent Escape." The article blasted the government for hiring "kids" to guard their prisons, teenagers straight out of high school who had few other options

for work, and who jumped at the signing bonus offered by the state. What can we expect when we send baby-faced teens to guard the worst? Should we really be surprised that someone like the Stranger would slip through the cracks? The article went on to list the recent escapes from all of Leavenworth's prisons, never mentioning whether the criminals were caught or not. Never saying if they were still walking among us.

My mother returned from the restroom. "You ready?"

"One second," I said, and carefully tore the article out of the paper.

"For your brother?" I nodded, and her face seemed to ease. "You guys still love that stuff, huh?" She grabbed the melted sundae. "All right, I guess a little excitement won't hurt anybody."

My mother made me sit up front, keep her company as we took the long way home. I didn't ask why we had to go the long way, but imagined that she felt bad for the van—locked up at the mechanic's for so long, not knowing when its owner would come to take it home—and wanted to make up for lost time.

We got off the main street and took one of the side roads, driving deeper into the city, to an area crowded with old houses, big and nice, but scary at night. Each had multiple floors, some with porches on both levels, and were inhabited by people whose families had been here since the beginning, my mother told me. We drove another few blocks, and my mother talked about how these people had watched the entire city grow around them, seen the good and the bad. They

were there when the Army rolled in the materials to build the military prison. At first the people weren't so sure, she said, and from their porches, they eyed the soldiers with suspicion. But the general in charge visited each family, traveling door-to-door to assure them that once the prison was built—by its future inhabitants, the prisoners themselves—nothing would change. No one was asking anyone to alter their ways.

Years later, there came word that the city was thinking about building a large prison of its own, instead of the state university originally planned. The people got off their porches for this. They took their wives and children down to the mayor's office to protest, their angry faces burning orange in the lamplight. But when they got there they were told sorry, they could not see the mayor. You can go home, it's already been decided. The prison would be good for the city's growth, it was said, good for the economy. In addition to all the jobs created, the inmates themselves would work for free at the nearby coal mines, giving the people of the city more time to spend with their families, more time to do fun things like fish and swim. And unlike a university, which could be afforded by few and came with no guarantees, the prison could always be counted on. Because as long as there were people, it was reasoned, there would be crime, and people to commit crime. And it would be our job to lock these people up, to watch over them every hour of every day and on through the night, to make sure those who had done wrong would never get out to do anything bad again.

"No one mentioned what the prison might do to the city's spirit," my mother said, finishing her history lesson, and I saw

another glimpse of why, before my parents split and my mother had to go full-time at the golf course, she wanted to be a teacher. "Sometimes I try to imagine what it would look like if they had built the school instead. How things would be different." A car sped by, its headlights washing over my mother's faraway face. "But who knows," she said. "It would probably all turn out the same."

We drove a few more blocks until I had no idea where we were. The van started to smell funny, like someone had poured pancake syrup on the engine. I rolled down my window, looked for a familiar landmark—the unpainted dinosaur at the abandoned fairgrounds, the big hill I never got to sled down—something to show us home.

"Where are we?" I said.

My mother wasn't listening. She was paying attention to the van, which had started to shake as we coasted down a narrow road. The shaking got worse when we stopped at a four-way stop sign. There were no cars around and the houses had their lights off.

The van gave a big shiver, and my mother patted the steering wheel. "It just needs a little help," she said. "That's all."

"I thought it was fixed."

"It is," my mother said. "I mean, it's supposed to be." But when she pressed the gas, the van didn't go. The engine gave one last cough and went still. The interior lights and dashboard warnings all came on at once.

"What? No," my mother said. She turned the key and pressed the pedal. When that didn't work, she closed her eyes and opened them again, like that would do something. She punched the horn, sending a sudden noise out into the surrounding silence. After the noise faded, she looked over at

me with her blue eyes, her blond hair almost touching the ceiling.

"Mom," I said.

"Please," she said, facing front again, "be quiet." She gripped the wheel with both hands, as if any moment the van would come back to life. "I have to figure this out. Damn mechanics."

I reached out. "Mom, it's OK."

She slapped my hand away and looked at me hard. "Don't tell me it's OK. You don't have to tell me that." She leaned over and unbuckled my seat belt. She put on the emergency lights and unlocked the door. "Get out."

Outside the air was buzzing with insects, and a strong wind rushed the road. My mother made me sit on the curb where she could see me. "Don't move," she said, and popped the van's hood. She put her hair up with the tie she always kept around her wrist. "I can't see a blessed thing," she said. Neither could I. The moon was covered by thick clouds, and we hadn't seen a streetlight for blocks. I looked both ways down the street. No cars were coming. None of the porch people were walking out with flashlights and toolboxes. There was no one here to help.

I held my knees and watched my mother work. She touched one part, wiggled another. I knew not to ask her what she was doing because she wouldn't want to admit that she didn't know. I wished my brother were here. He didn't know anything about cars, but he could help me pass the time. He would invent a game, take the scary world that was out there and turn it on its head. We would be danger-ous drifters, maybe, a traveling tag team. The night would be afraid of us, not the other way around.

I grew cold on the curb, so I walked over to the side of the van and peered in. The inside was a maze of dark parts. There was a thick smell of burning.

"I thought I told you to stay on the curb," my mother said. An entire arm of hers had disappeared into the engine and her face was wrinkled with strain.

"What are you trying to get?"

"What part of what I said don't you understand?"

"I want to help."

Her arm flinched like something bit her, and she screamed. She held her finger up, put it in her mouth to stop the bleeding.

"Are you OK?"

She turned to me angry. "You can't help, all right? I wish you could, but you can't. You can barely see over the hood. Now go sit."

"Maybe we should call Dad," I said.

"No. We're not going to call your dad every time we have a problem. We can't do that. That's the old story." She stepped away from the van and shook her head. She looked up at the sky again, checking the weather, maybe, or waiting for an answer.

"What are we going to do?" my mother said. "What are we going to do?" She stared at the clouds some more, as the wild wind stirred them in the sky. She stared for so long that I began to feel scared. It was like she wasn't there anymore, like it was just me with the van. No dad or brother to help.

"Mom," I said, but she didn't move. I called to her several more times, my voice growing louder. I tapped her on the hip. "Mom."

She slowly turned her face to me, and it took a second for her eyes to follow. "Yes?" she said.

I stared up at her until she snapped out of it.

"Yes. Yes, OK." She put her hand on my shoulder and looked around her, as though seeing it all for the first time. "OK, here's the plan. What does that street sign say? Run over and see."

I did as she told, though I couldn't see the sign until there was a flash of lightning.

"It says Pennsylvania. The other one says Tenth."

"Good," my mother said. "OK. Here's what we're going to do." She looked around, as if still unsure. "We're going to walk. That's it. That's just what we have to do."

"To our house?"

"No," she said. "That's too far. We'll have to get help from someone else. Are you ready? Here, take my hand. It's a bit of a hike, but we'll move fast. And we'll stick together, OK? Got it?"

Before I could reply she slung her purse over her shoulder and pulled me along. As we made our way down the road, I kept looking back. At where we were. Where we had been. Behind us, the van grew smaller the more we left it behind, and after walking a few blocks, it started to rain. A drizzle at first, one we told ourselves we could tolerate. But soon the clouds opened up, pouring all they had, not to be ignored. My mother put her purse over my head and told me not to worry, that it would be all right.

"Is it a tornado?" I yelled. I could barely hear myself over the rain.

"No," my mother said. "I don't know. But let's hurry." She squeezed my hand and began to run, dragging me as best

she could, our soaked shoes slapping the sidewalk. But as we picked up our pace, so did the rain. The drops grew fatter, faster, and after another block the only thing I could see was my mother's arm, tugging me forward, stretching farther and farther away as I tried to keep up. She shouted for me to come on, that we were almost there. I shut my eyes and pretended she was my brother. That we were back at the golf course, where it was dry and familiar, and we were ready to have an adventure.

When we came to a corner, my mother's hand slipped from mine. She had turned so quickly, and when I reached out for her again, she wasn't there. Just darkness and rain. I listened for her footsteps. Heard nothing. I called her name but the only sound that came back was the rain lapping my ear. I looked down at my clothes, drenched, painted on my body, and thought of the lake. I rubbed the water out of my eyes, and when I opened them again, a pale hand appeared out of the darkness. One of the lake people, I thought, come to claim me as their own.

"Hey," my mother said. "There you are. Come on, I think I found it."

She put her arm around me and we turned again, this time onto a narrow, flooded sidewalk. We passed through a gate that opened and closed with the wind and came upon a house. I could only see its outline at first, but as we approached the porch step, a motion light shot on, spotlighting my mother and me, and the square old home in front of us.

We got out of the rain and shivered under the porch, the wood of which was warped and pocked with holes. Under the front window were two lawn chairs, and under the chairs

a few empty bottles of beer, a soggy pack of cigarettes. My mother rang the doorbell. From inside, a dog barked.

The door opened and a big dog came wagging at me. Sandy yelled at it to get back in. Then she saw us. "Holy cow," she said. "Aggie."

"I'm sorry," my mother said. She pushed me in front of her and Sandy gasped again.

"Mother Mary. Well, get on in here."

Sandy had just made it home from work and was still in her cook clothes. Inside, the house was warm, but in our wet clothes it felt like we had just stepped out of the pool. Sandy showed us to the kitchen, disappeared to fetch some towels for me, a change of clothes for my mother. Her dog stayed behind, licking the rain off me, sniffing me with its cold nose. It was a long-haired mutt with a muddy snout, and it panted happily as I petted it.

"Sorry I don't have any clothes your size," Sandy said to me when she returned. My mother changed in the bathroom and came back looking funny in Sandy's sweats, which only went down to my mother's shins. The T-shirt she wore looked more like a cut-off tank top. "You either," Sandy said.

The two of them sat at down at the kitchen table, a long oval unlike our small square. I wrapped myself in the towels and stayed on the floor, next to the dog.

"That's Steamboat," Sandy said. "He used to have a brother, Tugboat. Are you a dog person?" she asked me.

"He is," my mother said. "I'm allergic. So, if I start sneezing and crying . . ."

I didn't know that about my mother. I didn't remember

her sneezing around Baron, though I didn't remember her petting him a lot either. Especially near the end.

I scratched Steamboat between his ears and he liked it.

"Look at that," Sandy said. "You've got a new friend." She got up from the table and took two glasses from the cupboard, set them in front of my mother. "You must be thirsty from your jog."

"A glass of water would be nice," my mother said, itching her nose.

"Yes, but would a glass of wine be even better?" Sandy opened the fridge and pulled out a box of wine left over from the party and poured two dark glasses. "There we go, something for our troubles." She sat back down and she and my mother each took a sip. "And for my soaked sailor, there are sodas in the garage. Right through there. Fridge is by the door."

I looked at my mother. Go on, she said, and started talking to Sandy about the van, what all we'd been through.

I had to go through the laundry room to get to the garage. A single bulb lit the entire room, which was packed with stacked boxes of junk. It looked like Sandy had just moved in, or she was getting ready to go somewhere. Except the boxes were worn, caving in on one another. I checked one with the hope of finding something rare, something I could borrow from Sandy if she wouldn't mind, and use to win back my brother if the Stranger article didn't do it. I found a photo of Sandy and a man who wasn't Cornbread. This man was white and wore a large hat that shadowed his face. Sandy was not wearing a hat. Her face was clear, and she looked much younger in the picture than she did now.

Her cheeks were smooth, her hair long and with no touches of gray.

I put the picture back and rummaged some more. There were more pictures of the man, of Sandy. In one photo Sandy was at a Halloween party, dressed in all yellow with a large hat that matched. In Sandy's arms was a crying baby dressed as a monkey, who seemed upset that someone had taken away its pacifier and given it a toy banana. Sandy's lips were pouted like she wanted to kiss the baby, or maybe she was shooshing it to be quiet. At the bottom of the box there was nothing but empty picture frames, a dusty rattle.

Steamboat met me at the door when I came back in. My mother's wineglass was almost empty, and Sandy's drink had gone from purple to clear.

"I know he's trying real hard," my mother said.

Sandy nodded. "And it doesn't bother you? What they say in the papers?"

My mother picked up her glass. "No, it doesn't," she said. "The dogs bark, but the caravan moves on."

Another one of her sayings. She once told me the same thing when I complained about my brother's name-calling. *There are always going to be mean people out there, people with bad hearts who mean you no good. I'm not saying your brother is one of them, but don't let what they say bother you. The dogs bark, but the caravan moves on.*

But whenever she said that to me, all I could think about was the dogs being left behind.

"That's good," Sandy said. She poured my mother a refill from the box.

"I mean, I know it's the city's reputation, blah blah blah.

But when it comes to that stuff, he always seems to come through." She stared into her glass of wine, as if it were a crystal ball and something would soon be revealed.

My mother sniffled, wiped her eyes.

"You know, it's funny. When I first moved here, I read about how Kansas was the worst allergy state in the country, made people absolutely miserable. But I never had a problem, not until we got that dog." Steamboat tilted his head, as if he knew my mother was talking about his kind.

"Well, don't worry, he'll catch him," Sandy said. "Sometimes it takes a day, sometimes longer, but they always catch them." My mother nodded. There were a few seconds of silence as Sandy held her glass in the air, suspended in thought. Finally she said, "I mean, where is there to go, really? Where can anyone go?"

My mother took a long gulp. "Nowhere comes to mind."

Sandy shifted in her seat and she put her hand over my mother's. "What I mean, sweetie, is there's no sense worrying about things you can't do a thing about."

"Yes," my mother said. "I know what you mean. You tell yourself not to worry, about money, prisoners, but it's always there. Hanging in the back of your mind when you lock the doors at night. It has a way of finding you."

"Like tornado season," Sandy said. "Like a tornado watch."

"Exactly," my mother said, taking another drink. "Except with kids, the watch is endless."

"Yes," Sandy said, "well."

She looked at her refrigerator. There were a lot of magnets, but no pictures or notes. Her eyes fell and she twirled

the stem of her wineglass between her thumb and pointer finger.

"Remember when you guys first came to town," Sandy said, "and there was that newspaper article. About that baby. They had your picture and everything." She paused, her gaze drifting upward, as if what she was picturing were written on the ceiling. "You sure looked beautiful. I remember that's all people talked about. How you were the most beautiful woman this city's seen."

"Right," my mother laughed.

"And that summer dress. Whatever happened to that dress?"

"Sold it," my mother said. "Last month when bills were due."

"Oh," Sandy said. "Sorry." She pinched the corner of the plastic tablecloth and made some joke about the golf course's wages. "What was it the baby was choking on?"

"A rubber nipple. It chewed the tip off and got it lodged in its throat."

"That's right. CPR on a baby." Sandy shook her head. "Your husband, the hero."

"Sandy," my mother said. "We don't have to talk about that."

Sandy poured another refill. This time she left the box on the table. "Well, sometimes I think it's best to discuss the worst." She swirled her wine around, making a tiny tornado. "At least, when you're among friends."

"Sure," my mother said, but under the table, where Sandy couldn't see, her feet were fidgeting. She drank more wine.

"But," Sandy said, "it doesn't have to be all gloom and doom. Let's talk about your new beau. Tell me what's it like, because I've got to tell you, I never would have figured you two."

Steamboat stretched out on the floor and groaned.

"Oh, I don't want to talk about that," my mother said.

"Well, he seems to be making you happy," Sandy said. "Isn't he? Are you happy?" I felt my mother look at me, so I acted like I wasn't listening. I lay down parallel to Steamboat and pretended we were having a conversation. I asked him if he'd ever seen a tornado, and could he believe this weather.

"I don't know," my mother whispered. "He's been such a help. The rides to work. Watching the kids at the course. And he really is a gentleman when he wants to be." Sandy didn't say anything. "Look, I know it could go either way. But if I'm wrong, I'm wrong. The way I see it, I deserve to be wrong. Everyone else gets to be wrong, why not me?"

"I don't know, honey," Sandy said. "But I can tell you from experience, being wrong is overrated."

The room went quiet, and I felt for sure I had missed an important gesture or look, up above.

"Yes, well, it's my decision to make, isn't it," my mother said. "No one else's."

"No, I guess not," Sandy said. "More wine?"

They drank a little more, and Sandy changed the subject back to my dad. Where did he fit in the picture? she wanted to know. What was his outlook like? My mother sighed, put her hand to her head, massaging her temple. She didn't know, she said, and looked at me again. This time I asked Steamboat what his plans were for tomorrow. If the weather was

right, how did he feel about a walk? Steamboat's ear perked up, and my mother resumed her talk.

She didn't know about my dad, my mother said. She wished she did. She took another sip. She said the worst was—it was this moment. There was a time, right after we learned I was, you know. Again. We were both lying in bed, watching some bad movie he rented, and I said, I don't know why, that maybe I shouldn't . . . see it through. It was something I'd been sort of thinking about for a while. I mean, we were living in a nice-enough house, but we had no money. So I started to think, about where we were headed, what our future looked like, and what I saw was us barely getting by for the rest of our lives. I saw myself never going back to school, staying in this city, in that house forever. As soon as I said it, though, I knew I could never go through with it. The words, they left this terrible taste. Still, they were already out there, waiting for a response. He paused the movie, sat up, and looked at me. He put his hand on my stomach and told me absolutely not, that I'd regret it for the rest of my life. And those were the right words, and he said them the right way, but something was wrong. I could tell he'd thought about it before. I could tell he was imagining it now. A life without . . . restrictions. In his mind he'd written an entirely different story for himself, one in which he could be anything, go anywhere, where the decisions he made didn't follow him around every day, nipping at his heels. I knew then he was ready to escape.

The room went silent. Under the table every leg was still. Steamboat got up, licked his chops. He stretched his back legs and went over to his empty dog bowl. He whined.

"Oh, hush," Sandy said. "You've already eaten."

"I've thought the same thing, to be honest," my mother said. "I mean, we were so young . . . but I never acted on it. That's the difference."

Steamboat walked over to Sandy and whined. "What? I don't know what you want," Sandy said. "You've had your fill. Go on."

"But now I think . . . I mean, I just don't know how long we can live like this. What if something goes wrong? What if the van has quit for good or something happens and we need to go to the doctor?" Sandy took my mother's hand. "We just, we need help," my mother said. "That's all."

"I know you do," Sandy said.

Above them the ceiling fan whirred. Steamboat put his head in Sandy's lap and whined, until she scratched his head and said OK. It's going to be OK.

When the wine box was empty, my mother said we should get going. She had an angry son at home.

"Do you want to call a cab?" Sandy said. "You don't want me driving."

My mother said no, she didn't have the money for that. But it was fine, she knew whom she could call. He should be off by now. Sandy showed her the phone in the living room, returned to the kitchen, where I was petting Steamboat. She asked me if we ever had a dog, and I said yes, but not anymore.

"He was a German shepherd," I said. "His name was Baron."

"How nice," Sandy said. "Was he a retired police dog?"

"I don't know. He was old."

"Well, I'm sure you were very kind to him. I bet you treated him like a brother, didn't you?"

My mother returned.

"He's on his way," she said. She gave Sandy a big hug, told her she could never thank her enough. Sandy said to hang in there and walked us to the door. She petted the side of my head like I petted Steamboat.

"I know it might not seem like you have much," she said, "at times. But you have this beautiful boy. And a bigger one just as good." She flipped on the porch light, so it wasn't so dark out there. "Let's let that count for something."

Outside, the rain had stopped. The sky had cleared in parts, forming small pools of stars, and a bright white moon lit the path ahead.

The van was where we left it, the way we left it, broken and alone. I rubbed its side mirror and said I was sorry for leaving it behind. I promised it wouldn't happen again.

Rick showed a few minutes later, windows rolled down, bad music blasting.

"Look who comes crawling back," he said. He grabbed a flashlight and some tools out of his trunk. "You two stay on the curb. Let Rick the fix-it take a look." But Rick didn't have any better luck than my mother, though he did know a good mechanic, someone who owed him a favor and would tow our piece of junk for free. He put his tools away and opened the door for my mother and me.

The back of the car was a disaster, full of greasy clothes, golf cart parts, used or stolen pro shop supplies. An air freshener in the shape of a racecar hung from the windshield, but

did little to mask the strong smell of gasoline. At the golf course, I once saw Rick show up early for his shift to fill gas cans he must've brought from home—pumping from the same white tank used for the golf carts—and sneak them off to his car when no one was looking. I never told my mother this or discussed it with my brother, imagining that if I ever got in trouble with Rick down the road, this information would be valuable. That I could somehow use it against him.

My mother sat in between Rick and me, so I could have the only working seat belt. After we got on the road, Rick put his arm around my mother and pinched my neck. "I thought testicles traveled in twos. Where's your bro?"

"At home," my mother said.

"Doing what?"

"Waiting."

"Oh, I get it. You're bonding with the baby," Rick said, and flicked my other ear, much harder than my brother ever would.

"Cut it out!" I yelled.

"Whoa, look at this guy. Look at how upset he gets when he's away from his brother. Do *not* separate the two."

My mother put her head back and closed her eyes. "Rick, my head is killing me."

Rick sniffled. At the golf course he always complained about his allergies, saying you had to be pretty stupid to make someone work a job they were allergic to. Then he'd laugh and say, but hey, that's the government for you.

"You didn't let me finish," Rick said. "I was gonna say him and his bro are lucky. I had a brother growing up, but we weren't thick as thieves like them two."

I tried to imagine a younger Rick, a Rick with a brother. I pictured the two of them riding around in Rick's cart, chucking water balloons at little girls and laughing.

"We were always at each other's throat. My dad used to throw shit at us, we got so loud." He sniffled again, wiped his nose on his arm. "My mom said we would grow out of it, but we never did. I hated my brother and I still do. I don't know where he is, and I don't care. If I saw him today, all he'd have to do is grin that shit-eating grin and my hate would be just the same."

We took a right at a stoplight, onto Limit Street. When we were a couple blocks away we saw a police car's reds and blues lighting up a family's driveway. An officer was talking to a father on the front step. A boy and a girl watched from behind the screen door, clutching their pillows as if they were precious treasure.

"Did your brother visit you in prison?" I said, and I could feel my mother open her eyes, alarmed at my question.

"No," Rick said. "Nobody did. That shit only happens in movies."

"What about your parents?"

"You don't have to answer that," my mother said to Rick. "He'll be quiet now. Won't you?"

Yes, I said, and we were silent the rest of the way. I put my cheek to the window and shut my eyes, not sleeping but not thinking either, until I heard the turn signal click and felt the familiar dip of our apartment's lot. My mother pushed me out, and we walked halfway to our building's door before she told me to stop.

"You didn't thank him, did you? Run back and thank

him. Hurry." I asked her if I had to, and she said yes. He helped us, didn't he? Since when do we not thank those who lend us a hand?

I ran to Rick's car, idling in the parking lot. He was watching us, waiting to see that we got in safe.

"Thank you," I said.

"Wasn't a thing," Rick said. He put the car in drive, but kept his foot on the brake. He leaned his head out the window and looked past me, at my mother. He sank back into his seat, gripped the steering wheel tight, like it was a balloon that would fly into the sky if he ever let it go.

"You've got a good mother," he said. "You like being with her, and so do I. But if you think she'd ever visit you or your brother in prison, you're dead wrong." He turned up the radio, reached for a seat belt that wasn't there. "Nobody wants to see living proof of the mistakes they've made."

nine

THE STRANGER STORY was ruined by the storm. It had slipped my mind until we stepped inside our building, the halls and stairwell buzzing with lights and things unseen. But as we made our way up the stairs, I remembered what we were returning to, my seething brother, waiting with closed fists for me, the liar. I pushed my hand into my pocket, so I could have the editorial ready to show him before he pummeled me. *Here*, I would say, hands up in surrender. *Don't shoot. Don't shoot.* In reality, what I pulled out of my pocket wasn't paper. It was a watered-down wad, a spitball that came apart in my hand when I tried to unfold it. I sighed. My evidence, my chance at forgiveness, was gone.

None of that mattered, though, at least not right away, because when we opened the door to our apartment, there was no brother. No lights were on, and when my mother called my brother's name, all we heard in return was the

hum of the fan. I didn't wait for my mother to bolt our door and find a place for her purse and keys. I went into the living room to see if my brother had made camp there. He hadn't. A blanket was in the right spot but there was no brother. The first place my mother looked was our room, but he wasn't in there, either.

"He's probably just hiding," I said, to punish us for leaving him for so long, coming back empty-handed. But I knew what I said wasn't true. I could tell my brother wasn't here. He was somewhere with Chris. Where, I didn't know. For now, it didn't matter. Because I wouldn't tell my mother anything. The next half hour our apartment was a one-man movie, starring me as the world's biggest liar.

"Show me all his spots," my mother said. "Show me where he could be."

I followed and helped her search, acting surprised when my brother wasn't behind the clothes in my mother's closet, or cocooned in her curtains.

"I don't know," I said. "He should be here."

While my mother searched the rest of the apartment, looking in desperate, silly places (inside the oven, under the kitchen sink), I opened the sliding glass door to let the air in. I gazed in the pool's direction and pictured the way it would look now. The automatic lights would have kicked on, giving the water a warm, sugary glow. All the chairs would be empty of belongings, except maybe one.

My mother came into the living room and asked what I was doing. I should be looking for my brother, she said. What kind of brother was I? She told me to recheck every spot I could think of.

"We have to keep searching, OK?" she said, and went to

the phone. She picked it up, returned it to the wall. "I'm going to check with the neighbors. You stay here and search. Don't go anywhere."

I said OK, but when she left I stayed by the sliding door. I imagined what it would be like to swim at night, to break the first pool rule. You would want to stay in the water, I thought, where it was warm. The sun wouldn't be there to comfort you, if you were just a spectator, a lowly stableboy. If you were on the diving board, you'd better know what move you wanted to do. You wouldn't want to spend too much time up there, exposed, where the air was free to get you.

I dazed off until I thought I heard a splash, so soft I wasn't sure if I had imagined it. I tried to get a better view of the pool. I slid open the screen door all the way and stepped onto our porch. Another splash. This one was louder, deeper. I stepped up on the porch's lower rail, leaned over the edge. I'm so close, I thought. Just a little higher. If I could get on the top rail, I could see it all.

"What are you doing, dummy?" a voice said.

I jumped down and turned around. It was my brother. He was not in his swimming suit. He had the same clothes on as before. He was dry, and I wanted to hug him.

"Mom is going to kill you," I said.

My brother smiled. "She'd never get away with it. Not in this city."

"Where were you?"

"You better get inside before Mom comes back," he said, and went inside and lay down in front of the fan. I sat on the couch, arms crossed.

"Where were you?"

"Nowhere."

"You're lying."

"You're right. What can I say, runs in the family."

He closed his eyes like he wanted to rest. As if wherever Chris had taken him, the two had traveled long and far. To what secret kingdom, I knew he would not say.

"I read a thing about the Stranger," I said.

My brother breathed deeply, his mouth open, and at first I thought he was asleep. "So?"

"So don't you want to know?"

"Know what?"

My mother returned. I heard her check our room again, then call from the hall, asking if I'd had any luck. I didn't answer. I let her step into the living room and see the scene herself. That's what I would have wanted, if I were her. I wouldn't want anyone to ruin the ending.

Her face twitched like it couldn't be sure of what it was seeing. After the shock passed, she ran to my brother. She told him to stand up so that she could give him a hug.

"Where have you been?" she said.

My brother pushed her arms away. "I waited for you. I stayed up and waited."

I watched his face closely, to see if it flickered when he started to lie. I couldn't tell my mother my brother's secrets, but maybe I could give her a clue.

"I'm sorry," my mother said, and she told him what happened, about the van and about Sandy. "But where were you when we came home? You weren't here, were you? As soon as I opened the door, I could tell the apartment was one boy short."

"I waited as long as I could." He put his head down. He wasn't answering the question.

"Stop ducking the question," I said. "He's ducking the question."

"You need to stay out of it," my mother said, though she seemed to take my point. "You were supposed to stay in your room."

My brother sat back down and faced the fan, turning his back to my mother like some proud villain. "I waited. But no one ever came to get me. I thought you forgot."

I rolled my eyes, mumbled, Give me a break.

"Then I got thirsty in there. So I came out for a glass of water." He paused there, either for effect or to give himself time to form his lie more fully. "That's when I heard the siren."

"Siren?" my mother said.

"Yes, I thought there was a tornado or something, so I went down to the laundry room, like you told us."

My mother looked at me. We had been outside for most of the night. If there was a siren, we would have heard it.

"We didn't hear anything," my mother said. "Are you telling me the truth?"

"I don't know," my brother said. "I don't know why you didn't hear anything, but that's what happened." The corner of his lip dipped a bit, almost forming a smile. "I swear."

His lip stayed dipped. He was lying, and he knew he would get away with it.

Our dad picked us up on Friday again, and again he was early. He came to the door and this time our mother was still around, though she had already started getting ready

for work. Still, she moved aside when our dad politely asked if he could come in, and the two sat at the kitchen table sipping cups of coffee in silence until he asked about the van breaking down again.

"How'd you know about that?" my mother said.

My dad coughed, took a sip of his coffee. "I have my sources."

My mother didn't mention anything about my brother, his disappearance. Maybe she didn't want my dad to worry. Or maybe, like me, she wanted to wait until the investigation was closed before making any judgment, releasing information to the public. But she did tell my dad to keep an eye on my brother. That he'd been acting out.

"Is that right?" my dad said. He took out a check, already made out to my mother. For the van, he said, and whatever else. My mother looked like she got socks for Christmas.

"Did you hear what I said?"

"Yes," he said. "Don't look so happy."

"How'd you know how much it costs?"

"I owe you," he said. "I want to owe you."

"Just watch him," my mother said. "OK? And don't expect anything in return." She magneted the check to our fridge, beneath a drawing my brother had done in school and our electric bill. Both were stamped *Outstanding*. "How's work? Anything on you-know-who?"

"I don't want to talk about work," my dad said.

"Then don't."

"Nothing's going to happen, Ag. Everyone thinks this guy's gonna come after their family, but that's never the case. I'm sure he couldn't care less."

"Yeah, but what about your job?"

"That's my problem. Nobody else's."

My brother stomped sleepy-eyed into the kitchen with his weekend bag, asked if we were going or what. My dad told him to wait his turn to talk, but my mother was already on her way to the front door.

"You'll pick them up before church?" my dad said, hanging in the doorway as my brother and I ran into the hall.

"In the morning. Yes."

"Hey, if the van isn't fixed, you know I can give you a lift on Sunday. I'm available for rides, or whatever else you need."

"I appreciate that," my mother said. "But the check is enough for now. I don't want you doing anything you don't want to do."

I looked at my dad. Her words hurt him, but he didn't take us and walk away. He stood in the open door and rebounded with a smile.

"Lucky for you I'm becoming a new man. All I do now are things I don't want."

"Ah," my mother said, "so you've been rehabilitated."

"Yep, the system works. Ask anybody at the station."

My mother looked at me, though I don't know why. She kissed the top of my head, rubbed my brother's back. "I just wonder if it's one of those things," she said. "Where it's meet the new, same as the old."

After we grilled out for dinner we didn't go to the video store. Our dad came downstairs in jean shorts and a polo shirt with our city's emblem on it. Holstered on his hip, for everyone to see, was his gun.

"Get in the car," my dad said. "I want to show you something."

He drove us out to a part of the city I wasn't familiar
with. We sped past the fenceless baseball fields and the city's
water tower, the trailer park where no one owned a shirt.
My brother and I kept our eyes out the window, watched the
falling sun flicker through the trees. Eventually we asked our
dad where we were going, but were glad when he wouldn't
tell us, when he said sorry, it's a secret.

We pulled into a small, loose-gravel parking lot packed
with squad cars. Again we asked where we were. He waved
us on and said to follow and be quiet. We walked up a hill
on a worn dirt path, me trailing my brother, my brother my
dad. When we got to the top, we saw a crowd of policemen
standing around with their guns out. Some were cleaning
their clips, others practicing taking aim. In the field behind
them was a row of shadow-shaped targets, hovering like
ghosts.

"Stay close," our dad said, leading us to the other officers.
Out of the seven policemen, only three were in uniform, but
they all had bulletproof vests strapped to their chests. Alan
came up to my dad, grinning. He asked my dad how he was
doing, and if he was going to come out to throw darts tonight. He didn't say anything about seeing us the other
day, whether or not they caught the burglar.

"Can't," my dad said, "got the boys."

"Bring them along!" Alan joked. "We could always use
another DD." He patted me on my shoulder and it stung.
"Seriously, though, we've missed you these past couple weekends. And we're not the only ones. I know a couple ladies
who put out an APB."

My dad stepped away from Alan and whistled for every-one's attention. The officers gathered around him, holstering their guns, and waited in silence for my dad to speak. My brother and I stood at my dad's side, like we were his best lieutenants.

"The Chief couldn't be here tonight. He had a council meeting with the mayor. But because we're all trained pro-fessionals . . . ," my dad said, and paused to let his men snicker, ". . . I know you all will be on your best behavior. Don't make a fool of me in front of my boys, OK?" He put a hand on our backs and I felt my face redden. "All right, let's line up."

Once everyone was in the proper place, lined up against the wooden railing, my dad explained how the drill would go. Each officer would empty two clips. The first would be freehand. Upon my dad's order, the officers would aim the gun at the shadowy bad guy and fire like it was any regular daytime shootout. But for the second clip, the officers would have to wait until the sun set. At that point my dad would give a signal, and the officers would flick on their black flashlights to light up the dark target, the unseen threat.

Our dad came over with two pairs of plastic earmuffs. "Take these," he said. I put the earmuffs on, but they were too big and kept sliding off my head, onto my neck. "I want you guys to watch from over there," he said, pointing to a splintery wooden bench, far away from the railing.

"That looks crappy," my brother said. "Why can't we stay by you?"

"These are live rounds."

"So?"

"Listen, you're not even supposed to be out here to begin

with. But the Chief's gone and I thought you'd might like to see this, see your old dad in action." My dad blinked his eyes, waiting for us to say something like cool or oh yeah. "You know, if your mom found out, she'd probably kill me. You'd have a dead dad on your hands."

He walked back to his men, the sun blinding him into a silhouette. I thought about his words, a dead dad on my hands. I imagined a miniature version of my dad. An action figure, small in my palm, the sad ending to one of my brother's warped plots.

We sat on the bench and watched our dad get everyone in position, help them settle in their stances. When everyone was in their proper place, he shouted, "Ready!" and the officers raised their guns, pointed them at the targets. For a second, I felt bad for the targets, the black, faceless blobs. They weren't holding a gun or a knife, or anyone hostage. What had they done? What was their crime? But before I could say anything, my dad yelled fire and, again, it was too late.

The sound wasn't the sound from our stupid movies. It was a long-lasting pop, one that blasted my ears and rattled my chest, making me feel hollow. It was the sound from the Stranger tape, and with it came everything I tried not to think about. I immediately put my hands to my head, pressing the earmuffs as hard as possible to shut out both thoughts and sound. But this trapped the noise inside me, so that the booms circled from my head to my heart in one continuous terrible loop.

I felt my brother nudge me, and when I looked over I saw that he was shaking with laughter. I didn't get what was funny until I realized he was laughing at me, his scared baby brother. I opened my mouth. I tried to tell him that he

was scared too. He thought of the same things I did, went to sleep each night with the same worry, and just because he had Chris and I didn't, that didn't mean he was any safer or better than me.

After every clip was empty, our dad gave the OK to retrieve the targets. The men held up their victims so the fading sunlight could shine through the holes where the bullets had hit. My dad examined each sheet, giving tips to those whose targets went untouched. The hand of one man, who hadn't hit a single thing, was bleeding badly and in need of a bandage. The gun's kickback had pinched the man on his first shot. He hadn't fired a gun since his training, he said. "Well, that's why we're here," my dad said, and grabbed a first-aid kit to patch the man up.

After the man's bleeding was stopped, our dad came over to see how we were doing. "What do you think, boys?"

I wanted to tell him that I didn't like this. The noise. The blood. And I didn't want to be here.

"Can I shoot a little?" my brother said, his eyes fixed on the men and their guns.

"No, son. This is official police practice."

"Official?" my brother said. "That guy's wearing a tank top."

"Some other time," my dad said, and put his hand to his gun, as if to double-check it was still there. He often did the same thing with his wallet, tapping his back pocket to make sure it hadn't been picked by a thief.

"Please," my brother said, "just one round."

My dad said no, asked my brother if he was hard of hearing. My brother dropped his earmuffs on the ground. He turned around and muttered.

"Excuse me?" my dad said.

"You heard me," my brother said, his words a little louder.

"Try me again."

"I said this is stupid."

"And why is that?"

"Because . . . they're shooting paper."

"That's a good thing."

"Yeah, but you're not even gonna shoot. You're just gonna stand around and tell everyone else what to do."

"That's my job."

"Then why did you bring your gun?" my brother asked.

My dad looked down at the gun on his side, to where his hand was resting, and it was obvious that he didn't have an answer. "I just thought you'd want to see what your old man does. That's all."

"Yeah," my brother said, and he turned away from my dad, so only I could see his smile, "but you don't *do* anything."

My dad's face hardened, and he looked at me as if I could explain why my brother was acting this way. But I didn't know what to say. I had questions of my own.

An officer called to my dad. They were ready to start the second round. "Just sit down and shut up," my dad said to my brother. "Next time you can stay at your mother's."

On the way home my brother sat in the back of the cruiser with me, and our dad kept glancing at us in the mirror, like we were a couple of criminals itching to escape.

"I have to run you home," our dad said. "I'm technically on duty now, so . . ." His voice trailed off as we came to a four-way stop. I knew where we were, and knew that if we went left, it would lead us to Limit Street, which we could

hop on and take to our mom's. We went straight. "You know," our dad said, "your mother's told me some things about you. How you've been acting." He was talking to my brother, who shook his head and rolled his eyes, but didn't say anything. "Hey," my dad said, "I'm talking to you."

My brother didn't respond. When it became clear he wasn't going to apologize without prompting, or admit to any wrongdoing, our dad didn't force him. He flipped on the police radio, and the car filled with garbled voices, battling back and forth. I stared out the window and tuned out the radio as best I could, until my thoughts were interrupted by my dad's voice. He had the radio to his mouth and had joined the conversation. He told the woman to show him responding, but didn't say responding to what.

My brother ceased his silent treatment. "What was that?"

"Nothing," our dad said. "Some idiot's trespassing. I've got to run by."

"Where?"

"The battery factory."

The battery factory was one of the biggest buildings in Leavenworth that wasn't a prison or a grain elevator. It was more than five stories tall, and painted a grassy green that had faded over time, after the factory was shut down and everyone lost their job. We'd driven by it only once or twice in my life, but each time we did our dad would shake his head and say what a shame. To my brother, the factory was an unexplored world, one of the few places big enough to house his imagination.

"Are we going?"

"I am," our dad said. "I'll drop you boys off first."

My brother grabbed the barrier in protest. "No way. Take us with you."

Our dad told him no. He wasn't taking his kids to a crime scene. Besides, it was nothing exciting. Probably just a couple of lonely-hearted high schoolers looking for a dark place to sneak off to.

"We won't do anything," my brother said. "We'll stay in the car and watch, won't we?" He nudged me until I said yes. "We just want to see."

When my dad didn't shoot him down right away, I knew my brother was onto something.

"Oh, I get it," our dad said. "So now what ye olde dad does is cool? Is that it?"

We stopped and a red light colored my brother's wide smile. "We'll be good," he said. "I promise."

Our dad looked in the rearview mirror. I couldn't see his mouth, but I saw his face rise, his eyes beam. He took a sharp turn, veering off our normal course, taking a side street off Main and up onto Marion, a street I'd never heard of.

It was dark when we pulled up. The streetlights weren't alive. There were no cars in front of the factory, or dusty bikes lying in the gravel. Whoever trespassed had traveled by foot. Our dad aimed the headlights at the front doors, chained shut with a dungeon lock. It felt like we'd stumbled into a movie someone else had rented. Our dad was the cop in the opening credits, the one who was just doing his job, and everyone knew would get it. *Wrong place, wrong time*, we would think, right before a monster snatched him from the rafters. I glanced at my brother, who was sitting on his feet

trying to get a better view. I didn't remember a single movie where the worthless cop brought his boys.

"Stay put," our dad said. "I'll be back in a second."

He rolled down our windows a little more than halfway and stepped out of the car. He didn't approach the chained door with his hand on his holster, like I thought he would. He walked up hands free and tried the doors, held fast by the chain. I kept waiting for the worst possible thing to burst through the doors, but the night remained quiet. Our dad stepped back from the building and looked up, as if the monster had scaled the walls and broken through one of the dirt-caked windows. I pictured the monster bashing the glass with a rock, not his fist, and suddenly the monster became the burglar. A criminal. And because I didn't know what the Stranger looked like, never got a good look at his face on the tape, in my mind I made Chris play the part.

Our dad took one last look at the police cruiser, at us, and ducked out of the headlights, into the darkness. I heard my brain shouting the same things it shouted when we watched a bad movie. The things I never said out loud, because if I did my brother would tell me to shut up. *They can't hear you*, he would say. *They're already dead.*

For a few minutes, we did as we were told. For a few minutes, we sat there and listened. But my brother grew bored. He stuck his head out the window to see if he could see anything. He wormed half his body out, and announced he was leaving. That he was going to help our dad and that I should stay here.

"Don't," I told him. "You know what'll happen."

My brother ignored me and slithered out the window.

"Dad needs backup," he said. "If you see or hear anything, the radio's right there." He poked his head through the window, and his arms dangled to the side, like he was seated at a guillotine, waiting for the blade to fall. "Now remember what Mom always says," he said, a sick grin stretched across his face. "Don't talk to the Stranger."

And with that, he left. He ran in the same direction as our dad, the gravel crunching under his feet. Soon I heard nothing, and the night opened before me, into what could have passed as an eternity. I tried my best to hide behind my dad's seat, glad at first that he had left the headlights on, a little night-light for this new and scary world. But as the minutes ticked away and neither my brother nor my dad returned, I wondered if I would be better off without the lights. If it would be better for me not to see whatever was coming. Still, I didn't close my eyes. I sat there. I watched the yellow oval the headlights made. Cover the front, I told myself. You can do that much.

A shadow streaked in front of the car. A flash of black. Before I could doubt what I'd seen, another flew by. Two shadows, flying through the headlights and back into the night. I grabbed the police radio, like my brother told me, and waited for the next thing to happen. Whatever it would be. But the shadows didn't return. They stayed in their shadow world, and the only sound I heard was the dispatch lady reporting another possible break-in, this one off Tenth and Limit, not far from where we lived. Where our mom was if she wasn't with Rick. Still, the thought of another criminal gave me comfort. For some reason, I found it hard to imagine two criminals at the same time. If the danger was on Limit Street, I thought, then we should be safe.

I heard a gunshot.

That sick pop. I closed my eyes. I imagined the sound of the shot bouncing off every empty room in the battery factory. I imagined the bullet finding its target, and could only hope that whatever shadow it sank into, it was the right shadow. It was the bad ghost, not the good. I put my hands together and prayed. Or I wished. I opened my eyes and realized I never understood the difference.

When neither shadow returned, standing tall and triumphant, or sinking low and clutching its gut, I decided to get out of the car. I couldn't breathe, so I wormed my way out like my brother.

The air didn't smell of smoke, like it did at the range. It smelled of mildew, of the river nearby. At I first I stayed next to the car. I walked around but made a deal that at all times I must keep a finger on the cruiser. I pretended it was a space shuttle and this was my first trip outside the ship. My first space walk after months of space crawl. But when I made it to the front, the lights were too bright, and without thinking I backed away. I floated out and someone cut my tether. I felt exposed, to the dangers and coldness of space. The universe was infinite and any part of it could get me.

I heard footsteps. I heard something being dragged on the ground. My mind made an axe, a sword, a maniac or monster lugging its deformed foot around. I saw a shadow drawing near, the bottom half of its outline like nothing I'd seen. Multiple legs, inkblot limbs limping toward me. I turned and ran, like I always swore I wouldn't if I was in this situation. I ran around the side of the factory and found a door propped open by a brick. I ducked inside, where it wasn't as dark as I'd thought. A big moon speckled its way

through the dirty windows, shining a light on the grimy floor. There were no rooms in the factory. All the walls had been torn down, leaving one enormous open space, where huge pieces of abandoned machinery waited for someone to spark them to life. A mad scientist. A deranged professor. If my brother made it this far, his imagination would have unfolded like a flower, blooming with possibilities. It was the type of place I imagined Chris would take him, if they kept taking their trips. It was the type of place where the Stranger would hide, make a home, until the cops gave up on the search. It was the type of place my brother would use for every story he ever told when playing with our Joes. The battery factory, with all its machines and secrets, was the perfect hideout for every bad guy my brother ever knew.

I accidentally kicked an empty bottle, sending a ting into the farthest corners of the building. I froze, remembering where I was, the shadows I was supposed to be running from. The bottle found a wall or a machine and knocked up against it, spinning loudly like a flicked quarter waiting to settle.

The side door lurched open behind me. I turned around and saw a shadow standing in the doorway. Normal-shaped, not the monster I'd seen before. But I couldn't make it match the bodies of anyone I knew. Not with my mind in its terrified state. I made the shadow the worst. I made it Chris with my brother in the woods. I made it Rick after discovering what we'd done to his course. I made it into the Stranger. I put myself in the tape.

"It's over," the shadow said.

I tried to run, but couldn't. I thought of my brother's phone call to the golf course: *Please . . . Send help . . . We're dying.*

The shadow floated toward me, drawing nearer and nearer. "C'mon," it said. "It's done. I've got your brother."

"No," I said. "Please, no. Leave my family alone."

"It's OK," the shadow said. "It's going to be OK."

It reached out toward me.

"Don't," I said. "We didn't do anything bad. You did. You hurt that woman. Not us."

The shadow didn't respond. Its hand came at me, like my mother's in the rain. So I let it have me, and told myself to think of my mother. Whatever happens, wherever it takes you.

"Ow," I said. The shadow's hand hooked itself under my arm and raised me to the shadow's face. The shadow's mustache.

"What the hell are you doing?" my dad said. "What did I tell you?"

He didn't wait for an answer. He started dragging me to the door, to the car. My dad threw me in the back, next to my brother, and when he released me I felt the immediate burn where his hand had hooked me hard.

"Buckle your goddamn seat belts," our dad said, and when my brother didn't move fast enough, our dad threw his hand to my brother's throat. He clasped his hook around my brother's neck and squeezed, until my brother's mouth opened involuntarily, begging for air. "Do not test me, son."

"Dad," I said, but he told me to shut up. Stay out of it. He held on to my brother for another long second, watching him struggle, clasp at my dad's wrist, before releasing him with the same violence he'd used to throw me in the car.

"Now," our dad said. "Seat belts."

———

Our dad would have to write a report. Not about the trespassing. There hadn't been one, or if there was, they were long gone by the time we arrived. There was no Stranger. No Chris. No shadowy monsters stalking me in the night. There was only my dad, my brother. There was only me. But every time an officer's weapon was discharged, my dad explained, a report had to be filed, detailing when and where and, of course, why. That last part was the one my dad said he would catch hell for. How could he explain what had just happened at the battery factory?

I cobbled together a hazy picture from the different things my dad shouted on the drive home: *What the hell were you thinking? After what I told you! After you promised to stay put!*

But my brother had not stayed put. That much I already knew. What I didn't know was that after my brother snuck out the window, he followed my dad. He pretended he was my dad's backup, his secret partner. He crept around, his finger the shape of a gun, slicing this pie, slicing that. How long was it before my dad noticed he was being followed? How long before he turned on my brother and beamed his flashlight in my brother's face? My brother would have put his hands up, instinctively, and pleaded his case. I just wanted to see, he would say. I just wanted to help. And maybe part of my dad forgave him. Maybe my dad lowered his flashlight and said, Well, that's OK. But this is no place for boys. Only trained professionals. Go back to your brother. I've got it covered.

What about your gun? my brother would say.

What about it?

Aren't you going to use it?

My dad would frown. We've been over this, he would say. Go to the car. Wait for me there.

I wasn't sure how my brother did what he did next. How he got the jump on our dad. I imagined after he was told to head back to the cruiser, he pretended to do so. He took a few steps, yes, but only enough to fool our dad. Now, as he followed him, my brother was more careful. He matched his pace to my dad's, so the crunch of their shoes canceled each other out. When my dad found the entrance to the battery factory, my brother waited a full minute before following. He had to be patient. He had to wait for the perfect opportunity, when my dad's mind was elsewhere, to sneak up on him. To, with one motion, pop the button snap on my dad's holster and swipe his gun.

Never in a million years.

Aimed the gun right at me.

You were right. Something is wrong.

These were the words my dad said to my mother. After he walked my brother to the basement, his holding cell, and dared him to move. My dad stretched the cord to the stairs, where he sat with his head in his hands, mumbling words of apology into the receiver as he finished the story. *I didn't say anything. I was so shocked. Never had a gun pointed at me. Yeah. Mm-hm. No, I don't think he knew what he was doing. He looked afraid. Like he'd realized what he'd done.*

My dad pulled the phone away from his face, and from my spot on the couch I could hear my mother's voice. I couldn't understand her words but I could hear their force. The way she launched them at my dad like missiles. I pictured my mother on the other end, pacing the entire apartment

with the cordless space phone, not bound by any tether. I saw her going into our vacant bedroom. Going out on the porch, staring at the moon. When she said all the mean things she could think to say, she gave my dad his punishment. His sentence, she would say, for being so thoughtless.

"I won't be seeing you guys for a while," my dad said. "Your mother's orders." This was after he made his appeal, was denied, and hung up the phone, defeated. We both sat there a while longer, in silence, my dad recovering from the one-sided fight he'd had with my mother. Me, trying to imagine not seeing my dad. No movies. No fast food or cop games. I imagined the Stranger showing up, looking to hurt my brother and me, my mother, what he thought was my dad's entire family, only to be disappointed when he found my dad, maybe drunk, definitely alone.

"Why'd you tell her?" I asked, somewhat angry.

"I almost didn't," my dad said. "But . . . that's what the old me would have done. Kept it a secret."

"What's going to happen now?"

"Tomorrow you'll go back to your mother's. You and your brother."

"That's it?"

"That's it."

My dad wrapped the phone around his neck like a noose, asked himself how he could be so stupid. I wondered if he would be fired. I pictured my dad in the Chief's office, head lowered in shame while the Chief raged at him like in the movies. My dad hadn't caught the Stranger, and now this. Again my dad would apologize, and again it wouldn't be enough. Heads need to roll, the Chief would say. Examples

must be made. He would extend an open hand, waiting for my dad's gun and badge.

"I just don't know what he was thinking," my dad said. "Do you? Hey, look at me. Is there something going on with your brother?"

I shook my head no, though the thought crept in of how easy it would be to say yes. How simple it would be to confess everything: what I saw the night of my mother's party, my brother's disappearance the night before, my theory about the pool and about Chris. The tape. What a relief it would be, I thought, to tell my dad all these things.

I looked at a picture my dad had on his wall. It was of my brother and me dressed as sailors, though we were so young we could barely walk, let alone steer a ship. My brother had his arm around my shoulder, and instead of facing the camera, he was facing me.

"He hasn't met any new friends?" my dad asked. "He's not hanging around any older boys who like to get in trouble?"

I kept my eyes on the picture, swallowed the dry in my throat. "I don't think so," I said, and was glad that we were sitting in the darkness.

My dad kept pressing me, asking me what we did the days our mother went to work. Did we go anywhere? We never left the complex, did we? I kept telling him no, we never went anywhere. We haven't met anyone. We haven't done anything.

"You're not lying to your dad?" he continued. "You're telling the truth? Because I would understand if you weren't. I know what it's like to want to protect somebody."

"I haven't done anything wrong," I said. "We don't know anything. Ask Mom."

At the mention of my mom, my dad went quiet again. He pulled himself off the stairs and hung up the phone with a resounding clack. He ate a slice of cheese straight out of the wrapper and went upstairs to change. When I heard his door shut, I went and sat at the kitchen table. My dad had left his police pad there, and I flipped through its pages so I could think about the crimes other people committed, the mistakes they made, and not the lies I had just told.

MW wrk.
MW liquor store.
MW home.
MWWR.
MW home.

These were the newest notes, but I didn't know what they meant. So I flipped backward, to the letters I could decipher. *B&E* meant breaking and entering. *DUI* we'd learned in school. *BK* I didn't know.

"Brian Kern," my dad said. I hadn't heard him descend the stairs. "Or as you and your brother like to call him, the Stranger. Now what did I say about going through my things?"

He grabbed his gun off the table, where he'd left it even after what had just happened. He put it in its holster, his badge on his hip.

"What about the rest?"

My dad snatched the pad from me, closed it. "The rest, you don't need to know," he said. "The rest is none of your business."

"But—"

"I said no, goddammit. Why are you and your brother so hard of hearing?" He grabbed his keys and wallet. "Now go to bed."

After he left, I sat on the couch wondering why my dad had told me the Stranger's full name, why that was my business but MW wasn't. Maybe he wanted me to know who he was in case I ran into him. Or maybe he wanted me to think of him as real, just another human being and not some scary monster out to get me. There are no monsters, my dad once told me. This when I couldn't sleep after watching a movie about a fish lady who ate her own kids. *Mother Guppy*, I think it was called. There are only people, my dad said. It's people you have to watch out for. But I won't let any of them hurt you. That's my job. I'm your dad.

This had calmed me at the time but now made things worse. A monster I could imagine, I could hold in my brain and toy with. A person, a real-life human being, I could never understand. Not fully. I could never grasp why my mother was with Rick. I couldn't understand why my brother kept leaving me for Chris, picking some guy we hardly knew over me, his only brother. A monster wouldn't do that. It would eat you, spit out your bones, but the only feeling it would ever force you to face was fear.

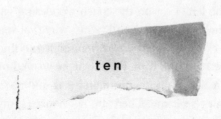

ten

THE SUMMER BEGAN to fall away. The city inched closer toward a nasty August heat, and the Stranger remained at large. After the battery factory, my brother refused to discuss anything about the Stranger. The only thing that interested him now, it seemed, was Chris.

But for a couple of weeks, Chris was unavailable, or my brother was unavailable to him. The morning after the shooting, our mother handed down my brother's sentence. In addition to not seeing our dad, my brother was grounded. Sentenced to the apartment for an undetermined amount of time. Maybe forever, my mother said, if he kept going the way he was going. Would there be time off for good behavior? There would not. Not for a crime as serious as my brother's.

So for what seemed like forever he did nothing. He stayed in our room most of the time, sleeping, reading, or doing push-ups. At first I visited him, pretending I was a variety

of people. I pretended I was family, not a brother but a distant cousin, come to show the black sheep support when everyone else had given up on him. I pretended I was a prison guard with a soft heart, the one who'd sneak an extra dinner roll from the mess hall. I pretended I was a detective. My dad's superior. I apologized for the way our dad had handled the case. That boy sure did bungle it, I said. But not to worry, we know you're innocent. We know you'd never hurt anyone. And I've made it my mission to find the people who did. So tell me the truth: Who did take that gun? Was it Chris? Did he tell you to do it? Or were you learning to protect yourself? Just in case.

"You're so stupid," my brother said, two weeks into his sentence. "Stop making shit up and leave me alone."

He threw a sock ball at my face. The guard should have searched his cell for weapons.

"Prison's changed you," I said. "That's the pen talking."

My brother shut the encyclopedia he was reading. Not A for anatomy. The letter E, for escape, I guessed. He grabbed a handful of my bottom-bunk sheets. "You think the Stranger's sheets had dinosaurs on them? This isn't a prison. It's a nursery. Now leave me alone, baby."

He wasn't going to talk. That was clear. One day his sentence would be served, and what then? I shut myself in the bathroom. I stared into the mirror and pretended the skinny kid with the bowl cut was someone else. A cop. A teacher. A guard. Anyone who knew what to do. Anyone who had an answer.

It's up to you, the reflection said, in a voice that was and wasn't my own. *You have to do it. Find out what's going on with your brother. Get him back on the force. It's the only way.*

———

I decided to tail him. If my brother wasn't going to volunteer the answers I wanted, I would have to get them some other way. But after following him around for a day without him noticing or caring, I realized I was more like a guy on the inside than I was a tail. I was the little brother, so it made sense for me to follow. I could walk by my brother's side, step where he stepped, and who would suspect a thing? To make sure my brother never got too far away, though, I acted like I was a dog and my brother was my owner. Inside the apartment I went room to room with him, plopped on the ground when he stopped, and panted or pretended to sleep. I imagined an invisible leash rung around my neck, and that my brother was walking me, and that we could only be as far apart as the leash stretched.

What I discovered was little. I learned that he didn't want to talk to me, that if I asked him what he was thinking while he stared out our sliding glass door, in the direction of the pool, at the woods, he had no problem putting me in a headlock, stuffing my head in the crack between the couch cushions. None of this was done in a playful way. He didn't smile to himself, the way one of his evil men would after drowning some hero's loved ones in the bathtub. He looked annoyed, and tired of me, of this apartment, the roaches. But we couldn't go anywhere. Our mother's boss was on post all week, so she couldn't take us with her to work. She called every thirty minutes to make sure we were there, and if I answered and said, Yes, we're doing fine, nothing is wrong, she said, OK, good. I believe you. Now put your brother on the phone. It was times like these I wished we had a second phone. So I could listen in on the other line,

hear my mother's instructions, instead of just my brother's half. *Yes. No. We won't. I won't. Goodbye.*

A couple of weeks into his sentence we went to the pool. But we didn't swim. We couldn't risk losing track of time and not being there when our mother called.

"Have you seen him?" I said. "Do you think he's gone?"

"No," my brother said. "He's not gone. I haven't been here. So."

"Will he come back?"

A hot breeze blew over the pool, and my brother put his arm through the pool gate, unlocked it.

"We can't," I said.

"I'm not." He opened the gate but did not enter. "But in case someone's looking," he said. "Now they know it's an open swim."

I didn't know what that meant, and my brother didn't explain. He left the gate open like that, for any chalk kid to wander in and fall in the water, to flail or worse. But I didn't shut it. I followed my brother like a good spy, and when we went into our apartment the phone was ringing. It'd been only ten minutes, but here was our mother, calling again. I just got this feeling, she said. I just got this feeling that something was wrong.

Trailing my brother became trickier the Sunday we went back to the golf course with our mother. Normally she didn't work Sunday mornings. That time was reserved for church. But the past month, we hadn't made it to a single mass. Instead, our mother slept in, after a long day of work or a long night out with Rick, who wasn't around when we arrived.

"He had an emergency, so you two have free roam of the course," she said. She stared at my brother as she spoke. She must have wanted to keep an eye on him, too.

"Emergency?" I said.

"Yes. He wasn't feeling well. But I expect you to be on your best behavior. Be back at the van before the cannon."

The cannon belonged to the fort. It fired every day at five, right after retreat was played over loudspeakers planted all over post. My brother and I didn't own watches, so our mother made us use the cannon to tell time. When the cannon sounded, my brother and I liked to clutch our chests and pretend we'd been shot. Fall to the ground, say woe is me.

We stopped by the cafeteria for a late breakfast. Sandy wasn't behind the counter or sitting in any of the empty seats.

"She must not be here," I said.

"She is too," my brother said. "She's hiding." He headed for the metal double doors that led to the kitchen, where we weren't allowed.

"We can't," I said.

"Watch us," my brother said.

"You just do what you want, don't you?"

"Yes. And I do what you want too, but are too baby to do." He pushed a door open and slid in without a sound. I thought about whether to follow, but couldn't make up my mind. A good undercover cop wouldn't hesitate, I knew. He would follow the mark wherever the mark went, do whatever the mark asked, until the line between right and wrong became blurred, and the cop began to wonder if there really was a good side and a bad, or if wrongdoing, as one bad movie had said, was in the eye of the beholder.

After a minute the door swung open and my brother's

head poked out. "You have to see this," he said before disappearing into the back again.

This time I did what a good cop would do, what I thought my dad would have wanted me to do. I followed him. I snuck through the door and hid behind an icebox that hummed like our box fan. I peeped around and took everything in, memorized the exits. The kitchen was dirtier than I had imagined. Old mop strings shed during the last scrub stuck to the floor. All the metal had a rust to it, and the walls and ceiling were yellow when it was clear they wanted to be white. We walked through a maze of boxes, stacked into towers that nearly touched the ceiling. My brother stopped me when we came to a corner and put his finger to his lips.

"Shh," he said. "Do not disturb." He waved me around the corner, and I stepped out in the open and saw what he wanted me to see. It was Sandy, sitting on a stack of huge sacks of popcorn kernels. Or, Cornbread sat on the sacks and Sandy sat in his lap, her back twisted, so I couldn't see what their faces were doing. Cornbread held her in his big arms, like my mother did when she wanted to pretend I was still a baby. Sandy rocked with him, cooed, moaned, and didn't shiver when Cornbread's hand drew circles on her naked knee.

I immediately thought of Rick and my mother, the night of the party. Cornbread's arms flexed harder, holding Sandy tight. Sandy's legs kicked in the air like she was swinging on a swing set, trying to get higher and higher. I watched for a moment longer, and walked away, in sort of a daze, until I reached the cafeteria, where my brother was waiting, laughing. "I know," he said. "It's stupid, isn't it?"

"I guess," I said, though I couldn't put into words what I just saw, or what seeing it made me feel.

"Don't you get it?" my brother whispered. "Nobody's watching. Rick's gone. Mom's working. Sandy and Cornbread are, well, you saw." He smiled at me, though in a way I didn't completely recognize. "We have the whole course to ourselves, dummy. We can do whatever we want."

He got up and walked out the cafeteria's side door, and I followed him outside, unsure what he meant. What could we do now that Rick was gone that we couldn't do while Rick was here, except relax, not worry about his leg pinch?

We went around back, down the long hill that led to the golf cart garage. The air was thick and dead. Coming in from the daylight, I rubbed my eyes to help them adjust to the darkness, while keeping up with my brother as he weaved from row to row, snaked through the endless sea of carts.

"What are we doing?" I said.

"We're doing what we always do," my brother said.

"I don't want to play hide-and-go-seek."

"Who said anything about that?" he said, and started to walk faster, to take sharper and more surprising turns. I tried to track his feet, but he was running now, darting toward the back, where it was all dark.

I had to stop to catch my breath. "Wait up," I said, but I could no longer hear my brother's footsteps. "Where are you?" The entire garage was still, buzzing with silence. Everything looked like it could come to life. "I told you I'm not playing."

I wound my way through several more rows. It got so dark that when I closed my eyes, there wasn't much of a difference. "Come out! I don't like this!"

No one returned my words. I sat down in the middle of a row and wondered what would happen if this was it. If I

was a dead boy. I imagined my face on a flyer tacked to the bulletin board at my dad's police station. The other officers would pat my dad on the shoulder, console him as he stared at my picture on his break, his face blank. They'll find him, Alan would say. They always do. When they did find me, when I was discovered by Cornbread or, more likely, Rick, my mother would collapse over my body. Don't touch him, she would say, running her hands through my hair, over my skin, which would be pale and pruney, like I had drowned in the pool. Don't any of you touch him. And Rick would slowly back away, slinking back into the shadows, because he had never had a son and couldn't know what to say. He would have to leave my mother alone.

I brought my legs to my chest and put my head down.

"Hey, c'mon," a voice said. "What are you doing?"

I looked up and saw my brother.

"Get up, would you?" he said. "I want to show you something."

"It's a cart," I said.

My brother had picked me up and walked me through rows of carts, leading me to what he wanted to show me. I held on to his shirt until we passed through what felt like the garage's center, where it was lighter and any sound echoed. We took turns hooting and shouting, letting our voices disappear into the dark, only to return to us a second later, tinny, like we were talking through a can.

"Here it is," he said, and sat down in a random cart, the last one in its row. I sat next to him in the passenger side, my butt on the edge so my feet could touch the floor.

"I don't get it," I said.

"Look." He pointed at the ignition, where someone had left a key. "It's Rick's. This is his cart." A green rabbit's foot dangled from the key ring, bright and unreal. I remembered something similar dangling from Rick's car keys. "Haven't you ever noticed? He always leaves his keys in his cart, like an idiot. But now everybody's gone. Now's our chance." I reached out to touch the rabbit's foot, which I had been too afraid to do in Rick's car. My brother slapped my hand away. "No way," he said. "You're too dumb to drive." He took a deep breath, moved his hand to the shifter, and put the cart in reverse. "If anyone's going to get us out of here, it's going to be me."

He twisted around so he could see what was behind him, and put his arm behind my neck, like our dad used to do to our mother when he drove our family around.

"Here we go," he said, and put his foot to the pedal.

The cart jerked backward. Fast, out of control, its little motor roaring.

"Shit!" my brother yelled. He kicked at the brake, and just as sharply as we started, we stopped, slamming me back into my seat.

A bead of sweat dripped off my nose and into my mouth, salting my tongue. For a moment I sat there, taking in what had just happened. I glanced over at my brother, who had both hands on the wheel, staring at it like it was an alien ship. The ship had crash-landed thousands of years ago, and we were the stupid humans foolish enough to think we could make it fly.

"Maybe we should stop," I said.

"We haven't done anything. Not yet."

I grabbed the rabbit's foot, combed back its hair to find its skin. I reminded myself that Rick was gone. He wasn't

working today. And with him out of the picture, there was no one here to punish us.

"Are you sure?" I said.

"Yes," my brother said. "Now's our chance to get out of this dump."

I scooted back in my seat. I took a breath, held on to the railing, and told my brother that I was ready. He put the cart in drive and inched us away from the wall. He drove slowly until the garage exit was in sight, like our mother did in school zones, even in the summer. But once we got out in the open, out of close quarters, he put his foot down hard and started to drive just like Rick.

We drove the cart all the routes Rick always went: up the hill to eighteen, down to five, across the rickety bridge to seven. Like Rick, and unlike any other driver I knew, when we started down a huge hill, instead of braking or letting the cart coast, my brother sped up. I grabbed the cart's side rail because I didn't have Rick's arm to hold on to.

We circled a water hazard, murky with algae and pond scum. We stopped and found the biggest rock to throw in. I found a small, weird-shaped stone and put it in my pocket. A golf club pinged somewhere far off, and a white dot drifted into the blue sky. We watched the ball land in the tall ragweed surrounding the pond, and we laughed, because we knew the owner would never find it. Rick once said tall grass was where golf balls go to die.

"It's nice not having to worry about Rick," I said. "His stupid leg pinch."

"We can go wherever we want," my brother said. "That's what's nice."

We got back in the cart and drove around some more. We drove all the places we could think to drive. I thought about the course map we made of all the places we explored—the one I spilled Kool-Aid on—how it took weeks to cover only a quarter of the course. If we had had the cart the whole time, we would have finished in one weekend. The whole thing seemed silly.

When we had gone everywhere else, my brother drove us to the abandoned scoreboard. The scoreboard stood to the side of where the eighteenth hole once was, back when eighteen was a par five. On one of our weekly rides, Rick explained that nobody could ever hit the ball far enough, so they moved the green and changed the hole to a four. Before that, the course was too tough, Rick said, especially for a city so short on talent.

We parked the cart behind a bush in case anyone showed up, though no one ever came out here but us. I raced my brother to the ladder, but when I looked back, he wasn't racing at all. He was walking. He let me climb the ladder attached to the scoreboard's back and took his time following. If you knew where to look, you could see the scoreboard from the cafeteria's corner window. From that distance, it seemed small, a toy, a real-life thing made miniature for toddlers. But up close was different. The scoreboard towered above us, an abandoned fortress, our own secret skyscraper.

At the top there was little room to stand, just a ledge you would fall to your death from if you weren't careful. I sidestepped across the scoreboard to the end of the other side, a spot usually reserved for my brother. I leaned over the edge, peered at the pool of dirt below.

"This is my favorite place," I said.

My brother sat down and let his legs dangle. "That's because you've never been anywhere." He had that jerkiness in his voice again. I tried to ignore him. I looked up at the horizon and tried to find the building farthest away. All I saw were prisons.

"Neither have you," I said. "Where have you been that I haven't?"

"Nowhere," he said. "I haven't been anywhere either." I watched him closely after he said this, but he didn't say anything more. The wind picked up, and I hugged the scoreboard. I thought about saying something mean, to tease more information out of my brother, but when I opened my mouth, there was a cloudless thunder.

"It's five," my brother said.

"What happened to the music?"

"We're too far away."

He didn't move. He just sat there, his back against the scoreboard, his eyes closed like he was sunbathing at the pool.

"We better get back," I said.

"She won't go anywhere without us," my brother said.

"She'll be mad."

"Of course she will."

"She will."

"Look, we're already late," he said, opening his eyes. "We still have to return the cart, right? We can't leave it here. So we're already late."

"You're going to make us later. You're going to get us into trouble again."

He stood up. "Again?" he said. "Us? *You* were never in trouble in the first place. You should have been." He walked

over to me quickly, crossing the narrow ledge without holding on to anything, or looking down to check his footing. "You know, I'm sick of you, you little liar. You follow me around, a little lying baby, doing what I do, wanting the things I want, but you're too afraid to go get them."

I bent my knees to brace myself. "No I'm not."

"You wanted to drive the cart, so I drove the cart. You wanted the gun, so I grabbed it." He grabbed me by the shirt. He could throw me off and there would be no witnesses. No one to call my brother out in court. "You wanted to go to the pool, to learn the Gainer and all the other cool pool moves, so I went and made friends with Chris."

"That's not what I wanted," I said.

"Liar," he said, and leaned me back, dangling me over the edge. I could feel the nothingness beneath me, the empty air between me and the ground. "You better tell me what I said is true," he said. "Or it's a long way down."

I tried to grab his arm. He leaned me back farther, until I was sure I'd fall.

"OK, OK," I said. "You're right. You're right."

"Say it. Say you're a baby."

"I'm a baby."

"A lying baby."

"I'm a lying baby."

"Say I'm smarter than you."

"You're smarter."

"Smarter than you'll ever be."

"You're smarter than I'll ever be."

He grinned at me and opened his mouth in fake shock, pretending he'd lost his grip. Don't, I said. He pulled me up

to him. "Ha. You really thought I was going to drop you, didn't you, dummy?"

He ruffled my hair, pushed my face. I punched him away. I sat down, swung my feet off the edge like I was at the pool, kicking them safely in the shallow end. I looked around until I found the cafeteria window, small, far away. I imagined someone watching what just happened from the window, my brother dangling me over the edge. It would look like something out of a movie, or one of my brother's epic toy plots. Me, the good guy in serious trouble. My brother, the bad. The villain who only won in the worlds my brother created.

My brother peered over the edge of the scoreboard, as if the pool waited below, waiting for his best move. It occurred to me I couldn't remember the last time I'd been in the pool, in the actual water.

"What do you guys talk about?" I asked my brother.

"Who? What do you mean?"

"You and Chris. Tell me what else you guys talk about, or I'll tell Mom what just happened. I'll tell her and Dad about you and Chris, sneaking out to the pool—everything."

There was a second of silence, and I felt my brother look at me. But I didn't look at him. I already knew the faces he was making. Anger, mixed with worry and disbelief.

"You're blackmailing me?" he said. I didn't know what that word meant, but felt I should say yes. My brother kept his back to me, and the sun baked his shadow into the scoreboard. "Unbelievable," he said.

He put his head down in thought, his hand on his chin, as if he were weighing the options.

"I can't tell you," he finally said. "I'm not supposed to."

I pulled up the tongue of my broken-laced shoe, got up, and walked over to my brother's side. I sat down and put my hand on his shoulder, as if to say, It's OK. It's me, your brother. If I were wearing a wire, this would be the part where I leaned in close and said, Don't worry, I won't tell a soul.

"Fine," he said. "But I can only tell you what isn't a secret. Got it?"

I nodded and scooted closer, so the only thing in between us was the wind. OK, my brother said, here is what you can know.

Chris was a lifeguard. Or he had been, at one time. This was the first thing my brother revealed. When he was a teenager, still in school, Chris spent summers working at the city pool. That's how he knew so much, so many moves. That's where he got those trunks. What happened? I asked. Why doesn't he work there now? Well, my brother said, he was fired. For what, I said, licking kids? No, he said, for falling in love. My brother blushed, embarrassed he'd used such a stupid word. This was Chris's story, he reminded me, not his. These are his words, not mine. Anyway, Chris met someone special. At the pool. Someone he couldn't live without. But he'd never had these feelings before. He didn't know what to do with them. He was too afraid to tell anyone, scared of what they might think or say, so he kept them to himself. What place is safer, more secret, he said, touching his chest, than right here? He didn't act. He waited. From his lifeguard perch, he studied the one he wanted, making sure they were worth the risk. Making sure his feelings weren't a fluke, some sick

joke the world was playing on him. But the feelings did not go away. They grew stronger. He couldn't concentrate. If the one he loved came for a swim, it became impossible for Chris to focus on anything else. His mind was right, but his heart felt like it was drowning.

What did he do? I asked.

He acted, my brother said. He took a chance.

And?

And it didn't work out. Chris left a note in their locker, tucked it into their pants pocket. That way they would find it later, Chris imagined, in their room when no one was looking. They would read it and finally know how Chris felt, how he'd fought and waited. How if he could love anyone else, he would.

The loved one never responded. Never met Chris at the park across the street from the pool. Never let Chris share a snow cone.

She ignored him? I said.

I guess. She stopped coming to the pool. Or she came once, but only to report Chris. To get him fired.

Oh, I said. That's sad.

There's more.

Before he left, Chris stole her membership card, with her name and address. He went to her house, at night. He brought flowers and candy. The neighborhood was quiet. No lights were lit. He climbed her porch and knocked on her window. Nothing. He waited and waited. He grew tired of waiting. He lifted the window and crawled inside.

My brother paused.

"What happened?" I said.

"I don't know," he said. "That's all he told me. Said he

would tell me the rest next time I saw him. But I haven't seen him since." He stood up and brushed off his shorts. "There, now you know some stuff. Happy?"

He started down the ladder, told me to hurry up. He didn't want to get grounded again. I climbed down and sat in the cart, and my brother put his arm around me and drove. I thought about the story he'd just told. How sad it made me feel, how it felt like a secret my brother shouldn't have shared. We rolled through the hills like this. Once in the garage, we parked the cart in the back, in the dark where it belonged. We left the key in the ignition, the rabbit's foot where we found it.

When we got to the pro shop, Rick was there, not our mother. His arm was in a blue sling that looked homemade from a pillowcase. This didn't stop him from pointing to his wrist, giving his big Rick grin.

"Hey, hey!" Rick said. "Look who it is!" He raised his good arm, readying the imaginary crowd for his grand announcement. "Gather 'round, everybody! They've returned! It's Duh and Little Duh, Duh's dumber brother!" We mumbled hello. "So where the hell have you been?" Rick said.

"Nowhere," my brother said.

"Ooh, that sounds nice. Have to go there sometime. Where is nowhere, by the way? A block away from nothing, down the street from wherever?"

"Leave us alone," my brother said. "We didn't do anything."

We tried to hurry by Rick, but he stepped in front of my brother, not letting us pass.

"That's funny, because earlier I stepped outside to have a

chew and you know what I saw? I saw two little shits driving my cart around. You shitheads know anything about that?"

"No," my brother said, and he looked right at Rick. His mouth didn't drop, giving away his lie.

"Oh, right, right, of course you don't. Because if you did, you know there'd be a whupping coming your way. You'd get a big old piece of Rick's wrath."

"Where's our mom?" my brother said.

"Hey, let's not get off subject now. I'm still curious about the cart."

"Is she in the van?"

Rick wrinkled his tan face, annoyed that my brother wasn't taking him seriously. "Listen," he said. "I saw you goons out there. Now 'fess up or we're gonna have problems. Even one-armed Rick is still a man you don't want to mess with."

My brother looked around. There were no customers nearby, no signs of our mother. "Fine," he said. "We drove the cart around a little bit. You're the dumb one who leaves your key in the ignition."

Rick nodded to himself, scratched the side of his stubbly face. He let out a big breath and I could smell the cheap cafeteria beer. Flecks of chew speckled his chin.

There was a pop, a wet smack.

I heard the slap before I saw anything, before I could realize what happened. I looked at my brother, now on the ground, rubbing his head. Rick stood over him, holding his good hand in the air. He turned to me. "You two think you can do whatever you want," he said. "Just like your dad. Where do you want it?"

I shook my head, even though it wasn't a yes-or-no question.

"Your punishment," Rick said. "Where do you want it? The head or your rear."

"I didn't do anything," I said.

"You didn't stop anything either. Know what that's called? Called an accomplice. Called guilty by association. You do time for that, too."

"Leave him alone," my brother said, still on the ground. He kept one eye closed, as if that would shut out the pain. "You can't punish us. You're not—"

"That's right. I most certainly am not," Rick said. "Know how you can tell? 'Cause I'm not a cheater. I would never do that to your mother. She might be a pain in the ass like you boys, but she's still one of the good ones." He adjusted the strap on his sling. "Besides," he laughed, "who'd want to be your dad right now? I've seen the paper. The man couldn't catch a cold."

The word *cold* made me think of my dad curled up on the couch, shirtless and alone.

"Shut up," I said.

Rick laughed. "Or what, retard? You gonna call the fuzz? He can't help you, OK?" He stuck out his hurt arm, the one he always used to pinch us, and poked my chest. "Face it, moron, Father Fuzz is a failure."

Later that night, when I was in my bed, my brother snoring above me, I replayed the day in my head. It was then I realized that it must've been me who screamed that high-pitched noise, announcing my attack. At the time, I only saw Rick's sling, swinging lazily in front of my face. Teasing me

until I couldn't take it anymore, until my mind must have gone white with rage. And then I must've screamed. All of this right before I grabbed Rick's hurt arm and pulled down as hard as I could.

Rick cried out in pain. His good arm flailed until he caught my head by my hair. I tried to twist away and find my brother, who was on the ground clutching his stomach. Rick must have hit him when I went for his arm. "Goddammit," Rick said. "Why the hell would you do that?"

"Let me go."

"No, no, no. I was gonna let you off easy. A smack on the ass or something. But now . . ." His grip on my hair tightened. My face felt like a mask Rick was ripping off. "Now you're in for a real treat. But don't worry, it's in your best interest. You won't do anything stupid any time soon."

He dragged me to the cafeteria and threw me in a chair. There was no one here either. The grill was no longer going.

"Man, did you step in it," Rick said. "Stepped in it big time." He let go of my head and began to undo his belt buckle, which he had welded in prison. "I'm doing this for your mother, you know. She may hate it here, but there are worse places. Worse things in life."

He licked his thumb and wiped a dirt spot off his buckle, twisted around to put it in his back pocket, already occupied by a puck of chew. This was my chance to escape. But when I tried to get up, Rick's good arm flew out and caught me by the thigh.

"Sit," he said, and his fingers sank into my leg like animal fangs, shooting a sharp shock down my entire side. "Stay."

He slid the belt off his waist and held it by its tail, like it

was a deadly snake ready to strike. I rubbed my leg, sure I would never use it again.

"What are you doing?" I said.

"Good question," Rick said. "Let me show you." He grabbed me by my neck and threw me over his lap, on top of his oil-stained jeans. "Think of it as preventative medicine," he said, and folded his belt in half in front of my face, so I knew exactly what was coming.

I closed my eyes and prayed for my brother. I hoped that he was faking hurt, that he would sneak up on Rick and put him in a choke hold, a combat move we had sort of learned from our dad, but were never supposed to use. Unless it was an emergency.

"Let him go," a voice said, soft. It couldn't belong to my brother. I opened my eyes and lifted my head. It was Sandy. Standing alone, her hair imprisoned by a hairnet, a small frying pan in her hand.

"Oh, mind your own damn business," Rick said. He wrapped the belt around his good hand, tested the tightness of his grip. "He broke the rules, so he gets punished. He gets the same treatment as me and you."

"Maybe," Sandy said. "But that's not up to you."

Rick stopped what he was doing. He rested both of his arms on my back and gave Sandy his attention. "What's that supposed to mean?"

"It means you should leave the punishment to the parents and go on about your business."

"Oh yeah?" Rick said. He pushed me off him and stood up. "Well, do you see his parents around anywhere?" Sandy slowly blinked her eyes. "Me either," Rick said. "But I'm here,

aren't I? I'm the one who's always around, OK. I see these brats more than their goddamn dad."

Sandy sighed, and for a moment it seemed she could see Rick's point. "It's not the same, Rick. You don't know what it's like."

Rick laughed to himself. For some reason, what Sandy said was funny to him. He unwrapped his hand and threw his belt over his shoulder. "Oh, so now you're an expert. On parenting." He sauntered over to Sandy, until the two were close enough to kiss. "You. Of all people. Is that right?"

Sandy met his eyes, her jaw clenched. "Don't."

"What?" Rick said, his voice dropping to a whisper. "You don't want to trade parenting tips?"

Sandy squeezed the frying pan's handle, and her arm veins popped up like little rivers.

"OK, how about a freebie?" Rick said, turning his back to Sandy and looking straight at me. "A free lesson from me to you, Sandy. Here it goes: If you ever have a baby that won't quit crying, don't shake it to make it stop." He turned around, smiled at me. "For God's sake, I mean, you don't treat a baby like a jug of juice."

Sandy's eyes dropped. She looked at me, biting her lip, as if she wanted to apologize with all her heart for burning my breakfast every day I ever knew her.

Rick licked his lips, proud of himself. "Nope, last time I checked they don't give out mother-of-the-year awards to a lady with a dead baby on her hands. I'm pretty sure they put people like that in jail."

Sandy lowered her head. Hit him, I thought. He isn't looking. Do it.

But Sandy didn't. She relaxed her grip on the pan, twirled it by its handle, and composed herself. "Are you sure you want to be airing each other's dirty laundry?" Rick stopped his cocky pacing. " 'Cause there are some things I heard about you, you know, things that you probably don't want getting out." My mind went to the gas cans Rick filled in secret, when he thought no one was looking.

Rick scratched his sling. "Bullshit. You don't know nothing."

"You're right," Sandy said. "I don't. But Cornbread does. He only told me a little, says there's some code among guys who've done time together. But I bet if I really wanted, I could get it out of him." She rolled her tongue in her mouth, combing her teeth, and her whole body loosened in a way I'd never seen before.

"Go ahead," Rick said to Sandy, "fetch your magic Negro. Just because we jailed together doesn't mean he knows shit."

"O-K," Sandy said, stretching out each letter. "Hey, maybe I'll fetch the boys' mother while I'm at it." Rick quickly turned around. I couldn't see his face, but I bet it was filled with fear. "How much does Aggie really know?" Sandy asked, her voice cold. "I'm sure she knows about the stupid things that landed you in jail. But does she know about what you did *in* prison? The stuff you did to survive?"

Rick walked away from Sandy and me and stood by a tall cafeteria window, his reflection milky in the glass pane. "She knows enough."

My brother came into the cafeteria, still holding his stomach. The mark on his face where Rick had hit him was easily visible.

"What's going on?"

Sandy and Rick exchanged a quick look.

"Nothing, sweetheart," Sandy said, and just like that she reverted to her former self, the ex-con cook who always treated me like I was the world's most precious metal. "Just having some words with Mr. Rick. But I think we're done."

Rick stayed by the window, gloomy. "I was just trying to help," he said, staring at his reflection, the only other person on his side. I liked to do the same thing when I was alone in our bathroom. I liked to whisper and watch my lips form the words. This is what I look like. This is what other people see.

Our mother was waiting in the van. Her big blond hair hung out the driver's window, soaking up the sun like Baron used to do on car rides. She had an hour to drive us home and feed us, she said, before she had to be back at work for the late shift. She didn't ask why we were late, where we had been, not until the van was parked and we were walking up to our building's pea-green door. "Why was I waiting?" she said. There were no sounds at the pool. The fireflies were out, lighting up what was left of the summer. "At the golf course, I mean."

"We were detained," my brother said.

My mother laughed a tired laugh.

"Detained?" she said. "That's a funny word for you. Hey, what happened to your face?"

"A golf ball hit me," my brother said. "I guess it was only a matter of time." He tried to pull open the building door, but my mother stuck out her long arm and held it shut.

"Hold it. You're not lying again, are you? Turn around."

My brother slowly spun around, and my mother brushed the hair covering his face. "I'm not ignorant," she said. "I know there was no siren that day. I canvassed the neighborhood. No one heard a thing." She cupped her hand on my brother's cheek and examined him, her thumb tracing his red mark, now a dark bump. I watched her and put my hand to my face, where my head had hit the patio door.

"The Bump Brothers," my mother said. She leaned in and gently kissed my brother's bump. "Listen, you don't have to tell me where you were that day, though you can if you want. Just tell me what happened to your face. And I don't want another lie. I've had enough lies to last a life."

My brother looked away.

"Rick did it," I said. "He hit him for no reason. That's why he has that mark."

"Rick did?"

"And he was going to hit me, but Sandy stopped him. He was going to beat me with his belt."

"He hit you," my mother repeated, sounding more confused than disapproving.

"What do you expect?" my brother said. "Working with prisoners."

"Ex-prisoners," my mother said, though that didn't sound any better. "OK, I'll talk to him."

"Yeah," my brother said, "talk."

Our mother waited until we were inside the apartment before she said any more. She wrapped a handful of ice cubes in a washrag and sat my brother down at the kitchen table, the ice pack pressed to his face. Across the living room the sliding glass door was open and I could hear a police car's

siren wailing down a nearby street. I pictured my dad racing across town, chasing down some bad guy. The Stranger.

"Listen," my mother said. "I'm sorry about your face."

"It's fine," my brother said. "Whatever."

"It's not fine. Rick is . . . complicated."

"We don't like him," I said.

"It's not that simple."

"He hurt him," I said. It was a simple statement, but true, and it stumped my mother for a long time. She sat there thinking. She repeated what I said, tried my words out on her lips. *He hurt him. He hurt him.*

Finally she said, "I'm sorry if Rick ever hurt either of you. But that's only because Rick has his own hurt." She took the ice pack off my brother's bump. The bump looked brighter, bigger. The swelling had gotten worse, not better. "It's like I always say, hurt people hurt people."

My brother slapped my mother's hand off his face, and the ice pack fell to the floor, scattering cubes across the kitchen. "I'm sick of your stupid sayings. You say all these things, but they never mean anything." He turned his bruised half away from us, showing only the good side, like he was giving us his best mug shot. My mother apologized again. "I don't care," my brother said. "Stop saying that. Stop saying you're sorry. You're sorry. Dad's sorry. It doesn't matter. Things keep happening."

"I know, I'm sorry." She put her hand to her mouth, to stop herself from apologizing. But she didn't know what else to say.

"Forget it," my brother said. He kicked the spilled ice out of the kitchen and onto the carpet, where it would melt

into dark pools I would accidentally step into later. He left. I sat in my chair, watching my mother think things through. Her hand in her big hair.

"He wouldn't hurt you for no reason," my mother said. "Rick isn't perfect, but he's got a good heart." I didn't know what she wanted me to say. If she wanted me to confess about the cart, that wasn't going to happen. I wasn't going to betray my brother again. She'd have to get it out of Rick.

"He didn't deserve that," I said. "We didn't do anything."

My mother nodded. She got up from the table to fix dinner: hot dogs and beans for the third time that week. She dumped the beans in one small pot, started water in another. Normally I would help her get everything ready. My mother would take down three plates and I would put a hot dog bun on each, opening them carefully so they didn't tear. I would get the ketchup out if we had any and turn it upside down, so whoever used it first didn't get the runny stuff. I would help my mother keep an eye on the hot dogs, which I knew were ready when they floated to the top, like the dead men we pretended to be at the pool.

But I didn't do any of these things. I couldn't make myself want to help. I kept thinking of Rick, of what he would say to us the next time we saw him, and the time after that.

"You've got your thinking face on," my mother said. She shut off the stove and put two plates on the table. One for me, one for my brother. Though my mother sat in his spot, the hot dogs drowning in the plate of beans in front of her. "What are you thinking about?"

I used my fork to make a mountain out of my beans. I dipped one of them in ketchup and it looked like blood. I said I wasn't thinking about anything.

"You know I meant it," my mother said, "when I said Rick's got his own issues. Did you see his sling?"

Yes, I saw it. I yanked it until I made Rick scream.

"Well, it wasn't an accident."

"What happened?" I asked. I pictured all the ways Rick could have hurt himself—falling off a ladder, the scoreboard, tripping down the stairs—and I couldn't help but smile. But my mother wouldn't say any more. How wasn't the point, she said. The point was someone hurt him. And now he had passed that hurt to me. To my brother.

"But it better stop there," she said. "You better stop it before someone stops it for you."

Before she went back to work our mother reminded us to take out the garbage. The trash men were coming tomorrow. I scraped the beans and dogs my brother never ate into the kitchen trash and tied the bag shut, replaced the old bag with a new one while my brother waited by the door. Outside, the complex was quiet, minus the buzz of bugs swimming around our building's exterior lights. The lights were set to a timer that turned them on at dusk, off at dawn. I imagined the bugs dreading the moment the sun started to show, leaving sad when the light went away.

My brother decided to swing by the pool before we went back in. I had never seen the pool at night. Not up close. It was different in person. Its sugary blue glowed brighter, so that the water looked like something from the future.

Something one of the men in my brother's plots would fall into and receive special powers from. My brother didn't open the gate. He ran his hand over the pool rules sign. No running. No horseplay. No swimming at night. But if that was a rule, why leave the pool lit up and uncovered? Why tempt us little bugs who didn't know any better?

My brother put one sneaker in the fence and hopped over. He opened the gate, but didn't wait for me to follow him through. I traced a path around the pool, to the shallow end where it was safe. Where if I fell in I could rescue myself. The water was still. No pumps were on. No wind formed a small tide, crashing waves against the pool's concrete side. There was no lapping. I got on my knees and bent over the water, until I saw myself staring back up at me. I waved to this other me, and when that wasn't enough, I reached out to touch my face. I wanted to feel this new water, feel something different. I wanted to wipe away my reflection, which hadn't changed at all since I studied it in the video store candy case. I was the same as I had always been. The water felt like it always did. Cold. Wet. There wasn't anything special about it. I sat back and looked up, first at the naked sky, then at the diving board, where my brother stood fully clothed, peering into the pool. The light from the maintenance shed outlined him as a shadow.

"What do you think?" he said. "Should I jump?"

I shook my head, but wasn't sure if he could see. From behind him, a second shadow emerged.

"I don't think it's a good idea," Chris said. "What good is the Gainer if no one's here to see it?"

Chris stuck out his hand and helped my brother down from the board. Even though it was night, he still wasn't

wearing a shirt. He gave my brother a hug and said it was good to see him again. He didn't say the same to me.

"What are you guys doing?" Chris said. "It's not safe to be out here alone. Not at night."

He and my brother walked over to where I was sitting on the shallow side. Chris was wearing the same trunks as last time, and had a hat on backward. "Then again, I guess you're not alone, are you?" Chris said. I could feel him smile, though not with the amount of energy I was used to. He sat down next to me and dipped his legs in the pool, like the first time we met. His tattoo shone in the pool's light. I stared at his trunks. I wanted to ask about his time as a lifeguard. I wanted him to finish the story.

"Where have you been?" my brother said.

"Oh, here and there," Chris said. "Trying to sort some things. You know how this world can be. One minute you've got it all figured out, the next you feel all wrong."

He craned his neck to the sky and sighed. And now? my brother said. What was Chris up to now?

"Just looking at the stars, my man. I like to come out when it's clear like this, check out the constellations. Look." He put his arm around my brother and pointed at the sky. "There's the Little Dipper. Ursa Major. There's Orion. And look at that, he's doing the Gainer."

Chris laughed a little, but his laugh sounded fake too. I looked at the stars, but couldn't see any of the things he pointed to.

"I'm just kidding," Chris said. "But did you know that Orion is the Hunter? He was a famous hunter who got stung by a scorpion . . . like this!" Chris turned his hand into a stinger and stung the back of my brother's neck. "And he

died. But the gods really liked him, so they brought him and the scorpion up to the sky. See, there's Scorpio." He drew another line with his fingers.

"That's cool," my brother said. "What else is out there?"

"Well . . . oh, I know. You'll like this." He tilted his head into my brother's, so their faces were nearly touching, their eyes set on the same spot. "You can't see them this time of the year, but to the right of Orion there are two super-big stars. Brothers." He planted two fingers in the sky, where the brothers should have been. "See? Those are their heads. And you can't tell, but they're always holding hands. Playing, having a good time. Always by each other's side."

He wiggled his fingers in the sky, made the brothers jump around.

"What are their names?" my brother said.

"Hmm," Chris said. "Good question. I forget."

"Is Orion their dad?"

Chris shook his head. "No. It's just the brothers. No stupid parents around, telling you what to do, where to go. Isn't that nice?"

Chris dropped his fingers and leaned back on his hands, and the three of us sat there like that, staring at the stars. I tried to make figures of my own out of the brightest dots, and stories to go with their shapes. Here was my mother, broke down by the van. Here was my father, fired by the Chief. Here was Rick. Here was Sandy. Here was Chris. I picked a star for everyone I knew.

"The cool thing," Chris said, "is that the stars are the same everywhere you go. That's what I like. No matter how you feel, no matter if you're up or down, they won't change."

How many things can you say that about? he said. He lay flat on the concrete, his hands resting behind his head. My brother and I did the same, until all we could see was the vast night, a blanket of black pocked with white.

"Chris," my brother said. "Are you OK?"

"Oh sure, Sir Knight. Sure I am. It's just . . ." His words trailed off. "Never mind."

A wisp of a cloud drifted into frame, pushed by a wind I couldn't feel. A few minutes passed and more wisps moved in, covering up the brother stars, tucking them in.

"See, that's the thing," Chris said. "The stars don't change, but you can't say the same about the world around them." He sat up quickly, as if struck by lightning, or some brilliant idea. "But," he said, "there are certain places clouds never touch. Places that . . . that . . . Why, in my travels, I've witnessed constellations few have ever seen."

He ran his hand across the sky, like a magician preparing his audience for the trick's final reveal. When he spoke again, he spoke like a shiny knight, not some sorcerer, and all his gloom had disappeared.

"I wonder," Chris said, "if these wonders interest any of you. I wonder—who amongst you is daring enough to face the most dastardly dangers? Who will look fear in the face and say, Not today, fiend, new worlds await." His hand dropped and he leaned back on his elbows, his voice crouching into a whisper. "Only the bravest will I lead, only the strongest of hearts may endure what is in store. Ask yourself, is that me? Am I ready to follow Chris to the ends of the earth? Am I ready to give my life, if asked? Weigh these questions heavily, dear friends, and do not reply until your soul is firmly resolved."

My brother was the first to stand up. "I am," he said. "I'm ready, Sir Chris."

"Bravo!" Chris said, abandoning his whisper. "But wait: Are you certain? Think long and hard. After all, you're not just going someplace new, you're leaving behind the old. You're abandoning the familiar for the strange. All your friends, all your valuables. Is that what you want?"

I looked at my brother, his weighing face. I thought of the list of valuables I made weeks ago, the treasured possessions I never wanted my mom to hock. I thought of the ones she'd already taken, the ones I'd crossed off the list and were gone forever.

"I have no more valuables," my brother said.

"Ah," Chris said. "I see. But what about your stableboy? Who will look after him, make sure he doesn't stray from his duties? Or worse yet, that he doesn't tell the world our secret whereabouts."

"He won't," my brother said. "He's sworn an oath of his own, haven't you?"

I didn't answer. I stared at the water, neon in the light. I wished it really were magical, some sort of potion or elixir, something that would give me the strength to do what I knew was right.

"Hey, stableboy," my brother said, "your knight is talking to you." He nudged me in the ribs with his foot. "You won't betray me again, will you?"

"No," I said. "I won't tell."

Good, my brother said. He said otherwise it would be off with my head. And in case I didn't know what that meant, he ran his finger across his throat: *Svvvt!*

"Then it's settled," Chris said, and he stood up to shake

my brother's hand. "Now you better get back to your castle, before the queen realizes you're missing."

My brother agreed, and I started toward the gate, but Chris called my brother back to him. He said hold on, he forgot to tell my brother something. He waved him close and said something louder than a whisper, but I couldn't hear it over the pool's cleaning pump, which had kicked on. My brother nodded to whatever Chris said, and Chris high-fived him and for a moment held on to his hand, swinging it by his side.

eleven

STORMS CAME AND WENT, threatened with rain and hail. Tornadoes dodged north and south of our city, biding their time, and we didn't see Chris, though every night I looked for him. We camped out in the living room and I lay facing the sliding glass door, waiting for Chris to climb in and finish the story. There were moments when I allowed myself to wonder if he and the Stranger were the same person. Chris snuck in and dragged his loved one out of her house, killed her in front of a camera, for the whole world to watch. This seemed beyond Chris, what he was capable of, but I couldn't stop myself from imagining them. Too many movies, any adult would say. Now go back to bed. Now shut your eyes.

During the day I busied myself hunting roaches. I did not tell my brother this, but I called myself Orion, only instead of scorpions it was something less scary. And instead

of killing them, I used the old coffee can as a temporary holding cell. This time, however, I didn't show them to my brother. I kept my collection to myself, and released the roaches into the woods alone, waiting until my brother had completed his push-up circuit and was in the shower, rinsing off his sweat.

Outside the sun assaulted my face, and I had to squint all the way to the woods, where I hugged a tree for shade. The roaches danced around the bottom of the can, happy to be out of the heat. I turned the can over and patted the bottom, watched as the roaches dropped to the ground. I blew on them and told them to go, to be free. I left the can in the woods, in case the roaches got homesick.

The apartment door was open when I returned. Inside, two low voices. I recognized one as my brother's but could not make out the second, other than it was a man. I put the voice in Chris's mouth, Chris's body in our kitchen table chair.

When I went into the kitchen, I saw it was our dad. Our dad, who wasn't allowed in here. Wasn't allowed to see his boys until our mother lifted her sentence, pardoned him for his parenting crimes. He looked tired, like the zombies had finally knocked down his door and bitten his brain. His face was pale and unshaven. What was once a mustache now bordered on a beard.

"You can't be here," I said, without thinking. My brain still saw Chris in the chair, not my dad. He told me to have a seat. He didn't look comfortable. His face and arms were sweating, and his uniform made him too big for our small chairs. His holster hung off the side, clacked the table when he shifted in his seat.

"I was just talking to your brother," he said. "Your mother's eased up a bit. You're going to spend the weekend with me. But just you."

I glanced at my brother to see what he made of this. He scratched at a dried flake stuck to the kitchen table. His face was far away.

"Don't worry, son," my dad said to my brother, "it'll all pass. She'll forgive me. She always does."

My brother didn't look up or say anything. Once the flake came off, he brushed it onto the floor. He got up from the table without a word and went into his room.

"He'll be OK," my dad said. His voice tilted up at the end, as if to say, "Won't he?"

I didn't know. I fiddled with the cereal bowl my brother left out from yesterday's breakfast.

"I bet your mother still cuts your hair with that bowl," our dad said. "She always loved doing that. She thought it made you look like something out of history. Like Shakespeare or something." He laughed, looked down for a while, lost in a memory.

"Ah, screw it," he finally said. "Grab your brother. Let's take a trip."

"To where?" I said. "Do you want to call Mom? Let her know where we'll be."

My brother came into the kitchen, head down, and my dad's brightness flickered away. "Yes," he said. "I suppose we should." I handed him the phone, but when he took it, he looked like I was handing him an object as cursed as the Stranger tape. He gave the phone back to me. "On second thought, let's let this be one of our secrets."

———

We drove around the city, and it was obvious my dad had no idea where he was going. We would stop at a light, and when it turned green he would veer off to the left or the right without any warning to the car behind us. When we hit downtown we rolled down the windows. People waved at my dad and he raised his hand in return, but we ignored the smiles that invited us to stop and chat. We drove on uncaring, an act some looked confused by.

We made a U-turn at the river and drove back through the city, past Limit Street and into a neighborhood with big houses we would never again afford. We took a right by a church I recognized. It wasn't one we ever attended, but I remembered it for some reason—its low triangle roof, the basketball hoop in the middle of the parking lot. We took a left on another street and that too, the act of turning at that spot, the angle at which we curved from one street to another, felt familiar. Once on this new street, I recognized all sorts of things: fire hydrants, mailboxes, the shapes and slopes of driveways.

"Where are we?" I said.

"God, you're dumb," my brother said.

We came to a cul-de-sac, circled around, and stopped across from a house. A warmness in my chest told me I had been here before. My dad put the cruiser in park. He turned off the radio and stared at the house.

"Is this our house?" I said. My dad didn't say anything. He continued to stare at the house, running his fingers over his mustache, his baby beard. This was our house. Or it once was. I was sure of it. I recognized the square windows, the one on the left for the hallway bathroom, the one on the right that went to the room my brother and I once shared. But it

also wasn't our house. The car in the driveway wasn't our van. The basketball goal was somebody else's, the birthday gift for some lucky kid.

"Why are we here?" my brother said. "Can we go?"

"It's weird, isn't it?" my dad said.

I stared at the house, trying to remember if it was always that light brown color.

"I'm bored," my brother said.

"You're bored?" my dad said. He wanted to stay a little longer, and so did I. "What if I do this?" He rolled up his window. We didn't get why we were supposed to be impressed. "Wait for it." He flipped a switch on a box attached to the center console. A steady static came out of the box's speaker. This seemed to encourage him, and he started playing with the dials.

"What are you doing?" my brother said.

My dad put his ear to the speaker. "Don't you hear that?"

"So what. Our TV does the same thing."

"Patience," my dad said, fiddling. "Patience perseveres."

He messed around for a minute more, until, suddenly, a voice broke through the static. A woman talking. Words popping in and out, crackling like fireworks.

"Is that a ghost?" I said.

My dad stopped messing with the box and stared out the window, at our old house. "Not a ghost," he said. "Now be quiet. We have to be quiet."

I covered my mouth. When that didn't work, I closed my eyes. I held my breath until the voice came back. This time clearer, but funny-sounding, like someone was sending words through a fan.

"He surprised me with it," the voice said. *"I was standing*

there chopping vegetables and he just came up and sat down by my leg. He said, 'Mom, I got it. Look.' And of course I thought it was something silly, so I didn't really look. But he kept on, saying, 'Look, Mom. Watch my shoe.' So finally I look down, and there he is, my baby boy, tying and untying his shoe like he's all grown up. Making the same face as his dad. That stupid face he makes when he's concentrating hard. Can you believe that?"

There was a silence. We couldn't hear the ghost on the other side.

"This one's a talker," my dad said.

"I know. So fast, right? . . . No, he wasn't here to see it. He was so mad when he got off work . . . No, mad that he missed it . . . He doesn't know about that . . . I know, but he's got to work, so what can we do? . . . I know. I pray every night that won't happen . . . Well, that's all I can do."

The speaker cracked again and fell into static. I closed my eyes, but the voices were gone. My brother and I sat up. Our dad didn't turn from the window.

"Who was that?" my brother said.

"Just some lady," my dad said.

"How can we hear them?"

"Sometimes we can hear people if they're talking on a cordless phone. That's all it is." He wasn't excited like us. He sounded like his football team had just lost a close one.

"Does she live in our house?"

"Who cares," my brother said.

I stared at the house's front door, hoping the lady would come out. "Can we go around back?"

My dad looked at me, his cheeks puffed up with pity. "We used to have fun back there, didn't we?"

"I'll take him," my brother said, "if that's what he wants."

Our dad turned to the house again, rubbed his chin. "OK," he said, "but be quick."

We got out and went around the car, my brother crossing the cul-de-sac without me. I hung back for a second. "Do you want to come too?" I asked my dad.

He put his arm in the window. "No, son. No parent wants a cop approaching their door."

I ran across the street and up the front yard. I laughed because it was funny; it was funny that my legs remembered running up this little hill. They knew exactly how many steps to take and when to tell my brain to stop. I ran around the side of our old house and into the backyard. It hadn't changed at all. Here was the porch, weathered and gray, where my dad used to grill. Here was the spot where grass refused to grow, season after season, the spot my brother and I used as home plate the day our dad bought us our wiffle ball and bat. We used a small bush as first, an old sandbag as second, and a porch pole as third. All these things remained. No one had bothered to change them since we left, or maybe nobody could.

My brother came around back. "It looks small," he said.

"What does?"

"Everything. It just looks smaller."

"It looks the same to me."

"What about the tree?" he said. "The tree is gone."

"I don't remember a tree."

He pointed at a mound at the edge of our property. "It was right there." He walked to the spot and put his hand to the ground. "See, there's the stump. Here, feel it."

I kneeled in the grass and spread my hand on the earth's

bump. It didn't feel familiar. "I don't remember any tree," I said.

"Well, it wasn't a big tree. More like a baby. Mom used to laugh at Dad because he would try to sit under it for shade. You don't remember that?"

"I think I remember," I said. "I mean, I want to."

My brother shrugged. Behind him there was movement at one of the house's windows. A hand parted a curtain, a woman's face. The woman stared down at us, and I couldn't help but think of my mother, even though this woman's hair was small and dark. She stepped back from the window, and a second later the porch door creaked open, the same way it always had. The woman stepped outside. She had a cordless phone in her hand and set it on the railing. She didn't say anything at first. She just watched as my brother circled the backyard, touching each base until he was home.

"That spot just won't grow," the woman said. Her voice was the same as the one that came out of our dad's box, only less staticky. "All the neighbor kids use it as base when they play hide-and-go-seek. You boys from around here?"

"We used to live there," my brother said, and pointed at the woman. Or, he pointed through the woman and at our old house. "But we don't anymore."

"Oh," the woman said. She twisted around and studied the house, as if she didn't already know what it looked like, as if she didn't live here every day. "Oh, OK. I didn't think I'd seen you before. Would you like to come in or something? Are your parents around?"

"We can't," my brother said. "Our dad's waiting."

"Oh," the woman said. "OK. Well." Her eyebrows arched

up, like she wanted to say more, or help in some way. Then her phone rang, startling the woman into a jump.

"That sounds like our phone," I said.

"Do you have one like it? I love the darn thing. I can take it anywhere! The only thing is that sometimes I pick up other people's calls." She laughed. "Makes me feel like a spy or something. Anyway."

I looked at the phone, at this woman who wasn't my mother. I looked at the cruiser parked out front, my dad listening in.

"We have to go," my brother said, and took off as the woman said it was nice meeting you. I followed slowly behind, wondering how my dad could do this.

We got in the car. The static box wasn't on. My dad put his notepad in my brother's lap. He told him to hold it, and put the cruiser in drive. Well, how was it? he wanted to know. I sat against the door and was glad I could stare out the window as we drove, happy that I didn't have to look at my dad. We stopped at a light across from the women's prison. A police cruiser exited the facility and drove past us, the driver nodding in our direction. Our dad nodded back. He asked again how it went. What did we think of the old place?

"It was OK," my brother said.

I kept my eyes on the prison. One woman was roaming the grounds, no guard in sight. I wanted to roll down the window, tell her to run.

"Look at that," my dad said. He shook his head. "That's somebody's mother, or wife maybe. Can you believe that? Man, if she were my wife—"

I took the notepad, still open to MW, resting in my

brother's lap, and studied the letters. "If she were my wife," my dad repeated, and again I didn't listen to the rest. I was too focused on the M and the W. In my mind I took the two letters and I separated them. I pulled them apart, putting enough space between them so that I could fill in the missing pieces.

"Son?" my dad said.

"What," I said.

"I asked you about the old house."

I closed the pad and looked out the window. The woman was still standing there, staring in our direction. She raised her hand and waved, turned on her heel, and walked back toward the prison. "It wasn't what I remembered," I said.

The light turned green and my dad eased off the brake. "No," he said. "I imagine it can't be."

My mother came home in a bad mood and yelled at us before I could even think about telling her what I had found out about my dad, how he had been using our phone to spy on her. Her face was tight and makeup-less, her mouth small, like she was ready for a fight. She paced around our small apartment like a cartoon bull or wolf, ready to blow the whole place down. Finally she grabbed the phone out of the kitchen, the new box of wine she'd brought home, and went to her room. Stay out and play, she said through the door. Give me peace.

We went to our room and played with our toys, but through our thin wall we could hear everything our mother said. She called Sandy and was complaining about Rick. She had confronted him about what had happened at the golf course. She told him in no uncertain terms to never touch us

again. That wasn't his place. Not his job. And Rick said, What is my job then? Whose job is it to make sure your little shits don't screw up their lives? Because it doesn't look like you're up to it. Or their asshole father. That's when my mother had slapped Rick. She didn't mean to, it wasn't premeditated or anything, but she had done it. Out of instinct, she said. And to be honest, it felt good. It seemed like a mistake now, not the way to handle things, but at the time nothing felt better.

She went quiet for a while on the phone, listening to Sandy and replying with the occasional "mm-hm" and "I know." I pictured my dad out in the parking lot, listening in. I pictured him jotting short notes in his police pad. R hit boys? MW slapped R. R & MW split? He would underline the last line, maybe draw a smile next to it.

I stopped listening and tried to play with my toys, like my brother was his. He was in the middle of one of his epic plots. One man had a tough decision to make. Should he go after the gang who wiped out his entire family, a journey he knew could take the rest of his life, cost him who knows what, or should he stay behind with his new bride, the sister of his fallen wife, and start a new family? The man was having a terrible time deciding. The sister pleaded with him to stay, to appreciate what he had here in front of him. There's nothing out there but more sorrow, she said. More misery. If you go, you'll never find anything good again.

My brother made the man nod, as if in agreement. He put the toy man's hand to his toy chin to make him think. He gave the man a monologue. Maybe it would be better to stay. Maybe his new wife was right. The man turned and looked at the wife. He extended his plastic hand and put it

to his wife's plastic cheek. He wants to stay, I thought. Make him stay.

There was a loud pounding on our apartment door. My brother and I were sleeping in the living room. The hallway light flicked on and through sleepy eyes we watched as our mother shuffled to the door in a tank top and short shorts. She undid the chain and told whoever was knocking to hold their horses.

Rick burst in. He brushed past my mother and turned on the kitchen and living room lights, stunning my senses.

"Hey," my mother said. "Hey, hey."

Rick ignored her. He stomped into the living room and almost stepped on my brother and me with his work boots. His eyes were red, I assumed from the gasoline he reeked of.

"You two rubes need to go to your room," he said. "Hear me?" My brother and I sat up, confused. I scooted my back to the box fan. "Hello?" Rick said, cupping his good hand over his mouth to make a megaphone. "Earth to morons. Come in, morons. Get your asses to your room. Your mother and I need to talk."

"Rick," my mother said, "we've done our talking for the day. Go home."

"I know that," he said. "But I didn't say what I wanted to say." He stepped around my brother and eased himself into the couch, careful not to bump his injured arm, wrapped in a new sling, a darker blue than the one before. "I feel like . . . I feel like I let my anger get the best of me. Earlier. But now I'm ready for a real sit-down." He patted the empty spot next to him. "So sit down."

My mother rubbed her arms like it was cold. "Boys, you better go to your room. Take your fort with you."

My brother stood up, pillow in hand like a shield. "Why do we have to go? We were here first."

"Just do it, OK?" my mother said, her voice remaining calm. "Because I said so."

"So," my brother said.

Rick laughed. "See, that's what I'm talking about. They don't listen." He leaned back in the couch and scratched the skin beneath his sling. "Boys need rules. That's what I was trying to tell you. If not, they run wild. Go down the wrong road."

"Oh, shut up," my brother said. "Nobody wants you here. You're just a jerk who won't leave."

Rick pushed himself out of the couch, his eyebrows raised. "What did you say to me?"

"You heard me. Jerk." My brother threw the pillow at Rick and Rick caught it.

"Stop it," my mother said.

Rick dropped the pillow and raised his hand to my mother. "It's OK." He stepped around the coffee table, toward my brother. "So you want a repeat of the golf course? Is that it?"

"I want you to leave," my brother said. "That's what I want."

Rick popped his good knuckles against his chest. "You need to go to your room. You need to take your baby bro and beat it, before it beats you."

"Rick," my mother said.

"See," my brother said, not backing down. "See how he is?"

"Oh, and how am I?" Rick said. "How am I exactly?"

"You're stupid. Too dumb for my mom."

There was a pause. Rick glanced at my mother, and for a moment it looked like he expected her to defend him, to say something nice about him so he wouldn't have to say something mean to my brother or hit him again. But my mother remained quiet.

"Oh, now I'm the dumb one?" Rick said. "This coming from the brothers with half a brain between them."

"That's half more than you got," my brother said. He smiled a bit, feeling confident now, sensing he was winning. "You have all your rules, but you don't get that nobody wants them."

"No?"

"No. Nobody cares."

"I care."

"So?" my brother said. "Nobody cares if you care. Nobody cares about you, either. You don't belong here."

Again Rick looked at my mother, who opened her mouth but still didn't say anything.

"Well, if I don't belong here, idiot, then where exactly do I belong?"

My brother took a step back, putting some distance between himself and Rick. He curled his lip like one of his villains, and I knew whatever he said next was going to be something mean, something he had wanted to say for a long time, but had been waiting for the right moment. Waiting for Rick to fall into his trap, for Rick to be his weakest.

"Isn't it obvious?" my brother said. "You belong in prison. With the rest of the scum."

Rick didn't look at my mother for help this time. He lunged at my brother, one arm raised like a crippled bear. But my brother was ready and easily jumped away.

"No!" my mother yelled, breaking her silence. She jumped in between them and stuck out her arms. "Cut it out! You," she said to Rick. "Sit down on the couch." She turned to my brother. "You, take your brother and go to your room. Now."

"Did you see that?" my brother said. "See what I mean? Tell him to leave."

My mother grabbed my brother by his arm and dragged him away from Rick, into the kitchen. She bent over him and put her finger in his face. "I've had enough of this. You need to say you're sorry and go to your room."

"No," my brother said. "I'm not going to say sorry. You don't even like him. You know you don't."

"It doesn't matter," my mother said. "You don't talk to people like that. I don't care who they are, or what they've done."

She shoved my brother toward the living room, and his face lost any sense of pride he felt from beating Rick. He walked over to Rick and stood in front of him, arms at his side. But he did not apologize. Instead he turned and kicked the box fan over, the same way our dad kicked our TV the day he left us for good. My brother looked at our mother a last time and went to our room, leaving me and our blankets behind.

"I'm sorry," my mother said to Rick. "I don't know what's gotten into him. He didn't mean it."

Rick slid off the couch's arm and into his original spot. He wouldn't look at my mother. He stared at our coffee table, thinking of things I could only guess. Prison, maybe. His cell. My mother went to him and sat in the spot he'd patted earlier. She took a throw pillow and slid it gently under his arm. Neither of them said anything, and the only noise

in the apartment came from the box fan, lying on its back from my brother's kick, whirring loudly like a vacuum lifted off the ground, begging for someone to put it down.

I stood the fan up. Part of its front plastic was broken off, and there was a hole big enough to fit my hand through.

"Go to your room," my mother said. "I won't say it again."

Exhausted from his anger, my brother fell asleep right away. I lay in bed listening to his heavy, troubled breathing for what I thought was an hour before realizing I was thirsty, that I could use a glass of mixed milk. When I opened our bedroom door, I knew Rick wouldn't be there. I could feel that he wasn't. In bed with the lights off, I hadn't heard my mother and Rick yell at each other, like I thought I would. My mother hadn't told Rick that he couldn't talk to us like that, that he shouldn't threaten to hit us, and that his way of doing things was wrong. Rick hadn't gotten mad and yelled back, like my dad might've done, shouting he was doing his best, and tough luck if she didn't like his methods. No one was told to get out, that they were through for good this time. No doors were slammed. The only sound that ever came was a call from my dad, fifteen minutes after Rick left, asking how my mom was, and if everything was all right.

My mother was in the kitchen, sitting at the table, drinking a cold cup of coffee. I opened the fridge and poured a glass of milk and tried not to look at her. When I finished my milk, I put my glass in the sink and turned to leave.

"Rinse your glass out," my mother said. She wasn't facing me, but knew I had forgotten. "You and your brother, you always forget. Or maybe you just don't listen." I rinsed the glass out and stood by the sink, watching the water swirl

down the drain, unsure what to do, what to say. "Come here," my mother said. "Come sit by me." She pulled a chair out with her foot. "Things haven't been good lately. Have they?"

I shrugged. Her breath tasted of coffee and wine.

"No, they haven't," she said. "I know that. I wish there was something I could do, you know, but I don't know what." She kicked me under the table, by accident. "Do you? Do you have any ideas?"

I could feel my mother's eyes on me, but I continued to not look at her. I focused on everything else in the kitchen instead. The empty cookie jar. The splintered square table. My mother's coffee cup. I closed my eyes and imagined each item disappearing, being sold by my mother when something bad happened and we needed the money. I imagined having to say goodbye to everything in the apartment, one by one.

"The pool," I said. "You could take us to the pool."

My mother laughed. "Is that it? Is that all you guys want?" I nodded. "All right, cute boy. If you think that'll do it, then the pool it is."

She sipped her coffee some more, and I got up to go back to bed. She kissed me on the cheek and said she loved me.

"You promise?" I said.

"I promise."

twelve

I WOKE BEFORE my brother. I didn't like doing this, being out in the world before him, but there was a sound. It was the dumb buzzing of my mother's alarm, beeping me out of my sleep. I closed my eyes and sent her a mental message to turn the thing off. The message didn't get there. I put my head under my pillow and fake suffocated myself. That didn't stop the sound either.

I stomped down the hall and knocked on my mother's door. Soft, then loud, then angry. I hated this. She slept like my brother, not lightly like me. I banged three more times and threw the door open, letting it whack the wall. I went straight for the alarm and mashed buttons until I found the snooze.

Another sound, this one from beyond our walls. It was the early chirp of a bird, calling to one of his buddies. My mother's window was open, and I could feel the morning

breeze fly by, puffing out the window's thin curtain. I breathed in the air, which smelled of chlorine, tasted like the pool.

I turned to the mess of covers in my mother's bed. It was dark in the room, blacker than the hall. "Are we still going to the pool?" I said. The lump didn't respond. "Mom." Nothing. I bumped the bed with my hip. "You promised," I said. "We've got new moves to show you. You've got to see our new moves."

When there was still no movement, I put my hand on the blanket where I thought her hip would be, but the covers caved. I felt all around, before diving into the cold blankets. She wasn't here. She was supposed to be, but she wasn't. I looked at the alarm to try to make sense of this. Its double zeros looked like surprised eyes.

I walked to the kitchen, knowing my mother wasn't there. My brother was there, though, sitting at the table, eating a big bowl of cereal.

"I used the last of the milk," he said.

"Where's Mom?"

He pointed his spoon at a sticky note on the fridge. She had arranged her words like a poem.

Boys, Rick is sick.
Had to run to work. Should be home
after lunch. Stay inside. Sorry
NO POOL.
I Love You.

I crumpled the note in my hand. "She said she would be here."

"What do you care, stableboy? Dad's picking you up later anyway."

I sat down and stared at my brother's cereal. "That isn't milk," I said. "I hate this."

"I know," my brother said.

"Rick was fine last night."

"I don't know."

"She told me."

"That's your problem," my brother said. "You've got to stop listening to her. She just says things." He stabbed a few flakes. "So does Dad. You know he's the one who messed up Rick? Yeah, I heard them talking last night. Rick was here until like two, begging. What a fucking baby."

He took a final violent bite of cereal. Two G.I. Joes from a forgotten plot lay in the middle of the table. I made the Army guy my dad. The guy with the metal head, I turned into Rick. Metalhead wouldn't tell my dad what he knew about the Stranger, so my dad had returned to the golf course, confronted him in the cafeteria, or in the golf cart garage. My dad said, Listen, Metalhead, you know what the Stranger has done, what he's promised to do. Stop playing games. Metalhead scoffed, twirled his keys around his finger, the rabbit's foot a green blur. I could help, he said, but I also could not. So the Stranger wants you out of the picture? Seems to me that's something we have in common. And maybe my dad would lunge for him then. Or maybe he'd ask him one more time, politely, with respect, before Rick—before Metalhead—told him to pound sand. You don't get it, he would say. I don't like you. I'm not like you. When I get ahold of something good, he would say, putting two fingers in my dad's face, shaping them into snake fangs, which would

paralyze my leg a few days later—when I get what I want, I don't let go.

"Dad pushed him," my brother said. "That's all I know."

A moment later there was a knock on our door, our dad telling us to let him in.

"What will you do?" I asked my brother. "When I'm gone."

A worm of a smile wiggled its way across my brother's face. He stood up, patted me on my shoulder. "The stable-boy is gone, so I guess I'll ready the horses."

My dad put me in the cruiser. As I waited for him to walk around and get in the driver's side, I looked out at our apartment building, its dull brown bleached light by the sun. Tall maples curtained the front windows. I tried to see through those curtains, through those walls and into our apartment, to guess what my brother was doing.

I saw nothing. I felt like I'd left recess early, and everyone was having fun without me.

I shook my head. I put Sandy's words in my mind and told myself my brother would be fine. *Where would he go? Where can anyone go?* When my thoughts began to clear, I saw the smoking lady, this ghost of early summer, by the dumpster. She was smoking and talking to someone. I couldn't tell who, not until my dad backed out and pointed the car away from the Frontiers. We drove too fast for me to be sure, but I was almost positive the person the smoking lady was talking to was Chris.

That night I was tucked in. I was put to bed and promised to. My dad wasn't going out. Not tonight. He patted the

blanket and asked if I wanted a story. No, I told him, which wasn't true. I wanted a story, just not from him.

In the middle of the night I was woken by water rushing through the pipes above the bed. My dad must've used the bathroom upstairs. Minutes later, he was standing over me. Son, he whispered. Son. He couldn't see me, or tell if I was sleeping, and for a moment I studied him, the way he waited, impatiently, his arms crossed, his body in full uniform.

"I have to run to work."

"Now?" I said. The word came out as more whimper than whisper.

"Yes, it's an emergency."

"Is it him?"

"Don't know what it is yet." I sat up, but held the blanket close. "You'll be fine," he said. "I'll lock the door and you'll go back to sleep."

"What if he comes?"

"He won't. He's far away."

"But—"

"Listen, if it is him, then that means he's not here, right? He can't be two places at once. No one can."

He patted me one more time and left, ascending the cheap, squeaky stairs.

I woke up the next morning with the world lapping around me. I ran upstairs to see my dad, to have him sit me down and say, Son, we got him. But the upstairs was empty. No notes, no poems, nothing. I made peanut butter toast and tried not to think about the worst possible things. I stayed away from the basement, where the spiders lived. I stayed away

from the stairs, which led to my dad's room, which led to his closet, and to the tape.

My dad came home a half hour later. The Stranger tip had been a bust. Some bored teen playing a prank. I pictured a swarm of patrol cars swooping in on the battery factory, only to find nothing. Or they found a boy, my brother, grinning, hands up in a fake apology.

But my dad had to go back to work. The false lead had angered the Chief, who didn't want to spend his last damn days on the job chasing a ghost. My dad needed to work hard, to work the morning after the night, if that's what it took.

"Are you close?" I asked him.

"I think so," my dad said. "Now grab your bag. I'll take you home."

The feeling in my chest was the lake without the dread. It was more excitement than fear, more last day of school than first. My dad could not drive fast enough; the streets were eternal. There seemed an unending number of houses and buildings, all in my way, all telling me to slow down, asking in Rick's voice, Where's the fire? Maybe that's what the feeling was, inside my chest. Something I had to put out, that would burn until I saw my brother and told him the Stranger was nearly caught. There was nothing to worry about.

When we finally pulled into the parking lot I forgot to tell my dad goodbye. I didn't answer when he said, Your mother's waiting inside, right?, and I didn't say I loved him. There was no time, there was a fire. There was me slamming the cruiser door, me sprinting the sidewalk, shouldering through the pea-green door. The stairs were as long as the city's streets.

They belonged to a tower, not a two-story apartment. I braved through. I climbed the ladder higher and higher, ignoring the flames, the thick musk of the smoking lady's smoke. And then I was at the door, and I was ready for whatever great thing was about to happen.

That my brother wasn't there didn't make sense. It didn't fit the story my brain had worked so hard to tell me. I was a hero ready to play my part, but no one else got the memo. There was a note in the kitchen, which I skimmed, something about my mother having to run out. To where and for how long it didn't say, and I didn't care. I crushed it in my hand and searched the rest of the apartment, the bedrooms I knew were empty. What was left but to look for clues, to pretend if I put the pieces together, they would all add up. There were new fingerprints, etched in the dust. In our bedroom, shirts missing. Shoes. My brother's favorite toys. The man torn between his family and revenge was long gone. He had chosen doom.

In the bathroom a towel was missing. A toothbrush. My brother's trunks were taken from the tub. I sat on the toilet and put my head in my hands. I closed my eyes and tried to think it through. I held up all the missing items in my mind. I put them in my brother's weekend bag. I put the bag on my brother's shoulders and, with a cry, sent him down the street.

All that was left was the pool.

The apartment was empty, the laundry room humming but the same. Outside, the summer was its hottest. A hot wind shook the trees but offered no relief. I took the longest way possible around the other apartment building before

finally taking a peek, seeing the thing I was most afraid to see.

Slicing the pie, I saw my brother. I poked my head around the far apartment building and I saw him. I saw Chris. They were not in the pool. They were behind it. They were at the top of the little hill and they were facing the woods. My brother had his bag around his shoulder, just as I had imagined, and was looking up at Chris, like a son would a father, like I would my brother. Chris put his arm around my brother. He squeezed him close. He took a look around, and as I saw his head twisting in my direction, I hid. I dissolved myself into the apartment bricks and prayed he had not seen me.

I caught my breath against the wall. I told myself to count to ten, then slice another piece of the pie. But like so many times before, when my brother was the hider and I was the seeker, I didn't count as high as I was supposed to. Because I couldn't wait. I had to look. I had to find him. I skipped a few.

If I had counted all the way to ten, I would have missed what happened next. I wouldn't have seen Chris take my brother's hand, hold his arm out, as if to say, This way, please. Are you ready? My brother nodded, but his mouth didn't open. He stepped toward the woods, took one last look back. If I had counted to ten, if I hadn't skipped three, five, and seven, I would have missed that look. That face that was so familiar. If I had counted to ten, I would have had no idea that my brother was afraid.

Many tens ticked away before I decided to act. How many it was hard to say. I was not counting. I was staring, at the hole

in the world my brother had disappeared into. The door in the woods Chris had opened and taken him through. Magic.

What could I do? I could walk to the pool. OK. I could climb the little hill, stand before the door. Done. But then what? I could turn around, yes, the same way my brother had done. And I could wonder. Not about the things he was thinking; I didn't want those thoughts. No, I wanted to know what was next. I wanted to know whether or not I should follow. My hand shielded my eyes from the sun, and I found our apartment. Our sliding glass doors. I could go inside, I realized, and call my mother, at Rick's or at work or wherever. I could call my dad. The police. But what would happen in the meantime? Where would Chris take my brother, while a phone cried in an empty room?

In the end, it was not that much different from my first dive in the pool. I faced the trees and I squared my shoulders. I took a deep breath and told myself a story. About me. About my long-lost brother, separated at birth when our family was lost at sea.

He is out there, I said.

He is waiting for you.

I stepped into the trees, the story's whisper tickling my ear.

Find him, it said. You have to find him.

Like my first dive, as soon as I stepped into the woods, I knew I had not fallen in right. Or, I had fallen in OK, but was in a place that was too big for me. Like the deep end, this was a place I didn't belong. The trees were not the trees surrounding the golf course, loose and spread out. These were longer, thicker with leaves and needles, and much closer

together. Some locked limbs or leaned into each other like they were sharing secrets. Insects buzzed from places unseen, alerting the world of my presence, warning the rest of the woods, and Chris.

I didn't have a plan. Not a real one, other than to run. To push my way through brush and grass until I caught sight of my brother. Our dad once taught us how to tail a suspect, but I couldn't remember how, not with my heart drowning my head, my chest swimming with worry. Only small pieces of memory found their way through. *Don't get too close . . . Blend in as best you can . . . Never work alone . . .*

I paused, out of breath, and let the rest come back to me. Never work alone. That always surprised me. A good tail, our dad said, works with a team: two or three partners to pick up the pursuit in case the mark makes you. If one of you gets too close, if the suspect gets suspicious, fall back, let another follow. But won't he see us? Won't he notice us both? No, he said. People are dumb. Most focus on one thing at a time. They get so fixed on one idea, they ignore the obvious other.

I ran some more, and for the first few minutes, none of what I remembered mattered. I didn't see anyone, any signs of Chris or my brother. I saw trees, bushes. I saw the sun disappear behind clouds, reappear heavy on my neck. I grew tired. My run became a walk, and I could feel the ache in my feet. In the movies, people kept running. They never ran out of breath. They tripped. They fell, flipped over on their hands and feet like a crab, and watched the axe fall on the last of their lives.

Keep going, my story told me. You're so close. I can see the shore.

I looked at my legs, these useless paddles. I looked back at where I came from, to see how much of the sea I'd swum. But I couldn't see my way back. I couldn't see anything. The trees had swallowed everything behind me. There's only forward, the story said. There's only Chris, your brother, and the end.

A fat gust of air ruffled my shirt, moved on, and the sea calmed. I took a long breath in, out, and began to row.

I changed from tens to twenties, to hundreds. Count to one hundred, I told myself, and if you don't see anything, run home. After the first hundred, I stopped and looked around for clues, for bent bush limbs or a secret signal fingered in the mud. There was nothing. No paths. The woods were untouched. When I came to the second hundred, I stopped again, but not as long. When I came to the third, the fourth and fifth, I didn't stop at all. I stopped counting before I gave up. I let a last number go, something in the high hundreds, but kept on walking. How long I'd been in the woods there was no way to tell, but it felt like forever and a second at the same time. Whichever it was, it became clear to me that the time needed for my sea story to tell itself had expired. Somewhere, in a world weirder and happier than my own, I was reunited with my brother. I braved a storm and crashed a shore, and in the morning I stumbled from my wreckage to find him sunbathing on the beach, dreaming up a list of moves to do off a nearby waterfall.

But in this world, under these trees, I sat down and cried. Softly, as if I might waken the woods. I pulled my knees to my face and sobbed, louder this time, not caring who heard. When my eyes were spent, I lifted my head from

my legs. The wet I left behind was a blob on my bony knee. I let my mind play the cloud game and tried to make a shape. Something that would cheer me up, replace my sea story. Something that would tell me to get on my feet, to keep moving. All I could think of, though, was the shape the chalk kid had drawn what seemed long ago. Before I learned the secrets of the Stranger. Before the kid and mom's apartment was robbed. Before Sandy and Rick, my dad, my mom, and everything else.

In the end I could make no shapes out of the pool on my leg or the chalk kid's sketch. No whales or hippos, ships or pirates, no secret islands in the sea. Nothing made sense, and all that was left was to keep going. To wipe my leg and walk on.

What felt like hours passed. I found footprints and they were my own. I was walking in circles, with no idea how to go home. It shouldn't be this hard, I kept telling myself. They weren't that far ahead. I started in a different direction. I saw trees I hadn't seen before, creeks I prayed were new. The sun glowed high above and wasn't close to quitting the day. I pretended I was in the desert and started making my own mirages. That creek was an oasis. That mud was silver, those rocks were gold. And what was that laughter? Where did those voices come from? From some bush that was my brother. From some splintered trunk that was Chris.

I shook my head, but the mirage didn't go away. I still heard voices. I heard Chris's laughter, close, and I ran to the sound. In the fall, I would have been noisy. I would have crashed through dead leaves breaking beneath my feet. But now, at the tail end of summer, the world was much louder

than me. Under the rush of wind pushing fat clouds across the sky, I ran, my feet drumming along to the beat of birdsong. I came to a faint path. A thin line of dirt stamped a lighter brown by two sets of footprints. I bent down and touched the smaller one, then sprinted the path until I saw my brother. Or the mirage that was my brother. My brother that was and wasn't real. Chris had taken his bag and carried it for him. His other hand held my brother's wrist.

I should have screamed right away, but the scene before me was a bad dream. Someone was standing over my bed, preparing to hurt me, and I couldn't open my mouth. The sleep world wouldn't let me. All I could do was moan, *Mmmmm*, like a mummy, and point. There. There it is. Somebody please make it stop.

I couldn't yell or talk, so I followed. More clouds moved in, a possible storm. My marks moved quickly. They didn't run, but they walked with long legs, their bodies in a hurry.

They paused at a hall of trees. A long, narrow clearing, with the towering woods lining each side. I had to tell my legs, so used to walking, to stop. I lay down on a muddy slope and listened, spied like I did on my parents in the dream about the tree.

"What?" my brother said. "Is this it?"

"Close," Chris said. "This is the road to it. A little farther."

"I don't get it. You keep your car out here?"

"No, not here, exactly."

My brother took his hand from Chris. "Yeah, but how did you get it here? Your car. It doesn't make sense."

Chris kept looking around, but not at my brother. "This isn't the time for questions, OK?"

"Yes, but—"

"I'm sorry, we have to keep moving."

My brother looked down at his sneakers, which he hadn't worn all summer.

"Remember," Chris said. "I asked you. I asked you if you were ready. I told you what it would mean. Remember? I made sure." He handed my brother his bag. "But it's up to you. You can take your bag and run back home, if you'd like, to your tiny apartment and your mom and dad, or we can stick to our plan. But I can't keep talking about it."

My brother cradled his bag to his chest, and Chris asked him what's it going to be, my liege, a hint of his early charm returning to his voice. But my brother wasn't so easily fooled. His body tightened and his mouth stayed straight. He wants to go home, I should have said. I should have stood up, revealed myself, and said, I've never seen that face, but that's what it says. Sorry, Chris. It's over. We're going home.

And this time I did stand up. This time I shook off my dream and my voice returned to my throat. But as I opened my mouth to speak, my brother handed Chris his bag. He said, Here. He said, I don't want to go back.

They walked a little longer. Chris kept his arm around my brother, though neither seemed to enjoy it. I tailed them without even trying. I didn't watch where I stepped or keep the proper distance. I sulked. I hoped I'd get caught, but had lost the courage or will to come out. What was the point? I didn't know where I was or how to get back, and there was no one around who cared enough to show me the way.

A bush stopped them. The size of a tree but not a tree. What is it? my brother said. A gate, Chris said. A passage to something special. Yes, my brain mocked, it's always

something special with Chris. He peeled back the bush and gestured my brother in. The gate was a mouth of darkness that led to a place unseen. But what did I care. This is the time to turn around, I told myself, to find your own way home. This isn't the time to worry about your brother. He didn't want to go back. This wasn't the time to wonder why you'd heard no sounds after Chris disappeared into the bush and the gate closed up. To wonder what was so great about this place, to let doubt creep in and poke you with stupid questions: What if this is something great and you're missing it? Or, what if it's the opposite? What if your brother needs you? What then? What would it be like to not be able to forgive yourself?

The bush's needles scratched at my face as I waded into the gate. I closed my eyes and followed the rustling in front of me, the brushing of branches and shuffling of feet. Almost there, I heard Chris whisper. Come on, come on, he sang, come a little closer. There. Isn't that better?

I opened my eyes and didn't understand. I was still in the bushes. This was not what I wanted. I pushed forward, harder, the needles tickling my skin with tiny cuts. It's OK, Chris said, it will only hurt at first. But already I could feel the burn of a scrape, the smear of my own blood. It's OK, Chris said again. It's fine. No one is here but us.

When I emerged from the bush, it took a moment for me to understand what was before me. To take it all in. I was in a clearing, yes. Naked of bushes and trees, but somehow shaded, somehow covered. And in the middle, impossible to miss, was a silo, twenty or thirty feet tall, a lonesome tower of block and cement. It was ancient and beautiful, but in bad shape. Its top was shattered; blocks cracked like broken teeth.

I circled the silo, tracing my hand against its grainy, uneven surface. Then my hand ran out of wall. I came to where there should've been a side, but there wasn't. There was a big gap, blown into existence by some disaster I couldn't imagine. I stepped through that gap and saw the tree. An oak. It was the biggest tree I'd ever seen and it stood dead center in the silo, where it made no sense to be. I craned my neck and followed the tree to the silo's top, where its branches had grown straight up, as if the tree were being robbed. How big. How strange. This was what Chris had promised. This, I understood, was a secret worth keeping.

Remember, Chris said to my brother, reading my mind. Remember what we said about secrets. Well, this is ours. OK? From now on, this is something only you and me know. Because, the thing is, I've tried this before, and it didn't work out. But that was my fault, understand. I rushed it. But this is different, right? You and me. I've waited. Those days at the pool. Our walks. Yes, that's right. So it'll be OK. We'll do what we need to do, then we'll be on our way, and everything will be just fine.

I couldn't see where Chris's words were coming from. They bounced around me, off the silo walls, and faded, fleeing out the gap. I sneaked around the tree. I told myself it was OK. Chris knows you're here. He's read your mind and he welcomes you. Leave the past at the pool. You belong here too. You belong with your brother.

On the other side of the tree was a darker shade. In that shade my brother was pressed against the wall, shirtless. Chris had the seat of his own shorts down and was leaning into him, pinning him to the silo like my brother was under arrest. One of Chris's hands handcuffed my brother's wrists

behind his head, and the other wrestled desperately with the double knot protecting my brother's trunks.

"You sure tie these tight," Chris said. "Afraid of losing them in the pool or something?"

My brother didn't answer. Chris's legs stretched out in a V and between them I saw my brother's legs, two pale sticks. They didn't struggle.

"Good thing I got long nails, huh?" Chris said. "There! Got that fat one."

I took a step forward, and my brother's leg gave a little kick. His knee buckled and his hips started to twist.

"Hold on," Chris said, and drove his hip into my brother's back until his body stopped ticking. "Almost finished."

There was the loud rip of the trunks' Velcro, and I stepped forward. With his free hand, Chris pushed down one side of my brother's shorts, then the other. My brother told him no, and I took another step forward. I opened my mouth and my brother said the word for me.

"Stop," he said. At first more of a whisper. "Stop. No. Please." He threw words out. Short words, words that traveled fast, became louder and louder. Don't. No. Stop. With each word, I took a step, like it was some sick game where I could move only when my brother was calling out for help. No, *step*. Chris, *step*. Please, *step*. Soon the words were coming so fast I was running. I was running to Chris, my hands in the air, and I was yelling for the whole world to make Chris leave my brother alone.

Chris yanked up his shorts and turned around. "You? What? Not you."

My brother pulled up his trunks and tried to run, but Chris caught him by the neck. "Whoa!" he said, wrestling

my brother's desperate, flailing arms. "Come on now." He finally got hold of one arm and used it to fling my brother against the silo wall. He pressed his hand into my brother's chest and with a fierce look commanded him to stay. "Jesus," Chris said, catching his breath. "What the hell? Just hold on a second, OK? Let's think this one through." My brother clawed at Chris's arms, his chest and wrist. Chris grabbed him by the shoulders and shook him into the silo wall, flexing his arms and shoulders with a strength I hadn't seen before. "What is wrong with you?" Chris said. "Cut it out!" He shook him one last time, then held him still. "Calm yourself. Are you calm?" I took another step but Chris warned me to stay back, that he'd deal with me in a second. Still, I could see my brother's face, reddened with hate, his mouth white with anger. It was what I must've looked like all those times my brother pinned me down with his knees, spit on me, or made me make promises I swore in my heart I would never keep.

"Promise me you'll calm down," Chris said. "You won't do that again."

My brother's eyes flashed at me. His jaw stuck out, in rage, in disbelief.

"Don't look at him," Chris said, and grabbed my brother's cheeks. "Look at me. Do you promise?"

My brother looked at Chris, his friend, our teacher. He nodded. He said he promised. He said, "Let me go."

Chris sized him up with one last look. He let him go. My brother's body relaxed, but he did not move from the wall. When Chris was satisfied that my brother wasn't a flight risk, he turned to me. "You're not supposed to be here."

I ignored him. I tried to ignore everything about Chris,

his loose trunks, his sick, milky limbs. I did my best to convince myself he was not here.

"Hey," Chris said. "I'm talking to you. You shouldn't be here."

"Dad got a tip," I said. "He's close to catching him."

Chris blinked his eyes quickly, batting away his confusion. He turned to my brother for answers. "What the hell is he talking about?"

I stepped away from Chris, so he was out of the scene and it was just me and my brother. I just needed a chance.

"Everything's fine," I said. "Everything will be OK."

Chris tried to touch my brother, and my brother slid away. My brother put his head down, hiding his face. I could tell by the shaking of his shoulders that he had started to cry. I reached out to my brother, to comfort him, but he shrank into a crouch, into the fetal position. He hid his head in his arms, in the cave between his knees.

"We don't have time for this," Chris said. He pushed me out of the way and bent down to my brother, brushed my brother's hair with the back of his hand. "It's OK. We can figure this out."

More winds rolled in, swirling the silo in a thudding rush. I looked at the circle of sky above me, at the puffy clouds moving in, dropping to the treetops. Chris caressed my brother's cheek, but shifted his stare to me.

"You realize you're coming too," Chris said. "I mean, you know I can't let you go back."

A drop of rain. I heard his words and immediately tried to unhear them. My brother lifted his face. He wiped his nose with his arm and through a sob told Chris no. "He shouldn't have to. Don't make him."

Chris walked over to the tree and broke off a piece of its bark.

"He doesn't know anything," my brother said. "I never told him."

Chris flipped the broken bark in his hands, tossed it against the wall, and watched it shatter. "He knows," Chris said. "Not a lot, but enough."

My brother backed into me, raised his arms, to keep Chris out. Chris said please. He looked at his hands, sticky with sap, and reminded us that although he wasn't much to look at, he was faster. He was stronger. He took a step toward us.

"Chris . . . ," my brother said, but there were no words to finish his thought.

"Stop calling me that," Chris said. "That's not my name."

My brother's arms drifted backward, closed around me. I peeked around his shoulder, at this man I didn't know.

"It really is you," I said. "You're the Stranger."

Chris cocked his head. "Stranger? C'mon, little man, you know me. So does your brother. I'm no stranger." He stuck out his hand, which still showed dots of what he'd done to the tree. "Now we're going to put this behind us. And you're gonna come with me, trust and all."

He drew nearer and I buried my face in my brother's back. No, I mouthed into my brother's skin. We can't.

"Isn't that what you want?" Chris said. "What we've all wanted all along?"

I felt his hand land on my brother's shoulder, his fingers crawl like spider legs into my hair. I felt his nails scratch at my scalp, digging their way in.

"No!" my brother shouted, and with a quick shove

knocked Chris to the ground. He grabbed my wrist and we started to run. But Chris was faster, as he promised, and beat us to the silo's gap. He blocked it with his body.

"I'm sorry. At this point, I really am. But we're too far. We're farther than I've ever been and I can't go back now. It might not be what you want, but the world has led you here. This must be what the world wants."

Then, as if the world had heard Chris, it answered. From the gray sky there came a low groan. A murmur at first, a rumble in my chest. But the sound grew greater and filled everything around us. Chris looked into the sky and frowned. It was our city's siren.

The rain picked up. Heavy drops splatted the big tree's leaves, made constellations on the ground. We saw this all, but heard none of it. The siren wailed around us, screaming an unthinkable volume. Chris covered his ears. He stepped away from the gap and I had every urge to run. We would have to move fast, bolt while Chris wasn't looking, but if we were lucky, maybe we could make it.

My brother pushed me away from Chris. He took me under the tree and stared. One more face I couldn't recognize. What was it saying to me now? He had a plan. Yes. A squint of his eye told me that. But there was more. There was a hardness in his cheeks, a tension I couldn't translate.

The siren sailed away, momentarily screaming its warning to someone else. Chris asked what we were doing. My brother ignored him. He pressed me into the tree the way Chris had pressed him. He took my head into his hands. He put his forehead to mine and started talking. Whispering things only I could hear. I told myself to keep my head up, my eyes in his. To not look at the scratch marks around his

waist, where Chris had desperately dug. On the other side of the silo Chris rose on his toes, trying to spy on our conversation. But he couldn't hear what we were saying. He couldn't understand our secret words. Only the long-lost brothers could.

My brother's plan was this: When the siren sounded again he would run past Chris and into the woods. Chris would chase him. When he did, I would run. I would find my way home, lock the door, and call our dad.

"Got it?" my brother said.

I didn't nod or shake my head. "I don't know the way. Where will you run?"

This close, his blue eyes were the size of planets. They didn't blink.

"I told you. The woods."

"No," I said. "Where will you hide?"

He dropped one of his hands and gave me his pity face. My mind had been trying to picture his plan. I saw him bursting past Chris, jumping into the woods again, half naked, desperate, like some sort of caveman. It didn't make sense. Chris knew the woods better than he did. And he was faster.

Then I realized my brother wasn't going to hide. That's what his face was saying. Hiding wasn't part of the plan. He squeezed me on the shoulder, and more water dripped down his face. He wasn't meant to escape.

The siren started to return.

"I can come with you," I said.

"No, you can't."

"Why?" I said. "Why can't I?"

My brother took his hand off my shoulder and turned to

Chris. But before the siren was completely back, he turned again and looked at me. He was wearing that smile, that classic brother smile that shot a sinking feeling into my stomach, and I knew exactly what he would say next. It was like the script was already written.

"You'd never make it," he said. "Out there is no place for a baby."

He turned and walked away. And I let him go.

Chris was leaning against the silo wall, next to the gap. His arms were crossed and his rain-soaked shirt clung to his skin.

"I'm sorry," he said. "I've tried being patient. Being the good guy. But we have to go."

Chris put his arm around my brother. He rubbed my brother's ear with his thumb, kissed his temple.

"Now call your brother," Chris said. "Tell him he can't hide forever. Tell him the world won't wait."

thirteen

MY ESCAPE BEGAN with a blur. One moment Chris was embracing my brother, waving me out from under the tree, telling me to hurry up. The train was leaving the station. The next my brother was slipping out of his grasp. He was throwing his bag in Chris's face and fleeing through the gap, disappearing into the woods. Chris never looked in my direction. He didn't say, You stay put or else, like I feared he would. Because I didn't matter. I wasn't the real prize.

Chris left my brother's bag and ran into the woods, forgetting all about me.

Alone, a strange calm settled over the silo. The siren left again and I could hear the crackle of branches breaking, twigs snapping in the deep woods as Chris chased my brother. When I couldn't hear them any longer, I made myself turn and run. I told myself, Don't think about what you want to think about—run as fast as you can.

I had no idea where I was running. I only knew that when I was following my brother here, the sun was behind me, so now I did my best to put it in front. This was mostly a guess. A family of clouds had moved in, deep gray and heavy with the weight of rain. The clouds swallowed the sun, only let it shine for a second before covering it once more. If I had stopped to think about it, the darkened sky would have worried me. But my mind only let me use the hovering storm as motivation. Hurry, my brain said, before more bad happens.

A break in the trees. A chain-link fence. The sight of the pool, a small miracle. I had run for seconds and I had run for hours. I had run for hours and I had run for days.

I was at the pea-green door. At our apartment. I was inside, the door locked behind me, my heart beating my entire body.

I grabbed the phone, took it to the sliding-glass door, and dialed my dad's number. As the dial played in my ear, I stared outside at the tops of the trees, waiting for an answer. I tried not to think about sharp branches clawing my brother's body, mud-covered rocks waiting like land mines. He has nothing, I thought. He's out there with nothing.

The phone continued to ring. My dad never bothered to get a new answering machine after my mother took the old one, and I imagined the phone hanging on his kitchen wall, repeating its ring throughout the duplex with no one there to pick up. I tossed the phone at the couch. The cushions. The cushion my brother elbow-dropped with excitement when we first learned we could go to the pool.

The pool. Chris. The Gainer.

Then, another blur. My hand was unlocking our apartment door. My eyes were ignoring the smoking lady. My

ears were filtering out her words, turning her question into the haunted whisper of a lonely ghost. *What . . . do . . . my . . . boy?* My legs were carrying me downstairs, outside. The siren was still going, and now I was running around the building, through the back field and to the edge of the woods. Now I stopped. I wiped the tears from my eyes and the world around me unblurred. The burning feeling returned, that lapping feeling that started in my stomach and swarmed my chest. The one that made me feel there was no hope, that made me want to run—-to and away from everything.

The siren did nothing to help, and the burning grew larger, but I didn't run into the woods to extinguish it. I was too afraid. I was scared I would sprint like a madman far into the woods before realizing I had no idea where I had run to, no clue where I was. Then there would be two boys lost in the woods. Two brothers. Tomorrow's local paper would say we ran away together. One writer would speculate it was because we couldn't take this place any longer. This city with no good jobs, where the streets were as cracked as the sidewalks, where everyone either ended up directly in prison, as the prisoner or the guard, or became tied to a prison in a hazy way, some way no one talked about or could put a finger on, which made it even worse.

I ran back inside. I called my dad again. I called the golf course. No one answered anywhere. There was only me again. There was the kitchen, its empty pantry. There was my mother's room, her swimsuit slung over the chair, dry and forgotten. There was our room. Missing toys, missing trunks. But there was the old wiffle-ball bat, long and bright yellow, and unused since that first weekend after the pool. I picked

it up. I looked at it like I expected it to tell me something. I told it to give me an answer. What was it doing in here? Why wasn't it out there, with my brother? It could have helped him. It could have hit Chris. The bat laughed, said it wasn't talking. I started beating the bed with it. I hit the railing as hard as I could. The bat twanged each time, vibrated in my hands and up my arms. I didn't care. I wouldn't stop. Who could stop me? No one. No one could.

Someone grabbed me from behind. They wrapped their arms around my waist. I knew who it was right away. I knew her arms by heart, but I still tried to swing the bat. Easy, she said. Baby boy, easy. It's just a test. She let me go. What are you doing? she said. What's wrong? I didn't turn around. She waited a second. She said, Where is your brother?

I faced her. She was on her knees, on my level, with her big blond hair, her worn-down eyes.

"Where is he?" she said. "Is he in the laundry room?" I looked at her shoes. She put her hand to my chest. "You can tell me. You don't have to protect him."

I kept my head down. I thought this might make things easier, but my eyes still became blurry.

"Hey," she said. The siren stopped. "Hey."

The scream dissolved into one long low note, like someone dying in slow motion.

"Look at me," my mother said. "One last time. Where is your brother?"

I turned toward our window, toward the woods. I bit my thumb and thought of the silo. "He's gone," I said. "He took him."

fourteen

I STAYED IN MY ROOM, the door shut and the lights off, but I could hear everything. The warble in my mother's voice when my dad picked up and she said his name. The ticking of our clock as she steadied herself and told him what happened. I heard the sobs that followed. I heard all these things in part because our apartment was quiet. There were no neighbors knocking around, no working A/C units sputtering on and off. But also because I had my eyes closed, which I knew for sure made me hear better.

When I opened my eyes, the room's dark was different. I had fallen asleep. I didn't know for how long. I had not dreamt.

There was someone sitting at the end of my bed, facing away from me. A slender, fit body. At first I thought it was my brother, returned to me once again. Maybe he had escaped after all. Maybe he knew a secret spot in the woods, more

secret than the silo. Maybe he had gone there, waited until the coast was clear, and simply strolled home.

"Hi, son," my dad said.

I sat up and leaned on his shoulder. He put his arm around me, like we were back at his place watching a bad movie. I put my head against his chest and felt the cold metal of his badge. He was in uniform.

"This will be hard," he said. "But I need you to help me. I need you to tell me everything about the man who took your brother." His gun, holstered on his side, dug into my hip. *Why aren't you out there right now?* I thought. *You should be out there, looking for him. We both should be.*

"I've got officers in the woods," he said, as if he knew exactly what I was thinking. "But you know how big those woods are. And soon it'll be dark."

He was right. I could see that through the window. The clouds had moved on, and the sun was still high in the sky, but so was the moon. Pink was peeking through the blue.

"Come on," he said, "let's go sit at the table. You can tell us all about it."

He took my hand and walked me to the kitchen, where my mother was sitting at the square table, her head in her hands.

"Aggie," my dad said.

My mother raised her head, showed me her red face. She pulled out a chair. "I made you some cereal," she said, sniffling.

I sat down and spooned the cereal. All the best bits were soggy; they had drowned waiting for me. My dad sat on the other side and opened his notepad.

"Tell us everything," he said. "Everything you ever saw. Everything that was ever said."

I could hear the desperation in his voice, the same panic that was on my mother's face, and that laced the air around us.

"Son," my dad said, "please. You have to help me."

I started at the beginning. I put in every detail I could think of. The tattoo. The trunks. The Gainer. I said his name was Chris, but then it wasn't. I took my time and chose my words carefully. I imagined I was my brother and tried to tell the story as if I were him. When I was done, my mother looked at me like I had fired acorns at every squirrel in our complex, until they all fell dead at the feet of their trees. My dad shook his head and said mercy. Mercy, he said. Over and over. He thanked me and told me to go to my room so he and my mother could talk. I nodded and left the kitchen, but didn't go into my room. I shut the door to fool them, and snuck back and spied from the hallway. I needed to hear them list what all I had done wrong. How I should have told them about Chris when my dad asked. How I should have stayed out of the woods. How I never should have left my brother alone.

"I have to go," my dad said. "I've got Tony and Alan in the woods, but that's all I got."

My mother said my dad's name. "You have to find him," she said. "He can't be out there like that. With that man."

I peeked around the hall wall, just enough to see my dad put his hand to my mother's hair. "I will bring him back," he said.

My mother nodded. She said she wanted to go with my

dad. She said all the things victims said in those bad movies we'd seen, the words that before never meant a thing.

My dad went to the door but stopped in the dark hall. "Aggie," he said. "I'm sorry."

"I know."

"No, I mean, you shouldn't be alone in this place, in this city. I never should have left."

My mother came out of the kitchen. But she didn't go to my dad. She went to the sliding glass door and stared at the woods. "I know," she said. "I know what you meant."

I found my mom standing at the glass door, still in her club shirt from work. She hadn't moved. The TV was on but the sound was off. A weatherman was pointing at various red blobs moving across the squares and rectangles that represented our corner of the state.

"This is bad," my mother said. "This is real bad." A few fat drops hit the glass. I put my arms around her and rested my head on her side. "I don't know whose fault this is," she said. "Whose fault is this?"

I knew I wasn't supposed to say anything, so I just squeezed my mother tighter. Her shirt smelled like sweat and club cleaner. The sky flashed and there was a quick pop, like a bulb had gone out. Little time between light and sound. My mother pushed me away from the glass. "The storm is close," she said. "We better watch the weather."

We sat on the couch and my mother put her arm around me. The weatherman zoomed in on our square. He pointed to the solid red mass southwest of us. He fast-forwarded the image behind him, showing us what our county would look like in a matter of minutes. What he showed was that our

county wasn't there. In its place was the red mass. The weatherman was doing his best to warn everyone. His gestures grew wilder, his eyes wider. But my mother and I couldn't make ourselves care. We sat on the couch and knew whatever was happening out there, whatever was coming our way, was going to happen, and that nothing we could do would make it stop. All we could do was wait.

I woke up because someone was shaking me. I opened my eyes but it was as if I kept them closed. All the lights were out. The city's siren blared.

"Come on, we have to go," my mother was saying. I was still on the couch. She struck a match and lit a candle. "This isn't a test."

She got me on my feet and led me to the door. The siren was louder out in the hallway, bouncing off our building's empty halls, the empty bedrooms. I couldn't see anything except my mother's worried face, yellow in the candle's glow.

The laundry room was humid and reeked of bleach. We were the only two down here. My mother pointed to a spot by a dryer. She didn't have to tell me what to do next. We had practiced this drill many times in school. An alarm would sound and the teacher would jump at her desk, drop her chalk, and lead us away from the classroom windows and into the hall. We would line up against the wall and they would tell us to get down on our knees. Ball up. Put your face between your legs and cover your head. They called it the fetal position, but none of us knew what that meant, unless we had an older brother who was smart and would tell us if we asked nicely. Still, we did what the teachers said. We huddled until our knees hurt from the tile, until we grew tired of

tasting our breath. When the drill was over and we were all back in the classroom, rubbing our necks and complaining, the teacher would say she was sorry. Some tornadoes like to take their time. But it's for your own good. In this part of the country, a drill like this can save your life.

"Stay down until I tell you," my mother said. I peeked out of my position and saw the black shape of my mother, leaning on a washer, watching the storm light up the stairwell wall. The siren was fainter down here, but we could hear the dark sky grumble, low and without pause. I tucked my head and covered my ears to shut out all the noise. I imagined the red mass passing our complex, and let myself believe the storm was over, that if there was a tornado, it had somehow skipped the Frontiers. But when I uncovered my ears the wind still howled, louder than I had ever heard it before. The walls shook and creaked, like a large hand was slowly wrenching out each nail. I looked for my mother again. She blew out the candle, got down, and balled herself up next to me. She started saying things, words I couldn't quite make out. I scooted closer so I could hear her. I put my head next to hers. Please, she said. Please. She wasn't talking to me. She was praying.

Something shattered. I heard the spray of broken glass. It was the stairwell window, finally giving in to the wind. The outside grew even louder, the low grumble now a relentless roar. In class, the day of each drill, we asked our teachers what it was like. What's it really like to be in a tornado? And each teacher had her own tale, her own set of memories. A green sky. A cloud like an infinite wall. But they all had one thing in common. When they described the sound of the tornado, it was always the same. It's like a train, they

would say. The shaking of the earth, the whistle of the wind. It's like someone laid tracks right where you live. You didn't notice because you were busy. Maybe you were at school or at work. Maybe you were picking up the kids. But when you finally did figure it out, when you heard the warning, it was too late. The train was coming through and you couldn't get out of the way.

My mother put her arm around me and pulled me into her. She covered my entire body with hers and whispered things I couldn't hear over the train's violent whistle. But they were nice things. They felt good in my ear. They got me away from my imagination, from thinking about what would happen if the roof fell, if the tornado picked me up and threw me somewhere nobody would ever find. Curled over me, my mother only let me think about her. We rode the train out like that.

The tornado went away before the siren did. The whistle faded. The walls rested. I asked my mother if it was safe. "Wait," she said. She stood, but kept her shoe on my back so I wouldn't move. The siren eventually died, restoring our apartment's silence. "OK," my mother said, "you can get up."

She helped me to my feet, and I followed her to the stairs. The lights flickered on and off, and it wasn't long before we saw the first sign of damage. At the ground level the window above the building's pea-green door was missing. The door itself hung by one hinge. I didn't have my shoes on, so my mother picked me up, carried me over the broken glass, and set me safely on the hall carpet. Be careful, she said.

Upstairs, the pictures of flowers had been knocked off the wall, their frames broken. We hurried into our apartment.

The electricity was out completely, so my mother lit each of us a candle. Let's see what's left, she said, and floated into the darkness. I took my candle and went my own way. From what I could see, everything looked the same. The bookcase stood, the encyclopedias were still in place. The sliding glass door remained closed, locked and intact. I walked into the kitchen. The square table hadn't moved either. My cereal bowl was right where I left it.

"It missed us," I said, out of shock, and went back into the living room, where my mother was looking up.

"No, it didn't," she said. She held her candle up to a gigantic crack in the ceiling, running diagonally corner to corner, spanning the entire living room. We could hear the wind breathing through the opening, invading our apartment. "This isn't safe," my mother said. "We have to go."

"Where?" I said. "Rick's?"

I didn't know why I said that, why I had guessed Rick's. I hadn't even thought about it, but now that the option was out there, the choice hung in front of us, a fork in the road.

"No," she said. "It'll have to be your dad's. For now."

"Why?" I said.

She looked at the ceiling's crack again, put her hand up to feel the cool air. "Because," she said. "Now go to your room and grab some things. And be quick."

When I opened the door to my room, I knew I would never live there again. There was no way. The gigantic crack from the living room tracked across our ceiling too, and the bedroom window was completely gone. In its place was a black square of night, through which a chill air seeped in. My brother's bunk bed had been knocked off mine and lay on

its side in the middle of the floor. I picked up his blanket and wrapped it around me. The outside temperature had dropped at least twenty degrees. In what was left of our ruined room, I realized I hadn't cried yet, about anything. I hadn't taken the time. But here, among the wreckage, I let the tears go.

When I was done, I put my shoes on and made my way around the mess. I tried not to look at what was once the room I shared with my brother, or think anymore about what this all meant. That time is over, I told myself, and packed my bag like I was going to stay the weekend with my dad. This is a normal weekend, I thought. This is an ordinary life.

On our way to my dad's we saw a glimpse of what the tornado had done. The damage it had left behind. Tall trees were shredded to splinters. Street signs lay broken, or spiked into front yards. The farther we drove, the more we realized how random the destruction was. How none of it made sense. The city would be pitch-black one block, perfectly lit the next. On one street every house had its roof ripped off. Then we took a left and everything seemed fine.

"What about the prisons?" I said. I imagined the tornado knocking down prison walls, letting loose the country's worst. I imagined the Stranger waving at his former roommates, laughing and saying our time has come.

"I'm sure they're fine," my mother said. "Those buildings are very old. In a time like this, a prison is probably the safest place to be."

From what we could see that night, it seemed she was right. None of the prisons had lost power. The federal penitentiary still shone on its hill, loomed over the rest of the

city. Other personal landmarks weren't as lucky. The city's grocery store had a parked car flipped through its front. At the city park, the tornado slide was bent in half, into an L. On almost every street we drove we saw debris, broken bits of somebody's property. Pieces of someone's life.

"This isn't half of it," my mother said. "We won't know how bad it really is until morning."

We turned onto my dad's street. The old people's home was still standing, though its fence, the one my brother and I once hit home runs over, was nowhere to be seen. It wasn't until we were four duplexes away from my dad's that we found it, coiled across the street like a big metal snake. We got out of the van and tried to move it, but we weren't strong enough, and no one came out to help. We left the van parked on the side and walked the rest of the way.

My dad's duplex was fine. The door was locked when I tried it, but my mother had a key. My dad had given it to her a long time ago, she said. Just in case.

We went inside and I felt like I had to show my mother around. So I showed her the kitchen, the grill out back, which miraculously hadn't moved. I took her upstairs and showed her my dad's room, the unmade bed where he slept. I figured she might want to go to sleep soon. I thought she was tired like me.

"I can't sleep now," she said. "But you can show me where you sleep. Maybe I'll lie next to you for a bit."

I took her downstairs, into the basement. I turned on the lamp and gestured toward my bed. A big daddy long-legs ran across the bedspread and disappeared under my pillow.

"You sleep here?" my mother said.

I found the spider and let it crawl on my hand. "It's not that bad."

"It's not that good, either," my mother said. She sat next to me on the bed. "You're so quiet." She brushed my bowl-shaped hair. "Don't you ever get scared?"

I lay down and thought about the question. I thought about what I felt when my brother and I were with Chris. I tried to remember how scared I was, but I couldn't. I thought of my brother out in the woods, alone or worse. I pictured Chris catching my brother, the two of them taking shelter in the silo. I imagined the tornado coming and taking Chris away. But as hard as I tried, I couldn't picture my brother coming back. I couldn't imagine what he would be like.

"I don't know," I said.

My mother put her head on the pillow next to me. She put one arm behind her head and wrapped me in the other.

fifteen

MY MOTHER WOKE ME. It was morning, though it looked the same in the basement. We went upstairs and there was no one there. My dad's police cruiser was not out front.

My mother made me an egg-and-cheese sandwich for breakfast. While I ate, I tried to remember pieces of the things I dreamed. But there was nothing I could hold on to. That world had fled, faded away. Now there was just the world in front of me, in which my mother sat watching me eat. Marveling at every bite like it was a small miracle. I tried not to stare back, not for too long. I stole glances at her makeup-less face, her dry, small eyes. When I was finished she put my plate in the sink and ran water over the yolk that had broken free of the egg and hardened. Something clogged the drain and I could hear the water slowly rise, forming a small pool.

"Go get your shoes," my mother said. "We need to move the van."

When I returned from grabbing my shoes in the basement, my mother wasn't waiting by the door. She was in the kitchen, looking in the fridge. I asked her what she was looking for. "Nothing," she said, and quickly slammed the door shut. She looked at me, then out the kitchen window, at me again. "Let's go. I have to get out of here."

Outside it was cold enough for a small jacket. The temperature had stayed down after the tornado. Dew wet the grass, and a thin fog descended on my dad's street. Summer was ending early. Once in the van I didn't know where my mother was taking me, but I didn't ask. It felt wrong to say more words than I had to. She drove with the radio off and I did my best to keep my mind blank, to not think about the empty basement back at my dad's place.

After we got onto Main Street, it became easier to think about things besides my brother. Because my mother was right: the tornado's damage was different in the light. The streets that had been without power the night before, the ones hidden in the dark, were the streets hit the hardest. Entire houses were crumbled, their frames warped and broken. Trees lay atop smashed cars, and random yards burned. Strangers walked up and down their once familiar neighborhoods, like zombies that had arisen from the dead after decades underground, who clawed their way out of their graves only to find everything they knew beyond recognition.

More than once we were forced to detour. On our way to wherever it was we were going. My mother sped from one street to another as though we were being chased, and as

soon as we thought we had escaped, a mountain of debris blocked our way. My mother punched the steering wheel each time we were cut off, made a U-turn, and peeled out in the opposite direction. This happened several times, until eventually we pulled into an unharmed gas station, with a liquor store attached. I couldn't remember being here before. My mother put the van in park.

"It's not open," she said. "After all that."

I looked where she was looking, at the *Open* sign, cursive and unlit. The insides of both stores were dark and unmoving. My mother slumped in her seat and closed her eyes. She started to cry. Loudly and without shame. Then, suddenly, she stopped, and although I thought she would feel better, she didn't.

"Why didn't you say anything?" she said. "You should have said something."

I turned from the window and faced my mother, her blue eyes reddened with sadness and disbelief. "This man, this Chris—all this time! You could have stopped him! Why didn't you tell anyone what was going on?"

"I didn't know."

"What do you mean you didn't know? Of course you knew."

I shook my head, the only thing my body would do.

"Oh, well, that's great," she said. "That helps a lot. You didn't know and look what happened."

She started crying again and I felt my mouth open. My cheeks tightened, but nothing fell. I stared at my mother, knowing I could offer nothing.

A car horn gave a quick honk from behind. I turned and saw it was a police cruiser. My dad's. He got out and walked

the few steps to the driver's side, like we'd violated some rule of the road and he was finally ready to take us in.

"We're still looking," he said. "But we're stretched thin because of the storm." I could hear the tired in his voice. From being in the woods all night. Calling out my brother's name, again and again with no reply.

"So what are you doing here?" my mother said.

"I saw you driving around. This street's closed, you know."

"No, I mean what are you doing *here*? Why aren't you out there? What the hell are you waiting for?"

"C'mon," my dad said, touching my mom's shoulder, "let's get you home."

She jerked away from him. "No! That's not what I need. I need you to be out there. I need you to find him."

"We will. Just—"

"Then do it! For God's sake, do something right for once in your life."

My dad's hand dropped. He backed away. For a moment, he looked like he'd been shot. The color left his face and his breathing stopped.

"Aggie," he said.

My mother sighed. She looked down at her hands, shaking the wheel. "I know," she said. "I know."

She started the van and we drove away.

I didn't know my mother snored until the first night we shared a bed. Not until I woke up, kicking her legs and calling my brother's name. Stop, I said. Would you stop.

I thought she would leave after that first night, after I made her remind me that my brother wasn't the one snoring. That my brother, her son, was gone. I thought she would

go upstairs and sleep on the couch, not stay down in the dark with the spiders. Though maybe that was the point. In the basement, it was always dark. There was no window well like at our old house, no light to leak in. My mother could pretend night lasted forever and stay in bed entire days, which she did.

My dad, he had no idea what to do. Those first few days he tried to coax my mother out, like she was some wild animal, scared but dangerous. But instead of biting or snapping her teeth, my mother did nothing. She said nothing. Only, I'm fine. Only, Please leave me alone.

My dad was the one who handled all the disappearance stuff. While my mother slept or didn't sleep, he did all the things I could never imagine doing. He talked to the KBI and the bordering counties' sheriff departments. Put up posters in the appropriate places. He went out into the woods every day and every night and came back with nothing. He found the silo and we talked about its tree, but that was it. There were no footprints showing him where to go. No broken limbs bent by a fleeing body. The storm, he said, washed everything away.

What about the smoking lady? I asked him. I had seen her talking to Chris, hadn't I? Whatever happened to her?

No sign, my dad said. Not since the tornado. We know she has no son listed, but we're tracking down her relatives. Nothing yet.

When my dad couldn't look anymore, he would come home. His eyes strained, his body tired and thinned with grief. If he was home at dinnertime, he grilled out. He stood alone on the porch and watched the open flame. He didn't move when the wind changed and the smoke drifted across

his face, already burned from hours spent wading through the woods. The last wave of the summer sun scorched him a sad brown, then a bright red, and each day he dried up and shrank a little. When the food was ready, my dad took a plate down to my mother, knowing she would eat next to nothing, if anything at all. He would murmur a few words to her, and slowly climb the stairs and return to the kitchen, where for the first time since we were all a family, he ate at the table. After the first week I stopped asking if he had found anything, if he'd picked up on any leads or discovered new clues. In those long hours we lingered in the living room, I learned to read my dad's face too.

When I was alone, my mind wanted comparisons. It wanted to make sense of the overwhelming emptiness I woke up to every morning, and carried with me through the day. It's like when Baron died, my mind told me. Remember? How strange and terrible it was to wander room to room and not be followed, to realize you would never hear the soft pant of his spent breath, the jingle of his collar clinking behind you. This is like that, don't you think? In some way? Doesn't that make it better?

The truth was it didn't. The truth was I knew that when I went downstairs each night and climbed into bed, my mother would be crying, and that I would clench my fists and flex my body as tight as I could in the stupid hope that I would not cry too. That will only make your mother sadder, I told myself, and haven't you done enough? The truth was I had dreams of the lake, only this time I was the one in the boat, and my brother was the one left in the water, with nothing to keep him afloat.

The city recovered. Or kept moving. So we would have something to talk about besides what we were avoiding, my dad kept up-to-date on the cleanup. Within a week the grocery store reopened. The car the tornado crashed through the front was removed, the windows replaced. Work crews cleared the streets of debris, filled dump trucks to their beds' rims. What they couldn't haul away they piled in yards, little hills of wrecked lives.

Still, the tornado wasn't a big one, according to the newspaper. Not when compared with others that had struck our state the same summer. Unlike those storms, which flattened entire towns off the map, ours had inflicted what the state labeled "manageable damage." Though many had been injured, though homes had been leveled or made unlivable, there were no known deaths.

"We'll get past this," my dad said one evening, his face hidden behind the paper.

I stared at the article on the back page of what he was reading, a blurb about another escape, this time from the women's prison. From what I could read, the article didn't mention anything about the Stranger. It was like the world had moved on and everything I cared about was forgiven or forgotten.

"How?" I finally said. How were things going to get better?

"Just give it some time, son. We don't know if things are the worst."

He put the paper down and tried to smile at me, then went downstairs to talk to my mother. I followed him to the door and listened to him plead with her. Tell her how he needed

her to be strong, to guide me through this while he was gone. Won't you come upstairs? my dad asked. If not for me, for him?

There was a lull. Until I heard my mother's voice. Soft, matter-of-fact. I heard her ask my dad if he'd found anything, if he knew who took her boy. When my dad said no, my mother said, Then you have my answer.

When my dad was gone, I hung out on his front step. There, I could think about whatever I wanted, or I could think about nothing. I could stay or I could go. I could sneak off and hurl a rock at a neighbor's door or I could be good. I could behave. I could sit and wonder why my brother chose not to, why he snuck out all the time, why he went into the woods with the man we thought was Chris. What was he after? I could ask myself. Where did he want to go?

All this because I couldn't watch TV anymore. I refused. I couldn't watch another fake family laugh their way through their fake problems. I couldn't watch the news and risk seeing a story about my brother. Only once did my dad suggest we go to the video store. No, I told him, but I didn't give him the reason why. I didn't tell him that, lately, there was only one tape I'd thought about watching. The one my dad kept upstairs, hidden in his closet. I didn't tell him that part of me still thought Chris and the Stranger were the same, and that if I could just make myself watch that tape one more time, at least some of my questions might be answered. I didn't tell him this because I was afraid. Because I couldn't imagine watching something so horrible again, and this time, without my brother.

———

I had forgotten about the smoking lady until my mother started to resemble her. This was the third week without my brother. Three weeks of my dad and me walking around like zombies. We no longer talked to each other. We chewed our food, he read the paper, and at the end of the day we silently nodded good night. A reality was sneaking up on us. A story I never wanted told.

I grew used to the quiet. When my dad was gone during the day and I had no desire to be outside with worthless birds chirping and the mocking sun, I lay on the couch. I crossed my arms like I was in a casket and stared at the ceiling, at nothing. I slept, and when I wasn't asleep, I thought of the worst things. And if I wasn't at peace I was at something like it, only sadder. There was the numbness of calm, but it came with a shadow. Lurking over me on the couch, saying, Don't get too comfortable.

So it was a shock when my mother came out of the basement during the middle of that third week. The middle of the day, even. I must've screamed when I saw her standing in the doorway. She startled and put her hand to her heart, wrapped herself tightly in the pink bathrobe she'd been wearing for weeks.

"Is your dad here?"

I shook my head, too mesmerized by her strange appearance to speak. She was new. She was once again transformed, but this time the change was bad. Her big yellow hair was limp, flat, matted to her head with sweat and grease. Purple circles hung under her eyes, puffed out from her bony, pale face. She looked like she was dying, or was already dead. Her hands would not stop fidgeting, a tic she must've picked up from the smoking lady.

"Did you have any breakfast?"

"No," I said. It was well past noon.

She slowly made her way to the kitchen and poured a glass of orange juice. She sat down and drank the glass with one long tilt, wiped her mouth with the back of her arm, and went downstairs, back into the basement. I did not see her the rest of the day.

One day my mother spent an entire morning upstairs, sipping her orange juice and staring out the back porch window. She didn't say anything to me and I didn't say anything to her. When my dad came home from an all-night shift and saw her sitting upstairs, he looked confused, like he came to the wrong home.

My dad sat down with my mom. She didn't seem to notice him at first, or if she did, she still didn't look in his direction. The two of them stared out the window, and although I knew neither would allow themselves to feel the smallest bit of happiness, for that fleeting second, the duplex lost a little of its gloom.

"She had a son," my dad said. "Your neighbor." My mother glanced up from her glass. "Not biological. The kid of the man she was with. But she raised him. He lifeguarded at the city pool."

"So," my mother said. "So what?"

She stared at my dad, her face desperately trying to make meaning of his words, trying not to jump to any conclusions. Finally her mouth opened, whispered, What? What is it?

"It seems he was fired," my dad said. "Nothing was ever proven, but there were charges . . . rumors that he"—he glanced cautiously at me—"*hurt* one of the kids."

"What do you mean?" my mother said. But then she seemed to realize something. The meaning behind my dad's words, his tone, the helplessness in his eyes, became clear.

My mother stood up. She looked at my dad hard, and left the kitchen, not wanting to hear any more. She was halfway down the basement stairs before she stopped and called back up to us.

"Do you know where she is?" she said. "Does this tell you where he might be?"

It didn't.

"Then don't," she said. "Don't you say it. Until you bring him back, don't you dare say what might've happened."

The last few stairs moaned under her feet. My mother didn't come up the rest of the week.

sixteen

MY DAD STILL did his job. He no longer spoke of a promotion, or seemed to hope or care about such a thing anymore, but he didn't miss a day. Unlike my mother, who never returned to the golf course, who never called Rick to let him know what was going on, my dad put on his uniform and went to work. He came home, changed and ate, went back out. Not to the bar, like before. Not to rent stupid movies. He went out looking for my brother, again and again. He never took me, and if I asked where he went and what he found, he wouldn't say, but I could see it all over him. I knew.

When it had been over a month, my dad got a call about the Stranger. Until then, it seemed the rest of the city had forgotten about the escape. For them, the threat had never become real. It became a waste of their time. There were no murders over the summer, nothing to satisfy the fears that buzzed the thick air. A prisoner had escaped. Yes. A

dangerous man made himself free, but he never went after their family. He did what my mother promised she would do, if she ever got half the chance. He left. He fled this city of prisons and little else, and he never looked back.

My dad hung up the phone and sat at the kitchen table. He didn't know I was in the living room, lying on the couch, in the dark. He opened his police pad, thumbed some pages, and shut the pad with a look of disgust. I imagined what he saw there, in his notes, the scribbles that told the story of this terrible summer. A few jots about the Stranger, yes. But most of the notes came from my dad spying. They were about my mother, with Rick, then without. If you read the pages closely, they showed what my dad really wanted.

My dad put on his gun and his badge.

"It's not him," I said, startling him from the darkness. "It can't be."

My dad came into the living room, saw me on the couch, my arms pulled into my shirt for warmth. "Sleeping here tonight?"

I nodded. I waited for him to shake his head, to say boys sleep in beds. But he pulled a blanket from the closet and draped it over me. He tucked me in and kissed me on the head.

"I love you, son. You know that."

I closed my eyes, unsure if his last words were a statement or a question. I told him I loved him, too, and listened to his footsteps move to the door, out into the night.

I woke at a painful hour. Too dark to be up, too light to go back to sleep. For a while I stared at the TV, blank and black. I tried to remember what day it was, what had happened

the night before and if any of it mattered. My dad had not come home. He was out chasing the Stranger lead, following the claim to its dead end. I tried to imagine what my dad would find when he arrived wherever the tip took him. An empty shack, perhaps. A stack of dirty dishes. In the sink an insulting note: *Sorry I missed you.* I pictured the disappointment on my dad's face, his hand crumpling the note or tearing it into a million pieces.

I poured a bowl of cereal before discovering the milk carton was empty. I went into the basement to tell my mother, as if this little tragedy would finally rouse her. I knelt by her side and listened to her light breathing. She wasn't asleep.

"What do you want?" she said, and I told her about the milk. "Be quiet," she said. "Come here." She moved over and pulled me onto the bed, wrapped me in both arms. She had taken on a certain smell these last couple of weeks, from rarely bathing, wearing the same robe day after day. She breathed into my neck. "Big spoon, little spoon," she said, and weaved a leg around me like a giant spider, squeezing me tight. "You know, when you were a baby this was the only way you would sleep. Just like this. Someone always had to be hugging you. Otherwise, you'd cry your head off."

She asked me if I remembered that, and when I said no, she said, Well, of course, you were just a baby.

"I don't remember when it stopped exactly," she said. "When you didn't have to be in bed with me or your dad." I felt her arms and legs flex with thought. "I guess it was when you were big enough to sleep by your brother." She sighed. "That makes the most sense."

She held me for a moment longer, then, as if satisfied

with the answer she gave to her own question, she released me. She lay on her back and stared at the black ceiling, a sky without stars, with no stories to tell.

"You stink," my mother said. "When's the last time you had a bath?"

I lied and said it was yesterday.

"Well, you need one now. Grab your things. Close the door behind you."

The bathroom was upstairs, next to my dad's bedroom. Since my mother and I had been staying here, the bedroom door was always closed. This morning, it was open, and an eerie daylight shone through the window blinds. I tried not to look, pretended that looking was also forbidden. But it was weird. The bed was made. Zero clothes were thrown on the floor, and the fan chair had been moved to the opposite side.

So there was a clear path to the closet, if I wanted it. I didn't want it. I put my clothes on the sink and started my bath. I waited for the tub to fill. I peed, flushed the toilet, and listened to the water move down the pipes, descending to the basement, rushing above where my mother lay in the dark. My dad was out there. My mother was downstairs. Everyone was somewhere else, and why couldn't I know? I deserved to know.

I kept the water running and tiptoed to my dad's closet. The box was still there. So was the tape. I waited until the bath was full before I snuck downstairs and put it in. I pressed rewind. I pressed play.

But there were no clues.

There was the woman. There was the gun. There was her face.

It's OK, the Stranger said. *They need to understand you deserve this.*

My wailing must've woken my mother, though I didn't realize it was me making those sounds until she appeared in the basement doorway.

"What's wrong with you?" my mother said.

I wiped the last bit of tears and snot off my face. I pointed to the VCR. The tape, done playing, half ejected itself, as if the VCR had spat it out, out of disgust.

"What is this?" my mother said.

I opened my mouth and wailed some more. "He's killed him," I cried. "I know it."

My mother dropped the tape. "What?" she said. "What are you talking about?"

The phone rang. In the story I accepted, the call was right on cue. It was an officer. It was my dad, calling to say he'd found another tape. With my brother. With Chris. You'd better come down here, he would say. To the station. It's over. It's all over.

On the way to the police station my mother would not say a word. I didn't blame her. I couldn't imagine myself ever wanting to talk again. Before we left I had thrown up, quickly, violently. Heaving all I had, and when all I had was gone, my body retched some more. Even though there was nothing left. No words. Only feeling terrible. Only the awful taste.

I sat in the back of the van. I would stay here. I would wait silently as my mother went into the station. Cars and clouds would roll by. A siren would shriek, and a minute later my mother would reappear, changed again.

My mother shook my knee to stir me from my daydream. We're here, she said, and stepped out of the van. Where we were wasn't the station. We were parked in an unfamiliar lot, behind a big brick building I'd never seen. Or I had seen it once, I was later told, but when my eyes were new and I entered our prison town for the first time, in the arms of my mother.

The hospital smelled like the school nurse's office, chemical and clean. My mother held my hand. A nurse gave her a number and my mother pulled me through a maze of halls. I peeked in a few of the rooms, saw serious-looking people standing over still feet. In one room I caught a man, not much older than my dad, pushing a pole to the bathroom. In another, an old woman slept in a chair, flowers in her hand, saggy balloons dying just above her head. Eventually we came to the door with the number. It was closed, and when my mother gently knocked, I heard my dad's voice call for us to come in.

The room was mostly dark. The lights were turned off, and only a few bars of daylight slipped through the blinds, striping the yellow walls white. My dad rose from the chair and greeted my mother with a hug, burying his puffy face in her neck, her yellow hair. He pulled away and whispered something that I couldn't hear or see behind my mother's head. But my mother nodded and the two turned to the opposite wall, to a bed I thought was empty until I stepped deeper into the room. In the bed I saw two feet and when I followed those feet I saw my brother.

It took a moment to recognize my brother in the body in the bed. I had to look past so much. His starved body, thin

as me. The long hair that swept over his shut eyes. He had bruises up and down his arms, dark purples stained on his neck and wrists. A tube snaked up his arm and disappeared in the hospital gown. His face looked sucked in, his cheekbones stuck out, and he was as white as a ghost. I didn't believe them when they said he wasn't dead.

My mother fell to her knees, rose with the help of the bed rails and my dad. He put his arm around us both and we watched my brother's chest rise and fall. We watched his mouth hang open, the drool that pooled off his lip. His face flinched as he slept. I wanted to put my finger in his mouth, to feel his breath. I wanted to dip my finger in the cave of his lips and watch him dream.

The next night we took him home. My mother's insurance ran out. My dad offered money but my mother wanted him out of here, she said. She wanted this to be over. A stern doctor cleared my brother, prescribing a lot of rest, food, and water. He looked at us with pity and sent us on our way.

All of this after my dad filed the police report. After my brother woke and answered my dad's questions. When he did wake, to me, he was a different person. Gone were the faces he made, the looks I recognized. He had no attitude or emotion and answered each question yes or no, or with the smallest of sentences.

Where were you kept? House.

Were you held against your will? Yes.

Where exactly? House.

Where in the house? Basement.

Did he hit you? Yes.

Where? My arms. Legs and face.

Were you tied up? Yes.

You could not move?

No.

For how long? All the time.

My mother held my brother's hand the entire interview, but this didn't seem to comfort him. He didn't look at her, or me. He looked at the window, even though the curtains were closed, and even if they weren't, the room's view was just another brick wall.

My dad continued.

This will be difficult, he said.

Did the man touch you, in an inappropri—? Yes.

—ate way? He did? Yes.

My mother stifled a cry.

OK, it's OK, son, my dad said. Can you tell me how many times? A few.

Can you show me where? My brother pointed. Down his front, between his legs. He rolled over and pointed down his back.

My dad let his head drop, but only for a second. "It's OK," he said again. "It's OK. It's over now." He took my brother's hand and rubbed his thumb over the bump where the IV entered his skin. "I just need you to do one last thing. When you're ready, I need you to come with me and identify the man. His body."

For the first time, my brother turned his gaze from the window.

"The Stranger's dead?" I said.

My dad turned and gave me a stern look. "Be quiet," he said. "No one's talking about that."

I looked at my brother, to see what this information did to his face, but he was through looking at any of us. Later, when I couldn't sleep, I let my mind imagine Chris's death. I put Chris in the woman's chair, instead of behind the camera. I made Chris take her place and I let the Stranger, whoever he was, whisper how I felt. *You need to tell them. They need to understand that you deserve this.* I made the Stranger put the gun to Chris's head. I made Chris beg and cry. You know me, he said. You know me. Do I look like a stranger?

I made the Stranger say shut up. I made him shoot and I watched Chris fall to the floor. *Do you know me?* the Stranger said. *Do you know me?*

After my dad put his notepad away, after my mother hugged my brother for hours and the doctor said we could go home, after my mother made my brother a bed on the couch and lay next to him, so he wouldn't have to sleep in the basement, so she could watch him—after all this, when it was just me in the basement, me and the spiders, I let the Stranger loose. I brought Chris back to life and let the Stranger kill him over and over. In all the ways I could think of. In all the ways I'd seen villains die in movies.

Nobody knows anybody, and if you think you do, this is what you get.

In my mind I made Chris suffer the worst, and I tried to make myself believe that this made things better.

You deserve this. You deserve this.

seventeen

THE STRANGER WAS FOUND weeks later, states away. My dad never mentioned the story, but it was all over the local news, the front page of the paper. He was caught hiding in an old barn on a random farm. The barn was rarely used, apparently, and had been all but abandoned. Boards were missing or cracked, the paint was worn off, and the roof had gaping holes and dents from suffering decades of storms. The land's owners might never have known about the Stranger had their teenage son not snuck a girl and some wine to the barn. They discovered the Stranger sleeping behind an old bale of hay, wild cats circling his head, meowing for food and water. The son told his dad and the dad, too old to deal with squatters anymore, told the sheriff. An hour later the Stranger was on his way back to Kansas. Back to Leavenworth.

We stayed with my dad, and the city continued to heal.

Every day the news ran a different heartwarming video telling the story of some small miracle related to the storm. A dog was picked up by the tornado and thrown two miles. Its owners gave up the dog for dead, until last week when they heard a whine at the door. The dog had crawled its way home, broken legs and all.

By September, when school was ready to start, there were few signs of the tornado's damage. You had to know where to look.

My mother took me by the apartment to gather the rest of our things. When I had put the last trash bag of our belongings in the van, I went to the pool. It too might've looked the same to someone who didn't know better. The water was calm and blue, and every pool chair was in its row. But the diving board was gone. Ripped out, I assumed, by the tornado. All that was left were rust-colored holes where the board had been bolted in. Four small circles that showed what once was.

Instead of going back inside the apartment when I was finished, as my mother instructed, I sat at the deep end. A dead leaf descended from some tree and floated in the water. I thought of Chris. How he died. My parents never told me directly, but of course there had been articles about my family in the paper. I wasn't allowed to read any of them except the one that told of my brother's return. It was brief and dealt only with facts, listing them in a way that didn't assign blame. The police officer's son had been found. Locked in the basement of a vacant house close to the city pool. Officers were led to the house after discovering the body of a twenty-year-old Leavenworth man, Adam Sharp, drowned in the city pool. An apparent suicide. A neighbor had seen Mr. Sharp

leaving the vacant house on several occasions, but thought nothing of it. The officer's son, my brother, was in stable condition.

So here was the leaf. Here was Chris, Adam, facedown in the pool. I thought of the time my brother and I went out to the apartment pool and found Chris in the same position. How we knew he was joking, but still grew worried. How when my brother swam out to make sure Chris was alive, Chris dove underwater like a shark and grabbed my brother's legs, pulling my brother down with him. I tried to imagine what it felt like when whoever found Chris poked at his body, waiting for him to roll over, to come to life. I thought of my brother, how he was changed, and tried to imagine what it would feel like when you realized someone was no longer alive.

My dad was waiting when we got back to the duplex. He eagerly helped us bring our leftover things inside, lapping us multiple times and carrying cartoonishly large loads. When the van was empty, he slammed the doors, and for the first time since my brother's disappearance, his mouth wasn't dragged into a frown.

"Well," he said, "is that it? We're all moved in?"

My mother and I looked at each other, at our dad, who was doing a terrible job hiding his excitement. Behind him the van rattled, even though it was parked and the engine was off. I grabbed the last bag out of my mother's hand.

"That's it," I said. "We sold all the rest. When you left and we were poor."

My dad's face fell. For a moment, I felt what my brother must have when he knocked Rick out with his words. For

some reason it felt good to hit my dad, and a part of me wanted more.

My dad checked the van's side door, to make sure it was locked. "I see," he said. "Well, I'll go clear some space inside."

He went in, and my mother followed him, but not before giving me a long, serious look. A warning maybe. Or a worry. Either way, she didn't say anything, and when I finally went in minutes later, I caught her and my dad whispering to each other in the living room. They shut up when they saw me.

My brother did not return to school with me. No one told me for how long, but for now he would be homeschooled by my mother, who ditched the bathrobe for slacks and her golf course polo, the closest thing she had to teaching attire. The encyclopedias were the schoolbooks, the kitchen was her classroom, and by the time I left each morning my mother and brother were sitting at the table, leaning over the day's lesson. The sound of my brother's voice was a comfort, but he still talked only when he had to. Every day I tried to think of something to say to him, something that would inch us back to the way we were, but every word or sentence I thought of sounded stupid in my head, worthless aloud. It was like the dialogue I forced upon my G.I. Joes, small and meaningless. Words that took up space and nothing more.

A few weeks into school I came home and my brother was in the basement. His things gone from the couch. I found my mother on the back porch, staring at the weather. The sky was gray, but the threats were gone. Storm season was over in Kansas. The dumb weathermen could relax.

"It was his idea," my mother said. "To go down there. I asked if he was sure."

I looked up at her. A light rain misted our faces.

"How was school?"

"Fine," I lied.

"You like your class?"

"I guess."

The rain stopped, started. The clouds watered the sun white, and my mother turned to me. "I got a call, you know. From Miss Scott. She says you're not paying attention. Not doing your work." I lowered my head. "Is this true?"

I turned my back toward her, thinking of the haze of each school day. The musty classroom. The windows pulled open. The low drone of my teacher's voice.

"It's not my fault," I said. "I don't get why I'm the only one who has to go."

My mother smiled. "Hm. I always loved school. Especially the beginning. The new books. The new supplies."

"Yeah," I said, as mean as I could. "Well, I'm not you."

I moved to the corner of the porch. Opposite my mother. I heard her drum her fingers on the porch railing for a moment.

"Come here," she said, and when I didn't move, she came to me. "Listen. You need to hear this." She turned me around and put my head in her hands, her palms cupping my cheeks. She looked me in the eye. She said, "You can't carry this with you."

"But—"

"No," she said. "I know how much you love him. But you have to leave it behind."

Rain ran down her forehead, dripped from the tip of her

nose. In another minute or two, we would be soaked, but my mother wouldn't let me go. Not until I met her stare and told her I understood. That everything that had happened, happened. That it was in the past and that the future, if we let it be, was open.

"Tomorrow is always different," she said. "Understand?"

I nodded, and through the rain did my best to meet her eyes, hardened over the summer, but still my favorite shade of blue. "Yeah, Mom," I said. "I get it."

"Good," she said.

When we ate dinner that week, we looked like a family. The TV was off, and my dad sat across from my mother, and I my brother. We chewed our food and my parents discussed their days. My dad talked of the Chief, who at the last minute pushed back retirement another six months. My mom spoke of my brother, telling my dad how smart he was, how studious. It was obvious she was hoping to spur him to speak, and when he didn't, she would look at me, eyes raised, my cue to try.

After dinner my brother would go straight to the basement and lie in the dark, sleeping or not, I couldn't tell, while my parents did the dishes in the kitchen. I didn't feel like I belonged in either place, so sometimes I went out back and sat on the porch, stared at the stars. If the night was clear, I found the constellations I knew, the ones I'd learned from Chris. The Little Dipper. Ursa Major. Orion the Hunter. And even though I knew the brother stars wouldn't come out for some time, I looked for them anyway. I found the hole in the night where I thought they belonged and wished for them to appear, holding my fingers in the sky. Two dots.

Though I didn't know what the stars looked like, or how far apart they really were.

My brother's birthday was the week of Thanksgiving. This year, it fell on the same Thursday. There was little fanfare for my birthday, but my mother made two pumpkin pies for my brother's, one for my dad and me and the other for the birthday boy. We gathered around the circle table and did our best to look happy. We sang, and when we were done my brother blew out the candles, the one and the one. There were no presents given. We couldn't think of a single thing my brother would want.

After dessert, we sat on the couch and watched a repeat of the parade. My mother convinced my brother to stay upstairs with us, at least for a little while. Have a second slice, she said. It's your special day. You deserve it. But five minutes later, when my brother's plate was clean, and he dropped it noisily in the sink and went to the basement without saying thank you or good night, it was clear that the second slice, him spending an extra moment upstairs, was his gift to us, not the other way around.

My mother poured herself a cup of coffee and sat on the love seat. She'd been sleeping there since my brother was found, but now that he was back in the basement, she had no real reason to. Or not the same reason. More than once I heard my dad invite her to sleep upstairs. To take his bed. He would gladly sleep on the couch. It'll be like old times, he said with a smile, you upstairs and me in the doghouse. But as comforting as a full bed sounded, my mother kept telling him no. She didn't want to be too far away from my brother.

The parade ended. The streets of that big scary city cleared and the floats were taken down. When it was all over, it was way past my bedtime. I closed my eyes, wanting to stay upstairs as long as I could. Not wanting to spend another night with my brother, listening to his troubled breathing, feeling his tossing and turning. I pretended I was asleep and listened to my parents talk close to each other. At first, they talked about anything they could so they wouldn't have to talk about my brother. They talked about things they read in the paper, things they heard. They talked about how the state was losing some of its funding and would have to let a few officers and guards go at the end of the year. They talked about my mom's job, what she wanted. They talked about my mother going back to school to get her teacher's degree, though she said she didn't know. She kind of missed her work, missed Sandy. They talked about other people I didn't know, places I had never seen or heard of. They talked about things I tried to understand.

But they couldn't ignore what was everywhere. The thoughts of my brother, their son, which drowned out our days, despite our best efforts to smile, to wade, to stay afloat.

My mother was the first to speak. "What are we going to do?"

A few weeks ago, my dad would've said, Give it time. Give him some space. But we had tried that and it had taken us only so far.

"Maybe he should talk to someone," my dad said.

"Like a therapist?"

"He won't say any more to me or you. We've tried."

"I know," my mother said. She lowered her voice to a

whisper. "Part of me doesn't want to make him relive it. But what else could he be doing down there?"

A week ago I woke up in the middle of the night, and I was happy because I couldn't place where I was, what life I was living. The feeling didn't last, however, and when I remembered all we'd been through, the burning returned to my chest and I sat up. My brother's half of the bed was empty. I thought about sneaking upstairs, spying on the world and finding my brother, who for some reason I assumed was sleeping on the couch again. Maybe he couldn't take it, I guessed. Maybe being down here with me was too much after all.

But when I put my foot to the floor, I heard a noise from the wall by the stairs. A hiccup. A choked sob. My eyes adjusted to the dark and I saw the shadow of a boy, balled up in the fetal position. I went to him, part of me thinking this was still a dream. And when I touched him, he didn't slap my hand away and his heavy breathing told me I was right; this was a dream. But it was my brother who was dreaming, not me. He was the one who couldn't wake. Who moaned and moaned, terrified by some unseen force. I tried to put my arm around him, but that only made him wail louder. A siren, calling closer and closer. I didn't know what else to do, so I ran back to bed and hid under the covers. I listened to him cry for several hundreds, as I counted sheep after sheep, praying for someone to take me to sleep.

In the morning I woke and found my brother dressing, preparing for his lessons with my mother. He didn't say a word to me. And I didn't know what to say to him.

But now, maybe, an idea. Something I could do.

"You're right," my mother said. "He needs to talk. He needs to tell someone his story." Then she repeated what she said to me. "He can't carry it alone."

My dad agreed, and it was decided they would call someone in the morning. Set up something for after the holiday. But that wasn't soon enough, was it? My brother needed to talk now, and not to some stranger.

My mother finished her coffee. My dad shook me awake from my fake sleep. Both said they loved me. Both, Boys sleep in beds.

My brother was already asleep. I thought about waking him. Whispering, It's OK. You can tell me. I know what you did for me. And I will never forget.

Where to start? In my mind I went over what I knew. I skipped past the beginning, meeting Chris. The middle, Chris growing closer to my brother. I skipped past what could have been the end. The story would have to start with Chris catching my brother in the woods. The bad guy capturing the good. If it were a movie, we would see Chris tie my brother's hands, maybe with the rope he used to tie the desk chair to the pool fence. We would see a strip of duct tape stretched across my brother's mouth. We would watch Chris march my brother miles into the woods, until they emerged in a part of the city I didn't recognize. It would be the middle of the night, and they would walk to a silent street full of old empty houses. For Sale signs would creak in the wind. Chris would lead my brother to one of these vacant places, inside which were stacks of stolen items, cans of food and toiletries taken from the chalk kid's apartment, nearby houses.

Chris would crack open a back window and shove my brother inside. He would throw a leg over the sill, take one last look around to make sure no one was watching, that no one would interrupt what he was about to do. He wouldn't smile. He wouldn't look at the camera. He would pull his other leg into the darkness, shut the window, and the screen would go to black.

But my brother's story couldn't end there.

I rolled over and stared at the ceiling, the water pipes that ran beneath the floor above. The first weekend we stayed at the duplex, my brother and I had contests to see who could hold on to the pipes the longest. The loser had to get back up and hold the pipes some more, while the winner pretended he was an evil prison warden, sent by the state's corrupt governor to torture the inmates for information. The warden would whip the prisoner's ribs with a pillow, or drill him in the stomach with a sock ball, until he got the answers he wanted.

They would have to bring my brother in, I realized. In the movie, to fill in the rest of the story, they would drag my brother down to the station. We need to know what happened, they would say. What exactly this man did to you. We need to know why he drowned himself and not you. We need answers. For our sake and yours.

My brother wouldn't talk. He would give them the same thousand-yard stare he'd walked around carrying for months now. The police would get mad. Out of anger, they would treat him as a hostile witness, not the victim he was. They would bring in the good cop so they could bring in the bad. But it wouldn't matter. No one would get my brother to

describe what he'd been through. No amount of pressure or force. They could beg. They could plead, and they would. *We just want to understand. Why did you go with this man? Why do something we told you never to do?* Still, my brother wouldn't talk. Everyone would throw up their hands. A cop would kick over a chair. You know, this is for your own good, they would say. We're doing this for you.

And when all hope was lost was when I came in. The long-lost brother everyone forgot about. The ex-partner who could read the victim inside and out. At first, no one would notice me. I would slide into the room unseen while the others continued with their questions. These last-ditch efforts. You're a smart kid. Your dad's a cop, for God's sake. You should have known what this man was up to. Surely you felt it, the more time you spent with him. Surely you knew he was leading you down a bad path. So why stick by his side? Why not tell anyone? Why follow him down that road, unflinching?

My brother shook his head. Under the hot lamp, he said he didn't know. And maybe he was telling the truth. Maybe he didn't understand why he stuck by Chris's side no matter what. Why, for that small window of time, he would follow Chris to the ends of the earth, if Chris asked, despite the feeling deep in my brother's heart that told him where you are going, where he is taking you, is someplace wrong.

Just tell us why, the cops said. Let's start there.

I stood in the corner, looking at my reflection in the two-way glass. I smiled with the realization. The reasons I understood, even if he didn't.

Why? the cops begged. Please, just tell us why.

In the real world I took my brother's hand. I squeezed it. In the imaginary world, I turned dramatically away from the glass. I faced my brother and my brother smiled back at me.

I think I know, I said. Maybe I can help.

acknowledgments

It's not enough, but thank you to Claudia Ballard, my agent, dream maker, and champion. To my editor, Emily Bell, the raddest woman I know. Whiskey's on me, EB, *ad aeternam*. To Marie-Helene Bertino and everyone at *One Story*, who published my first story and gave me the encouragement to continue writing.

To the amazing English teachers whose classrooms I was lucky enough to wander into over the years: Ginny Scott, Tom Lorenz, and Deb Olin Unferth. In most of your classes I was the quiet kid, but I was always listening, and am thankful that I did.

To my brilliant MFA classmates at the University of Kansas: especially Robert J. Baumann, Iris Moulton, Dan Rolf, and Chloé Cooper Jones.

To my family: My mom and dad. If anyone asks if this book is about you, tell them only the parts in which the

narrator looks at his parents with an ocean of love and pride. That's how I think of you every day. My step-dad, Gary. *Step-dad* is a stupid word. *Hero-dad* is better, and more fitting. My sister, Candi. Thank you for being more proud of me than I will ever be. My brother Brent. In the world of brothers, you're over 9000. My brother Brett: my role model, my favorite writer, and my best friend.

To all my pets, and in particular my dog Buckley. Thank you for reminding me that there's a world outside of writing, waiting to be explored and sniffed.

And to my wife, Nicole. I sat behind you in Miss Scott's high school English class. The only way I could get you to talk to me was to make bets on who would do better on our vocabulary quizzes. Here are words I could define but you could not: *lugubrious, obdurate, acerbic.* Thus, I won. In the years since, here are words you have helped me understand: *life, love,* and *family.* I guess I won again.